THE
COLLECTED TALES
OF
A. E. COPPARD

Alfred Edgar (handwritten annotation over "OF")

To Earl E. Fisk of Green Bay

THE
COLLECTED TALES
OF
A. E. Coppard

ALFRED A KNOPF

NEW YORK

1951

FOREWORD

In preparing this American omnibus collection of my tales I debated whether to risk saying one or two things about them— and myself. For there are dangers either way. Twenty years ago my *Collected Poems* were published by Mr. Knopf and in the introduction I committed the indiscretion of stating that I had nothing much to say about my poems except that I liked them myself. This unbearable effrontery annoyed some reviewers; you might truly have thought I had tried to sell the American public a lot of junk, which I now immodestly declare was then, and still is, very far from being my opinion.

So now about these tales: I refrain from owning that I like them myself merely as a precautionary measure, justifiable on the grounds of previous experience and present expedience, and not as an indication of my regard for them one way or the other. My blatant humility is urging me not to leave it at that, but there are just two things I really must say about short stories in general and their principles of manufacture. First, I want to crush the assumption that the short story and the novel are manifestations of one principle of fiction, differentiated merely by size, that the novel is inherently and naturally the substantial and therefore the important piece of work, the bale of tweed— you may suppose—out of which your golfer gets his plus-four suit, the short story being merely a remnant, the rag or two left over to make the caddie a cap. In fact the relationship of the short story to the novel amounts to nothing at all. The novel is a distinct form of art having a pedigree and practice of hardly more than a couple of hundred years; the short story, so far from being its offspring, is an ancient art originating in the folk tale, which was a thing of joy even before writing, not to mention printing, was invented. Put the beginning of English printing in the last quarter of the fifteenth century and you light on a date when the folk tale lost its oral or spoken form and issued as a printed short story. Moreover, it was only through that same device of printing that the novel became even a possibility; it did not materialize until the eighteenth century, its forerunners being *Pilgrim's Progress* and *Gulliver's Travels*.

The folk tale ministered to an apparently inborn and universal desire to hear tales, and it is my feeling that the closer the modern short story conforms to that ancient tradition of being spoken to you, rather than being read at you, the more acceptable it becomes. One of the earliest delights of childhood is to be told a tale, and the queer pleasure does not lessen or leave us until we ourselves are left in the grave. Cut off a person from all contact with tales and he will assuredly begin to invent some—probably about himself. I don't know why this is, or what is the curious compulsion that urges some to take to the job of telling the tale, that unconscionable lying which is styled the Art of Fiction, but for good or ill I seem to have been that sort of liar. It has been a pleasant business for me, and I hope it will not be too bad for those about to receive these fabrications.

The second principle I would like to urge is that unity, verisimilitude, and completeness of contour are best obtained by plotting your story through the mind or consciousness of only one of your characters, a process that I used to think might be the secret hinted at in Henry James's tale "The Figure in the Carpet."

Of course one does not adhere to literary principles any more than one does to political or moral ones—we accept them for guidance, not for use in dictatorship. As long as mine served and were not too difficult to embody, I was virtuous; whenever they became irksome or incurred some loss of interest, I took the primrose path and hoped for the best.

A. E. COPPARD.

CONTENTS

CONTENTS

THE
COLLECTED TALES
OF
A. E. COPPARD

A·E· C OPPARD

THE HIGGLER

On a cold April afternoon a higgler was driving across Shag Moor in a two-wheeled cart.

H. WITLOW

DEALER IN POULTRY

DINNOP

was painted on the hood; the horse was of mean appearance but notorious ancestry. A high upland common was this moor, two miles from end to end, and full of furze and bracken. There were no trees and not a house, nothing but a line of telegraph poles following the road, sweeping with rigidity from north to south; nailed upon one of them a small scarlet notice to stone-throwers was prominent as a wound. On so high and wide a region as Shag Moor the wind always blew, or if it did not quite blow there was a cool activity in the air. The furze was always green and growing, and, taking no account of seasons, often golden. Here in summer solitude lounged and snoozed; at other times, as now, it shivered and looked sinister.

Higglers in general are ugly and shrewd, old and hard, crafty and callous, but Harvey Witlow though shrewd was not ugly; he was hard but not old, crafty but not at all unkind. If you had eggs to sell he would buy them, by the score he would, or by the long hundred. Other odds and ends he would buy or do, paying good bright silver, bartering a bag of apples, carrying your little pig to market, or fetching a tree from the nurseries. But the season was backward, eggs were scarce, trade was bad—by crumps, it was indeed!—and as he crossed the moor Harvey could not help discussing the situation with himself.

"If things don't change, and change for the better, and change soon, I can't last and I can't endure it; I'll be damned and done, and I'll have to sell," he said, prodding the animal with the butt of his whip, "this cob. And," he said, as if in afterthought, prodding the footboard, "this cart, and go back to the land. And I'll have lost my fifty pounds. Well, that's what war does for you. It does it for you, sir," he announced sharply to the vacant moor, "and it does it for me. Fifty pounds! I was better off in the war. I was better off working for farmers; much; but it's no good chattering about it, it's the trick of life; when you get so far, then you can go and order your funeral. Get along, Dodger!"

The horse responded briskly for a few moments.

"I tell ye," said Harvey adjuring the ambient air, "you can go and order your funeral. Get along, Dodger!"

Again Dodger got along.

"Then there's Sophy, what about Sophy and me?"

He was not engaged to Sophy Daws, not exactly, but he was keeping company with her. He was not pledged or affianced, he was just keeping company with her. But Sophy, as he knew, not only desired a marriage with Mr. Witlow, she expected it, and expected it soon. So did her parents, her friends, and everybody in the village, including the postman, who didn't live in it but wished he did, and the parson, who did live in it but wished he didn't.

"Well, that's damned and done, fair damned and done now, unless things take a turn, and soon, so it's no good chattering about it."

And just then and there things did take a turn. He had never been across the moor before; he was prospecting for trade. At the end of Shag Moor he saw standing back in the common, fifty yards from the road, a neat square house set in a little farm.

Twenty acres, perhaps. The house was girded by some white palings; beside it was a snug orchard in a hedge covered with blackthorn bloom. It was very green and pleasant in front of the house. The turf was cleared and closely cropped, some ewes were grazing and under the blackthorn, out of the wind, lay half a dozen lambs, but what chiefly moved the imagination of Harvey Witlow was a field on the far side of the house. It had a small rickyard with a few small stacks in it; everything here seemed on the small scale, but snug, very snug; and in that field and yard were hundreds of fowls, hundreds of good breed, and mostly white. Leaving his horse to sniff the greensward, the higgler entered a white wicket gateway and passed to the back of the house, noting as he did so a yellow wagon inscribed

Elizabeth Sadgrove
Prattle Corner

At the kitchen door he was confronted by a tall gaunt woman of middle age with a teapot in her hands.

"Afternoon, ma'am. Have you anything to sell?" began Harvey Witlow, tilting his hat with a confident affable air. The tall woman was cleanly dressed, a superior person; her hair was grey. She gazed at him.

"It's cold," he continued. She looked at him as uncomprehendingly as a mouse might look at a gravestone.

"I'll buy any mottal thing, ma'am. Except trouble; I'm full up wi' that already. Eggs? Fowls?"

"I've not seen you before," commented Mrs. Sadgrove a little bleakly, in a deep husky voice.

"No, 'tis the first time as ever I drove in this part. To tell you the truth, ma'am, I'm new to the business. Six months. I was in the war a year ago. Now I'm trying to knock up a connection. Difficult work. Things are very quiet."

Mrs. Sadgrove silently removed the lid of the teapot, inspected the interior of the pot with an intense glance, and then replaced the lid as if she had seen a black-beetle there.

"Ah, well," sighed the higgler. "You've a neat little farm here, ma'am."

"It's quiet enough," said she.

"Sure it is, ma'am. Very lonely."

"And it's difficult work, too." Mrs. Sadgrove almost smiled.

"Sure it is, ma'am; but you does it well, I can see. Oh, you've some nice little ricks of corn, ah! I does well enough at the dealing now and again, but it's teasy work, and mostly I don't earn enough to keep my horse in shoe leather."

"I've a few eggs, perhaps," said she.

"I could do with a score or two, ma'am, if you could let me have 'em."

"You'll have to come all my way if I do."

"Name your own price, ma'am, if you don't mind trading with me."

"Mind! Your money's as good as my own, isn't it?"

"It must be, ma'am. That's meaning no disrespects to you," the young higgler assured her hastily, and was thereupon invited to enter the kitchen.

A stone floor with two or three mats; open hearth with burning logs; a big dresser painted brown, carrying a row of white cups on brass hooks, and shelves of plates overlapping each other like the scales of fish. A dark settle half hid a flight of stairs with a small gate at the top. Under the window a black sofa, deeply indented, invited you a little repellingly, and in the middle of the room stood a large table, exquisitely scrubbed, with one end of it laid for tea. Evidently a living-room as well as kitchen. A girl, making toast at the fire, turned as the higgler entered. Beautiful she was: red hair, a complexion like the inside of a nut, blue eyes, and the hands of a lady. He saw it all at once, jacket of bright green wool, black dress, grey stockings and shoes, and forgot his errand, her mother, his fifty pounds, Sophy—momentarily he forgot everything. The girl stared strangely at him. He was tall, clean-shaven, with a loop of black hair curling handsomely over one side of his brow.

"Good afternoon," said Harvey Witlow, as softly as if he had entered a church.

"Some eggs, Mary," Mrs. Sadgrove explained. The girl laid down her toasting-fork. She was less tall than her mother, whom she resembled only enough for the relationship to be noted. Silently she crossed the kitchen and opened a door that led into a dairy. Two pans of milk were creaming on a bench there, and on the flags were two great baskets filled with eggs.

"How many are there?" asked Mrs. Sadgrove, and the girl replied: "Fifteen score, I think."

"Take the lot, higgler?"

"Yes, ma'am," he cried eagerly, and ran out to his cart and fetched a number of trays. In them he packed the eggs as the girl handed them to him from the baskets. Mrs. Sadgrove left them together. For a time the higgler was silent.

"No," at length he murmured, "I've never been this road before."

There was no reply from Mary. Sometimes their fingers touched, and often, as they bent over the eggs, her bright hair almost brushed his face.

"It is a loneish spot," he ventured again.

"Yes," said Mary Sadgrove.

When the eggs were all transferred her mother came in again.

"Would you buy a few pullets, higgler?"

"Any number, ma'am," he declared quickly. Any number; by crumps, the tide was turning. He followed the mother into the yard, and there again she left him, waiting. He mused about the girl and wondered about the trade. If they offered him ten thousand chickens, he'd buy them, somehow, he would. She had stopped in the kitchen. Just in there she was, just behind him, a few feet away. Over the low wall of the yard a fat black pony was strolling in a field of bright greensward. In the yard, watching him, was a young gander, and on a stone staddle beside it lay a dead thrush on its back, its legs stiff in the air. The girl stayed in the kitchen; she was moving about, though, he could hear her; perhaps she was spying at him through the window. Twenty million eggs he would buy if Mrs. Sadgrove had got them. She was gone a long time. It was very quiet. The gander began to comb its white breast with its beak. Its three-toed feet were a most tender pink, shaped like wide diamonds, and at each of the three forward points here was a toe like a small blanched nut. It lifted one foot, folding the webs, and hid it under its wing and sank into a resigned meditation on one leg. It had a blue eye that was meek—it had two, but you could only see one at a time

—a meek blue eye, set in a pink rim that gave it a dissolute air, and its beak had raw red nostrils as though it suffered from the damp. Altogether a beautiful bird. And in some absurd way it resembled Mrs. Sadgrove.

"Would you sell that young gollan, ma'am?" Harvey inquired when the mother returned.

Yes, she would sell him, and she also sold him two dozen pullets. Harvey packed the fowls in a crate.

"Come on," he cried cuddling the squalling gander in his arms, "you needn't be afeared of me, I never kills anything afore Saturdays."

He roped it by its leg to a hook inside his cart. Then he took out his bag of money, paid Mrs. Sadgrove her dues, said: "Good day, ma'am, good day" and drove off without seeing another sign or stitch of that fine young girl.

"Get along, Dodger, get along wi' you." They went bowling along for nearly an hour, and then he could see the landmark on Dan'el Green's Hill, a windmill that never turned though it looked a fine competent piece of architecture, just beyond Dinnop.

Soon he reached his cottage and was chaffing his mother, a hearty buxom dame, who stayed at home and higgled with any chance callers. At this business she was perhaps more enlightened than her son. It was almost a misfortune to get into her clutches.

"How much you give for this?" he cried, eyeing with humorous contempt an object in a coop that was neither flesh nor rude red herring.

"Oh crumps," he declared when she told him, "I am damned and done!"

"Go on with you, that's a good bird, I tell you, with a full heart, as will lay in a month."

"I doubt it's a hen at all," he protested. "Oh what a ravenous beak! Damned and done I am."

Mrs. Witlow's voice began indignantly to rise.

"Oh well," mused her son, "it's thrifty perhaps. It ain't quite right, but it's not so wrong as to make a fuss about, especially as I be pretty sharp set. And if it's hens you want," he continued triumphantly, dropping the crate of huddled fowls before her, "there's hens for you; and a gander! There's a gander for you, if it's a gander you want."

Leaving them all in his cottage yard he went and stalled the horse and cart at the inn, for he had no stable of his own. After supper he told his mother about the Sadgroves of Prattle Corner. "Prettiest girl you ever seen, but the shyest mottal alive. Hair like a squirrel, lovely."

"An't you got to go over and see Sophy tonight," inquired his mother, lighting the lamp.

"Oh lord, if I an't clean forgot that. Well, I'm tired, shan't go tonight. See her tomorrow."

II

Mrs. Sadgrove had been a widow for ten years—and she was glad of it. Prattle Corner was her property, she owned it and farmed it with the aid of a little old man and a large lad. The older this old man grew, and the less wages he received (for Elizabeth Sadgrove was reputed a "grinder"), the more ardently he worked; the older the lad grew, the less he laboured and the more he swore. She was thriving. She was worth money, was Mrs. Sadgrove. Ah! And her daughter Mary, it was clear, had received an education fit for a lord's lady; she had been at a seminary for gentlefolk's females until she was seventeen. Well, whether or no, a clock must run as you time it; but it wronged her for the work of a farm, it spoiled her, it completely deranged her for the work of a farm; and this was a pity and foolish, because some day the farm was coming to her as didn't know hay from a bull's foot.

All this, and more, the young higgler quickly learned, and plenty more he soon divined. Business began to flourish with him now; his despair was gone, he was established, he could look forward, to whatever it was he wanted to look forward, with equanimity and such pleasurable anticipation as the chances and charges of life might engender. Every week, and twice a week, he would call at the farm, and though these occasions had their superior business inducements they often borrowed a less formal tone and intention.

"Take a cup of tea, higgler?" Mrs. Sadgrove would abruptly invite him; and he would drink tea and discourse with her for half an hour on barndoor ornithology, on harness, and markets, the treatment of swine, the wear and tear of gear. Mary, always present, was always silent, seldom uttering a word to the higgler; yet a certain grace emanated from her to him, an interest, a light, a favour, circumscribed indeed by some modesty, shyness, some inhibition, that neither had the wit or the opportunity to overcome.

One evening he pulled up at the white palings of Prattle Corner. It was a calm evening in May, the sun was on its downgoing, chaffinches and wrens sung ceaselessly. Mary in the orchard was heavily veiled; he could see her over the hedge, holding a brush in her gloved hands, and a bee skep. A swarm was clustered like a great gnarl on the limb of an apple tree. Bloom was thickly covering the twigs. She made several timid attempts to brush the bees into the skep but they resented this.

"They knows if you be afraid of 'em," bawled Harvey. "I better come and give you a hand."

When he took the skep and brush from her she stood like one helpless, released by fate from a task ill-understood and gracelessly waived. But he liked her shyness, her almost uncouth immobility.

"Never mind about that," said Harvey, as she unfastened her veil, scattering the white petals that had collected upon it; "when they kicks they hurts; but I've been stung so often that I'm 'noculated against 'em. They knows if you be afraid of 'em."

Wearing neither veil nor gloves he went confidently to the tree and collected the swarm without mishap.

"Don't want to show no fear of them," said Harvey. "Nor of anything else, come to that," he added with a guffaw, "nor anybody."

At that she blushed and thanked him very softly, and she did look straight and clearly at him.

Never anything beyond a blush and a thank-you. When in the kitchen, or the parlour, Mrs. Sadgrove sometimes left them alone together Harvey would try a lot of talk, blarneying talk or sensible talk, or talk about events in the world that was neither the one nor the other. No good. The girl's responses were ever brief and confused. Why was this? Again and again he asked himself that question. Was there anything the matter with her? Nothing that you could see; she was a bright and beautiful being. And it was not contempt, either, for despite her fright, her voicelessness, her timid eyes, he divined her friendly feeling for himself; and he would discourse to his own mother about her and her mother:

"They are well-up people, you know, well off, plenty of money and nothing to do with it. The farm's their own, freehold. A whole row of cottages she's got, too, in Smoorton Comfrey, so I heard; good cottages, well let. She's worth a few thousands, I warrant. Mary's beautiful. I took a fancy to that girl the first moment I see her. But she's very highly cultivated—and, of course, there's Sophy."

To this enigmatic statement Mrs. Witlow offered no response; but mothers are inscrutable beings to their sons, always.

Once he bought some trees of cherries from Mrs. Sadgrove, and went on a July morning to pick the fruit. Under the trees Mary was walking slowly to and fro, twirling a clapper to scare away the birds. He stood watching her from the gateway. Among the bejewelled trees she passed, turning the rattle with a listless air, as if beating time to a sad music that only she could hear. The man knew that he was deeply fond of her. He passed into the orchard, bade her good morning, and lifting his ladder into one of the trees nearest the hedge began to pluck cherries. Mary moved slimly in her white frock up and down a shady avenue in the orchard, waving the clapper. The brightness of sun and sky was almost harsh; there was a little wind that feebly lifted the despondent leaves. He had doffed his coat; his shirt was white and clean. The lock of dark hair drooped over one side of his forehead; his face was brown and pleasant, his bare arms were brown and powerful. From his high perch among the leaves Witlow watched for the girl to draw near to him in her perambulation. Knavish birds would scatter at her approach, only to drop again into the trees she had passed. His soul had an immensity of longing for her, but she never spoke a word to him. She would come from the shade of the little avenue, through the dumb trees that could only bend to greet her, into the sun-

light whose dazzle gilded her own triumphant bloom. Fine!
Fine! And always as she passed his mind refused to register a
single thought he could offer her, or else his tongue would refuse to utter it. But his glance never left her face until she had
passed out of sight again, and then he would lean against the
ladder in the tree, staring down at the ground, seeing nothing or
less than nothing, except a field mouse climbing to the top of a
coventry bush in the hedge below him, nipping off one thick leaf
and descending with the leaf in its mouth. Sometimes Mary
rested at the other end of the avenue; the clapper would be silent
and she would not appear for—oh, hours! She never rested near
the trees Witlow was denuding. The mouse went on ascending
and descending, and Witlow filled his basket, and shifted his
stand, and wondered.

At noon he got down and sat on the hedge bank to eat a snack
of lunch. Mary had gone indoors for hers, and he was alone for
a while. Capriciously enough, his thoughts dwelt upon Sophy
Daws. Sophy was a fine girl too; not such a lady as Mary Sadgrove—oh lord, no! her father was a gamekeeper!—but she was
jolly and ample. She had been a little captious lately, said he was
neglecting her. That wasn't true; hadn't he been busy? Besides,
he wasn't bound to her in any sort of way, and of course he
couldn't afford any marriage yet awhile. Sophy hadn't got any
money, never had any. What she did with her wages—she was
a parlour-maid—was a teaser! Harvey grunted a little, and said
"Well!" And that is all he said, and all he thought about Sophy
Daws then, for he could hear Mary's clapper begin again in a
corner of the orchard. He went back to his work. There at the
foot of the tree were the baskets full of cherries, and those yet
to be filled.

"Phew, but that's hot!" commented the man, "I'm as dry as a
rattle."

A few cherries had spilled from one basket and lay on the
ground. The little furry mouse had found them and was in-
dustriously nibbling at one. The higgler nonchalantly stamped
his foot upon it, and kept it so for a moment or two. Then he
looked at the dead mouse. A tangle of entrails had gushed from
its whiskered muzzle.

He resumed his work and the clapper rattled on throughout the afternoon, for there were other cherry trees that other buyers would come to strip in a day or two. At four o'clock he was finished. Never a word had he spoken with Mary, or she with him. When he went over to the house to pay Mrs. Sadgrove Mary stopped in the orchard scaring the birds.

"Take a cup of tea, Mr. Witlow," said Mrs. Sadgrove; and then she surprisingly added: "Where's Mary?"

"Still a-frightening the birds, and pretty well tired of that, I should think, ma'am."

The mother had poured out three cups of tea.

"Shall I go and call her in?" he asked, rising.

"You might," said she.

In the orchard the clappering had ceased. He walked all round, and in among the trees, but saw no sign of Mary; nor on the common, nor in the yard. But when he went back to the house Mary was there already, chatting at the table with her mother. She did not greet him, though she ceased talking to her mother as he sat down. After drinking his tea he went off briskly to load the baskets into the cart. As he climbed up to drive off, Mrs. Sadgrove came out and stood beside the horse.

"You're off now?" said she.

"Yes, ma'am; all loaded, and thank you."

She glanced vaguely along the road he had to travel. The afternoon was as clear as wine, the greensward itself dazzled him; lonely Shag Moor stretched away, humped with sweet yellow furze and pilastered with its telegraph poles. No life there, no life at all. Harvey sat on his driving board, musingly brushing the flank of his horse with the trailing whip.

"Ever round this way on Sundays?" inquired the woman, peering up at him.

"Well, not in a manner of speaking, I'm not, ma'am," he answered her.

The widow laid her hand on the horse's back, patting vaguely. The horse pricked up its ears, as if it were listening.

"If you are, at all, ever, you must look in and have a bit of dinner with us."

"I will, ma'am, I will."

"Next Sunday?" she went on.

"I will, ma'am, yes, I will," he repeated, "and thank you."

"One o'clock?" The widow smiled up at him.

"At one o'clock, ma'am; next Sunday; I will, and thank you,"
he said.

She stood away from the horse and waved her hand. The first
tangible thought that floated mutely out of the higgler's mind as
he drove away was: "I'm damned if I ain't a-going it, Sophy!"

He told his mother of Mrs. Sadgrove's invitation with an air
of curbed triumph. "Come round—she says. Yes—I says—I 'ull.
That's right—she says—so do."

III

On the Sunday morn he dressed himself gallantly. It was
again a sweet unclouded day. The church bell at Dinnop had
begun to ring. From his window, as he fastened his most ornate
tie, Harvey could observe his neighbour's two small children in
the next garden, a boy and girl clad for church-going and each
carrying a clerical book. The tiny boy placed his sister in front of
a hen-roost and, opening his book, began to pace to and fro before her, shrilly intoning: "Jesus is the shepherd, ring the bell.
Oh lord, ring the bell, am I a good boy? Amen. Oh lord, ring
the bell." The little girl bowed her head piously over her book.
The lad then picked up from the ground a dish that had contained the dog's food, and presented it momentarily before the
lilac bush, the rabbit in a hutch, the axe fixed in a chopping block,
and then before his sister. Without lifting her peering gaze from
her book she meekly dropped two pebbles in the plate, and the
boy passed on, lightly moaning, to the clothes-line post and a
cock scooping in some dust.

"Ah, the little impets!" cried Harvey Witlow. "Here, Toby!
Here, Margaret!" He took two pennies from his pocket and
lobbed them from the window to the astonished children. As
they stooped to pick up the coins Harvey heard the hoarse voice
of neighbour Nathan, their father, bawl from his kitchen: "Come
on in, and shut that bloody door, d'y'ear!"

Harnessing his moody horse to the gig Harvey was soon
bowling away to Shag Moor, and as he drove along he sung

loudly. He had a pink rose in his buttonhole. Mrs. Sadgrove received him almost affably, and though Mary was more shy than ever before, Harvey had determined to make an impression. During the dinner he fired off his bucolic jokes, and pleasant tattle of a more respectful and sober nature; but after dinner Mary sat like Patience, not upon a monument but as if upon a rocking-horse, shy and fearful, and her mother made no effort to inspire her as the higgler did, unsuccessful though he was. They went to the pens to look at the pigs, and as they leaned against the low walls and poked the maudlin inhabitants, Harvey began: "Reminds me, when I was in the war . . ."

"Were you in the war!" interrupted Mrs. Sadgrove.

"Oh yes, I was in that war, ah, and there was a pig . . . Danger? Oh lord bless me it was a bit dangerous, but you never knew where it was or wat it 'ud be at next; it was like the sword of Damockels. There was a bullet once come 'ithin a foot of my head, and it went through a board an inch thick, slap through that board." Both women gazed at him apprehendingly. "Why, I might 'a' been killed, you know," said Harvey, cocking his eye musingly at the weather-vane on the barn. "We was in billets at St. Gratien, and one day a chasseur came up—a French yoossar, you know—and he began talking to our sergeant. That was Hubert Luxter, the butcher: died a month or two ago of measles. But this yoossar couldn't speak English at all, and none of us chaps could make sense of him. I never could understand that lingo somehow, never; and though there was half a dozen of us chaps there, none of us were man enough for it neither. 'Nil compree,' we says, 'non compos.' I told him straight: 'You ought to learn English,' I said, 'it's much easier than your kind of bally chatter.' So he kept shaping up as if he was holding a rifle, and then he'd say 'Fusee—bang!' and then he'd say 'cushion'—kept on saying 'cushion.' Then he gets a bit of chalk and draws on the wall something that looks like a horrible dog, and says 'cushion' again."

"Pig," interjected Mary Sadgrove, softly.

"Yes, yes!" ejaculated Harvey, "so 'twas! Do you know any French lingo?"

"Oh yes," declared her mother, "Mary knows it very well."

"Ah," sighed the higgler, "I don't, although I been to France. And I couldn't do it now, not for luck nor love. You learnt it, I suppose. Well, this yoossar wants to borrow my rifle, but of course I can't lend him. So he taps on this horrible pig he'd drawn, and then he taps on his own head, and rolls his eyes about dreadful! 'Mad?' I says. And that was it, that was it. He'd got a pig on his little farm there what had gone mad, and he wanted us to come and shoot it; he was on leave and he hadn't got any ammunition. So Hubert Luxter he says: 'Come on, some of you,' and we all goes with the yoossar and shot the pig for him. Ah, that was a pig! And when it died it jumped a somersault just like a rabbit. It had got the mange, and was mad as anything I ever see in my life; it was full of madness. Couldn't hit him at all at first, and it kicked up bobs-a-dying. 'Ready, present, fire!' Hubert Luxter says, and bang goes the six of us, and every time we missed him he spotted us and we had to run for our lives."

As Harvey looked up he caught a glance of the girl fixed on him. She dropped her gaze at once and, turning away, walked off to the house.

"Come and take a look at the meadow," said Mrs. Sadgrove to him, and they went into the soft smooth meadow where the black pony was grazing. Very bright and green it was, and very blue the sky. He sniffed at the pink rose in his buttonhole, and determined that come what may he would give it to Mary if he could get a nice quiet chance to offer it. And just then, while he and Mrs. Sadgrove were strolling alone in the soft smooth meadow, quite alone, she suddenly, startlingly, asked him: "Are you courting anybody?"

"Beg pardon, ma'am?" he exclaimed.

"You haven't got a sweetheart, have you?" she asked, most deliberately.

Harvey grinned sheepishly: "Ha ha ha," and then he said: "No."

"I want to see my daughter married," the widow went on significantly.

"Miss Mary!" he cried.

"Yes," said she; and something in the higgler's veins began to pound rapidly. His breast might have been a revolving cage and his heart a demon squirrel. "I can't live for ever," said Mrs. Sadgrove, almost with levity, "in fact, not for long, and so I'd like to see her settled soon with some decent understanding young man, one that could carry on here, and not make a mess of things."

"But, but," stuttered the understanding young man, "I'm no scholar, and she's a lady. I'm a poor chap, rough, and no scholar, ma'am. But mind you . . ."

"That doesn't matter at all," the widow interrupted, "not as things are. You want a scholar for learning, but for the land . . ."

"Ah, that's right, Mrs. Sadgrove, but . . ."

"I want to see her settled. This farm, you know, with the stock and things are worth nigh upon three thousand pounds."

"You want a farmer for farming, that's true, Mrs. Sadgrove, but when you come to marriage, well, with her learning and French and all that . . ."

"A sensible woman will take a man rather than a box of tricks any day of the week," the widow retorted. "Education may be a fine thing, but it often costs a lot of foolish money."

"It do, it do. You want to see her settled?"

"I want to see her settled and secure. When she is twenty-five she comes into five hundred pounds of her own right."

The distracted higgler hummed and haa-ed in his bewilderment as if he had just been offered the purchase of a dubious duck. "How old is she, ma'am?" he at last huskily inquired.

"Two and twenty nearly. She's a good healthy girl for I've never spent a pound on a doctor for her, and very quiet she is, and very sensible; but she's got a strong will of her own, though you might not think it or believe it."

"She's a fine creature, Mrs. Sadgrove, and I'm very fond of her, I don't mind owning up to that, very fond of her I am."

"Well, think it over, take your time, and see what you think. There's no hurry I hope, please God."

"I shan't want much time," he declared with a laugh, "but I doubt I'm the fair right sort for her."

"Oh, fair days, fair doings!" said she inscrutably, "I'm not a long liver, I'm afraid."

"God forbid, ma'am!" His ejaculation was intoned with deep gravity.

"No, I'm not a long-living woman." She surveyed him with

her calm eyes, and he returned her gaze. Hers was a long sallow face, with heavy lips. Sometimes she would stretch her features (as if to keep them from petrifying) in an elastic grin, and display her dazzling teeth; the lips would curl thickly, no longer crimson but blue. He wondered if there was any sign of a doom registered upon her gaunt face. She might die, and die soon.

"You couldn't do better than think it over, then, eh?" She had a queer frown as she regarded him.

"I couldn't do worse than not, Mrs. Sadgrove," he said gaily.

They left it at that. He had no reason for hurrying away, and he couldn't have explained his desire to do so, but he hurried away. Driving along past the end of the moor, and peering back at the lonely farm where they dwelled amid the thick furze snoozing in the heat, he remembered that he had not asked if Mary was willing to marry him! Perhaps the widow took her agreement for granted. That would be good fortune, for otherwise how the devil was he to get round a girl who had never spoken half a dozen words to him! And never would! She was a lady, a girl of fortune, knew her French; but there it was, the girl's own mother was asking him to wed her. Strange, very strange! He dimly feared something, but he did not know what it was he feared. He had still got the pink rose in his buttonhole.

IV

At first his mother was incredulous; when he told her of the astonishing proposal she declared he was a joker; but she was soon as convinced of his sincerity as she was amazed at his hesitation. And even vexed: "Was there anything the matter with this Mary?"

"No, no, no! She's quiet, very quiet indeed, I tell you, but a fine young woman, and a beautiful young woman. Oh, she's all right, right as rain, right as a trivet, right as ninepence. But there's a catch in it somewheres, I fear. I can't see through it yet, but I shall afore long, or I'd have the girl, like a shot I would. 'Tain't the girl, mother, it's the money, if you understand me."

"Well, I don't understand you, certainly I don't. What about Sophy?"

"Oh lord!" He scratched his head ruefully.

"You wouldn't think of giving this the go-by for Sophy, Harvey, would you? A girl as you ain't even engaged to, Harvey, would you?"

"We don't want to chatter about that," declared her son. "I got to think it over, and it's going to tie my wool, I can tell you, for there's a bit of craft somewhere, I'll take my oath. If there ain't, there ought to be!"

Over the alluring project his decision wavered for days, until his mother became mortified at his inexplicable vacillation.

"I tell you," he cried, "I can't make tops or bottoms of it all. I like the girl well enough, but I like Sophy, too, and it's no good beating about the bush. I like Sophy, she's the girl I love; but Mary's a fine creature, and money like that wants looking at before you throw it away, love or no love. Three thousand pounds! I'd be a made man."

And as if in sheer spite to his mother; as if a bushel of money lay on the doorstep for him to kick over whenever the fancy seized him; in short (as Mrs. Witlow very clearly intimated) as if in contempt of Providence, he began to pursue Sophy Daws with a new fervour, and walked with that young girl more than he was accustomed to, more than ever before; in fact, as his mother bemoaned, more than he had need to. It was unreasonable, it was a shame, a foolishness; it wasn't decent and it wasn't safe.

On his weekly visits to the farm his mind still wavered. Mrs. Sadgrove let him alone; she was very good, she did not pester him with questions and entreaties. There was Mary with her white dress and her red hair and her silence; a girl with a great fortune, walking about the yard, or sitting in the room, and casting not a glance upon him. Not that he would have known it if she did, for now he was just as shy of her. Mrs. Sadgrove often left them alone, but when they were alone he could not dish up a word for the pretty maid; he was dumb as a statue. If either she or her mother had lifted so much as a finger, then there would have been an end to his hesitations or suspicions, for in Mary's presence the fine glory of the girl seized him incontinently; he was again full of a longing to press her lips, to lay down his doubts, to touch her bosom—though he could not think she would ever allow that! Not an atom of doubt about *her* ever visited him; she was unaware of her mother's queer project. Rather, if she became aware he was sure it would be the end of him. Too beautiful she was, too learned, and too rich. Decidedly it was his native cunning, and no want of love, that inhibited him. Folks with property did not often come along and bid you help yourself. Not very often! And throw in a grand bright girl, just for good measure as you might say. Not very often!

For weeks the higgler made his customary calls, and each time the outcome was the same; no more, no less. "Some dodge," he mused, "something the girl don't know and the mother does." Were they going bankrupt, or were they mortgaged up to the neck, or was there anything the matter with the girl, or was it just the mother wanted to get hold of him? He knew his own value if he didn't know his own mind, and his value couldn't match that girl any more than his mind could. So what *did* they want him for? Whatever it was, Harvey Witlow was ready for it whenever he was in Mary's presence, but once away from her his own craftiness asserted itself; it was a snare, they were trying to make a mock of him!

But nothing could prevent his own mother mocking him, and her treatment of Sophy was so unbearable that if the heart of that dusky beauty had not been proof against all impediments, Harvey might have had to whistle for her favour. But whenever he was with Sophy he had only one heart, undivided and true, and certain as time itself.

"I love Sophy best. It's true enough I love Mary, too, but I love Sophy better. I know it; Sophy's the girl I must wed. It might not be so if I weren't all dashed and doddered about the money; I don't know. But I do know that Mary's innocent of all this craftiness; it's her mother trying to mogue me into it."

Later he would be wishing he could only forget Sophy and do it. Without the hindrance of conscience he could do it, catch or no catch.

He went on calling at the farm, with nothing said or settled, until October. Then Harvey made up his mind, and without a word to the Sadgroves he went and married Sophy Daws and gave up calling at the farm altogether. This gave him some feeling of dishonesty, some qualm and a vague unhappiness; likewise he feared the cold hostility of Mrs. Sadgrove. She would be terribly vexed. As for Mary, he was nothing to her, poor girl; it was a shame. The last time he drove that way he did not call at the farm. Autumn was advancing, and the apples were down, the bracken dying, the furze out of bloom, and the farm on the moor looked more and more lonely, and most cold, though it lodged a flame-haired silent woman, fit for a nobleman, whom they wanted to mate with a common higgler. Crafty, you know, too crafty!

V

The marriage was a gay little occasion, but they did not go away for a honeymoon. Sophy's grandmother from a distant village, Cassandra Fundy, who had a deafness and a speckled skin, brought her third husband, Amos, whom the family had never seen before. Not a very wise man, indeed he was a common man, stooping like a decayed tree, he was so old. But he shaved every day and his hairless skull was yellow. Cassandra, who was yellow too, had long since turned into a fool; she did not shave, though she ought to have done. She was like to die soon, but everybody said old Amos would live to be a hundred; it was expected of him, and he, too, was determined.

The guests declared that a storm was threatening, but Amos Fundy denied it and scorned it.

"Thunder p'raps, but 'twill clear; 'tis only de pride o' der morning."

"Don't you be a fool," remarked his wife, enigmatically, "you'll die soon enough."

"You must behold der moon," continued the octogenarian; "de closer it is to der wheel, de closer der rain; de furder away it is, de furder der rain."

"You could pour that man's brains into a thimble," declared Cassandra of her spouse, "and they wouldn't fill it—he's deaf."

Fundy was right; the day did clear. The marriage was made and the guests returned with the man and his bride to their home. But Fundy was also wrong, for storm came soon after and rain set in. The guests stayed on for tea, and then, as it was no better, they feasted and stayed till night. And Harvey began to think they never would go, but of course they couldn't and so there they were. Sophy was looking wonderful in white stockings and shiny shoes and a red frock with a tiny white apron. A big girl she seemed, with her shaken dark hair and flushed face. Grandmother Fundy spoke seriously, but not secretly to her.

"I've had my fourteen touch of children," said Grandmother Fundy. "Yes, they were flung on the mercy of God—poor little devils. I've followed most of 'em to the churchyard. You go slow, Sophia."

"Yes, granny."

"Why," continued Cassandra, embracing the whole company, as it were, with her disclosure, "my mother had me by some gentleman!"

The announcement aroused no response except sympathetic, and perhaps encouraging, nods from the women.

"She had me by some gentleman—she ought to ha' had a twal' month, she did!"

"Wasn't she ever married?" Sophy inquired of her grandmother.

"Married? Yes, course she was," replied the old dame, "of course. But marriage ain't everything. Twice she was, but not to he, she wasn't."

"Not to the gentleman?"

"No! Oh no! He'd got money—bushels! Marriage ain't much, not with these gentry."

"Ho, ho, that's a tidy come-up!" laughed Harvey.

"Who was the gentleman?" Sophia's interest was deeply engaged. But Cassandra Fundy was silent, pondering like a china image. Her gaze was towards the mantelpiece, where there were four lamps—but only one usable—and two clocks—but only one going—and a coloured greeting card a foot long with large letters KEEP SMILING adorned with lithographic honeysuckle.

"She's hard of hearing," interpolated Grandfather Amos, "very hard, gets worse. She've a horn at home, big as that . . ." His eyes roved the room for an object of comparison, and he seized upon the fire shovel that lay in the fender. "Big as that shovel. Crown silver it is, and solid, a beautiful horn, but"—he brandished the shovel before them—"her won't use 'en."

"Granny, who was that gentleman?" shouted Sophy. "Did you know him?"

"No! No!" declared the indignant dame. "I dunno ever his name, nor I don't want to. He took hisself off to Ameriky, and now he's in the land of heaven. I never seen him. If I had, I'd 'a' given it to him properly; oh, my dear, not blay-guarding him, you know, but just plain language! Where's your seven commandments?"

At last the rain abated. Peeping into the dark garden you could see the fugitive moonlight hung in a million raindrops in the black twigs of all sorts of bushes and trees, while along the cantle of the porch a line of raindrops hung, even and regular, as if they were nailheads made of glass. So all the guests departed, in one long staggering, struggling, giggling, guffawing body, into the village street. The bride and her man stood in the porch, watching, and waving hands. Sophy was momentarily grieving: what a lot of trouble and fuss when you announced that henceforward you were going to sleep with a man because you loved him true! She had said good-bye to her Grandmother Cassandra, to her father and her little sister. She had hung on her mother's breast, sighing an almost intolerable farewell to innocence—never treasured until it is gone—and thenceforward a pretty sorrow cherished more deeply than wilder joys.

Into Harvey's mind, as they stood there at last alone, momentarily stole an image of a bright-haired girl, lovely, silent, sad, whom he felt he had deeply wronged. And he was sorry. He had escaped the snare, but if there had been no snare he might this night have been sleeping with a different bride. And it would have been just as well. Sophy looked but a girl with her blown hair and wet face. She was wiping her tears on the tiny apron. But she had the breasts of a woman and decoying eyes.

"Sophy, Sophy!" breathed Harvey, wooing her in the darkness.

"It blows and it rains, and it rains and it blows," chattered the crumpled bride, "and I'm all so bescambled I can't tell wet from windy."

"Come, my love," whispered the bridegroom, "come in, to home."

VI

Four or five months later the higgler's affairs had again taken a rude turn. Marriage, alas, was not all it might be; his wife and his mother quarrelled unendingly. Sometimes he sided with the one, sometimes with the other. He could not yet afford to install his mother in a separate cottage, and therefore even Sophy had to admit that her mother-in-law had a right to be living there with them, the home being hers. Harvey hadn't bought much of it; and though he was welcome to it all now, and it would be exclusively his as soon as she died, still, it was her furniture and you couldn't drive any woman (even your mother) off her own property. Sophy, who wanted a home of her own, was vexed and moody, and antagonistic to her man. Business, too, had gone down sadly of late. He had thrown up the Shag Moor round months ago; he could not bring himself to go there again, and he had not been able to square up the loss by any substantial new connections. On top of it all his horse died. It stumbled on a hill one day and fell, and it couldn't get up, or it wouldn't—at any rate, it didn't. Harvey thrashed it and coaxed it, then he cursed it and kicked it; after that he sent for a veterinary man, and the veterinary man ordered it to be shot. And it was shot. A great blow to Harvey Witlow was that. He had no money to buy another horse; money was tight with him, very tight; and so he had to hire at fabulous cost a decrepit nag that ate like a good one. It ate—well, it would have astonished you to see what that creature disposed of, with hay the price it was, and corn gone up to heaven nearly. In fact Harvey found that he couldn't stand the racket much longer, and as he could not possibly buy another it looked very much as if he was in queer street once more, unless he could borrow the money from some friendly person. Of course there were plenty of friendly persons but they had no money, just as there were many persons who had the money but were not what you might call friendly; and so the higgler began to reiterate twenty times a day, and forty times a day, that he was entirely and absolutely damned and done. Things were thus very bad with him, they were at their worst—for he had a wife to keep now, as well as a mother, and a horse that ate like Satan, and worked like a gnat—when it suddenly came into his mind that Mrs. Sadgrove was reputed to have a lot of money, and had no call to be unfriendly to him. He had his grave doubts about the size of her purse, but there could be no harm in trying so long as you approached her in a right reasonable manner.

For a week or two he held off from this appeal, but the grim spectre of destitution gave him no rest, and so, near the close of a wild March day he took his desperate courage and his cart and the decrepit nag to Shag Moor. Wild it was, though dry, and the wind against them, a vast turmoil of icy air strident and baffling. The nag threw up its head and declined to trot. Evening was but an hour away, the fury of the wind did not retard it, nor the clouds hasten it. Low down the sun was quitting the wrack of storm, exposing a jolly orb of magnifying fire that shone flush under eaves and through the casements of cottages, casting a pattern of lattice and tossing boughs upon the interior walls, lovelier than dreamed-of pictures. The heads of mothers and old dames were also imaged there, recognizable in their black shadows; and little children held up their hands between window and wall to make five-fingered shapes upon the golden screen. To drive on the moor then was to drive into blasts more dire. Darkness began to fall, and bitter cold it was. No birds to be seen, neither beast nor man; empty of everything it was, except sound and a marvel of dying light, and Harvey Witlow of Dinnop with a sour old nag driving from end to end of it. At Prattle Corner dusk was already abroad: there was just one shaft of light that broached a sharp-angled stack in the rickyard, an ark of darkness, along whose top the gads and wooden pins and tilted straws were miraculously fringed in the last glare. Hitching his nag to the palings he knocked at the door, and knew in the gloom that it was Mary who opened it and stood peering forth at him.

"Good evening," he said, touching his hat.

"Oh!" the girl uttered a cry, "higgler! What do you come for?" It was the longest sentence she had ever spoken to him; a sad frightened voice.

"I thought," he began, "I'd call—and see Mrs. Sadgrove. I wondered . . ."

"Mother's dead," said the girl. She drew the door farther back, as if inviting him, and he entered. The door was shut behind him, and they were alone in darkness, together. The girl was deeply grieving. Trembling, he asked the question: "What is it you tell me, Mary?"

"Mother's dead," repeated the girl, "all day, all day, all day." They were close to each other, but he could not see her. All round the house the wind roved lamentingly, shuddering at doors and windows. "She died in the night. The doctor was to have come, but he has not come all day," Mary whispered, "all day, all day. I don't understand; I have waited for him, and he has not come. She died, she was dead in her bed this morning, and I've been alone all day, all day, and I don't know what is to be done."

"I'll go for the doctor," he said hastily, but she took him by the hand and drew him into the kitchen. There was no candle lit; a fire was burning there, richly glowing embers, that laid a gaunt shadow of the table across a corner of the ceiling. Every dish on the dresser gleamed, the stone floor was rosy, and each smooth curve on the dark settle was shining like ice. Without invitation he sat down.

"No," said the girl, in a tremulous voice, "you must help me." She lit a candle: her face was white as the moon, her lips were sharply red, and her eyes were wild. "Come," she said, and he followed her behind the settle and up the stairs to a room where there was a disordered bed, and what might be a body lying under the quilt. The higgler stood still, staring at the form under the quilt. The girl, too, was still and staring. Wind dashed upon the ivy at the window and hallooed like a grieving multitude. A crumpled gown hid the body's head, but thrust from under it, almost as if to greet him, was her naked lean arm, the palm of the hand lying uppermost. At the foot of the bed was a large washing-bowl, with sponge and towels.

"You've been laying her out! Yourself!" exclaimed Witlow. The pale girl set down the candle on a chest of drawers. "Help me now," she said, and moving to the bed she lifted the crumpled gown from off the face of the dead woman, at the same time smoothing the quilt closely up to the body's chin. "I cannot put the gown on, because of her arm, it has gone stiff." She shuddered, and stood holding the gown as if offering it to the man.

He lifted that dead naked arm and tried to place it down at the body's side, but it resisted and he let go his hold. The arm swung back to its former outstretched position, as if it still lived and resented that pressure. The girl retreated from the bed with a timorous cry.

"Get me a bandage," he said, "or something we can tear up."

She gave him some pieces of linen.

"I'll finish this for you," he brusquely whispered, "you get along downstairs and take a swig of brandy. Got any brandy?"

She did not move. He put his arm around her and gently urged her to the door.

"Brandy," he repeated, "and light your candles."

He watched her go heavily down the stairs before he shut the door. Returning to the bed he lifted the quilt. The dead body was naked and smelt of soap. Dropping the quilt he lifted the outstretched arm again, like cold wax to the touch and unpliant as a sturdy sapling, and tried once more to bend it to the body's side. As he did so the bedroom door blew open with a crash. It was only a draught of the wind, and a loose latch—Mary had opened a door downstairs, perhaps—but it awed him, as if some invisible looker were there resenting his presence. He went and closed the door, the latch had a loose hasp, and tiptoeing nervously back, he seized the dreadful arm with a sudden brutal energy, and bent it by thrusting his knee violently into the hollow of the elbow. Hurriedly he slipped the gown over the head and inserted the arm in the sleeve. A strange impulse of modesty stayed him for a moment: should he call the girl and let her complete the robing of the naked body under the quilt? That preposterous pause seemed to add a new anger to the wind, and again the door sprang open. He delayed no longer, but letting it remain open, he uncovered the dead woman. As he lifted the chill body the long outstretched arm moved and tilted like the boom of a sail, but crushing it to its side he bound the limb fast with the strips of linen. So Mrs. Sadgrove was made ready for her coffin. Drawing the quilt back to her neck, with a gush of relief he glanced about the room. It was a very ordinary bedroom, bed, washstand, chest of drawers, chair, and two pictures—one of deeply religious import, and the other a little pink print, in a gilded frame, of a bouncing nude nymph recumbent upon a cloud. It was queer: a lot of people, people whom you wouldn't think it of, had that sort of picture in their bed-rooms.

Mary was now coming up the stairs again, with a glass half full of liquid. She brought it to him.

"No, you drink it," he urged, and Mary sipped the brandy.

"I've finished—I've finished," he said as he watched her, "she's quite comfortable now."

The girl looked her silent thanks at him, again holding out the glass. "No, sup it yourself," he said; but as she stood in the dim light, regarding him with her strange gaze, and still offering the drink, he took it from her, drained it at a gulp, and put the glass upon the chest, beside the candle. "She's quite comfortable now. I'm very grieved, Mary," he said with awkward kindness, "about all this trouble that's come on you."

She was motionless as a wax image, as if she had died in her steps, her hand still extended as when he took the glass from it. So piercing was her gaze that his own drifted from her face and took in again the objects in the room, the washstand, the candle on the chest, the little pink picture. The wind beat upon the ivy outside the window as if a monstrous whip were lashing its slaves.

"You must notify the registrar," he began again, "but you must see the doctor first."

"I've waited for him all day," Mary whispered, "all day. The nurse will come again soon. She went home to rest in the night." She turned towards the bed. "She has only been ill a week."

"Yes?" he lamely said. "Dear me, it is sudden."

"I must see the doctor," she continued.

"I'll drive you over to him in my gig." He was eager to do that.

"I don't know," said Mary slowly.

"Yes, I'll do that, soon's you're ready. Mary," he fumbled with his speech, "I'm not wanting to pry into your affairs, or anything as don't concern me, but how are you going to get along now? Have you got any relations?"

"No," the girl shook her head, "no."

"That's bad. What was you thinking of doing? How has she left you—things were in a baddish way, weren't they?"

"Oh no." Mary looked up quickly. "She has left me very well off. I shall go on with the farm; there's the old man and the boy —they've gone to a wedding today; I shall go on with it. She was so thoughtful for me, and I would not care to leave all this, I love it."

"But you can't do it by yourself, alone?"

"No. I'm to get a man to superintend, a working bailiff," she said.

"Oh!" And again they were silent. The girl went to the bed and lifted the covering. She saw the bound arm and then drew the quilt tenderly over the dead face. Witlow picked up his hat and found himself staring again at the pink picture. Mary took the candle preparatory to descending the stairs. Suddenly the higgler turned to her and ventured: "Did you know as she once asked me to marry you?" he blurted.

Her eyes turned from him, but he guessed—he could feel that she *had* known.

"I've often wondered why," he murmured, "why she wanted that."

"She didn't," said the girl.

That gave pause to the man; he felt stupid at once, and roved his fingers in a silly way along the roughened nap of his hat.

"Well, she asked me to," he bluntly protested.

"She knew," Mary's voice was no louder than a sigh, "that you were courting another girl, the one you married."

"But, but," stuttered the honest higgler, "if she knew that, why did she want for me to marry you?"

"She didn't," said Mary again; and again, in the pause, he did silly things to his hat. How shy this girl was, how lovely in her modesty and grief!

"I can't make tops or bottoms of it," he said, "but she asked me, as sure as God's my maker."

"I know. It was me, I wanted it."

"You!" he cried, "you wanted to marry me!"

The girl bowed her head, lovely in her grief and modesty. "She 'was against it, but I made her ask you."

"And I hadn't an idea that you cast a thought on me," he murmured. "I feared it was a sort of trick she was playing on me. I didn't understand, I had no idea that you knew about it even. And so I didn't ever ask you."

"Oh, why not, why not? I was fond of you then," whispered she. "Mother tried to persuade me against it, but I was fond of you—then."

He was in a queer distress and confusion: "Oh, if you'd only tipped me a word, or given me a sort of look," he sighed. "Oh, Mary!"

She said no more but went downstairs. He followed her and immediately fetched the lamps from his gig. As he lit the candles: "How strange," Mary said, "that you should come back just as I most needed help! I am very grateful."

"Mary, I'll drive you to the doctor's now."

She shook her head; she was smiling.

"Then I'll stay till the nurse comes."

"No, you must go. Go at once."

He picked up the two lamps and, turning at the door, said: "I'll come again tomorrow." Then the wind rushed into the room. "Good-bye," she cried, shutting the door quickly behind him.

He drove away in deep darkness, the wind howling, his thoughts strange and bitter. He had thrown away a love, a love that was dumb and hid itself. By God, he had thrown away a fortune, too! And he had forgotten all about his real errand until now, forgotten all about the loan! Well; let it go; give it up. He would give up higgling; he would take on some other job; a bailiff, a working bailiff, that was the job as would suit him, a working bailiff. Of course, there was Sophy; but still—Sophy!

Fishmonger's Fiddle (1925)

THE CHERRY TREE

THERE was uproar somewhere among the backyards of Australia Street, so alarming that people at their midday meal sat still and stared at one another. A fortnight before, murder had been done in the street, in broad daylight, with a chopper; people were nervous. An upper window was thrown open and a startled and startling head exposed.

"It's that young devil Johnny Flynn again! Killing rats!" shouted Mrs. Knatchbole, shaking her fist towards the Flynns' backyard. Mrs. Knatchbole was ugly; she had a goitred neck and a sharp skinny nose with an orb shining at its end, constant as grief.

"You wait, my boy, till your mother comes home, you just wait!" screamed this apparition, but Johnny was gazing sickly at the body of a big rat slaughtered by the dogs of his friend George. The uproar was caused by the quarrelling of the dogs, possibly for honours, but more probably as is the custom of victors, for loot.

"Bob down!" warned George, but Johnny bobbed up to catch the full anger of those baleful Knatchbole eyes. The urchin put his fingers promptly to his nose.

"Look at that for eight years old!" screamed the lady. "Eight years old 'e is! As true as God's my maker, I'll—"

The impending vow was stayed and blasted for ever, Mrs. Knatchbole being taken with a fit of sneezing, whereupon the boy uttered some derisive "Haw haws!"

So Mrs. Knatchbole met Mrs. Flynn that night as she came from work, Mrs. Flynn being a widow who toiled daily and dreadfully at a laundry and perforce left her children, except for their school hours, to their own devices. The encounter was an emphatic one, and the tired widow promised to admonish her boy.

"But it's all right, Mrs. Knatchbole, he's going from me in a week, to his uncle in London he is going, a person of wealth, and he'll be no annoyance to ye then. I'm ashamed that he misbehaves, but he's no bad boy really."

At home his mother's remonstrances reduced Johnny to repentance and silence; he felt base indeed; he wanted at once to do something great and worthy to offset it all; he wished he had got some money, he'd have gone and bought her a bottle of stout —he knew she liked stout.

"Why do ye vex people so, Johnny?" asked Mrs. Flynn wearily. "I work my fingers to the bone for ye, week in and week out. Why can't ye behave like Pomony?"

His sister was a year younger than he; her baptismal name was Mona, but Johnny's elegant mind had disliked it and so one day he rebaptized her; Pomona she became and Pomona she remained. The Flynns sat down to supper. "Never mind, mum," said the boy, kissing her as he passed, "talk to us about the cherry tree!"

The cherry tree, luxuriantly blooming, was the crown of the mother's memories of her youth and her father's farm; around the myth of its wonderful blossoms and fruit she could weave garlands of romance, and to her own mind as well as to the minds of her children it became a heavenly symbol of her old lost home, grand with acres and delightful with orchard and full pantry. What wonder that in her humorous narration the joys were multiplied and magnified until even Johnny was obliged to intervene:

"Look here, how many horses *did* your father have, mum— really, though?"

"Oh—lots, Johnny; any amount of 'em!"

"But what *sort* of horses, mum?"

"Sort! Oh—they were—they were—piebald horses—like circus horses."

Johnny looked fearfully unconvinced.

"But what did you *do* with them, mum?"

"Oh," Mrs. Flynn was very blithe, "I used to drive out with them, Johnny. Every morning before breakfast I used to drive out with my piebald horses and sit on the front seat, 'long with the butler. And we had a plum-pudding dog too, to trot under the axle . . ." But here Mrs. Flynn became vague, cast a furtive glance at this son of hers, and suddenly screamed with laughter. She recovered her ground with: "Ah, but there *was* a cherry tree, Johnny, truly!"

"What sort of a cherry tree, mum?"

"Well—a cherry tree, a beautiful cherry tree."

"A big one?"

"It was nearly as big as the house, Johnny."

"And cherries on it?"

"Cartloads, cartloads of cherries on that tree, Johnny. Cartloads! All sorts. Every kind of cherry you can think of. It *was* a lovely cherry tree."

Well, they got on with their supper, and grand it was—a polony and four or five potatoes—because Johnny was going away shortly, and ever since it was known that he was to go to London they had been having something special, like this, or sheep's trotters, or a pig's tail. Mother seemed to grow kinder and kinder to him. He wished he had some money, he would buy her a bottle of stout—he knew she liked stout.

Johnny went away to live with his uncle, but, alas, he was only two months in London before he was returned to his mother and Pomony. Uncle was an engine-driver who disclosed to his astounded nephew a passion for gardening. This was incomprehensible to Johnny Flynn. A great roaring boiling locomotive was the grandest thing in the world, Johnny had rides on it, so he knew. And it was easy for him to imagine that every gardener cherished in the darkness of his disappointed soul an unavailing passion for a steam engine, but how an engine-driver could immerse himself in the mushiness of gardening was a baffling problem. However, before he returned home he discovered one important thing from his uncle's hobby, and he sent the information to his sister:

Dear Pomona,

Uncle Henry has got a alotment and grow veggutables. He says what makes the mold is worms. You know we puled all the worms out off our garden and chukked them over Miss Natchbols wall. Well you better get some more quick a lot ask George to help you and I bring som seeds home when I comes next week by the xcursion on Moms birthday

Your sincerely brother

John Flynn

On mother's birthday Pomona met him at the station. She kissed him shyly and explained that mother was going to have a half-holiday to celebrate the double occasion and would be home with them at dinner-time.

"Pomony, did you get them worms?"

Pomona was inclined to evade the topic of worms for the garden, but fortunately her brother's enthusiasm for another gardening project tempered the wind of his indignation. When they reached home he unwrapped two parcels he had brought with him. One was a bottle of stout and the other a bag of cherries. He explained a scheme to his sister and he led her into the garden. The Flynn's backyard, mostly paved with bricks, was small and so the enclosing walls, truculently capped by chips of glass, although too low for privacy were yet too high for the growth of any cherishable plant. Johnny had certainly once reared a magnificent exhibit of two cowslips, but these had been mysteriously destroyed by the Knatchbole cat. The dank little enclosure was charged with sterility; nothing flourished there except a lot of beetles and a dauntless evergreen bush, as tall as Johnny, displaying a profusion of thick shiny leaves that you could split on your tongue and make squeakers with. Pomona showed him how to do this, and Pomona and he busied themselves in the garden until the dinner siren warned them that mother would be coming home. They hurried into the kitchen and Pomona quickly spread the cloth and the plates of food upon the table, while Johnny placed conspicuously in the centre, after laboriously extracting the stopper with a fork and a hairpin, the bottle of stout brought from London. He had been much impressed by numberless advertisements upon the hoardings respecting this attractive beverage. The children then ran off to meet their mother and they all came home together with great hilarity. Mrs. Flynn's attention having been immediately drawn to the sinister decoration of her dining-table, Pomona was requested to pour out a glass of the nectar. Johnny handed this gravely to his parent, saying:

"Many happy returns of the day, Mrs. Flynn!"

"Oh, dear, dear!" gasped his mother merrily. "You drink first!"

"Excuse me, no, Mrs. Flynn," rejoined her son, "many happy returns of the day!"

When the toast had been honoured, Pomona and Johnny looked tremendously at each other.

"Shall we?" exclaimed Pomona.

"Oh yes," decided Johnny; "come on, mum, in the garden, something marvellous!"

She followed her children into that dull little den, and happily the sun shone there for the occasion. Behold, the dauntless evergreen bush had been stripped of its leaves and upon its blossomless twig the children had hung numberless couples of ripe cherries, white and red and black.

"What do you think of it, mum?" cried the children, snatching some of the fruit and pressing it into her hands. "What do you think of it?"

"Beautiful!" said the poor woman in a tremulous voice. They stared silently at their mother until she could bear it no longer. She turned and went sobbing into the kitchen.

Clorinda Walks in Heaven (1922)

THE POOR MAN

ONE of the commonest sights in the vale was a certain man on a bicycle carrying a bag full of newspapers. He was as much a sound as a sight, for what distinguished him from all other men to be encountered there on bicycles was not his appearance, though that was noticeable; it was his sweet tenor voice, heard as he rode along singing each morning from Cobbs Mill, through Kezzal Predy Peter, Thasper, and Buzzlebury, and so on to Trinkel and Nuncton. All sorts of things he sang, ballads, chanties, bits of glees, airs from operas, hymns, and sacred anthems—he was leader of Thasper church choir—but he seemed to observe some sort of rotation in their rendering. In the forepart of the week it was hymns and anthems; on Wednesday he usually turned to modestly secular tunes; he was rolling on Thursday and Friday through a gamut of love songs and ballads undoubtedly secular and not necessarily modest, while on Saturday—particularly at eve, spent in the tap of the White Hart—his program was entirely ribald and often a little improper. But always on Sunday he was the most decorous of men, no questionable liquor passed his lips, and his comportment was a credit to the church, a model even for soberer men.

Dan Pavey was about thirty-five years old, of medium height and of medium appearance except as to his hat (a hard black bowler, which seemed never to belong to him, though he had worn it for years) and as to his nose. It was an ugly nose, big as a baby's elbow; he had been born thus, it had not been broken or maltreated, though it might have engaged in some prenatal conflict when it was malleable, since when nature had healed, but had not restored it. But there was ever a soft smile that covered his ugliness, which made it genial and said, or seemed to say: Don't make a fool of me, I am a friendly man, this is really my hat, and as for my nose—God made it so.

The six hamlets that he supplied with newspapers lie along the Icknield Vale close under the ridge of woody hills, and the inhabitants adjacent to the woods fell the beech timber and, in their own homes, turn it into rungs or stretchers for chair-manufacturers who, somewhere out of sight beyond the hills, endlessly make chair, and nothing but chair. Sometimes in a wood itself there may be seen a shanty built of faggots in which sits a man turning pieces of chair on a treadle lathe. Tall, hollow, and greenly dim are the woods, very solemn places, and they survey the six little towns as a man might look at six tiny pebbles lying on a green rug at his feet.

One August morning the newspaper man was riding back to Thasper. The day was sparkling like a diamond, but he was not singing, he was thinking of Scroope, the new rector of Thasper parish, and the thought of Scroope annoyed him. It was not only the tone of the sermon he had preached on Sunday, "The poor we have always with us," though that was in bad taste from a man reputed rich and with a heart—people said—as hard as a door-knocker; it was something more vital, a congenital difference between them as profound as it was disagreeable. The Rev. Faudel Scroope was wealthy, he seemed to have complete confidence in his ability to remain so, and he was the kind of man with whom Dan Pavey would never be able to agree. As for Mrs. Scroope, gloom pattered upon him in a strong sighing shower at the least thought of her.

At Larkspur Lane he came suddenly upon the rector talking to an oldish man, Eli Bond, who was hacking away at a hedge. Scroope never wore a hat, he had a curly bush of dull hair. Though his face was shaven clean it remained a regular plantation of ridges and wrinkles; there was a stoop in his shoulders, a lurch in his gait, and he had a voice that howled.

"Just a moment, Pavey," he bellowed, and Dan dismounted.

"All those years," the parson went on talking to the hedger; "all those years, dear me!"

"I were born in Thasper sixty-six year ago, come the 23rd of October, sir, the same day—but two years before—as Lady Hesseltine eloped with Rudolf Moxley. I was reared here and I worked here sin' I were six year old. Twalve children I have had (though five on 'em come to naught and two be in the army) and I never knowed what was to be out of work for one single day in all that sixty year. Never. I can't thank my blessed master enough for it."

"Isn't that splendidly feudal," murmured the priest, "who is your good master?"

The old man solemnly touched his hat and said: "God."

"Oh, I see, yes, yes," cried the Rev. Mr. Scroope. "Well, good health and constant, and good work and plenty of it, are glorious things. The man who has never done a day's work is a dog, and the man who deceives his master is a dog too."

"I never donn that, sir."

"And you've had happy days in Thasper, I'm sure?"

"Right-a-many, sir."

"Splendid. Well—um—what a heavy rain we had in the night."

"Ah, that *was* heavy! At five o'clock this morning I daren't let my ducks out—they'd a bin drowned, sir."

"Ha, now, now, now!" warbled the rector as he turned away with Dan.

"Capital old fellow, happy and contented. I wish there were more of the same breed. I wish . . ." The parson sighed pleasantly as he and Dan walked on together until they came to the village street, where swallows were darting and flashing very low. A small boy stood about, trying to catch them in his hands as they swooped close to him. Dan's own dog pranced up to his master for a greeting. It was black, somewhat like a greyhound, but stouter. Its tail curled right over its back and it was cocky as a bird, for it was young; it could fight like a tiger and run like the wind—many a hare had had proof of that.

Said Mr. Scroope, eyeing the dog: "Is there much poaching goes on here?"

"Poaching, sir?"

"I am told there is. I hope it isn't true for I have rented most of the shooting myself."

"I never heard tell of it, sir. Years ago, maybe. The Buzzlebury chaps one time were rare hands at taking a few birds, so I've heard, but I shouldn't think there's an onlicensed gun for miles around."

"I'm not thinking so much of guns. Farmer Prescott had his warren netted by someone last week and lost fifty or sixty rabbits. There's scarcely a hare to be seen, and I find wires wherever I go. It's a crime like anything else, you know," Scroope's voice was loud and strident, "and I shall deal very severely with poaching of any kind. Oh yes, you have to, you know, Pavey. Oh yes. There was a man in my last parish was a poacher, cunning scoundrel of

the worst type, never did a stroke of work, and *he* had a dog, it
wasn't unlike your dog—this is your dog, isn't it? You haven't
got your name on its collar, you should have your name on a
dog's collar—well, he had a perfect brute of a dog, carried off my
pheasants by the dozen; as for hares, he exterminated them. Man
never did anything else, but we laid him by the heels and in the
end I shot the dog myself."

"Shot it?" said Dan. "No, I couldn't tell a poacher if I was to
see one. I know no more about 'em than a bone in the earth."

"We shall be," continued Scroope, "very severe with them. Let
me see—are you singing the Handel on Sunday evening?"

"*He Shall Feed His Flock,* sir, *like a Shepherd.*"

"Splendid! *Good* day, Pavey."

Dan, followed by his bounding, barking dog, pedalled home
to a little cottage that seemed to sag under the burden of its own
thatch; it had eaves a yard wide, and birds' nests in the roof at
least ten years old. Here Dan lived with his mother, Meg Pavey,
for he had never married. She kept an absurd little shop for the
sale of sweets, vinegar, boot buttons, and such things, and was a
very excellent old dame, but as naïve as she was vague. If you
went in to her counter for a newspaper and banged down a halfcrown she would as likely as not give you change for sixpence—
until you mentioned the discrepancy, when she would smilingly
give you back your halfcrown again.

Dan passed into the back room, where Meg was preparing
dinner, threw off his bag, and sat down without speaking. His
mother was making a heavy succession of journeys between the
table and a larder.

"Mrs. Scroope's been here," said Meg, bringing a loaf to the
table.

"What did *she* want?"

"She wanted to reprimand me."

"And what have *you* been doing?"

Meg was in the larder again. " 'Tis not me, 'tis you."

"What do you mean, mother?"

"She's been a-hinting," here Meg pushed a dish of potatoes to
the right of the bread, and a salt-cellar to the left of the yawning

remains of a rabbit pie, "about your not being a teetotal. She says the boozing do give the choir a bad name and I was to persuade you to give it up."

"I should like to persuade her it was time she is dead. I don't go for to take any pattern from that rich trash. Are we the grass under their feet? And can you tell me why parsons' wives are always so much more awful than the parsons themselves? I never shall understand that if I lives a thousand years. Name o' God, what next?"

"Well, 'tis as she says. Drink is no good to any man, and she can't say as I ain't reprimanded you."

"Name o' God," he replied, "do you think I booze just for the sake o' the booze, because I like booze? No man does that. He drinks so that he shan't be thought a fool, or rank himself better than his mates—though he knows in his heart he might be if he weren't so poor or so timid. Not that one would mind to be poor if it warn't preached to him that he must be contented. How can the poor be contented as long as there's the rich to serve? The rich we have always with *us,* that's *our* responsibility, we are the grass under their feet. Why should we be proud of that? When a man's poor the only thing left him is hope—for something better; and that's called envy. If you don't like your riches you can always give it up, but poverty you can't desert, nor it won't desert you."

"It's no good flying in the face of everything like that, Dan, it's folly."

"If I had my way I'd be an independent man and live by myself a hundred miles from anywheres or anybody. But that's madness, that's madness, the world don't expect you to go on like that, so I do as other folks do, not because I want to, but because I a'nt the pluck to be different. You taught me a good deal, mother, but you never taught me courage and I wasn't born with any, so I drinks with a lot of fools who drink with me for much the same reason, I expect. It's the same with other things besides drink."

His indignation lasted throughout the afternoon as he sat in the shed in his yard turning out his usual quantity of chair. He sang not one note, he but muttered and mumbled over all his anger. Towards evening he recovered his amiability and began to sing with a gusto that astonished even his mother. He went out into the dusk humming like a bee, taking his dog with him. In the morning the Rev. Mr. Scroope found a dead hare tied by the neck to his own door-knocker, and at night (it being Saturday) Dan Pavey was merrier than ever in the White Hart. If he was not drunk he was what Thasper calls "tightish," and had never before sung so many of those ribald songs (mostly of his own composition) for which he was noted.

A few evenings later Dan attended a meeting of the Church Men's Guild. A group of very mute countrymen sat in the village hall and were goaded into speech by the rector.

"Thasper," declared Mr. Scroope, "has a great name for its singing. All over the six hamlets there is surprising musical genius. There's the Buzzlebury band—it is a capital band."

"It is that," interrupted a maroon-faced butcher from Buzzlebury, "it can play as well at nine o'clock in the morning as it can at nine o'clock at night, and that's a good band as can do it."

"Now I want our choir to compete at the county musical festival next year. Thasper is going to show those highly trained choristers what a native choir is capable of. Yes, and I'm sure our friend Pavey can win the tenor solo competition. Let us all put our backs into it and work agreeably and consistently. Those are the two main springs of good human conduct—consistency and agreeability. The consistent man will always attain his legitimate ends, always. I remember a man in my last parish, Tom Turkem, known and loved throughout the county; he was not only the best cricketer in our village, he was the best for miles around. He revelled in cricket, and cricket only; he played cricket and lived for cricket. The years went on and he got old, but he never dreamed of giving up cricket. His bowling average got larger every year and his batting average got smaller, but he still went on, consistent as ever. His order of going in dropped down to No. 6 and he seldom bowled; then he got down to No. 8 and never bowled. For a season or two the once famous Tom Turkem was really the last man in! After that he became umpire, then scorer, and then he died. He had got a little money, very little, just enough to live comfortably on. No, he never married. He was a very happy, hearty, hale old man. So you see? Now there is a cricket club at Buzzlebury, and one at Trinkel. Why not a cricket club at Thasper? Shall we do that? . . . Good!"

The parson went on outlining his projects, and although it was plain to Dan that the Rev. Mr. Scroope had very little, if any, compassion for the weaknesses natural to mortal flesh, and attached an extravagant value to the virtues of decency, sobriety, consistency, and, above all, loyalty to all sorts of incomprehensible notions, yet his intentions were undeniably agreeable and the Guild was consistently grateful.

"One thing, Pavey," said Scroope when the meeting had dispersed, "one thing I will not tolerate in this parish, and that is gambling."

"Gambling? I have never gambled in my life, sir. I couldn't tell you hardly the difference between spades and clubs."

"I am speaking of horse-racing, Pavey."

"Now that's a thing I never see in my life, Mr. Scroope."

"Ah, you need not go to the races to bet on horses; the slips of paper and money can be collected by men who are agents for racing bookmakers. And that is going on all round the six hamlets, and the man who does the collecting, even if he does not bet himself, is a social and moral danger, he is a criminal, he is against the law. Whoever he is," said the vicar, moderating his voice, but confidently beaming and patting Dan's shoulder, "I shall stamp him out mercilessly. *Good* night, Pavey."

Dan went away with murder in his heart. Timid strangers here and there had fancied that a man with such a misshapen face would be capable of committing a crime, not a mere peccadillo—you wouldn't take notice of that, of course—but a solid substantial misdemeanour like murder. And it was true, he *was* capable of murder—just as everybody else is, or ought to be. But he was also capable of curbing that distressing tendency in the usual way, and in point of fact he never did commit a murder.

These rectorial denunciations troubled the air but momentarily, and he still sang gaily as beautifully on his daily ride from Cobbs Mill along the little roads to Trinkel and Nuncton. The hanging richness of the long woods yellowing on the fringe of autumn, the long solemn hills themselves, cold sunlight, coloured berries in briary loops, the brown small leaves of hawthorn that had begun to drop from the hedge and flutter in the road like dying moths, teams of horses sturdily ploughing, sheepfolds already thatched into little nooks where the ewes could lie—Dan said—as warm as a pudding: these things filled him with tiny ecstasies too incoherent for him to transcribe—he could only sing.

On Bonfire Night the lads of the village lit a great fire on the space opposite the White Hart. Snow was falling; it was not freezing weather, but the snow lay in a soft thin mat upon the road. Dan was returning on his bicycle from a long journey and the light from the bonfire was cheering. It lit up the courtyard of the inn genially and curiously, for the recumbent hart upon the balcony had a pad of snow upon its wooden nose, which somehow made it look like a camel, in spite of the huddled snow on its back, which gave it the resemblance of a sheep. A few boys stood with bemused wrinkled faces before the roaring warmth. Dan dismounted very carefully opposite the blaze, for a tiny boy rode on the back of the bicycle, wrapped up and tied to the frame by a long scarf; very small, very silent, about five years old. A red wool wrap was bound round his head and ears and chin, and a green scarf encircled his neck and waist, almost hiding his jacket; gaiters of grey wool were drawn up over his knickerbockers. Dan lifted him down and stood him in the road, but he was so cumbered with clothing that he could scarcely walk. He was shy; he may have thought it ridiculous; he moved a few paces and turned to stare at his footmarks in the snow.

"Cold?" asked Dan.

The child shook its head solemnly at him and then put one hand in Dan's and gazed at the fire that was bringing a brightness into the long-lashed dark eyes and tenderly flushing the pale face.

"Hungry?"

The child did not reply. It only silently smiled when the boys brought him a lighted stick from the faggots. Dan caught him up into his arms and pushed the cycle across the way into his own home.

Plump Meg had just shredded up two or three red cabbages and rammed them into a crock with a shower of peppercorns and some terrible knots of ginger. There was a bright fire and a sharp odour of vinegar—always some strange pleasant smell in Meg Pavey's home—she had covered the top of the crock with a shield of brown paper, pinioned that with string, licked a label: "Cabege Novenbr 5t," and smoothed it on the crock, when the latch lifted and Dan carried in his little tiny boy.

"Here he is, mother."

Where Dan stood him, there the child remained; he did not seem to see Mother Pavey, his glance had happened to fall on the big crock with the white label—and he kept it there.

"Who ever's that?" asked the astonished Meg with her arms akimbo as Dan began to unwrap the child.

"That's mine," said her son, brushing a few flakes of snow from the curls on its forehead.

'Yours! How long have it been yours?"

"Since 'twas born. No, let him alone, I'll undo him, he's full up wi' pins and hooks. I'll undo him."

Meg stood apart while Dan unravelled his offspring.

"But it is not your child, surely, Dan?"

"Ay, I've brought him home for keeps, mother. He can sleep wi' me."

"Who's its mother?"

" 'Tis no matter about that. Dan Cupid did it."

"You're making a mock of me. Who is his mother? Where is she? You're fooling, Dan, you're fooling!"

"I'm making no mock of anyone. There, there's a bonny grandson for you!"

Meg gathered the child into her arms, peering into its face, perhaps to find some answer to the riddle, perhaps to divine a familiar likeness. But there was nothing in its soft smooth features that at all resembled her rugged Dan's.

"Who are you? What's your little name?"

The child whispered: "Martin."

"It's a pretty, pretty thing, Dan."

"Ah!" said her son, "that's his mother. We were rare fond of each other—once. Now she's wedd'n another chap and I've took the boy, for it's best that way. He's five year old. Don't ask me about her, it's *our* secret and always has been. It was a good secret and a grand secret, and it was well kept. That's her ring."

The child's thumb had a ring upon it, a golden ring with a small green stone. The thumb was crooked, and he clasped the ring safely.

For a while Meg asked no more questions about the child. She pressed it tenderly to her bosom.

But the long-kept secret, as Dan soon discovered, began to bristle with complications. The boy was his, of course it was his—he seemed to rejoice in his paternity of the quiet, pretty, illegitimate creature. As if that brazen turpitude was not enough to confound him, he was taken a week later in the act of receiving betting commissions and heavily fined in the police court, although it was quite true that he himself did not bet and was merely a collecting agent for a bookmaker who remained discreetly in the background and who promptly paid his fine.

There was naturally a great racket in the vestry about these things—there is no more rhadamanthine formation than that which can mount the ornamental forehead of a deacon—and Dan was bidden to an interview at the "Scroopery." After some hesitation he visited it.

"Ah, Pavey," said the rector, not at all minatory but very subdued and unhappy. "So the blow has fallen, in spite of my warning. I am more sorry than I can express, for it means an end to a very long connection. It is very difficult and very disagreeable for me to deal with the situation, but there is no help for it now, you must understand that. I offer no judgment upon these unfortunate events, no judgment at all, but I can find no way of avoiding my clear duty. Your course of life is incompatible with your position in the choir, and I sadly fear it reveals not only a social misdemeanour but a religious one—it is a mockery, a mockery of God."

The rector sat at a table with his head pressed on his hands. Pavey sat opposite him, and in his hands he dangled his bowler hat.

"You may be right enough in your way, sir, but I've never mocked God. For the betting, I grant you. It may be a dirty job, but I never ate the dirt myself, I never betted in my life. It's a way of life, a poor man has but little chance of earning more than a bare living, and there's many a dirty job there's no prosecution for, leastways not in this world."

"Let me say, Pavey, that the betting counts less heavily with me than the question of this unfortunate little boy. I offer no judgment upon the matter, your acknowledgment of him is only right and proper. But the fact of his existence at all cannot be disregarded; that at least is flagrant, and as far as concerns your position in my church, it is a mockery of God."

"You may be right, sir, as far as your judgment goes, or you may not be. I beg your pardon for that, but we can only measure other people by our own scales, and as we can never understand one another entirely, so we can't ever judge them rightly, for they all differ from us and from each other in some special ways. But as for being a mocker of God, why, it looks to me as if you was trying to teach the Almighty how to judge me."

"Pavey," said the rector with solemnity, "I pity you from the bottom of my heart. We won't continue this painful discussion, we should both regret it. There was a man in the parish where I came from who was an atheist and mocked God. He subsequently became deaf. Was he convinced? No, he was not—because the punishment came a long time after his offence. He mocked God again, and became blind. Not at once: God has eternity to work in. Still he was not convinced. That," said the rector ponderously, "is what the Church has to contend with; a failure to read the most obvious signs, and an indisposition even to remedy that failure. Klopstock was that poor man's name. His sister—you know her well, Jane Klopstock—is now my cook."

The rector then stood up and held out his hand. "God bless you, Pavey."

"I thank you, sir," said Dan. "I quite understand."

He went home moodily reflecting. Nobody else in the village minded his misdeeds, they did not care a button, and none condemned him. On the contrary, indeed. But the blow had fallen, there was nothing that he could now do, the shock of it had been anticipated, but it was severe. And the pang would last, for he was deprived of his chief opportunity for singing, that art in which he excelled, in that perfect quiet setting he so loved. Rancour grew upon him, and on Saturday he had a roaring audacious evening at the White Hart, where, to the tune of *The British Grenadiers,* he sung a doggerel:

> Our parson loves his motor car,
>   His garden and his mansion,
> And he loves his beef for I've remarked
>   His belly's brave expansion;
> He loves all mortal mundane things
>   As he loved his beer at college,
> And so he loves his housemaid (not
>   With Mrs. parson's knowledge).

> Our parson lies both hot and strong,
>   It does not suit his station,
> But still his reverend soul delights
>   In much dissimulation;
> Both in and out and roundabout
>   He practises distortion,
> And he lies with a public sinner when
>   Grass widowhood's his portion.

All of which was a savage libel on a very worthy man, composed in anger and regretted as soon as sung.

From that time forward Dan gave up his boozing and devoted himself to the boy, little Martin, who, a Thasper joker suggested, might have some kinship with the notorious Betty of that name. But Dan's voice was now seldom heard singing upon the roads he travelled. They were icy wintry roads, but that was not the cause of his muteness. It was severance from the choir; not from its connoted spirit of religion—there was little enough of that in Dan Pavey—but from the solemn beauty of the chorale, which it was his unique gift to adorn, and in which he had shared with eagerness and pride since his boyhood. To be cast out from that was to be cast from something he held most dear, the opportunity of expression in an art which he had made triumphantly his own.

With the coming of spring he repaired one evening to a town

some miles away and interviewed a choirmaster. Thereafter Dan Pavey journeyed to and fro twice every Sunday to sing in a church that lay seven or eight miles off, and he kept it all a profound secret from Thasper until his appearance at the county musical festival, where he won the treasured prize for tenor soloists. Then Dan was himself again. To his crude apprehension he had been vindicated, and he was heard once more carolling in the lanes of the vale as he had been heard any time for these twenty years.

The child began its schooling, but though he was free to go about the village little Martin did not wander far. The tidy cluster of hair about his poll was of deep chestnut colour. His skin—Meg said—was like "ollobarster": it was soft and unfreckled, always pale. His eyes were two wet damsons—so Meg declared: they were dark and ever questioning. As for his nose, his lips, his cheeks, his chin, Meg could do no other than call it the face of a blessed saint; and, indeed, he had some of the bearing of a saint, so quiet, so gentle, so shy. The golden ring he no longer wore; it hung from a tintack on the bedroom wall.

Old John, who lived next door, became a friend of his. He was very aged—in the vale you got to be a hundred before you knew where you were—and he was very bent; he resembled a sickle standing upon its handle. Very bald, too, and so very sharp.

Martin was staring up at the roof of John's cottage.

"What you looking at, my boy?"

"Chimbley," whispered the child.

"Oh ah! that's crooked, a'nt it?"

"Yes, crooked."

"I know 'tis, but I can't help it; my chimney's crooked, and I can't putt it straight, neither, I can't putt it right. My chimney's crooked, a'nt it, ah, and I'm crooked, too."

"Yes," said Martin.

"I know, but I can't help it. It *is* crooked, a'nt it?" said the old man, also staring up at a red pot tilted at an angle suggestive of conviviality.

"Yes."

"That chimney's crooked. But you come along and look at my beautiful bird."

A cock thrush inhabited a cage in the old gaffer's kitchen. Martin stood before it.

"There's a beautiful bird. Hoicks!" cried old John, tapping the bars of the cage with his terrible fingernail. "But he won't sing."

"Won't he sing?"

"He donn make hisself at home. He donn make hisself at home at all, do 'ee, my beautiful bird? No, he donn't. So I'm a-going to chop his head off," said the laughing old man, "and then I shall bile him."

Afterwards Martin went every day to see if the thrush was still there. And it was.

Martin grew. Almost before Dan was aware of it the child had grown into a boy. At school he excelled nobody in anything except, perhaps, behaviour, but he had a strange little gift for unobtrusively not doing the things he did not care for, and these were rather many unless his father was concerned in them. Even so, the affection between them was seldom tangibly expressed, their alliance was something far deeper than its expression. Dan talked with him as if he were a grown man, and perhaps he often regarded him as one; he was the only being to whom he ever opened his mind. As they sat together in the evening while Dan put in a spell at turning chair—at which he was astoundingly adept—the father would talk to his son, or rather he would heap upon him all the unuttered thoughts that had accumulated in his mind during his adult years. The dog would loll with its head on Martin's knees; the boy would sit nodding gravely, though seldom speaking: he was an untiring listener. "Like sire, like son," thought Dan, "he will always coop his thoughts up within himself." It was the one characteristic of the boy that caused him anxiety.

"Never take pattern by me," he would adjure him, "not by me. I'm a fool, a failure, just grass, and I'm trying to instruct you, but you've no call to follow in my fashion; I'm a weak man. There's been thoughts in my mind that I daren't let out. I wanted to do things that other men don't seem to do and don't want to do. They were not evil things—and what they were I've nigh forgotten now. I never had much ambition, I wasn't clever, I wanted to live a simple life, in a simple way, the way I had a mind to—

I can't remember that either. But I did not do any of those things because I had a fear of what other people might think of me. I walked in the ruck with the rest of my mates and did the things I didn't ever want to do—and now I can only wonder why I did them. I sung them the silly songs they liked, and not the ones I cherished. I agreed with most everybody, and all agreed with me. I'm a friendly man, too friendly, and I went back on my life, I made nought of my life, you see, I just sat over the job like a snob codgering an old boot."

The boy would sit regarding him as if he already understood. Perhaps that curious little mind did glean some flavour of his father's tragedy.

"You've no call to follow me, you'll be a scholar. Of course I know some of those long words at school take a bit of licking together—like 'elephant' and 'saucepan.' You get about half-way through 'em and then you're done, you're mastered. I was just the same (like sire, like son), and I'm no better now. If you and me was to go to yon school together, and set on the same stool together, I warrant you would win the prize and I should wear the dunce's cap—all except sums, and there I should beat ye. You'd have all the candy and I'd have all the cane, you'd be king and I'd be the dirty rascal, so you've no call to follow me. What you want is courage, and to do the things you've a mind to. I never had any and I didn't."

Dan seldom kissed his son, neither of them sought that tender expression, though Meg was for ever ruffling the boy for these pledges of affection, and he was always gracious to the old woman. There was a small mole in the centre of her chin, and in the centre of the mole grew one short stiff hair. It was a surprise to Martin when he first kissed her.

Twice a week father and son bathed in the shed devoted to chair. The tub was the half of a wooden barrel. Dan would roll up two or three buckets of water from the well, they would both strip to the skin, the boy would kneel in the tub and dash the water about his body for a few moments. While Martin towelled himself Dan stepped into the tub and after laving his face and hands and legs he would sit down in it. "Ready?" Martin would ask, and scooping up the water in an iron basin he would pour it over his father's head.

"Name o' God, that's sharpish this morning," Dan would say, "it would strip the bark off a crocodile. Broo-o-o-oh! But there: winter and summer I go up and down the land and there's not— broo-o-o-oh!—a mighty difference between 'em, it's mostly fancy. Come day, go day, frost or fair doings, all alike I go about the land, and there's little in winter I haven't the heart to rejoice in. (On with your breeches or I'll be at the porridge pot afore you're clad.) All their talk about winter and their dread of it shows poor spirit. Nothing's prettier than a fall of snow, nothing more grand than the storms upending the woods. There's no more rain in winter than in summer, you can be shod for it, and there's a heart back of your ribs that's proof against any blast. (Is this my shirt or yours? Dashed if they buttons a'nt the plague of my life.) Country is grand year's end to year's end, whether or no. I once lived in London—only a few weeks—and for noise, and for terror, and for filth—name o' God, there was bugs in the butter there, once there was!"

But the boy's chosen season was that time of year when the plums ripened. Pavey's garden was then a tiny paradise.

"You put a spell on these trees," Dan would declare to his son every year when they gathered the fruit. "I planted them nearly twenty years ago, two 'gages and one magny bonum, but they never growed enough to make a pudden. They always bloomed well and looked well. I propped 'em and I dunged 'em, but they wouldn't beer at all, and I'm a-going to cut 'em down—when along comes you!"

Well, hadn't those trees borne remarkable ever since he'd come there?

"Of course, good luck's deceiving, and it's never bothered our family overmuch. Still, bad luck is one thing and bad life's another. And yet—I dunno—they come to much the same in the end, there's very little difference. There's so much misunderstanding, half the folks don't know their own good intentions, nor all the love that's sunk deep in their own minds."

But nothing in the world gave (or could give) Dan such flattering joy as his son's sweet treble voice. Martin could sing! In the dark months no evening passed without some instruction by the proud father. The living-room at the back of the shop was the tiniest of rooms, and its smallness was not lessened, nor its tidiness increased, by the stacks of merchandise that had strayed from Meg's emporium into every corner, and overflowed every shelf in packages, piles, and bundles. The metalliferous categories—iron nails, lead pencils, tintacks, zinc ointment, and brass hinges—were there. Platoons of bottles were there, bottles of blue-black writing fluid, bottles of scarlet—and presumably plebeian—ink, bottles of lollipops and of oil (both hair and castor). Balls of string, of blue, of peppermint, and balls to bounce were adjacent to an assortment of prim-looking books—account, memorandum, exercise, and note. But the room was cosy, and if its inhabitants fitted it almost as closely as birds fit their nests, they were as happy as birds, few of whom (save the swallows) sing in their nests. With pitchpipe to hand and a bundle of music before them Dan and Martin would begin. The dog would snooze on the rug before the fire; Meg would snooze amply in her armchair until roused by the sudden terrific tinkling of her shop-bell. She would waddle off to her dim little shop—every step she took rattling the paraffin lamp on the table, the coal in the scuttle, and sometimes the very panes in the window—and the dog would clamber into her chair. Having supplied an aged gaffer with an ounce of caraway seed, or some gay lad with a packet of cigarettes, Meg would waddle back and sink down upon the dog, whereupon its awful indignation would sound to the very heavens, drowning the voices even of Dan and his son.

"What shall we wind up with?" Dan would ask at the close of the lesson, and as often as not Martin would say: "You must sing 'Timmie.'"

This was "Timmie," and it had a tune something like the chorus to "Father O'Flynn":

> O Timmie my brother,
> Best son of our mother,
> Our labour it prospers, the mowing is done;
> A holiday take you,
> The loss it won't break you,
> A day's never lost if a holiday's won.
>
> We'll go with clean faces
> To see the horse-races,
> And if the luck chances we'll gather some gear;

But never a jockey
Will win it, my cocky,
Who catches one glance from a girl I know there.

There's lords and there's ladies
Wi' pretty sunshadies,
And farmers and jossers and fat men and small;
But the pride of these trips is
The scallywag gypsies
Wi' not a whole rag to the backs of 'em all.

There's cokernut shying,
And devil-defying,
And a racket and babel to hear and to see,
Wi' boxing and shooting,
And fine highfaluting
From chaps wi' a table and thimble and pea.

My Nancy will be there,
The best thing to see there,
She'll win all the praises wi' ne'er a rebuke;
And she has a sister—
I wonder you've missed her—
As sweet as the daisies and fit for a duke.

Come along, brother Timmie,
Don't linger, but gimme
My hat and my purse and your company there;
For sporting and courting,
The cream of resorting,
And nothing much worse, Timmie—come to the fair.

On the third anniversary of Martin's homecoming Dan rose up
very early in the dark morn, and leaving his son sleeping he
crept out of the house followed by his dog. They went away from
Thasper, though the darkness was profound and the grass filled
with dew, out upon the hills towards Chapel Cheary. The night
was starless, but Dan knew every trick and turn of the paths, and
after an hour's walk he met a man waiting by a signpost. They
conversed for a few minutes and then went off together, the dog

at their heels, until they came to a field gate. Upon this they
fastened a net and then sent the dog into the darkness upon his
errand, while they waited for the hare which the dog would drive
into the net. They waited so long that it was clear the dog had
not drawn its quarry. Dan whistled softly, but the dog did not
return. Dan opened the gate and went down the fields himself,
scouring the hedges for a long time, but he could not find the dog.
The murk of the night had begun to lift, but the valley was filled
with mist. He went back to the gate: the net had been taken
down, his friend had departed—perhaps he had been disturbed?
The dog had now been missing for an hour. Dan still hung
about, but neither friend nor dog came back. It grew grey and
more grey, though little could be distinguished, the raw mist
obscuring everything that the dawn uncovered. He shivered with
gloom and dampness, his boots were now as pliable as gloves,
his eyebrows had grey drops upon them, so had his moustache and
the backs of his hands. His dark coat looked as if it was made of
grey wool; it was tightly buttoned around his throat and he
stood with his chin crumpled, unconsciously holding his breath
until it burst forth in a gasp. But he could not abandon his dog,
and he roamed once more down into the misty valley towards
woods that he knew well, whistling softly and with great caution
a repetition of two notes.

And he found his dog. It was lying on a heap of dead sodden
leaves. It just whimpered. It could not rise, it could not move, it
seemed paralysed. Dawn was now really upon them. Dan wanted
to get the dog away, quickly, it was a dangerous quarter, but
when he lifted it to his feet the dog collapsed like a scarecrow. In
a flash Dan knew he was poisoned, he had probably picked up
some piece of dainty flesh that a farmer had baited for the foxes.
He seized a knob of chalk that lay thereby, grated some of it into
his hands, and forced it down the dog's throat. Then he tied the
lead to its neck. He was going to drag the dog to its feet and
force it to walk. But the dog was past all energy, it was limp and
mute. Dan dragged him by the neck for some yards as a man
draws behind him a heavy sack. It must have weighed three
stone, but Dan lifted him on to his own shoulders and staggered
back up the hill. He carried it thus for half a mile, but then he

was still four miles from home, and it was daylight, at any moment he might meet somebody he would not care to meet. He entered a ride opening into some coverts and, bending down, slipped the dog over his head to rest upon the ground. He was exhausted and felt giddy, his brains were swirling round—trying to slop out of his skull—and—yes—the dog was dead, his old dog dead. When he looked up, he saw a keeper with a gun standing a few yards off.

"Good morning," said Dan. All his weariness was suddenly gone from him.

"I'll have your name and address," replied the keeper, a giant of a man, with a sort of contemptuous affability.

"What for?"

"You'll hear about what for," the giant grinned. "I'll be sure to let ye know, in doo coorse." He laid his gun upon the ground and began searching in his pockets, while Dan stood up with rage in his heart and confusion in his mind. So the Old Imp was at him again!

"Humph!" said the keeper. "I've alost my notebook some-wheres. Have you got a bit of paper on ye?"

The culprit searched his pockets and produced a folded frag-ment.

"Thanks." The giant did not cease to grin. "What is it?"

"What?" queried Dan.

"Your name and address."

"Ah, but what do you want it for. What do you think I'm doing?" protested Dan.

"I've a net in my pocket which I took from a gate about an hour ago. I saw summat was afoot, and me and a friend o' mine have been looking for 'ee. Now let's have your name and no nonsense."

"My name," said Dan, "my name? Well, it is—Piper."

"Piper is it, ah! Was you baptized ever?"

"Peter," said Dan savagely.

"Peter Piper! Well, you've picked a tidy peppercarn this time."

Again he was searching his pockets. There was a frown on his face. "You'd better lend me a bit o' pencil too."

Dan produced a stump of lead pencil, and the gamekeeper,

smoothing the paper on his lifted knee, wrote down the name of Peter Piper.

"And where might you come from?" He peered up at the miserable man, who replied: "From Leasington"—naming a village several miles to the west of his real home.

"Leasington!" commented the other. "You must know John Eustace, then?" John Eustace was a sporting farmer famed for his stock and his riches.

"Know him!" exclaimed Dan. "He's my uncle!"

"Oh ah!" The other carefully folded the paper and put it into his breast pocket. "Well, you can trot along home now, my lad."

Dan knelt down and unbuckled the collar from his dead dog's neck. He was fond of his dog, it looked piteous now. And kneeling there it suddenly came upon Dan that he had been a coward again, he had told nothing but lies, foolish lies, and he had let a great hulking flunkey walk roughshod over him. In one astonishing moment the reproving face of his little son seemed to loom up beside the dog, the blood flamed in his brain.

"I'll take charge of that," said the keeper, snatching the collar from his hand.

"Blast you!" Dan sprang to his feet, and suddenly screaming like a madman: "I'm Dan Pavey of Thasper," he leaped at the keeper with a fury that shook even that calm stalwart.

"You would, would ye?" he yapped, darting for his gun. Dan also seized it, and in their struggle the gun was fired off harmlessly between them. Dan let go.

"My God!" roared the keeper, "you'd murder me, would ye? Wi' my own gun, would ye?" He struck Dan a swinging blow with the butt of it, yelling: "Would ye? Would ye? Would ye?" And he did not cease striking until Dan tumbled senseless and bloody across the body of the dog.

Soon another keeper came hurrying through the trees.

"Tried to murder me—wi' me own gun, he did," declared the big man, "wi' me own gun!"

They revived the stricken Pavey after a while and then conveyed him to a policeman, who conveyed him to a jail.

The magistrates took a grave view of the case and sent it for trial at the assizes. They were soon held, he had not long to wait, and before the end of November he was condemned. The assize court was a place of intolerable gloom, intolerable formality, intolerable pain, but the public seemed to enjoy it. The keeper swore Dan had tried to shoot him, and the prisoner contested this. He did not deny that he was the aggressor. The jury found him guilty. What had he to say? He had nothing to say, but he was deeply moved by the spectacle of the Rev. Mr. Scroope standing up and testifying to his sobriety, his honesty, his general good repute, and pleading for a lenient sentence because he was a man of considerable force of character, misguided no doubt, a little unfortunate, and prone to recklessness.

Said the judge, examining the papers of the indictment: "I see there is a previous conviction—for betting offences."

"That was three years ago, my lord. There has been nothing of the kind since, my lord, of that I am sure, quite sure."

Scroope showed none of his old-time confident aspect, he was perspiring and trembling. The clerk of the assize leaned up and held a whispered colloquy with the judge, who then addressed the rector.

"Apparently he is still a betting agent. He gave a false name and address, which was taken down by the keeper on a piece of paper furnished by the prisoner. Here it is, on one side the name of Peter Pope" ("Piper, sir!") "Piper: and on the other side this is written:

3 o/c race.   *Pretty Dear*, 5/- *to win*.   *J. Klopstock*.

Are there any Klopstocks in your parish?"

"Klopstock!" murmured the parson; "it is the name of my cook."

What had the prisoner to say about that? The prisoner had nothing to say, and he was sentenced to twelve months' imprisonment with hard labour.

So Dan was taken away. He was a tough man, an amenable man, and the mere rigours of the prison did not unduly afflict him. His behaviour was good, and he looked forward to gaining the maximum remission of his sentence. Meg, his mother, went to see him once, alone, but she did not repeat the visit. The prison chaplain paid him special attention. He, too, was a Scroope, a

huge fellow, not long from Oxford, and Pavey learned that he
was related to the Thasper rector. The new year came, February
came, March came, and Dan was afforded some privileges. His
singing in chapel was much admired, and occasionally he was allowed to sing to the prisoners. April came, May came, and then
his son Martin was drowned in a boating accident, on a lake, in
a park. The Thasper children had been taken there for a holiday.
On hearing it, Pavey sank limply to the floor of his cell. The
warders sat him up, but they could make nothing of him, he was
dazed, and he could not speak. He was taken to the hospital
wing. "This man has had a stroke, he is gone dumb," said the
doctor. On the following day he appeared to be well enough, but
still he could not speak. He went about the ward doing hospital
duty, dumb as a ladder; he could not even mourn, but a jig kept
flickering through his voiceless mind:

> In a park there was a lake,
> On the lake there was a boat,
> In the boat there was a boy.

Hour after hour the stupid jingle flowed through his consciousness. Perhaps it kept him from going mad, but it did not
bring him back his speech, he was dumb, dumb. And he remembered a man who had been stricken deaf, and then blind—
Scroope knew him too, it was some man who had mocked God.

> In a park there was a lake,
> On the lake there was a boat,
> In the boat there was a boy.

On the day of the funeral Pavey imagined that he had been
let out of prison; he dreamed that someone had been kind and
set him free for an hour or two to bury his dead boy. He seemed
to arrive at Thasper when the ceremony was already begun, the
coffin was already in the church. Pavey knelt down beside his
mother. The rector intoned the office, the child was taken to its
grave. Dumb dreaming, Pavey turned his eyes from it. The day
was too bright for death, it was a stainless day. The wind seemed
to flow in soft streams, rolling the lilac blooms. A small white

feather, blown from a pigeon on the church gable, whirled about like a butterfly. "We give thee hearty thanks," the priest was saying, "for that it hath pleased thee to deliver this our brother out of the miseries of this sinful world." At the end of it all Pavey kissed his mother and saw himself turn back to his prison. He went by the field paths away to the railway junction. The country had begun to look a little parched, for rain was wanted—vividly he could see all this—but things were growing, corn was thriving greenly, the beanfields smelled sweet. A frill of yellow kilk and wild white carrot spray lined every hedge. Cattle dreamed in the grass, the colt stretched itself unregarded in front of its mother. Larks, wrens, yellow-hammers. There were the great beech trees and the great hills, calm and confident, overlooking Cobbs and Peter, Thasper and Trinkel, Buzzlebury and Nuncton. He sees the summer is coming on, he is going back to prison. "Courage is vain," he thinks, "we are like the grass underfoot, a blade that excels is quickly shorn. In this sort of a world the poor have no call to be proud, they had only need be penitent."

> In the park there was a lake,
> On the lake . . . . boat,
> In the boat . . . . . .

The Black Dog (1923)

THE BALLET GIRL

On the last night of Hilary term Simpkins left his father's shop a quarter before the closing-hour in order to deliver personally a letter to John Evans-Antrobus, Esq., of St. Saviour's College. Simpkins was a clerk to his father, and the letter he carried was inscribed on its envelope as "Important," and a further direction, "Wait Answer," was doubly underlined. Acting as he was told to act by his father, than whom he was incapable of recognizing any bigger authority either in this world or, if such a slight shrinking fellow could ever project his comprehension so far, in the next, he passed the porter's lodge under the archway of St. Saviour's and, crossing the first quadrangle, entered a small hall that bore the name J. Evans-Antrobus with half a dozen others neatly painted on the wall. He climbed two flights of wooden stairs, and knocking on a door whose lintel was marked "5, Evans-Antrobus," was invited to "Come in." He entered a study and confronted three hilarious young men clothed immaculately in evening dress, a costume he himself privily admired much as a derelict might envy the harp of an angel. The noisiest young gentleman, the tall one with a monocle, was his quarry; he handed the letter to him. Mr. Evans-Antrobus then read the letter, which invited him to pay instanter a four-year-old debt of some nine or ten pounds which he had inexplicably but consistently overlooked. And there was a half-hidden but unpleasant alternative suggested should Mr. Evans-Antrobus fail to comply with this not unreasonable request. Mr. Evans-Antrobus said: "Damn!" In point of fact he enlarged the scope of his vocabulary far beyond the limits of that modest expletive, while his two friends, being invited to read the missive, also exclaimed in terms that were not at all subsidiary.

"My compliments to Messrs. Bagshot and Buffle!" exclaimed the tall young man with a monocle angrily; "I shall certainly call round and see them in the morning. Good evening!"

Little Simpkins explained that Bagshot and Buffle were not in need of compliments, their business being to sell boots and to receive payment for them. Two of the jolly young gentlemen proposed to throw him down the stairs, and were only persuaded not to by the third jolly young gentleman, who much preferred to throw him out of the window. Whereupon Simpkins politely hinted that he would be compelled to interview the college dean and await developments in his chambers. Simpkins made it quite clear that, whatever happened, he was going to wait somewhere until he got the money. The three jolly young gentlemen then told little Simpkins exactly what they thought of him, exactly;

omitting no shade of denunciation, fine or emphatic. They told him where he ought to be at the very moment, where he would quickly be unless he took himself off; in short, they told him a lot of prophetic things that, as is the way of prophecy, invited a climax of catastrophic horror.

"What is your name? Who the devil are you?"

"My name is Simpkins."

Then the three jolly young gentlemen took counsel together in whispers, and at last Mr. Evans-Antrobus said: "Well, if you insist upon waiting, Mr. Simpkins, I must get the money for you. I can borrow it, I suppose, boys, from Fazz, can't I?"

Again they consulted in whispers, after which two of the young gents said they ought to be going, and so they went.

"Wait here for me," said Mr. Evans-Antrobus, "I shall not be five minutes."

But Mr. Simpkins was so firmly opposed to this course that the other relented. "Damn you! come along with me, then; I must go and see Fazz." So off they went to some rooms higher up the same flight of stairs, beyond a door that was marked "F. A. Zealander." When they entered Fazz sat moping in front of the fire; he was wrapped as deeply as an Eskimo in some plaid travelling-rugs girt with the pink rope of a dressing-gown that lay across his knees. The fire was good, but the hearth was full of ashes. The end of the fender was ornamented with the strange little iron face of a man whose eyes were shut but whose knobby cheeks fondly glowed. Fazz's eyes were not shut, they were covered by dim glasses, and his cheeks had no more glow than a sponge.

"Hullo, Fazz. You better today?"

"No, dearie, I am not conscious of any improvement. This influenza's a thug; I am being deprived of my vitality as completely as a fried rasher."

"Oh, by the by," said his friend, "you don't know each other: Mr. Simpkins—Mr. Zealander."

The former bowed awkwardly and unexpectedly shook Mr. Zealander's hot limp hand. At that moment a man hurried in, exclaiming: "Mr. Evans-Antrobus, sir, the dean wants to see you in his rooms at once, sir!"

"That is deuced awkward," said that gentleman blandly. "Just excuse me for a moment or two, Fazz."

He hurried out, leaving Simpkins confronting Mr. Zealander in some confusion. Fazz poked his flaming coal. "This fire! Did you ever see such a morbid conflagration?"

"Rather nice, I thought," replied Simpkins affably; "quite cool tonight, outside, rather."

The host peered at him through those dim glasses. "There's a foggy humidity about everything, like the inside of a cream tart. But sit down," said Fazz, with the geniality of a man who was about to be hung and was rather glad that he was no longer to be exposed to the fraudulent excess of life, "and tell me a bawdy story."

Simpkins sank into an armchair and was silent.

"Perhaps you don't care for bawdy stories?" continued Fazz. "I do, I do. I love vulgarity; there is certainly a niche in life for vulgarity. If ever I possess a house of my own I will arrange—I will, upon my soul—one augustly vulgar room, divinely vulgar, upholstered in sallow pigskin. Do tell me something. You haven't got a spanner on you, I suppose? There is something the matter with my bed. Once it was full of goose feathers, but now I sleep, as it were, on the bulge of a barrel; I must do something to it with a spanner. I hate spanners—such dreadful democratic tools; they terrify me, they gape at you as if they wanted to bite you. Spanners are made of iron, and this is a funny world, for it is full of things like spanners."

Simpkins timidly rose up through the waves of this discourse and asked if he could "do" anything. He was mystified, amused, and impressed by this person; he didn't often meet people like that, he didn't often meet anybody; he rather liked him. On each side of the invalid there were tablets and bottles of medicine.

"I am just going to take my temperature," said Fazz. "Do have a cigarette, dearie, or a cigar. Can you see the matches? Yes; now do you mind surrounding me with my medicines? They give such a hopeful air to the occasion. There's a phial of sodium salicylate tabloids, I must take six of them in a minute or two. Then there are the quinine capsules; the formalin, yes; those lozenges I suck—have one?—they are so comforting, and that depressing laxative; surround me with them. Oh, glorious, benignant, isn't it? Now I shall take my temperature; I shall be as stolid as the sphinx for three minutes, so do tell me that story. Where is my thermometer, oh!" He popped the thermometer into his mouth, but pulled it out again. "Do you know L. G.? He's a blithe little fellow, oh, very blithe. He was in Jacobsen's rooms the other day—Jacobsen's a bit of an art connoisseur, you know, and draws and paints, and Jacobsen drew attention to the portrait of a lady that was hanging on the wall. 'Oh, dear,' said L. G., 'what a hag! Where did you get that thing?' just like that. Such a perfect fool, L. G. 'It's my mother,' says Jacobsen. 'Oh, of course,' explained L. G., 'I didn't mean *that,* of course, my dear fellow; I referred to the horrible treatment, entirely to the horrible treatment; it is a wretched daub.' 'I did it myself!' said Jacobsen. You don't know L. G.? Oh, he is very blithe. What were you going to tell me? I am just going to take my temperature; yesterday it was ninety-odd point something. I do hope it is different now. I can't bear those points, they seem so equivocal."

Fazz sat with the tube of the thermometer projecting from his mouth. At the end of the test he regarded it very earnestly before returning it disconsolately to the table. Then he addressed his visitor with considerable gloom.

"Pardon me, I did not catch your name."

"Simpkins."

"Simpkins!" repeated Fazz, with a dubious drawl. "Oh, I'm sorry, I don't like Simpkins, it sounds so minuscular. What are you taking?"

"I won't take anything, sir, thank you," replied Simpkins.

"I mean, what schools are you taking?"

"Oh, no school at all."

Fazz was mystified. "What college are you?"

"I'm not at a college," confessed the other. "I came to see Mr. Evans-Antrobus with a note. I'm waiting for an answer."

"Where do you come from?"

"From Bagshot and Buffle's." After a silence he added: "Bespoke boots."

"Hump, you are very young to make bespoke boots, aren't

you, Simpkins, surely? Are you an agnostic? Have a cigar? You
must, you've been very good, and I am so interested in your
career; but tell me now what it exactly is that you are sitting in
my room for?"

Simpkins told him all he could.

"It's interesting, most fascinating," declared Fazz, "but it is
a little beyond me all the same. I am afraid, Simpkins, that you
have been deposited with me as if I were a bank, and you were
something not negotiable, as you really are, I fear. But you
mustn't tell the dean about Evans-Antrobus, no, you mustn't, it's
never done. Tell me, why do you make bespoke boots? It's an
unusual taste to display. Wouldn't you rather come to college,
for instance, and study—er—anthropology—nothing at all about
boots in anthropology?"

"No," said Simpkins. He shuffled in his chair and felt uneasy.
"I'd be out of my depth." Fazz glared at him, and Simpkins
repeated: "Out of my depth, that would be, sure."

"This is very shameful," commented the other, "but it's interesting, most fascinating. You brazenly maintain that you
would rather study boots than—than books and brains!"

"A cobbler must stick to his last," replied Simpkins, recalling
a phrase of his father's.

"Bravo!" cried Fazz, "but not to an everlasting last!"

"And I don't know anything about all this; there's nothing
about it I'd want to know, it wouldn't be any good to me. It's no
use mixing things, and there's a lot to be learnt about boots
—you'd be surprised. You got to keep yourself to yourself and not
get out of your depth—take a steady line and stick to it, and not
get out of your depth."

"But, dearie, you don't sleep with a lifebelt girt about your
loins, do you now? I'm not out of my depth; I shouldn't be
even if I started to make boots. . . ."

"Oh, wouldn't you?" shouted Simpkins.

"I should find it rather a shallow occupation; mere business is
the very devil of a business; business would be a funny sort of
life."

"Life's a funny business; you look after your business and that
will look after you."

"But what in the world are we in the world at all for, Simpkins? Isn't it surely to do just the things we most intensely want to do? And you do boots and boots and boots. Don't you ever get out and about?—theatres—girls—sport—or do you insist on boot, the whole boot, and nothing but the boot?"

"No, none of them," replied Simpkins. "Don't care for theatres, I've never been. Don't care for girls, I like a quiet life. I keep myself to myself—it's safer, don't get out of your depth then. I do go and have a look at the football match sometimes, but it's only because we make the boots for some of your crack players, and you want to know what you are making them for. Work doesn't trouble me, nothing troubles me, and I got money in the bank."

"Damme, Simpkins, you have a terrible conviction about you; if I listen to you much longer I shall bind myself apprentice to you. I feel sure that you make nice, soft, watertight, everlasting boots, and then we should rise in the profession together. Discourse, Simpkins; you enchant mine ears—both of them."

"What I say is," concluded Simpkins, "you can't understand everything. I shouldn't want to; I'm all right as it is."

"Of course you are, you're simply too true. This is a place flowing with afternoon tea, tutors, and claptrap. It's a city in which everything is set upon a bill. You're simply too true, if we are not out of our depth we are in up to our ears—I am. It's most fascinating."

Soon afterwards Simpkins left him. Descending the stairs to the rooms of Evans-Antrobus he switched on the light. It was very quiet and snug in those rooms, with the soft elegant couch, the reading-lamp with the delicious violet shade, the decanter with whisky, the box of chocolate biscuits, and the gramophone. He sat down by the fire, waiting and waiting. Simpkins waited so long that he got used to the room, he even stole a sip of whisky and some of the chocolate biscuits. Then to show his independence, his contempt for Mr. Evans-Antrobus and his trickery, he took still more of the whisky—a drink he had never tasted before—he really took quite a lot. He heaped coal upon the fire, and stalked about the room with his hands in his pockets or examined the books, most of which were about something called

Jurisprudence, and suchlike. Simpkins liked books; he began reading:

That the Pleuronectidæ are admirably adapted by their flattened and asymmetrical structure for their habits of life, is manifest from several species, such as soles and flounders, etc., being extremely common.

He did not care much for science; he opened another:

It is difficult indeed to imagine that anything can oscillate so rapidly as to strike the retina of the eye 831,479,000,000,000 in one second, as must be the case with violet light according to this hypothesis.

Simpkins looked at the light and blinked his eyes. That had a violet shade. He really did not care for science, and he had an inclination to put the book down as his head seemed to be swaying, but he continued to turn the pages.

Snowdon is the highest mountain in England or Wales. Snowdon is not so high as Ben Nevis. Therefore the highest mountain in England or Wales is not so high as Ben Nevis.

"Oh, my head!" mumbled Simpkins.

Water must be either warm or not warm, but it does not follow that it must be warm or cold.

Simpkins felt giddy. He dropped the book, and tottered to the couch. Immediately the room spun round and something in his head began to hum, to roar like an aeroplane a long way up in the sky. He felt that he ought to get out of the room, quickly, and get some water, either not or cold warm—he didn't mind which! He clapped on his hat and, slipping into his overcoat, he reached a door. It opened into a bedroom, very bare indeed compared with this other room, but Simpkins rolled in; the door slammed behind him, and in the darkness he fell upon a bed, with queer sensations that seemed to be dividing and subtracting in him.

When he awoke later—oh, it seemed much later—he felt quite well again. He had forgotten where he was. It was a strange place he was in, utterly dark; but there was a great noise sounding quite close to him—a gramophone, people shouting choruses and dancing about in the adjoining room. He could hear a lady's voice, too. Then he remembered that he ought not to be in that room at all; it was, why, yes, it was criminal; he might be taken for a burglar or something! He slid from the bed, groped in the darkness until he found his hat, unbuttoned his coat, for he was fearfully hot, and stood at the bedroom door trembling in the darkness, waiting and listening to that tremendous row. He *had* been a fool to come in there! How was he to get out—how the deuce was he to get out? The gramophone stopped. He could hear the voices more plainly. He grew silently panic-stricken; it was awful, they'd be coming in to him perhaps, and find him sneaking there like a thief—he must get out, he must, he must get out; yes, but how?

The singing began again. The men kept calling out "Lulu! Lulu!" and a lady's gay voice would reply to a Charley or a George, and so on, when all at once there came a peremptory knock at the outer door. The noise within stopped immediately. Deep silence. Simpkins could hear whispering. The people in there were startled; he could almost feel them staring at each other with uneasiness. The lady laughed out startlingly shrill. "Sh-s-s-sh!" the others cried. The loud knocking began again, emphatic, terrible. Simpkins's already quaking heart began to beat ecstatically. Why, oh why, didn't they open that door?— open it! open it! There was shuffling in the room, and when the knocking was repeated for the third time the outer door was apparently unlocked.

"Fazz! Oh, Fazz, you brute!" cried the relieved voices in the room. "You fool, Fazz! Come in, damn you, and shut the door."

"Good gracious!" exclaimed the apparently deliberating Fazz, "what is that?"

"Hullo, Rob Roy!" cried the lady, "it's me."

"Charmed to meet you, madame. How interesting, most fascinating; yes, I am quite charmed, but I wish somebody would kindly give me the loose end of it all. I'm suffering, as you see, dearies, and I don't understand all this, I'm quite out of my depth. The noise you've been making is just crushing me."

Several voices began to explain at once: "We captured her,

Fazz, yes—Rape of the Sabines, what!—from the Vaudeville. Had a rag, glorious—corralled all the attendants and scene-shifters—rushed the stage—we did! we did! everybody chased somebody, and we chased Lulu—we did! we did!"

"Oh, shut up, everybody!" cried out Fazz.

"Yes, listen," cried the voice of Evans-Antrobus. "This is how it happened: they chased the eight Sisters Victoria off the stage, and we spied dear little Lulu—she was one of those eight Victorias—bolting down a passage to the stage entrance. She fled into the street just as she was—isn't she a duck? There was a taxi standing there, and Lulu, wise woman, jumped in—and we jumped in too. (We did! We did!) 'Where for?' says taximan. 'Saviour's College,' say we, and here you are—Lulu!—what do you think of her?"

"Charming, utterly charming," replied Fazz. "The details are most clarifying; but how did you manage to usher her into the college?"

"My overcoat on," explained one voice.

"And my hat," cried another.

"And we dazzled the porter," said a third. There were lots of other jolly things to explain: Lulu had not resisted at all, she had enjoyed it; it was a lark!

"Oh, beautiful! Most fascinating!" agreed Fazz. "But how you propose to get her out of the college I have no more notion than Satan has of sanctity—it's rather late, isn't it?"

Simpkins, in his dark room, could hear someone rushing up the stairs with flying leaps that ceased at the outer door. Then a breathless voice hissed out: "You fellows, scat, scat! Police are in the lodge with the proctors and that taximan!"

In a moment Evans-Antrobus began to groan. "Oh, my God, what can we do with her? We must get her out at once—over the wall, eh, at once, quick! Johnstone, quick, go and find a rope, quick, a rope."

And Fazz said: "It does begin to look a little foolish. Oh, I am feeling so damn bad—but you can't blame a fool for anything it does, can you? But I am bad; I am going to bed instantly, I feel quite out of my depth here. Oh, that young friend of yours, that Simpkins, charming young person! Very blithe he was, dear Evans-Antrobus!"

Everybody now seemed to rush away from the room except the girl Lulu and Evans-Antrobus. He was evidently very agitated and in a bad humour. He clumped about the room exclaiming: "Oh, damnation, do hurry up, somebody. What am I to do with her, boozy little pig! Do hurry up!"

"Who's a pig? I want to go out of here," shrilled Lulu, and apparently she made for the door.

"You can't go like that!" he cried; "you can't, you mustn't. Don't be a fool, Lulu! Lulu! Now, isn't this a fearful mess?"

"I'm not going to stop here with you, ugly thing! I don't like it; I'm going now, let go."

"But you can't go, I tell you, in these things, not like that. Let me think, let me think, can't you! Why don't you let me think, you little fool! Put something on you, my overcoat; cover yourself up. I shall be ruined, damn you! Why the devil did you come here, you . . . !"

"And who brought me here, Mr. Antibus? Oh yes, I know you; I shall have something to say to the vicar, or whoever it is you're afraid of, baby-face! Let me go; I don't want to be left here alone with you!" she yelled. Simpkins heard an awful scuffle. He could wait no longer; he flung open the door, rushed into the room, and caught up a siphon, the first handy weapon. They saw him at once, and stood apart amazed.

"Fine game!" said the trembling Simpkins to the man, with all the sternness at his command. As nobody spoke he repeated, quite contemptuously: "Fine game!"

Lulu was breathing hard, with her hands resting upon her bosom. Her appearance was so startling to the boy that he nearly dropped the siphon. He continued to face her, hugging it with both hands against his body. She was clad in pink tights—they were of silk, they glistened in the sharper light from under the violet shade—a soft white tarlatan skirt that spread around her like a carnation, and a rose-coloured bodice. She was dainty, with a little round head and a little round face like a briar rose; but he guessed she was strong, though her beauty had apparently all the fragility of a flower. Her hair, of dull dark gold, hung in loose tidiness without pin or braid, the locks cut short to her neck, where they curved in to brush the white skin; a deep straight fringe of it was combed upon the childish brow. Grey were her surprised eyes, and wide the pouting lips. Her lovely naked arms—oh, he could scarcely bear to look at them. She stood now, with one hand upon her hip and the other lying against her cheek, staring at Simpkins. Then she danced delightfully up to him and took the siphon away.

"Look here," said Evans-Antrobus to Lulu—he had recovered his nerve, and did not express any astonishment at Simpkins's sudden appearance—"he is just your size, you dress up in his clothes, quick, then it's simple."

"No," said the girl.

"And no for me," said Simpkins fiercely—almost.

Just then the door was thrust partly open and a rope was flung into the room. The bringer of it darted away downstairs again.

"Hi! here!" called Evans-Antrobus, rushing to the door; but nobody stayed for him, nobody answered him. He came back and picked up the rope.

"Put on that coat," he commanded Lulu, "and that hat. Now, look here, not a word, not a giggle even, or we are done, and I might just as well screw your blessed neck!"

"Would you?" snorted Simpkins, with not a little animosity.

"Yes, would you!" chimed Lulu, but nevertheless she obeyed and followed him down the stairs. When she turned and beckoned, Simpkins followed too. They crossed a dark quadrangle, passed down a passage that was utter darkness, through another quad, another passage, and halted in a gloomy yard behind the chapel, where Evans-Antrobus struck a match, and where empty boxes, bottles, and other rubbish had accumulated under a wall about ten feet high.

"You first, and quiet, quiet," growled Evans-Antrobus to Simpkins. No one spoke again. Night was thickly dark, the stars were dim, the air moist and chill. Simpkins, assisted by the other man, clambered over the rickety boxes and straddled the high thick wall. The rope was hung over, too, and when the big man had jumped to earth again, dragging his weight against it, Simpkins slid down on the other side. He was now in a narrow street, with a dim lamp at one end that cast no gleam to the spot where he had descended. There were dark high-browed buildings looming high around him. He stood holding the end of the rope and looking up at the stars—very faint they were. The wall was much higher on this side, looked like a mountain, and he thought of Ben Nevis again. This was out of your depth, if you like, out of your depth entirely. It was all wrong, somehow, or, at any rate, it was not all right; it couldn't be right. Never again would he mess about with a lot of lunatics. He hadn't done any good, he hadn't even got the money—he had forgotten it. He had not got anything at all except a headache.

The rope tightened. Lulu was astride the wall, quarrelling with the man on the other side.

"Keep your rotten coat!" She slipped it off and flung it down from the wall. "And your rotten hat, too, spider-face!" She flung that down from the wall, and spat into the darkness. Turning to the other side, she whispered: "I'm coming," and scrambled down, sliding into Simpkins's arms. And somehow he stood holding her so, embracing her quite tightly. She was all softness and perfume, he could not let her go; she had scarcely anything on—he would not let her go. It was marvellous and beautiful to him; the glimmer of her white face was mysterious and tender in the darkness. She put her arms around his neck:

"Oh—I rather love you," she said.

The Black Dog (1923)

ARABESQUE—THE MOUSE

In the main street amongst tall establishments of mart and worship was a high narrow house pressed between a coffee factory and a bootmaker's. It had four flights of long dim echoing stairs, and at the top, in a room that was full of the smell of

dried apples and mice, a man in the middle age of life had sat
reading Russian novels until he thought he was mad. Late was
the hour, the night outside black and freezing, the pavements
below empty and undistinguishable when he closed his book and
sat motionless in front of the glowing but flameless fire. He
felt he was very tired, yet he could not rest. He stared at a picture on the wall until he wanted to cry; it was a colour print by
Utamaro of a suckling child caressing its mother's breasts as she
sits in front of a black-bound mirror. Very chaste and decorative
it was, in spite of its curious anatomy. The man gazed, empty
of sight though not of mind, until the sighing of the gas jet
maddened him. He got up, put out the light, and sat down again
in the darkness trying to compose his mind before the comfort of
the fire. And he was just about to begin a conversation with himself when a mouse crept from a hole in the skirting near the
fireplace and scurried into the fender. The man had the crude
dislike for such sly nocturnal things, but this mouse was so
small and bright, its antics so pretty, that he drew his feet carefully from the fender and sat watching it almost with amusement. The mouse moved along the shadows of the fender, out
upon the hearth, and sat before the glow, rubbing its head, ears,
and tiny belly with its paws as if it were bathing itself with the
warmth, until, sharp and sudden, the fire sank, an ember fell,
and the mouse flashed into its hole.

The man reached forward to the mantelpiece and put his hand
upon a pocket lamp. Turning on the beam, he opened the door
of a cupboard beside the fireplace. Upon one of the shelves there
was a small trap baited with cheese, a trap made with a wire
spring, one of those that smashed down to break the back of
ingenuous and unwary mice.

"Mean—so mean," he mused, "to appeal to the hunger of any
living thing just in order to destroy it."

He picked up the empty trap as if to throw it in the fire.

"I suppose I had better leave it though—the place swarms
with them." He still hesitated. "I hope that little beastie won't
go and do anything foolish." He put the trap back quite carefully, closed the door of the cupboard, sat down again, and extinguished the lamp.

Was there anyone else in the world so squeamish and foolish about such things! Even his mother, mother so bright and beautiful, even she had laughed at his childish horrors. He recalled how once in his childhood, not long after his sister Yosine was born, a friendly neighbour had sent him home with a bundle of dead larks tied by the feet "for supper." The pitiful inanimity of the birds had brought a gush of tears; he had run weeping home and into the kitchen, and there he had found the strange thing doing. It was dusk; mother was kneeling before the fire. He dropped the larks.

"Mother!" he exclaimed softly. She looked at his tearful face.

"What's the matter, Filip?" she asked, smiling too at his astonishment.

"Mother! What are you doing?"

Her bodice was open and she was squeezing her breasts; long thin streams of milk spurted into the fire with a little plunging noise.

"Weaning your little sister," laughed mother. She took his little inquisitive face and pressed it against the delicate warmth of her bosom, and he forgot the dead birds behind him.

"Let me do it, mother," he cried, and doing so he discovered the throb of the heart in his mother's breast. Wonderful it was for him to experience it, although she could not explain it to him.

"Why does it do that?"

"If it did not beat, little son, I should die and the Holy Father would take me from you."

"God?"

She nodded. He put his hand upon his own breast. "Oh, feel it, Mother!" he cried. Mother unbuttoned his little coat and felt the gentle *tick tick* with her warm palm.

"Beautiful!" she said.

"Is it a good one?"

She kissed his upsmiling lips. "It is good if it beats truly. Let it always beat truly, Filip, let it always beat truly."

There was the echo of a sigh in her voice, and he had divined some grief, for he was very wise. He kissed her bosom in his ecstasy and whispered soothingly: "Little mother! little mother!"

In such joys he forgot his horror of the dead larks; indeed, he helped mother to pluck them and spit them for supper.

It was a black day that succeeded, and full of tragedy for the child. A great bay horse with a tawny mane had knocked down his mother in the lane, and a heavy cart had passed over her, crushing both her hands. She was borne away moaning with anguish to the surgeon, who cut off the two hands. She died in the night. For years the child's dreams were filled with the horror of the stumps of arms, bleeding unendingly. Yet he had never seen them, for he was sleeping when she died.

While this old woe was come vividly before him he again became aware of the mouse. His nerves stretched upon him in repulsion, but he soon relaxed to a tolerant interest, for it was really a most engaging little mouse. It moved with curious staccato scurries, stopping to rub its head or flicker with its ears; they seemed almost transparent ears. It spied a red cinder and skipped innocently up to it . . . sniffing . . . sniffing . . . until it jumped back scorched. It would crouch as a cat does, blinking in the warmth, or scamper madly as if dancing, and then roll upon its side rubbing its head with those pliant paws. The melancholy man watched it until it came at last to rest and squatted meditatively upon its haunches, hunched up, looking curiously wise, a pennyworth of philosophy; then once more the coals sank with a rattle and again the mouse was gone.

The man sat on before the fire and his mind filled again with unaccountable sadness. He had grown into manhood with a burning generosity of spirit and rifts of rebellion in him that proved too exacting for his fellows and seemed mere wantonness to men of casual rectitudes. "Justice and Sin," he would cry, "Property and Virtue—incompatibilities! There can be no sin in a world of justice, no property in a world of virtue!" With an engaging extravagance and a certain clear-eyed honesty of mind he had put his two and two together and seemed then to rejoice, as in some topsy-turvy dream, in having rendered unto Cæsar, as you might say, the things that were due to Napoleon! But this kind of thing could not pass unexpiated in a world of men having an infinite regard for Property and a pride in their traditions of Virtue and Justice. They could indeed forgive him his sins

but they could not forgive him his compassions; so he had to go
seek for more melodious-minded men and fair unambiguous
women. But rebuffs can deal more deadly blows than daggers;
he became timid—a timidity not of fear but of pride—and grew
with the years into misanthropy, susceptible to trivial griefs and
despairs, a vessel of emotion that emptied as easily as it filled,
until he came at last to know that his griefs were half deliberate,
his despairs half unreal, and to live but for beauty—which is
tranquillity—to put her wooing hand upon him.

Now, while the mouse hunts in the cupboard, one fair recollection stirs in the man's mind—of Cassia and the harmony of
their only meeting, Cassia, who had such rich red hair, and eyes,
yes, her eyes were full of starry inquiry like the eyes of mice. It
was so long ago that he had forgotten how he came to be in it,
that unaccustomed orbit of vain vivid things—a village festival,
all oranges and houp-la. He could not remember how he came
to be there, but at night, in the court hall, he had danced with
Cassia—fair and unambiguous indeed!—who had come like the
wind from among the roses and swept into his heart.

"It is easy to guess," he had said to her, "what you like most
in the world."

She laughed. "To dance? Yes, and you—?"

"To find a friend."

"I know, I know," she cried, caressing him with recognitions.
"Ah, at times I quite love my friends—until I begin to wonder
how much they hate me!"

He had loved at once that cool pale face, the abundance of her
strange hair as light as the autumn's clustered bronze, her lilac
dress and all the sweetness about her like a bush of lilies. How
they had laughed at the two old peasants whom they had overheard gabbling of trifles like sickness and appetite!

"There's a lot of nature in a parsnip," said one, a fat person of
the kind that swells grossly when stung by a bee, "a lot of nature
when it's young, but when it's old it's like everything else."

"True it is."

"And I'm very fond of vegetables, yes, and I'm very fond of
bread."

"Come out with me," whispered Cassia to Filip, and they

walked out in the blackness of midnight into what must have been a garden.

"Cool it is here," she said, "and quiet, but too dark even to see your face—can you see mine?"

"The moon will not rise until after dawn," said he, "it will be white in the sky when the starlings whistle in your chimney."

They walked silently and warily about until they felt the chill of the air. A dull echo of the music came to them through the walls, then stopped, and they heard the bark of a fox away in the woods.

"You are cold," he whispered, touching her bare neck with timid fingers. "Quite, quite cold," drawing his hand tenderly over the curves of her chin and face. "Let us go in," he said moving with discretion from the rapture he desired. "We will come out again," said Cassia.

But within the room the ball was just at an end, the musicians were packing up their instruments and the dancers were flocking out and homewards, or to the buffet, which was on a platform at one end of the room. The two old peasants were there, munching hugely.

"I tell you," said one of them, "there's nothing in the world for it but the grease of an owl's liver. That's it, that's it! Take something on your stomach now? Just to offset the chill of the dawn?"

Filip and Cassia were beside them, but there were so many people crowding the platform that Filip had to jump down. He stood then looking up adoringly at Cassia, who had pulled a purple cloak around her.

"For Filip, Filip, Filip," she said, pushing the last bite of her sandwich into his mouth, and pressing upon him her glass of Loupiac. Quickly he drank it with a great gesture, and flinging the glass to the wall, took Cassia into his arms, shouting: "I'll carry you home, the whole way home, yes, I'll carry you!"

"Put me down!" she cried, beating his head and pulling his ears, as they passed among the departing dancers. "Put me down, you wild thing!"

Dark, dark was the lane outside, and the night an obsidian net, into which he walked carrying the girl. But her arms were looped around him, she discovered paths for him, clinging more tightly as he staggered against a wall, stumbled upon a gulley, or when her sweet hair was caught in the boughs of a little lime tree.

"Do not loose me, Filip, will you, do not loose me," Cassia said, putting her lips against his temple.

His brain seemed bursting, his heart rocked within him, but he adored the rich grace of her limbs against his breast. "Here it is," she murmured, and he carried her into a path that led to her home in a little lawned garden where the smell of ripe apples upon the branches and the heavy lustre of roses stole upon the air. Roses and apples! Roses and apples! He carried her right into the porch before she slid down and stood close to him with her hands still upon his shoulders. He could breathe happily at the release, standing silent and looking round at the sky sprayed with wondrous stars but without a moon.

"You are stronger than I thought you, stronger than you look, you are really very strong," she whispered, nodding her head to him. Opening the buttons of his coat she put her palm against his breast.

"Oh, how your heart does beat! Does it beat truly—and for whom?"

He had seized her wrists in a little fury of love, crying: "Little mother, little mother!"

"What are you saying?" asked the girl, but before he could continue there came a footstep sounding behind the door, and the clack of a bolt. . . .

What was that? Was that really a bolt or was it . . . was it . . . the snap of the trap? The man sat up in his room intently listening, with nerves quivering again, waiting for the trap to kill the little philosopher. When he felt it was all over he reached guardedly in the darkness for the lantern, turned on the beam, and opened the door of the cupboard. Focusing the light upon the trap, he was amazed to see the mouse sitting on its haunches before it, uncaught. Its head was bowed, but its beadlike eyes were full of brightness, and it sat blinking, it did not flee.

"Shoosh!" said the man, but the mouse did not move. "Why doesn't it go? Shoosh!" he said again, and suddenly the reason of the mouse's strange behaviour was made clear. The trap had not caught it completely, but it had broken off both its forefeet, and the thing crouched there holding out its two bleeding stumps humanly, too stricken to stir.

Horror flooded the man, and conquering his repugnance he plucked the mouse up quickly by the neck. Immediately the little thing fastened its teeth in his finger; the touch was no more than the slight prick of a pin. The man's impulse then exhausted itself. What should he do with it? He put his hand behind him, he dared not look, but there was nothing to be done except kill it at once, quickly, quickly. Oh, how should he do it? He bent towards the fire as if to drop the mouse into its quenching glow; but he paused and shuddered, he would hear its cries, he would have to listen. Should he crush it with finger and thumb? A glance towards the window decided him. He opened the sash with one hand and flung the wounded mouse far into the dark street. Closing the window with a crash, he sank into a chair, limp with pity too deep for tears.

So he sat for two minutes, five minutes, ten minutes. Anxiety and shame filled him with heat. He opened the window again, and the freezing air poured in and cooled him. Seizing his lantern he ran down the echoing stairs, into the empty street, searching long and vainly for the little philosopher until he had to desist and return to his room, shivering, frozen to his very bones.

When he had recovered some warmth he took the trap from its shelf. The two feet dropped into his hand; he cast them into the fire. Then he once more set the trap and put it back carefully into the cupboard.

Adam and Eve and Pinch Me (1921)

ALAS, POOR BOLLINGTON!

"I WALKED out of the hotel, just as I was, and left her there. I never went back again. I don't think I intended anything quite so final, so dastardly. I had not intended it, I had not thought of doing so, but that is how it happened. I lost her, lost my wife purposely. It was heartless. it was shabby, for she was a nice woman, a charming woman, a good deal younger than I was, a splendid woman, in fact she was very beautiful, and yet I ran away from her. How can you explain that, Turner?"

Poor Bollington looked at Turner, who looked at his glass of whisky, and that looked irresistible—he drank some. Bollington sipped a little from his glass of milk.

I often found myself regarding Bollington as a little old man. Most of the club members did so too, but he was not that at all, he was still on the sunny side of fifty, but *so* unassertive, no presence to speak of, no height, not enough hair to mention— if he had had, it would surely have been yellow. So mild and modest he cut no figure at all, just a man in glasses that seemed rather big for him. Turner was different, though he was just as bald; he had stature and bulk, his very pince-nez seemed twice the size of Bollington's spectacles. They had not met each other for ten years.

"Well, yes," Turner said, "but that was a serious thing to do."

"Wasn't it!" said the other, "and I had no idea of the enormity of the offence—not at the time. She might have been dead, poor girl, and her executors advertising for me. She had money, you know, her people had been licensed victuallers, quite wealthy. Scandalous!"

Bollington brooded upon his sin until Turner sighed: "Ah well, my dear chap."

"But you have no idea," protested Bollington, "how entirely she engrossed me. She was twenty-five and I was forty when we married. She was entrancing. She had always lived in a stinking hole in Balham, and it is amazing how strictly some of those people keep their children; licensed victuallers, did I tell you? Well, I was forty, and she was twenty-five; we lived for a year dodging about from one hotel to another all over the British Isles, she was a perfect little nomad. Are you married, Turner?"

No, Turner was not married, he never had been.

"Oh, but you should be," cried little Bollington. "It's an extraordinary experience, the real business of the world is marriage, marriage! I was deliriously happy and she was learning French and Swedish—that's where we were going later. She was an enchanting little thing, fair, with blue eyes, Phoebe her name was."

Turner thoughtfully brushed his hand across his generous baldness, then folded his arms.

"You really should," repeated Bollington, "you ought to, really. But I remember we went from Killarney to Belfast, and there something dreadful happened. I don't know, it had been growing on her I suppose, but she took a dislike to me there, had strange fancies, thought I was unfaithful to her. You see, she was popular wherever we went, a lively little woman, in fact she wasn't merely a woman, she was a little magnet, men congregated and clung to her like so many tacks and nails and pins. I didn't object at all—on the contrary, "Enjoy yourself, Phoebe," I said, "I don't expect you always to hang around an old fogey like me." Fogey was the very word I used; I didn't mean it, of course, but that was the line I took, for she was *so* charming until she began to get so bad-tempered. And believe me, that made her angry, furious. No, not the fogey, but the idea that I did not object to her philandering. It was fatal, it gave colour to her suspicions of me—Turner, I was as innocent as any lamb—tremendous colour. And she had such a sharp tongue! If you ventured to differ from her—and you couldn't help differing sometimes—she'd positively bludgeon you, and you couldn't help being bludgeoned. And she had a passion for putting me right, and I always seemed to be so *very* wrong, always. She would not be satisfied until she had proved it, and it was so monstrous to be made feel that because you were rather different from other people you were an impertinent fool. Yes, I seemed at last to gain only the pangs and none of the prizes of marriage. Now, there was a lady we met in Belfast to whom I paid some attention . . ."

"Oh, good lord!" groaned Turner.

"No, but listen," pleaded Bollington, "it was a very innocent friendship—nothing was further from my mind—and she was very much like my wife, very much, it was noticeable, everybody spoke of it—I mean the resemblance. A Mrs. Macarthy, a delightful woman, and Phoebe simply loathed her. I confess that my wife's innuendoes were so mean and persistent that at last I hadn't the strength to deny them, in fact at times I wished they were true. Love is idolatry if you like, but it cannot be complete immolation—there's no such bird as the phœnix, is there, Turner?"

"What, what?"

"No such bird as the phœnix."

"No, there is no such bird, I believe."

"And sometimes I had to ask myself quite seriously if I really hadn't been up to some infidelity! Nonsense, of course, but I assure you that was the effect it was having upon me. I had doubts of myself, frenzied doubts! And it came to a head between Phoebe and me in our room one day. We quarrelled. Oh, dear, how we quarrelled! She said I was sly, two-faced, unfaithful, I was a scoundrel, and so on. Awfully untrue, all of it. She accused me of dreadful things with Mrs. Macarthy and she screamed out: "I hope you will treat her better than you have treated me." Now, what did she mean by that, Turner?"

Bollington eyed his friend as if he expected an oracular answer, but just as Turner was about to respond, Bollington continued: "Well, I never found out, I never knew, for what followed was too terrible. "I shall go out," I said, "it will be better, I think." Just that, nothing more. I put on my hat and I put my hand on the knob of the door when she said most violently: "Go with your Macarthys, I never want to see your filthy face again!" Extraordinary, you know, Turner. Well, I went out, and I will not deny I was in a rage, terrific. It was raining but I didn't

care, and I walked about in it. Then I took shelter in a bookseller's doorway opposite a shop that sold tennis rackets and
tobacco, and another one that displayed carnations and peaches
on wads of coloured wool. The rain came so fast that the streets
seemed empty, and the passers-by were horridly silent under
their umbrellas, and their footsteps splashed so dully, and I tell
you I was very sad, Turner, there. I debated whether to rush
across the road and buy a lot of carnations and peaches and take
them to Phoebe. But I did not do so, Turner, I never went back,
never."

"Why, Bollington, you, you were a positive ruffian, Bollington."

"Oh, scandalous," rejoined the ruffian.

"Well, out with it, what about this Mrs. Macarthy?"

"Mrs. Macarthy? But, Turner, I never saw her again, never.
I—I forgot her. Yes, I went prowling on until I found myself at
the docks and there it suddenly became dark; I don't know,
there was no evening, no twilight, the day stopped for a moment
—and it did not recover. There were hundreds of bullocks
slithering and panting and steaming in the road, thousands;
lamps were hung up in the harbour, cabs and trolleys rattled
round the bullocks, the rain fell dismally and everybody hurried.
I went into the dock and saw them loading the steamer, it was
called s.s. *Frolic,* and really, Turner, the things they put into the
belly of that steamer were rather funny: tons and tons of monstrous big chain, the links as big as soup plates, and two or three
pantechnicon vans. Yes, but I was anything but frolicsome, I
assure you, I was full of misery and trepidation and the deuce
knows what. I did not know what I wanted to do, or what I was
going to do, but I found myself buying a ticket to go to Liverpool on that steamer, and, in short, I embarked. How wretched
I was, but how determined! Everything on board was depressing
and dirty, and when at last we moved off, the foam slewed away
in filthy bubbles as if that dirty steamer had been sick and was
running away from it. I got to Liverpool in the early morn, but
I did not stay there, it is such a clamouring place, all trams and
trolleys and teashops. I sat in the station for an hour, the most
miserable man alive, the most miserable ever born. I wanted
some rest, some peace, some repose, but they never ceased

shunting an endless train of goods trucks, banging and screeching until I almost screamed at the very porters. Criff was the name on some of the trucks, I remember, Criff, and everything seemed to be going criff, criff, criff. I haven't discovered to this day what Criff signifies, whether it's a station or a company, or a manufacture, but it was Criff, I remember. Well, I rushed to London and put my affairs in order. A day or two later I went to Southampton and boarded another steamer and put to sea, or rather we were ignominiously lugged out of the dock by a little rat of a tug that seemed all funnel and hooter. I was off to America, and there I stopped for over three years."

Turner sighed. A waiter brought him another glass of spirit.

"I can't help thinking, Bollington, that it was all very fiery and touchy. Of course, I don't know, but really it was a bit steep, very squeamish of you. What did your wife say?"

"I never communicated with her, I never heard from her, I just dropped out. My filthy face, you know, she did not want to see it again."

"Oh come, Bollington! And what did Mrs. Macarthy say?"

"Mrs. Macarthy! I never saw or heard of her again. I told you that."

"Ah, yes, you told me. So you slung off to America."

"I was intensely miserable there for a long while. Of course I loved Phoebe enormously, I felt the separation. I— Oh, it is impossible to describe. But what was worst of all was the meanness of my behaviour, there was nothing heroic about it. I soon saw clearly that it was a shabby trick, disgusting, I had bolted and left her to the mercy of—well, of whatever there was. It made such an awful barrier—you've no idea of my compunction —I couldn't make overtures—"Let us forgive and forget." I was a mean rascal, I *was* filthy. That was the barrier—myself; I was too bad. I thought I should recover and enjoy life again. I began to think of Phoebe as a cat, a little cat. I went everywhere and did everything. But America is a big country, I couldn't get into contact, I was lonely, very lonely, and although two years went by I longed for Phoebe. Everything I did I wanted to do with Phoebe by my side. And then my cousin, my only relative in the world—he lived in England—he died. I scarcely ever saw him, but still he was my kin. And he died. You've no comprehension, Turner, of the truly awful sensation such a bereavement brings. Not a soul in the world now would have the remotest interest in my welfare. Oh, I tell you, Turner, it was tragic, tragic, when my cousin died. It made my isolation complete. I was alone, a man who had made a dreadful mess of life. What with sorrow and remorse. I felt that I should soon die, not of disease, but disgust."

"You *were* a great ninny," ejaculated his friend. "Why the devil didn't you hurry back, claim your wife, bygones be bygones? Why, bless my conscience, what a ninny, what a great ninny!"

"Yes, Turner, it is as you say. But though conscience is a good servant, it is a very bad master, it overruled me; it shamed me, and I hung on to America for still another year. I tell you my situation was unbearable, I was tied to my misery, I was a tethered dog, a duck without water—even dirty water. And I hadn't any faith in myself or in my case; I knew I was wrong, had always been wrong, Phoebe had taught me that. I hadn't any faith, I wish I had had. Faith can move mountains, so they say, though I've never heard of it actually being done."

"No, not in historical times," declared Turner.

"What do you mean by that?"

"Oh, well, time is nothing, it's nothing, it comes and off it goes. Has it ever occurred to you, Bollington, that in five thousand years or so there will be nobody in the world speaking the English language, our very existence even will be speculated upon, as if we were the anthropophagi? Oh, good lord, yes."

And another whisky.

"You know, Bollington, you were a perfect fool. You behaved like one of those half-baked civil-service hounds who lunch in a dairy on a cup of tea and a cream horn. You wanted some beef, some ginger. You came back, you must have come back because there you are now."

"Yes, Turner, I came back after nearly four years. Everything was different, ah, how strange! I could not find Phoebe, it is weird how people can disappear. I made inquiries, but it was like looking for a lost umbrella, fruitless after so long."

"Well, but what about Mrs. Macarthy?"

Mr. Bollington said, slowly and with the utmost precision: "I did not see Mrs. Macarthy again."

"Oh, of course, you did not see her again, not ever."

"Not ever. I feared Phoebe had gone abroad too, but at last I found her in London. . . ."

"No," roared Turner, "why the devil couldn't you say so and done with it? I've been sweating with sympathy for you. Oh, I say, Bollington!"

"My dear Turner, listen. Do you know she was delighted to see me, she even kissed me, straight off, and we went out to dine and had the very deuce of a spread and we were having the very deuce of a good time. She was lovelier than ever, and I could see all her old affection for me was returning, she was so—well, I can't tell you, Turner, but she had no animosity whatever, no grievance, she would certainly have taken me back that very night. Oh dear, dear . . . and then! I was anxious to throw myself at her feet, but you couldn't do that in a public café, I could only touch her hands, beautiful, as they lay on the white linen cloth. I kept asking: 'Do you forgive me?' and she would reply: 'I have nothing to forgive, dear, nothing.' How wonderful that sounded to my truly penitent soul!—I wanted to die.

" 'But you don't ask me where I've been!' she cried gaily, 'or what I've been doing, you careless old Peter. I've been to France, and Sweden too!'

"I was delighted to hear that, it was so very plucky.

" 'When did you go?' I asked.

" 'When I left you,' she said.

" 'You mean when I went away?'

" 'Did you go away? Oh, of course, you must have. Poor Peter, what a sad time he has had!'

"I was a little bewildered, but I was delighted; in fact, Turner, I was hopelessly infatuated again, I wanted to wring out all the dregs of my detestable villainy and be absolved. All I could begin with was: 'Were you not very glad to be rid of me?'

" 'Well,' she said, 'my great fear at first was that you would find me again and make it up. I didn't want that, then; at least I thought I didn't.'

" 'That's exactly what I felt,' I exclaimed, 'but how could I find you?'

" 'Well,' Phoebe said, 'you might have found out and followed me. But I promise never to run away again, Peter dear, never.'

"Turner, my reeling intelligence swerved like a shot bird.

" 'Do you mean, Phoebe, that you ran away from *me?*'

" 'Yes, didn't I?' she answered.

" 'But I ran away from *you*,' I said. 'I walked out of the hotel on that dreadful afternoon we quarrelled so and I never went back. I went to America. I was in America nearly four years.'

" 'Do you mean you ran away from me?' she cried.

" 'Yes,' I said, 'didn't I?'

" 'But that is exactly what *I* did—I mean, I ran away from you. *I* walked out of the hotel directly you had gone—*I* never went back, and I've been abroad thinking how tremendously I had served you out and wondering what you thought of it all and where you were.'

"I could only say: 'Good God, Phoebe, I've had the most awful four years of remorse and sorrow—all vain, mistaken, useless, thrown away.' And she said: 'And I've had four years—living in a fool's paradise after all. How *dared* you run away? It's disgusting!'

"And, Turner, in a moment she was at me again in her old dreadful way, and the last words I had from her were: 'Now I *never* want to see your face again, never, this *is* the end!'

"And that's how things are now, Turner. It's rather sad, isn't it?"

"Sad! Why, you chump, when was it you saw her?"

"Oh, a long time ago, it must be nearly three years now."

"Three years! But you'll see her again!"

"Tfoo! No, no, no, Turner. God bless me, no, no, no!" said the little old man.

The Black Dog (1923)

DUSKY RUTH

At the close of an April day, chilly and wet, the traveller came to a country town. In the Cotswolds, though the towns are small and sweet and the inns snug, the general habit of the land is bleak and bare. He had newly come upon upland roads so void of human affairs, so lonely, that they might have been made for some forgotten uses by departed men, and left to the unwitting passage of such strangers as himself. Even the unending walls, built of old rough laminated rock, that detailed the far-spreading fields, had grown very old again in their courses; there were dabs of darkness, buttons of moss, and fossils on every stone. He had passed a few neighbourhoods, sometimes at the crook of a stream, or at the cross of debouching roads, where old habitations, their gangrenated thatch riddled with bird holes, had been not so much erected as just spattered about the places. Beyond these signs an odd lark or blackbird, the ruckle of partridges, or the nifty gallop of a hare had been the only mitigation of the living loneliness that was almost as profound by day as by night. But the traveller had a care for such times and places. There are men who love to gaze with the mind at things that can never be seen, feel at least the throb of a beauty that will never be known, and hear over immense bleak reaches the echo of that which is no celestial music, but only their own hearts' vain cries; and though his garments clung to him like clay it was with deliberate questing step that the traveller trod the single street of the town, and at last entered the inn, shuffling his shoes in the doorway for a moment and striking the raindrops from his hat. Then he turned into a small smoking-room. Leather-lined benches, much worn, were fixed to the wall under the window and in other odd corners and nooks behind mahogany tables. One wall was furnished with all the congenial gear of a bar, but without any in-

tervening counter. Opposite, a bright fire was burning, and a
neatly dressed young woman sat before it in a Windsor chair,
staring at the flames. There was no other inmate of the room,
and as he entered, the girl rose up and greeted him. He found
that he could be accommodated for the night, and in a few
moments his hat and scarf were removed and placed inside the
fender, his wet overcoat was taken to the kitchen, the landlord,
an old fellow, was lending him a roomy pair of slippers, and a
maid was setting supper in an adjoining room.

He sat while this was doing and talked to the barmaid. She
had a beautiful but rather mournful face as it was lit by the firelight, and when her glance was turned away from it her eyes had
a piercing brightness. Friendly and well spoken as she was, the
melancholy in her aspect was noticeable—perhaps it was the dim
room, or the wet day, or the long hours ministering a multitude
of cocktails to thirsty gallantry.

When he went to his supper he found cheering food and drink,
with pleasant garniture of silver and mahogany. There were no
other visitors, he was to be alone; blinds were drawn, lamps lit,
and the fire at his back was comforting. So he sat long about his
meal until a white-faced maid came to clear the table, discoursing
to him about country things as she busied about the room. It was
a long, narrow room, with a sideboard and the door at one end
and the fireplace at the other. A bookshelf, almost devoid of
books, contained a number of plates; the long wall that faced the
windows was almost destitute of pictures, but there were hung
upon it, for some inscrutable but doubtless sufficient reason, many
dish-covers, solidly shaped, of the kind held in such mysterious
regard and known as "willow pattern"; one was even hung upon
the face of a map. Two musty prints were mixed with them,
presentments of horses having a stilted extravagant physique and
bestridden by images of inhuman and incommunicable dignity,
clothed in whiskers, coloured jackets, and tight white breeches.

He took down the books from the shelf, but his interest was
speedily exhausted, and the almanacs, the county directory, and
various guide-books were exchanged for the *Cotswold Chronicle*.
With this, having drawn the deep chair to the hearth, he whiled
away the time. The newspaper amused him with its advertise-

ments of stock shows, farm auctions, travelling quacks and conjurers, and there was a lengthy account of the execution of a local felon, one Timothy Bridger, who had murdered an infant in some shameful circumstances. This dazzling crescendo proved rather trying to the traveller; he threw down the paper.

The town was all as quiet as the hills, and he could hear no sounds in the house. He got up and went across the hall to the smoke-room. The door was shut, but there was light within, and he entered. The girl sat there much as he had seen her on his arrival, still alone, with feet on fender. He shut the door behind him, sat down, and crossing his legs puffed at his pipe, admired the snug little room and the pretty figure of the girl, which he could do without embarrassment, as her meditative head, slightly bowed, was turned away from him. He could see something of her, too, in the mirror at the bar, which repeated also the agreeable contours of bottles of coloured wines and rich liqueurs—so entrancing in form and aspect that they seemed destined to charming histories, even in disuse—and those of familiar outline containing mere spirits or small beer, for which are reserved the harsher destinies of base oils, horse medicines, disinfectants, and cold tea. There were coloured glasses for bitter wines, white glasses for sweet, a tiny leaden sink beneath them, and the four black handles of the beer engines.

The girl wore a light blouse of silk, a short skirt of black velvet, and a pair of very thin silk stockings that showed the flesh of instep and shin so plainly that he could see they were reddened by the warmth of the fire. She had on a pair of dainty cloth shoes with high heels, but what was wonderful about her was the heap of rich black hair piled at the back of her head and shadowing the dusky neck. He sat puffing his pipe and letting the loud tick of the clock fill the quiet room. She did not stir and he could move no muscle. It was as if he had been willed to come there and wait silently. That, he felt now, had been his desire all the evening; and here, in her presence, he was more strangely stirred in a few short minutes than by any event he could remember.

In youth he had viewed women as futile, pitiable things that grew long hair, wore stays and garters, and prayed incomprehensible prayers. Viewing them in the stalls of the theatre from

his vantage-point in the gallery, he always disliked the articulation
of their naked shoulders. But still, there was a god in the sky, a
god with flowing hair and exquisite eyes, whose one stride with
an ardour grandly rendered took him across the whole round
hemisphere to which his buoyant limbs were bound like spokes
to the eternal rim and axle, his bright hair burning in the pity of
the sunsets and tossing in the anger of the dawns.

Master traveller had indeed come into this room to be with this
woman, and she as surely desired him, and for all its accidental
occasion it was as if he, walking the ways of the world, had suddenly come upon what, what so imaginable with all permitted
reverence as, well, just a shrine; and he, admirably humble, bowed
the instant head.

Were there no other people within? The clock indicated a few
minutes to nine. He sat on, still as stone, and the woman might
have been of wax for all the movement or sound she made. There
was allurement in the air between them; he had forborne his
smoking, the pipe grew cold between his teeth. He waited for a
look from her, a movement to break the trance of silence. No
footfall in street or house, no voice in the inn but the clock, beating away as if pronouncing a doom. Suddenly it rasped out nine
large notes, a bell in the town repeated them dolefully, and a
cuckoo no farther than the kitchen mocked them with three
times three. After that came the weak steps of the old landlord
along the hall, the slam of doors, the clatter of lock and bolt, and
then the silence returning unendurably upon them.

He rose and stood behind her; he touched the black hair. She
made no movement or sign. He pulled out two or three combs
and, dropping them into her lap, let the whole mass tumble about
his hands. It had a curious harsh touch in the unravelling, but
was so full and shining; black as a rook's wings it was. He slid
his palms through it. His fingers searched it and fought with its
fine strangeness; into his mind there travelled a serious thought,
stilling his wayward fancy—this was no wayward fancy, but a
rite accomplishing itself! (*Run, run, silly man, y'are lost!*) But
having got so far, he burnt his boats, leaned over, and drew her
face back to him. And at that, seizing his wrists, she gave him
back ardour for ardour, pressing his hands to her bosom, while

the kiss was sealed and sealed again. Then she sprang up and picking his scarf and hat from the fender said:

"I have been drying them for you, but the hat has shrunk a bit, I'm sure—I tried it on."

He took them from her and put them behind him; he leaned lightly back upon the table, holding it with both his hands behind him; he could not speak.

"Aren't you going to thank me for drying them?" she asked, picking her combs from the rug and repinning her hair.

"I wonder why we did that?" he asked, shamedly.

"It is what I'm thinking too," she said.

"You were so beautiful about—about it, you know."

She made no rejoinder, but continued to bind her hair, looking brightly at him under her brows. When she had finished she went close to him.

"Will that do?"

"I'll take it down again."

"No, no, the old man or the old woman will be coming in."

"What of that?" he said, taking her into his arms. "Tell me your name."

She shook her head, but she returned his kisses and stroked his hair and shoulders with beautifully melting gestures.

"What is your name? I want to call you by your name," he said. "I can't keep calling you Lovely Woman, Lovely Woman."

Again she shook her head and was dumb.

"I'll call you Ruth, then, Dusky Ruth, Ruth of the black, beautiful hair."

"That is a nice-sounding name—I knew a deaf and dumb girl named Ruth; she went to Nottingham and married an organ-grinder—but I should like it for my name."

"Then I give it to you."

"Mine is so ugly."

"What is it?"

Again the shaken head and the burning caress.

"Then you shall be Ruth; will you keep that name?"

"Yes, if you give me the name I will keep it for you."

Time had indeed taken them by the forelock, and they looked upon a ruddled world.

"I stake my one talent," he said jestingly, "and behold it returns me fortyfold; I feel like the boy who catches three mice with one piece of cheese."

At ten o'clock the girl said:

"I must go and see how *they* are getting on," and she went to the door.

"Are we keeping them up?"

She nodded.

"Are you tired?"

"No, I am not tired." She looked at him doubtfully.

"We ought not to stay in here; go into the coffee room and I'll come there in a few minutes."

"Right," he whispered gaily, "we'll sit up all night."

She stood at the door for him to pass out, and he crossed the hall to the other room. It was in darkness except for the flash of the fire. Standing at the hearth he lit a match for the lamp, but paused at the globe; then he extinguished the match.

"No, it's better to sit in the firelight."

He heard voices at the other end of the house that seemed to have a chiding note in them.

"Lord," he thought, "is she getting into a row?"

Then her steps came echoing over the stone floor of the hall; she opened the door and stood there with a lighted candle in her hand; he stood at the other end of the room, smiling.

"Good night," she said.

"Oh no, no! come along," he protested, but not moving from the hearth.

"Got to go to bed," she answered.

"Are they angry with you?"

"No."

"Well, then, come over here and sit down."

"Got to go to bed," she said again, but she had meanwhile put her candlestick upon the little sideboard and was trimming the wick with a burnt match.

"Oh, come along, just half an hour," he protested. She did not answer, but went on prodding the wick of the candle.

"Ten minutes, then," he said, still not going towards her.

"Five minutes," he begged.

She shook her head and, picking up the candlestick, turned to the door. He did not move, he just called her name: "Ruth!"

She came back then, put down the candlestick, and tiptoed across the room until he met her. The bliss of the embrace was so poignant that he was almost glad when she stood up again and said with affected steadiness, though he heard the tremor in her voice:

"I must get you your candle."

She brought one from the hall, set it on the table in front of him, and struck the match.

"What is my number?" he asked.

"Number-six room," she answered, prodding the wick vaguely with her match, while a slip of white wax dropped over the shoulder of the new candle. "Number six . . . next to mine."

The match burnt out; she said abruptly: "Good night," took up her own candle, and left him there.

In a few moments he ascended the stairs and went into his room. He fastened the door, removed his coat, collar, and slippers, but the rack of passion had seized him and he moved about with no inclination to sleep. He sat down, but there was no medium of distraction. He tried to read the newspaper that he had carried up with him, and without realizing a single phrase he forced himself to read again the whole account of the execution of the miscreant Bridger. When he had finished this he carefully folded the paper and stood up, listening. He went to the parting wall and tapped thereon with his fingertips. He waited half a minute, one minute, two minutes; there was no answering sign. He tapped again, more loudly, with his knuckles, but there was no response, and he tapped many times. He opened his door as noiselessly as possible; along the dark passage there were slips of light under the other doors, the one next his own, and the one beyond that. He stood in the corridor listening to the rumble of old voices in the farther room, the old man and his wife going to their rest. Holding his breath fearfully, he stepped to *her* door and tapped gently upon it. There was no answer, but he could somehow divine her awareness of him; he tapped again; she moved to the door and whispered: "No, no, go away." He turned the handle, the door was locked.

"Let me in," he pleaded. He knew she was standing there an inch or two beyond him.

"Hush," she called softly. "Go away, the old woman has ears like a fox."

He stood silent for a moment.

"Unlock it," he urged; but he got no further reply, and feeling foolish and baffled he moved back to his own room, cast his clothes from him, doused the candle and crept into the bed with soul as wild as a storm-swept forest, his heart beating a vagrant summons. The room filled with strange heat, there was no composure for mind or limb, nothing but flaming visions and furious embraces.

"Morality . . . what is it but agreement with your own soul?"

So he lay for two hours—the clocks chimed twelve—listening with foolish persistency for *her* step along the corridor, fancying every light sound—and the night was full of them—was her hand upon the door.

Suddenly, then—and it seemed as if his very heart would abash the house with its thunder—he could hear distinctly some-one knocking on the wall. He got quickly from his bed and stood at his door, listening. Again the knocking was heard, and having half-clothed himself he crept into the passage, which was now in utter darkness, trailing his hand along the wall until he felt her door; it was standing open. He entered her room and closed the door behind him. There was not the faintest gleam of light, he could see nothing. He whispered: "Ruth!" and she was standing there. She touched him, but not speaking. He put out his hands, and they met round her neck; her hair was flowing in its great wave about her; he put his lips to her face and found that her eyes were streaming with tears, salt and strange and disturbing. In the close darkness he put his arms about her with no thought but to comfort her; one hand had plunged through the long harsh tresses and the other across her hips before he realized that she was ungowned; then he was aware of the softness of her breasts and the cold naked sleekness of her shoulders. But she was crying there, crying silently with great tears, her strange sorrow stifling his desire.

"Ruth, Ruth, my beautiful dear!" he murmured soothingly. He

felt for the bed with one hand, and turning back the quilt and
sheets, he lifted her in as easily as a mother does her child, replaced the bedding, and, in his clothes, he lay stretched beside
her, comforting her. They lay so, innocent as children, for an
hour, when she seemed to have gone to sleep. He rose then and
went silently to his room, full of weariness.

In the morning he breakfasted without seeing her, but as he
had business in the world that gave him just an hour longer at
the inn before he left it for good and all, he went into the smoke-
room and found her. She greeted him with curious gaze, but
merrily enough, for there were other men there now—farmers,
a butcher, a registrar, an old, old man. The hour passed, but not
these men, and at length he donned his coat, took up his stick,
and said good-bye. Her shining glances followed him to the door,
and from the window as far as they could view him.

Adam and Eve and Pinch Me (1921)

THE OLD VENERABLE

Down in the village the women called him "the dirty old man,"
the children did not seem to notice him, and their fathers called
him "the Owd Venrable," or old Dick, with a sigh as of vague
envy. There was little cause for that, he living in a wood in a
little old tent shanty built of boughs and string and tarpaulin,
with a heap of straw to sleep on. Outside the tent was his fire,
and he had dwelt there so long that the mound of wood ash had
grown almost as big as his house. Seventy years old he was, an
old venerable ragged crippled man using two sticks, with a
cheery voice and a truculent spirit, but honest as spring water,
sharing his last drop with the last man or the first—he invariably

shared theirs. When he was drunk he sang, when he was not drunk he talked for evermore about nothing, to nobody, for his tent was in a wood, a little clearing in a great wood, and the wood was away, a long way, from anywhere, so that he lived, as you might say, on air and affability and primed his starved heart with hope. A man like that could hope for anything, and a mere anything—twopence—would bring him bliss, but his undeviating aspiration, an ambition as passionate as it was supine, was to possess a donkey. He had pestered many sympathetic people who had the means; often he had sent out that dove of his fancy from the ark of his need, but it had never returned, at least not with a donkey; and never an ass fell like a bolt from heaven. If it had done, it would surely have taken no hurt, such a grand wood it was, miles of it, growing up and down the hills and hills, and so thickly bosomed that if you had fallen from a balloon into the top of that wood it would have been at the last like sinking into a feather bed. And full of birds and game. And game-keepers. The keepers did not like him to be there, it was un-natural to them, but keepers come and go, the shooting was let to a syndicate, and he had been there so long that new keepers found him where the old ones had left him. They even made use of him; he swept the rides and alley-ways for the shooters, marked down the nests of pheasants, and kept observation on rabbits and weasels and the flocks of pigeons which anybody was welcome to shoot. Sometimes he earned a few shillings by plash-ing hedgerows or hoeing a field of roots, but mostly he was a "kindler," he gathered firewood and peddled it on a hand-truck around the villages. That was why he dreamed of donkey and nothing but donkey; a creature whose four feet together were not so big as one of its ears, would carry double and treble the load of kindling and make him a rich man.

One day he tramped right over to the head keeper's house to deliver a message, and there Tom Hussey had shown him a litter of retriever puppies he was tending. They had a pedigree, Tom Hussey said, as long as the shafts of a cart; the mother her-self was valued at fifty golden guineas, but the sire belonged to Lord Camover and bank-notes wouldn't buy that dog, nor love nor money—not even the crown of England. There they were, six puppies just weaned and scrambling about, beautiful bouncing creatures, all except one that seemed quiet and backward.

"That one?" Tom Hussey said; "I be going to kill her. Sha's got a sort of rupture in her navel."

"Don't do that," said old Dick, for he knew a lot about dogs as well as birds and lambs and donkeys. "Give it to I." And Tom Hussey gave him the pup then and there, and he took it home to his tent and bandaged it artfully with a yard strip of canvas, and called it Sossy because it was so pert.

Every day the old man attended to that bandage round Sossy's stomach—he knew a whole lot about dogs—and the dog throve and grew, and every night nuzzled in the straw beside him; and Dick rejoiced. They lived heartily, for Dick was a nimble hand with a wire, and rabbits were plentiful, and he was always begging for bones and suchlike for his Sossy. Everywhere in that wood he took Sossy with him and he trained her so in the arts of obedience that she knew what he wanted even if he only winked one eye. After about six months of this he took off her bandage for the last time and threw it away. There she was, cured and fit and perfect, a fine sweet flourishing thing. What a glossy coat! What a bushy tail! And her eyes—they made you dream of things!

Awhile after that Tom Hussey came into the wood to shoot some pigeons. There was always a great flock of them somewhere in the wood, and when they rose up from the trees the whirr of their thousand wings was like the roar of a great wave. Well, Tom Hussey came, and as he passed near the tent he called out the good of the morning to old Dick.

"Come here," cried Dick, and Tom Hussey went, and when he saw that dog you could have split him with a lath of wood he was so astonished. Sossy danced round him in a rare flurry, nuzzling at his pockets.

"She's hungry," he said.

"No, she ain't. Get down, you great devil! No, she ain't hungry, she's just had a saucepan full o' shackles—get down!—that saucepan there what I washes myself in."

When Tom Hussey shot a pigeon she stood to the gun and brought the bird back like an angel.

"Dick, you can swap that dog for a donkey whenever you've a mind to," Tom Hussey said.

"Ain't she got a mouth? I tell you," Dick cried joyfully.

"Like silk," was the rejoinder.

"It's a gift."

"Born," chanted Tom Hussey.

"It's a gift, I tell you."

"Born. She's worth twenty pounds. You sell that bitch and get you a donkey, quick."

"No," deliberated the veteran. "I shan't do that."

"Twenty pound she's worth, of good money."

"I shan't have 'ee, I tell you."

"You sell that bitch and get you a donkey. That's my last word to you," Tom Hussey said as he stalked away.

But that "Owd Venrable" was a far-seeing sagacious creature, a very artful old man he was, and when the time came for it he and Tom Hussey conjured up a deal between themselves. It would have been risky for Tom Hussey, but as he was changing to another estate he chanced it and he connived and Sossy was mated on the sly to one of his master's finest retrievers, as good as ever stepped into a covert, and by all accounts the equal of Lord Camover's dog that had begot Sossy. So when Tom Hussey departed, there was old Dick with his valuable dog, looking forward to the few weeks hence when Sossy would have the finest bred puppies of their kind in the land. He scarcely dared to compute their value, but it would surely be enough to relegate the idea of a donkey to the limbo of outworn and mean conceits. No, if all went well he would have a change of life altogether. He would give up the old tent; it was rotting, he was tired of it. If things came wonderful well he would buy a nag and a little cart and a few cokernuts and he would travel the round of the fairs and see something of the world again. Nothing like cokernuts for a profitable trade. And perhaps he might even find some old "gal" to go with him.

This roseate dream so tinted every moment of his thoughts that he lived, as you might say, like a poet, cherishing the dog, the source and promise of these ideals, with fondness and joy.

The only cloud on the horizon of bliss was the new gamekeeper, a sprag young fellow, who had taken a deep dislike to him. Old Dick soon became aware of this animosity, for the new keeper kept a strict watch upon his neighbourhood and walked about kicking over Dick's snares, impounding his wires, and complaining of his dirty habits and his poaching. And it was true, he *was* dirty, he had lost his pride, and he *did* poach, just a little, for he had a belly that hungered like any other man's, and he had a dog.

Early one morning as Dick was tending his fire the new keeper strolled up. He was a wry-mouthed slow-speaking young chap, and he lounged there with his gun under his arm and his hands in his pockets. Neither spoke for a while, but at last the keeper said:

"It burns well."

"Huh, and so would you burn well," grinned the old man, "if I cut you atop of it."

For fully two minutes the young keeper made no retort, he was a rather enraging young keeper. Then he said: "Ah, and what do you think you may be doing round here?"

The old man flung a few pinches of tea into a can of boiling water.

"You get on with your job, young feller, and I'll get on with mine."

"What *is* your job?"

The "Owd Venrable" eyed him angrily.

"My job? I'll tell you—it's to mind my own business. You'll learn that for yourself later on, I 'spects, when you get the milk outer your mouth—you ought to, however. Wait till yer be as old as I."

"Ah," drawled the keeper, "I don't mind waiting."

"I met chaps like you before," the old man began to thunder. "Thousands on 'em. D'you know what happened to the last one?"

"Died of fleabites, I shouldn't wonder," was the placid rejoinder.

"I had him on the hop. When he warn't thinking," the old

man, ruminating, grinned, "I wuz! I give him a kick o' the stomach as fetched him atween wind and water, and down he went, clean as a smelt. D'you know what I did then?"

"Picked his pocket, I shouldn't wonder."

"Yah! Never stole nothing from no man, 'cept it was my own. Clean as a smelt, I tell you."

"Well," the new keeper slowly said, shifting his gun from the left arm to the right, "I can take a hiding from any man. . . ."

"Ah, and from any old woman, too, I should say."

". . . from any man," continued the imperturbable one, "as can give it me—if you know of one." He began to pick his teeth with a matchstick. "Did you get my message?" he more briskly added.

"What message?"

"I sent you a message."

"Then you sent it by a wet hen. I an't had no message."

"I know you had it, but I'll tell you again. I've got orders to clear you out of this wood, you and your dog. You can take your time, don't want to be hard on you, but out you goes, and soon, you and your dog."

"Well, we can go, my cunning feller, we can go."

"That's right, then."

"We can go—when we've a mind to. But who's a-going to look arter my job?"

"What job's that?"

"Huh, what job!" the old man disgustedly groaned. "Why, who's a-going to keep an eye on things, and they poachers, thousands on 'em, just waiting for to catch I asleep! But they can't do it."

"Naw, I shouldn't think anyone *could* sleep in a hole like that!"

"Yah, I could sleep, I could sleep a sack o' taters rotten! And who's a-going to clear up when the storms been shamracking about the place? I cleans up the paths, I cleans 'em for one and all, and I cleans 'em for you. Some I does it right for and some I does it wrong. If I did it right for all, I'd be out of this world, seemly."

"Who asked you to? Nobody asked you to, we can do without

it, and we can do without you. So now I've told you." With that the young keeper sauntered airily away.

"Yah!" the Old Venerable called after him. "Clean as a smelt, I tell you, clean as a smelt"; and as long as his adversary remained in view he continued to remind him of that excellent conclusion.

But despite his contempt the old man was perturbed; he knew the game was up, he would have to seek a lodging elsewhere. By the grace of fortune the blow had come just when it could least concern him; all he wanted was time for Sossy to rear her pups, and then he would go; then he would go gaily, driving his horse and cart like a man of property all over that Berkshire and that Oxfordshire, along with some old "gal."

A week later Sossy was safely delivered of nine puppies. Miracles are possible—they must be—but it is not possible to anticipate a miracle: a litter of nine! They were born in the tent beside the man, and they all—Dick, Sossy, and the nine morsels —slept together, and in a few days, although Sossy, despite heroic feeding, began to grow lean, the pups were fat as slugs.

When they were seven days old the man got up one morning to go to a job of hedging. It was a bright, draughty March morn, and he noted the look of the early pink clouds. A fine day promised, though some of the clouds had a queer shape like a goose with its head turned backwards. That boded something! The blackies and thrushers sang beautiful. After Sossy had fed somewhat daintily from the same pot of "shackles" as himself, old Dick hung the sack over the tent opening and left her mothering the pups. He limped off to work. The hedge he was laying was on an upland farm that overlooked his wood. At midday when he lunched he could sit and stare over the vast stern brownness that was so soon to unbend in unbelievable trellises of leaves. Already the clearings and banks were freckled with primroses, the nut thickets hung with showers of yellow pods, and the pilewort's cresset in the hedge was a beam to wandering bees. In all that vastitude there was one tiny hole into which he had crept like a snail for years and years, but it was too small to hide him for ever and ever. So now they would go, he and Sossy,

Just beside him was a pond and the barns of the farm. Two white horses were nuzzling each other in the croft, and a magpie watched them from the cone of a stack. A red ox at the pond snuffled in the water, and as it lifted its head to stare at the old man streams of water pattered back from its hairy lips. Deftly the ox licked with its tongue first one nostril, then the other, but water still dribbled from its mouth in one long glutinous stripe. A large cloud hung above the scene, brooding, white and silent as a swan. Old Dick rose and stretched himself; the wind had died. When the afternoon had worn on he ceased work and turned home. Half-way through the woods he came to a clearing full of primroses, and on a bank, with her muzzle in a rich clump of the blooms, lay his dog, shot through the breast. The old man knelt down beside his dog, but there was nothing he could do, she had been dead a long time. He recalled hearing the shot of a gun, hours ago, not a sharp report, but sullen. Perhaps she had gone out for a scamper and had been chasing a rabbit, or perhaps she had left her litter in order to come to him. The keeper had shot her, shot a poor man's dog, shot her dead. There was nothing he could do, the doom had come crushing even time in its swiftness.

"Fizzled and mizzled I am now," he said forlornly, "and that's a fact."

He left her there and, conversing angrily, pottered home to his tent. Two of the pups were already dead. The others were helpless, and he was helpless; there was nothing he could do for them, they were too young to feed by hand, and he had nothing to feed them with. He crawled out of the tent to suck a long drink from the bucket of water that stood outside, and then he knelt there gazing without vision at the smouldering fire.

"I know, yes, I know what I can do," he mumbled, picking up his long, heavy billhook. "Just a smack o' that behind his ear-hole and he won't take no more hidings from e'er a man or a woman neither. Tipet, I says, and he'd be done, he'd be done in a couple o' minutes, ah, quicker, quicker'n you could say smoke." He dashed the billhook to the earth and groaned. "Oh, I be fair fizzled and mizzled now, I be, ah." He sat up and pulled the bucket between his legs. Picking up one of the pups he plopped it into the bucket. "There's your donkey," he gurgled, "huh, huh, huh! And there"—as he plopped the others in one by one —"goes your cob and your cart and your cokernuts. And there" —as he dashed the last one violently in—"goes the old gal. Huh!"

After a while the old man rose and emptied the drowned bodies into a heap of bushes; the clash of the bucket as he flung it back only fretted the silence of the wood for a few moments.

The Field of Mustard (1926)

ADAM AND EVE AND
PINCH ME

. . . and in the whole of his days, vividly at the end of the afternoon—he repeated it again and again to himself—the kind country spaces had *never* absorbed *quite* so rich a glamour of light, so miraculous a bloom of clarity. He could feel streaming in his own mind, in his bones, the same crystalline brightness that lay upon the land. Thoughts and images went flowing through him as easily and amiably as fish swim in their pools; and as idly, too, for one of his speculations took up the theme of his family name. There was such an agreeable oddness about it, just as there was about all the luminous sky today, that it touched him as just a little remarkable. What *did* such a name connote, signify, or symbolize? It was a rann of a name, but it had euphony! Then again, like the fish, his ambulating fancy flashed into other shallows, and he giggled as he paused, peering at the buds in the brake. Turning back towards his house again, he could see, beyond its roofs, the spire of the church tinctured as richly as the vane: all round him was a new grandeur upon the grass of the fields, and the spare trees had shadows below that seemed to support them in the manner of a plinth, more real than themselves, and the dykes and any chance heave of the level fields were underlined, as if for special emphasis, with long shades of mysterious blackness.

With a little drift of emotion that had at other times assailed him in the wonder and ecstasy of pure light, Jaffa Codling pushed through the slit in the back hedge and stood within his own garden. The gardener was at work. He could hear the voices of the children about the lawn at the other side of the house. He was very happy, and the place was beautiful, a fine white many-windowed house rising from a lawn bowered with plots of mould, turreted with shrubs, and overset with a vast walnut tree. This house had deep clean eaves, a roof of faint-coloured slates that, after rain, glowed dully, like onyx or jade, under the red chimneys, and half-way up at one end was a balcony set with black balusters. He went to a French window that stood open and stepped into the dining-room. There was no one within, and, on that lonely instant, a strange feeling of emptiness dropped upon him. The clock ticked almost as if it had been caught in some indecent act; the air was dim and troubled after that glory outside. Well, now he would go up at once to his study and write down for his new book the ideas and images he had accumulated —beautiful rich thoughts they were—during that wonderful afternoon. He went to mount the stairs and he was passed by one of the maids; humming a silly song she brushed past him rudely, but he was an easy-going man—maids were unteachably tiresome—and reaching the landing he sauntered towards his room. The door stood slightly open and he could hear voices within. He put his hand upon the door . . . it would not open any further. What the devil . . . he pushed—like the bear in the tale—and he pushed, and he pushed—was there something against it on the other side? He put his shoulder to it . . . some wedge must be there, and *that* was extraordinary. Then his whole apprehension was swept up and whirled as by an avalanche— Mildred, his wife, was in there; he could hear her speaking to a man in fair soft tones and the rich phrases that could be used

only by a woman yielding a deep affection to him. Codling kept
still. Her words burned on his mind and thrilled him as if
spoken to himself. There was a movement in the room, then
utter silence. He again thrust savagely at the partly open door,
but he could not stir it. The silence within continued. He beat
upon the door with his fists, crying: "Mildred, Mildred!" There
was no response, but he could hear the rocking armchair com-
mence to swing to and fro. Pushing his hand round the edge of
the door he tried to thrust his head into the opening. There was
not space for this, but he could just peer into the corner of a
mirror hung near, and this is what he saw: the chair at one end
of its swing, a man sitting in it, and upon one arm of it Mildred,
the beloved woman, with her lips upon the man's face, caressing
him with her hands. Codling made another effort to get into the
room—as vain as it was violent. "Do you hear me, Mildred?" he
shouted. Apparently neither of them heard him; they rocked to
and fro while he gazed stupefied. What, in the name of God
. . . What this . . . was she bewitched . . . were there such
things after all as magic, devilry!

He drew back and held himself quite steadily. The chair
stopped swaying, and the room grew awfully still. The sharp
ticking of the clock in the hall rose upon the house like the
tongue of some perfunctory mocker. Couldn't they hear the
clock? . . . Couldn't they hear his heart? He had to put his hand
upon his heart, for surely, in that great silence inside there, they
would hear its beat, growing so loud now that it seemed almost
to stun him! Then in a queer way he found himself reflecting,
observing, analysing his own actions and intentions. He found
some of them to be just a little spurious, counterfeit. He felt it
would be easy, so perfectly easy to flash in one blast of anger and
annihilate the two. He would do nothing of the kind. There was
no occasion for it. People didn't really do that sort of thing, or, at
least, not with a genuine passion. There was no need for anger.
His curiosity was satisfied, quite satisfied, he was certain, he had
not the remotest interest in the man. A welter of unexpected
thoughts swept upon his mind as he stood there. As a writer of
books he was often stimulated by the emotions and impulses of

other people, and now his own surprise was beginning to intrigue him, leaving him, oh, quite unstirred emotionally, but interesting him profoundly.

He heard the maid come stepping up the stairway again, humming her silly song. He did not want a scene or to be caught eavesdropping, and so turned quickly to another door. It was locked. He sprang to one beyond it; the handle would not turn. "Bah! what's *up* with 'em?" But the girl was now upon him, carrying a tray of coffee things. "Oh, Mary!" he exclaimed casually, "I . . ." To his astonishment the girl stepped past him as if she did not hear or see him, tapped upon the door of his study, entered, and closed the door behind her. Jaffa Codling then got really angry. Hell! were the blasted servants in it! He dashed to the door again and tore at the handle. It would not even turn, and, though he wrenched with fury at it, the room was utterly sealed against him. He went away for a chair with which to smash the effrontery of that door. No, he wasn't angry, either with his wife or this fellow—Gilbert, she had called him—who had a strangely familiar aspect as far as he had been able to take it in; but when one's servants . . . faugh!

The door opened and Mary came forth smiling demurely. He was a few yards farther along the corridor at that moment. "Mary!" he shouted, "leave the door open!" Mary carefully closed it and turned her back on him. He sprang after her with bad words bursting from him as she went towards the stairs and flitted lightly down, humming all the way as if in derision. He leaped downwards after her three steps at a time, but she trotted with amazing swiftness into the kitchen and slammed the door in his face. Codling stood, but kept his hands carefully away from the door, kept them behind him. "No, no," he whispered cunningly, "there's something fiendish about door-handles today, I'll go and get a bar, or a butt of timber," and, jumping out into the garden for some such thing, the miracle happened to him. For it was nothing else than a miracle, the unbelievable, the impossible, simple and laughable if you will, but having as much validity as any miracle can ever invoke. It was simple and laughable because by all the known physical laws he should have collided with his gardener, who happened to pass the window

with his wheelbarrow as Codling jumped out on to the path.
And it was unbelievable that they should not, and impossible
that they *did* not collide; and it was miraculous, because Codling
stood for a brief moment in the garden path and the wheelbarrow
of Bond, its contents, and Bond himself passed apparently
through the figure of Codling as if he were so much air, as if he
were not a living breathing man but just a common ghost. There
was no impact, just a momentary breathlessness. Codling stood
and looked at the retreating figure going on utterly unaware of
him. It is interesting to record that Codling's first feelings were
mirthful. He giggled. He was jocular. He ran along in front of
the gardener and let him pass through him once more; then
after him again; he scrambled into the man's barrow and was
wheeled about by this incomprehensible thick-headed gardener
who was dead to all his master's efforts to engage his attention.
Presently he dropped the wheelbarrow and went away, leaving
Codling to cogitate upon the occurrence. There was no room for
doubt, some essential part of him had become detached from the
obviously not less vital part. He felt he was essential because he
was responding to the experience, he was reacting in the normal
way to normal stimuli, although he happened for the time being
to be invisible to his fellows and unable to communicate with
them. How had it come about—this queer thing? How could
he discover what part of him had cut loose, as it were? There
was no question of this being death; death wasn't funny, it
wasn't a joke; he had still all his human instincts. You didn't get
angry with a faithless wife or joke with a fool of a gardener if
you were dead, certainly not! He had realized enough of himself
to know he was the usual man of instincts, desires, and prohibi-
tions, complex and contradictory; his family history for a million
or two years would have denoted that, not explicitly—obviously
impossible—but suggestively. He had found himself doing things
he had no desire to do, doing things he had a desire *not* to do,
thinking thoughts that had no contiguous meanings, no meanings that could be related to his general experience. At odd times
he had been chilled—ay, and even agreeably surprised—at the
immense potential evil in himself. But still, this was no mere
Jekyll and Hyde affair, that a man and his own ghost should

separately inhabit the same world was a horse of quite another colour. The other part of him was alive and active somewhere . . . as alive . . . as alive . . . yes, as *he* was, but dashed if he knew where! What a lark when they got back to each other and compared notes! In his tales he had brooded over so many imagined personalities, followed in the track of so many psychological enigmas that he *had* felt at times a stranger to himself. What if, after all, that brooding had given him the faculty of projecting this figment of himself into the world of men! Or was he some unrealized latent element of being without its natural integument, doomed now to drift over the ridge of the world for ever? Was it his personality, his spirit? Then how was the dashed thing working? Here was he with the most wonderful happening in human experience, and he couldn't differentiate or disinter things. He was like a new Adam flung into some old Eden.

There was Bond tinkering about with some plants a dozen yards in front of him. Suddenly his three children came round from the other side of the house, the youngest boy leading them, carrying in his hand a small sword, which was made, not of steel, but of some more brightly shining material; indeed, it seemed at one moment to be of gold, and then again of flame, transmuting everything in its neighbourhood into the likeness of flame, the hair of the little girl Eve, a part of Adam's tunic; and the fingers of the boy Gabriel as he held the sword were like pale tongues of fire. Gabriel, the youngest boy, went up to the gardener and gave the sword into his hands, saying: "Bond, is this sword any good?" Codling saw the gardener take the weapon and examine it with a careful sort of smile; his great gnarled hands became immediately transparent, the blood could be seen moving diligently about the veins. Codling was so interested in the sight that he did not gather in the gardener's reply. The little boy was dissatisfied and repeated his question: "No, but Bond, *is* this sword any good?" Codling rose, and stood by invisible. The three beautiful children were grouped about the great angular figure of the gardener in his soiled clothes, looking up now into his face and now at the sword, with anxiety in all their puckered eyes. "Well, Marse Gabriel," Codling could hear him reply, "as far as a sword goes, it may be a good un, or it may be a bad un, but, good as it is, it can never be anything but a bad thing." He then gave it back to them; the boy Adam held the haft of it, and the girl Eve rubbed the blade with curious fingers. The younger boy stood looking up at the gardener with unsatisfied gaze. "But, Bond, *can't* you say if this sword's any *good?*" Bond turned to his spade and trowels. "Mebbe the shape of it's wrong, Marse Gabriel, though it seems a pretty handy size." Saying this he moved off across the lawn. Gabriel turned to his brother and sister and took the sword from them; they all followed after the gardener and once more Gabriel made inquiry: "Bond, is this sword any *good?*" The gardener again took it and made a few passes in the air like a valiant soldier at exercise. Turning then, he lifted a bright curl from the head of Eve and cut it off with a sweep of the weapon. He held it up to look at it critically and then let it fall to the ground. Codling sneaked behind him and, picking it up, stood stupidly looking at it. "Mebbe, Marse Gabriel," the gardener was saying, "it 'ud be better made of steel, but it has a smartish edge on it." He went to pick up the barrow, but Gabriel seized it with a spasm of anger and cried out: "No, no, Bond, will you say, just yes or no, Bond, is this sword any *good?*" The gardener stood still and looked down at the little boy, who repeated his question—"just yes or no, Bond!" "No, Marse Gabriel!" "Thank you, Bond," replied the child with dignity, "that's all we wanted to know," and, calling to his mates to follow him, he ran away to the other side of the house.

Codling stared again at the beautiful lock of hair in his hand and felt himself grow so angry that he picked up a strange-looking flowerpot at his feet and hurled it at the retreating gardener. It struck Bond in the middle of the back and, passing clean through him, broke on the wheel of his barrow, but Bond seemed to be quite unaware of this catastrophe. Codling rushed after, and, taking the gardener by the throat, he yelled: "Damn you, will you tell me what all this means?" But Bond proceeded calmly about his work unnoticing, carrying his master about as if he were a clinging vapour, or a scarf hung upon his neck. In a few moments Codling dropped exhausted to the ground. "What . . .

Oh hell . . . what, what am I to do?" he groaned. "What has happened to me? What shall I *do?* What *can* I do?" He looked at the broken flowerpot. "Did I invent that?" He pulled out his watch. "That's a real watch, I hear it ticking, and it's six o'clock." Was he dead or disembodied or mad? What was this infernal lapse of identity? And who the devil, yes, who was it upstairs with Mildred? He jumped to his feet and hurried to the window; it was shut; to the door, it was fastened; he was powerless to open either. Well! well! this was experimental psychology with a vengeance, and he began to chuckle again. He'd have to write to McDougall about it. Then he turned and saw Bond wheeling the barrow across the lawn towards him again. *"Why* is that fellow always shoving that infernal green barrow around?" he asked, and, the fit of fury seizing him again, he rushed towards Bond, but before he reached him the three children danced into the garden again, crying, with great excitement: "Bond, oh, Bond!" The gardener stopped and set down the terrifying barrow; the children crowded about him, and Gabriel held out another shining thing, asking: "Bond, is this box any good?" The gardener took the box and at once his eyes lit up with interest and delight. "Oh, Marse Gabriel, where'd ye get it? Where'd ye get it?" "Bond," said the boy impatiently, "is the box any *good?"* "Any good?" echoed the man. "Why, Marse Gabriel, Marse Adam, Miss Eve, look yere!" Holding it down in front of them, he lifted the lid from the box and a bright-coloured bird flashed out and flew round and round above their heads. "Oh," screamed Gabriel with delight, "it's a kingfisher!" "That's what it is," said Bond, "a kingfisher!" "Where?" asked Adam. "Where?" asked Eve. "There it flies—round the fountain—see it? see it!" "No," said Adam. "No," said Eve.

"Oh, do, do, see it," cried Gabriel, "here it comes, it's coming!" and, holding his hands on high, and standing on his toes, the child cried out as happy as the bird which Codling saw flying above them.

"I can't see it," said Adam.

"Where is it, Gaby?" asked Eve.

"Oh, you stupids," cried the boy. *"There* it goes. There it goes . . . there . . . it's gone!"

He stood looking brightly at Bond, who replaced the lid.

"What shall we do now?" he exclaimed eagerly. For reply the gardener gave the box into his hand and walked off with the barrow. Gabriel took the box over to the fountain. Codling, unseen, went after him, almost as excited as the boy; Eve and her brother followed. They sat upon the stone tank that held the falling water. It was difficult for the child to unfasten the lid; Codling attempted to help him, but he was powerless. Gabriel looked up into his father's face and smiled. Then he stood up and said to the others:

"Now, *do* watch it this time."

They all knelt carefully beside the water. He lifted the lid and, behold, a fish like a gold carp, but made wholly of fire, leaped from the box into the fountain. The man saw it dart down into the water, he saw the water bubble up behind it, he heard the hiss that the junction of fire and water produces, and saw a little track of steam follow the bubbles about the tank until the figure of the fish was consumed and disappeared. Gabriel, in ecstasies, turned to his sister with blazing happy eyes, exclaiming:

"There! Evey!"

"What was it?" asked Eve, nonchalantly, "I didn't see anything."

"More didn't I," said Adam.

"Didn't you see that lovely fish?"

"No," said Adam.

"No," said Eve.

"Oh, stupids," cried Gabriel, "it went right past the bottom of the water."

"Let's get a fishin' nook," said Adam.

"No, no, no," said Gabriel, replacing the lid of the box. "Oh, no."

Jaffa Codling had remained on his knees staring at the water so long that, when he looked around him again, the children had gone away. He got up and went to the door, and that was closed; the windows, fastened. He went moodily to a garden bench and sat on it with folded arms. Dusk had begun to fall into the shrubs and trees, the grass to grow dull, the air chill, the sky to muster its gloom. Bond had overturned his barrow, stalled his tools in the lodge, and gone to his home in the village. A curious cat came round the house and surveyed the man who sat chained to his seven-horned dilemma. It grew dark and fearfully silent. Was the world empty now? Some small thing, a snail perhaps, crept among the dead leaves in the hedge with a sharp, irritating noise. A strange flood of mixed thoughts poured through his mind until at last one idea disentangled itself, and he began thinking with tremendous fixity of little Gabriel. He wondered if he could brood or meditate or "will" with sufficient power to bring him into the garden again. The child had just vaguely recognized him for a moment at the waterside. He'd try that dodge, telepathy was a mild kind of a trick after so much of the miraculous. If he'd lost his blessed body, at least the part that ate and smoked and talked to Mildred . . . He stopped as his mind stumbled on a strange recognition. . . . What a joke, of course . . . idiot . . . not to have seen *that*. He stood up in the garden with joy . . . of course, *he* was upstairs with Mildred, it was himself, the other bit of him, that Mildred had been talking to. What a howling fool he'd been!

He found himself concentrating his mind on the purpose of getting the child Gabriel into the garden once more, but it was with a curious mood that he endeavoured to establish this relationship. He could not fix his will into any calm intensity of power, or fixity of purpose, or pleasurable mental ecstasy. The utmost force seemed to come with a malicious threatening splenetic "entreaty." That damned snail in the hedge broke the thread of his meditation; a dog began to bark sturdily from a distant farm; the faculties of his mind became joggled up like a child's picture puzzle, and he brooded unintelligibly upon such things as skating and steam engines, and Elizabethan drama so lapped about with themes like jealousy and chastity. Really now, Shakespeare's Isabella was the most consummate snob in . . . He looked up quickly to his wife's room and saw Gabriel step from the window to the balcony as though he was fearful of being seen. The boy lifted up his hands and placed the bright box on the rail of the balcony. He looked up at the faint stars for a moment or two, and then carefully released the lid of the box. What came out of it and rose into the air appeared to Codling to be just a piece of floating light, but as it soared above the roof he saw it grow to be a little ancient ship, with its hull and fully set sails and its three masts all of faint primrose flame colour. It cleaved through the air, rolling slightly as a ship through the wave, in widening circles above the house, making a curving ascent until it lost the shape of a vessel and became only a moving light hurrying to some sidereal shrine. Codling glanced at the boy on the balcony, but in that brief instant something had happened, the ship had burst like a rocket and released three coloured drops of fire which came falling slowly, leaving beautiful grey furrows of smoke in their track. Gabriel leaned over the rail with outstretched palms, and, catching the green star and the blue one as they drifted down to him, he ran with a rill of laughter back into the house. Codling sprang forward just in time to catch the red star; it lay vividly blasting his own palm for a monstrous second, and then, slipping through, was gone. He stared at the ground, at the balcony, the sky, and then heard an exclamation . . . his wife stood at his side.

"Gilbert! How you frightened me!" she cried. "I thought you were in your room; come along in to dinner." She took his arm and they walked up the steps into the dining-room together. "Just a moment," said her husband, turning to the door of the room. His hand was upon the handle, which turned easily in his grasp, and he ran upstairs to his own room. He opened the door. The light was on, the fire was burning brightly, a smell of cigarette smoke about, pen and paper upon his desk, the Japanese book-knife, the gilt matchbox, everything all right, no one there. He picked up a book from his desk . . . *Monna Vanna*. His bookplate was in it—*Ex Libris—Gilbert Cannister*. He put it down beside the green dish; two yellow oranges were in the green dish, and two most deliberately green Canadian apples rested by their side. He went to the door and swung it backwards and forwards quite easily. He sat on his desk trying to piece the thing together, glaring at the print and the book-knife and the smart matchbox, until his wife came up behind him exclaiming: "Come along, Gilbert!"

"Where are the kids, old man?" he asked her, and, before she replied, he had gone along to the nursery. He saw the two cots, his boy in one, his girl in the other. He turned whimsically to Mildred, saying: "There *are* only two, *are* there?" Such a question did not call for reply, but he confronted her as if expecting some assuring answer. She was staring at him with her bright beautiful eyes.

"Are there?" he repeated.

"How strange you should ask me that now!" she said. . . . "If you're a very good man—perhaps . . ."

"Mildred!"

She nodded brightly.

He sat down in the rocking-chair, but got up again saying to her gently: "We'll call him Gabriel."

"But suppose—"

"No, no," he said, stopping her lovely lips, "I know all about him." And he told her a pleasant little tale.

Adam and Eve and Pinch Me (1921)

THE PRESSER

Two or three years after the first Jubilee of Queen Victoria a small ten-year-old boy might have been seen slouching early every morning along the Mile End Road towards the streets of Whitechapel. Johnny Flynn was a pale boy of pinched appearance—for although his black coat was a size too large for him, his black trousers were a size too small—he was not very well, and he was tired. Plodding along from his aunt's house miles away in Hackney, he sometimes drowsily ran into things; things like sauntering policemen (who were ductile and kind) or letter-boxes (which were not). A policeman genially shook him.

"Ay! Where ye going?"

"Going to work, sir."

"Work! What work do ye work at?"

"Mr. Alabaster's, a tailor, sir."

"Oh, a tailor! Mind he don't put ye under a thimble and suffocate ye. Get along with it, and don't go knocking people down 's if ye was popping off to Buckingham Palace!"

Johnny wanly smiled as he said: "No" and "Good morning, sir."

It was generally a letter-box, though, and after such a mishap one day he had gone into a public lavatory. There he had seen a bad word chalked upon the wall—a very bad word. Johnny Flynn knew all about bad words although he had never uttered them; his mind shrank from them as a snail shrinks when you spit on it. But this time he went on his way with the bad word chanting in his mind—he could *not* but listen to it, he was absorbed by it; and the very next letter-box he came to he said it out boldly and loud, seven times, to the letter-box. And one day he dropped his packet of dinner into the mouth of one of those letter-boxes.

Well, when he came to Whitechapel, there was Leman Street, and off Leman Street there were other streets full of shops with funny names over the windows, like Greenbaum, Goldansky, Finesilver, and Artzbashev, and shops full of foreign food that looked nasty and smelled, or full of objects that seemed vaguely improper. There were hundreds of clattering carts bedazing him, and women who were drunk at eight o'clock in the morning sat on doorsteps with their heads in their hands. And they smelled, too. Very soon now he reached a high dull building that hoarded a barracks of prolific Jewish families, and ascending one flight of its sticky stone stairs he came to a standstill outside a door in a dark passage. There he had to wait until Mr. Sulky, who was the presser and had the key, arrived. Mr. Sulky was a big dark young man with a pale pitted face, who lodged in an eating-house, and went for long walks on Sundays, and passed for a misogynist. The rest of his time he spent in pressing trousers with a large hot-iron goose.

Johnny said: "Good morning, sir."

Mr. Sulky said: "Huh!" but he always said it with a faint smile.

The first business in the tailor's workshop was to light the fire, a great fire maintained with coke. Then to sweep the room clean of its countless fragments of cloth and cotton. Heaping these in a wooden box, the boy staggered with it across the dark passage into a smaller apartment with a window, the very symbol of gloom, looking down into a dank yard where he could see people all day long going to the privy. The room contained only a colossal pile of cloth clippings covering the whole floor, and it was his unending task to sort these into their various kinds. The pile never lessened, it seemed to grow with absorbent inexorable growth. Sometimes he could scarcely enter the door to get into the room; and the implacable mountain of rags was watered with the tears of his childish hungers and despairs. He emptied the box and returned to the workshop.

Eight or nine women came in and began their work of making trousers. A massive table stood in the middle; the women sat round three sides of the room on old empty boxes—these were less comfortable than chairs, but more convenient. The room was large and well lighted from two windows. In summer the windows were a blessing to the women, the hot fire an affliction; in winter it was otherwise. Sometimes they sweated, and sometimes they sneezed or they coughed, but they never shivered. Each woman had a pad of needles tacked to her bodice, a pair of scissors and skeins of thread in her lap, and her hands were busied with the garments of men she knew nothing about. Each had a wedding ring on her nuptial finger, the beginnings of a hump on her shoulders, and the deuce knows what emotions in her heart. They were mostly young women, but they looked old, whereas Mr. Sulky and Mr. Alabaster were young and looked young. It reminded Johnny of the question propounded by a famous advertisement:

WHY DOES A WOMAN LOOK OLD
SOONER THAN
A MAN?

And the answer was something to do with soap.

His favourite was certainly Helen, she was handsomest. Johnny liked her, she had a pretty, freckled face and a big bosom, and was tall and fair. Johnny admired her, though she was not kind to him and effusive like old Mrs. Grainger. Indeed, she was in some ways, he thought, rather unkind and slightly haughty, but her smile was lovely. She was married to a bottle-washer named Smithers, and they had a little girl Hetty, six or seven years old, with weak eyes and heavy boots, who often came and sat on the stairs waiting for her mother. Mrs. Grainger was a wrinkled crone who got drunk on Saturday nights in order to import cheer into her fading hours. Beer, she declared, was better than hot soup in her belly. When Johnny first same to work with them she catechized him.

"You're a weeny little chap. What's your age?"

Her hands were shiny and lumpy; she was thin, but she had a plump behind.

"I'm ten years," replied the flustered boy.

"God's my mercy! You ought to be at school, your age. Why don't you go to school?"

"I'm not well," said Johnny.

"Nobody's well in this world. We're all alike."

The old woman hawked and spat into her snuffy handkerchief. "What's the matter with you?"

"I don't know," Johnny Flynn confessed.

"How d'ye know you're not well, then?"

"I can feel," said Johnny.

"What can you feel?"

"In my liver," the boy whispered. "Inch and half lower than it ought to be, and we can't alter it. My mother's a widow."

"So your father's dead?"

"Yes; she lives in the country."

"And where do you live?"

"With my aunt and uncle. Down at Hackney. He's an engine-driver."

"That's grand! D'ye like it?"

The boy reflected. "I don't know," he said slowly.

"Well, God's my mercy!" tittered the old woman. "You must go out in the fresh air all you can."

In the corner a girl sat machining seams. Mr. Sulky took a hot goose from the fire to the table and pressed trousers under a damp rag that soon rotted the air with the odour of steaming cloth. This was a necessary evil, for although all the others were engaged in cutting out, preparing, stitching, binding, button-holing, and generally compounding trousers, the art of finishing the garment lay with the presser, the prince of a tailor's work-shop—and that was Mr. Sulky. No civilian, from a bookbinder to a bishop, would dream of donning a pair of trousers that had not been pressed. A Hottentot might, or a skipjack—yes, conceivably even a bookbinder might—but certainly not a bishop. Let it have buttons of gold, fabulous fabric, silky seams, and trimmings of rapture, fused in a noble equilibrium of cut, but until it had been baptized with a wet rag and punched with a hot iron it is nothing.

Mr. Sulky (who passed for a misogynist) whistled airily as he bumped and hissed with his iron, and then began to chaff the women.

"Well, ladies!"

Heavy scarlet lips gave him the pout of a sardonic man, but his face was a kind face, very pale and very bare. Not a hair or the sign of it was to be seen on his chin. Or on his arms. At work he cast off his coat, waistcoat, and collar and wore only a striped shirt and a belt round his trousers. He kept on his neat buttoned boots, turned up his stiff cuffs, and his cuff-links tinkled as he jerked his arms.

"What devilry have you all been at since yesterday?"

The ladies glanced at each other and tittered.

"Nothing, Ernie, so help me God," cackled Mrs. Grainger. "Ask Helen."

"Bah!" The presser clouted his goose down upon some innocent trousers.

"Oh dear, ladies," cried the provoking old woman, "he's got a wink over his eye this morning."

Mr. Sulky, somewhat baffled, stuttered: "Born devils! And you're the worst of the lot."

"No, Ernie, no." The old woman's glasses twinkled reas-suringly at him. "I had my dues, thank God, years ago."

"Your dues!"

"Many a time, and I can't deny it," said the old woman.

"Ah, devils born, I tell you," groaned the presser.

"And the men! Dear Lord!" Mrs. Grainger shot at him. "You can't even make your own trousers."

Mr. Sulky made a rude reply, and the women laughed quietly though they pretended not to. It made Johnny laugh, but at the same time he was ashamed to laugh—and he pretended not to. Once a boy at school had told him a rude joke, and it was such a cunning comical joke that he had to tell it in a whisper to his father. Father had giggled. "Don't tell mother," implored the boy. And father had said: "Pooh, no. No fear!" But Johnny was sure that he had gone and told mother at once, and he could not bear to think of it.

There was no more joking after Mr. Alabaster came in, for he was the master. Mr. Alabaster had short bow legs, a pink face, and florid hair that curled dandily. So did his voice, for he lisped. Very cheerful he looked, and was seldom harsh to anyone. At the table opposite Mr. Sulky he stood with a measuring tape around his shoulders, a pair of shears or a piece of pipeclay in his right hand; and having made chalk marks on whatever piece of cloth was before him, he cut trousers out of serge, flannel, duck, vicuña, tweed, any mortal cloth you could think of, all day long. A very clever fellow. A thoughtful man, too. He would never allow Johnny Flynn to stay in the workshop during the dinner hour. Summer or winter, rain or shine, out he had to go.

"You muth get the fresh air into you," Mr. Alabaster said. "Itth good for the lining of the stomach, or I shall have the poleeth on me. You can go under the railway arch if it rainth,"

No one but Mr. Sulky had the privilege of staying in the workshop during dinner-time; that was the edict, the injunction, the fixed rule. Then how was it that Mrs. Smithers stayed there sometimes, Johnny would like to know. Mr. Alabaster did not know of it, but Johnny knew and the women knew; what was more, although they never enjoyed that favour themselves, they were glad when Helen did. Johnny was glad too, in a way, because of course her husband was a nasty cruel man who slogged her about, and it was best for her not to go home more often than she had to. Mrs. Grainger used to advise her about Smithers:

"Give him in charge, my gal, turn him out, or sling your hook.

He's a dirty foul thing, and the Lord gave him to you for a walking wickedness."

"How can I do that?" asked Helen. "I'm married to him, and there's little Hetty."

"Oh, God's my mercy!" Mrs. Grainger was baffled, but still emphatic. "Give him in charge and sling your hook. What with the men and their women and the holy marriage bells, you can't tell your head from your elbow. It ought to be made impossible, and then there'd be some sense in Christianity."

Well, the boy would go and walk in the streets. Unless it rained he avoided the railway arch because someone had done murder there, and someone else had painted a white skeleton on the wall; so he walked about. There was the dreadful den where the Jews brought their fowls to be strangled; knots of gabbling women dangling dead birds or birds that were going to be dead, the pavement dribbling blood, and feathers falling, sticking in the blood. And in the bakehouse next door you could watch a man flinging limp matzos, like pieces of white velvet, into a big oven, and another man drawing them out as stiff as china plates. Soon he opened his package of food—wedges of bread and slips of meat folded in a sheet of newspaper. Scrupulously he sniffed the meat, and not caring for that smell he dropped the meat into a gutter and chewed the bread with resentment. Yesterday it was pickled pork, and the day before; it would be pickled pork to-morrow, and the day after, and the day after that. Whatever it was, he had it for a week; six days it savoured, and did all that it was not expected to do. His aunt was a wise and busy woman who could not prepare a fresh meal for him every day; it was not to be thought of and it was not necessary. Every Saturday night she bought for his separate and sole consumption a little joint of meat, cooking it specially for him on Sundays; and every week his stomach turned sour on it after a day or two. This image of that evil ort of flesh reposing undiminishably in the larder tormented him even in dreams. It never entered his mind to complain to his aunt, and if it had done so he had little of the spirit of complaint. If he was not exactly a Spartan, he was, you might say, spartanatical. Things happened to you; they were good, or they were bad—and that was the truth about everything.

Now, this neighbourhood was full of little Jew boys, and it was the custom of little Christians to submit such heathens to mockery, often to ill-treatment. In the early days there Johnny Flynn had called after some of them: "Sheeny! Sheeny!" Sweet knowledge, how we live and learn! It was no joke to be the one pure Christian boy in a street full of belligerent bloody-minded Hebrew serpents who pretended to run away when you made a face at them, but who, as soon as you pursued them, turned diabolically upon you and dashed your Christianity into discomfiture and blood. Perhaps it was these very misfortunes that made Johnny Flynn so fond of evangelical hymns. Whenever he experienced any joy—and that was not seldom—he would lift up his heart and sing to himself that he was

> Sweeping through the gates of the New Jerusalem,
> Washed in the blood of the Lamb.

Or if it were sorrow that he felt—and that, too, was not seldom— he would murmur the

> Sweetest carol ever sung:
> Jesus, blessed Jesus.

But maybe it was really an emotional gift from his mother. Always on Sunday eve she had taken him to an undenominational chapel run by some hooded sisters and a preacher with gaunt eyes who sometimes preached himself into a fit. At some stage of the service the sisters would come round and interrogate the worshipper.

"Are you saved?"

"Yes, ma'am, thank you," Mrs. Flynn would reply.

"Praise God. Is your little boy saved?"

"Yes, ma'am," said mother, with bright hope in her eyes, "I *think* he is."

"Praise God, sister."

But when the lady had passed on Johnny would bend and growl at his mother:

"What d'you tell her that for?"

"Well, you *must* be saved, Johnny, you know you must."

"I ain't going to be," he would say wretchedly; "never, I won't be."

"Now, don't you be a bad boy, Johnny, or you'll go to the fire. Of course you must be saved; what ever next!"

Then, seeing him so cross, she would press his hand fondly and he would love her again, so that when they stood up to sing "Sweeping through the gates," he would join in quite happily and admire her sweet voice.

Ah, in such matters he was on the side of his father. Father was an atheist, he had even joined the Skeleton Army—a club of men who went about in masks or black faces, with ribald placards and a brass band, to make war upon the Salvation Army. Yet when his father had died—twelve months ago—and a friend had made a small wooden cross, painted black, to put on his grave, Johnny had painted his name and dates on the cross in white paint with a thin brush that vexed him to madness, for the hair of the brush kept sticking out at the angle of the pressure applied and looked like an L. Moreover, Johnny had decided that his father should have an epitaph; so he cut up a piece of a cardboard box, gave it a border of black ink, composed a verse, and tacked the card to the cross with some little nails.

> I am not gone I am only a sleep.
> Where Jesus heavenly mansions keep.
> Grieve not for long nor trouble be
> And love each other because of me.
>   J. F.

He wept while he composed this piece of deathly poetry, and whenever he recalled it afterwards he wept again. His mother, too, liked it so very much that tears came into her eyes. In a few weeks rain had soaked the card on the cross; the sun had bleached it and discoloured the ink so that it could hardly be read. When some of the tacks came out the card curled over and exposed an advertisement on its back of somebody's baking powder.

Long ere day was over, the boy regretted his rash disposal of the meat; devastating hunger assailed him and he yearned for any scrap, even a dog's. At such times it was the joy of heaven to him if Mrs. Grainger beckoned at tea-time.

"Johnny, I want you to go and get me a ha'p'orth of tea, a ha'p'orth of sugar and a farthingsworth of milk. There's three-ha'pence—you can have the farthing for yourself."

Nice, nice old woman! With his farthing he would buy a few broken biscuits; and he would borrow a pinch of her sugar and dip his biscuits in her milk. That did not happen every day. At other times it was a desperate joy to stand in front of a grocer's window, to divide the display in half, and to ponder long and exquisitely which half he would have if a choice were given him. Would you have marmalade, potted tongue, cocoa, and condensed milk—things like that—or would you have pineapple, corn beef, and split peas—candles being no good? Desperate schemes for obtaining any of these, or anything else eatable, simply assaulted his longing, but he had no courage to test them again after he had once stolen a salted gherkin that made him vomit. He would turn away and glare along the pavements and gutters, hoping to find an apple-core or a rotten orange. Once he had the odd chance to pick up a playing-card, which he tore in pieces. Mother had warned him against the sin of card-playing; she had warned him against everything immoderate and immodest—strong drink, little girls, stealing, smoking, swearing, and such-like. Yet whenever Mr. Alabaster or Mr. Sulky sent him out in the evening for a can of beer he could not resist taking a stealthy gulp or two of the liquid. Hunger was awful. In a daze he soaped seams for Mr. Sulky or sewed buttons for Helen and Mrs. Grainger. If there was nothing else to be done he had to go to the rag-room and sort clippings from that maddening pile. Kneeling down beside his box among the soft rags, he would dream over the fine doings he had had on Queen Victoria's Jubilee day. That *was* a day! All the scholars went to school in the morning to pray, to implore God to confound and frustrate certain name-less nations, to receive a china mug with the Queen's face twice on it, a medal with her face again—in case the mug got broken—and a paper bag containing half a sausage pie and a great piece of cake. Lord, how grand! He ate them all over again and again. Then you marched out to the park with flags, and the park was full—millions of kids. There were clowns and jokers and sports, and you had your mug filled with tea from a steam-roller. Hundreds of steam-rollers. And then he forgot everything and fell asleep sprawling amongst the rags until he was awakened by angry Mr. Alabaster.

"Hi! hi! Thith won't do, you know. I don't pay you for thleeping, it will bankrupt me. It won't do at all. You and I muth part. God bleth, aren't you well?"

"Yes, sir."

"Well, then! God bleth, do you think I am a millionaire with hundredth of pounds? I can't understand you, and it won't do. You and I will part, my man."

But at the end of the day the kind Mr. Alabaster would sometimes give him a penny to ride part of the way home in a tram. With his penny Johnny hurried off to buy a cake or a pie, and thereafter walked cheerfully home. Often that penny became such a mighty necessity to him that as he knelt alone among the rags in the gloomy room, the pose, the quiet, and the need induced a mood in which he mumbled dozens of prayers.

"O God, make him give me a penny tonight, only a penny; make him give me a penny, please God. Amen."

As if to impregnate his pleas with suitable flavour, he crooned over the hymns he knew. Then again: "Please God, make him give me a penny. This once, like you did before, and I won't ask again. Amen."

Not often were these prayers answered, and directly their failure became apparent, he would descend weakly to the street, his whole body burning with ferocity against so frightful, so callous, so unseeing a god; and he would gasp out horrible blasphemies, until he came to a shop window where he could pause for a long rest, divide up its delicacies, and mystically devour them. In such delight he always forgot his anger against Jehovah.

One morning Helen came to the workroom at a very late hour. Mr. Alabaster regarded her sternly as she came in, until he saw she had a black eye horribly bruised, and knew she had been crying. She whispered a few words to Mr. Alabaster before going to her seat, and he lisped: "Oh yeth, yeth. Dear me! Itth dreadful, yeth. Dear, dear me. All right."

Mr. Sulky did not utter a sound, not one terrible word, and the whole room became silent. After his first and only glance at the disfigured woman, Mr. Sulky pounced upon his task with a fermenting malignity, the wrath of one whose soul has been split by a shock that drained him of charity and compunction, and his hot iron crashed upon the apparel before him as though it contained the body of a loathed enemy. Windows trembled at each mighty jar, implements on the table spitefully clattered, and paper patterns fluttered off the walls as if casting themselves to perdition. Mr. Alabaster looked across protestingly.

"My word, Ernie! I thay!"

The presser ignored him. Snatching the iron from its stand, he flashed across the room, flung the cooling goose into the heart of the fire, took another in its place, tested it with a spit of saliva that ticked and slid into limbo, and resumed his murderous attack on the trousers.

"Stheady, Ernie! God bleth, you'll have the theiling down on uth!"

Mr. Alabaster's pipeclay was jolted from the table by the next concussion. Mr. Alabaster was master there, but he was a timid man; Sulky could eat three of him, and Sulky was a pearl amongst pressers; so Mr. Alabaster put on his coat. If Sulky was going mad he could go mad in peace and comfort.

"Muth go up the town this morning. Be back after dinner. Look after everything, Ernie. You know. Don't—ah—don't break anything, Ernie."

The ignoring Mr. Sulky signalized his master's departure by a volley of ferocious clouts upon the garment he was handling. Then he stopped. Although the sewing-machine whirred in its corner, the quietness of the women was perceptibly tense. Helen bent low over her work. Johnny knew that she was still crying, and he could not bear to see this, so he tiptoed away from the workshop into the room across the passage and flung himself into the melancholy business of sorting the clippings. Canvas, buckram, silesia, cotton, silk, tweed, serge, flannel, and vicuña all fetched different prices in the rag market and had to be separated into heaps. The main heap was impregnable; it was a job that never could be finished, for the pieces always accumulated faster than the boy could sort them. It was a tide that ebbed lightly and flowed greatly, and the spirit of the boy was drowned in it. Once he had read a fairy tale about a prince in captivity who was given a barn full of canary seed to sort out in a single night or else he was to be turned into a donkey. But the prince had a fairy god-mother who set some earwigs on the job, and they finished it while the prince went off to a ball and married a poor girl who was lovely and good and had cured the fairy godmother of tooth-ache. But there were no fairy godmothers in Whitechapel, and earwigs were no use—not with cloth. And Johnny's head be-haved strangely nowadays. Sometimes his head would go numb and he would feel as if he were falling out of his body and sink-ing into the void. Or if he only heard the ping of an omnibus bell in the city, even that gave him a horrible blow in his heart, and his heart would rattle madly. The sound of the bells was so shocking to him that when he went up to the city he always stuffed pieces of wadding in his ears. And the sight of the room full of rags affected him in much the same way: his head swam, his knees trembled, and his heart rocked.

Suddenly the door was dashed open and Mr. Sulky appeared.

"Oh," he said, seeing Johnny there. Then: "Get out of this!"

The boy slunk out into the dark passage. Helen stood at the door; she held a handkerchief to her eyes.

"Come," said Mr. Sulky, and Helen followed him into the rag-room. They did not fasten the door. Johnny lingered outside; he did not know what else to do, he was a stupid boy. Hearing nothing within the room and being somewhat bewildered, he pushed open the door. Helen and Mr. Sulky were folded tightly in each other's arms, silent.

"Where shall I go?" the boy timidly whispered.

The presser turned his white face towards him and with his great teeth bared he snarled:

"Go away, you idiot!"

Out shot his foot and the door slammed in Johnny's face. The boy felt that his indiscretion had been vulgar. There was some-thing in the surprising embrace of the two people—the figure of the piteous Helen and her tender cherishing by Mr. Sulky—that seemed almost holy. He crept back to the workroom, where the women were talking aloud.

"Here, Johnny," cried Mrs. Grainger. "Just run out and get me a pennyworth of pills at the post office. My consumption's so bad this morning it's murdering me. Ask them for rhubarb pills. I don't suppose they'll do me any good—the only cure for me is a dose of poison; but God Almighty made the medicine, and I might be lucky. A pennyworth of rhubarb pills, Johnny. And tell the man with the crooked nose they're for a lady that's got a delicate stomach. Don't forget that, there's a good boy."

When he returned from this errand of mercy Helen and Mr. Sulky were back in the workshop again, looking as if nothing particular had occurred. Helen seemed cheerful. Mr. Sulky whistled softly and did not bang his irons about very much.

This was one of the days on which silly Johnny had thrown his dinner away, and as time wore on, the old hunger brought him to his old despair. At seven o'clock Mr. Alabaster and Mr. Sulky tossed up to see who should pay for supper, and Mr. Sulky won—he always did. Johnny fetched them a small loaf, some cheese, a tin of lobster, and a can of beer. He tore off as much of the loaf's crust as he dared; if he could only have got at the lobster he would have gone to prison for it. He placed the food on the table.

"Good night, sir. Good night, Mr. Sulky," then he said, moving slowly towards the door. The two men were laughing and cracking jokes.

"Hi! Here, Johnny, hereth a penny for the tram!"

Oh my, it was very blissful then! Fatigue and despair left him; down the stairs he went leaping and fled to a cookshop in the Mile End Road. It was some distance away, but it was there you could buy such marvellous penny cakes, of a size, of a succulence, reeking with sweet fat and crusted with raisins. Never a thought of the Lord, never a thanksgiving prayer. Johnny unwrapped the cake and stood gazing at it, seeking the loveliest corner of entry, when a large boy came to him from an alley near by and accosted him.

"Give us a bite, young 'un."

"Gives nothing." Master Flynn was positive to the point of heartlessness.

"I've had nothing to eat all day," the large boy said mournfully.

Johnny intimated that he was in the same unfortunate case himself.

"Give us half of it, d'ye hear," the other demanded in truculent tones, "or I'll have the lot."

Johnny shook his head and hiked a shoulder. "No you won't."

"Who'd stop me?" growled the bandit.

"Inky," replied young Flynn. And then, as he lifted the cake to his mouth and prepared to bite a great gap in it, the absolute and everlasting end of the world smote him clump on the ridge of his chin. He heard the rough fellow grunt: "There's the upper cut for yer"; the cake was snatched from his paralysed grasp. "And there's another for civility." Again the end of the world crashed upon his face from the other side. Johnny felt no pain, not the faintest scruple of a physical twinge, but there was such a frantic roaring in his ears that he had to bend down with his head in his hands and stare abstractedly at the pavement. Scores of people were passing, but none seemed to have noticed this calamity; and when he looked up, the fellow was gone, and the cake was gone. Dazed Johnny, after an interval for recovery, and after imprinting upon his mind the exact spot of the occurrence and the situation of that darksome alley, walked on grinding his teeth and registering a vow. He would train for a whole week on puddings made of blood—and then! Arabs gave their horses cakes made with mutton fat and they would fly over the desert, mad, all day long; but for people it had to be blood—and then you could blind anyone. He'd get some blood, a lot.

The next day was cold, with a frozen mist niggling in the streets, and when Johnny returned from an afternoon journey to the city it was almost dark. As he ascended the stairs he could just discern the little girl Smithers sitting there.

"Hullo, Hetty," he said; and she said: "Mind where you're coming!" She was nursing a black kitten.

"Your mother ain't done yet, Hetty, not for hours."

The child hugged her kitten more closely, making no reply.

"Why don't you go home?" Johnny asked.

The child looked up at him, as if wondering at his foolishness.

"Somebody 'ull kick you," he went on, "sitting down. What you sitting there for?"

A voice from the head of the stairs called: "Hoi!"

Johnny looked up. "It's me," he said.

Down came Mr. Sulky. "Is that Hetty?"

The child stood up and the man put an arm round her shoulders. "Hallo, Hetty. Cold, aren't you? Want some tea?"

Hetty tucked the kitten under her arm and said: "Yes," very softly. So Mr. Sulky put his hand in his pocket and jingled some money. Then he turned to Johnny. "You want some tea?"

"No, not much," lied the boy.

"Well, here's sixpence. Take Hetty out to some coffee-shop and give her a good tea, anything she likes, and have some yourself if you want any. Will you do that?"

"Yes," said the boy.

"There you are, Hetty," Mr. Sulky said; "you go along of Johnny. He'll take you. And then come back here with him." Bending down, Mr. Sulky astonishingly kissed the child.

She and Johnny clattered down the stone stairs together and out into the street.

"You can't bring that kitten," Johnny pointed out, "not in a shop."

"Why?" asked the little girl.

"They won't serve you, not in a shop."

Dully the child answered: "Yes, they will."

"They'll laugh at you," protested Johnny. "They'll—they'll cut its head off."

"No, they won't," Hetty said.

And in point of fact they did not, although the first thing they saw on entering the coffee-house was a man in a white apron sharpening a long thin knife—a very large man. They sat down in a compartment, rather like a church pew, and the large man soon came up to them and tapped on the table with his ferocious knife.

"Well?" said he, very affably.

"Two cups of coffee, please, and two dorks, please," young Flynn timidly ordered.

Soon the large man returned with these things.

"Two coffee, two slices," he said, and pushed a basin of brown sugar towards them. Johnny thereupon gave him the sixpence, and the man gave him threepence change.

"It's nice in here, ain't it?" said Johnny. And indeed it was;

warm and savoury, with the mingled odours of fish and bacon and the sawdust on the floor. Most of the other compartments had men in them, but they took no notice at all of the children or the kitten. Hetty dropped some spoonfuls of coffee into her saucer and stood the kitten on the table. It lapped a few drops and then sat upon its haunches to gaze at the ceiling.

"Going to have some more coffee?" inquired the boy.

Hetty nodded her head and said: "You?"

"Na!" Johnny was contemptuous. "I don't want any more coffee. What else d'you want?"

"Jam turnover," replied the child.

The boy made a wry face. "You don't want that. Nothing in 'em," he declared. "If I was you I'd have a lump of Tottenham cake. Have some Tottenham cake?"

Hetty picked the kitten off the table. "Ernie said I could have what I like. . . ."

Johnny took her empty cup and walked off to the counter, returning with the cup refilled, a jam turnover, and a triangle of cake that had a pink bile-provoking veneer upon it. "Tottenham," said Johnny. They lingered on for some time until everything had disappeared, and Johnny had to explain to incredulous Hetty that all the money was gone.

"Where d'you live?" he asked her, and she replied that she lived in Bermondsey, that her father was a bottle-washer.

"I ain't got no father," said Johnny Flynn dismally.

"He gets drunk every day," continued Hetty.

"I ain't got no father at all," repeated the boy, leaning his elbows on the table and looking mournful.

"And slashes mum," said she.

"What for?" The boy was awed, but curious.

"He keeps on trying to kill us."

"Yes, but what for?"

"I dunno," said the little girl. "Mum says he's gone into bad habits."

"When my father got drunk," Johnny Flynn expanded, "he was grand."

"And 'e's a noremonger," Hetty added.

"What's that?"

"I dunno," Hetty went on, stroking her kitten. "I wish we'd got another one; I don't like him. More does mum."

"But you can't have another father! Course you can't, silly," commented Johnny Flynn.

"Yes, you can; and mum says we will, soon. We'll have to."

Just then a quarrel arose in a compartment near them, between a man with a peg-leg and a man with a patch over one eye. They were sitting opposite each other.

"You're a liar!" bawled the wooden-leg man.

"Oh, am I!"

"Yes. There you are. Now you know. I don't care what company I'm in, or what company I ain't in, that's straight from my bloody heart."

"I'm a liar, am I?" Patch-eye shouted.

"Yes, there you are!"

"And there *you* are!" cried the other, and he walloped his accuser over the head with a jar of salt.

The large man in the white apron dropped his knife and rubbed his hands together, yelling: "Hi! Drop it. Devil and hell, where d'ye think you are—in the bull ring?"

And he hurled himself competently upon the brawlers.

"Drop it, d'ye hear! Or I'll have the guts out of you for my garters. Drop it!"

Both combatants subsided into their benches.

"D'ye see where he hit me?" said the peg-leg man, pointing with his finger to a spot on his head. "Feel that!"

The fat host plunged his fingers amongst the greying hair. "Jesus wept!" he murmured. "There's a lump like St. Paul's Cathedral. I'm surprised at you, Patchy."

"Called me a liar," the aggressor explained callously.

"Pooh, that's only his ignorance!"

"Ignorance!" moaned the afflicted one. "He's broken my brain-pan. That's done me a lot of good, ain't it?"

"Ay, it's just his playful heart, that's all! Now behave your-selves," the host went on, with emollient raillery, ". . . or! You know what I'll do to you—ha, ha! You know that, don't you? I'm the king of the castle here, and an Englishman's castle's his birthright all the world over. A king can do no wrong."

"Why not?"

"It's just a law, like everything else," mine host explained, "but of course it's kept private."

"Oh," said the one-eyed man resignedly, "give him another cup of cawfee!"

During this tumult Hetty trembled fearfully, and at last Johnny had to usher her out of the place.

"I don't like these dark streets," said she, clutching Johnny's hand and tucking the kitten under her arm.

"That's nothing," Master Flynn assured her. "I like fighting. Don't you like fighting? I had a scrap with a bloke last night in the Mile End Road, and I split his head open in six places. Do you know what Peter Jackson does when he trains himself? He's the champion of the world, he is."

Miss Smithers did not know.

"He drinks blood," Johnny informed her.

When they approached the workshop they met Hetty's mother standing in the doorway at the foot of the stairs, so Johnny told her of the grand tea they had had. And while he was also telling her about the quarrel Mr. Sulky came tripping down the stairs.

"Hallo!" he cried, greeting them as if he had just met them for the first time. "Here we are, then. This way, Nell. Good night, Johnny. Come on, Hetty." And before Johnny could explain how he had spent the whole sixpence Mr. Sulky took Helen's arm and Hetty's hand, and the three of them walked off together. And Johnny heard Hetty exclaiming:

"Mum! Look at the dear little kitten!"

Johnny never saw Helen again. Apparently she had gone away, and she would be happier now. At the end of the week the women had a "whip round" and collected a small sum of money to buy Mr. Sulky a teapot. He was setting up housekeeping—Mrs. Grainger said. And when she gave him the teapot she said God bless him, and wished him the best of luck.

In a little while Johnny's tribulation came to a happy end. His mother wrote that she could not bear to be parted from him any longer; he had been away a year; he must come home to her now. His aunt was deeply annoyed at such ingratitude and wanted him to refuse to go home; but Johnny gave his notice in to Mr.

Alabaster, who said he was very sorry to part with him, and declared that he "wath the beth boy he ever had." When the joyous last day came Mr. Alabaster wished him good-bye and gave him some good advice. Mr. Sulky did the same and presented him with sixpence as well.

"Good-bye, little Johnny," whispered old Mrs. Grainger—and she gave him two new pennies. Johnny kept them sacredly in a box for many a long day.

Silver Circus (1928)

THE GREEN DRAKE

In the village of So-and-so lived an old woman, Rebecca Cracknell, who had a dog with an odd eye and the name of Jack, a kitten with an odd tail and the name of Jack, and a green drake with odd ambitions that was called Jack. The old woman's only son was young Jack, and her husband, long since dead, had been known as old Jack. They began by having different names, every one of them, but the forces of habit were so strong in the good old woman that she always called everything and everybody by that one name. The drake was a middle-aged duck, cooped up in a yard as dry as the deserts of Egypt. Sometimes it tried to go sporting out into the great wet world of gutters and puddles and pools, but Rebecca could not bear to see it behaving so untidily, so she confined it, and there in the dry yard it pined and lived.

One day her son Jack tucked the drake under his arm.

"Jacky, my lad, I do believe today is your birthday!" And off he went with the drake under his arm for a mile or more until he came to a field with a barn in it and a pond beside, whose grassy banks, so moist and green, sloped gently into the water. The water itself was only a dark bronze liquid that stank, but there were three or four chestnut trees close by, just casting their pure blooms into it. How bright the day! And how the wind blew!

Into this pond the young man Jack threw Jack the drake, and the drake became demented with joy. It heaved the water up with its beak and cast it over its back. It trod and danced, or flew skimming the pond from shore to shore. It tried to bury itself in the waters, to burst down through them into that duck paradise that lies at the bottom of all ponds, but half of him—and the worst half—always remained quivering in the common world above.

The lad Jack said he would leave him there to enjoy himself, because it was his birthday, and he would come again and fetch him before nightfall. So the drake was left alone on the pond and swam about quacking incessantly in his pride and excitement. How bright the day and how the wind blew, dashing among the chestnut trees until their heavy foliage seemed a burden to them and they snowed their white petals upon the bosom of the pond! A crow came chattering in the trees, to scoff at the buffoonery and bad manners of the drake. Intoxicated it was!

Later on, a man in the prime of life with a brown face and a weather-coloured hat came passing by. He'd a moleskin suit on with the breeches belted below the knees, and a wicker bag slung across his shoulder. He had drunk ale in the sweetness of the morning. One hand rested in the broad belt round his belly, with the other he took out his pipe—and spat fulsomely.

"Hey, my cocky!" he cried when he saw the drake, and he stood viewing its antics with meditative eyes.

The drake replied: "Quack."

"Quack to me!" cried the man in surly tones. "Where's your manners?"

So the drake knew he was not conversing with a common creature, but one who might be a god or a gentleman, and he answered him then with care and addressed him with respect.

"Hey, my hearty!" the man exclaimed, "you's as fine a young feller of a duck as ever I see."

It was—the drake informed him—his birthday.

"Hi up!" cried the man, and at once he squatted down upon a

hump on the bank of the pond, a great castle of a place that some ants had built—ants are such ambitious creatures.

"Hi up!" repeated the man, and he said it was his birthday too. "Allecapantho!" Now wasn't that curious?

"So I stops me at home this morning," he continued, "but my old woman kept growling and groaning until I had to ask her, very civil-like: 'What ever's come over you?' I asks her, 'on my birthday? You're like a dog with a sore nose,' I says, 'and I can't do with you and I can't stand your company, not on my birthday. You're nought but a bag o' mutton,' I says; 'you go and pick the fleas out of your tail,' I told her, and I went off to my allotment and cultivated a few chain of the earth. And now my neck's as stiff as a crust a beeswax. Cold winds and sweat, I suppose. Misfortune was ever following me, I tell you. Misfortune was my downfall, and so it is, I can tell you. If you wants to know my history I can tell you: I was born honest, so I shall die poor."

The drake snoozed upon the water, blinking with affability and deep enjoyment. Never had anybody taken so much notice of him before, or flattered him with so much kindly attention. And here he was now! The man sat on the ant-hill dividing his attention in three parts: by puffing at a cold pipe, by trying to light it again, by talking genially to the duck on the pond.

"You's as pretty a little duck as ever I seed. I couldn't say no fairer if I'd a mind to."

"But," the drake sorrowfully sighed, "I am only an orphan."

"Pooh! What about it? Anyone can be an orphan if they like. Anyone. 'Cept royalty. You mustn't run away with any funny notions, young feller," the bluff man declared. "What part are you from?"

The drake told him that he came from the village of So-and-so.

The man knew the place very well. "Hi up! yes," he said, "but there's not a mortal thing in that village to attract a sunny soul, neither bliss nor blessing. There's not a man of that sort nor a woman of that sort; there's not a house of that sort, nor an inn of that sort, not a child, pony, hog, dog, or hen of that sort. All poor bred uns they be."

The drake confessed that life there was very dull, yes; often it had desired to change its habitation.

"Dull!" roared the other. "Why, I could not bear to live in that hole, not if the streets was paved with crystal and there was gold on every floor. No, I live in a better place nor that."

"Pardon me, sir," said the polite little drake. "I do not know your name, or where you dwell."

"Ha, ha! Allecapantho!" returned the man. "Appercrampus! You would like to know my pedigree? There's a touch of Muscovy about you, I should say, with a brush of Indian blood. Oh, I can see it, you're a good bred un. So am I; there's few can trace their ancestors back to history like me, not straight forward they can't. That's sound truth, speak it or be shamed. Two stones in Barclay Buttle churchyard—d'ye know it? No! Two stones in Shimp churchyard—d'ye know it? No! There used to be four in Shimp but two on 'em fell over (or was pushed over, if truth be known), and Fiddler Kinch stole 'em for his hog-pen, but he never had no more luck with a pig till the day he died after it. Bolted his food, he did. It's true; everyone can tell you truth as knows it; but if it ain't known it can't be revealed. Two stones in Shimp, two stones in Barclay Buttle, brass plate with a skull's head on it in Tooby chancel. What's amiss in that for pedigree? Tooby, Shimp, and Barclay Buttle? Came over with the king of the Busbys and we're still hereabouts. William Busby." Here the man smote his bosom with pride, and thus the duck learned that his friend's name was W. Busby, and not allecapantho or appercrampus.

"When Fiddler died the reverend Saxby discovered they stones where they were—course he'd known all along. Parson took 'em up in the dead a night and transferred them. If you want to see they stones you just lift up the cloth and you'll see 'em on top of the altar in Shimp church, all fixed and fast and consecrated upside down. What's amiss in our tribe? You never heard nothing against the family of Busby—not as a family. I could show you the stone now, if you had the time, of the Busby twins, Hezekiah and Joseph, who met untimely ends (just what it says) from the sting of a viper coming from church after being confirmed. 1766. Hi up! God bless us, I remember my old great-grandfather as used to tell me about William the Conqueror, all about that man he told me, every word. The Busbys are a great nation of chaps, they're everywhere, high up and well breeched, please God. I heard a one up in the county of Nottinghamshire as owns a row of houses with a shaving-shop at one end and a coastguard station at the other! And all belongs, all belongs—a master man, ye know. He used to stuff birds and fishes and one thing and another, could stuff 'em well, like life. Used to stuff for the Duke of What-evers-the-name-of-the-feller, and for royalty. Years and years—rows of houses—till his eyes give out and he got old and his spirits sunk. Kidneys, I shouldn't wonder; I be troubled the same myself. Master man! They've got it up here."

With his finger Busby indicated a position in the middle of his forehead, and then appeared to swallow something. "Appercrampus!" he added mystically.

The little drake smiled, and quacked his delight at the conversation of Mr. Busby, who now stood up, surveyed the surrounding field with deliberation, and then sat down upon the ant-hill again, drawing a tobacco-box from his pocket. A pipe was filled and ignited, and for a while Mr. Busby puffed and gazed dreamily at the pond and the drake and listened to the wind threshing in the chestnut trees. Ah, a lovely day!

"Who do you live with in So-and-so?" the man inquired.

"I live with Jack Cracknell," answered the gentle duck, "do you know him?"

"Know him! Allecapantho! I knew his father; we were at school together. He always said he was younger than me, but I can't understand how that could be because he left school afore I did and went and drove plough for the sleepy girl's husband. I kept on at school for another six months, and then I became a thatcher. All the Busbys be master men. They got it up here." The man took his pipe from his mouth and pointed with it to his forehead again and then spat richly over his shoulder to defeat the play of the wind.

The drake asked him another question: "Who was the sleepy girl?"

"Eli Sadler's daughter," replied Busby. "She dropped off to sleep one day and she slept so's they couldn't rouse her no more. There were two girls and Eli and their mother. Of course Eli died, and there was Mary and there was this Annie. Mary was in service at the squire's, but Annie went to sleep and didn't wake up for seven years. She lay in her bed for seven unconscious years, and she didn't wake up and she did not die. People came from all parts of the world to look at her and stick pins in her—dukes and schoolmasters and members of Parliament—but they could not wake her up, nobody couldn't. Seven years is a long time, ye know. Mystery. Her mother made a fortune a money out a that girl, a fortune, sacks of it. But of course the mother died, and everyone said to Mary: 'Mary, you'll have to come home and look arter your sleepy sister.' Mary said no, she wouldn't have that caper. 'Why not?' they says to her, 'she's your sister,' they says, 'helpless and dependent on your care.' 'Because,' says Mary, 'I shall damn soon wake her up.' And that's what she did do—woke her up! And Annie went and got married and had ten children in next to no time. Never went to sleep no more. Sleeping beauty, they called her. Huh. She was the biggest fraud as ever stepped on England's ground, the biggest fraud within forty thousand miles. And old Jack Cracknell began work for the sleepy girl's husband. Well, upon my soul, there's all sorts a dodges for getting a living, and if you wants a thing in this world you must get it by force or by fudge. Force and fudge rule this sinful world, my cocky; everything's for someone's selfish pleasure—never your own. D'ye know what my advice is to you? My advice to you, sir, is this: if your pleasure brings more harm to another than it brings in joy to you—and it very often will—then you must do the best you can with your pleasure. If"—Busby pointed with his pipe straight at the attentive little duck—"if so be you are the sort as don't stop to think, you won't know of the harm you do, and you won't pause, and you won't care. Mind you, if you are of the other sort, the sort that *do* care as man to man, my advice would be wasted—for of course you wouldn't follow it, you could not. Such is human nature," Busby said, applying yet another match to his pipe, "and such" (puff) "is life."

"Yes, that is very true," sighed the happy drake.

"And another thing," continued the philosophizing thatcher. "We may not get all we asks for, but you may lay your life we'll get all that's coming to us, and I shan't be far away from my own funeral. Nor will you, my cocky. Force and fudge, I

tell you, rule this sinful world. If you can tell the tale, grief will
never be your master. Take Jack Cracknell, as worked for sleepy
girl's husband: I never did trust that man Cracknell. For one
thing, he'd talk the skin off your nostrils! I never trusted anyone
from the village of So-and-so, I never liked 'em; poor bred uns,
all. Young Jack's the same. And my advice to you is: don't return there any more, preserve your independence now you've
got it, and don't own him, don't listen to him, don't follow him.
Never let misfortune be your downfall. My lad, I like you, I will
be your friend for life. There's my hand on it."

Busby stood up, surveyed the landscape with care, spat a good
spit, rubbed his right hand upon his haunch, and went to the
water's edge. So the little drake swam in to accept of his friendship.

"Hey, my cocky!" The man's hand closed tightly round the
duck's neck, and the bird was snatched from the water. In a few
moments its neck was limp; it fluttered no more, it spake no
more, it lived no more.

"Nice li'l bird," commented Busby, feeling its breast and back,
"beautiful bird." And putting the body in his bag, he slung the
bag over his shoulder again.

"Appercrampus!" he joyously murmured as he walked away.
"Allecapantho!"

Nixey's Harlequin (1931)

ABEL STAPLE DISAPPROVES

A LITTLE harbour at the mouth of an Anglian river. On the far
side, a mile away, a tiny town gleaming quietly in the sunset,
with two church towers, an ecclesiastical college, and a home for

ancient mariners. On the near side, wharves, huts, sand dunes, and a solitary inn called the Ferry, which had some daffodils in its half-a-perch of front garden; beyond that, pastoral heaths, wind-mills, and hamlets.

Evening was placidly enfolding the harbour. A few rugged smacks nudged amiably at the wharves, fumes of tar and fish drifted from the blocks, cordage, and tackle, and sea odours rose from the fallen tide in the river. A man by the name of Billings who was squatting on a bollard got up and slouched away into the bar of the Ferry Inn. There is no keeping some people out of some public-houses, and Billings had the mystical compulsion. He also had a seafaring hat with a red paper flower fastened at the corner of the peak, and gold rings in his florid ears; a fair man, a tall man, a man in a blue jersey, with brine in his voice and long wading-boots up to his thighs—in short, a fisherman. Into the Ferry goes Billings, and "Good evening" to him says the landlord, Alan Starr, a fraternally dapper person with avid eyes and a waxed moustache; his white shirt-sleeves were rolled up above his elbows.

"A pint," replied Billings.

"Nice evening, Edward," repeated the landlord, and Billings grunted: "Ah!" When he had taken a good quaff of ale he said: "You ain't seen my brother-in-law yet?" And he lounged easily against the counter—he was the sort of man that always leans.

"No, bor; I ain't seen Abel for three or four days."

"I'm expecting him by and by."

It was a dim faded taproom and seemed too shy ever to have been painted—it had been cleaned so well. A couple of tables scrubbed to the bone, some hard chairs, and framed photographs on the walls of wedding groups twenty years ago, beanfeasts, and cricketers wherein Alan Starr might be guessed at as the knowing young man with cap cocked awry and a ball in his fist. But the worn linoleum on the floor, streaked grey and white, had a sug-gestion about it of the entrails of some glutinous leviathan. There was not a great deal of profit to be made out of the custom of the Ferry Inn, and Mr. Starr augmented his income by crafty deals in antique clocks and life-saving dogs.

Two flat-faced, tidy strangers sat at one table, stoutish, with pipes protruding from their faces. The landlord, addressing them, resumed an interrupted yarn:

"Well, it was in the time of the Fenians—"

"Just fill that mug again," one of the stout strangers commanded.

"Yes, sir!" cried Alan with ferocious alacrity. As he gave the handle of the beer engine a coaxing pull he repeated: "In the Fenian days it was—" He set the pot in front of the customer, who then asked to be obliged with a postage stamp. Alan disappeared into his private parlour in search of a postage stamp.

"It's a good tale, this Fenian tale," the one man remarked to his companion.

"It *was.*" The other puffed at his pipe stolidly.

"But it wants telling, you must realize that. It wants *telling,* in a certain *way,* delicate."

"Yes, yes; and I heard it twenty years ago," said the other with an air of contempt.

"So've I. Five thousand times. But a good tale is worth hearing over and over again, Harry, so long as it's well told. It's the art of it."

"That's right enough, Sam, and I had a queer experience once, I did."

"It *is* funny how experience keeps on cropping up!"

"A very funny experience."

"Wherever you go, experience is a great thing, Harry. It carries you through all the troubles and trials of life. And you never forget it."

"I was there for three weeks once."

"Where?"

"Edinburgh."

"Don't I know it! I been there. A noble city, wide streets—ain't they?—and very well educated I should say, such a lot of bookshops."

"The streets are all blooming granite and the books are all religious, but I was only there for three weeks and three days, I was."

"Just long enough, Harry. Just long enough to love what you like. That's the main factor, ain't it?"

"I was ordered to go on guard. . . ."

"D'ye know, that's a duty I always liked when I was a soldier. Most chaps didn't, but I did. I liked being on guard." Sam swilled down a hearty draught. "Go on, you tell your tale, Harry, you tell it."

"Well, it's a good 'un. Just give me half a chance, Sam; if you'll only listen, and my God it's good."

Then Harry began to mumble so secretively to Sam that Billings could not overhear any more. Back came the landlord.

"There you are, sir!" he cried, and laid a postage stamp before the inquiring man, who thereupon tendered him sixpence. The two friends waited mutely until the change was brought. The landlord then, after a furtive glance round, rested his hands oratorically upon their table and began: "As I was just about to tell you—"

A woman with a jug came in at the door and stepped up to the bar counter.

"It was in the time of the Fenians," shouted the landlord, retreating to his lair. "I'll tell you in a minute. Yes, ma'am?" He picked up the woman's jug and hovered over his handles. "In the time of the Fenians— Beer, did you say, ma'am?"

"Stout," answered the woman wearily, counting some coppers from her purse.

"Pint, ma'am? No—half a pint, of course." He pulled and paused. "Stout, I think you said, ma'am? Lumme, this cask is nearly empty; I must go and see to it." And after serving the woman he trotted down into his cellar.

Harry resumed his colloquy with Sam, while Billings still leaned, watching for his brother-in-law, Abel Staple. Tap, tap, tap; the landlord was adjusting his barrels. His wife, an unpleasant woman with red hands and an agate brooch, came into the taproom and lit a hanging lamp. The two men ceased their whispering until she had finished. Then a labourer entered.

"A pint, missus," he muttered.

As she was supplying the drink, the labourer said quietly to her: "I just been along to see Albert, and, oh, he's dying fast; he can't last another hour."

"Oh, oh," the landlady intoned distressfully, and quickly put the pot on the counter. The man drew it towards him and laid down his pence. She pushed the money away. "No, no, I could not take it. I'm very grateful to you for coming and telling me. I must run along at once and see the poor thing."

She flung on a cloak and bonnet and called down to her husband in the cellar that Cousin Albert was just dying. As she and the labourer left the taproom together, Alan Starr came up to the bar again.

"Poor old Albert!" he said to Billings. "How that man have suffered! Operation after operation, in and out of hospital like a bee in a hive. It's a funny thing, though, but if your bladder's got a slit in it, it grows with a sort of selvedge edges and won't come together again. Stands to reason, flesh won't grow together unless it's raw. There's no arguing about that; you can put your two fingers side by side, like that, but they won't join up—not unless you skin 'em, mind you, and scrape the flesh raw and bind 'em tight together. *Then* they might, but not without. Poor Albert, it's a funny business! Dear me! Poor old Albert!"

Turning briskly towards Harry and Sam, he cried: "Well, gents, about these here Fenians—"

Both men instantly rose.

"Must bid you good evening," said Sam.

"What! Are you off, gentlemen?"

"Yes, we are off."

"We got to go," added Harry.

"Ay, ay. Good evening," Alan said, "and thank you."

In silence after their departure the landlord meditatively filled his pipe; having lit it, he marshalled his hopes once more with a sigh and leaned upon the counter:

"Did I ever tell you that tale about the Fenians, Ted? I don't think I did, did I?"

Billings slowly shook his head. "I can't call to mind I ever heard it."

The landlord glanced at the clock.

"Well, it was in the time of the Fenians—"

"Just a bit," the tall fisherman interposed. "Give us another pint, will you?"

"Pint, Ted? Certainly."

Billings drew some coins from his pocket and selected a shilling. The landlord pushed the filled pot towards him. "Yes, it was in the Fenian days—" But the coin slipped from Alan's wet fingers and went rolling and wriggling across the taproom floor as though escaping from some dire tyranny.

"Hoi! Hoi!" The landlord trotted round after it. "Now where are you gone to?" He stooped, peering under the hard chairs and the tables after the lost coin. "Did you see where he went, Ted?"

No, Ted had not observed that. Alan sank upon one knee and struck a match, searching here and there.

"Come out, you shameful thing!"

But the shilling lay low, and the landlord was soon exhausted by the pressure of his belt and the constriction of his breeches.

"Well, may I be boiled alive!" he cried. " 'S gone hopping off like a frog in a tunnel. Must be here somewhere."

"I di'n' see it go," Billings said. "You had it."

"Yes, I had it, but I di'n' see it go neither. I'll find it," he said, rising, "tomorrow morning. It must be there, I know it's there."

Returning to the bar, he composed himself once more. "Well, I was going to tell you—"

Again Billings interposed: "What about my change?"

"Your change! Ah! What was it you give me, Ted?"

"I give you that shilling."

"Oh, ah," sighed Alan, "that darned thing!" He glared into the dark corner of the room where the coin was last seen. "I know it's just there, I see it go. Let me get a candle; I'll soon have him out of that."

So with a lit candle he searched, and after much gaping and groping and groaning he found the shilling just as the door was thrust open and Abel Staple came in.

Staple was a clean-shaven ruddy countryman, clad in fawn corduroy that reeked of sheep, and his shrill voice was so powerful that it produced tangible vibrations in the air. He lived in a village a few miles off, where his wife, Fanny, a sister of Ted Billings, had died the year before.

"How goes it, Abel?" was the landlord's greeting as he returned to his counter.

"Oh—there's beef and butter, and the bread's none so bad!" grinned Abel.

"Ain't seen much of you lately."

"Well, what with the time o' year and the time o' life and the time o' day I can't stand the pressure of these late nights. Five o'clock in the morning you'll see me in my bloom! A pint, please."

"Pint? Five o'clock, eh? The Almighty never put it in my power to behave like that, Abel. I could not do it, not for the Emperor of China and fifteen pound a week."

"You can always get up if you got anything to get up arter."

"Pooh," replied Alan, "it's only a habit!"

Abel paid him from a leather purse and then turned to his brother:

"I got a rabbit for you, Ted."

"I got a dozen herring for you," answered Ted.

"This rabbit ought a bin a hare."

"They're longshore uns, but half of 'em has tidy roes."

The two men moved over to a table in the corner farthest from the bar counter and sat down side by side.

"What about my change, Alan?" Billings sternly called.

"Di'n' I give it you?"

"If you did I ain't seen it."

"If you ain't seen it, Ted my boy, then I reckon I can't have given it to you."

He brought the change and handed it to Billings. "Nothing like honesty and a free mind." Then he went humming away to sit in his private parlour.

Night had grown dark outside; there were no sounds from the harbour or the sea, for the wind was still. The old clock in the bar was ticking loudly.

"Have you thought of any little thing to put in the paper?" Abel asked in a lowered voice. "Any little bit of a jink that's nice and proper?" And Billings, extracting two or three scraps of paper from somewhere under his jersey, replied: "I got one or two snatches here."

They were proposing to insert a joint notice in the "In Memoriam" column of the local newspaper; Billings read out from one of his paper scraps:

> *In fond memory of Fanny Staple who fell*
> *asleep May 12. Gone but not forgotten. From*
> *her sorrowing husband Abel and her brother*
> *E. Billings.*

The sorrowing husband emitted a doubtful "Humph!"

"I think that's a good one," Billings declared. "Don't you? It 'ull cost two shillings. Or you could have a verse of a hymn or a text from the Bible and that 'ull be half a crown."

"I don't much like that 'fell asleep' talk," the widower commented.

"It's only a manner of speaking, Abel."

"Yah. But sleeping is sleeping, and when you're in your grave it's something else or different. I go to sleep, but I get up again. Five o'clock of a morning, my angel, year in, year out."

"It's only a manner of speaking."

"I know that; but, dammit, she died, didn't she!"

"Well, all right; what about a hymn?" her brother suggested. "Fanny was always partial to hymns—it runs in our family. I like a song myself."

"God bless us and well I knows of it! She'd howl her eyes out over a hymn."

"You mustn't forget she had a tender heart," Billings maintained. "Right from girlhood she had."

"No call to! Not as I could ever see."

"I dunno—I dunno. Some has a smile for one thing and a sob for another and you can't understand the reason for either." Billings seemed to be mournfully affected by some recollection. "If we could understand that, Abel, we should know a lot more than we do."

"You's looking for the place where the cat put her paws, Teddy. You know she's bin and collared the cream, so what does it signify? Fanny was as good a wife as ever trod on this earth, cooking, washing, mangling, mending—every mortal thing the heart could wish for—except a child—and that she never had. That was her downfall. She come to me in her prime, pretty as a lamb, a laughing girl, but she soured early and took to other ways. I tell you honest, Ted, she gave me a fair sickener of hymns and tears. You can cry tears till your breast is wet and you dream of nothing else; you can drop your tears all over the furniture—I've seen the spatters, ah!—and then you can go and drop them all over the garden, but tears don't make the beans to grow. So much psalming is all very well and we has to put up with it, but out of season is out of reason, I say. I've been religious and soulful, too, in my day—we all of us have, ain't we? In my young time forty year ago, when I was a boy, Parson Froggett took me through my confirmation and he was a good old Christian vicar as ever tipped a shoe. I can remember him marching us all off from the schoolhouse one fine morning to go for the blessing of the lord bishop. (Just such another day, it was, as that fine Whitsun when Fanny and I got wed; lilacs, laburnums, and the grass sweet as an apple.) I can remember him now! Off we goes across the fields to the church, boys in front and the gals behind all dressed in their white muslins. And we boys got the devil in us somehow that morning, it was such a pink of a day, and the bell ringing, and we rooshed along over stiles and through hedges till the gals puffed and blowed and tore their frocks to tatters, and old Froggett—he was very fat, fine old face, stuttered a bit —he calls out: "S-s-s-steady, boys, steady; n-n-n-not so fast in front there!" But we boys got the devil in us that morning and we made their backs sweat for 'em. He were a good old Christian man, Froggett; kept up a good house though he was never married hisself; cook, coachman, two maids, and Eva Martin's daughter cleaned his boots for years and got tuppence a week for it; but I'm blammed if he didn't go and poison hisself arter all. I liked old Froggett."

The fisherman ruminated, with puff puff puff at his pipe.

" 'Twarn't so much the eyes," he said, "it was the mind weeping."

"I shouldn't ha' said she was weak-minded, Ted."

"Nah, well," Billings sighed. "What are you going to put in this notice? We got to put in something or other—or ain't you going to, arter all?"

"Sure!" cried Abel, "I be game enough."

" 'Cause if you ain't," Billings declared, "I'll put it in myself."

"You've no call to say that," Abel soothingly answered. "You've got a brother's full heart, I know, I know you have, but she was my wife, whether or no, and I'm not renagging."

"There's this one, then." Billings fingered another paper scrap: *"Till we meet again."*

"Well, ye know, that's pretty much of a hymn, too!"

"She was fond of hymns, very fond," Billings steadfastly declared.

"She was, oh, she was, Ted; but my heart was never a crock for that sort of pickle. Let's have something cheerful and a bit different now it's all over. *Peace, perfect Peace,* I reckon is the best. We don't want a lot of palaver about a silent tear and that sort of chatter. It's all over. Let's have *Peace, perfect Peace.*"

The brother was silent. After waiting some moments Abel inquired:

"What do *you* say, Ted?"

And Ted said: "Oh, have it your own way. I'm agreeable."

"All right, now," Abel answered. "That's settled then: *Peace, perfect Peace.* Of course, next year, if God spares us, you can put in whatever you've a mind to; that's only fair. Now you look arter it, Ted, will you, and see it goes in the paper the proper time? When *is* the date of it?"

"Week after next."

" 'Course it is! What ever was I thinking about! Times flies so. *Peace, perfect Peace,* then. Landlord!"

Abel rapped loudly upon the table with his empty pot. Alan came forward. "Give us a couple a pints."

The beer was drawn. Alan Starr pocketed the money and lingered with a smile on his face as the men gulped deeply; then, suddenly leaning upon the table, he began once more: "It was in the time of the Fenians." It would be unmeet, however, to pursue that story to its close, though the prospects of impropriety, however reprehensible, are very alluring. At its conclusion the two men prepared to go home.

"Here's your herring," said Ted to Abel.

"Ay, ay; here's your rabbit," Abel replied.

"And what about paying for the memorial notice? Half and half you said, Abel."

"That's right, I was near forgetting. Tell ye what, Ted: I don't mind tossing ye to see who pays the lot."

"Call to me," said Ted grimly.

Abel called and lost.

"My, if that ain't a blow from a pig's tail!" he cheerfully cried, as he handed Billings a two-shilling piece.

Dunky Fitlow (1933)

PURL AND PLAIN

AT ten o'clock one summer night Father Corkery was in his study devouring a fine large governmental report on Population when his housekeeper tapped and told him that a gentleman was wanting to see him, and very anxious. Father Corkery was a good citizen of the world, a little plump now, a little bald now, a little lazy now, for at sixty you become more impressionable to the blandishments of Time, but he was also a good priest, so he received the gentleman at once, a rich young gentleman, and his name it was Robert Moriarty. It is your business to understand now that this Mr. Moriarty was not only an Irishman, he was an enthusiastic Irishman, his servants were Irish, and he had just now sought out Father Corkery because he was an Irish priest. Mr. Moriarty was married to an agreeable English lady, a creature of beauty! and both she and her husband were newly come to the borough of Clapham, where Father Corkery was in holy orders. By the grace of God (and the connivance of Mr. Moriarty) this lady was even now being brought to bed of a child, so would his reverence come along at once to baptize the child as soon as it should be born. "Will a duck swim!" says Father Corkery.

Off they went together to a new nice house in the borough of Clapham, where they were let in by a pretty Irish servant, and her name it was Mary O'Sullivan. Her master inquired: had anything come along while he was away? "No, Mr. Bob," says she, "not a finger of it yet." So young Mr. Moriarty—a very nice affable fellow, a bit distracted, but who wouldn't be at such times?—he bowed his reverence into a nice room and sat him in an armchair. He took his black bag away from him and put it under a sofa, but then he picked it up out of that again and set it on the piano. The room was used as a dining-room, or it was used as a drawing-room, but now it had the air of having temporarily suppressed its customary spirits. It smelled faintly of tomato sauce and was filled with dark heavy orderly furniture, a sideboard with a canopy reaching the ceiling, armchairs of leather, a grandfather's clock as big as a coffin, and a long rectangular table covered with a cloth of patterned rose and brown. The only frivolous objects in the room were the electric lights and a white elephant of china that stood on the mantelpiece where a clock ought to have been.

Father Corkery and Mr. Moriarty then conversed gently with each other as Mr. Moriarty told the story of his marriage. And this was the way of that. A year ago he had been married—to the finest woman in Ireland. He had been born and bred a good Catholic, but he had been overpowered with love for a lady who was only a Protestant. It was a little bit of an obstacle, that difference of religion, but "Jewel," says he, "my heart's in your pocket." There could be no other obstacle, both of them being young and ripe for marriage, their incomes were agreeable and their relations obliging. "I, Robert, take thee, Millicent, to my wedded wife." And it was agreed there and then that any boys born of their marriage were to become good little Catholics (or they should), and any girls might become little Protestants, and so here they were now waiting for the first child to be born. The doctor was upstairs, the nurse was there, the priest was here. . . .

"So if it's a girl," said Father Corkery, "my time is wasted and I'll not be wanted?"

Mr. Moriarty walked over the room, took the priest's black bag off the piano and put it on the whatnot.

"I was going to tell you about that, Father," he began. He was deeply obliged to his reverence for coming; he had dearly wanted an Irish priest, for, as his reverence knew, there were only two sorts of people in the world—the Irish and those others. "I was going to tell you about that," repeated Mr. Moriarty, when the door was knocked and Mary O'Sullivan came ushering in a young curate and said: "Mr. Caspin, Mr. Bob."

"Hey, hey, come along," said Mr. Moriarty. The curate, who had the complexion of a fair girl and the mouth of an old man, went up to Father Corkery very close, said: "Good evening," and shook him violently by the hand. And then, as he took off a light overcoat, revealing himself dressed in a cassock like Father Corkery, he remarked again that it was a pleasant evening. Like his reverend brother he, too, had brought a little black bag with him, and in this they both resembled the doctor, except that *he* was supervising the child's entry into this world while they were already concerning themselves about its entry into the next. Mr. Moriarty took Mr. Caspin's bag and went to put it on the what-not, until he noticed another bag there, and so he bent down and shoved it under a chair.

"No, not yet," said Mr. Moriarty to the curate, "but almost any moment now. Will you seat yourself, sir? . . . Father Corkery, this is the Reverend Caspin against it's a girl—you mind what I told you. And, Mr. Caspin, this is Father Corkery against it's a boy—you mind what I told you earlier on? Excuse me now, reverend gentlemen."

Pressing a handkerchief to his brow, the young man left the two clerics sitting opposite each other before the empty fireplace. Almost immediately Mr. Moriarty rushed in again, opened a cupboard, and placed on the table a decanter of port and two glasses.

"Help yourselves, gentlemen, please," said he, and rushed away again.

"I never touch it," the curate said.

Father Corkery was pouring out a good glass.

"Forgive me, gentlemen!" cried Mr. Moriarty, rushing in once more in great agitation, "cigars!" From the same cupboard he brought a box of cigars.

"I never touch them," the curate said. Father Corkery said he would use his pipe, and he began to fill his pipe as Mr. Moriarty went away again.

"I suspect," then said the one to the other, "that we have a long wait before us."

"Is the poor lady in difficulties?" inquired Mr. Caspin.

Father Corkery nodded into his tobacco pouch and replied: "Oh, so-so. A trying day, ye know, is the day of birth, and for a while the heart pines for oblivion. But in a very short time she will discover, what every mother discovers early or late, that she has been divinely chosen to give birth to one of the world's prodigies."

To the Reverend Ferdinand Caspin, this homely and familiar notion sounded strange; perhaps it was because he thought Father Corkery used the word "protégés," a word that at such a time, on such an occasion, had certain unnamable sectarian connotations. Pressing the tips of his fingers together in the immemorial symbol of curacy he leaned forward.

"Tell me, sir: do you approve of these family arrangements? Do you think it right for a child's religion to be decided by the mere accident of its sex?"

Father Corkery puffed his pipe in the immemorial grandeur of reflection. Then he said:

"For us to approve or not to approve makes devil a bit of difference; it's like putting a lock on a cardboard door. On the other hand, sex is no accident at all; it comes, I suppose, by the grace of God. All the important things of life are decided by sex, and maybe it's as good a guide as any other."

"Oh come, I say," Mr. Caspin almost gasped, "really now!"

"Well," laughed his reverence, "I admit I have sometimes thought it would not be a bad thing if all men were Christians, and all women heathens. Indeed, I fancy Nature intended something of the kind and that we have blundered."

"By Jove," exclaimed the curate, "do you know, sir—have you read the ninth volume of Thatchbason's *Commentaries*?"

Well, now, Father Corkery had never even heard of Thatchbason.

"Upon the Epistles!" the curate insisted. "By Jove, really; he has something absolutely new to say about Saint Augustine, as well as Saint Paul. He propounds, expounds, and defends a thoroughly new position, and a very brilliant position."

"Something new? Ay?"

"Entirely. And, of course, sir, one is forced to recognize that the female sex is definitely inferior in moral stability—not to be trusted."

"Oh, I like a woman to be reasonably unreliable," said Father Corkery, replenishing his glass and pushing the decanter towards Caspin, who however reminded him that he never touched it.

"Oh," said Father Corkery, "I was thinking it was tobacco you never touched."

"Tobacco, too," confessed the curate, blushing.

"Ah, you don't touch tobacco! Humph. Yes," continued Father Corkery, "that is rather my own feeling about woman. I was in Venice once—were you ever in Venice?"

Mr. Caspin nodded enthusiastically. "Oh, a fascinating place! I shall never forget—"

"Have you a match?" interrupted Father Corkery.

Mr. Caspin handed a box across to his confrère and repeated: "I shall never forget—" when Father Corkery again slid the decanter towards him and ejaculated: "Port!"

"No, no, thank you," Mr. Caspin replied, and was then silent.

After a few moments Father Corkery asked him *what* it was he would never forget.

"Oh, I only wanted to say," the curate said, "that I shall never forget the oleanders on the Lido and the charming little lizards flashing about under the dried seaweed."

"Oh, I never saw them. While I was there," Father Corkery proceeded, "I once went into a great beautiful church, very quiet and lonely. As I went in at the door I heard voices singing, but sounding far away, as if in some chamber, muffled, but extraordinarily beautiful. I stood rapt and the saintly sound brought tears to my eyes. When I looked about I could not discover where the singing came from. Suddenly the door of the sacristy opened, and then it shut. For a moment I caught a full wave of that rich singing. Then I saw a young girl who had come out of that doorway, and she walked across to the high altar and fetched an armful of candlesticks. I could still hear the music, faintly, but the girl had got on those loose slippers the Italian women wear and the flapping of her heels made a very sharp clatter. When she reached the door again, she could not open it because her arms were full of the candlesticks, so she kicked on it, crying angrily for it to be opened. I was quite near her, so I went and pulled open the door, and then the song burst on me in great fullness. I could see a dozen women inside, old and young, sitting at a long bench cleaning the holy plate. But what smote me, like a cudgel on a drunken head, was the thing they were all singing, with the gusto of a happy choir in beautiful unison. Do you know what it was? I could hear it clearly, and I had heard it before. It was a song of the last conceivable bawdiness! Too wicked for anything."

Ferdinand Caspin sighed: "Good heavens! Dear me!"

"And yet," Father Corkery went on, lolling easily in his chair, "I never think of Venice but I recall the sweet emotion that their fine singing gave me. Oh, they were happy innocent women. And I can see that young girl now, kicking the door, with her arms full of candlesticks, and calling harshly: 'Open!' "

Father Corkery glanced across at the other, who was mute, and then he gurgled with laughter.

"Is that a box of dominoes I see over on the sideboard? If it is I will play you a game."

Mr. Caspin thought it was not a box of dominoes. And in any case he did not play dominoes.

"I thought we might be here a long time," said his reverence.

After Father Corkery had taken another swig at the wine, Mr. Caspin said:

"I suppose you really approve this arrangement of the Moriartys about their children?"

Father Corkery took his pipe from his mouth. "I am rather old now to approve things. At my time of life it is much easier to condemn anything, only condemnation so often upsets the kidneys, ye know."

"Indeed, sir," said the other, "I thought age brought a—a—a more mellow wisdom."

"It may bring wisdom," Father Corkery agreed, "but wisdom isn't mellow; what is mellow is one's indifference. Wisdom must be critical, or what is the use of having it at all? On the other hand, we often fall into the error of believing that criticism itself is wisdom when it may only be bad temper. It is impossible to exercise wisdom in regard to women, for instance, and to criticize them is merely bad taste. Woman is most prone to superstition—so she worships man. She is a great gambler—so she bears his children. It's a pity you don't play dominoes. What do you think—will it be a boy or a girl tonight?"

Mr. Caspin intimated that he could not tell, but they would be bound to know before very much longer.

"I bet you," Father Corkery said, "that it's a girl."

"No, no." The other shook his head. "I never gamble."

"Not! Why not?"

"To me," said Mr. Caspin, but he made it plain that his present objection was quite impersonal, "to me gambling is superstition, dissatisfaction, greed, and idolatry."

"Well," said Father Corkery, "we are already dissatisfied and greedy and superstitious, all of us, women more so than men—"

"Exactly," interjected the curate.

"And that," his reverence continued, "may be because they have more to fear—as observed by your Mr. Thatchbason. But now give a guess; d'ye *think* it will be a boy, or d'ye *think* it will be a girl?"

Mr. Caspin was disinclined to prophesy, but he had an intuition. "My intuitions," he declared, "very seldom fail me."

"Ha, ha!" Father Corkery rallied him. "Some people can't resist 'em; it's like cards and horse-racing."

"Well, if you insist," said the curate, "my intuition is that the child will be a boy."

"Is that so?" murmured Father Corkery. "Now I will tell you my intuition. Today is the seventh day of the seventh month, and as I walked here with Mr. Moriarty we passed very few people; all told, there were seven—and all of them were women. Now what d'ye think of that for a female tip!"

Mr. Caspin was bound to laugh at him. "I think," he replied, looking at the clock, "it is very likely that this child will be born on the eighth day. Now I will tell you something. After Mr. Moriarty called on me this evening about this matter, I went to my study. In my brief absence somebody had been into my room and tidied up, for on the mantelpiece my own photograph stood confronting me—upside down!"

"Well," temporized the other, "what d'ye make of that?"

"Surely," smiled the curate, "that I am losing my time in this case, that the child will be a little boy."

"That's a grave omen," said Father Corkery with a twinkle. "It probably will be little, but I bet you—" Pausing, he raked in his pocket and inspected some coins he found there. "—I bet you a solid two shillings that it's a female child."

"No, certainly not," Mr. Caspin replied, a little wanly.

"As you will," retorted the other.

For some time both were silent, Father Corkery puffing imperturbably, Mr. Caspin clasping his knees with folded hands and gazing into anything but the present and at anything but the priest. The house grew so oppressive in its quiet that when the clock struck eleven the air boomed and oozed with its reverberations; they poured through door and ceiling and burst upon the roof to shock the dreaming chimneys.

"I was interested in a case recently of a sailor," then began Mr. Caspin, "who fell off the rigging in the Bahamas. He was on a ship in the Bahamas, I think it was, but I'm not sure at the moment where it was—humph!"

Father Corkery chanted: "Where the remote Bermudas ride."

"No, it *was* the Bahamas," continued Mr. Caspin, "and broke his leg so badly that it had to be amputated and he had to be discharged. He came home and had to be an attendant in a men's public lavatory, one of those underground places, in the parish of a friend of mine, a man I know very well. The sailor's wife had disappeared; I don't know anything about that matter, but no one knew where or why she had gone, so the sailor had to lodge with his married daughter. Every day at one o'clock that young woman, a very respectable creature, had to take her father's dinner to him at that place. She had to stand at the top of the steps and call out 'Father!' until he came up to her. Awful, you know. My friend was vicar of the parish, and such a thing was most distasteful to him, as you can understand. Every day this young married woman was subject to all the ribald remarks of any men coming or going in such a place. So my friend had to take steps and he tried to put a stop to it one way and another, and at first he couldn't, though at last he succeeded. He arranged for one of his choir boys who lived in the same street to take the man's dinner every day. But the extraordinary thing was that the young woman was very angry and would never enter my friend's church again! Very touchy, these people," concluded Mr. Caspin.

"Asperity has many friends." Father Corkery conceded that it was a picturesque case. "What did the sailor do about that?"

"Oh," Mr. Caspin was confused, but he gloomily continued, "he was a bad lot after all. Some quite unmentionable traffic went on between them, I never knew what, something indelicate, and it was found out."

"Between whom?" asked Father Corkery.

"The sailor and the choir boy," returned the other. "Of course the man was discharged and the boy was sent to a home. Detestable! Why are men so weak? Tell me," he cried, "the past was heroic, why is our own age so vulgar?"

Father Corkery brushed his hand over his benignant baldness. "Ah, my friend, we are superstitious and dissatisfied and greedy. We are endowed, you know, with far more prejudice than judgment. Man enjoys his sinful manhood until he comes to a conviction of sin. Then he reforms and enjoys his reformation until he comes to a conviction of foolishness. That's the way of his life, alternations, a sort of purl and plain woven into the figure of him."

Mr. Caspin murmured that this was painfully true.

"It helps," Father Corkery added, "to make a pattern, just as it does in knitting. But what is that?" he asked sharply. "Listen!"

They listened, and they heard the thin cry of a new-born babe. Father Corkery put down his pipe and crossed himself. Mr. Caspin jumped up, went to his bag, and wriggled into his surplice while the priest went on whispering a prayer. Then Father Corkery opened his own bag and put on his own surplice.

"This water I have here," he said, "is from the River Shannon; a colleague sent me a quart of it a little while ago. I've brought it specially because our friend is an enthusiastic Irishman. To him the Irish are the greatest people in the world."

"Dear, dear, this racial pride is fantastic," said Caspin. "Do you know, the Japanese believe they are actually descended from the gods?"

"There is really nothing fantastic about that," his reverence answered, "for every devout Christian necessarily believes the same."

At that moment young Mr. Moriarty came rushing in with a very happy look on him.

"It is a girl," he shouted.

The two clerics looked at each other. "There now!" laughed Father Corkery. "I should have won my bet! Ah well, the blessing of God on it all, Mr. Moriarty; I congratulate you from the bottom of my soul. From the bottom of my soul," he repeated, raising his arms and struggling to get out of his surplice. "And may the wee thing grow up as beautiful as Helen, as wise as Pallas, and as chaste as, as—who was that other one, Caspin? Ah, never mind! And is your wife doing well?"

"Splendid, Father, the cream of creation," cried Mr. Moriarty with gleeful pride. "Splendid! But don't be so hasty now, your reverence. It's what I have to tell you, I have to tell something to both of you and I don't know how to tell it to either of you. But it's about Milly—that's herself—she's renagged, at the last moment, of her own will. Yes, Father, will you keep your surplice on? There was the babe in the basket by her side, and she looking at it like a pot of gold, and I'm telling her you both were ready for the baptizing. 'I'd forgotten about all that,' says she. 'But you remember the arrangement, Milly,' says I, 'the boys for me, the girls for you!' 'Sure, I'd forgotten entirely,' says she, 'and now it's a girl after all.' 'Jewel,' I says, 'I've the Protestant man downstairs.' 'No,' she says, 'I was never cracked about religion, but 'twould be a sin for a child to be different from her father and her brothers.' 'Then it's Catholic, you mean,' says I. 'Catholic it is,' says she."

Mr. Moriarty could not conceal, even from Mr. Caspin, his glee at the way things turned out, but he said to him:

"A hundred thousand pardons for disturbing you, sir, and troubling you for nothing at all. It's the women, sir, are the queer creatures."

Mr. Caspin put his clothes off and into the bag and begged him not to mention it. In a few moments he bade them both good night.

"Mr. Moriarty," Father Corkery said, "God has blessed you with a very fine wife."

"True for you," the happy husband beamed, "and you don't even know her like I do."

"God has blessed you," repeated his reverence, "with the finest wife in the world."

"True it is, Father; but you can't tell what they'd be wanting from one hour to another. The devil himself, saving your presence, don't know where he is with the creatures."

"No," asserted Father Corkery as they went upstairs together. "God alone knows."

Silver Circus (1928)

A BROADSHEET BALLAD

At noon the tiler and the mason stepped down from the roof of the village church which they were repairing and crossed over the road to the tavern to eat their dinner. It had been a nice little morning, but there were clouds massing in the south. Sam, the tiler, remarked that it looked like thunder. The two men sat in the dim little taproom eating, Bob, the mason, at the same time reading from a newspaper an account of a trial for murder.

"I dunno what thunder looks like," Bob said, "but I reckon this chap is going to be hung, though I can't rightly say for why. To my thinking he didn't do it at all; but murder's a bloody thing and someone ought to suffer for it."

"I don't think," spluttered Sam as he impaled a flat piece of

beetroot on the point of a pocket-knife and prepared to contemplate it with patience until his stuffed mouth was ready to
receive it, "he ought to be hung."

"There can't be no other end for him though, with a mob of
lawyers like that, and a judge like that, and a jury too—why the
rope's half round his neck this minute; he'll be in glory within a
month, they only have three Sundays, you know, between the
sentence and the execution. Well, hark at that rain then!"

A shower that began as a playful sprinkle grew to a powerful
steady summer downpour. It splashed in the open window, and
the dim room grew more dim and cool.

"Hanging's a dreadful thing," continued Sam, "and 'tis often
unjust I've no doubt, I've no doubt at all."

"Unjust! I tell you—at the majority of trials those who give
their evidence mostly knows nothing at all about the matter;
them as knows a lot—they stays at home and don't budge, not
likely!"

"No? But why?"

"Why? They has their reasons. I know that, I knows it for
truth—hark at that rain, it's made the room feel cold."

They watched the downfall in complete silence for some
moments.

"Hanging's a dreadful thing," Sam at length repeated, with almost a sigh.

"I can tell you a tale about that, Sam, in a minute," said the
other. He began to fill his pipe from Sam's brass box, which was
labelled cough lozenges and smelled of paregoric.

"Just about ten years ago I was working over in Cotswold
country. I remember I'd been in to Gloucester one Saturday
afternoon and it rained. I was jogging along home in a carrier's
van; I never seen it rain like that afore, no, nor ever afterwards,
not like that. B-r-r-r-r! it came down. Bashing! And we come to
a cross-roads where there's a public-house called the Wheel of
Fortune, very lonely and onsheltered it is just there. I see'd a
young woman standing in the porch awaiting us, but the carrier
was wet and tired and angry or something and wouldn't stop.
'No room,' he bawled out to her, 'full up, can't take you!' and
he drove on. 'For the love of God, mate,' I says, 'pull up and

take that young creature! She's—she's—can't you see!' 'But I'm all behind as 'tis,' he shouts to me; 'you know your gospel, don't you—time and tide wait for no man?' 'Ah, but dammit all, they always call for a feller,' I says. With that he turned round and we drove back for the girl. She clumb in and sat on my knees; I squat on a tub of vinegar, there was nowhere else, and I was right and all, she was going on for a birth. Well, the old van rattled away for six or seven miles; whenever it stopped, you could hear the rain clattering on the tarpaulin, or sounding outside on the grass as if it was breathing hard, and the old horse steamed and shivered with it. I had knowed the girl once in a friendly way, a pretty young creature, but now she was white and sorrowful and wouldn't say much. By and by we came to another cross-roads near a village, and she got out there. 'Good day, my gal,' I says, affable like, and 'Thank you, sir,' says she— and off she popped in the rain with her umbrella up. A rare pretty girl, quite young, I'd met her before, a girl you could get uncommon fond of, you know, but I didn't meet her afterwards, she was mixed up in a bad business. It all happened in the next six months while I was working round these parts. Everybody knew of it. This girl's name was Edith and she had a younger sister, Agnes. Their father was old Harry Mallerton, kept the British Oak at North Quainy; he stuttered. Well, this Edith had a love affair with a young chap, William, and having a very loving nature she behaved foolish. Then she couldn't bring the chap up to the scratch nohow by herself, and of course she was afraid to tell her mother or father: you know how girls are after being so pesky natural, they fear, oh, they do fear! But soon it couldn't be hidden any longer as she was living at home with them all, so she wrote a letter to her mother. 'Dear Mother,' she wrote, and told her all about her trouble.

"By all accounts the mother was angry as an old lion, but Harry took it calm like and sent for young William, who'd not come at first. He lived close by in the village, so they went down at last and fetched him.

"'All right, yes,' he said, 'I'll do what's lawful to be done. There you are, I can't say no fairer, that I can't.'

"'No,' they said, 'you can't.'

"So he kissed the girl and off he went, promising to call in and settle affairs in a day or two. The next day Agnes, which was the younger girl, she also wrote a note to her mother telling her some more strange news.

"'God above!' the mother cried out, 'can it be true, both of you girls, my own daughters, and by the same man! What ever were you thinking on, both of ye! What ever can be done now!'"

"What!" ejaculated Sam, "both on 'em, both on 'em!"

"As true as God's my mercy—both on 'em—same chap. Ah! Mrs. Mallerton was afraid to tell her husband at first, for old Harry was the devil born again when he were roused up, so she went for young William herself, who'd not come again, of course, not likely. But they made him come, oh yes, when they told the girls' father.

"'Well, may I go to my d-d-d-damnation at once!' roared old Harry—he stuttered, you know—'at once, if that ain't a good one!' So he took off his coat, he took up a stick, he walked down the street to William and cut him off his legs. Then he beat him until he howled for his mercy, and you couldn't stop old Harry once he were roused up—he was the devil born again. They do say as he beat him for a solid hour; I can't say as to that, but then old Harry picked him up and carried him off to the British Oak on his own back and threw him down in his own kitchen between his own two girls like a dead dog. They do say that the little one, Agnes, flew at her father like a raging cat until he knocked her senseless with a clout over head; rough man he was."

"Well, a' called for it, sure," commented Sam.

"Her did," agreed Bob, "but she was the quietest known girl for miles round those parts, very shy and quiet."

"A shady lane breeds mud," said Sam.

"What do you say?—Oh ah!—mud, yes. But pretty girls both, girls you could get very fond of, skin like apple bloom, and as like as two pinks they were. They had to decide which of them William was to marry."

"Of course, ah!"

"'I'll marry Agnes,' says he.

"'You'll not,' says the old man. 'You'll marry Edie.'

" 'No I won't,' William says; 'it's Agnes I love and I'll be married to her or I won't be married to e'er of 'em.' All the time Edith sat quiet, dumb as a shovel, never a word, crying a bit; but they do say the young one went on like a—a young—Jew."

"The jezebel!" commented Sam.

"You may say it; but wait, my man, just wait. Another cup of beer. We can't go back to church until this humbugging rain have stopped."

"No, that we can't."

"It's my belief the 'bugging rain won't stop this side of four o'clock."

"And if the roof don't hold it off, it 'ull spoil they Lord's commandments that's just done up on the chancel front."

"Oh, they be dry by now." Bob spoke reassuringly and then continued his tale. " 'I'll marry Agnes or I won't marry nobody,' William says, and they couldn't budge him. No, old Harry cracked on, but he wouldn't have it, and at last Harry says: 'It's like this.' He pulls a halfcrown out of his pocket and 'Heads it's Agnes,' he says, 'or tails it's Edith,' he says."

"Never! Ha! Ha!" cried Sam.

" 'Heads it's Agnes, tails it's Edie,' so help me God. And it come down Agnes, yes, heads it was—Agnes—and so there they were."

"And they lived happy ever after?"

"Happy! You don't know your human nature, Sam; where ever was you brought up? 'Heads it's Agnes,' said old Harry, and at that Agnes flung her arms round William's neck and was for going off with him then and there, ha! But this is how it happened about that. William hadn't any kindred, he was a lodger in the village, and his landlady wouldn't have him in her house one mortal hour when she heard of it; give him the right-about there and then. He couldn't get lodgings anywhere else, nobody would have anything to do with him, so of course, for safety's sake, old Harry had to take him, and there they all lived together at the British Oak—all in one happy family. But they girls couldn't bide the sight of each other, so their father cleaned up an old outhouse in his yard that was used for carts and hens and put William and his Agnes out in it. And there they had to bide. They had a couple of chairs, a sofa, and a bed and that kind of thing, and the young one made it quite snug."

" 'Twas a hard thing for that other, that Edie, Bob."

"It was hard, Sam, in a way, and all this was happening just afore I met her in the carrier's van. She was very sad and solemn then; a pretty girl, one you could like. Ah, you may choke me, but there they lived together. Edie never opened her lips to either of them again, and her father sided with her, too. What was worse, it came out after the marriage that Agnes was quite free of trouble—it was only a trumped-up game between her and this William because he fancied her better than the other one. And they never had no child, them two, though when poor Edie's mischance came along I be damned if Agnes weren't fonder of it than its own mother, a jolly sight more fonder, and William—he fair worshipped it."

"You don't say!"

"I do. 'Twas a rum go, that, and Agnes worshipped it, a fact, can prove it by scores o' people to this day, scores, in them parts. William and Agnes worshipped it, and Edie—she just looked on, 'long of it all, in the same house with them, though she never opened her lips again to her young sister to the day of her death."

"Ah, she died? Well, it's the only way out of such a tangle, poor woman."

"You're sympathizing with the wrong party." Bob filled his pipe again from the brass box; he ignited it with deliberation; going to the open window, he spat into a puddle in the road. "The wrong party, Sam; 'twas Agnes that died. She was found on the sofa one morning stone-dead, dead as a adder."

"God bless me!" murmured Sam.

"Poisoned!" added Bob, puffing serenely.

"Poisoned!"

Bob repeated the word "poisoned." "This was the way of it," he continued. "One morning the mother went out in the yard to collect her eggs, and she began calling out: 'Edie, Edie, here a minute, come and look where that hen have laid her egg; I would never have believed it,' she says. And when Edie went out, her mother led her round the back of the outhouse, and there on the top of a wall this hen had laid an egg. 'I would never have believed it, Edie,' she says; 'scooped out a nest there beautiful, ain't she? I wondered where her was laying. 'Tother morning the dog brought an egg round in his mouth and laid it on the doormat. There now, Aggie, Aggie, here a minute, come and look where the hen have laid that egg.' And as Aggie didn't answer, the mother went in and found her on the sofa in the outhouse, stone-dead."

"How'd they account for it?" asked Sam after a brief interval.

"That's what brings me to the point about that young feller that's going to be hung," said Bob, tapping the newspaper that lay upon the bench. "I don't know what would lie between two young women in a wrangle of that sort; some would get over it quick, but some would never sleep soundly any more, not for a minute of their mortal lives. Edie must have been one of that sort. There's people living there now as could tell a lot if they'd a mind to it. Some knowed all about it, could tell you the very shop where Edie managed to get hold of the poison and could describe to me or to you just how she administrated it in a glass of barley water. Old Harry knew all about it, he knew all about everything, but he favoured Edith and he never budged a word. Clever old chap was Harry, and nothing came out against Edie at the inquest—nor the trial neither."

"Was there a trial, then?"

"There was a kind of a trial. Naturally. A beautiful trial. The police came and fetched poor William. They took him away and in due course he was hanged."

"William! But what had he got to do with it?"

"Nothing. It was rough on him, but he hadn't played straight and so nobody struck up for him. They made out a case against him—there was some onlucky bit of evidence which I'll take my oath old Harry knew something about—and William was done for. Ah, when things take a turn against you it's as certain as twelve o'clock, when they take a turn; you get no more chance than a rabbit from a weasel. It's like dropping your matches into a stream, you needn't waste the bending of your back to pick them out—they're no good on, they'll never strike again. And

Edith, she sat in court through it all, very white and trembling and sorrowful, and when the judge put his black cap on, they do say she blushed and looked across at William and gave a bit of a smile. Well, she had to suffer for his doings, so why shouldn't he suffer for hers? That's how I look at it."

"But God-a-mighty—!"

"Yes, God-a-mighty knows. Pretty girls they were, both, and as like as two pinks."

There was quiet for some moments while the tiler and the mason emptied their cups of beer. "I think," said Sam then, "the rain's give over now."

"Ah, that it has," cried Bob. "Let's go and do a bit more on this 'bugging church or she won't be done afore Christmas."

Clorinda Walks in Heaven (1922)

SILVER CIRCUS

HANS SIEBENHAAR, a street porter, is basking on his stool in a fine street of Vienna, for anybody to hire for any sort of job. He is a huge man with a bulbous hairless face that somehow recalls a sponge, and this sponge is surmounted by a flat peaked hat encircled by a white band bearing these words in red: *Wiener Dienstmann*. His voice, which we shall hear later on, is a vast terrifying voice that seems to tear a rent in Space itself. At fifty years of age Hans is a conspicuous man. But a street porter! Not a profitable way of life, yet it must serve, and must continue to serve. It is a hot July morn, tropical; there are many noises, but no one speaks. The fruit-stall women are silent and hidden; they have pinned newspapers around the edges of their big red umbrellas. It is stifling, languorous; one thinks of lilac, of cool sea, of white balloons; the populace tears off its hat, fans itself desperately, sips ice in the cafés, and still perspires. The very street sounds are injurious to the mind. The drivers of carts wear only their breeches, their bodies are brown as a Polynesian's and lovely to behold.

Just such a day it was as the day twelve months gone when Mitzi Siebenhaar, his second wife, had run away with that Julius Damjancsics. Yes, please very much, she had left him. Hans took off his hat. After contemplating its interior as though it was a coffer of extraordinary mystery, he sighed huskily into it. How was it possible to understand such an accident? Smoothing his brown bald skull with the other hand, he collected so much sweat upon his hairy freckled fingers that as he shook them the drops simply splashed upon the pavement. Young Mitzi! It was her youth. Ah, God bless, she had the pull of him there, a whole fifteen years, fifteen years younger; youth as well as beauty, beauty as well as youth. At thirty-five she was as lovely as a girl, fitful and furious just like a girl, so he was only able to keep her for one little year; that is to say, keep her faithful, to himself. One little year! That is not long, but for a man of fifty it is so difficult, yes; but then Julius Damjancsics was just as old. And she had gone off with him! What could she see in Julius Damjancsics? How was it possible to understand such an accident? They had all been friends together, and Julius could play the mandolin, but Hans could pound him into dust. What could she see in Julius Damjancsics? He could crush him in one fist, like a gherkin. If he had caught them—but that was difficult too. Belgrade he had gone to, for Julius Damjancsics was a Serbian, and Buda-Pesth he had gone to, for Mitzi was Hungarian, but this Julius was a wandering fellow and very deceitful. So. Well, it was pitiful to think of in such hot weather, there was nothing to be done, he had come back to Vienna. And now here he was brooding, here he was groaning; pitiful to think of. At last he said to himself: "Let us wipe our tears and forget that Christ died. *Gloria Patri et Filio et Spiritu Sancto,*" he murmured, for he was a good Catholic man, as Father Adolf of Stefans Dom could testify.

"Porter!" cried a voice.

Hans looked up quickly and put on his hat.

"Sir," said he.

A big man, with a big important foreign face and fat and flourishing appearance and shiny black boots with grey cloth tops stood as it were examining the porter. Although the boots were fastened with what appeared to be pearl buttons, they were rather uncared for, but to offset this a large gold watch-chain was lavishly displayed, with jewelled tiepin and studs. The man's fists were in his trousers pockets; he twirled a long, thin cigar between his rich red lips. Immense and significant, he might have been a Turk or a Tartar, but he was neither; he was the boss of a Rumanian Circus.

"Come with me, I want you," and the huge Hans followed the circus man to a *Biergarten,* where another man was waiting who might have been a Tartar or a Turk. He called him Peter, he was certainly his brother, and Peter called him Franz. All three sat down and drank together.

"Tell me, Hans Siebenhaar," said Franz, "you are a strong man?"

"Yes, I am a strong man, that is so."

"You have a good voice?"

"Please—" Hans paused. "I am no singer, not much."

"Ah! No, no, no. You have a strong voice to speak, to shout, you can make great sounds with your voice?"

"Oh, ay," Hans agreed. "I have a strong voice, that is so, very strong, I can make a noise." And there and then he accorded them a succession of hearty bellows in testimony. There was only one other occupant of the *Biergarten,* a man with an Emperor Franz-Josef sort of face and white whiskers like the wings of an easy chair, who sat smoking a china pipe under an acacia tree. And he seemed to be deaf, for he did not take the slightest notice of the appalling outcry. Two waiters rushed with alarm into the garden, but Franz waved them away.

"Good," said Franz reflectively. "Listen now." And sitting there between the brothers Hans heard them propound to him a scheme that smote him with amazement and bereft him of sympathy; it filled him indeed with any and every emotion but that of satisfaction. They wanted him, in brief, to become a tiger.

"No." Hans was indignant, and he was contemptuous. "I do not understand, but I do not do this."

Not at once, they cried, not today. No, no. Plenty of time, a week's time in fact. And they would instruct him in the art of impersonating a tiger, they would rehearse him, and for a single performance, one night only, they would give him two hundred Austrian shillings. Peter the Turk declared it was far too much money. Franz the Tartar invoked his God.

There is more in this, thought Hans, than strokes my ear; I have to beware of something. Aloud he inquired: "Two hundred shillings?"

"Two hundred," said Peter.

"Shillings," echoed Franz, scratching the table with a wooden toothpick.

"And, please very much, I am to do?"

They told him what he was to do. He was to be sewn up in the skin of a tiger; he was to enact the part of a tiger in their menagerie; he was to receive two hundred shillings. Very, very simple for a strong man. Hans Siebenhaar was to be sewn up in the tiger's hide for two hundred shillings; he was to prance and fight and hideously roar in the best way he knew so that the hearts of the audience be rocked within them and fly into their throats—and the two hundred shillings was his. It was his voice, it was because of his great bellowing tigerish voice that they had come to him. Such a voice was worth some riches to them, and so they were going to pay two hundred shillings for his services.

"Two hundred shillings?" murmured Hans.

"Two hundred," said Peter, and Franz said: "Two hundred."

It is not, thought Hans, to be sneezed at, but there is more in this than strokes my hearing; I must be wary.

"Why do you not have," he asked them, "a real tiger?"

"But we had!" they both cried.

"And now he is dead," said Peter.

"A real proper tiger," Franz declared.

"But now he is dead," repeated his brother. "Ah, he had paws like a hassock."

"And the ferocity!"

"Beautiful," said Peter. "He died of grief."

"No, no, no," objected Franz. "I would not say that of this tiger."

"But yes," affirmed Peter. "Of grief. He loved me, and lately I married again."

"The heart was broken, yes, perhaps," Franz admitted.

"His voice died away like a little whistle." There was sorrow in Peter's eyes. "No fury."

"Two hundred shillings," said Franz.

"Brrr-o-o-o-owh!" Hans suddenly roared, and skipping up he began capering and pawing madly about the garden. "Ookah, pookah, boddle, oddle, moddle, miowh!" he roared.

The deaf old gentleman with the Franz-Josef whiskers gently laid his china pipe on the table before him; he neither observed nor heeded Hans, he only put his fingers into his mouth and extracted his false teeth. These he calmly examined, as though they were a foreign substance he had never noticed before and was wondering how it came to be there. Hans began crashing over the tables and chairs; waiters rushed into the garden and, flinging themselves upon the perspiring maniac, rolled him over into a corner.

"That is good," cried Franz, "very good!"

"Absolutely," Peter said, "absolutely!"

Three waiters clung to Hans Siebenhaar with the clear intention of throttling him.

"Enough!" shouted Franz. "Let him go," and with his powerful hands he dragged two of the waiters from the prostrate body of Hans as you would draw two pins from a pincushion, and likewise did Peter do with the other waiter.

"It is all right," said Franz, and Peter said it was quite all right. They gave the waiters a few coins and soothed them. In the meantime Hans had resumed his seat, and the deaf old gentleman was replacing his teeth.

To Hans the brothers said: "Listen," and Hans listened. Their circus-menagerie was now on view in the Prater, and at the festival next week they had contemplated to stage a novel performance, nothing less than a combat between a lion and a tiger —ah, good business!—but just at this critical moment what does their tiger do?

"It dies," suggested Hans.

"Dies," agreed Franz. "It dies. So now!"

"Yes, now?" Hans said, and nodded.

"You must be our tiger, that is the simple fact of the business. You have the voice of a tiger, and the character. You will get the two hundred shillings. Hooray! It is like lapping honey, yes."

"But what is this?" cried Hans. "To fight a lion!"

"Pooh," Peter said. "It is more friendly and harmless than any kitten."

"No," said Hans. "No."

"Yes," said Franz. "Yes. It is, it is but a caterpillar, I tell you."

"No!" shouted Hans.

"It has no teeth."

"Not I," cried the intended victim.

"It has been in our family for a hundred years."

"Never," declared Hans with absolute finality, and he got up as if to go. But the brothers seized each an arm and held him down in his chair.

"Have no fear, Mr. Siebenhaar; it will love you. Two hundred and fifty shillings!"

"No, I will not—ha!"

"Mr. Siebenhaar, we can guarantee you. Three hundred shillings," said Peter.

"And fifty," added Franz.

"Three hundred and fifty!" repeated Hans. "So? But what? I cannot fight a lion. No, no. I am not a woman, I have my courage, but what is three hundred and fifty shillings for my life's blood and bones?" In short, a lion was not the kind of thing Mr. Siebenhaar was in the habit of fighting.

"Ach! Your blood and bones will be as safe as they are in your trousers. You will not have to fight this lion—"

"No, I will not—ha!"

"—you have only to play with it. This lion does not fight, Mr. Siebenhaar; it will not, it cannot."

"Why so?"

"It is too meek, it is like a lamb in a meadow that cries baa. You have only to prance about before it and roar and roar, to make a noise and a fuss. It will cringe before you. Have no fear of him. A show, you understand, make a show."

"I understand a show," said Hans, "but, please very much,

permit me, I will not make a spectacle of my blood and bones."

"So help me Heaven!" shouted Franz, exasperated, "do you think we want your bones?"

"Not a knuckle!" cried Hans.

Peter intervened. "You misunderstand us, Mr. Siebenhaar; we desire only entertainment, we do not want a massacre."

"You do not want a massacre!"

"A massacre is very well in its way, perhaps, in its time and place," Peter continued, "but a massacre is one thing, and this is another."

"Thank you," said Hans, "it is very clear, that is very good."

And Franz and Peter intimated that they were simple men of business whose only care it was to bring joy and jollity into the life of the Viennese populace; that the fury of the lion was a figment, its courage a mockery, its power a profanation of all men's cherished fears. If there was one animal in the world more deserving the kindness and pity of mankind, more subservient, more mercifully disposed than any other, Franz assured him, it was a lion. And if there was one lion among all lions more responsive to the symptoms of affection, added Peter, it was this identical lion. Was three hundred and fifty shillings nothing to him?

"No," Hans conceded.

"Is it a bunch of beans?"

"No, no."

"Three hundred and fifty shillings is three hundred and fifty shillings, is it not?" Peter questioned him; and Hans replied: "For what is past, yes; but for what is yet to come, no. The future —pardon, gentleman, does not lie in our behinds."

"Three hundred and fifty shillings is three hundred and fifty shillings, it is not a bunch of beans," said Franz severely. They had men in their employ who implored him on their knees to be honourably permitted to enact the part of this tiger, but they had not the physique, they had not the voice, and, if Mr. Siebenhaar would pardon him, they had not the artist's delicate touch. One thing he, Franz, was certain of: he knew an artist when he saw one, hence this three hundred and fifty shillings.

At the end of it all Hans once more determined to wipe his tears and forget that Christ died. In effect, he agreed to be sewn

up on such and such a date in the tiger's hide and to make a
manifestation with Messrs. Franz and Peter's ingenuous lion, on
the solemnest possible undertaking that no harm should befall
his own blood and bones.

"Thunder and lightning! What could harm you?"

"Good."

And after parting from Hans, and when they were well out of
hearing, Mr. Franz said: "Ha, ha!" and Mr. Peter said: "Ho,
ho!"

II

Hans Siebenhaar had several rehearsals before the eventful
day. Submitting himself to be sewn up in the tiger's skin, he
dashed his paws upon the floor, pranced, gnashed, snarled,
whirled his mechanical tail, and delivered himself of a gamut of
howls eminently tigerish. Perfectly satisfactory.

"Where," Hans would ask, "do you keep this old lion?"

"Yes," the brothers always replied, "he is not well, he is sleeping; you see him next time."

And thus it happened that Hans did not see his adversary until
they met in the cage of battle. The morning of that day was dull
and Hans too was dull, for on awakening he felt so strange, so
very unwell, that he greatly feared he would have to send Franz
word that he could not come to perform his tiger; but as the day
wore on and brightened, Hans, sitting on his stool in the sunny
street, brightened with it, and while thinking of the three
hundred and fifty shillings his sickness left him. A nice sum of
money that! And what would he do with it? Ah, please very
much, what would he not have done if Mitzi, the shameless one,
had not forsaken him! They might have gone again, as they had
gone of old, on one of those excursions to the Wiener Wald. He
liked excursions, they were beautiful. With their happy companions they could climb the mountains, prowl in the forest for
raspberries and mushrooms, and at noon they would sit under
the chestnuts in the *Biergarten* at the Hunter's Meadow and lap
the rich soup and gulp lager and talk of love and wealth and food
and childhood. That was life, that was wonderful! Then they
would all go and loaf in the grass and Mitzi would throw off her

frock and lie half naked, browning her sleek shining body, while Julius Damjancsics thrummed his mandolin and they all murmured songs. Ah, such music! She loved it. She had a dimple behind each shoulder, a rare thing, very beautiful. In the cool of the evening there would be dancing, and they would be at Dreimarkstein in time to see the fireworks go up from the Prater—he liked fireworks, lovely. Or to the trotting races, they might go and win some more money, for when luck was on you the fancy could never deceive; beautiful horses, he loved horses. Or to the baths at Gänsehaufel—the things one could do with a little money! But there was no longer any Mitzi, she had gone with Julius Damjancsics. Gone wife, gone friend; there were no more journeys now. But a man with three hundred and fifty shillings need never lack companions, there was a lot of friendship in three hundred and fifty shillings. But that Mitzi—she was very beautiful, that little Mitzi.

So the day wore on and the evening came and the Prater began to sparkle with the lights of its many booths and cafés, to throb with its much music, for youth was gallant and gay and there was love and money in the world. It was the hour at last. Hans had been sewn up in the tiger's skin. Now he crouched in a corner of a shuttered cage, alone, trembling in darkness, seeing no one and seen of none. There was a door in the side of his cage that led into a large empty lighted cage, and beyond that was another like his own in which walked a lion. At a certain moment the doors of the end cages would be opened and he would have to go into that central cage and face that other beast. But no, he could not, he was limp with fear. To the stricken man came the excited voices of the people coming in to witness his calamity, and the harsh tones of the trumpeting band playing in pandemonium outside on the platform, where there was a large poster of a combat between a tiger and a lion. Hans recalled that the lion's teeth were buried in the tiger's belly amid the gushing blood, and it seemed that his very heart violently cried: "No! No! Let me out!"

Beating upon the walls of his cage he gasped: "In Christ's name, let me out!" but nobody heeded, no one replied, and although he tore at his tiger-skin, his paws were too cumbersome for him to free himself. He was in a trap, he knew now he had been trapped. For an eternal anguishing time the clamour went on, then that dreadful side door which led into the central cage slid quietly open. Hans saw that this cage was yet empty, the lion's door was still closed, he was to be the first to enter. But he averted his eyes, he lay in the corner of his trap and would not budge from it. Almighty Heaven! was he going to sacrifice himself for a few pitiful pieces of silver that he had never seen and never would see? He was not fit to do it, he was an old man, even his wife, Mitzi, had left him for another man—did they not know that! And all day long he had been unwell, sick as a dog. As he lay in his corner, refusing to budge and sweating most intensely, a sharp iron spear came through the bars and pricked him savagely in the behind. With a yell he leaped up, trying to snatch the spear. He would use it, it would save him—but he could not grasp it with his giant paws. Then came bars of red-hot iron searing him, and more spears; he was driven screaming into the central cage. The door closed behind him and he was left alone behind those terrible bars with a vast audience gazing at him. Then, ah then, in a frenzy, an epilepsy of fear, he dashed himself so violently against the bars that the crowd was spellbound. The band played riotously on, drowning his human cries. The other side door slid open, there was silence in that other cage, but he dared not turn to meet whatever was there; he crouched half swooning, until he caught sight of a face in the audience that he knew. Wonder of God! It was Mitzi, she herself! Oh, but there was something to fight for now and he turned resolutely. As he did so, there was a titter in the audience that surged into general laughter—the lion had come into the cage. Truly, it was a cadaverous lion. Without the least display of ferocity or fear it stepped quietly into that cage and fixed its strong eyes upon the eyes of its enemy. Not a leap did it make, not a roar did it give, it padded forwards quietly, and the tiger retreated before it. Thus they circled and circled round the cage. Would that mocking laughter never stop?

God! Hans could bear it no longer, he turned and faced the lion, in appearance bold, though trembling in his soul. The lion paused too.

"Pater noster qui es in cœlis," Hans gasped involuntarily.

To his unspeakable astonishment he heard the lion answer:

"Et ne nos inducas in tentationem. Sed libera nos a malo."

In an incredible flash Hans realized that the lion also was a spurious creature like himself; his fears vanished, he knew now the part he had to play, and he hurled himself upon the lion, howling:

"Brrr-o-o-owh! Ookah, pookah, boddle, oddle, moddle, miowh!"

Over they rolled, lion and tiger, together, and the onlookers shook with mirth.

"Not so rough, brother!" cried a voice from inside the lion, and the tones struck a strange echo in the mind of Hans Siebenhaar. They disengaged and stood up on all fours facing each other. From the moment's silence that ensued there issued a piercing cry of fear from a woman in the audience. Hans turned. The lion turned. It was Mitzi, shrieking: "Julius! Watch out!" Hans's throbbing mind caught at that fatal name, Julius. By all the gods, was it possible! Heaven and hell, he would tear the heart out of *that* lion! *Not so rough, brother!* Ha, ha, he knew it now, that voice! Ho, ho! and with a cruel leap he jumped with his heels savagely in the middle of the lion's back, the back of Julius Damjancsics, thief of Mitzi, the beloved of Hans, and down sank the lion with the tiger tearing at its throat as fearfully as any beast of the jungle. Ah, but how the people applauded; this was good in spite of the deception! They had paid to see a real lion and a real tiger contending, and they felt defrauded, insulted; but this was good, yes, it was very comical, good, good. When they noticed a man's hand appear outside the flapping paw of the tiger their joy was unbounded.

"Tear him!" they cried, as one cries to a hound with a fox. "Ha, ha, tear him!" And Hans's loosened hand ripped up the seam in the lion's neck, and his hand went searching within the rent for a throat to tear. At once the teeth of Julius ground themselves upon it; in a trice Hans's smallest finger was gone, severed. But Hans never uttered a cry, he gripped the throat with his wounded hand and crushed everlastingly upon it, moment after moment, until he knew that Julius Damjancsics was gone, and for ever, to hell or glory, whatever destiny had devised for him. The lion moved no more, it lay on its back with its hind legs crooked preposterously, it forelegs outspread like one crucified. The people hushed their laughter as Hans slunk trembling and sweating from that droll oaf wrapped in a lion's skin. He was afraid of it now and he crawled on all fours to the bars of the cage. The thing behind him was awfully still. The onlookers were still. They were strange, as strange as death. Mitzi was there, craning forward, her face as pale as snow. Hans caught hold of the cage bars and lifted himself to his feet. The onlookers could hear wild tormenting sobs bursting from the throat of the tiger as it hung ridiculously there. The door of Hans's first cage now slid open again, it was finished, he could go. But Hans did not go.

Silver Circus (1928)

LUXURY

EIGHT o'clock of a fine morning in the hamlet of Kezzal Predy Peter, great horses with chains clinking down the road, and Alexander Finkle rising from his bed singing: "Oh, lah, soh doh, soh lah me doh," timing his notes to the ching of his neighbour's anvil. He boils a cupful of water on an oil stove, his shaving-brush stands (where it always stands) upon the window ledge ("Soh lah soh do-o-o-oh, soh doh soh la-a-a-ah!"), but as he addresses himself to his toilet the clamour of the anvil ceases and then Finkle too becomes silent, for the unresting cares of his life begin again to afflict him.

"This cottage is no good," he mumbles, "and I'm no good. Literature is no good when you live too much on porridge. Your writing's no good, sir, you can't get any glow out of oatmeal. Why did you ever come here? It's a hopeless job and you know it!" Stropping his razor petulantly as if the soul of that frustrating oatmeal lay there between the leather and the blade, he continues: "But it isn't the cottage, it isn't me, it isn't the writing—it's the privation. I must give it up and get a job as a railway porter."

And indeed he was very impoverished, the living he derived from his writings was meagre; the cottage had many imperfections, both its rooms were gloomy, and to obviate the inconvenience arising from its defective roof he always slept downstairs.

Two years ago he had been working for a wall-paper manufacturer in Bethnal Green. He was not poor then, not so very poor; he had the clothes he stood up in (they were good clothes) and fifty pounds in the bank besides. But although he had served the wall-paper man for fifteen years that fifty pounds had not been derived from clerking, he had earned it by means of his hobby, a little knack of writing things for provincial newspapers. On his thirty-first birthday Finkle argued—for he had a habit of conducting long and not unsatisfactory discussions between himself and a self that apparently wasn't him—that what he could do reasonably well in his scanty leisure could be multiplied exceedingly if he had time and opportunity, lived in the country, somewhere where he could go into a garden to smell the roses or whatever was blooming and draw deep draughts of happiness, think his profound thoughts, and realize the goodness of God, and then sit and read right through some long and difficult book about Napoleon or Mahomet. Bursting with literary ambition, Finkle had hesitated no longer: he could live on nothing in the country —for a time. He had the fifty pounds, he had saved it, it had taken him seven years, but he had made it and saved it. He handed in his notice. That was very astonishing to his master, who esteemed him, but more astonishing to Finkle was the parting gift of ten pounds that the master had given him. The workmen, too, had collected more money for him and bought for him a clock, a monster; it weighed twelve pounds and had a brass figure of Lohengrin on the top, while the serene old messenger man who cleaned the windows and bought surreptitious beer for the clerks gave him a prescription for the instantaneous relief of a painful stomach ailment. "It might come in handy," he had said.

That was two years ago, and now just think! He had bought himself an inkpot of crystalline glass—a large one, it held nearly half a pint—and two pens, one for red ink and one for black, besides a quill for signing his name with. Here he was at Pretty Peter and the devil himself was in it! Nothing had ever been right, the hamlet itself was poor. Like all places near the chalk hills its roads were of flint, the church was of flint, the farms and cots of flint with brick corners. There was an old milestone outside his cot, he was pleased with that, it gave the miles to London and the miles to Winchester; it was nice to have a milestone there like that—your very own.

He finished shaving and threw open the cottage door; the scent of wallflowers and lilac came to him as sweet almost as a wedge of newly cut cake. The may bloom on his hedge drooped over the branches like crudded cream, and the dew in the gritty road smelled of harsh dust in a way that was pleasant. Well, if the cottage wasn't much good, the bit of a garden was all right.

There was a rose bush too, a little vagrant in its growth. He leaned over his garden gate; there was no one in sight. He took out the fire shovel and scooped up a clot of manure that lay in the road adjacent to his cottage and trotted back to place it in a little heap at the root of those scatter-brained roses, pink and bulging, that never seemed to do very well and yet were so satisfactory.

"Nicish day," remarked Finkle, lolling against his doorpost, "but it's always nice if you are doing a good day's work. The garden is all right, and literature is all right—only I live too much on porridge. It isn't the privation itself, it's the things privation makes a man do. It makes a man do things he ought not want to do, it makes him mean, it makes him *feel* mean, I tell you, and if he feels mean and thinks mean he writes meanly, that's how it is."

He had written topical notes and articles, stories of gay life (of which he knew nothing), of sport (of which he knew less), a poem about "hope," and some cheerful pieces for a girls' weekly paper. And yet his outgoings still exceeded his income, painfully and perversely after two years. It was terrifying. He wanted success, he had come to conquer—not to find what he *had* found.

But he would be content with encouragement now even if he did not win success; it was absolutely necessary, he had not sold a thing for six months, his public would forget him, his connection would be gone.

"There's no use though," mused Finkle as he scrutinized his worn boots, "in looking at things in detail, that's mean; a large view is the thing. Whatever is isolated is bound to look alarming."

But he continued to lean against the doorpost in the full blaze of the stark, almost gritty sunlight, thinking mournfully until he heard the porridge in the saucepan begin to bubble. Turning into the room, he felt giddy, and scarlet spots and other phantasmagoria waved in the air before him.

Without an appetite he swallowed the porridge and ate some bread and cheese and watercress. Watercress, at least, was plentiful there, for the little runnels that came down from the big hills expanded in the Predy Peter fields, and in their shallow bottoms the cress flourished.

He finished his breakfast, cleared the things away, and sat down to see if he could write, but it was in vain—he could not write. He could think, but his mind would embrace no subject; it just teetered about with the objects within sight—the empty, disconsolate grate, the pattern of the rug, and the black butterfly that had hung dead upon the wall for so many months. Then he thought of the books he intended to read but could never procure, the books he had procured but did not like, the books he had liked but was already, so soon, forgetting. Smoking would have helped and he wanted to smoke, but he could not afford it now. If ever he had a real good windfall he intended to buy a tub, a little tub it would have to be, of course, and he would fill it to the bung with cigarettes, full to the bung, if it cost him pounds. And he would help himself to one whenever he had a mind to do so.

"Bah, you fool!" he murmured, "you think you have the whole world against you, that you are fighting it, keeping up your end with heroism! Idiot! What does it all amount to? You've withdrawn yourself from the world, run away from it, and here you sit making futile dabs at it, like a child sticking pins into a pudding and wondering why nothing happens. What *could* happen? What? The world doesn't know about you, or care, you are useless. It isn't aware of you any more than a chain of mountains is aware of a gnat. And whose fault is that—is it the mountain's fault? Idiot! But I can't starve and I must go and get a job as a railway porter, it's all I'm fit for."

Two farmers paused outside Finkle's garden and began a solid conversation upon a topic that made him feel hungry indeed. He listened, fascinated, though he was scarcely aware of it.

"Six-stone lambs," said one, "are fetching three pounds apiece."

"Ah!"

"I shall fat some."

"Myself I don't care for lamb, never did care."

"It's good eating."

"Ah, but I don't care for it. Now, we had a bit of spare rib last night off an old pig. 'Twas cold, you know, but beautiful. I said to my dame: 'What can mortal man want better than spare rib off an old pig? Tender and white, ate like lard.'"

"Yes, it's good eating."

"Nor veal I don't like—nothing that's young."

"Veal's good eating."

"Don't care for it, never did, it eats short to my mind."

Then the school bell began to ring so loudly that Finkle could hear no more, but his mind continued to hover over the choice of lamb or veal or old pork until he was angry. Why had he done this foolish thing, thrown away his comfortable job, reasonable food, ease of mind, friendship, pocket money, tobacco? Even his girl had forgotten him. Why had he done this impudent thing? It was insanity, surely. But he knew that man has instinctive reasons that transcend logic, what a parson would call the superior reason of the heart.

"I wanted a change and I got it. Now I want another change, but what shall I get? Chance and change, they are the sweet features of existence. Chance and change, and not too much prosperity. If I were an idealist I could live from my hair upwards."

The two farmers separated. Finkle, staring haplessly from his window, saw them go. Some schoolboys were playing a game of marbles in the road there. Another boy sat on the green bank quietly singing, while one in spectacles knelt slyly behind him trying to burn a hole in the singer's breeches with a magnifying glass. Finkle's thoughts still hovered over the flavours and satisfactions of veal and lamb and pig until, like Mother Hubbard, he turned and opened his larder.

There, to his surprise, he saw four bananas lying on a saucer. Bought from a travelling hawker a couple of days ago, they had cost him threepence halfpenny. And he had forgotten them! He could not afford another luxury like that for a week at least, and he stood looking at them, full of doubt. He debated whether he should take one now; he would still have one left for Wednesday, one for Thursday, and one for Friday. But he thought he would not, he had had his breakfast and he had not remembered them. He grew suddenly and absurdly angry again. That was the worst of poverty—not what it made you endure, but what it made you want to endure. Why shouldn't he eat a banana? Why shouldn't he eat *all* of them! And yet bananas always seemed to him such luxuriant, expensive things, so much peel, and then two, or not more than three, delicious bites. But if he fancied a banana—there it was. No, he did not want to destroy the blasted thing! No reason at all why he should not, but that was what continuous hardship did for you, nothing could stop this miserable feeling for economy now. If he had a thousand pounds at this moment he knew he would be careful about bananas and about butter and about sugar and things like that; but he would never have a thousand pounds, nobody had ever had it, it was impossible to believe that anyone had ever had wholly and entirely to himself a thousand pounds. It could not be believed. He was like a man dreaming that he had the hangman's noose around his neck; yet the drop did not take place, and it would not take place. But the noose was still there. He picked up the bananas one by one, the four bananas, the whole four. No other man in the world, surely, had ever had four such fine bananas as that and not wanted to eat them? Oh, why had such stupid mean scruples seized him again? It was disgusting and ungenerous to himself, it made him feel mean, it *was* mean! Rushing to his cottage door he cried: "Here y'are!" to the playing schoolboys and flung two of the bananas into the midst of them. Then he flung another. He hesitated at the fourth, and tearing the peel from it, he crammed the fruit into his own mouth, wolfing it down and gasping: "So perish all such traitors."

When he had completely absorbed its savour, he stared like a fool at the empty saucer. It was empty, the bananas were gone, all four irrecoverably gone.

"Damned pig!" cried Finkle.

But then he sat down and wrote all this, just as it appears.

Clorinda Walks in Heaven (1922)

THE FAIR YOUNG WILLOWY TREE

At the side of a long road winding high over a lonely moor stood a fair young willowy tree. Alone it grew on the verge of the road, the one tree in that solitary place; there was no other within the compass of an eye, not a hedge or house or bush to greet a stumbling traveller, only the vast hummocks of the moorland.

The tree was a little scattery sort of thing but it was graceful. When soft breezes played she waved her arms happily to the sky, but in squally weather she shrank from the wind and squealed at its roughness. The fogs, too, wearied her, so that she drooped and wept; often she sighed at the loneliness of her lot and longed for a companion.

"If only I had a friend to give me greetings and to talk with about the great matters of the world I should be the happiest of creatures; but I am alone, alone, all alone."

She grew and grew until she was twelve feet high and then

one day, while peeping from her topmost twigs, she saw far down the road a wagon filled with huge black poles, and a gang of men beside it engaged in merry activities. They returned the next day and the next and for many more days; each day seemed to bring them all nearer to her and at last she was able to see what it was they were about. They were digging pits by the roadside and hoisting a tall black pole in every one, and along the tops of the poles they were hanging bright wires for a new telegraph line. Oh joy! Wild with delight and hope, she watched the lengthening column of tall black poles advancing steadily across the lonely moor, ever nearer and nearer, until at last they were so close that she could hear the shouts of the men and the thumping of their gear as they shovelled and dug. When they were close at hand the men came and dug a hole just beside the fair young willowy tree and hoisted a sturdy blackamoor of a pole upright in it, then filled in the hole and rammed the earth tight at its foot. They put back the turf so neatly, left the pole standing beside her, and went on, farther and farther, planting giant poles across the moor.

The fair young willowy tree was filled with gladness.

"Now at last I have a dear companion!" and she laughed and spoke to the sturdy telegraph pole.

For a while the poor thing was gloomy, he was new to that country and felt lost in his surroundings, but he soon settled down and became friendly. Unhappily, however, a nasty odour of tar drifted from him to the fair young willowy tree whenever the wind was set to her quarter, and this offended her delicate senses. As such times she shrank from his neighbourhood as far as her station would permit—though this of course was not very far; indeed, it was not far enough for her happiness, and she would rail at her companion for a stinking interloper.

"Oh what a stench you have brought to the flavour of this highway!" she complained to the telegraph pole. "I cannot bear your company; you are a common low thing, stuck there and reeking with smells and defiling my air. And look at your stupid stumpy arms, and your skinny wires that groan and moan without stopping! What am I to do about it!"

"Alas!" the pole sighed. "It is true that my appearance is nothing to boast about now; in my figure I take no pride; but I am not now as once I was. You should have seen me then! Oh no indeed, I have been maimed and put to uses I was never educated for. I have travelled the wide world over, but I take no credit for that—have you ever travelled, my dear?"

"No," replied she. "I should scorn it. I do not want to go else-where. This is my real home."

"Oh, but it broadens the mind," he said. "One should travel when one is young. I did."

"I have no wish to travel." The fair young willowy tree tossed her head disdainfully and at the same time looked most beautiful with her trim leaves and sweet slender boughs.

"No, of course not," the sturdy pole answered. "Neither had I. I was reared in the northern land beyond the sea. I had a thousand companions around me there, and I had my branches too, but I was not graceful and delicate like you—I was only sturdy and brave. All the same, you could not have endured the life, you could not have survived the fury of the weather and the bitterness of those crags where I had my home. My! How the wind came screaming over the icy isles! All day long and all year long the roaring waves came crashing upon our shore and I could watch the swirl of the last foot of foam hissing at the last foot of shingle. Oh, so good! So good! But you, my dear—your delicate body would have soon perished there, yes, indeed. It did not daunt me, though; nothing could uproot me."

"How vain you are!" taunted the fair young willowy tree. "I love the wind. I do not fear it, it is my joy. I hold out my arms and it embraces me and I hear the voices of angels, the sun pours its beams among my leaves."

So then the tall black pole began to brag of his travels: "I have travelled the wide world over, by ship and by wagon."

But the fair young willowy tree only laughed at him: "Pooh! You had to be carried! You had no choice. You were cut down and sold. A fine traveller indeed! You cannot travel now, you are just a post stuck in the ground, you can neither turn nor move. Ha, ha, ha!"

Such hilarity vexed him, it was so unkind, and he retorted sourly: "And how, pray, did you come to be rooted where you are? You cannot travel anywise at all, you cannot stir from this spot. You did not plant yourself, you have no will, no pride, no use—you have only vanity!"

"No use!" she cried indignantly. "No use! Listen!" she shook her branches and a sweet bird appeared upon one of the swaying boughs and began to sing its song, for in the bosom of the fair young willowy tree it had woven a nest, and in the nest were five golden eggs.

"You see, stupid thing! Birds come to me for shelter and love. What bird would ever, or could ever, build its nest upon you!"

"But, but, but," the sturdy pole protested, "such birds are of no account. In my country birds are as big as hounds; eagles, condors, alabatrossers; even the swan is just nothing."

"But can they sing, any of them!" cried she.

"Now why," the pole asked. "should an eagle sing? Do be reasonable. Tiny birds hop about and chipper and eat worms, or they go into private gardens and dig up the seeds, or steal the cherries before anyone else can pick them. It is dreadful, they are a great nuisance until the cat catches them. That is the only thing cats are good for."

Time and again they would squabble, which was a pity because they had no other friends, not a hedge nor a house nor a bush nor a tree, and the other poles were as poles apart, business-like fellows with no nonsense about them. She was often petulant and overbearing, yet she was so very young and beautiful that he always soon forgave her and in the pleasant summer breezes she would dance for him alone. When the foggy autumn weather hung over them, and she was drooping in despair as her leaves fell from her, and her twigs dripped with weeping, he would comfort her childish tears.

How solitary they were! Sometimes in all a week only a coach would go by—but then it would be a coach of blue with yellow wheels and four white galloping horses and a man in red to blow the long copper horn! If the day were fine the passengers might even be singing, and that was most sweet to hear.

"How good it is! Yes, yes, it is grand!" the sturdy pole would say, although his heart was despairing for he had begun to be in love with the fair young willowy tree and saw no hope for himself.

Or a flock of sheep might cross the road at evening chased by a shepherd whistling and a dog that harried them. How their tough little hoofs scattered the dust!

"This is most enjoyable and exciting," he would cry. "Life is sweet, is it not, my dear? Tell me now, what would you like best to be in all the world?" And he was hoping she might say she would like to be his wife!

"To be? Oh, if I could have my choice," laughed the fair young willowy tree, "I would like to feel bright flowers growing upon me everywhere, blossoms on every twig, of many different colours —yes, and each flower to turn at last into a yellow quince. What now would you most care to be?"

"Me? If I could have my choice," he answered, "I would be the mast on some tall leaning ship, with my white sails trimmed and my ropes to hold me fast, so I could peer far down into the crystal waters and note the wonders of the deep."

"Of the deep!"

"Yes. The billowing forests that are there, the vast ocean fungi, the caverns in the coral, the dreaming weed swaying in its dream; sponges like palaces, the fish going and coming all in silver and gold like princes' children."

"No, I would rather be as I am," said the fair young willowy tree. And that was wise of her, for then she could wave her arms merrily in the way she most liked to do, day in, day out, and every day, and dance as well as her station allowed—although that was not so very well because she was rooted in the soil. All the same, that does not matter if nobody sees you. There was only herself to please, and the sturdy pole had grown so fond of her that he thought it was perfection. One bright day he summoned up his courage and said:

"I would like to marry you."

"Oh, but you are dead," said she. "Aren't you? You have no twigs, no branches, only those stupid wires; you are not even alive."

"I may be dead, young lady," was his sorrowful rejoinder, "but I am still useful."

"Not useful to yourself, Mr. Pole."

"To others." He sighed. "The dead are of no use to themselves."

"Nor useful to me. I am alive, alive!" she cried. "Pray do not speak of this again, it upsets me. I have other hopes for myself."

"You have certainly little else," he retorted with an insolent sniff.

That made her quite angry and she cried out: "Why are you so stupid, tell me that, you fool!"

"Pardon me," he loftily replied, "is that a serious question?"

"You can make what you like of it."

"Well, I can't make sense of it," said he.

"Try again, you great big blackamoor," she said in her most aggravating tone.

"Is it a joke?" he asked. "I am quite unable to laugh at it."

"But who wants you to laugh! I am only asking you a simple question."

"I am not a dictionary," the proud pole responded.

"And I don't think that so very funny either!" said the fair young willowy tree. Oh, she was very furious! And most provoking.

But the sturdy pole went on: "Let me tell you it is honourable and good to be useful when you are dead. And I am not really dead, not yet. I am only half dead. You see, I have been painted with the nasty-smelling stuff in order to preserve me for a span of usefulness, and I am glad of it too, for otherwise I should have been chopped up for a fire probably."

"Ugh! Do not speak of fire!" She quivered to her very roots. "I hate it. I abominate it. The very thought of it makes me tremble."

"But fire is good," said he soothingly. "In a way it is very valuable. It has a long history, it is most useful and is highly esteemed in the highest circles."

"I don't care," she answered, "I hate it! I hate it!"

"And those wires you dislike so, which I carry on my shoulders: they are my veins! My life blood! Without them I should be nothing at all. They carry the news of the great world and, do you know, sometimes I can actually hear them whisper the messages from the King!"

"I have my own veins," said she. "I have no need of messages and news. I can dance with my branches in the rays of the sun, I can whistle with the wind, I have a hundred arms, I have more twigs than there are stars in the sky, my leaves are full of joy and they dream in the moonlight."

"Ah, my dear," murmured the poor black pole, "ah, my dear." It was all he could say, and he did not propose to hear any more.

Time, which cannot hold back, passed over the moor in the breath of happy winds, in the flight of gloomy clouds. Lone as the sky itself, the heather on the moor budded, bloomed, and faded. Sharp winter came harrying the world, and the fair young willowy tree lost her leaves again; they flew away from her and she shivered forlorn in the icy blast. But the tall black pole did not shiver. Valiant and unconcerned, even when the snow pillowed itself thickly round half his spine, he did his duty without complaint.

Not until Shrovetide did the young tree recover her spirits and begin to grow gay again. At Eastertide she was quite lighthearted, for her twigs were covered with tough little purple buds. By Whitsuntide the buds had broken into tender twinkling leaves, the birds were at nest again in her bosom, and she sang in the wind and danced in the sun, and her leaves dreamed in the moonlight. Moreover, she grew, she was shaping into a tall tree; her topmost branches strained upwards, and one day the sturdy pole felt her highest twigs tapping against the wires close to his head, very tenderly, very soothingly,—Oh, it was most blissful. And she was joyful too; they became the dearest of friends and dreamed in the moonlight together, all the bright year, all spring, all summer, all autumn.

And then, one day, an officer of state was passing by and he saw that the branches of the fair young willowy tree were mingled with the wires of the telegraph.

"That is dangerous," said he. "That cannot be allowed. I must attend to that."

And he sent a man with a shining broad axe, who cut down the fair young willowy tree without a word of apology. Not content with that, the man hacked off her beautiful arms, hewed her trunk into seven separate pieces, piled her remains in a heap together on the spot where once she grew, and went away and left her there.

Thus it was, and there she lay, destroyed and forgotten, until

many months afterwards, when cold, cold hours were blighting
the moor and a poor tinker man came traveling along who saw
the heap of fuel and settled down there and, wanting a fire to
thaw the ice from his bones, burned the remains of the fair young
willowy tree into fine white ash and little black cinders. And
when the fire was done and all was cold again, he travelled on,
leaving the ashes there. For long after he was gone the heap of
ash remained, black and sad, the winter through, at the foot of
the sturdy pole. The poor pole almost wept to see it, but he could
not quite weep—he could only stand and mourn.

By and by the spring came again. And the birds came, but
alas, the fair young willowy tree was gone, quite gone; only the
heap of ash remained. And even then the grass around was
growing so high that it soon covered up the ashes, and then no
one, not even the sturdy pole, could see it any more.

And so he forgot her.

You Never Know, Do You? (1939)

MY HUNDREDTH TALE

It is many years since I came to live in this forest, to live in solitude in a miserable hut. Well, no, the hut is not miserable; its
wooden walls are warped, and in places knawed by idiotic rats
who imagine I have something secreted from them, but I have
enjoyed much of my life here, and indeed perhaps I still enjoy it.
It is hard to find the truth about your own emotions. I can look
back with joy upon times when I fancied I was unhappy, but I
know now that one enjoys all experiences, whether happy or
not. You want me to tell you why I came to this wood? Well, I
will tell you; yes, and I will tell you why I remain here although

the original motive has long ceased to animate me. Yes, I will tell you, I swear I will tell you, but I must tell all this in my own way. You know I am thought to be a shy retiring silent person; that is my general character, that is how I am known, a man with nothing to say. But that is all wrong, it is not true; I have an ocean of thoughts to pour out—but not to any listener. Oh no. I am a retiring inarticulate person, but God knows how my brain goes round ceaselessly. It goes round like a squirrel in its cage, it will not stop, it never gives me rest, and what is more, it does not like to be interrupted or distracted or contradicted. When I am alone, as I always desire to be, I let my spinning mind pour out its thoughts, its everlasting ruminating profusion, good thoughts sometimes, bad thoughts often, but thoughts of anger and love, thoughts, thoughts, thoughts about everything, anything—even thoughts about nothing. Did you know that? You can have thoughts about nothing? There was a man I knew, a writer who had a great vogue in his day—though I could never understand why until I asked him to explain it to me. He was then a man of airs that might once have been graces, and graces that were merely airs; he moved in a world of poets, painters, and performers on the fiddle.

"Well, the plain truth of the matter is," he said to me, with a compassionate grin, "that you can never become a successful writer without intuition and training. I for one began by writing about anything and everything—locusts, bad eggs, Abernethy biscuits—it was all one to me. That was my training. But at last I perceived that the grand secret was to write, and write authoritatively, about nothing."

"Nothing!"

"Nothing at all. That was my intuition. So then I began to sit and think of nothing, and ever since I have written most sincerely and persuasively about that."

"But nothing?"

"Just that, nothing but nothing. But not *for* nothing, ha, ha! That's the way to teach people to think that they know."

"Know what?"

"Why," he cried plaintively, "something they did not know until they read me, of course."

That was what he told me, and I can tell you that he was a man who managed to convey quite a sense of their inferiority to those who had hardly realized as much before. He suggested things about me that were quite untrue—at least I should be sorry if they were not. A brute of a man!

No, no, I am sure he was wrong. The soul of man is like a tree that in autumn is shedding its leaves, the golden fruit of his ideals. Oh, vanity! They fall softly, serenely covering the sweet soil until they are trodden by some hoof or scattered by winds. A few lie safe in nooks and crannies—until they rot. But the tree lives on.

But I am going to tell you about myself and the forest and why I came here. O yes, I swear I will tell you, but be patient—life has hurried past me so, let me be leisurely for once. There are tens of thousands of trees in this forest, and on every tree each year there are thousands of leaves, but not one leaf of one tree in the forest has ever conveyed one single intimation to me. But they are my companions, I love them. They too are lonely and silent, nothing grows beneath them but moss and a silly green useless herb called dog's mercury. Few birds haunt these glades, and few animals. The trees sometimes die and fall and rot, but most of them in time are cut by axe and saw and hustled away to be changed into furniture for a clown's kitchen or a king's castle. And I swear there are things the trees wish to say, but they cannot say them to me, they cannot say them.

My age—I should have told you my age—is forty. I am a grown-up responsible man, you see, but now I want to begin at the beginning of everything. I am going to be garrulous, to say what I like, just anyhow. It will mean nothing to you, it may be tiresome for you, but to me it will be my life, and my only heaven. I tell you I am forty years old, living alone in this forest, and so now (in the way of modern stories) having begun at the end I dart back to my childhood, my eldorado that I carry with me.

> Fair Quiet, have I found thee here,
> And Innocence, thy sister dear?

My earliest recollections are concerned with a sense of continuous sunshine—how the window-blinds used to flutter in the bright

Easter winds!—and my mother, beautiful as an angel. (She often described angels to me. They seemed to be neither male nor female, and they wore no boots, but they had white gowns and musical instruments, feathers like birds, and features like my mother.) There was also a tall ship in a harbour, and a tiny man aloft in the cross-trees as remote as a pigeon on a steeple. And there was Sugarloaf Hill, on whose top I knelt and worshipped God because I dared not look up into His sky. My mother, so like an angel in spirit, wore a bustle, and my father, who much resembled God, had a thick chestnut beard. I have never suffered either of these appendages to appear on my person, but they were really fashionable then.

In those good old days when young men wore beards and ladies wore bustles my father, both before and after he became my father, spent most of his leisure and a large part of his other life in the company of a certain Bill Brown, a man of his own age, profession, inclination, and pursuits. You might hardly believe that two married tailors could find enjoyment in poaching fish or hares or birds, in card-playing, in strange vagrant women, or in gathering mushrooms, but there it was; they worked together, played together, and infallibly got drunk together. Our room always had some cages of live birds like goldfinches and linnets, often some jars of wildflowers, and in autumn there was a large crock of home-made ketchup stored under the bed.

Like, it is said, begets like, and there may be truth in it, for when I was ten years old I was mates with a lad of the name of Bill Brown. He was fatherless, his mother had a printed card in their window: *"Robes et Modes,"* and he had a sister Carlotta who was a year younger than me. She was shy and slender, with pale cheeks, and pale hair that hung as beautifully from her crown as a waterfall from a rock. Whenever I kissed Carlotta she would turn her face gently away and not look at me, never look at me. My Bill and my Carlotta were well cared for; their mother was prosperous, they had good boots and Sunday clothes, but my father was ill and my mother was poor; indeed, she was glad to do odd jobs for Bill Brown's mother.

We dwelt in a cot that stood in the shadow of a gigantic via-

duct, whose brick piers rose from our side like a cliff above a
bathing-hut. Once or twice an hour a train came snoring across
the viaduct with a racket that tore the sky and made the orna-
ments topple on the mantelpiece. A few other cottages were
ranged about us, and on a scrap of waste land a caravan stood
—it was there for years, was never moved in my time—the
home of some gypsies. They were deemed to be wealthy and
were spoken of by our neighbours as king and queen of the
gypsies, though they never made such a claim themselves in my
hearing. Their caravan was a tiny palace on red wheels with
big brass bosses; inside and out it was painted in that incomprehensible fashion known as "graining," adorned with soft-
shining brass that gleamed without a blur in all its pillars and
bands and rails, though who polished them was unknown to
us. Witchcraft, I suspect. The king was indeed a kingly figure,
tall, with emphatic belly and emphatic voice that was never
heard unless he was bawling at somebody. He wore a pepper-
and-salt bobtail coat, tight-fitting trousers to match, smart boots,
and a brown billycock hat. I never saw him handling a horse,
but he invariably carried a driving-whip. On his fat neck his
head grew proud and high; he buried his hands in the cross-
pockets of his breeches and sidled the whip under his arm. And
the queen, a famous fortune-teller, was his magnificent mate, as
tall, as stout, with a lovely brown romany face and black curls
as long and stiff as candles. Their grown-up son wandered
about the country fairs on business of his own, which I fancy
was thimblerigging, but he often visited his parents. He had a
tenor voice more piercing than any piccolo, but he sang only
one song, called *The Queen of the Earth*, and he could not sing
that more than once of an evening because its sustained chro-
matics so completely debilitated him that he had been known
to swoon after it. Sabrina, their twelve-year-old daughter, was a
dusky Circe with the accents of a deep-sea fisherman. All of
them were illiterate, and I used to go of an evening to their caravan to read to them in their newspaper the accounts of Jack-
the-Ripper murders. I would sit on a stool in the caravan, facing
the stove, the daintiest fitting imaginable with fire-guard and

poker of brass, kettle of copper, and saucepans of the same. The lamp itself was copper, and there were cushions, curtains, and pots of fuchsias.

"Read that bit again, boy."

And I would read: "The ab-do-men was much mu-ti-lated and certain parts of it were missing."

The king stared at the queen, the queen at the king. Pointing with his fat finger, he whispered huskily:

"What's that—Abdiman?"

I did not know, but when I got home I asked Mother and she said "Belly"; so the next evening I told the king.

Each evening they gave me a ha'penny for my services. Sabrina sometimes came to our cottage when I was not there and left things for me, such as a penknife, which my mother would hand over to me, a pencil-case or a top or a ball or a finger-ring, all of which my mother would hand over to me, often murmuring something about a "little bitch"; but most often Sabrina would leave a threepenny bit, which I regret to say my mother never would resign. Sabrina neve. gave a thing to me personally, but when she met me she would ask if I had received her presents. Despite their failure to reach me she continued to ply my mother with threepenny bits. Was that magnificent generosity or magnificent subtlety? I suppose I was an innocent child. I was small for my ten years, and she was much bigger. How she alarmed and abashed me! Often she waylaid me in the dark and cuddled me with contemptuous ardour, or she would throw me down and do most shameful things to me with a violent vulgarity that distressed me even more than her fearful language. I told Bill Brown about her. I always told Bill Brown about everything: he was the kind of person you did tell things to, and although he never told *me* any secrets—I was the kind no one ever told anything—I was quite proud of having so much to tell *him*. And then, suddenly, Sabrina stopped noticing me. No more gifts, no more threepenny pieces for mother, no more scandalous caresses; but sometimes Bill Brown would casually display a new knife, a new top, even cigarettes, and although he never let on, I was only too painfully aware of how he came by them. For now that I was discarded I began to long for what I had lost; not the gifts—indeed, no—but the wild affection of the princess.

About that time I was put to work under an ugly man. With a pony-cart and a dog we vended paraffin oil, soap, hearthstone, soda, firewood, and other such sundries in the streets of our town. I had an important property, a shrill piping voice which invited the attention of customers to our approach. (But oh, with what shame I hailed our wares in the street where golden-haired Carlotta dwelt!) My shortcomings throughout this appointment were very grave. I was often late, frequently lazy, and my master more than once found me sleeping in the cart. Upon our travels no injunctions of mine could induce his decrepit pony to move a hoof if she happened to stop, while if she were moving, no command from me ever persuaded her to stand at ease; sometimes, too, the dog in a forgetful mood bit me as if I was a stranger to him. All this was so annoying to an official in my position that I became careless of the customers' demands, reckless in my dispensation of good measure, and above all forgetful of my master's money—though try as I would I never succeeded in embezzling a single ha'penny, he was such a cute one. In short, I became a nuisance to my master and was soon discharged.

Toppling upon this disaster, which involved my family in a total loss of sixpence a day, my father now at the end of his long illness began to die. An uncle of mine, a monumental mason, wanted to adopt me and apprentice me to his funereal enterprise, and I was anxious to assist him at interments and carve epitaphs upon tombstones. At the back of his mind there was also the idea, dim but audacious, of arraying me as a child mute, in black, with gloves and a tall hat flounced with crape, for use as a special and novel attendant at infants' funerals. With this bright ambition, and in the callous egotism of boyhood, I hoped that my father would die. Other such caprices, as inhuman and ungovernable, have harassed me throughout my life; I have hidden them in some dungeon of the mind, but they still cover me with shame, and upon the gay picture of myself advancing years and wisdom have inflicted deep and tarnishing revenges. At times a recollection of that father who died unlamented thirty years ago comes upon me with a shock of tears. I scarcely knew him. What were the interesting human things about him? His conceptions, his prejudices, desires, commonplaces of phrase and act, his humour? I would give many precious things to know them now, for I have come to have a deep paternal regard for his memory. Yes, paternal! Am I not already much older than he was when he died, a young man in the prime of years? What was that mysterious forebear, I mean in the soul of him? Swayed by what rude ideas, flouted by what experiences, dominated by what passions, what genial futilities? I deeply divine. I could hold out a hand across the grave and the years and hail with almost impudent familiarity that young man who was my father.

My mother honoured her bereavement with the usual imprudent orgy of mourning. She clapped upon my head a black bowler hat so unspeakably ill-fitting that it turned my mysterious tears of grief into those of mortification. A kind but ill-instructed friend hatched out for me a suit of black. I was now my mother's principal relative. I was to attend my father's obsequies garbed for the first time in trousers, and offensive trousers they were; large in capacity but restricted in range, they reached only to my boots tags. Though I was small the jacket was smaller, fitting as tightly as a pair of stays. In this vain gear I was to follow my father to his grave, and thankful I am that he could not see me; for he, poor man, was a tailor with a reverence for his art. When the fatal moment came for mother to don the bonnet of widowhood, she broke into pitiable grief. The hearse stood at the door, and he lay waiting in it under a few sprays of flowers. Poor father. Poor mother. For some time she would not put on this bonnet; she ran into the scullery away from the assembled friends. They pursued her into the tiny garden. All their condolations there would have been useless had not some cute neighbour urged me forward. I am persuaded that at first, what with her tears and my own astonishing appearance, my mother did not recognize me. But the intervention was successful—I could always incline my mother to what I wanted. All other details of the interment have faded out of memory except that upon our return the mourners were treated to small glasses of wine, "Tarrigony, very good," and pieces of cake, seed cake; to my mother's mind seed was more decorous than plum.

II

I grew up in the companionship mainly of Bill Brown, whom I loved, or it seemed to me that I loved him. When first we met he was not very handy at games and such things, except the game of marbles, which he played with such devastating accuracy as to sow a permanent bitterness in my soul. I was always a sort of pioneer for Bill Brown, a pioneer whom he consistently ousted and excelled. He was fair and freckled. I did not like freckles, but my heart concealed its distaste from him, just as it concealed a contempt for many of the things he did; and although his accomplishments, when he accomplished anything, were undeniable, I chafed at his methods, which seemed pervaded by a mysterious unfairness. I do suspect now that I did not love him at all, and that my emotion was but a reflection of another I indulged in, my timid silent worship of his tender silent sister, Carlotta. He was freckled, and I could not endure freckles. He had simply no fingernails, they were gnawed off, and he knew a lot of dirty songs that a cabmaster named Babstock taught him. At that time I did not like dirty songs—not until many years afterwards.

When we were sixteen I had discovered in myself a fondness and aptitude for running. I longed to become fleet as a roe; often I imagined that I was. The desire may have grown out of a poem I learned at school:

> My heart's in the Highlands, my heart is not here,
> My heart's in the Highlands a-chasing the deer;
> A-chasing the wild deer and following the roe,
> My heart's in the Highlands wherever I go.

I could go out alone upon the South Downs and take them for my mountains, with deer in every valley and a castle on every crown. There was never a buck in that thymy wonderland—I

knew it so well!—though there were flocks of a thousand sheep
looking no more than a few gnats in all the manifolding graciousness that seemed to swoon from one end of the shire to
the other. Limitless and lonely the uplands rose in the east and
lay down in the west, unconquered. The long fawn-hued grass
that the sheep never cropped was mingled in their season with
small frail flowers like the harebell or by robuster blooms,
toadflax, ramshorn, and cowslip. Above all were the vast dens
of furze, inviolable, beloved of the rabbit, the fox, the finch;
dew-pounds, with their unclean drink; old thorn trees casting
a rare shade. Often I saw Colonel Hamilton with his team of
greyhounds on the hills. He was said to be vastly immoral—he
"lived with" a lovely lady. Or I might come across Paishy Gor-
ringe, the squinting hunchback, decoying birds into his net
with a mealy redpoll. I learned to run wildly up on these
uplands, where the heart was never known to tire nor the limbs
to fail; or I would lie and gaze at the lovely land, my mind
flowering with thoughts that have borne no frunt. Fluid tender
hours!

After I had won a race or two, my Bill Brown decided to take
up running, and soon he became altogether fleeter than me. In
races he was always my master, though in truth I was never
satisfied, and explained to others with ineffable sincerity that I
was really and truly not merely faster than him but very much
his superior in everything.

There was another youth, Ike Smart, with a face like an ape,
who could play the mouth organ divinely well and run like a
hound. I was fond of him, and he of me. He worked as a rag-
picker for the McQuires, who were scrap merchants. Two of the
McQuire sons were boxing champions, and although I idolized
their prowess I could not pass them in the street without a glint
of fear. I longed to say "Hullo, Joe," "Hullo, Alec," to them, yet I
never presumed so far. Boxing soon became more than a fancy
to me; the great long-armed black man, Peter Jackson, often
trained on our highway, and I knew an old rascal called The
Admiral (he kept the Ship Tavern) who had only one eye. Tom
Sayers had some time lodged with him, and The Admiral used to
demonstrate a particular Sayers punch which he called "the

auctioneer." Insidious incentives! Ike Smart learned all sorts of
tricks from the boxing McQuires, and we used to practise them
together, until my own proficiency delighted me. Upon which
my Bill Brown, noting my growing passion for this ungentle art,
took up the gloves and developed a cordial and inexplicable
capacity to punch the guts out of me. (There was nothing of
Pylades about Bill Brown.) It was impossible for me to understand this, and I was never able to explain it. It was against
science, against all expectation, and against the laws of nature,
so he must have put a spell on me. He was always my master.

Then there was Alice. I got to know her first, long before Bill.
She was not pretty—*she* had freckles—but she was a very mature
girl, and reputed to be an ardent Venus with a reckless disposition. Pooh, how do such tales get spread about? I could never
understand how such stories come into circulation. When I
walked out with Alice she was cold and unresponsive, I could
not account for it. Well, perhaps she was not cold, but she laughed
at me, she only laughed. I found her first, and for a while she
was really my Alice, until Bill Brown took her just as he had
taken Sabrina; and in the course of time I learned that she was
all, more than all, the erotic fancy had painted her, and I had
either deceived myself, or been deceived. I could not account
for it.

Alice was going to have a baby, and Bill told me he was the
father. I was horrified; we were all three only sixteen years old.

"What did your mother say when she heard it?"

"Christ!" said Bill, "she did go on!"

"What she say?"

"She said: 'Willie, you must 'a forgot yourself.'"

"And what d'you say?"

"I said: 'Yes, ma, I did.'" Goodness, how we laughed, Bill
and me!

"But what are you going to do, Bill, about it?"

"I dunno," he said coolly; "what can I do?"

"What's Alice going to do?"

"That's her look-out," said Bill. "I got enough troubles of
my own."

"Ain't you going to—to—see her any more?"

My Bill Brown closed one eye in an expressive wink and began to chant some of old Babstock's dirty doggerel:

> There was an old Quaker
> As lived in Jamaica.

And then, as we were thus talking at the corner of a street, who should chance to go by in a private carriage drawn by a pair of horses but our princess, Sabrina! She was magnificently attired, and she saw us, she saw us both, but her fierce gaze flashed over and beyond us as if nauseated. "Lousy bitch!" commented Bill.

At eighteen Sabrina had left home in order to live adventurously with an elderly Russian duke, who for the good of his country or his private soul was dwelling in Hampshire; but she was still the darling of her royal parents and she was just come from visiting them.

"Do you know what I'd like to do to her?" Bill savagely inquired.

I told him I did not want to know, but he told me all the same. How foolish to be so bitter!

Well, that's enough of bawdy girls and boys. God send us all our fortunes and temper the wind to born fools. I never saw Sabrina again, or Alice again, nor for the matter of that did I ever see Bill again, for his mamma at once scurried him off to an aunt at Birmingham. I was not surprised to find myself bearing the loss of Bill with indifference; for long I had wondered if I loved him any more—I could not be sure about it. But because of his absence I was not likely to see much of Carlotta, my golden-haired, as our meetings had been confined to the times I had called at their house for Bill. I had not tried to entice her into walking out with me, I could never be so daring; and Bill would have been nasty about it, I was sure. He would not, for instance, suffer any friendship between Carlotta and Alice, or between Carlotta and Sabrina, and at that time I thought it was beautifully high-minded of him; indeed, it was years before I guessed he was only afraid the girls would gossip to his undoing. Carlotta was quiet; like a beautiful statue steeped in silence she waited for something to happen to her.

And so I fell in love with other girls, one after another, or with some together—it is so easy; fancy turns you round and about like a cock on a church, this way, that way. My mother always seemed to know about these passions that I thought were secret and desired to keep sacred. By what divination it came to pass I never knew, but my mother, who had the heart of courage, the soul of duty, but whose mind was as responsive to taste as a tuft of weed on a rock, always with a deft nudge toppled my idols from their pedestals. How did she know that I had a queasy mind and was terrified by ugliness or vulgarity? I did not know it myself then!

Of Myra Stogumber, lively little dark-eyed Myra, who was as kind as she was uncouth—for she had not a vice except in her vocabulary alone—she merely remarked: "Her legs are bandy. Like a jockey's. She couldn't catch a pig in a pantry."

Thenceforward my figure of Myra was indissolubly merged with pigs and crooked legs. And I was not sorry for Myra's undoubted misfortune. I was merely ashamed—as if I had been caught playing with her legs; which, indeed to God, I had not!

Violet Mutton—sacred Cæsar, what a name!—Violet Mutton was so sylphlike, so Egyptian; there was not a crook in her bones and she walked with the grace of a queen. Oval olive face, teeth like snow, and such black cursed hair. A brainless Cleopatra; but do you know if I still had the luck to go to paradise there would be little there to look at as fine as she was, and nothing finer.

"There's lice in her hair, you can watch 'em," said my mother.

A really nice girl was Honor Clapperton; she was plump and large, with a violent soprano voice and a habit or hobby of being jocular about the Scriptures. You would never have guessed that she took a Sunday-school class, and even when she began to recite things like collects and litanies and psalms you would not imagine that she ever really prayed. I never did, she was far too plump and large and jolly, but she must have prayed in large quantities, one way and another.

"But what a trial it is to her mother!" said my mother to me.

"What?" I asked.

"You know, don't you? What a funny boy you are!"

"But I don't know."

"They say she can't help it, but all the same—"

"What, mother?"

"You must have heard, Johnny. She wets the bed."

And Rose Tilack was fresh and pink and fair, but devastatingly common. The neatest, cleanest girl, clean as new bread and neat as a reel of cotton, but with a scatological mind that would have shamed a monkey.

Things are never what they seem, they are merely what they are; pitiful, for how splendid are our dreams!

> Have you seen but a bright lily grow
> Before rude hands have touched it?

Myra, Violet, Honor, Rose, they were there in perfection to me, yet a sigh from my mother blew their beauty away and I was hoist like a herring from its shoal in the streaming seas, a spectacle for myself to gaze upon. As I *did* gaze, feeling that I ought to be crushed with sorrow! But not a tear rose to the brink of my eyes, nor a groan out of my bruised bosom. I was vaguely ashamed of this.

III

As I was walking home through the town one night it was windily snowing and I waited at a bookseller's shop that had an open window under an awning. Pictures delighted me more, but I had always been fond of books, any sort of a book that could be read at all. If it could be borrowed, well and good, for I could never afford more than a twopenny purchase. Snow drifted on some of the shelves not covered by a sack, the gas flames roared in the draught, the bookseller's name was Kisstruck, and my feet were cold, but I bought a "Penny Poet" because of a nice piece of poetry it contained. I could not understand the title of it, but I was fascinated by its lovely melancholy:

> The sedge has withered from the lake,
> And no birds sing.

At eighteen one begins to care for poetry if it is going to be cared for at all, and from thence onwards poetry coloured my days and thoughts with a hazy glamour that at times was pretty much of a fog. Often at night I would wake from sleep in a mania of composition, chanting words that had no meaning and lines that merely scanned, like the rumble of an engine, noise, abracadabra, token of youth's fantastic exaltations. It played fast and loose with me; it harboured all my joy, it nurtured all my pride, so that I could no longer fall in love; I had grown into a superior being and the nymphs of my once fond fancy declined into dowdy trollops, so vulgar to my eyes. One of them, I remember, had married a tram-conductor, and I saw her wearing his cast-off cap. I regretted the tram-conductor, it is true, but I had become very superior now, I had heard the voice of the siren, of *La Belle Dame sans merci,* and I tried to find her again in the groves of the public library, where I gulped down Johnson's *Poets* in endless little brown volumes. None of my friends ever read poetry, and what was more, if that trifle of singularity had not already sufficed to make a coxcomb of me, none of them had ever begun to write a book—as I was doing.

How does one ever come to embark upon anything so audacious as the writing of a book? Even a book like this, full of half-truths—truths as I see them, the other halves hidden from me yet so very plain to you? Is it for fame, honour, immortality? Or for the sake of beauty or truth? Why does an ass bray? What is truth? It is like, yes, it is like that caravan of Sabrina's royal parents, where fortunes were told (and collected) by people who had no alphabet, but a good deal of wit. On the roof of their van was a gaudy shallow box in which reclined a stuffed puma that peered over the hood at you with a ferocity the years did nothing to diminish and little to expose, while underneath the van a mild-looking dog, whom nobody trusted, was kept perpetually chained.

Not for any of these reasons did I begin to write. Not for the sake of fame, which a soap-boiler can buy with a poster. Their immortality is nothing to dead men. Beauty is a trade for museum guides, and honour is a fortune the vulgar cannot win—my father was a tailor, my mother a housemaid. Poetry played fast and loose with me for years until I sported with prose. *La Belle Dame* had made me a prig, but it is a pity to be a prig for ever. Or for nothing. And so I began to write, and I wrote and wrote until a whole book was done. In time it was published, and it was a success:

The Immortal Target
A NOVEL
BY
John Flynn

It was no sort of book to be bragging about. It had the usual number of pages and I can't pretend that genius germinated there, that felicity curled from every comma, or sense from every phrase. No academic salvos greeted it, and the Thames remained serenely cool, but its creation had been a tortuous delight. I had fashioned a group of people, imaginary persons, and filled them with passions and humours, with virtue, vulgarity, and laughter, with blood, bones, tears, bad temper, and love. Their emotions were not my own, they were spurious, and yet I had lived with these figments so closely, brooded over them so long, that I myself helplessly assumed the protean dooms I inflicted on them, suffering the foul and rejoicing at the fair when I permitted them a respite from my slings of outrageous fortune.

Of all human characteristics I divined most keenly the thing called vulgarity, a sorry human foible that can drive poetry, or love, or even passion, into disguising or suppressing itself. I lived in it, had recognizably lived in it and not outside it, all my life. *La Belle Dame* taught me that. *La Belle Dame* discovered the prig in me, and *The Immortal Target* gave the figure rope, though not enough to hang it by. I had been bred and born of people who had common virtues and even common vices. I saw it and was shamed. My tiny scutcheon of new grandeur was smudged by what I had sprung from. Useless to pretend a pride in humble origins. A tailor might devour his cabbage with a soup-spoon and fart in front of his wife and still serve God with humility, but your poet would rather shoot himself than imitate the tailor. And so, I thought, would I. As long as my elation supported me and I could prance or pose, it was bearable, but as soon as the mood collapsed, as it almost daily did, the world in which I continued to dwell became a marsh peopled by troglodytes and smelt like a shoemaker's hut. I cursed my common fellow man and feared my common fellow woman; hideous were their faces and forms and minds, vulgar their clothes and habits, their amiable jokes, their tears at funerals, their passions for food, politics, and propriety. I was a castaway bleeding among cannibals; they would eat the head off you before you were aware.

But there was a world beyond this trumpery barrel of chopped chaff in which I was living, a sweeter world, wiser, of fairest nature made, a world of summer solitude where one could lie alone and have peace to dream of things that could never be forgotten, because they never lived; they crept like pearly clouds along the halcyon horizons of the mind. There, beside the harebells in the tawny grass, I could behold the dream ripen from flower to fruit and from fruit to everlasting glory.

And then, suddenly, I would be walking open-eyed in my own real world again, rejoicing in its meagre comfort, the decent kindly people no longer hideous, and vulgar no more. The men were again my friends, the women my adored, their joys mine, mine their trivial hopes and appetites, and mine their silly sufferings too. I saw that those who ignorantly live may yet profoundly die. They died their deaths, and with them I died often.

Did I really die? Did I really so suffer and enjoy? You need not believe it at all. Or you may. I swear I cannot tell whether those thoughts were really mine or whether I am at my old trick again of writing about things that eluded me, or aping some protean image that bore my likeness. I came from nothing, and it may be I was never anything more than a contrivance for recording emotions I would fain have taken for my own, but could not—life passed me by.

And now this forest hems me in. Ten million trees or ten thousand—what does it matter? they cannot be numbered, they are there—a floral bastion that leans and dreams in unimaginable beauty against the void. And why are they there? For what purpose do they grow? I will tell you: it is that chairs may be made! Nothing but chairs! All these majestic things, that like the sky above are never contemptible or contemptuous but always tender and dignified, must in time be cloven into chairs on which the vast buttocks of the world may be seated to drink its tea or nurse its weeping child.

As to how and why I came to the forest? Forgive me, this is a story I am telling you, it is not merely a conversation. I do not like to be interrupted.

I wrote another book, and again it passed off well, though it did not bring me wealth. I grew tired of the silly people I lived amongst, who knew little of me and nothing of my fine fame. I wanted them to love my books, they were my own people, my tribe; but no one ever read me there, and it seemed that only in London would I ever meet the fine people who would recognize and love me. My parents were dead, I was alone in the world, so to London I went, and for years I lived in suburbs that were blank as the mind of Lot's wife, walked in public parks that grew grass to look at, plodded through museums and galleries that belled you out before twilight, and visited sights, sounds, un-used churches, and places where notices screamed at you to ad-just your dress before leaving. I felt more alien than ever. I could not find my world. There was never a friend to be met in high-way or by-way, the fine men were always in a hurry, the fine women already in love. Soon, soon I was yearning for my own sort of place, my own sort of people, but only after years had gone by was I borne on waves of love once more to my native town.

IV

Impossible hopes! Having no longer a home, I lived in a board-ing-house there. Alas, the Myras and Honors, the Roses and Violets were already blown and hung fading on the bosoms of detestable males. The lads of my time were now men with sallow faces, preposterous moustaches, bald heads. They were pushing perambulators about. People called me Sir. Home was gone. Turning my back on this, I wandered after a sweeter world, wiser, of fairest nature made, and one day I entered this forest and found it fair "as the coral round Calypso's cave." Beseemingly it lured me—and confounded me, so low. Here was a little green clearing and an old little house with a well beside it. All round were trees. Here I made my home. A mile away were farms and villages and people, though I never knew them well. Save for poachers and gamekeepers and old women gathering sticks the forest was almost my own. But man was not made to live in solitude, however beautiful, and after a while I paid a visit to my home town again, and when I returned to the forest I brought back a woman with me.

Her name does not really signify, and for that matter neither does her appearance, but she was small and fair and I called her Dove. Her husband was a seaman, but for reasons into which I did not probe he was fast fixed in Mexico, where at some undetermined date Dove was to join him. For a while, a little while, all went merry as a marriage bell—though that is an unseemly image. My pretty Dove was lively when passionate, but at other times she was merely dull. For myself I did not mind that, I was writing still another book, but for her there was no such diversion. She was not very wise, the solitude of the forest began to oppress her, while the trifle of housework to be done left her with so much leisure that she was constantly coming to me, like a kitten, to be petted and fondled. It was the misfortune of our lives that at such times I was often in the throes of writing, a mood so altogether prejudiced and absorbed that it can turn a playfellow into a boor without taste for board and bed; while at other times when I had finished a spell and wanted to be gay she would as like as not curl up on the sofa and sleep. She was always falling asleep. It was another misfortune that our house had only three rooms, a large living-room, a bedroom, and a kitchen. It was happy enough when I lived there alone, but when Dove came I had nowhere else to work in private, so I wrote while she mooned or snoozed at the other end of the living-room, a disturbing presence that was jealous of my divided concern.

"What's the good of all your everlasting writing?" she asked.

"I just earn my living by it, that's all."

"I know that; but what's the good of books?"

"Oh, they interest people, sometimes they influence them."

"But what use is that? A baker earns his living, but he makes bread, you can eat it. And a farmer grows things for us, and a carpenter makes things we must have, but what can you do with books?"

"My dear Dove, they keep the farmers and bakers and carpenters from going mad."

"Oh, do they! They're not so silly as to read 'em. I don't."

Later on, when she woke up again and saw me still writing, she

cried out: "Still at that wretched book!" and complained of the
monotony of life.

So I proposed a holiday in London, but she said:

"God! D'ye want the whole world to know we're living together?"

"But how could anybody there know we are not married,
my Dove?"

"They always know," said she. "And I've got friends in
London."

"So have I, but they would not mind."

"Mine would," she said; "they're pretty respectable, I can
tell you."

"Well, we need not go to London. Let us go somewhere else,
anywhere you like."

"I don't want to go. I'm all right. It's only—" She paused, and
I asked:

"Only what?"

"Oh, be kind to me!"

I sat by her side and she leaned her head against my breast.
Pretty golden hair, tearful eyes. Fond foolish man.

"Be kind to me. I'm so lonely."

"My dear! What do you mean—be kind?"

She sighed. "You don't understand, you don't understand at
all. Try to understand, won't you? Oh, my lamb, be kind to
me."

"But what is there to understand?" I asked her. She gave a puff
of derision and turned away from me.

I said: "If you are lonely and don't want to go away, suppose
we invite some of your friends here?"

"I can't, stupid. Don't you see, I can't!"

"Why not?"

"Because I am not supposed to be here, am I? And they would
write and tell my husband, wouldn't they?"

"Well, and what if they did? You are done with him. You
can't go to him now."

"What are you saying? Of course I must go to him, if he
wants me!"

I was silent. Stupefied and angry though I was, I knew better than to argue with a woman about another man. But it was impossible to keep silent for long. I asked her:

"Shall I invite some friends of mine to come and spend a few days here?"

"Can if you like," she answered moodily. "It's your house. But I should go away."

"Why?"

"Oh, you always make me feel such a fool when anyone else comes here. You do, you know you do! Besides, I don't like your friends, not what I've seen of 'em."

Dove curled up again as if to go on sleeping, and so I went to the table and began to fiddle once more with a pen and paper. I was startled by a shriek.

"Oh, stop that blasted drivel!" she screamed. "What's the good of it!"

She sat up raging as I turned in my chair.

"Stop it! I hate it! I hate it! I can't read it! It's all soppy. You're mad!"

Ah, she knew how to knife me. I sprang up and blared:

"Get away, you ignorant vulgar idiot! Who wants you to read it? Be off! Go to hell! Go to bed!"

In a flash she jumped up from the couch and flung her arms around me, rejoicing in my anger.

"Oh, you devil," she murmured, "put me to bed."

I stood like a stock, taut and cold to her cleaving lips.

"Yes, yes! Go on!" she urged, her eager brightness enfolding me. "I love it when you are mad with me. Go on! Do you hear? Undress me!"

Relentingly I half-undressed her; then she quivered in my arms and beseechingly whispered:

"Oh, my heart's darling, be a Cossack! Crush me, bruise me, give me a beating!"

What could I make of this? Cossack and convertite! I was to be kind, I was to be cruel, the devil knows what. But I was no Cossack—more's the pity.

Such interludes came often and often, until I was distracted. I could not tell her to be gone, it was beyond my courage, and I knew I would have to bear it until she herself put an end to our pitiful sentiment. But there were other times when I thought I should die if she ever left me, just as I thought I would kill her if she did not, so incalculable are our wretched passions. Tinker, tailor, soldier, sailor; I hate her, I love her, I don't seem to care! When I loved her I thought her beautiful, but love is not like a two-shilling piece which you can rap on the counter and get change for at any odd moment. The hands of a clock, although it is telling the right time, are often upside down or at an angle of degrees. When poor Dove was the sport of one of the numerous indelicacies of existence and her body blossomed with red spots, which she scratched and made bloody, I found it hard to conceal my distaste. I chanted to myself: "You spotted snake with double tongue," but took care that she did not overhear me! At other and cooler times I thought her merely dull, a kitten that slept, scratched itself, and mewed in boredom.

It all ended simply enough. Her husband ordered her to Mexico at last, and she with alacrity obeyed, though full of grief at our actual parting.

"I won't go. I will stay with you."

I hung my head in sympathetic misery.

"Why don't you ask me to stay? Or shall I just go, and then come back to you?"

How incredible it sounds!

A day later I was whole and cheerful again, as if a log had been lifted from a limb, and I doubted not my pretty Dove was the same. Twice she wrote me letters from abroad, and once she sent me, of all things, a small parcel of books! So I sent her a Bible. The letters gave me twinges of shame, they were so badly composed, and they annoyed me because they were inspired by a reproachful sense of my wickedness. I had never envisaged Dove as a prude, or myself as a mere rascal, but apparently it was so! Well, well. The sum of intimate knowledge behind any judgment is hard to count, there are so few facts and so many fancies. She had loved amiss and judged awry; I had perhaps done the same in reverse. I still owe the books she gave me the duty of my attention.

V

By the time my new story was finished and disposed of I had grown restless. The year was falling into decay, and in the forest there is nothing between the fall of the leaves and the coming of the primrose. The primroses come, and after them there is the blue bugle. The wild parsnip runs to seed (I rub it on my hands because I love its curious scent), and then the leaves fall off trees and the year is over. Now, like the prodigal son, I wanted to gather my rags about me and turn home, for the habits of home are the things we measure life by—but I had no other home.

Often I thought of Dove. Something of her lay in my heart as she had once lain in my arms, but the memory was not pleasant. If she had died I should have heard the news unmoved, if she had come back I should have been aghast, but I could not keep from thinking of her, and pitying her. She had measured me by her standard of romance, and I had failed her. I had measured her by my standard— Oh, I do not know what my standard was, but whatever it was she was as far from it as fustian from the fleece, common, not good enough. I was common, vulgarity was my birthright, but surely all women were not vulgar? She had been merciless, too, but there was nothing of the highborn tragic glory of *La Belle Dame sans merci,* nor the beautiful menace of her desire in our embarrassing squabble.

The book finished, and my mind loitering over the old fond graces and endearments of childhood, I went off again to visit my town, still a harbour of blissful memories. But bliss wavered on the spot before exposures that were as trivial as burnt-out matches. Was this home! Yes, this was home; these columns of shabby houses, the chapel by the viaduct, the viaduct by the cemetery. Here were the folk, the playmates and parents, among whom I was reared—though they were mine no longer. The treacherous years had covered all with squalid dust or reared a change that knew no brightness. In the old ha'penny shops things were now sold by the pound in paper bags and no longer by the pint measure straight into your pocket; the lovely red factory where I had worked so long wore a pinched sour look; the hills around seemed conscious of disgrace; even the gypsies had built themselves a cottage, and the old caravan was rotting in a barn. Where was that man with the balloon-like brow who sold striped sweets for a farthing and dissented on Sundays with terrible conviction in a white waistcoat at the corner of our road? Or the midnight man with basket on head who hawked sheep's feet garnished with mustard, which he called Trottile? Where? Why? Who? When? What? Stupendous questionings. Pitiful answers. Sabrina, who sleeps with you? Alice, where art thou? Bill Brown? And what had happened to me? Poor Bill Brown, I had a pastime now that he could never take from me. He had taken so much, but none of these people would take, or want to take, that. If I had told them I wrote books they would have laughed, compassionately. Yet I deeply wanted them to read and like them, for they were my people, my own sort.

These intimations of disaster did not crowd upon me at once, but were accumulating during the dismal days I quarried in every quarter of the town, from the sea to the hills, musing in taverns and old rendezvous where I had no friends to meet.

One evening a wet tempest blew, and I wandered down to the sea to watch its great waves. The wind and the waters roared, the rain slewed in gushes along the esplanade where the tall lights glinted on the pavement, leaving a gloss so vivid that the seaward blackness beyond the shore rose like an appalling terrace from chaos to the ridge of eternity. The pier and its pavilion were only half-lit, for the season was late and visitors few, but as the wind swayed I could sometimes hear the music of the band trailing its melancholy airs across the storm. I slouched along in a mood of vicious enjoyment until I became aware that I was strangely alone, even on such an evening as this. From end to end of the long lighted parade, coming or going, I could see no other figure; but by and by I heard shouting, there, down on the beach at the sea's edge. I saw a crowd of people hauling a boat, and I ran down some steps and hurried across the beach towards them.

"What is the matter?" I heard someone cry, and a voice answered: "Ship on fire!" Then I saw a speck like a star far away on the horizon, but as I gazed it flashed like no star I had ever seen before. In that shocking moment I also saw men close by me hauling on a capstan and a great empty lifeboat creeping up the shingle back to its shed. The rescue had been abandoned; for hours the huge seas had baffled all attempts at launching, and the lifeboat was creeping back to its shed. Our shallow beach had an evil name for launchings, and this had proved beyond human effort. The lifeboatmen sat exhausted in a group on the beach drinking something out of cups, dim hooded men with rings in their ears. A crowd stood by them despite the downpour, watching the fiery ship.

"What are they drinking?" someone asked.

"Cocoa," said another.

The gale harried the sea as a taskmaster lashes his men, but the great waves slounched up the shore like ponderous oafs and swilled derisively back. Far out, beyond our aid, drifted that flaring Tophet, and I saw rocket after rocket spout up into the sky and pause and fall as if in despair. Again I could hear the strains of the oblivious pier band. I even recognized the tune they were playing: it was called *Distant Greeting*.

In time I left the beach, but I could not go home, it was as if I too were burning alive. I wandered along the coast for miles, watching the ship that drifted so very fast, making for a shore that offered only a choice of dooms. Suddenly it disappeared, I saw it no more, and in that certainty of its final engulfment my own horror left me. Poor tragic seamen. Weary with pity I turned home; and throughout the dark journey, whether to spur my lagging footsteps or in sheer mitigation of thought, what could I do but whistle! And of all the tunes I could whistle, why was there only one to purr so persistently on my lips—that *Distant Greeting?*

Next morning I slept late, and woke with a pang as heavy as if my own death confronted me. Yet it was a mild bright morning. I went off to the bathroom but found three servants sitting there, with a board laid across the bath, having their breakfast. They said they were sorry, the bath should be ready in five minutes.

"All right," I said, "could you get me a newspaper?"

"Have this," said one of the girls, holding out the local *News*.

"There was a ship on fire last night. I saw it," I said, "it was a dreadful sight."

"Um," said the girl, an angular creature with red hair and a black mole near her lips.

"They could not get the lifeboat out to them," I went on. "Is there anything about it here?"

"I didn't notice, sir. What would you like for breakfast?"

"Oh, anything. What is there to have?"

"Would you like fish, sir? Fresh caught."

Fish! Fish from that sea! "Oh, God, no. Anything but fish."

"Kidneys and mushrooms, sir?"

But there it was, staring on the front page, a marvellous rescue from a burning ship by a lifeboat from a harbour some miles west of our town! Seven Swedes and an Irishman. All's well! Fish if you like! And tootling away at *Distant Greeting,* I marched back to my room.

VI

That bright day was so much brighter for its defeat of tragedy and it ended as it began, with a prolonged sweetness of surprise. At night I had gone into the public library where I had once spent so many rapt hours on a hard chair beneath a heavy-tongued clock that was all too swift for my absorption, and I sat down at a table opposite a young woman who was turning over the pages of some picture papers. To me she seemed marvellously beautiful, and she was elegantly clad in a way that befitted her beauty. I, too, shuffled the magazines, while now and again the young woman wrote a line or two in a notebook with a little gold pencil. On one of her fingers was a golden ring with a large faint-blue stone in it. I should have known her even apart from the golden hair, though I had not seen her for fifteen years—since she was a girl. She was no longer a girl, she was thirty or thereabouts, but the gentle shy air still attended her. I would have known her at once among ten thousand. Presently she fastened up her notebook, pushed the pencil in its socket, and rose to go. As she went to pass me I called quietly, for her ears alone: "Carlotta!"

Without turning in any gesture of recognition, she paused for me to join her, and I walked out into the street at her side. There she turned and smiled.

"It is nice to see you. What are you doing here?"

I made a sort of explanation. "Are you going home?"

"Yes. We still live in the same old street. Come along and see mother, she will be surprised. Yes, she is quite well."

"And Bill?"

"Bill too. He's an ironmonger now, you know."

"Ah! He sells pails and nails and packets of flea-powder, does he?"

"Yes, things like that," she answered gravely. "Don't you ever write to him?"

"No, I never had his address."

"I can give you it," said Carlotta brightly. "He would like to hear from you."

Oh, it was woeful conversation, but she was beautiful beyond the promise of her childhood or the images that had flowered in my boyish heart. She was a lily, swaying; she was, somehow— fragrant.

"And what are you doing in the world, Carlotta, now?"

"*Robes et Modes,*" she laughed; "do you remember? It's mother and I, now."

Yes, I remembered. (Why couldn't she say "dressmaking?") And it appeared they had quite a good business, with a workshop and a dozen girls and Carlotta as an expert designer. She was an enthusiast, practising her art upon gores and gussets, pleats and seams.

"There was a ship on fire last night," I said. "I saw it; it was a dreadful sight."

And I told her about the ship.

"Do you remember," said she, "the wreck *Vandalia*?"

Yes, soon I remembered. In our childhood a ship full of oranges had gone ashore on our coast and burst. For days the fruit rolled unceasingly along the shore, and the boys of the town collected oranges, oranges, oranges, as they were washed up by the tide. Carlotta remembered that I had brought many to her.

I went home with her, and I saw her mother in the kitchen-like sitting-room where years ago I had kissed the child her daughter, and we talked about Bill and Mr. Babstock and Carlotta's flourishing business and my books.

Mrs. Brown still had a girlish manner, though she was something more than half a century old, and her hair was as light in colour and as finely spun as Carlotta's. I fancy she wore some sort of a wig, but that is not surprising, for by the time you are fifty you have probably brushed and combed your hair twenty thousand times.

"It would be nice," said Mrs. Brown, "if you wrote something very good and became famous some day."

I said: "There was a ship on fire last night. I saw it. It was a dreadful sight."

"Dear me!" said Mrs. Brown. Her husband had died, or disappeared, before we knew her, but she never made any reference to him and I suspect he was a bad man, or if not—he must have been unsatisfactory.

Carlotta gave me some cake and port wine. I stayed for an hour, and when I made to come away Carlotta lingered with me in the dim porch outside and said we should meet again tomorrow. With a kind of drowsy smile she gave me kisses for kisses, hundreds it seemed, and I could not bear to leave her.

Tomorrow we met, and for many days after. Our meetings were always timed for the evenings; she was so conscientious about her precious business that I could not prevail upon her to come holiday-making by day. I did not go to her home any more; I would see her to the dim porch where we lingered, but she did not invite me in. Once or twice on a Sabbath we went by steamer to the Isle of Wight. The Isle of Wight is a silly place, and so is a steamer, but my love was charmed with such things, and I adored her. And she liked going to exhibitions at night where people gave you samples of soap powder, or hooks and eyes, or sold you a thimbleful of jam for twopence. To the library we would often go, where she would scan the periodicals and make notes of the products of fashion in her notebook with the gold pencil. I loved her devouringly, but she was so full of modesty, shyness, and reserve that I was far from realizing my desire, and we seemed never to go anywhere where we could breathe in the freedom of love.

Then one day—it all happened so unexpectedly—she was sweet and desirous and I made her my own. Alas for me! Passion has nocturnal instincts, it shuns the light, but Carlotta and I loved at noon as we lay one Sabbath morn in a hollow of my long and lovely hills. Autumn was scarcely to be noticed there, for the furze still bloomed, the sun beamed on us, the tawny grass was our resting-place. Carlotta wept long and unconsolably. I could not discover why. I only knew that an irresponsible shame that will not be hidden may flush the most devoted, even the most legal, lovers. I felt no shame, nothing but a deeper love, a precious tenderness; but my endearments could not charm the guilty look from her averted eyes. Yet she was not a virgin. For that I adored her all the more. In silent sorrow she walked home by my side.

As we were parting I told her how I would meet her again, the time and place, but Carlotta said she could not meet me again, not for a while, and perhaps not for ever.

"No, Johnny; Johnny, no."

Gaily I told her she would love again as sweetly tomorrow.

"No, Johnny; Johnny, no."

And that was all I could get out of her there. She said she would write to me, she had something to explain, to confess, something she ought to have told me long ago.

I could not let her go then. I made her come apart with me, and we walked in some town gardens where good Sunday people were throwing buns to ducks on a pond. Some ducks took the buns, but most were topsy-turvy on the water, groping for God knows what.

"Tell me now," I urged her as we went meandering on.

"I cannot tell you, not here. Let me write to you."

"Tell me now, my dear. Don't be shy. I can guess what you want to say: you have had a lover before. Well, what of it? So have I!"

"You!" she whispered. "Oh, my God!" It was pitiful to hear.

Of course I had guessed aright, but she had more to reveal; she was engaged to marry the man. He was a manufacturer who lived in the midlands and made tape—pink tape, white tape, green tape, black tape, tape for documents, window blinds, dresses, and underwear; for every conceivable use to which tape could be put that man made it. And he was coming to marry her.

"Perhaps he won't come," was all the comfort I could think of.

"He will," answered Carlotta, "it is certain."

"But you don't want him now!"

"I gave my word to him."

"You didn't know me then!"

"I know you well enough now."

"Well enough to marry me? Instead of him?"

"No, Johnny; Johnny, no. It can't be altered."

"Nonsense! Is it fair to go and marry him now?"

"Whatever it is worth, he thinks me good, and he thinks me true. And I must keep so."

"But you are not!"

"It's a pity," said Carlotta.

"Will you tell him what we've done?"

"No," Carlotta murmured, "never."

"He may be doing the same, you know."

"Let him," said she.

Had the place we were in held less of a raging swarm of idiotic people, if my passion had had less pride or my courage less diffidence, I would have smothered her foolishness with my fondness then and there in front of them all; but the cursed ducks and buns had detained a flock of people, they were trooping everywhere around us, and so I could only take Carlotta's arm and press it decorously, so powerful are the proprieties we disdain. I argued, wrangled, scolded, and cajoled, but—exquisite dialectic!—she would not break her word to him. It was borne upon me, too, that if I had but asked her to marry me before we became lovers, the problem might have been simpler for her: a mere matter of a choice between two men—and she had loved me as a boy, loved me now. But it was a matter of choice no more, it was a question of reparation, and it led her to mortify her own soul: since she had so broken her troth the incomprehensible creature conceived it her sacred duty to repair it in secrecy and pretend it had suffered no damage.

"What are you thinking of! This is lunacy!" I cried.

But to all my pleas she gave the same sad answer: "No, Johnny; Johnny, no."

Was it wrong to leave her so? Day after day I tried to turn her will, but I ended by becoming a convert to her madness and came to believe that her renunciation was an atonement of mystical nobility. Then I left her. And oh, there is an abounding logic in our illusions; I believe she is very happy in her married life. For a long time afterwards I used to buy myself bundles of tape, pink or green or white, wherever I saw them displayed. I had no use at all for it, I did not want it, but you see it might somehow have been touched by her fingers. I have a boxful stowed away somewhere. If I plaited it all together I could make a rope to hang myself by, easily.

VII

It is humiliating to describe my feelings—they were idiotic but they had a meaning—when at last I gave up in despair (as I thought) and came back to live in the wood and forget as quickly as might be. I loved Carlotta—I could have sworn—devotedly, but now I cannot be sure even of that, though I am sure I loved her distractedly. Our emotions are secrecies of some inner stimuli we do not understand. Was I in despair? I dare not protest I was, but I know I felt I could die. And why should I die? I could have died—let me confess it—not of love, but of shame; shame at being rejected for a tape-maker! Of course he would be a low-class fellow, he was bound to be, and I was conscious (Heaven forgive me!) of my superior quality. Not my superior class! Oh no, my class was common enough, common as spawn, and it had betrayed me once again. I had been a fool: if one must be immoral he should at least be immoral with an air, with taste, with quality, and keep his vulgar affinities in subjection. I vowed to have no more traffic with vulgar women. Love Carlotta! Faugh, does the hawk mate with a wagtail! It was impossible to forgive Carlotta's preference for a tapeworm. She too was as vulgar as Dove. Surely all women were not vulgar, surely some could transcend the accidents of poor birth and environment—or what hope was there for the world? Carlotta was beautiful, was adored, was as pure as could be expected, but she had failed me; she had failed in courage, and everything was ruined by that deficiency.

And I swear I cannot tell you whether these mean lucubrations of that time were sincere or not, whether their exposure of my shame was genuine, or whether I used them as a sort of purge for the abdominal futility of life. One cannot think for one hour alike; one only feels, and then the whole gamut of nature is quaveringly touched and tried: love, hatred, quiescence; heat, cold, zero; love turns to ice, hatred to fire, and zero is but death. I had no fancy for death then, but I could savour its efficacy, and even admire the courage of a girl who used to sit at the cash desk of a man that made a heap of money by dealing in hams. I met their van-driver in the inn one day, and he told me she had cut her throat. It was inexplicable.

"Terrible!" he said. "She made a good job of it though. Nearly had her head off. A good girl and a splendid girl. Many a time she helped me out of a muddle with my accounts when another would have got me the sack. Cut her own throat. Yesterday morning. In bed. After eating her breakfast, too! Can't understand it. No embezzlement, no love affair, nothing wrong anywhere. Mere dislike of life. And I'm very sorry."

Poor bleeding neck! And Carlotta, Carlotta! She had gone to sit by another hearth and loved not me. Why could I not be loved as I desired to be? Why was I so frustrated, so outcast? Was it possible that I was a bird of the same feather as Easy Nurick, the cattle-drover? He was a man of thirty who had no home, but stayed always in or near the village of his youth, slept in sheds or stacks or sties, and begged boots or old clothes from sympathetic people. On Sunday nights in winter he would go to chapel, where it was warm and comforting; there was nothing else to do in the cold dark world. He always put a halfpenny in the bag and would come away with a tract that he could not read. Then he would wander along the black road, and if he saw a woman he would stalk up to her and say "Good evening, miss. May I have the pleasure?" But he never had the pleasure, for he smelt badly, and when you could see him you noticed he had a squint and looked sly. You either liked him enough to pity him or loathed him enough to want to kill him. But your emotions about

him availed nothing. Was I like him? There were horrible re-
semblances.

Well, it was not long before I began to laugh at my anger, to
despise my love, and to ridicule my miseries and fears. I had
come to doubt all the fine paraphernalia of emotions, good or
bad, and the more I pondered, the stronger my doubt grew,
until I was conscious of a mockery in all my thoughts, a cynicism
in all that attended me, and the cause of this unhappy state grew
clear; I understood.

I had lived so intently in my world of fictitious shadows, writing of people who had no existence, aping emotions and postures
that had no real play, counterfeiting violence and imitating
peace, that when I touched this real thing of my own, imagination twirled up like a cloudy witness and warned me that I was
lost indeed, that I was but a fictionmonger, a dealer in illusions
and masquerade. I had lost my self in the shadows. I was a
nonentity, my being was a myth. I had no love, I could only pretend a passion that had never stirred a ripple in my blood. Anger
was an imposture, I had never been angry; you could only work
yourself up into an angry mood, and that was foolish. If I felt the
hackle of jealousy I let the feeling surge and pervade me, savour-
ing its bitter heat, its terrible pleasure, until I knew all its tricks.
As for grief, I was a mere sponge that sucked up other people's
tears and squeezed them out as my own for pounds, shillings, and
pence. I had endured anguish, throbbed with felicity: I too had
lived in Arcadia, even Acheron was familiar, but only by means
of those protean proxies—the mood of fiction, the brooding mind,
the deceiving phrase. These had been my guides, but now they
had stolen my birthright of joy and pain and betrayed me. I was
no longer the play, I was merely the book of words. Something
had been drawn from me as a glove is drawn from the fingers
and it had left me void. Only in the things I could write was I
ever alive or sincere; elsewhere in the world I was but a hollow
reed echoing the wind's will, never my own.

When that blinding revelation burst on me I was shaken by a
real and profound emotion indeed! I could no longer pharisaically
thank God I was not as other men are, I could only envy all
who were not like me, in whose faithful hearts love at least might

find a home. That soft visitor had once flown into my breast, but it had not liked the place, it had not nested there. To lose faith in one's own human feeling is pitiful, but it seemed to me then and there that I had lost it, though one sneck of toothache might prove me sophist in a shrug of time. And base is he who shrinks from those he has loved because some fleering folly hints that they are beneath him. That was my doom. And if that ignominy had descended on me, if my senses had indeed lost all real momentum and my response to life was vested in mere words, was it any wonder that love gave me the go-by? It was no wonder, it was but just.

Do you think I am agitated about all this? Not at all! Remember, when the mind has become artificial it is easy enough to think tempestuously.

Besides, there came a time when my fate was tried once more and I was raised like a Lazarus from my self-made grave. But that was not for some years. For five long years yet the cot in the woods was my constant home, and I had no wish to leave it for a world full of disorder in thought and act. The world revolves in untidiness. Rooms are crammed with chairs and tables and books and photos and bottles and ink and matches and clothing and crumbs and papers. It cannot be borne, this chaos, it infuriates me: I must fling things into the fire and things out of the window before I can sit down. I must tear up my life by the roots from such futilities. And then? Then I just sit down to enjoy this tidiness, it is sweet. Serenely I contemplate what the next move shall be, and am contented with myself, having as good a right as most men to be so contented. Sins? Of course, of course I have my sins. If you glance at them they look terrific, but if you survey them with a clear cool mind they are not so bad. I suppose I have lied about myself, even here, about my real character—it is difficult to know. I have said things I would like to be true; if I had my way they *would* be true, perhaps there will be time to prove them yet. The mirror we hold up to ourselves deceives us from childhood. Whenever I saw my mother's face in the looking-glass it seemed to me one-sided. I told her so, and I am sure she never forgave me.

Five years went laggingly by, and in each year I wrote a new book and each book did passably well, though their fate one way or the other has seldom kept me from my sleep. By the end of that time I had grown sour and unhappy. There was no longer any horizon to my life, nothing but the ends of little views and vistas close at hand: a line of poplars, a sunny hedge, twelve o'clock, haymaking, the royal mail, the smell of tobacco, Sundays. But I was too dead to move on from these things. What lay beyond them was possibly sweet: singing birds, a pool, harmony in the wind, but all was inherently changeless, everywhere. You swapped the poplars for an oak, the hedge for a wall: duties, appetites, cheesemongers, ten o'clock, Tuesdays—all were there as here. The invariety of existence was cloying, but it was vain to move on. Oh, the all-pervading sameness! From what feeble moments had I come, to what eternity must I go? If only the earth itself would burst like a rocket; if the sea would but leap into the sky and become a new Niagara, or the hills upheave their bosoms and twirl upon their own paps! Some cosmic umbrage, some terraqueous prank—for my sweet sake! But no. Men came to put tar and stones on the roads, or it rained a couple of showers, and that was all.

Dear, dear, what thoughts a dull mood will put into a man's preposterous cranium! I tore myself out of the forest and went to London.

VIII

It was spring and the hour was noon as I sauntered along a city avenue. I came to a big office where men were painting some iron railings. One of the painters was gilding the images on top of the principal posts—they were twelve little lions squatting on their behinds and gazing ferociously at a shirt shop opposite. As soon as the painter completed the gilding of one he clapped a paper bag over it to keep naughty boys from smudging it with their fingers. I stood watching this until I saw a man approaching us; he had a blue handkerchief round his neck. Farther off, at a street corner, a policeman stood doing nothing in a policemanly way. I heard the sound of a shot; the man with the blue handkerchief lifted one knee very high, stopped, let down his leg again, and sprawled on his face. I ran towards him, so did the painters and a score of other people, but we all stopped some way off the prostrate man, encircling him, all staring, all whispering: "Who did it?" A detachable starched cuff had slipped from his sleeve and covered the one outstretched hand. He was very bald. Then the policeman came, and the crowd hid him and I never saw his face or understood his end, for a young lady of lovely appearance stood pale and trembling beside me on the fringe of the crowd. Was she about to swoon? It looked like it. "Come away," I said, and I took her arm.

Somehow I got her into a café near by, where we sat together and sipped brandy. She had no stately height, yet was noble in her bearing. When she pulled off the close-fitting hat her short locks fluttered out with the foxy glow of new chestnuts; lips of coral, teeth of pearl, mournful eyes; a faint rose began to brighten the refined face, and a faint rose odour was wafted from her figure. Perfumed and richly dressed, she was a rare thing, with an aloofness, a hauteur, that seemed to intimate: "I am not for any mean man's love." But it was her love that I—starved booby—was already intent upon.

"What happened to that poor devil?" she asked.

"Someone shot him, I think."

"Who?"

"I do not know, no one saw that."

"Killed, was he?"

"I think so, he lay so still."

She gave me a cigarette and lit one herself.

"The blood made me feel sick," she explained. "Foolish of me."

After a while, when I had ordered luncheon, she asked: "Who are you?"

I told her my name.

"What are you?"

I told her, and it was pleasant to hear that she knew of my books.

"My name is Livia Portadyne," she said.

"And what are you?" I asked.

She frowned, a little comically. "I am only what you see."

"What do you do?"

"I live in a hotel in Kensington, and mourn the passing days."

It was my turn to frown.

"I have nothing else to do," she quickly explained; and I gathered briefly that her family was, as she put it, moderately aristocratic, that she had a sufficiency of income and few close relatives.

I never discovered more than that about the origin of Livia Portadyne; there was perhaps some mystery about her birth and present isolation, but whatever it was I concealed my curiosity, and she did not explain.

At the end of lunch she invited me to dine with her that same evening at her hotel in Kensington.

"Come and tell me about yourself, will you?" she said, "if you have nothing else to do; have you?"

No, I had nothing else to do, and even if I had . . . and so on and so forth.

"Let's go," Miss Portadyne said; so we went into the street and I found a taxi for her. When she was seated in it, she leaned to the open window and suggested: "Why not come along with me now—to tea?"

I got in beside her. I fancy she said: "That's topping!" She would have said something of that sort, it was characteristic of her, but I do not remember clearly anything about that journey. Her rooms were just the rooms of a hotel in Kensington, a large sitting-room lavish with rugs and settees, a screen near the fireside, mirrors on the wall, and vast china vases in every nook.

"I do not care for them very much," she said, "but they serve."

There was a little case of books, but it contained none of mine. I suppose we smoked and talked of trivial things until tea arrived. After tea Miss Portadyne said: "Now, you will come back and dine with me?"

I did not want to leave her, even for an hour, but I said yes and went away wondering why she wanted to be rid of me. There seemed no reason for whisking me off, but I concluded it was the custom of people who lived in that way. Stupid custom! A vague idiotic resentment fluttered in my mind and I thought I would not go back at all. But I did, punctually.

She was in evening dress, and I realized I should have been so too, but it had not occurred to me, and she showed no surprise.

The dinner was wonderful, though we did not eat much of it. We seemed to drink quantities of wine, and after the meal when we sat on a settee in front of the fire the king of the world himself would have been flattered by her attentions. I remember her leaning her head on my shoulder with cajoling fondness. "Tell me more about yourself, won't you, Johnny?"

We had continued drinking wine, much wine. She was Livia, I was Johnny. Embraces, kisses, and words I had thought I could never utter again. I felt that I was acting, that she too had her allotted part, and what was happening was a phase in a brief charming comedy; yet the old intimations, crude and primitive, flowed between us, and I wanted her to love me. That I could love her truly I did not feel, but imagination lent me ardour and craft as well as words.

"Oh," she murmured, "how wicked you are—and how you delight me!"

When I asked her if she really loved me, she answered: "Oh, quite distinctly yes!"

"Already?"

"Rather much, indeed. And isn't it marvellous that we should fall upon each other like this? . . . Oh, isn't that rich!" She rippled with the first laughter between us. "But like this—suddenly—out of the sky! Where do you come from, Johnny?"

"From the most beautiful place in the world," I told her, and I spoke of the deadly forest as if it was Eden itself, from month to month the wood using its gradual grace to mark the seasons by: early blossoms, the grey buds on the black bough of the whitebeam, the green veil, betrothal to summer, birds, blooms, and leafy bowers, enchantment in every glade; then berries and nuts and the long bright vines in the bushes.

"It sounds like dreamland," Livia cried. "It must be frantic fun!"

I was a happy Adam, I told her, but there was no Eve.

"I'd like to go there."

"Come, then," said I.

"I will. Do you mean it? May I come?"

"If you'll love me."

"Do you really mean it?" she urged.

Caught in my own garrulous net, I could only say: "It's spring-time, and hard to live alone."

"Take *me* there, Johnny!"

"Shall I?"

"Take me soon."

"When will you come, Livia?".

She turned sharply to look at the clock on the mantelpiece, then leaned staring at it for quite a while as if calculating before she answered, almost with a sigh: "Tomorrow, I suppose."

It was not until hard upon dawn, as I was getting into my own bed, that I recalled that man with the blue handkerchief. So horrible. I had forgotten him until then and I did not think of him for very long. Livia was coming to live with me.

In the morning I was depressed, and I determined not to call for her. It was absurd to suppose that a wonderful creature like Livia would want to come and stay with a man she had only known for a few hours. It was true we had already loved, and I had not even flattered her—it must have been the drink we had taken. I admired her, she was superb in her breeding, her ac-ceptance, but was I in love with her? Could I ever be truly in love? Had I not lost my birthright? Ah, but my starving soul yearned to be loved by someone, truly, again; it would be a token that I was still a man alive; it would ward off—for how long? for a little longer?—the pang of my inadequacy. To this mean and selfish desire I succumbed, and she came to live with me in the forest.

From the very beginning there were revelations. Love might be a myth, yet the woes that fringed the beauteous illusion were still mine to feel. Innocence was no bridal gift of Livia's.

"Yes, I have loved men before. And you? You have had your women, I suppose? But for me this is all different, you are so much better. My dear, you make me very fond of you."

Flushed with strange annoyances, I laughed crudely. With a bright smile and a quick caress she said: "I suppose you think I have said the same to them all?"

"All!" I cried. "No. No, I was merely thinking that it is just what I have said to others.

"And it's true!" Livia declared eagerly.

"Yes, it is true enough," I agreed.

Yet for one so careless of convention she had surprising qualms. She angrily refused to let me hire a servant to attend us there, insisting that she preferred to live with me in my own primitive way, fending for ourselves. I knew it was really because she did not want a witness of our affair. Such a simple matter contributed to our downfall, for she had not a scrap of domestic art, and the burden of housekeeping fell on me. That was easy when I lived by myself, even pleasant, but her gastronomic standards alone put a strain on my time and patience; cooking was a long-drawn-out rite. Moreover she had none of my feeling for tidiness and order. It was as if she had been brought up with the expectation of a smooth soft clean world that ran itself, in which nothing could impede her. No doubt her life had been lived in that way, but that was her secret, which I did not intrude upon. Now if a thing lay in her path she would fall over it. If a thing was to be tenderly handled she would drop it. She never shut a door, or closed a window, or replaced anything she used. She was eager to help, but I could not stand her helplessness and waved her brusquely away. Down to the village she would go and bring back a bag of buns, for which she had a revolting fondness. They were things I could not bear to eat, but she never remembered this. There were stale and staler buns all over the place, on shelves, in cupboards and tins, and so one day when she came in with another supply I pointed to a notice I had written and pinned up on the wall:

There are some
BLOODY BUNS
in the cake tin!

Livia took a pencil and wrote on the notice a word that would have enraged even a cabman; then, turning to me with a smile, said:

"You are right. Yes, you are always right, damn you. You ought to have been a butler."

In a week or two she went off on a visit—God knows where. I asked her, but her answer was vague. It was something about things she had to do that must not be neglected.

"My honour is at stake," she whimsically said.

"Humph!" I grinned, "So is my sense of humour, I suppose."

Anyway, there were family affairs, lawyers, and other great bothers of that kind; she would be back soon.

Her absence lasted a week, yet she did not write me a line. There were, indeed, many of these mysterious flights into the unknown, where it was clear I was forbidden to follow or even to peer. Not once did she ask me to accompany her, nor did I venture any offer to do so; on her return I was too joyous to risk any disaster by complaining. We were happy together, that was enough. What do you think love is? Do you suppose it is a simple thing? It is not. Livia and I were often moved in opposing directions by the same cause; I was governed by emotions she seemed never to experience, and she by fancies I could hardly tolerate; yet we were happy together. Love is not a carefully calculable thing built up on devotion, fine principles, candour, confidence, and goodness knows all the rest of it. You might build a house for a dog that way—it would be fit for a dog. Love is mysterious, unprincipled, tender, fierce, sublime, brutish, delicate, and devastating, all fire and frailty, with less substance than a rainbow and eternally desirable. Let it remain at that. Pry no more, ladies, pry no more. The cobweb, sinister and lovely, will survive a storm, but succumb to the prod of any poking investigator. I wanted to be loved, and I was proud of the love she gave, proud too of the high breeding that could stoop to mate with me. It ministered to both pride and joy. I was not yet dead.

At times, though, I felt my manners distressed her, I was a fork-fumbling, hand-shaking, dumb sort of oaf, inelegant, ill-bred. Uncouth bearing, boorish ways—were they the reasons why she never made me the friend of her friends? She *had* friends, many people wrote to her, but I knew not even their names. Once she twitted me with my ignorance of social customs; she would teach me, they were so easy to learn!

"I don't want your instruction," I said.

"What is it you do want?"

"Only your love, Livia." I can remember even now the way my voice quivered with emotional foolery as I said it. Long ago it was, four years, five years, but if she came to me now, I could but say the same and feel the same. I wanted her to regard my wounded heart and soothe its injury, but all she said was:

"Stupid! It has nothing to do with love."

"Then it is not worth my while."

"Why not? To a gentleman"—Livia was positive—"it is worth much."

"I'm no gent."

She stared at me, slightly baffled, as one is on hearing a platitude that cannot be resolved.

"I'm an artist," I continued pompously. (You know the kind of thing: "My mind to me a kingdom is," and all the flattery that poetry subserves.) "An artist is born, not made."

"Perhaps so," she answered, "but all the same I think he ought to go to school."

This wood, as you can see, is full of flowers. There they are, you can see from the window how they breathe in freedom to the very door, yet she must needs go outside and pick posies to put in tumblers on table and shelves. And she brought a kitten that was always micturating on the hearthrug. Why do people do these heinous things? Discontent began to shadow me, and a doubt to grow. If I knew not what to make of my own love, how could I trust hers? Doubt is so easy when the mind knows its own shortcomings. There was fire in my heart, but it was fanned by mere words, its fuel was only the stubble left from my harvest of literary imagination. I thought so then, I think so now—and yet?

At the end of a year Livia was subtly changed. To outward seeming she was all she had ever been to me, but my inward-groping eyes lit upon dreadful torments. Her caresses seemed cheerless, her love perfunctory. I was constantly suing for assurances and she would give them, but I was not reassured. I could not be. When I brought her to the verge of a quarrel she always eluded me and smiled with genteel compassion upon my fuming. Yet despite all her kindness and forbearance the sure and certain intimations of a cleavage wrung my heart and I grew sick with jealousy. There was an intangible wall between us now; I could not reach beyond it, nor feel her gentle presence: sometimes it seemed a wall of rock that I could not scale, sometimes a wall of wool that I tore at and grappled with until it enveloped and suffocated me, sometimes a wall of glass through which I could perceive only her infidelity, so crude are the means by which the soul divines its fate.

I came upon a letter she had written to a man. I never knew his name, it had no envelope, she had gone out to buy some. She had written it and folded it, but could find no envelope and had put it into a drawer that I had no right to open. But I opened it and read the letter. I had not known the letter would be there, but the instant I saw its folded leaves I knew it for the bolt whose shattering glare would illumine all my darkness. Listeners hear no good of themselves, and he who reads a letter not intended for his eyes may get the shock he deserves. But no truth, however cruel, can be so unbearable as the misery of suspicion.

It was a warm affectionate letter, written in a tone of intimate confidence. Had it been for me I would have wept with joy to receive it, but it was not mine, though it contained much about me. Some of it I could not understand, but one part of it was brutally clear:

He torments me asking do I love him, and why do I and how do I. It's like as if he were pulling out my brain with his fingers, like a mass of dough, and it won't come out and he turns my answers into ridicule. I can't tell how long I shall go on staying here. I would like to leave at once only that would be too crude, but I must do it soon. He is miserable, and I can't help but pity him. Else I'd have left him long ago. No love for me, I don't think he has ever loved anybody. He continues to deceive himself, but I am not deceived; he often repels me. But he needs me quite dreadfully, that is why I want to let him down lightly. Of course he does not say so, he is too proud. Proud, mind you! His people were just rabbits, he has no education and is so uncivilized, in fact just vulgar, so you can imagine how dull I am now until I get your letters—don't forget that. Love me always. You, and only you, know all my thoughts.

No man knows what image of himself lies in the heart of the woman he loves. It is different, oh, far different, from what he fondly supposes or hopes or desires or deserves.

When she came in with her envelopes and her buns, I told her what I had done. I put the letter in her hands. "I've read this."

For a moment or two she did not comprehend, then she realized and exclaimed:

"That's a pretty low trick. It's depressingly vulgar. Seems to confirm what I've written."

"I think you ought to have told me."

"I couldn't tell you that."

"That's why I had to find out. I felt it. I knew."

She seemed touched to some distress by that.

"Will you do me a favour?" she asked, staring at the letter. "I will if I can."

"Take me out and kill me."

"Good lord!" I could laugh at that. "Why so drastic?"

"I hate you, hated you for a long time."

"It would have been kind to have told me sooner."

"Oh, there are so many things to hate in the world, one would never be done speaking of them."

Within an hour she had left me for good and all.

> Mother Eve, when she was chidden,
> Turned and flaunted out of Eden;
> Father Adam, much less wise,
> Hung around his paradise.

She left me face to face with an inadequacy I had never before been able to look squarely in the eye. I look at it now, I have much time; for five years I have stared myself almost blind by not doing anything else. She had found me vulgar, not merely because I had abjured life by imitating joys and sorrows that were never really mine—a parvenu in a suit of words—but because I had been *born* vulgar. And now I have lost my place, there is no place for me either here or there. With the women of my own class love had been nipped by *their* deficiencies, with Livia it was ruined by my own. Do you understand the tragedy? They had love to give that I could only despise; she had love to give that I could not win. I had sneered in secret at Dove, at Carlotta, because of their common tone, and preened myself in secret because of Livia's superior favour—until she found in me all that I hated in them. Ah, that was good justice!

I do not write books now, I suppose my mind is bored. What a mind! One might suffer so from sorrow, melancholy, love, or a hundred other such ills—but boredom! For five years I have done nothing, I am getting poor again, and I suppose I shall die soon in some idiotic way. But it does not matter, nothing really matters: the gnat has a piercing tooth, but great calamities calm us.

A wren was nesting in a niche outside the door. She used to chirp at me. Carelessly I left a large box standing there, so that at night a weasel climbed upon it and caught the bird and its young. I heard the mother screaming and I could not sleep. This morning a wren fledgeling flapped in at the door and fluttered round and round the room; at last it came and settled on my head. But I can do nothing for it, I can do nothing for myself. I am a lost ship waiting for a wind that will never blow again.

Nixey's Harlequin (1931)

RING THE BELLS OF HEAVEN

To every man his proper gift
Dame Nature gives complete.

I

THE sun was glaring over a Suffolk heath that spread on either side of a sandy road thick with dust. The heath had two prevailing colours—the hue of its bracken green and tall, the tint of its flowering ling. These colours were clearly denoted and merged in isolated tracts, as though in the comity of vegetation one had commanded: thus far the purple, and the other: thus far the green. At the edge of the green ferns, haunt of heath fleas and lady-birds, some brown skeletons of last year's foliage, blown there by mournful airs, lay clinging to their youthful offspring as if to say: "Dream not, but mourn for us." On this July afternoon the blue of the sky was swart and clear although some stray clouds, trussed like the wool on a sheep's back, soared over a few odd groups of pine and a white windmill turning on a knoll.

And along the road came padding a small black pony swishing its tail; wisps of dust puffed up from its hoofs, and bareback upon the pony sat a small uncomely boy about ten years old, carrying on his arm a bright tin bucket half full of red currants. The boy, who had the queer name of Blandford Febery, though he commonly answered to the call of "Cheery," was off to meet his father, who had gone to market. The pony pranced along the heath road for a mile or so until they came to the town and so into the market. Mr. Febery was sitting at a table in the cool courtyard of the Tumble Down Dick inn with a group of men clad in cutaway coats and gaiters. He got up, took the bucket of currants from his son, and set it down by the table. "That's my Cheery boy!" he cried gaily, lifting his son from the pony. "Now you jest slip along to Mrs. Farringay's and leave her those currants from me while I put pony in stall, and I'll wait here for you."

"They be large currants, Albert," said George Sands, as Blandford carried them away.

"A fairish sample, George," shouted Mr. Febery, leading the pony off; "but my stomach can't never abide such traffic, it turns on 'em, it do. And all our family be the same."

"Has he got a large family?" asked Henry Ottershaw, a man with a big rosy face and a black patch over one eye.

"He's got two boys," replied George; "two boys and a gal. That one's the oldest."

"He's the very image of his father, whether or no."

"Oh, ay," George answered; "Albert might have spit 'e out of his blessed mouth."

This was only externally true. Albert Febery was a small yeoman farmer of cheerful disposition, for in those days—the 1880's —farming was still a pretty business, and farmers, like his friends bluff George Sands and Henry Ottershaw, were spruce men whose wants were modest and their cares few. But his son was morose, and his wants were not modest.

The sky had grown overcast. Around the inn the air was full of protesting sounds and the smell of ordure, for the cattle were being routed out of the pens and screaming pigs were being lugged into carts. The market was over, though some stall-holders were still trading briskly in sweets and shoddy clothing.

The boy returned from his errand before his father had finished stalling the pony, and he sat himself silently down on the bench beside George Sands.

"I was a-going to begin cutting our oats tomorrow," said Henry Ottershaw, casting a glance at the sky, "but I don't like the look o' they raggedy clouds; they can't hold their water, we shall have a dirty Thursday. I think I do know when rain's about—I can smell it."

"Teasy weather," remarked Sands. "Weather is teasy, you can never be sure: I had ten pole of early potatoes this year in my kitchen garden; sweet and blooming they was. Come a frost in May and cut 'em off like a soot sack."

Ottershaw held up an admonishing finger. "We shall have a hard winter, George, mark you. Last week I was digging up a nut hazel bush and there was a frog and a toad under the root of it. 'Ho, ho,' I says, 'there's a hard weather brewing, you mark my words, people.' I recollect two year ago a man prophesying as this very winter before us now was going to be the worst known for two hundred year. 'Oh my,' I says to him, 'how ever can you recollect all that?' 'Never you mind,' he says, 'it's the God's truth I'm be telling you.' "

"Who was that, Henry?"

"Maybe you don't know him—Will Goodson?"

"Oh, ah! Went bankrupt, didn't he?"

"That's the chap. And owed me thirteen pound ten. He come and told me one day, leaned on the back of his cart and cried till the tears rolled all along the tailboard and dropped on to the road. I saw 'em, couldn't take my eyes off 'em, George."

"Cried! That man Goodson!"

"Like a girl, George."

Sands shook his head and pursed his lips derisively: "A must have put pepper in his eyes."

Young Blandford went into the inn to seek his father. The taproom was empty. On the wall hung a theatre poster:

THE MARKET HALL
TONIGHT

The boy went to it at once and stood intently transcribing its meaning. He made out that it was the bill of a benefit performance with all sorts of attractions for that night only, such as scenes from *The Lady of Lyons* and *The Dumb Man of Manchester,* including a recitation (illuminated with lantern slides) by the world-renowned tragedian, Caesar Truman (*Hamlet, Belphegor, The Duke's Motto,* etc., etc.). At the bottom of the bill was a small woodcut, the picture of a carter with a long whip pulling at a horse that looked tired, and a verse beginning:

"The curfew tolls the knell of parting day."

Mr. Febery came in. "Hallo!" he said. The boy did not answer, and his father peered over his shoulder at the bill.

"That's a nice bit of poetry. Yes, it is; and you'll be able to read it all if you live long enough."

The boy still silently studied it, while his father rambled on: "My! You could hear some grand reciting twenty years ago. You never hear anything like it now. They'd frighten you, they would! They'd make the tears pour out of your eyes, they would then."

"Father," said the boy, "it's tonight, let us go."

"Oh, we can't do that," his father gruffly answered. "No, no, we must have a cup of tea and then cut along home. It's going to rain, I think."

To his amazement his son's eyes were brimmed with tears!

"Oh, father, take me!" cried the boy. "Take me, I *must* go!"

"Hoi! hoi! What's amiss?" the elder sternly asked. "You're too young for that sort of canter, Cheery."

The youngster bent his head, drew his sleeve across his snivel-
ling nose, and sobbed.

"Why, Blandford! What's this ado? Shut up, now, shut up and
come and have your tea."

But the boy was inconsolable.

"I tell you we cannot go," the father angrily expostulated. "We
cannot go. Your mother would die of fright not knowing where
we were."

"I must! I must!" raged the unhappy boy.

George Sands came in and stared alternately at father and at
son. "Why, what's he been up to?"

"This infant wants me to take him to the theayter!" Albert
explained. "Crying fit to burst! Look at him. Did you ever?"

"Well," Mr. Sands commented, "what a God's the harm of it?"

" 'Tain't the harm. Had I known on't I could 'a' told Susan this
morning, but Susan don't know; she'd worry herself into her
grave afore dark."

"You know," Mr. Sands said, "I like to see a bit of good play-
acting myself. If you go I'll come with ye. You can send word
to your missus—Jim Easby passes your door within a hundred
yards almost. I'll be seeing him in a few minutes."

The elder Febery hovered exasperatingly over this simple solution, but at last gave way and consented.

"All right, George. If you do, see Jim and tell him to tell my
missus, will you, as Cheery and me have gone to the performance
and won't be home till late. Now dry up!" he exhorted the boy.

"Oh, father!" In a passion of thankfulness the youngster threw
his arms around his father's hips.

"God bless my soul!" Mr. Febery was bewildered.

Father and son then went into the parlour and sat down to a
tea served with ham and pickled cabbage, for the Tumble Down
Dick was an ancient inn, lacy, leathery, and agreeably musty,
famed for its good fare. If you halted there and for a moment
doubted, you had but to open the precious album of beanfeast
tributes that lay on the parlour table and you could doubt no
longer. The very first page recorded the immense gratification of
the Dredging Department of the London & So-&-So Railway, and
not far off was the eulogy of the policemen from Plaistow: "To

satisfy thirty-one policemen is no mean feat. We are confident there is no more comfortable hostel place to put up at than Tumble Down Dick's. Signed Sergeant Trepelcock. X Div."

The Feberys ate gustily until George Sands came back after instructing Jim Easby, and then George Sands sat down to eat too. And he told Cheery what a lot of fine things and comic things and terrible things they would be sure to see at the play; murders and daggers and pistols going off bang, and strangulation and poison, and bushels of blood flowing, enough to perish his little bones; but it would not do for him to be frittened, there was no call to be frittened, for it was all false as the devil's heart. That was what everyone liked—the Lord knew why—it was a corker!

"But I do love a good drama, Albert. A good drama is what I do love."

"Oh, ah!" said Mr. Febery.

"It's education."

"That's it."

"And I reckon it 'ull do him a smartish bit of good. There's ghosts and what all, Cheery. Are you feared of ghosties?"

The boy shook his head, his mouth was full of onion.

"Nor me, neither," said Mr. Sands. "I likes to see a good ghost or two; it brings the hereafter before you, don't it?"

Mr. Febery averred that it certainly did that.

They went to the skittle alley at the back of the inn and the two men began to play a match, but Blandford soon tired of watching them heave the clumping cheeses at the fat ninepins and he stole away. When they had finished their game they found him standing in front of the theatre bill, moving his forefinger slowly along the words of the verse, spelling out those difficult lines about the curfew and the lowing herd. What *was* a curfew, or a knell? And those other words? His untutored mind was bothered, but none the less something had brushed his fancy with magic wings, had touched it indelibly. It set up some astonishing absurdities, and he could not ask his father to explain them.

"Let's be off," cried George, "there's bound to be a crowd if we want a good place."

Across the square they went to the Market Hall and stood for half a weary hour in a crowd clustered about the door, while everyone said jovial pleasant things until the doors were opened, but when the doors were opened all the men fought like tigers and swore and blasted and shoved and screamed. Somehow everybody got into the hall at last and although breathless and bruised they were jovial and pleasant once more. The hall had a blue-washed indigent interior, but there was a platform at one end hidden by curtains of real red velvet with golden tassels, and in front of that a smiling man with a melodeon, a man with a clarionet, and a boy with a triangle and a drum sat and played agreeable music. The boy was no bigger than Cheery, but he performed—as George Sands declared—remarkable well.

"Now you watch," Mr. Febery enjoined his son when the music ceased. "You mustn't say a word, and don't be scared, 'cause it is not real at all. Watch!"

The curtain rolled up. There was nothing to be scared about. It was a short play, all about a clergyman being lathered for a shave by a black footman with a whitewash brush out of a bucketful of soapy suds. The audience rocked with laughter.

"What d'ye think o' that?" panted Mr. Sands as the curtain descended.

The boy smiled a little wanly. "When will they do that bit about the curfew?"

"Curfew? Curfew? Oh, the curfew! Yes, that's the last of all; presently."

The next piece was all about a poor orphan boy named Frankie, and he was adopted by a rich lady and gentleman who had no children of their own. Frankie was not a bit bigger than Blandford Febery; this rich lady and gentleman treated him very, very kindly, and he was being educated for a higher station in life. One evening this rich lady and gentleman left him alone in the study doing his home lessons and went upstairs to their parlour to have a little music. And while he was studying his home lessons and counting on his fingers, a nasty burglar crept through a window behind Frankie and began crawling on his hands and knees towards the gentleman's safe where he kept all his gold and silver. This ugly burglar had a horrible knife in his hand and went crawling very quiet like a snake to steal all the gold and silver, but Frankie happened to catch sight of him and said: "Hoi!" The burglar sprang up. "Silence!" he hissed. But Frankie was too brave for him: "I cannot allow you to pass," he cried. "Silence!" the burglar hissed again, "or I shall cut your head off with my knife." "No," replied Frankie, "I shall not keep silent. You are on mischief bent. You are about to rob my benefactor, to whom I owe everything that is dear." And he called out: "Help! Police!"

Then the burglar jumped on him and stabbed him in the chest. Frankie fell down on the hearthrug, and the burglar felt rather sorry because it was only a child. He bent down and said: "You're not hurt, are you?" Just then the rich lady rushed in and flung herself on top of Frankie and screamed, and Frankie said he was dying and feeling very cold. So the lady said: "Help!" and her rich husband came hurrying in just as Frankie breathed his last. "Merciful Heaven!" moaned the rich man when he saw that all was over. He turned to the burglar, and pointing to the orphan's body on the hearthrug, he asked him very haughtily: "Was yours the hand that struck this innocent youth that deadly blow?" The burglar shuffled and snivelled and then he tearfully said: "I couldn't help it, guvnor; I couldn't, on my honour." But that was not good enough for the rich gentleman; he went to the window and shut it down with a bang. Then he latched it. Then, in a terrible voice, he said to the burglar: "You shall expiate your crime upon the scaffold." And he would have done, too, only, after all, Frankie was not dead, he had only fainted away and was not hurt at all, not the least little bit.

"Damn my heart!" Mr. Sands huskily said. "But that boy acted very remarkable well."

"Of course," Mr. Febery intimated, "it wasn't a boy at all, it was a gal dressed up in boy's clothes."

"I felt perhaps it was," agreed Sands. "No boy could act so noble as that. It ain't in 'em. Later on, a man if you like, but not a boy, no. Well, that was a marvellous good piece o' drama, like life itself, very enjoyable. It moved you, Albert."

"Oh, ah!" said Mr. Febery.

"It did *me*, anyhow."

Cheery sat between them, smitten with dumb wonder as the

grandeurs of Thespian art unfolded themselves before his eyes.
Filled with immensity, with inexplicable emotions, he wanted at
once to be the boy with the triangle, to roll his marvellous drum.
He wanted to be Frankie, to be stabbed, to lie down, to die for
ever, and then rise again to confound the wickedness of man.
But the last piece was now preparing. The curtain rolled up, revealing an empty stage with a white sheet, and on the sheet a
circle of light shone with dazzling splendour in the paramount
darkness.

"Magic lanterns," whispered Blandford's father.

A pretty picture appeared on the sheet, of some fields and
cattle with a thin moon rising; a bell boomed solemnly far off.

"Curfew," Febery whispered.

And then Blandford became aware that the great Caesar Truman was on the stage. He emerged mysteriously from darkness,
and now a light followed him wherever he moved. Melodiously
his great vibrating voice began to thrill the soul of young Febery
with the words of the poem he had read upon the bill. And how
beautiful they sounded!

"*The ploughman homeward plods his weary way.*" With what
infinite weariness that line was intoned!

"*And leaves the world to darkness,*" declaimed Caesar Truman.
There was a long pause of surprise ere the great tragedian added
in a soft whisper: "*and to me.*"

Then, after the actor had burst forth again into: "*Now fades
the glimmering landscape on the sight,*" he spread his arms wide,
hissing with bated breath: "*And all the air a solemn stillness
holds.*"

Behind him on the screen the pictures were withdrawn and
changed. There was an owl, a churchyard, a farm, men ploughing
or reaping or chopping down trees, and then the churchyard
again. But few were mindful of these, for the great Caesar Truman had cast them all under his spell. Not least the boy, in whom
the voice of the old tragedian was arousing strange incommunicable recognitions. To declare that the uncomely Blandford
Febery was never the same again would be no more than saying
"Heaven is high" or "The sea is wide." He had not lived till then;
the creature we are to know was born in that hour.

The show being over, the two men went across to Tumble Down Dick's to share a quart of ale. George Sands then mounted his saddle cob and rode away. Febery lit his two gig lamps, led out his harnessed mare, and backed her into the gig, while Cheery brought the little pony and tied its halter to a ring on the tailboard. Silently they drove out of town, but Febery, half-way across the dark heath, bent to his son. "That was a rum come-up, Cheery, eh!"

"We didn't see any ghosts," the boy sullenly responded.

"Naw, we didn't neither! Better luck next time, eh!"

At that moment they saw a green light ahead of them, strangely swaying.

"What's that, in the name of God!" Mr. Febery sat bolt upright and pulled guardedly at the reins. An old bearded man carrying a lantern and leading a white mule came stalking out of the bracken.

"It's only old Barnaby; my God, I thought—"

The man with the mule waved his lantern as they drove past him.

"Good night, Ginger!" Mr. Febery yelled, and turned to see if the pony was still securely hitched to the cart tail.

"I'm going to be an actor," said the boy suddenly.

"Are you?" gurgled his father. "You'll make a fine actor, upon my soul you will. Oh, ah!"

II

The boy was robust enough, no illness molested him, but he had never displayed any relish for the work of the farm and after his momentous visit to the theatre he manifested a deep dislike. Although he did not care much for school he now became studious, made himself a proficient reader, and was generally found with his head stuck in some book or other, any sort of book, borrowed from anybody. It annoyed his father.

"All that truck will make a fool of him! It's nonsense. He'll never be able to turn his hand to any darn thing!"

"Leave him alone," said Mrs. Febery, "he's got a headpiece, and that's what he wants."

But the father was unconvinced. "Susan, it's folly, you know

that well. Your headpiece is good and all for the sense that may
be in it, but your feet must be set firm afield and your hands
guiding the plough. What all can he get from this here *Pilgrim's
Progress* and that Shakespeare?"

"Give him a chance, Albert!" protested Susan. "He's young
yet."

"At fourteen years of age! Young! Why, my grandfather was
married then!"

"Don't lie so, Albert!"

"Well, he was—very nearly! And I started work myself when
I was ten. But him! Oh no, I can't make anything out of him."

But at last he made him a corn chandler, and for four or five
years Blandford Febery worked in the office of some millers in
the market town, lodging during the week with some relations
who also dwelt there.

On market days Albert would pop into the office and greet his
son, but Blandford derived little pleasure from the visits; he disliked being kissed so childishly in front of his fellow clerks, and
was restless until his chattering father said: "Well, so long,
Cheery; see you Sunday." And on Sundays Cheery would trudge
over the heath to the farm for the day, to kiss his mother and eat
mighty meals and be driven back in the gig by his father at night.

After a year, however, he did not visit the farm so often; he
was still madly reading, spending all his leisure on book after
book. And what for?—what for? some people would privately
ask, and answer themselves with a "God knows!"

By the time he was twenty the morose youth had begun to
emerge from his uncouthness into the style of a carefully dressed
and not unconfident young man. There were rather sullen eyes
in his palish face, his lips were unpleasantly thick, and despite his
contact with a variety of people he seemed unable to cotton on to
any acquaintance, male or female, of more than passing note. But
on a sudden—it was during the Boer War—he resigned his post
at the millers' office, wrote to his mother saying that he was off to
seek his fortune—and disappeared! His mother took the news
with fortitude. his brother and sister grew up, his father went on
ploughing and sowing and reaping.

Cheery never saw any of them again, he never went back. They
thought he had gone off to fight the Boers, but it was not so; he

was journeying around the north country with a circus! Knowing something of horses and forage, he was given a job, but he developed an unsuspected talent for announcing the performances of the circus, and so his scope was enlarged. He was not the ring master, he was the gentleman in a tall silk hat who with whip in hand strutted on the platform outside the great tent and harangued the hesitating mob in a picturesque rodomontade that was impressive, and therefore convincing. His perorations commonly produced a rush to the pay-box. This phase did not last a year, for he found an opportunity to join a travelling theatre company and Blandford Febery became an actor, an actor in plays of the kind that the great Caesar Truman himself had once adorned. His rise was rapid indeed; in a year or two he became a line on the bills of the play; soon he became the top line. Then a whole bill was given up to him until you might have thought the play itself was Febery, and nothing but him. Good God, what impossible changes this world does contrive—as if a toad could turn into a giraffe! That taciturn exterior had been harbouring a muffled but burning magniloquence, whose liberation made Blandford Febery.

"A youth to fortune and to fame unknown," the idol of provincial audiences. And the man himself changed with his fortunes. No longer merely a dumb observer and reader, eloquence flowed from his person in gestures as in speech; he was the eccentric, the admired, the envied comrade of his fellow players.

Though not exactly witty, he was stimulating, and often there was a gush of mystical inspiration from him that awed them. Pity it was that he could not retain their pleased regard, but envy accrued against him, and all too soon, conscious of their misjudgment, he grew overbearing, dictatorial, a passionate cantankerous fellow who could flay the rest of the company with contemptuous criticisms. And the company had to suffer him; they thought him a poseur—but a genius none the less; he was a spoiled ass, but a golden one at that. Yet in truth it was not merely success that had turned Blandford Febery's head; not that alone. He was a creature freed who had once been caged, and he was intoxicated by this realization. Having found a talent long buried in a napkin, he imagined that all had talents that they kept secretly hidden, or were too stupid to seek for, still creeping in their cages, wilfully unfree. He wanted something of them, but they could not understand what he wanted, any more than he could understand their want of understanding.

Perhaps he wanted them to be better than they were, better as actors and better as men, for he swore that only by becoming good actors could they become good men. Hoots! Toots! they would answer; they were all as good as good could be! Once Febery felt a violent urge, a quite burning desire, to call them the miserable drunkards, cowards, gamblers, and fornicators he supposed them to be, but he modified the extreme indictment: they were merely liars and shameful toadies! Whereat the oldest member of the company, a man with harsh eyes and turbulent lips who oft-times played Polonius, rebuked him:

"That won't do, Mr. Febery. All the world's a stage, and we have to play the play. In my time," said Polonius, "I have played many parts. I don't mean as an actor but as a citizen of the world, Mr. Febery. Each part gave me an inkling about the truth, and I took my cue from it. My own father used to exhort me when I was a boy at school: 'Never be ashamed to speak the truth.' He told me, instructed me, and impressed it upon me, never to be ashamed of truth. But I soon found that it was the one thing that *did* profoundly shame me! I took my cue from that, I did. D'you understand? To tell lies shamed me to myself perhaps, but that was far, far better than shaming myself to other people, or shaming them. I soon gave it up. Yes, and whatever I said I stuck to as long as it was necessary—it was never very long. So I say what I say now, true or false, devil or no, simply because it suits me best, pleases them, and injures nobody."

Febery sighed, helpless before such abasement.

Pride goes before a fall, it is said, but you must not blame pride for the disaster; Blandford Febery's downfall was due to other causes. One night he got a little tipsy at a leave-taking party— someone was off to America—and Febery fell into a dock at Liverpool, damaging one of his feet so hideously that it could not be properly repaired. Febery was an extremely abstemious man, he had never been drunk before; if one believed in omens and signs it was indeed a warning. As it turned out, the leave-taking party might have served him for his own, for in hospital he was soon made to realize that he would never again be able to strut heroically before the footlights; never any more. Hamlet with a club-foot and a walking-stick was unthinkable. Never any more. Farewell to the stage. The company resigned him, with tears, with sincere lamentations, with good wishes, and the company passed on. Febery never encountered his old actor friends again, for his life seemed to divide itself into segments having no relation to anything that had gone before.

After a sorry spell of months in hospital he endured a month or two of crutches; then, with a stick and the fanciful cloak he always wore, he obtained a temporary lodging at the house of a successful nonconformist draper, one Scrowncer, who had a nonconformist mission in life. In heart Mr. Scrowncer was a kind, kind creature, but in the tactics of conversion he was a regular Mahomet for militancy and yearned to put the devil and all his minions to the edge of the battleaxe of song and salvation.

Mr. Scrowncer knew his man, realized his predicament, and found a use for his unimpaired gift of eloquence. Febery was taken by him to some very emotional services and soon became profoundly meditative. Paying scrupulous attention to Mr. Scrowncer's suggestions—for he was now confronted by a serious monetary dilemma—he appeared at a chapel entertainment and recited Gray's *Elegy* with miraculous effect. Oh, what an instrument for holy work! The draper declared his conviction that the Lord had put Blandford Febery into his hands for His peculiar purpose, and when Mr. Scrowncer outlined that purpose to him Blandford Febery began to believe it too, and was soon put to the proof by Mr. Scrowncer.

Febery was one of those to whom the sensations of things, rather than their meanings, were important. Inspired by occasions that yielded his cherished gift to eloquence a grander scope than ever, he exhorted with the sombre fire and fearful passion so necessary to bring sinners to their penitential knees until the draper was no longer merely certain. Miracles and marvels were to be wrought! It was a divine appointment! Blandford Febery was an angel and minister of grace!

"What do you require of me?" asked Febery.

And Mr. Scrowncer cried: "To speak the truth, and shame the devil!"

The devil! Shame the devil! Some features of oblivion must

have rolled over Mr. Febery. Thrilled by his own emotions, he could believe that he himself believed.

"When I was a boy," he said impressively, "my father always exhorted me to speak the truth. He told me, instructed me, and impressed it on me; never to be ashamed of truth. I will, to the best of my power, do what you wish."

In short, he embarked upon the career of a revivalist preacher under the direction of Abner Scrowncer, whose organizing powers as to gimp, cotton flannel, and hairpins were as nothing compared to his genius in such a tremendous Cause. Not at all unmindful of Febery's theatrical renown, Mr. Scrowncer caused the circuits to blaze with posters announcing the new evangelist. Febery did his part with a degree of secular skill not less than his admonitory gifts. It was no uncommon thing for him to appear at midday in the square of some market town uttering the weird incantation:

"Ring the bells of heaven! Reuben Ranzo's gone! Follow me!"

There was plenty to mock at in his appearance, a slightly unshorn, slightly dissolute-looking man. Aided by a stick, he limped along in a curious black cloak. He wore no hat, and his thin sandy hair hung down to his collar. The eyes gleamed and the lips were heavy and thick, there always seemed to be some saliva on them as though some demon possessed him. But there were few that mocked.

"Give way there! By your leave," he would cry, raising a histrionic hand. Open-mouthed the housewives gazed at his fantastic figure, the children shrank, the cattle-drover paused with uplifted stick as Febery went by, and crowds would follow him to an appointed place in the open air to listen to his denunciation of their godless state:

"Listen to me. Do you suppose for one moment that you are the result of some conscious call into the world? You are *not!* It is true that you stand here now—in a bowler hat and corduroy trousers, with a cotton shirt and a moustache copied from a comedian—but do you suppose that *that* was the figure explicit or implicit in the glow of procreative ardour from which you were begotten? It was *not!* All nature grins at you. Nobody, not one, that knew you when you were born could recognize you now. Nobody could imagine the beginning who sees this curious culmination. We are the result of evil tuition, evil environment, and a faculty for imitation. And now," he would quote with soft irony, *"now on this spot we stand with our robust souls."* With both arms menacingly raised he would cry: "All nature grins at you! Here are we, in the midst of teeming life, clinging to existence like a barnacle on a ship's bottom, without a care for our divine meaning. All of us doing business; one way and another, business; some chopping suet, others selling beans. But I will tell you this about your business: one man's meat is another man's poison, one man's evil is another man's good, what profits some is a fraud to many. From its innocent beginning in Eden, our world has turned into a topsy-turvy world. Sometimes it is comically so, but more often it is tragic, and tears arise, and there seems no consolation possible; we feel tender towards our poor silly fellow creatures."

Febery paused, adjusted his cloak, and shifted his stick from the left hand to the right.

"But you must pardon me, you people, if I seem to treat you as though you were simple little children. For you are *not!* We are none of us innocent now, not you, not I, none. We are all blackguards, one time or another, and all responsible for the measure of evil we create. What is to be the issue of it? How shall we escape from this damnation? You say you are helpless in the toils, that life uses us in this way; you tell me that the devil tempted you. Bah! I tell you: every heart conceives its own sin."

"It's true, it's true!" murmured some of the eldery hearers, and though the younger were silent and perturbed, they seemed to agree.

"Do not come whining that the devil tempted you. Don't try to hang your misdeeds on *that* hook—it is overloaded already! You are merely robbing Peter in order to pay Paul. The gospel of redemption may never find the devil, but it *can* find you! Let me tell you a story:

"There was once a rich man who had received many favours from the Enemy of Mankind, and when in the fullness of time he was brought to bed of a sickness, he sent for a notary to make him a will. The notary got out his pen and his ink-horn. 'Sir, what have you got to dispose of?' The man said he desired to leave his body to corruption, his good works to the devil, and his soul to God. 'But—er—you can't make a will like *that!*' said the notary. 'Not! Why not?' asked the sick man. The notary hummed and haaed, and said it was the first time he had ever heard of such a request. 'That's nothing to the point,' the sick man said, 'it's the first time I've had to die, isn't it? Do as I bid you.' So the notary, not daring to enrage the man in his precarious state, wrote out the will and it was properly attested. The man then bade farewell to all his friends and died soon after, and was buried amid great lamentations. But when the will came to be read—my goodness! The fat was in the fire! His friends exclaimed against it, the family declared against it, and everyone said it was scandalous. Long and bitterly they disputed. They swore it was all a machination of the devil, and determined to bring the devil to book about it, they carried the matter to law. But when the judge and jury took the case in hand it was learnt that the devil was not present in court, and what was more—he never *would* be! 'Why, what is this?' the judge asked very sternly; 'has he not been cited to appear?' 'My lord,' said the clerk, 'we have tried to notify him, but it has been found that you can't serve a writ against the devil.' The judge took a peep into his register and saw that this was truly the law of the land. 'So,' said he, 'the will must stand as a good and proper will. His soul must go to God—nobody will deny him that. His body must go to corruption—nobody can dispute it—while his good works must go to the devil; I do not see what can prevent it, anyway! *Fiat justitia*,' he said, 'you can't serve writs against the devil.' "

Although dubiously swayed, the listening crowd was absorbed in him; as the harangue moved on, his denunciations ceased and were exchanged for promises of mystical bliss. "Oh, blessed are the pure in heart." There came a dying fall, and he spoke with tender urgency of a heaven that opened at the gates of Belief, filled with everlasting beauty, the sports of angels, the delight of kings, and every joy familiar as Eve's paradise.

The man's success as a religious orator was as striking as his success as an actor; it spread over an even wider range, curving like a meteor in evangelical orbits from Milford Haven to The Wash, from Carlisle to Canterbury. People flocked to hear him and were straightway smitten with a hysteria in which miracles and marvels indeed were wrought. Nobody was ever cured of a sickness by him—Blandford Febery never attempted that—but he undeniably did influence the lives of thousands of people, ordinary everyday people, those lambs who had no thought of evil until Blandford Febery expounded it, and thereafter no hope of mercy until he came to save them. Even others, some of the notoriously evil, became unnerved, voluntarily confessed their crimes, and went to prison; while a few of the notoriously good, hopeless of attaining any futher sanctification, simply went mad and were conveyed to the appropriate asylums. The Scrowncer fraternity revered him as a creature of ultra-human destiny—prophet, saint, perhaps even an archangel! A long period of proselytizing triumphs inspired Mr. Scrowncer with the colossal ambition of founding a new church with a new iconoclastic creed, but Blandford Febery was not so eager.

"No, friend, no; don't make a church of me!" he cried. "I'd rather go psalm-singing in the tropics. Every church, you know, contains the seeds of its own infamy, snares for its own delusion. The way of the Church is to proselytize, to organize, to subsidize; and then, while it stuffs itself with metaphysical mendacities, it suffers its holy inspiration to sicken and die. Do you not see that? Do you not realize that in a short time the sap perishes and the trunk alone is fostered and cherished? It becomes a valuable property—oh, they must keep it in good repair! It becomes a golden casket indeed, though it has never a gem inside! For that is the fate of all organizations, whether of law, religion, politics, patriotism, or commerce; to play the felon Jacob to its brother Esau, over and over again. The idolaters are worshipping a crown, a cross, a button, or a flag. Bah! No churches for me; I'll beat the highways and the hedges."

III

One autumn night, in the Town Hall of a south-coast town where a thousand people had thronged to hear him, he received a new summons. In the forefront of the hall sat an attractive young woman, with another girl beside her not so attractive. Throughout his discourse the pretty girl observed him with a rapt attention that was possibly not entirely devotional, and her appearance, simple, sweet, and perplexed, was just as magnetic to Febery. His eyes constantly encountered her eyes, confronting him with an appeal he had hitherto scarcely allowed himself to recognize. The choir from the local brotherhood broke into his address at designed stages with hymns. At the singing of *Rock of Ages* a stout widower stumbled weeping from the hall, overcome at the remembrances aroused by the hymn, which had been sung at his late wife's funeral. The massed sympathy of the audience flamed into massed worship, and Febery called aloud for penitents. With closed eyes he waited, one skirt of his cloak cast over one shoulder, leaning both hands heavily upon his stick in exhaustion. Moment after moment ticked by; the hesitant people sobbed, groaned, and sighed; no one responded to his call.

Suddenly he beckoned with his finger in the direction of the pretty girl: "Come, lady; come!" At once she rose. There was a slight scuffle with her companion, who tried to retain her, but with averted head she walked to the little room set apart for those who desired the preacher's private intercession. And there, alone, at the close of the meeting Febery found her awaiting him.

Her name was Marie Shutler and her eyes were beautiful. The room was odd as to shape, having the design of a harp, and odd as to its furniture, which was a big table with a red cloth upon it and coconut matting under it. One wall had a brass bracket with a gas lamp, and on the other were old oil paintings of the unknown ancestors of many living sinners. The charming girl stood meekly before him, answering his questions. She was—well—perhaps twenty-one or twenty-two. On one of her clasped fingers was an engagement ring with pearl stones. Febery closed his eyes, the girl did the same, and they stood immobile as though awaiting some pentecostal sign. Yet while still communing the girl peeped at him. At last he asked:

"Do you feel happiness now?"

"No," said the girl.

Febery asked her if there was anything she didn't understand, and the girl began to rack her brains, right and left, but could think of nothing to say—she could *not!*

"Sister," he entreated, "let—"

At that moment there came a knock upon the door and a stout bonneted, corseted, beaded dame bustled in.

"Marie! What ever is the matter? Everybody has gone home, long ago. You must come now." And turning to Febery she continued with a wry smile: "I must tell you, sir, that my daughter is already converted—aren't you, dear? Long ago, ever since childhood, she always has been. And I am, too, and so is my husband—all of us! I can't think what made her do this. What ever will people think of us, Marie! It is quite a mistake, sir, she is a really good girl, and she is going to be married soon to a sound Christian man. Come along now, Marie, we must go. I'm sorry she has troubled you, sir. Quite unnecessary!"

And seizing the pretty pentitent firmly by the arm, Mrs. Shutler led her daughter away. Febery was conscious of something very much like annoyance—not with the girl; even her pusillanimity was charming!—but with the mother. The bugbear! the bugaboo!

The mission was continuing for a week, and on the following day, as Febery was limping along under a sunless sky, he saw the girl sitting on a bench above the sea wall. He was thrilled to meet her there, though not with surprise: love has no surprises commensurate with its anticipations. He sat down with her.

"What made you respond last night?"

She did not reply at first, but he insisted:

"Why? You must tell me why."

The girl answered: "I do not know what made me do it."

"But," he said sternly, "you *must* know!"

"It was silly of me, I was all wrought up," she lamely explained. "And I told my friend not to let me go if I felt like that, and I did not think I should want to, but somehow, after all, I *did* want to, and I really don't know why. She tried to stop me—"

"I saw that," he interjected. "You snatched your hand away."

"It was wrong of me," said the girl.

"Why wrong?"

"I was all wrought up," she had no other interpretation, and sat watching the mild little waves splashing on sad little stones, and people throwing sticks for mad little dogs. Her eyes were beautiful. At length she burst out with: "I hate being good!"

It was Febery's turn to be puzzled.

"Just as much as I hate being bad," Marie continued.

"Those two hatreds cancel each other!" he exclaimed.

She shook her head decidedly. "No."

"Then what is it you want to do, or be?"

It appeared she hardly knew, but she thought she would like to go out into the wide, wide world and study art.

"Art!"

She loved art; it all had such immense significance, didn't he think?

"I have not studied it," he mused. "I have looked at it, some of it, and some of it I like; but I can't understand how one can like it because it is art."

Oh, but *she* understood that perfectly! And then she plied him with so many questions about his old theatrical career that the morning wore away and she had to hurry home.

They met again, they met daily throughout his stay and talked, recklessly, of things that had no connection with the object of the mission. About her approaching marriage, for instance, to the young flourishing ironmonger.

"I do not really want to marry him," the girl confessed.

"But you are engaged!" said the preacher.

"Yes, I suppose I must."

"It is wrong of you."

"I hate being good."

"That is no reason for marrying *him*—marry me!" the preacher said.

For days he had been ruminating angrily about her marriage to the ironmonger, pious though he was said to be, and although he, Febery, was pious too—in fact, all three of them!—his thoughts insidiously dwelt upon marriage, marriage, marriage, and in the company of the girl his mind was conscious of proprieties that his body demurred at. And Marie, too, was tempted, but: "No," she sadly said. "It would not do, it is too late now, I can't now; I hate being bad."

He implored, he wooed, they wrangled. "No, no, no. It is silly of me," she sighed. But at their final good-bye she kissed him fondly.

Away went Febery on his endless mission, and from the far-off towns he was reviving, still deeply impassioned, he importuned her in numerous letters. But Marie was obdurate, tenderly, even pleadingly, so; her vow to the ironmonger had completely enmeshed her timid soul. Or was it the old disparity of youth and age, Febery being now about thirty-five? Or was it that insubstantial fear which, in the guise of steadfastness, rules so many lives? She hated to be bad, and in a few months she married her ironmonger.

Still, the correspondence continued. Her part was affectionate while his, though more formal now, was deeply flattering to a feminine heart. After a year she grew mysteriously unwell and became a partial invalid. He gave her consoling tittle-tattle of the far-off towns he visited, while she wrote to him of her bath-chair. None the less she was still acutely disturbing to him. Alas, there were other disturbances in Blandford Febery now. He had begun to doubt—well, everything: the message he had to preach; the validity of the penitence he could so easily evoke; the minds, wills, and habits of the sheep who so soon relapsed into the old rank pastures; and, saddest reflection of all, he doubted even himself until he was less concerned about ultimate truths, or the truths of other people, than with the black truth about Blandford Febery. It was a figure stuffed into a false heroic semblance! These flashing gleams that stirred the multitudes no longer stirred *him*. They portended a holy fire, but the fire was never seen, and none knew better than he that it had never flamed in him, but had burned out of vapours that he conjured for a fee—it was but a mirage. Not love, not righteousness, moved them at all—it was fear! Without the fear of annihilation there could be no religion, and the fear had seduced and subdued mankind. What it had seduced them from did not matter the toss of a ha'penny!—it had seduced them. For its own ends religion, that social flunkey, had traded upon man's fear of extinction and had promised him an eternal reward for a temporary conformity. Not for the sake of being good was goodness wrought, but from fear of everlasting punishment. Faugh! What reality could ever arise from such Thespian fudge!

It was not long before he was at loggerheads with the fraternity in general and with Mr. Scrowncer in particular. Blandford Febery was indisputably the head and front of their great spiritual revival, but Scrowncer was the alloy that shaped it, the hidden plinth of its structure, the provider of the means whereby it throve, and Scrowncer had grown uneasy, become alarmed, and at last appalled, at Febery's recusancy. He pleaded, he protested, he argued, he demonstrated clearly that even an ordinary clergyman could confute these new dogmas with one twist of his cloven tongue. He stormed, he ridiculed, he forbade; but Febery believed, and believed violently, that no one saw things as clearly as himself, or felt so deeply as he. Fortitude, he claimed, was his prime virtue. The truth! The truth alone! He would shame the devil still, though it brought him to the stake!

"The devil!" Mr. Scrowncer said. "You do not shame the devil, my poor man, you only shame us all!"

"Well, if the cap fits," roared Febery, "wear it!"

"God forgive you, Febery," then said Mr. Scrowncer, "this is the end. We have come to the parting of the ways."

They had indeed, and Febery was cast out of the fraternity. Sadly the circuits were notified, meetings were cancelled, and the great mission for the time being came to an end. In the numerous windows of the Scrowncer emporiums, amid their displays of the latest things in linoleum blankets and lingerie, appeared the announcement:

SPECIAL NOTICE
I have nothing more to do with
Blandford Febery.
(*Signed*) A SCROWNCER

His fall was complete.

Hard upon this debacle there came the saddest news from Marie, still suffering from her long-standing malady. It had been thought that marriage would effect a cure, but it had not done so, and now, after four years of wedlock, she was despairing and begged to see him once again—it might be for the last time. Without an hour's delay he went off by train to her seaside town. Bright was the day; the summer had been long and dry, yet seemed in no mood to change, mellow breezes were crimping the blue water of the streams, and as he journeyed Febery felt as elated as the pilgrim who had thrown a burden from his back.

At times he was ashamed of this joy, but he continued to rejoice. From the station he limped out to the villa where Marie dwelt, with a sardonic smile upon his heavy face, for the long-haired "ginger" preacher was known to many of the passers-by and his cloaked appearance brought caustic comments from others more staidly clothed than he.

Her house had a garden in front with a tennis lawn and a dell under some trees. There was a summer hammock strung up in the dell, but the garden and the hammock were empty. The window blinds were drawn. "She may be away, or gone out," thought Febery as he gave a gentle knock upon the door.

It opened immediately. Her husband and his brother came out, and the door was shut quietly behind them.

"She is sleeping," muttered the husband, while his brother groped in a nook under the windows and brought out three folding chairs, which they opened and stood upon the lawn.

"She is very ill," her husband said moodily, "but she will not take to her bed as she ought now. She is lying down in the room there. Sit down, please, or is it too hot here?"

They sat down and talked of her condition in low tones. Was she so ill! It seemed to Febery that they were disinclined to let him see her again. Of course he had written to her about his loss of faith and his disagreement with Scrowncer, and she had sympathized, she had praised him, but it was clear that her husband deeply disapproved and was antagonistic. Marie had sent for him, a pathetic invitation, and he had flown in response to her. So this was her husband, the successful tradesman! His expensive clothes somehow hung cheaply upon him, and his pale sour face oppressed the visitor. Ten sombre minutes had passed when the door opened quietly and she herself stood there, her soft eyes blinking in the sharp sunlight, her mouth curved in a wry smile. Her dress was creased upon her, for she had been lying down. Malignant Time! How she had changed! Illness had scooped into her beauty, the contours of her face were angular now, and her hair hung in wispy locks. But the prime design was still there, it was beauty in a cloud—Febery's beauty. She walked slowly up to him as he rose, and they exchanged timid greetings.

Quickly her husband led her out of the sunlight to the dell

under the trees, and as she sank down into the hammock she bade Febery bring his chair. He did so. The husband and his brother—partners in ironmongery—did not rejoin them, they went strolling up and down the far side of the lawn as though by intention leaving the two friends together. The dell was screened by its trees, the hammock hidden by them.

"Do you like him?" Marie whispered.

"Who?" he asked doubtfully.

"My husband," she said.

Febery made a shrugging gesture.

"You do not like him!" She smiled as though it were no matter.

"Because you married him," he ventured, "and I still love you."

Marie stared at him. Then she groped for his hand and pressed it fondly. She closed her eyes and turned her face away.

"Ha ha ha!" laughed her husband, and "He he he!" his brother tittered in echo. They were apparently telling each other peculiar stories. With a glance at them through the screen of leaves, Febery bent over Marie and kissed her. She opened her eyes.

"Too late," she whispered. All her graceful frailness smote him with grief and longing. There was a small spider running across her bosom; it had jade-green legs and a lemon-coloured body with a brown disk upon it. Febery brushed it away and let his hand glide along her hip.

"Too late," she murmured again. "And I hate being good!"

"Ah, but when you are well?" he said softly, "when you recover—!"

"No use," she sighed. "I'm done for. Can't last much longer. They're only waiting for me to die. Quick, kiss me again—I don't care!"

They heard her husband chortling across the lawn: "Oh dear! Oh dear!" and his brother replying: "That's good, *very* good!"

The stupefied Febery stared over the back of his chair at the scorched grass of the lawn; the tennis net had slackened, the air was full of gnats. Sweat hung upon Febery's brow. How incredible it was! Of course it *could* not be true! What vital men those two looked prancing over there, though their clothes seemed to sag upon them and their shoes were dusty! Marie was wearing slippers of blue leather with white fur on the edges; her stockings were of silk to the knee, and a little beyond. It was piteous, it was impossible, she *could* not be dying—now!

"Tell me," she said. "What you are going to do now you have broken with old Scrowncer?"

"I have no plans," he answered, "I can think only of you."

"And there'll be no more plans for me, either." She spoke with a gay rally. "Lord, I have done nothing, been nothing, seen nothing—and there's Paris, and all those Alps, and the Kremlin, and the Suez Canal!"

He wanted to comfort her with kisses but feared to excite the frail sick woman and sat on despairingly by her side, wondering whether the predicament of Tantalus was not after all said and done more applicable to her than to him.

"You will not go preaching again?"

"Never any more," he said.

"I am glad of that!"

"I feel no gladness, Marie," he averred. "Far from it."

"Ah, don't fail me now, my dear." She smiled, but added ruthlessly: "I never believed in you as a preacher!"

"Not?"

"Of course not."

"I believed in myself."

"As a preacher of the truth! But you don't now, do you?"

What *was* it he *did* believe, or had *once* believed, or could ever believe again? How explain to her, dying as she was, that he had found out he had been preaching—oh, vanity of vanities!—to God and not to man! It was too piteous now to disturb her simple faith. Not now, not now.

"You don't believe in it now?" she iterated urgently, as though a paramount consolation hung upon his expected answer; and moved by her insistence, he conceded:

"I have no—what you call—beliefs, but—"

"Neither have I!" she interjected triumphantly. "Never. I supposed I had—till I met you. Then I knew I had none. They know it too," she whispered.

"Who?"

She nodded towards the lawn. "I am tired of it all. He worries me. He knows I am fond of you and think just as you think, and he wants me to believe now and be good—good!"

"Then why not, Marie?"

She was startled and half rose from the hammock.

"What! Why do you say that—now?"

Febery hesitated; again she urged him: "Why?"

The miserable man said: "You have nothing to lose—now—if—if—"

"You mean now I am dying?" She turned her face away, murmuring: "Yes, I know that. But it would be mean, now, don't you think?"

"Pooh!" he exclaimed.

"Ah, don't fail me now!" she protested with damnable caressing archness. "You have no faith, you never had any at all."

He could not bring himself to utter a reply, but she understood his silence; it confirmed her.

"Nor have I," she said. "I can't have. What is the use of pretending now? I'm just sorry."

Later in the afternoon Febery went away into the town and took a lodging. Her husband did not ask him to stay with them, and indeed Febery shrank from lingering there. He promised Marie that he would call every day, every day—until—yes, he would come every day.

He called the next day, but she was not to be seen, she was sleeping. Again he called, but she was sleeping, sleeping; her husband almost shooed him away. For three days he hung around the closed house. Then she died.

IV

For months Febery drifted about like a dead leaf at the will of the winds, limping on foot from town to town, doing little or nothing, until he was reduced to beggary and the winter days came on.

"It is time now," said he, "to take my fate in hand." And he thought and thought and went on thinking until his brains were woolly and the soles of his boots worn thin. Forlorn and unshaven, he was no longer fitted for business, from acting he was bitterly resigned, and religion had cast him out. "Is there nothing to which I can turn my hand?" he mournfully mused. "Am I only a spouter of hyperbole and fudge?"

Well, on a Sunday morning he tramped into a little town. By the grace of God it was a fine day, with no sharpness wherever the sunlight lay, and where it lay brightest and best was on a small green common with an old gibbet conserved in its centre. There were men idling about there, plenty of men waiting for the taverns to open, so Febery walked up to the gibbet, took a stand upon its knoll, and began calling the men to come listen to him. And when they came he began to preach to them of the virtues of temperance and the sin of indulgence in strong drink. Having sworn vows against it ever since he had broken his foot in the dock at Liverpool, no drop of the evil had again passed his stubborn lips. Inspired now by necessity rather than any moral urge, he harangued so passionately, so despairingly, and yet so amusingly that his hearers were moved to applaud him. It was not his theme that arrested and impressed them so much as his appearance; they were enlivened by his gestures and tickled by his style, so that his appeal for a collection at the close met with a generous response, and he left the common with a new hope in his breast while they left it mostly for the purpose of whetting the whistle with an ironical relish. That was one to Febery; he had preached temperance, and the intemperate had paid him jovially. Well, it was no use preaching to the temperate!

He came to another town at evening and again attracted a large audience for his sermon on the evils of drink, with still more profitable results. There was something hoarsely command-ing about the man; wild-eyed and with uplifted hands, he seemed to denounce the whole world in most hearty fashion, and the spittle came spurting from his lips.

Some of his hearers were impressed, others were visibly moved, but all were fascinated. When they flung questions at him his repartee delighted them—oh, they liked to be bullied!—and into a handkerchief he had spread on the ground before him their pence fell like showers of leaves on windy autumn days. It was a long, long time before Febery realized that this largesse was not the reward of virtue communicated or acclaimed, but was be-stowed upon him because he was a most impressive *amusement*. By then, however, he was launched upon his new career and, uncontrolled by any executives, spoke wherever he happened to be, in any fashion he chose, and with a lugubrious philosophy that deepened as the months rolled by. Now and again offers were made to him by wealthy societies who required him to lecture for them, but he declined, roughly, rudely. Disliking organizations, he chose to live in haphazard fashion on his itinerant alms. That made a hard life of it, and to the wandering man it seemed as though winter would never pass away. Yet neither spring nor summer brought any ease to the sorrow that laboured in his heart, a sorrow that was often mingled with a mysterious resentment. Poor Marie! It was sad—poor baffled woman! She was—good Lord above—she was—well—she had been born a romantic, a romantic without wings! She had had the flame in her breast, but not the wit to fly!

It was not alone the loss of Marie that fretted and consumed him: there was something within *himself,* loneliness and intolerance, that also consumed, that was all of a piece with his strange appearance. The glitter of heaven had dulled, it was no longer desirable; he was of the world, and yet the world disgusted him; he wanted to love it, love it madly, yet he could take no part in it at all. He was cast out, he too was baffled, and his despairing isolation fumed and quavered at his speeches:

"One enters a tavern at night— Stop! Why have you entered here? The mind stammers at the question; it knows there is a subtle answer, but it cannot enunciate it. To drink, to talk, to rest? Bah! Not these alone! One's journey is long, with an end no man knows, from a beginning that none remembers, and on either hand the Green Dragons and the Black Lions and the Pink Ptarmigans blazon their foolish symbols. One enters a tavern at night—to lounge over a bar counter and be absorbed. Absorbed! What do you mean? Absorbed in what? Well, in a twist of harmonious chaos, minute parochial chaos, torn from immensities of isolation. But what are these figures standing here or sitting there, babbling incessantly in gay tones? There is beer before them on the tables. They have hats on. Their faces are ruddy or sallow. They are arrayed in suits with soiled handkerchiefs in the pockets, matches, tobacco, money, and all the intimate revelations of a gnat. They discourse of work, wenching, and horse-racing, or they are immersed in mysteries to which I have no clue. It is a world of shirt-button joys, and griefs that would drown in a single tear. How fatuous! What waste, what profanation! I hear a voice that cries: 'Begone! You may not enter here!' Yet the heart pleads for some charity that the soul ever denies, and I long to enter there, to merge myself humbly with these, and be one with its cheap oblivion. 'Begone! Begone! You may not enter here!'

"The world is my tavern. Am I excluded, or is it I that exclude myself? Are there cherubim at the gate of that paradise from which I have known neither expulsion or exclusion, or is that flaming sword merely my own? I know, I know, for it scorches my hand and heart!"

Two winters followed two summers, and careless of personal welfare, Febery slept often in barns or among the heather, but in the end his self-consuming flame and the quite needless privations he incurred did their work: he was stricken with a fever and carried helpless into a hospital attached to a convent. A convent! There was no escape for Febery, he was dying. The quiet nuns besought him to take the final consolation. Febery declined. There was bliss in all this restful illness, the small white ward, the immaculate nuns, the comfort, the soft passage of the daylight hours. It was a community of gentle women, sisters of mercy indeed. But the nights were full of mortal anguish and fear of what might lie ahead when there were nights no more. A young monk came to sit by his bedside and spoke earnestly. He too seemed to be lit with gleams of that urgent holy rapture that had once been Febery's joy, and the mind of the sick man faltered under his persuasions; at the core of his dying heart an ash of warmth began again to flicker. What beauteous visions still hung in that curious creed! And he had only to submit himself, to cast away his human pride, and say simply and humbly—yes! The word sang in his heart and had almost trembled from his lips when the voice of poor dead Marie came murmuring to his ears:

"Ah, do not fail me now!"

And Febery remembered. He had led her from the cross; they

had agreed! Despite everlasting hell he *could* not fail her now. He dared not. With a grim gurgle he recalled an incident at one of the great Scrowncer revivals. A shoemaker on crutches, with both of his legs partially paralysed, had shuffled up to them, a derelict ugly outcast.

"Tell me this," said the poor wretch to a lady helper. "If I get to heaven at last, shall I have a good pair of legs?"

"Oh yes," she answered with gay conviction. "You will have a good pair of legs. You will be hale and hearty and clean and you'll live for ten thousand years."

"And," said the poor shoemaker, cogitating wistfully, "will there be any gals up there?"

The devout young monk spoke on, hopefully, consolingly, but Febery's life was ebbing away in dreams of heaths with windmills on them, and green marshes with blue brooks and old wooden bridges; of a day when a small boy rode on a black pony into market with a basket of plums or something, and his father had taken him to a theatre.

Polly Oliver (1935)

NIXEY'S HARLEQUIN

I MUST explain about Sally and me before I tell you the terrible thing that happened. I ought to tell you about the terrible thing first, I ought to begin with that because it is what the story is about, and desperately tragic, I can tell you. But as it happens there are two men named Wilson concerned, one of them very wickedly concerned, and my name is Wilson. It is a common enough name, you couldn't have anything commoner than Wilson, and I have told everybody that I am not the guilty Wilson; I am indeed as innocent as a new-born lamb, but nobody believes me, they just grin.

And why grin? In *any* case, why grin? Suppose I *were* the guilty Wilson, is that anything to grin at? Would they grin then? I suppose they would; it seems natural to some razor-faced individuals to grin at pain and shame—but why! I told the police it must be the other Wilson who was to blame, and they told me that that was just what *he* said about *me!* You see, my name is Thomas and his name is also Thomas. I cannot think why people are allowed to have similar names at all; your name ought to be sacred to you, as private as your own fingernails, but here is this fellow born certainly ten years later than me. . . . And at the age of forty, let me tell you, one has come to respect one's name; I mean one's name is one's own title and I like to preserve a good title—I don't mean merely being praised by inconspicuous clergymen. . . . And here's this fellow has taken my name, the same in every letter, what is called my cognomen, and dragged my character in the mire. What is more, he has fobbed off a dreadful responsibility on me. He is married, I am not. They seem to think that makes all the difference, in his favour. Now I ask you, what difference could that really make when you know the facts? Not an inch! Man is man, as I'm almost tired of telling them. And I am not that kind of man at all; in fact, I enjoy rather poor health, always did.

I can remember one day I was in the shop where Sally worked when this very Wilson came in, this other Tom Wilson. I admit I had been there some little while passing the time o' day to Sally, but what of it! She was one of the handsomest young women ever seen behind a counter; short fair hair that curled a little, cheeks as pink as roses, healthy as a wild bird. In came this Wilson, one of your hearty, cocksure, unpleasant sort of men, and when Sally asked: "What would you like, Mr. Wilson?" he out and said: "A kiss, and the afternoon off with you!" Just like that. Of course I suppose it was the perfect answer to make to pretty Sally, it consorted so with her charming primness and her general bloom. In a way it was genius. Or, though I don't know, it may have been a mere common tag, the sort of thing that men like that are always saying to girls in shops like that, but I *do* know that *I* could never bring myself to utter such fancies, or so blatantly either. I would *like* to, mind you. Oh please, very much! Make no mistake about that, I certainly would like; but there you are, I—can—not. I have plenty of words and things I *could* say to girls like Sally, but not that sort of thing. For instance: the indiarubber mat on the glass counter was half worn out by the coins of customers who never bought anything but tobacco; well, I could have asked if she never grew tired of seeing the same oafs buy the same brand of tobacco for the same price at the same hour daily, giving them exactly the same change from exactly the same coins, and all to be stuffed in the same pipes or be chewed by the same rotten teeth.

I use tobacco myself, of course. Men are alike, very much alike in habit and instinct; I am in some ways much like other men, and I haven't the moral imagination to wish myself any better than I am. Still, I have always preferred cigarettes, and I dare say shall continue that form as long as it suits me; in fact, I have no doubt about it at all at present.

You know, men of a certain type imagine things about girls like Sally, and—and—and there you are! I could never have said that sort of thing to her, but I confess that afterwards I sometimes imagined myself to ask her:

"What would you like, Sally?"

And she was to reply:

"A kiss, and the afternoon off with you, Mr. Wilson."

Or perhaps she would say "Tom."

Of course I never never never *did* ask her any such thing; pardon, it is quite out of keeping with my character; but I did have a feeling, often and very often, that that was what she *would* have said if I had ever put it so to her. Yes, exactly; but of course I did not. I had—indeed, I don't mind confessing it—an idea that the poor girl was really rather fond of me in a tobacconist-shop sort of way, but I never made up to her at all, never stroked her fingers as she gave me my change—it is—you will pardon me— I honestly do not think myself capable of such a thing.

And yet I got tangled up in the whole matter, one of the most frightful affairs a man could possibly be mixed up with, extremely repellent to me, and all because my name is Wilson—and not only that, but Thomas besides. You know, you will never be able to persuade me that such things are the mere *accidents* of life: I don't know what they *are*, but they are not that. I had known Sally Burden for at least a year, perhaps nearly two years, when she died suddenly while on a visit to a relative in London. Very mysterious it was, an inquest and all that was found to be necessary. Believe me, I did not hear of the poor girl's death, I did not even know about the inquest, until I heard my barber talking of that to Filkins the ironmonger two days after it had taken place. In London it was. I seldom read newspapers, in any case we have no local sheet; and though our town is a small town, there are at least fifty persons you do *not* know for every one you *do,* and so it was in no way surprising that I had remained so completely in the dark about a matter that was destined to concern me so seriously. Poisoning it was, the girl had died of poisoning, and I gathered it could not have been suicide because a man had been arrested, so the poor thing must have been murdered. That was the conclusion I came to. I bought newspaper after newspaper but I could not find any reference to Sally's case. I went up and down all the columns, but I need not have wasted my time and pence on the stupid things, for inquests, it seems, are as common in the metropolis as prayer meetings. I was to hear all—or nearly all—in the course of a few hours, and even that was much more than I wanted to hear, or had ever thought of hearing. To be brief—for I detest those people who beat about the bush, trying to beguile you into sympathizing with them before they reveal to you the crime they have committed—I myself was visited by the police, and interrogated about my relationship with that poor dead girl, closely and pointedly questioned. Most disagreeable and unnerving it was.

Perhaps you have already guessed the mystery? Poor lamb, she had been seduced I am sorry to say that is the whole explanation. Now, when a girl finds herself in such a plight she generally ends by marrying the man in a right and proper way, but poor Sally *could not* marry the man, even if they had both been willing, because she had a husband already!

I tell you, that *was* a startler to begin with, the revelation that Sally was a wedded wife; but there was more to come—oh, I'll not deceive you, that was nothing. A Mrs. Burden she was—not Miss at all, her maiden name had been Golightly—and married to a soldier, this Burden, who had gone abroad on foreign serv-

ice, Seringapatam or some such place—I couldn't tell you, really
—but he had been gone for two years and looked like staying for
ever. He'll never come back now, that's certain.

One of the most extraordinary things is that difference—I can't
tell what it is, I wish I could—between a woman who is married
and a woman who is not, when you do not know *which* she is;
but there are men who *do* seem to know, and Sally, poor lamb,
had fallen in love again with one, the wretch who had soon
brought this trouble upon her. I am not going to defend her, nor
am I going to blame him: I am not in a position to do so, for my
ignorance on subjects of this nature is reasonably profound, and
I hope will continue to be so; but I do feel there was something
rather too casual about this Seringapatam marital arrangement.
Even so, I'm not going to hold her entirely blameless. Having a
husband somewhere in the offing, she ought to have refrained
from associating with this other person; but the reasons why
women fall in love with some particular men are inscrutable;
men with the faces of mice and the hearts of centipedes, indecently hairy men, or razor-faced men who blather to them about
the right to self-fulfilment. Some such oaf had caught Sally's
fancy, and the soldier in Seringapatam was betrayed.

And what had I to do with all this? A moment, please; I am
coming to that.

The poor lamb was dead. Up in London she privily visited
some quack in the underworld who throve on such cases, and he
sold her something to remove the disgrace. In two days she was
dead. The quack was traced and arrested. They could not find
Sally's guilty lover; they did not know who he was, though there
was plenty of suspicion; indeed to God there was altogether too
much! That secret died with the girl, but she left a whole bushel
of other secrets lying about. Because, the strange thing is, she had
kept a diary—though that is not strange in itself—which was
found by the police, and it told them all about her secret life and
love ever since the departure of her husband. There was a great
deal of it, with very intimate details. Why do some people delight
to confess to themselves in secret those things they would rather
die than outface in public—as Sally did indeed die? Beauty like
hers is glory, but it is a peril too, for her diary revealed the story

of her illicit amours, not merely with the defaulting lover but with twenty-two different men, at various times and places. She had left an almost complete record, and she had left their names. In truth she was one of the most beautiful creatures in the bright world, and yet she had to do with some queer men, ugly fellows rather, and low characters, although one of them, I assure you, was the mayor of the town—but *he* had a wooden leg. Holy God, there is wickedness everywhere! I am a man of independent means myself, though I fraternize with the poorer orders and others because, of course, I realize that education is merely the means of enabling you to do easily the things you find difficult or do not care so much about; yet it is hard for me to understand that book. Still, many new ideas are born into God's world, and I am told it is not very hard to explain.

One of these men had brought her to her death. Which one? Several of the episodes in her diary implicated Tom Wilson, and, as I have already told you, there are two Thomas Wilsons in our town. I swear I am not the one referred to in the diary. I am *not*, I know my innocence as well as that viper with my name must know his own bitter sin, but there was nothing else to guide the police beyond those names written in the book of a girl who was dead and couldn't explain, and so we *both* had to go. The other names did not give any trouble; they, too, were common enough, like Meakins, Hoar, Tuckwell, Cox, Rowbotham—every man jack of them came from our town—and all were traced home and all, like the two Thomas Wilsons, protested their ignorance of the case. Nevertheless, we were all cited to appear and answer if called upon at the trial of this quack who had killed our Sally. For such a large party it was obviously possible, as well as wise, to make special arrangements; there were twenty-four all told, including the police inspector and me, and so we chartered a charabanc and rode up to London together.

I am not likely to forget a journey so noted in my memory, from that calm peerless morn down by the harbour, where I joined the charabanc, a cockily painted motor-coach christened *Nixey's Harlequin,* until night, when it brought me back again— a marked man. The coach was but half full when I entered, the

detective-sergeant stood at the door, and those within sat moodily
staring seawards while we waited there for stragglers. There is
no harbour really, nothing but a few stone piers left of a project
abandoned before I was born—a hurricane killed it, I fancy.
The giant mast that gives such a nautical air to the open space
fronting the sea was only designed to support a flag on the King's
birthday. Two black, speckled pigeons were bobbing on the
pavement outside the fishmonger's. There were lilacs out in that
garden next door to the blind umbrella-maker's. In so soft and
warm an air, by so genial a sea, at so placid an hour, it seemed a
world without end. People strolled on indolently with one hand
on their hips, and the old postman with blue spectacles on
rambled unhurriedly in and out of shops and gardens. Upon the
flat sea long slender rolls of water, smooth and soft as a bosom,
would arise and slowly glide, and then begin to hurry as if tiptoeing to the shore, but they soon tired and subsided and never
curled into rich waves.

The last arrival was this man Wilson, wearing a geranium in
his buttonhole and carrying an umbrella and a suitcase. He was
always noted for a sort of vile affability, and as he came into the
coach he grinned expansively at us all and bawled:

"Now then, naughty boys, whad yeh all bin up to, eh?"

Nobody answered, all were stricken with consternation, for
most of them were endeavouring by a gloss of unconcerned de-
tachment to impress their fellow travellers with the sense that
they were there by the purest of accidents and not at all as
culprits.

"Ha, ha," gurgled Wilson as he found a seat and sat down.
Pulling a green silk handkerchief from his breast, he smeared
his mouth with it.

"Naughty boys! Whad yeh gunna do about it, eh?"

The detective looked round and delivered what I think in the
circumstances was a correct and perfectly proper rebuke to him:

"If you please, we don't want any of that."

"Oh, all right," sneered Wilson, "pass me the password,
Reginald. That's all I want."

The audacity of the fellow! And the sergeant's name was not

Reginald at all. But I am bound to say he was quiet for the remainder of the journey.

The sergeant counted us, and as we were all aboard he gave the signal to start. But I felt my soul sicken at going where I was going with such men, sharing their wretched plight, and, remembering that they had all embraced her, breathing in their shame. For the shame, somehow, was not in her at all, it was in *them,* and they were going to deny her. It did not seem to matter a bit that she had been—well—had been—unusual; to have seen her and enjoyed her beauty was a thing to be grateful for. I looked to see who amongst them had honoured her memory with a sign of mourning; there were only three or four wearing black ties, and these I perceived were the unmarried ones—they had nothing to fear from wives! Nearly all were of the artisan class, a carpenter, a fishmonger, a dairyman, an engineer, a clerk, the driver Nixey himself; Wilson was an insurance agent, and of course you could tell the mayor by his wooden leg. And it seemed as if all these men, except the sergeant and me, had had a hand in this crime. Perhaps it was the burden of that reflection that kept them all furtively mute until we got to London and disembarked at the court.

I can never make out why justice is chambered in such uncouth shape, in courts of absurd proportions, gloomy, unsavoury, moth-eaten, the concrete distillation of inconvenience, and staffed by attendants who seemed to have served their apprenticeship at some low menagerie. Nothing is in accord with the honour of justice, there is only a purposeless harmony with the misery of the delinquent. For hour after hour we sat in two rows at the back of the court, listening to the accusation and the denial and the examination of witnesses who infuriated the judge because they did not "speak up." A young woman in the witness-box, rather a pretty creature as things go, kept pressing her handkerchief to her mouth; the poor wretch was sweating with emotion. And at last the judge, whose face had the complexion of sliced ham, addressed her in lofty tones:

"Have you by any chance got toothache, or a cough, or a sore throat, or what? No! Then put that handkerchief away," he bellowed. "If your tonsils are not in a state of decay I want to hear them *booming* at me, you understand."

The girl's replies to the next two or three questions were uttered in such a mere waif of sound that his lordship dashed his pen upon his desk and glared at her.

"Oh, this is intolerable! Shout at me, please, witness!"

The witness hung her head as if in tears.

"Will you do me the favour," he roared, "of shouting at me? Shout! Shout as if you were at one end of a telephone speaking to someone in the north of Scotland who couldn't hear you."

Then, quite audibly, the voice of the witness rose:

"I don't know anybody in Scotland, sir."

"That's right. Much better. Keep it up, now."

But a few moments later he was again admonishing her:

"Oh, if you would only *scream* at me!"

So the case went on, and although time was consumed in trivialities and by a clerk who wrote down reams of evidence very slowly in a fair copyright hand, the hours passed so speedily that the end of the day was almost upon us before counsel reached the vital question of the diary.

"Where is it?" asked the judge.

The book was handed up to him and he perused it for some minutes, while the barrister folded his hands behind him under his black gown and engaged in confident meditation with the ceiling.

"How many did you say?"

Counsel sank upon his brief with alacrity:

"Er—twenty-two, my lord."

"Have you any testimony to put forward in regard to this book? Were you proposing to call these men?"

"That is for you to decide, my lord. They are in attendance here"—and he waved a bland hand in our direction—"all of them."

And the judge said he didn't want to hear us; the judge actually said we were nothing to do with the case! He gave a sort of ruling—though I must say I do not understand the law—he gave a ruling (*a*) that the diary was *said* to have been written by the woman who was now dead, but there was no proof forthcoming that it had *indeed* been written by Mrs. Burden; in any case she could not be cross-examined about it. (*b*) The entries might or might not be true, but counsel was unable to substantiate them. (*c*) Even if counsel had been in a position to do so, the entries themselves had no bearing whatever on the charge he was trying. So he said he must rule it out. And he ruled it out! Yes, we were ruled out just as if nothing of this had the slightest relation to a person who had died.

We all waited until the court rose, but nothing more happened because the trial was not concluded; in fact, I was told, it lasted most of the following day. All my time and expense had been wasted, to say nothing of the trouble, for I was not given a chance of clearing myself of this odious suggestion. Things were left just as they were, just as, in fact, they are now, for I have never been able to make plain to anybody, public *or* private, that I was taken there under a misapprehension. No one would listen to me, no one paid me the slightest attention. I might have been a child complaining of a lost rattle. But I am a man not easily balked, I determined to say my say and uphold my character. I have a natural regard for honest conduct, and I resolved to speak to the judge if I could, or if not him, then somebody else in authority, and so when I saw the prosecuting barrister passing out of the hall I ran after him and told him everything. He stopped whistling and said:

"Well, what do you want *me* to do?"

"Can't you see, sir, I am entirely innocent of all this?"

"No one has said otherwise," he answered.

"But the police brought me here!"

"They will take you back again," he said.

"I am not the T. Wilson referred to in the diary," I told him.

"Still," he says, "you have not been charged with anything, have you?"

"No, but I come of a family that has always been esteemed," I explained. "My father was a master apothecary; he patented a cure for palsy and owned his own property. People do not like these millstones to be hung round their necks."

"Neither do I," says he; and off he struts, whistling again.

I shouted after him: "It is a *most despicable, most* despicable business." For though I am certainly not easily balked, and with me difficulties come only to be *over*come, when it comes to being baffled by sheer absence of comprehension it is not so simple; you are balked or baffled not by a difficulty so much as a complete void. And what do you do with a void? I could do nothing; I could do nothing then, I have been able to do no more to this very day.

Do you know, not a word was spoken about the case during the whole return journey. Would you believe it! We stopped at a public-house half-way home to wet the whistle, as they say; one of those places of bloated service where the piano plays for a penny, and there I tried to wrestle out the mistake with this T. Wilson, but he was impervious. I kept saying to him: "Look here, you know," but I've no care to make a public show, my wish is to live and die private. He stood in the midst of that saloon-crowd holding a glass of whisky up in his right hand; the bloom of the geranium in his coat had been shattered to its sprigs.

"Not my drink, boys, by rights. I guarantee to say I don't drink a bottle of whisky a year. You know what I mean, not of my own drinking. If I am out with the boys, good men, one of ourselves, that's different, but I guarantee to say I do not, *not* in a year, not a *bottle,* not on my own. I mean to say of course if I'm out with friendly men, that's another matter, that's ex gratia; we're all sports, or we hope we are, you know what I mean. But apart from that, taking it all round, year in and year out, I guarantee to say a bottle of whisky does not pass my sacred lips."

"Look here," I began again.

"And what's more," said he, "it won't neither."

"Listen here," I said. "I want you to explain to everybody here that I am not the T. Wilson mixed up in this."

But he soothered me with a lot of odious verbiage, neither quite denial nor quite admission; what we know we *know,* and what we *don't* know is done with, and all that. Ah, the cockroach! You'd have thought *he* was the mistaken, the misunderstood, and *I* the bad one! It was impossible to counter the vile and tricky affability of that man, and the others applauded him.

It was the same at the melancholy end of the journey. The harbour was in a drift of haze, foul with insipid moonlight, and the twenty-two parted as though there was something they had all conspired to suppress, to deny, to ignore, to cast out and bury deeply. But whatever they thought or said or did, shame is shame and you can't hide it in your pocket. Like Cain's mark it is on the brow, and I—my God!—I've got my unlucky share of it.

Nixey's Harlequin (1931)

JUDITH

I

THIS is the story of a great lady who did a great wrong to a mere man, a man so nearly insignificant and uncouth as to be almost unworthy of the honour. He was—may Heaven determine his rewards—a village schoolmaster, she the great dame of their part of the Suffolk county, and her name was Judith. Of high but untitled birth, she had been married young to a baronet of greater age, whose family distinction was as high, and whose life was devoted to the timely destruction of ferocious things in field and flood and air, by gun or hound or angle. Master of hounds and owner of choice coverts, he was a Nimrod; when birds were coming freely over, his loader had more than once seen—left, right; left, right—the four birds falling in the air at the one time. Often! Duffy Dallow tell you the same. Sir Gulistan Leeward was a tall thin man with a seared and apparently vexed face; though his chest was not broad, his lungs were powerful, for he spent a great part of each hunting day around the coppices yodelling a piercing tenor cry: "Barley! Barley! Barley! Barley!" in a voice whose demoniacal lustre must have added a mile a minute to the pace of absconding foxes. "Flew wind him in there!" he would cry with passion, "flew wind him, my beauties!"

and if some silly Cressid or Rampart ambled from the thicket to wag a tail at him, the thong of his whip would crack at their misguided behinds.

For ten years Judith shared in his sport and enjoyed his company "reverently, discreetly, advisedly and soberly, duly considering the causes for which Matrimony was ordained," but by the time she was thirty there was an ache in her bosom—she had no child. Sir Gulistan Leeward may have regretted this, but whether the omission was hers (as he had no doubt), or the lapse his (as Judith believed), he was not profoundly concerned, and being by this time fifty years old, he declared that his burning desire to shoot hippopotami—and possibly anthropophagi—in the swamps of Africa must be immediately realized or for ever relinquished, heaven itself being no place for hippo. Judith did not accompany him upon that happy business, and it was during his twelvemonth's absence that this little episode of the schoolmaster occurred.

Early one hunting morn, a crisp morn full of hoar-frost and slanting sunlight that laid shadows of trees half-way across fields, the bay she was riding had refused a hedge that everything else took easily, and she was left alone. Judith coaxed and scolded and clouted her timid gelding, but he was feckless—perhaps he was not properly awake. Blast the wretch! they had only just cast off. The lady realized soon that she was entirely alone, the hunt had swept on, there was not a sight or sound of it; she was inimitably, almost terribly, alone. So they went at it again, but the devil took the hedge so timorously that he only landed half-way across it and stuck there like a fool with his forelegs on one side and his hind legs on the other, while Judith had flown haplessly over his head into a lane. She dropped on some boggy turf, still clutching the bridle, but she had wrenched her stirrup foot. Very ruffled and shaken, she adjusted her hat and then sat huddled up, clutching her knee, although it was her foot that tortured her. The horse soon wriggled himself free from the hedge and stood before her, snuffing the rank herbage, until Judith terribly told him the unmentionable truth about his behaviour. He tossed his head, champed, and briskly flourished his cropped tail. The lady pulled herself up by the bridle and stood on her sound foot, but as soon as she began to hop towards the saddle, the beast sidled away from her.

"Ach, cantankerous offal!" she sighed.

Then, startled by her strange approaches, the bay wrenched itself away from her altogether and galloped down the lane.

A little way off it passed a cottage with a smoking chimney, standing back a little from the road, and Judith saw a man run out from the cottage and stare after the flying horse. Then the man turned and looked in Judith's direction. She had sunk down on the grass again. She waved her crop at him. The man stared doubtfully for a while, with one hand upon his hip, but when Judith gave a faint shout he ran down the road towards her. He was only half-dressed, in grey trousers and white shirt, he had no coat or waistcoat on, there was a brown belt round his waist. He did not run strenuously or excitedly, but with a long casual lope that brought him quickly.

"What's the matter?"

He was tall and lean, fair and shaven, with mild eyes and a blunt nose; perhaps thirty years old; his face had a country tan. Judith could not quite tell if he were a gentleman, but he was very friendly and sympathetic.

"My horse threw me, I've hurt my foot, I can only stand on one leg. . . ."

"Like a heron," he grinned.

Certainly no gentleman.

"You can't walk, then?" he asked.

"No. I want you to send for my car."

He stared down at her, she up at him. The man apparently did not know her!

"I'm Lady Leeward," she said, a shade too casually perhaps.

"Leeward? Oh—from the park! Dear—that's two miles away. You'd better come along to my cottage."

"But I can't walk, you see," explained the lady. "If you'll send to the park and tell them to bring the car—"

"I've no one to send."

"Haven't you a bicycle?"

"No, I think bicycles are such—"

"If you aren't gone too long I can stop here. Would it be putting you to—" Her head began to sag and her mind to grow hazy; "—if you aren't gone long."

"I think I'd better not leave you," interrupted the man, quickly bending. "Not like this. I can see you are sweating with pain. I must carry you, it's just along there, two minutes, you can see it. Let me help you to get up."

"I wish you wouldn't," she muttered pettishly, but somehow she was tilted upon to her sound foot. Then she swooned away and was remotely aware that he was carrying her huddled across his shoulders, like a sick sheep, for hours and hours. When she revived she could hear a loud steady noise—boom, boom, boom— and she was lying on a couch in his cottage. The man was sitting beside her, his left arm was around her, her head was against his breast, and she was sipping from a cup of water in his right hand. She did not want to move, she was aware of a fine log fire on the open hearth, and a kettle boiling. There was her hunting hat lying upside down under the table. Boom, boom, boom. The door was open, she could see the sunlight blazing on the asters in the garden. It was blazing, too, diagonally across the white cloth on the table, on the teapot and mug and jug and loaf and plate of red apples. Such yellow butter, too! Boom, boom . . . why, yes, that was his heart beating.

"How did I get here?" she murmured, and stirred; she took the cup from him.

"Pulling round now?" asked the man.

"How did I get here?"

He told her he had carried her.

She sipped the water, then gave him the cup again. He reached down and put it on the floor beside him.

"A weight," sighed Judith.

"Pooh! a feather," he laughed. "But it was lucky you had stood up. You fainted, you know, and I had to carry you like—like a sack of corn."

She sat up, away from him now. She had beautiful hair, a dark gold, and there was a perfume in it. Her hat lay under the table.

"Yes," the man nodded briskly, "I was the lost shepherd—no, I was the shepherd and you the lost lamb, on my shoulders. Really! But there was nobody passing. If your foot is swelling,

I'd better take your riding-boot off at once, or it may be difficult."

"I can do it." Judith took off her gloves, still with a good deal of languor, but tugging at the boot made her giddy and he had to kneel down and assist her. Then he drew off her stocking and looked at the swollen ankle.

"I've got some liniment, what about that?" he suggested.

"My—car—" suggested she.

"Ah, yes." But he got up from his knees, went to a shelf, and brought a bottle of oil. The man hovered over the naked foot and rubbed oil upon the swelling. His fingers were long and thin, their touch was soothing. Occasionally he hurt her, but she was stoical and leaned back on the couch watching his bent head. The fair hair was thick and tousled, his features brown and pleasant, a nice creature.

"It feels much better now," said Judith. "Do you live here? But of course you do."

"Yes," said he.

"Always?"

"Always."

"Alone?"

"Alone."

He was laconic. Judith sighed. "I wonder where my beast of a horse is?"

"Oh, he's galloped right out of the story," said the man. After a moment or two he continued: "Yes, alone. It is my habit to do so, it suits me."

Judith meditated. "Well, you have friends to visit you. It would be lonely otherwise."

"I have no friends." He gave the foot its final massage.

"Is that because you don't want them?" Judith was staring interestedly at her foot. "I'm sure that must be the reason."

He was picking up the cork and replacing it in the liniment bottle.

"Oh no, no," he said. "I do, I do."

Then he glanced at the clock on the shelf, it was nearly nine o'clock.

"I must go now, I am the schoolmaster," he explained, rising to his feet. "Directly I get to school I'll send a boy over to the park and your car ought to be here in half an hour. You'll be quite all right here until then."

"I am very much obliged to you," said Lady Leeward.

He put on a coat and a hat, and took a stick from the corner. "Shall I leave the door open?" He paused.

"Please," the lady answered.

"You might shut it when you go," he added.

"I will, yes," Judith nodded brightly.

"Good-bye. You'll be all right. Half an hour."

"Thank you so very much," said Judith.

She lay on the couch for a while, then she sat up. There were no pictures on the walls, but there was a shelf of books close at hand. Astronomy he appeared to like, and moths. A lot of books about philosophy and history, and, yes, Socialism—dozens. Judith drew on her stockings. There was a horrid bulge at the ankle but it was much easier now. And the horse had galloped out of the story! No friends: *My mind to me a kingdom is.* What story? The lost lamb—over nine stone, too! Must be strong, never turned a hair.

The car came with her maid and a footman, they had come instantly without hats or coats. Her ladyship explained her accident and then with their aid limped out to the car. The maid took the riding-boot, the footman the hat from under the table.

"Wait a minute," cried Lady Leeward. "There's a bottle of liniment on the table. Just fetch it, Maude, will you?"

When the liniment was safely stored the car turned and took them all away.

Had they telephoned for a doctor?

"No, my lady."

"Why not!" What fools servants were! "Well, it doesn't matter, don't." A hundred of them were not worth one sensible friend; they were willing but stupid, it was all a question of love. Oh dear, I did not even ask his name.

No, Maude did not know his name, but the footman said the schoolmaster's name was Jones. Judith sighed. How awful! It must be terrible for him. It would be impossible, utterly impossible to like a person with the name of Jones. Bones, groans, moans.

"Jones," she echoed.

"Yes, m'lady." The footman enlarged: "Christopher Jones."

"Oh," the lady mused, "Christopher. Yes." The car entered the lodge gates and soon drew up at the Hall. Oh, there was a thing she had forgotten! And the chauffeur was sent flying back to close the door of Mr. Jones's cottage.

II

A few days later a letter was posted and delivered.

Old Hall, Leeward Park
Thursday, Nov. 1

Lady Leeward presents her compliments to Mr. Jones and desires to thank him for his recent great kindness. Her foot is almost well, but the injury still prevents her calling to thank Mr. Jones personally. If Mr. Jones could find it convenient to take tea with her on Saturday afternoon Lady Leeward would esteem it a very great pleasure.

The reply was as follows:

Rose Cottage, Frogmoor Lane

Mr. Jones begs to acknowledge Lady Leeward's letter of the 1st, but regrets he is unable to accept her kind invitation. Mr. Jones is glad to hear of Lady Leeward's recovery from her mishap.

"Heavens above!" gasped Judith. And there the matter might very well have rested. But Fate himself would have a meagre business if human nature did not probe and prove him. The pitcher may go once too often to the well, but until that date there are no other such delightful journeys. What is a pitcher for —if not to fill? Or a well—but for the use we may make of what lies in the bottom of it?

Old Hall, Leeward Park
Nov. 6

Dear Mr. Jones,

I am sorry that I chose an unsuitable date. I am the most unlucky person in the world. May I try again? Will you come

*over at any time convenient to yourself? I should be so
pleased.*

Yours sincerely,

Judith Leeward

The answer ran:

Dear Lady Leeward,
    *It is very kind of you, but I feel sure that there are (if I could
only think of them!) many reasons why I am unable to come to
tea at Old Hall. Please excuse me. Good luck to your foot.*

Sincerely,

Christopher Jones

"What the—the deuce does that mean! Many reasons—unable
—luck to your foot. Why foot! It's an extraordinary Jonesy letter, complete Jones—bones, moans, groans—Christopher, friendless man. Oh well, thank you, Jones, thank you very much."

So the next evening Lady Leeward drove herself over in the
small car to Rose Cottage, Frogmoor Lane. It was some distance
away from the village; why did the man poke himself away in
such an absurd place, all by itself? It was as much as she could
do to find it in the dark. She stopped the engine at his gate and
hooted. There was a light from the window, but nobody answered
her call. She had to get out of the car and walk up the black path,
slipping off her gloves as she did it, and knock the door smartly
with her knuckles.

"Come in," his voice cried, and she opened the door. There was
a splendid fire on the hearth, a green silk shade on the lamp, it
was cosy. And he—he was sewing! Sewing a piece of yellow
stuff. With cotton and a needle.

"Do excuse me bursting in on you like this," began Lady Leeward, half in and half out of the doorway.

He quickly stood up, dropped the sewing on the chair behind
him, and went towards her with a smiling "Good evening."
She found herself shaking hands with him as he said: "Come in"
again.

"No no, I only came to—"

"There's a draught," he said, glancing at his lamp flickering on
the table. And so Lady Leeward walked in.

"What am I doing with this thimble?" she asked brightly. "I found it in my hand." She set a thimble on the table.

"It slipped off my finger," he explained, shutting the door. "Won't you sit down?"

"And it slipped into my hand!" She laughed again. "How funny!"

"Well, you write with a pen, you know, instead of your finger —won't you sit down?—and you sew with a thimble for the same reason."

"But it's funny to see a man sewing at all!"

"I don't do it often," he replied, "but I believe I follow all the rules. I can hemstitch, herring-bone, and make a seam." He picked up the yellow stuff and showed her what he had been doing.

"It's quite good," said Lady Leeward. "What is this you are making—curtains!"

"For my window," he added.

Said the lady, bending over the sewing: "You must let me give you some."

"Oh no, no, no." So decidedly, she might have been offering him some infectious fabric. "Thank you, no, I prefer these home-made things."

"But I mean I will make them for you myself."

"Thank you," he smiled, "but these will be all I want. Yes, thank you."

The lady looked astoundingly handsome, though exceedingly berobed in a heavy grey corduroy cloak with dark fur at the neck and wrists. A perfume seemed to float from her copper-coloured hair, and her fine features had a rosy glow. She was not wearing a hat.

"Ah, yes." With a mock sigh she shrugged her shoulders. "You are a self-sufficient man. That's why you have no friends."

"No friends!"

"You told me you had none."

"Oh, that was just bunkum." He moved a chair for her to use, as she still stood, rich and gracious, in the low-ceilinged room. She seemed to tower in and pervade his home.

"No, thank you," said Lady Leeward. "I've only just run over

to bring you this. I stole all your liniment, it was so good, and
I've brought you another bottle. Thank you, so much."

"Oh," he murmured, with a deprecating gesture.

"My foot is quite well now—"

"Good," he said.

"—and that is entirely due to your treatment. I did not even
call our doctor in."

"Risky, wasn't it?" suggested the schoolmaster.

"Was it? Well, I didn't want to," she said, "I was in your
good hands, and the lost lamb is very grateful to you." She moved
to the door. "Good evening," she said, smiling and very handsome. He held her proffered hand for a moment and then unlatched the door for her. The asters down the pathway glared
lividly in the sudden light thrown upon them; her heavy cloak
brushed them as she walked by. Outside his gate she stopped and
glanced up and down the road, then at the sky. Miles away, a
cloud hanging low over a lighted town shone like a cushion of
luminous wool. He had followed her quietly down the path. It
was a cold clear night, the stars rippled in the sky like diamonds
on a bed of dark velvet. A wind threshed gently in the trees, and
dry leaves ticked along the road, running across the path of the
headlights like little brisk tumbling gnomes. Lady Leeward
squeezed herself into the little car and the schoolmaster fastened
the door for her. Then she leaned towards him from under the
hood, and it seemed as if all her imperious beauty had become
tender in that close secrecy of the dark vehicle. He heard her
whisper: "Come for a ride."

Instantly he said: "Yes," ran back to the cottage, put on an
overcoat, turned down the lamplight, pulled to the door, and so
back to her and away.

He could not tell whether they rode for an hour or for five
minutes. They were fleeing from darkness, with a light under
their feet—and they talked of the price and condition of hay.
They discoursed of hay, sanfoin, clover, and old meadow, but
they never chopped it into chaff. They were too absorbed for
that. Of the price of hay, this year's, last year's, next year's hay,
they speculated and prophesied; the time to mow it, and the way
to make it. They found themselves hopelessly enmeshed, buried

and swaddled in a great cock of hay. Like the ass-headed weaver they had a great desire, it seemed, to a bottle of it. So at last the lady stopped the car by the roadside, and turning to the man, she said:

"Don't you think Mahomet might come to the mountain now?"

Mahomet prevaricated: "What do you mean?"

"I mean you did me a great kindness. I want to show that I'm not ungrateful."

"It isn't worth," he wavered, "not worth a cup of tea."

"No? Not to you. But I have my own sense of it."

He was silent, she was silent. Both stared ahead along the road where the farther trees seemed to cringe from their light.

"Are you hungry?"

He was, yes, a little bit hungry; rushing through the air gave you an appetite.

"Good," she cried. "So am I. Now I'll take you to the Hall and we'll have a meal straight away."

"My—excuse—no, no," he ejaculated, stirring as if about to leap out of the car.

"Why not?"

He did not answer.

"Do come."

"You see," he said, fumbling for words, "I'm not used to such things. You must let me off. I'm not dressed. I'm plebeian. You must excuse me. Some other time. I'm not used to such things."

"What things!" she cried. "There's nobody to meet, not a single visitor." She brushed a strand of hair back from her cheek. "I'll get them to scrape up a meal for just you and me. We'll have something up on a tray, in my own room. Yes, yes, that's quite settled."

She edged in the clutch, and the car ran on again, turned into the great park at the lodge gates, and drew up at Lady Leeward's home. A shaft of light gleamed from the hall. A footman ran down the steps and stood by the car while they alighted.

"How bright the stars are!" Lady Leeward said. Jones did not answer, although he too looked up into the sky. The footman looked up into the sky and smiled. He followed them up into the huge hall that seemed all grey and white tiles, barometers, long clocks, shining brass and mahogany. The bewildered schoolmaster was bereft of his coat and hat by the footman, and then Lady Leeward ushered him along to the library, a room furnished in dark heavy sumptuousness, leather and black oak, with sere busts on the tops of the bookcases, glasses of stuffed fish hanging in recesses, and family portraits huge and gloomy. A bright fire was there.

"What will you drink?" she asked, opening a cupboard where there were decanters.

"I—no, thank you."

"A cigarette?" There was a silver box.

"No, thank you."

"There are a few books." She nodded towards the cases as she lit a cigarette for herself. "Can you amuse yourself with them for ten minutes—there are lots of astronomy and history—until supper is ready? I don't know about philosophy, but I'm sure there's no Socialism."

"Yes, I will—see what I can see," he grinned.

"I must go and change," said Lady Leeward. "Excuse me for ten minutes."

The schoolmaster sat down and for a while pored mindlessly over an old volume of *Punch*. There was not a sound to be heard anywhere save the faint ticking of a china clock in a glass cover. He wondered if he might get up and steal away. The box of cigarettes was still open on the table beside him. He began to count them, but there were too many. His watch was three minutes ahead of that clock. He leaned forward and sat holding his head in his hands.

"Supper is ready, sir." The footman stood in the doorway. Jones got up and followed him along a corridor, with the incomparable and tragic timidity of a nervous cricketer walking out from the pavilion to take his innings. In the midst of that green desert lurk eleven white sardonic harpies, and he walks as a man into the trap of death, one against many, but he dare not hurry and he may not lag.

At the end of another corridor across the hall he was shown into a room furnished with a heavy but bright sumptuousness. It was oblong, with huge white chimneypiece, pink silk lights, a smallish table laid with silver dishes, and wine. And Lady Leeward was standing by the fire dressed in a gown of black silk, pale stockings, black shoes with high red heels. He hovered vaguely in the room. The footman pulled out a chair at the table, and the lady came half-way across the room.

"Well," she asked, "did you find any disgraceful books?"

"I looked at *Punch,*" he replied, sitting down as she indicated.

"I like *Punch,*" remarked his hostess.

"Enthralling," the schoolmaster exclaimed.

There was a plate of cold pheasant and tongue before him. The servant helped him to salad.

"Claret, sir?" murmured the footman, and Jones nodded.

After putting another log of wood on the fire the footman went away, and the schoolmaster by constant sipping drank up his glass of claret.

"I am so glad you came."

"I did not come," he ventured, "I was abducted."

"Oh no, you were not!" She pushed the wine towards him and he refilled his glass. "Besides, what was I to do! You don't mind now?"

He laughed. "No, I am quite quite happy."

"Glad I am not so terrifying, after all."

He had begun to look about the room, at the couch of green velvet, the little black piano, the water-colours on the wall. But his glance came back to her and her sweetly innocent eyes. The red-gold hair that slightly curled was bunched in a thick casual roll on her neck. The black dress gave a lustre to the pale moulding of her shoulders and the graceful arms. There were a few jewels on her fingers, and from each ear hung a tiny chain of gold ending in a golden hollow ball; he could hear the tinkle of the pellets in them when she sharply moved her head.

"It was not you, no, no," he began to explain, "it was myself, my plebeian self. I never go out anywhere. I do not even know how to address you."

Lady Leeward fumbled with her bread; it seemed to amuse her.

"Formally?" she asked, then looking at him keenly with her marvellous eyes. "But what is it you want to say?"

"I mean your title, yes, and that sort of thing," he added, lamely.

She was really amused. "Oh, but my dear man! The servants say "M' lady." My friends call me what they like." She pushed her empty wineglass towards him. "I've a dozen nicknames— give me a new one. Have some trifle?"

"Please," said he. He filled her glass and his own and took the plate of trifle she handed him.

"Well?" She took up her dessert-spoon. "What is my name to be?" Her elbows rested on the table, she was smoothing the spoon with her finger and thumb. "Do you know, I don't care very much for your name."

The schoolmaster swallowed a portion of his trifle and laid the spoon carefully back on his plate.

"Which one?" he inquired.

Lady Leeward said: "Jones."

"That is not really my name," the schoolmaster replied.

She looked at him inquiringly: "Not!" And then eagerly: "You are going to tell me you are a prince in disguise! I guessed it!"

"Ha, ha, no. My real name is a hideous one. So I changed it many years ago."

"But 'Jones!' Why did you change to Jones? It's so—so—I mean it's like jumping out of the frying-pan into the stove."

And Mr. Jones mused: "Humph, perhaps so. But it was a question of good taste, I did not want to make spurious capital out of that opportunity. I chose the commonest name I could think of."

"What *is* your dreadful name?"

"My name?" He paused to drink again, then with burlesque solemnity he said: "My name is Death."

Her vivacity was a little quenched. "Really?" She peered earnestly at him, spinning the stem of her glass between finger and thumb, and he bowed assent. "How lugubrious! Yes, you were right to change it—for anything."

They had finished with the trifle and were bedevilling the

oranges and nuts. The perfume she exhaled came, he thought, from her splendid hair—may-blossom after warm showers.

"My maiden name was Catterick."

"Scotch?" he inquired.

"No. Suffolk," said the lady.

"Well," he was picking a stubborn nut from its shell. "I can't call you that."

"No." She was parting an orange in her plate; her gaze was concentrated upon that object.

"I can't stand calling you Lady Leeward. I hate titles."

"Socialist! But yes, they are a great bore. Don't you like my Christian name?"

"No."

"Why not?" asked Judith, still intent upon her orange.

"She cut off the head of her lover."

Lady Leeward stared up uncomprehendingly for some moments. "Oh—you mean that Judith—in the Bible—and that Holofernes man. Ah, I promise not to do that."

In the tingling silence that followed she began to blush, and to cover her confusion she raised her glass towards him.

"Here's to you—Christopher!"

He raised his until it clinked with hers, and he murmured: "To you, Judy." She sought his hand across the table.

And then the footman arrived with the coffee, and a maid to clear the table.

Coffee was served to them on the green velvet couch, and while the servants were clearing the table the lady chatted to Mr. Jones of those interesting things in her house which she desired to show him on some other occasion. It was an old house, an admiral had built it after the naval victory at La Hogue. William and Mary's reign. Sixteen ninety something. "You like old furniture?"

"No," said the schoolmaster. The servants withdrew so quietly that he did not perceive their going.

"Are there any legends about the place?" he asked.

"No, there are none that I know of."

"Or ghosts?"

"No. No legends or ghosts. The Leewards have always, as they say, feared God and honoured the King. Always. Doing nothing magnificent and no wrong thing."

Jones put his coffee cup carefully aside and said:

"Your neighbours, you know, do just the opposite." He leaned back into a corner of the couch, crossed his legs, and clasped his hands across one high knee. A sort of wry grin appeared upon his face. Lady Leeward had already noticed that his features seldom presented anything so soft, so tender, as a smile. Yes, he was a satirical creature, downright and indubitable; and there was a lack of breeding even in the expression of his sympathies, they did not flow in a gentle crystal spring, but in a fountain of brine. And yet. . . . When she asked him who, precisely, he meant by her neighbours, he retorted:

"The country folk, the poor, Hodge, the cowman, the ploughman. They do everything magnificently, but they do nothing right—the poor preposterous poor!"

Lady Leeward took a cigarette, the guest refused one. "Oh, the villagers! You are unjust to them, aren't you?" She waited for Jones to offer her a light, but he did not notice this. "What have they done wrong? On the whole I find them charming, yes, very industrious. Oh no, oh no. What do you find wrong about my neighbours?"

Jones said: "They've kept the cuckoo in their nest."

She struck a match and puffed meditatively at the cigarette. "Cuckoo!" It puzzled her; there were one or two cases of infidelity in the village, it was true, but . . . "What on earth do you mean?"

"I mean that the village pipits have maintained and cherished the Leeward cuckoo for—so you tell me—over two hundred years."

She blew out a long puff of smoke. "Oh, I get your meaning. Humph, you *are* a Socialist! I'm the wicked cuckoo, then. That is not very complimentary to me."

"Neither is it," he said grimly, "complimentary to them."

"And you think it is all wrong?"

"Both grand and wrong," said Jones.

"Nature," continued Lady Leeward, "created the real cuckoos, that's a natural precedent."

"Ah," he sighed, "you're still in a state of nature rather than of grace."

"It is no bad thing if you are born to be a Leeward. I prefer it. One might have been a Jones—or a Brown or Robinson. There had to be a cuckoo."

"Yes, that's the grandeur of it," murmured he.

"You see," she went on eagerly, "you can't all be leaders, some must be servants in a world like ours. And as the Bible says, *They also serve who only stand and wait.*"

"Bible! Bah! They always wait who only stand and serve!"

"You're an atheist, too, then?"

"No, I'm not," the schoolmaster's tone was gruff. "It isn't in the Bible, it's Milton."

"I must own that I prefer a gentleman to a peasant. In the long run you'll find he is the better. Breeding counts. The important thing in life is to be well-bred."

"Ah! Take care of the parents and the offspring will pay for it-self."

Nothing could be more charming than her patience. "These village people are nice things to have in a landscape, or to read about in books, but what is there inside them? They have mean souls, mean minds, they are musty in body and brain. They lie and shuffle, steal, scandalize, flatter, and deceive. And that is because their souls are mean."

"Or how else," he blandly inquired, "could you have deceived them for so long? Whether the pipit was made for the cuckoo, or the cuckoo for the pipit, cuckoos there are and they thrive on the blood of the poor. Hasn't the cuckoo a mean soul? Does it not live meanly?"

"Do you really think that's the sort of person I am?" Her voice was soft, velvety.

He replied, with the nearest thing to a smile that he ever achieved: "I assure you I am speaking quite impersonally."

Judith shook her head distrustfully. "No, you are not. But what do you take us for? We have the best of things because we are the better people. We have the advantage because we have developed the finer type; it's like the flower of a tree, what comes to the top after centuries, the seed of culture, courage, integrity, all the higher things the race is capable of. I don't mean that we alone possess them, but that we have promoted and conserved them. And that would only be possible in a leisured class, the possibility of it even would be gone without us. . . ."

He intervened: "In one word you mean the gentry are a national profit?"

She hesitated. "I don't like that one word, but in general we haven't mean souls, we can be trusted, we are staunch, our word is a pledge to death. Esprit de corps, and so on. But I suppose you would deny that?"

He would: "To add my weak word to the verdict of history, justice, and common sense," he said, "would be superfluous."

Was he angry? She could not tell. She felt angry, but she was sure it was not with him. Yet you could scarcely be angry with yourself.

"Oh, stop this, please!" she suddenly cried. "Why, what are we arguing about? Why have we drifted into such a discussion? It's snobbish of me."

Judith went over to the little black piano and let her fingers ripple over the keys. Without turning round she called to him:

"I did not mean one word of what I said about them."

As he made no answer she played a pretty phrase or two over and over again, then stopped and facing him said:

"Neither did you."

Ah, but he did! And there was no doubt that he meant it. Again primping on the piano, she exclaimed:

"I wish you did not think such things, you are wrong about us, you know. I wonder when I shall see you again. You look on me as 'the enemy,' I suppose. I am going away soon."

At last he stood at her side, saying he must go, yes, really he must go.

"Bannerman shall take you in the car," said Lady Leeward.

"No, no," protested Christopher Jones. He preferred to walk, much, yes, truly.

Lady Leeward then put on a cloak of yellow velvet trimmed

with white fur and went along to the hall with the schoolmaster. He put on his coat and then the lady said she would walk with him to the lodge gates for a breath of air if the night were fine. The night was fine. The lodge gates were a quarter of a mile away, and the road dark though the sky was sparkling. It lay between trees and he walked slowly, warily, as if at any moment he might put his foot through the crust of the earth into the next world. The lady slipped her arm into the schoolmaster's and immediately they began to hurry. They walked quickly, step to step.

"Why are you going so fast?" whispered Judith.

Then they stopped, quite still, and without a word the schoolmaster pulled her quickly to him with both his arms.

"Oh, be careful, Jones! Chris, be careful," murmured the lady, returning his kisses. "Why—you have gone mad, anyone could see me in this cloak."

The madman only pressed her lips more fondly, with little moans of tenderness.

"Listen," she breathlessly gasped. "I'll write to you. Will you write to me? Chris, Chris! I must go. Oh, be careful, I must. Good-bye, I will write."

She swung out of his arms and began to walk steadily back to the Hall, while he stood watching her, mumbling: "Lovely she is. I am a boor, she is a queen."

For ten days he hungered, in fevers of anticipation, for that something which hung in the air between them. As to what it was, Jones would not permit himself to gaze too deeply: was it a flame too bright for his eyes, or a mere mist of ecstasy? Jones only knew that his mind and emotions, thought, desire, and fear were charged with an image of her splendour, her friendliness and frankness. Of course she had been right to defend her class from his trite gibes, she herself was the living proof against him. No pharisee, no, she was no pharisee, though she was surely "not as these others are." The poor *were* mean, and the high-born *were* fine, though the claim of the under-class was age-old and unconfutable. But she did not write to him, why did she not write to him? And he could not see her again, she was beyond his reach; he did not even hear of her, she was beyond his range. Yes, and beyond him in everything—beauty, position, pride, and beyond him—oh, unalterably!—beyond him in love. How had it come about that he, a son of the people—yes, that was his own grandiloquent appellation—should have leaned to take one step in an intrigue, a dishonourable intrigue, with one of the class he had been born to despise? As the days slunk by, his fervour, unabated, swerved to meet his own cynical challenge; she had been only too right about social quality and tone, it was he who had been the offensive snob, he had begun it, he had scoffed at the "honour" of her class and he had paraded the "honour" of his own. And then he had tempted her! What a lesson! You could not trust a boor with an agreeable lady. Judith had dropped him like a hot coal. And how that coal still flamed! *My name is Death!* Bah, you fine phrasing fellow, now you have caught a tartar. What a lesson, oh, what a lesson!

And then there came a letter. From abroad. From the south of France. She did not explain that annihilating transit, but she called him her dear Chris. He was, she wrote, so wise, so experienced, so sympathetic about the poor, it had moved her very deeply, and she longed to know more, and much more about himself. He was to tell her all about himself. And she signed: *Yours, Judy.*

In his quick reply he threw serenity to the dogs, gave pride, gave scruple, the discard—his bubbling, baffled blood told him he was lost—he wanted passionately to know why she had gone, and when she was coming back.

Lady Leeward moved serenely eastwards in the south of France, and at Christmas she had gone into Switzerland for the winter sports. She was travelling with friends. Many letters passed between them; hers were tender, his were ardent. It was unwise, she wrote, for him to keep her letters. She entreated him to burn hers as soon as read, just as she was doing. He obeyed, with the feeling of a devout man forced to commit a violent sacrilege. Then she went on to Italy, and the despairing schoolmaster feared that she would not come back again until Sir Gulistan was home from his hunting in Africa. But he did not ask her about that; he dared not ask himself why he feared Sir Gulistan's return. February went, March went, April came. At last she was coming home! By then the tree-tops in the lane were just heaps of waving buds, petulant when the skies were grey or white, but when the sun shone and the breezes blew them in that bold cerulean air they were angelic, unearthly; the twirl of the universe was in their movement. And they would ripen, when she came, as if their whole body was one enchanting fruit. The schoolmaster set his small house in order, day by day, with marvellous care. When he laid his white sheets on the grass to air they had an immensity that surprised him. And when May was near, Judith came home once more to the Hall in the park.

III

The western bounds of Leeward Park were determined by a wide dense wood, and from the wood stretched a heathery moor wherein lay many dells of greensward and dens of furze. In the middle of the moor, at a distance of nearly a mile from Old Hall rose a small grassy hill crowned with a dozen dark pines. Whatever its geological significance might have been, Black Knoll had no known historical or legendary affiliations; its contour was comely, its situation singular, and its loneliness endowed it with charm or the reverse according to the mood of the passer-by. It was this remote spot that Judith indicated for their place of meeting, enjoining the utmost secrecy and caution upon the schoolmaster. He was to be there at eight o'clock, there would be a moon, and she would come to him by the pathway through Leeward Wood that led from the park to the moor. On the appointed evening he stole there by uncustomary paths, avoiding the village. The evening air was so mild that it quivered when the evening bells of St. Nicholas shook their melancholy note into it, and a long shroud of white fume from the allotment fires dispersed laterally without movement, meditating. After a while the schoolmaster came to a road leading from the village. A young bedraggled woman was sitting on a bank there as if waiting for someone. At Jones's approach she got up and walked a few yards behind him.

"Mister!" she whined, "will you give me something for a night's lodging?"

He stopped and gave her a shilling. Then they walked on together for a few moments in the dusk until someone advanced along the road towards them. The woman stopped and turned fearfully. "Christ, is that Jimmy?" she whispered. The school-master looked ahead. "That's the shoemaker," said he. "Oh," sighed the woman, relieved, "is it?" Jones laughed and the woman laughed and they moved on again.

"Good night, George," said Jones in reply to the passing shoe-maker, and the beggar-woman commented:

"Shoemaker! Well, it don't much matter what it is, to get a living is all a worry."

"Ah," agreed the schoolmaster. "But I turn off here, good night."

"God bless you," said the woman, and he left her in the road and took a footpath beside a hedge. He did not hear her footsteps resume their march along the road; perhaps she was watching him, but he could not tell if this was so because of a bend in the hedge path. By and by he came to another road, and beyond it Leeward Great Wood began, shaped in a half-circle curling round the park. Jones did not enter the wood, but advanced along its outside contour until he came to the moor, and there, suddenly closer, loomed Black Knoll. He climbed its easy slope and reached the pines, and there he waited. The moon was high aloft in the windless air. Passionate moon! The man waited and the lady came wrapped in a dark cloak.

Oh, for weeks this promised assignation had been their fiery secret, and now the encounter was cool—How d'ye do?—almost polite, but once they moved into the shadow of the grove they seemed to leap and melt into a wordless unity, a thing of lips but no tongue. But what is this? He swung her back to the light again to behold her beautiful hair cropped in a new foreign fashion. At the edge of the trees they sat side by side on a thick mat of pine needles, conversing about her travels, but in a little while, when they had fallen to whispering, they lay down to-gether. Her arms stole round his neck, and his hands went rudely, caressingly, about her until Judy threw off her cloak and they took the ultimate embrace.

At a later moment the lady sat up and uttered a sound of dis-may. "Somebody has been watching us!" A dark figure was running from the shadows of Leeward Wood towards them.

Twice it stopped and looked, its face a pallid spot before the moonlight, and then ran stumbling on, skirting the knoll until it passed out of their sight, lost among the bushes.

"Who is it?" asked the startled Judith.

"He saw nothing," her lover assured her, "he was too far away. He was unaware of us, a poacher, I fancy. Something in the wood alarmed him, perhaps. He could not see us."

"I hope not; it must never be known, Chris. Let us go now."

Jones lifted her to her feet with tender joy, she put on her cloak again, and they descended the hill and crossed over the moor to Leeward Wood. He was to go with her as far as the wall on the other side. They entered the dark glades, away from that passionate moonlight, and walked in the paths steadily, never speaking, but only clasping each other. In a quarter of an hour they came to the wall and the private door into the park. Judith took a key from a pocket in her cloak and unlocked the door, and the holy radiance of the moon burst on them again. There lay the smooth choice park with its flint wall stretching right and left of them and trees curving benignantly over it, and across the grass, a quarter of a mile away, was her home, the great Hall. There were lights shining in a few of the windows in the wing that was in shadow.

"I do not want to go there," Judith murmured. "I could stay here for ever with you," and she pulled him back behind the dark secrecy of the wall and hung silently against his breast.

"You will never speak of this, dear Chris, not to a living soul. You'll swear it."

"How could you imagine it of me!" he asked reproachfully.

"I know, I know; but men do love to boast of their conquests."

"Not I."

"I trust you, beloved. Think of my reputation. Are you—aren't you hungry?"

He laughingly reminded her that she had asked him the same question on their first night together in the car. But he had eaten little today.

"Nor I. I was too excited. I knew," she whispered, "I knew we were going to love." She peeped into the park again. "It isn't far. Wait. Will you wait? I will go and fetch something to eat and

we will have a moonlight picnic, eh? You must be starved, poor
dear. What is the time?"

It was ten o'clock.

"Keep the door shut while I am gone," said she, "and wait only
a tiny time."

She stepped boldly and quickly across the park. Carefully
Jones closed the door and waited behind it in the shadow thrown
by the wall, listening to little scratching movements in the under-
growth. The moonlight glared above the wall and there was a
sort of terror in the unshaking shadows of some of those skeleton
trees; that radiance from aloft lay upon their trunks like scrofula.
But there was a wild cherry tree blooming alone there; the moon-
beams caressed its bosomed whiteness with a lustre infinitely
precious and pure. To the waiting anxious lover it seemed that
his lady had gone out of this fantasy of time and the miracle of
space; it was not possible that she would return, but he would
wait and wait, under the wild white cherry tree. It had the gleam
of her breasts and her smooth tremulous limbs. And though all
her beauty and richness had been crumpled in passionate dis-
array, she had been strangely triumphant. How nonchalant that
witnessing moon!

Across the park she came flitting back to him. Under her cloak
Judith had brought a bag with slices of plum cake.

"Look!" she whispered gaily; there was a bottle.

"What is it?" he asked.

"Hock," said she breathlessly. "Isn't it a lark! I couldn't get
anything else without making a fuss. We'll go just inside the
park, it's lighter, and we can sit under a yew tree; the grass is
dry. Chris, break the neck off the bottle in here, quietly, and then
come over to the yew tree."

Judith darted off into the park. "And, Chris, shut the door after
you," she cautiously called. Having done these things, he joined
her under the tree and they quaffed the wine from her collapsible
drinking-cup. For an hour they lay and lingered there, and before
parting, there had been a repetition of that flaring passion of the
pine knoll.

"Chris, have I given myself too easily—will you despise me?"

Her melting tenderness exalted him. "Judy, Judy!"

"Oh, take care!"

"I'll be mum as the grave."

"My dear secret lover!"

Jones drew off her shoe and stocking and kissed the foot he had once comforted.

"Take," she whispered at last, "that empty bottle with you and heave it somewhere into the wood; mustn't leave it here. And, Chris, remember: be discreet, I am far too fond of you."

As she stole away from him he stood in the shadow of the tree, with the bottle clutched in his hands, watching her all the way until she was lost in the gloomy angle of the Hall. What was the curious fear in his heart as he turned away? That this was the end of it, that she would never, never come again, and he was lost, lost, lost for evermore! By the time he had got safely into the wood again he was happy, and in his exhilaration he flung the bottle with all his might among the trees. Stupid ass! He flung it carelessly and gashed the palm of his hand on its splintered neck. The blood streamed. Wrapping his handkerchief against his palm, he hurried on. There was no pain, nothing could pain him now, with all that fostering bliss in the heaven of a world. Sometimes he broke into a run, so exhilarated was he. When he reached home it was midnight and, going at once to bed, he fell into a dreamless sleep.

Three days later he was arrested for murder.

IV

In Leeward Great Wood the body of an unknown woman of the tramping class had been found; she had been violated and then murdered by a cruel blow from a stake on the back of her skull. It would be tedious to follow in detail the process by which suspicion fell upon the schoolmaster, but it will be seen that he was himself largely to blame for the position he was in when the local court committed him. Briefly, the woman was the beggar woman to whom he had given a shilling, and she was killed on the night he and Judith had met on Black Knoll. Absolutely nothing was known of the woman; it was as if she had just sauntered into the world of Christopher Jones for a few moments and blasted it. The salient pieces of incriminating evidence were these. A shoemaker, as we know, had seen Jones walking with the woman on the fatal evening. Jones explained that matter. He had gone out for a stroll and the woman, a complete stranger, had accosted him and begged a shilling from him. He had given her a shilling and left her standing in the road. He did *not* know that she had, as the shoemaker declared, followed him down the hedge path to Leeward Great Wood. The accused man declared that he had walked past Leeward Wood, quite alone, and gone to the Black Knoll. While resting there, he had seen a man run out of Leeward Wood in a suspicious way, but he had not passed close enough for Jones to recognize him or describe him; then he had returned home. Another witness had seen Jones enter the wood with a woman between nine and nine thirty on that night. Jones emphatically denied that. It was certainly himself and Judith who had been seen, but he dared not implicate her. Witness was certain it was Jones he saw, but the woman was a stranger; it was full moonlight and he had been sitting on a stile not twenty yards from the entrance to the wood. Another person had seen Jones near his home just before midnight. He was running. It seemed to Jones that the world that night had been crowded with spying eyes. He swore that he had reached his home at nine o'clock. Then a handkerchief of his, soaked with blood, had been found in the path not very far from the body. Jones could not deny that the handkerchief was his, but he could not explain that he must have dropped it while running, or that it was his own blood.

Jones was bewildered by the astounding circumstances that implicated him. It was unthinkable that an innocent man could be convicted of this crime, but it looked as though Judith might be drawn into it if he was not very careful. Otherwise he was not unduly alarmed. He was, indeed, more deeply moved because he was hurried into prison just as he had attained a topmost peak of joy. Until the trial was over, the intolerable separation must be endured. Pending any move from Judith—and he could not know what course she would be desirous of pursuing —he maintained this untrue version of his movements. There was time enough, if the worst incredibly came to the worst—

well . . . of course . . . then . . . well, they would have to see. . . .

So Christopher Jones endured the ordeal of his trial with stoicism, if not with a quite clear conscience. None knew of his secret meeting with Judith on Black Knoll, and not all the King's horses nor all the King's men should drag that knowledge from him until she signified her submission to his supreme need. And he had never a doubt of her, only a vague wonder, until he was condemned to be hanged by the neck until he was dead. The crashing doom, the appalling certainty, moved him only to a grinding silent ironic commination of the great lady who feared God and honoured the King. The queenly thing was a carcass stuffed with rags. It was not God alone, then, whom she so falsely feared, and if she honoured the King she could yet shame the King's justice! This was what *her* breeding, culture, courage, integrity came to when encountering a terrific fact that could not veil their shame. As for *his,* he would have to teach her a lesson, a great lesson. Horrible! Her infatuation with her "good name" had doomed him to death. Ancient Judith cut off her lover's head! Her pride of caste was a tyrannous fiction, a foible, without ultimate quality. Honour, fine thinking, fine doing, were in the blood of those she despised. His pride should triumph. Perhaps, in the end, it was less pride than pity, and more love than either. He had but to lift a finger, a little tiny finger—but let her be comforted! For her to have declared the truth would have been a glory indeed. For him to declare it would be infamy. That was how it worked. Poor, poor Judith, she had failed. Poor heroic dunce, need he fail too?

The whole village was saddened by his fate; even those villagers who had betrayed him believed in him, somehow, against all reason. All remembered his kindness, his honesty, his queerness. Pots of paint! Every month he had given the best boy in his classes a pot of paint. "If you have no other use for it," he would say to the boy, "you could paint your front door with it." Each month the paint was of a different colour, and that was how the cottage doors had come to have the bright hues that so surprised casual visitors. He had painted the village not red, but green and

purple, blue and orange. Butterflies! At the summer fete a year
or two ago Lady Leeward had presented the prizes, and at the
close of that function half a dozen of Jones's boys had come forward, each bearing a cardboard box. As they came up to her
ladyship the boys had opened the boxes—they were full of living
butterflies. The boys had cast the butterflies into the air above the
great lady, and while they hovered, fluttered, and wandered about
her the people had cheered. But pots of paint and butterflies are
no defences against the assaults of misfortune.

Meanwhile Judith had lived in such anguish of love and shame,
and agony of fear so great, that her beauty melted from her like
a white cloud in the blaze of noon. With a thousand equivoca-
tions she cajoled her conscience. Perhaps, after all, he *had* committed the foul crime. She did not, could not, know, no one
would ever know. The evidence was overwhelming, and he had
not communicated with her, he had lied and lied and lied. To
save such a man she would have to betray her husband and their
kindred—far-reaching subtle ruin. Why need she reveal anything
yet? Not yet, all might yet be cleared up and he would be saved
without her sacrifice. He would be sure to disclose the truth
sooner or later, and when *he* did so she would accept it, confirm
it, she would not deny it. But one white fact shone through all
her sophistries with blinding ray—he had not betrayed her. Perhaps her one sincere but deeply hidden wish was that he *would*
tell; beyond that one possibility of escape for him her mind could
not dare to grope. When she learned the dreadful issue of the
trial she determined to flee away, she could not rest, neither night
nor day, with such a sword plunging into her heart, but after
making preparations flesh and blood failed her, her spirit was
wrecked, and she was carried to her bed, and her physician
summoned from London. He was an old bachelor, a friend of
Sir Gulistan's, and he slept at the Hall for a while. On the day
before Jones was to die Judith gulped down a dose of poison—
veronal or some such drug to which high-born women seem to
have easy access. On the table by her bedside she had left a sealed
letter addressed to the doctor marked: *"Open immediately."*
When it was discovered what Judith had done, Dr. Paton Cope,
an exceedingly capable man despite the fact that he had himself

suffered from hernia for twenty years, plunged after the poisoned woman as Orpheus plunged after Eurydice. He saw the letter and he scrambled it into his pocket. She lay in a state of coma for three days, and if the spirit really goes awandering at such times, Heaven knows what frightful visitation the soul of Judith made. This was her letter: the doctor read it when he was quite alone, in Sir Gulistan's study.

"Dear Paton:

"I am going to poison myself. There is no way out, a horrible thing is killing me, so horrible that it is only a question of a few hours one way or the other. I shall die in any case. There is nothing more for me to do except write this letter and confess everything. That is so difficult. I made the acquaintance of Christopher Jones some months ago; he did me a great kindness when I was thrown once at hunting. I liked him at once, he was curiously *good,* a high-minded though low-spirited man. And he was friendless, and I was lonely. Now he has been convicted of the murder of a wretched tramp-woman. Well, he had nothing whatever to do with that, but I am the only person who knows it. He has been wrongly condemned. He is *innocent.* He knows that I know it, but he will not call me because my own evidence would involve me so seriously. It would be so easy for him. When I was abroad we wrote long loving letters, we were in love, and when I came back I was mad to see him again. I do not love him now, I hate him. I hate his fearful generosity. I am in a trap. I am angry, not sorry at all, angry that I have got to die, more angry that I have got to die because of some stupid mistake, and most angry of all because it is no use dying unless I tell you why. It is impossible to tell a thing like this and go on living. And I can't live any longer. There are times when that hysterical statement is true. On the night of this horrible murder we had arranged to meet at Black Knoll at eight o'clock. We had not seen each other for months and we had been writing—oh, the things men and women do write! We met there, the most beautiful evening in all time. Moonlight and spring. It was wonderful. Kisses and caresses were not enough, it was all wild and impetuous, and there we were lovers. You *understand,* real lovers. I gave everything, will-

ingly. It was no time to think of honour. After all, my honour is
my own, to do what I like with. That is why I throw it away
now, for *nothing*. I loved him passionately then. I do not love
him now. I hate him as I hate myself. Afterwards we saw a man
break out from the wood and run away as if he were afraid of
something. It must have been *that* man who killed the woman.
She was killed while we were loving. We walked back together
in the lovely moonlight, through Leeward Park to the gate in the
park wall, and then we did not want to leave each other. Even
then. He said he was hungry, so I went across to fetch something
from the house. I could only get a bottle of wine and some cake.
We sat under a yew tree just inside the park, and after we had
drunk the wine it was all so magical and still, the grass cold and
soft. A long way off, a bird was making a long frantic purring
noise. Again there was kissing and embracing, and once again
we were lovers. So you see it was impossible for him to have done
this thing to that woman, for twice that night he had been my
lover. He was with me. She was already dead. She was lying in
the wood beyond the wall, dead, as I shall be dead in an hour. It
was past eleven o'clock when I left him. I told him to take the
empty bottle away and throw it in the wood, and I see it must
have been that bottle which gashed his hand so dreadfully. I have
not seen him since. I dared not go to the trial, I dared not, I dared
not, you must realize that. There is another thing besides. I know
now that I am with child. If I lived I should have *his* child. Gulistan has been away for months. I am in a trap whichever way I
turn. What mad, mad irony! Do you see, that child itself is the
proof of its father's innocence.

"This is all true, quite true, the whole truth, so help me God. I
am not mad, I am quite calm, I do not love him now. I have no
feeling but rage, rage against these evil circumstances, everything is so stupid, stupid, stupid. I can only free him by doing
what I am going to do. You must take all the necessary steps, old
friend, at once. He has risked everything to keep my name out of
this affair, but that must not matter now. As I said, my honour
is my own. I did what I liked with it. This is all I can do now.
Tell him from me that he was right after all, he will remember
and understand.

"Good-bye, Paton.

"Good-bye, Gulistan.

"These are the last words of Judith Leeward.

"Good-bye, Chris.

"PS.—I *did* love him, and O my God I love him *now*.

The doctor was confounded. He was a tall, slightly stooping, rather ascetic man, with high, bare brow and pince-nez. Sour though his features looked, he had a pleasant voice and pleasant manner. He was highly esteemed.

"It's preposterous," he murmured, "of course, it's preposterous." Again he read the letter, and again certain passages.

"Pooh, impossible, my dear Judith, impossible. Sheer neurotic dementia. If ever there was a woman free from erotomania I should have said it was Judith, you know. It's this long separation from Gulistan, ought to have gone with him. Highly strung, nervous state, sex hallucinations playing the devil. They play the devil with you."

Once more he read the letter.

"By Jove, yes, it *is* impossible. Never was a clearer case against a scoundrel. I'll get rid of this."

Paton Cope stooped over the fire and dropped the letter in. It burnt to a grey trembling ash.

"Neurotic dementia," repeated the doctor. "Must get Gulistan back at once. Neurotic dementia."

The following day he began efforts to get into touch with Judith's husband, but they proved to be all in vain, for poor Sir Gulistan had been stung by a poisonous insect in East African territory and suffered a most unhappy end. The great lady was ill for a week or two longer, then she recovered. At a safe interval, much later, Paton Cope questioned her about the letter. What letter? She did not understand, did not quiver an eyelid. He dropped the subject and congratulated himself. Paton Cope was fond of her. Certainly she never had a child. Perhaps some day she will marry him.

The Field of Mustard (1926)

FATHER RAVEN

The old priest, Father Raven, was a dear and a darling, a little prancing man somewhat big in the belly, though you wouldn't call it a paunch, it was a plumpness that betokened a good appetite and caused the crucifix and holy medallion on his watch-chain to tinkle as he trotted along with smiles coming out of his nice old face. And he had a way with him that betokened a kind heart towards the unsaintly as well as the dutiful and any other whatever. He loved little children and nice women and good men, and as shepherd of his little flock he led them right and he led them true. His mind was at rest with God, and when he slept he was visited by proper and beautiful dreams—angels and so on.

Did you hear what happened to him then on the Day of Judgment?

He and his flock had gone as they thought, poor dears, on their annual outing to the seaside, the entire concourse of the parish, all the men, the women, the children, and a dog or two, the whole forty of them; not a creature stayed at home in that scrimp of a place barring the pigs and a pack of hens, so when the postman tramped into it at one o'clock, although it was warm and sunny with the trees just waving and the dust of the lane just rising, every window in the parish was fastened, every wicket shut, every door locked. It was silent and deserted, it was blank and hollow—like a city of the dead, the postman thought, and he wasn't at all easy in his mind until he was out of the place again.

And there they were all at the seaside, gone in three wagonettes hired for the day from Broadribb's Hotel; the drivers wore tall hats with coloured ribbons dangling, and the two Hatfall men, Jake and Johnny, with their little sister, Nym, played music. Johnny had a glib finger for the melodeon and his brother Jake jingled and thumbed a tambourine while little Nym, a lovely fair pippit of seven years, rippled away with them on the triangle. So when they were disporting themselves along the shore in good enjoyment, Father Raven walked a little way off and stretched himself on the beach stones to have a quiet look at the small waves tumbling in and sliding back again.

"All the same water," thinks he, leaning on his elbow, "but never the same wave."

And then on a sudden, nobody knows the how and why or the least little fore and aft of it, it was very queer, but all in a twink Father Raven found himself marching like a drum major at the head of his flock, the whole forty of them marching behind him, on the road to Paradise. The Last Call had come and that is the place they were bound for, Paradise. The way was long, but all was sweet and mild with the trees just waving above them, the dust of the road just rising under them, and bells from some golden towers set on a hill ahead of them trailing a distant clamour. White roads stretched unendingly in all directions on each side of them, crowded with people travelling afoot to Paradise. Plain it was to see, its towers so glittered, yet although they kept travelling onwards it still seemed far away.

"Keep your courage up, now," Father Raven called out. "We shall soon be there."

Most of them were light-hearted and hopeful already, though one or two were uneasy. Father Raven told them to quit flinching and flushing.

"There's nothing to fear as yet," he said. "Fair play is a jewel, I can promise you that. You've a clean slate with me anyway. I expect we shall have to wait our turn, there's such a deuce of a crowd everywhere."

There was! A diggins of a crowd! The noise of all the footsteps going the selfsame way was like the flutter of a forest when the rain sobs on it. On they go, on and on, and not a one felt any trifle of weariness, not even little Nym, the youngest and least and last of all her family. Brothers and sisters had grown up, she was unlike the rest, and all said she was a pure and fragrant child. As far as that goes it might be true, though the Most High knows that only archangels and the like of that could be really so; but little Nym was as near it as makes no odds—here below at any rate. Some of the parish began to feel some of the things in their past lives looming up on them, and Aby Purvis murmured that in all his seventy and seven years he had never had a thing he had ever wanted and didn't look like getting it now, by crumps he did not! Dearo, dearo, dear, when your grandson's going bald, things are getting on with you.

"What in hell d'ye expect?" Cattermutt asked with a sneer.

The Widow Usher cried out at that: "Shoosh, Mr. Cattermutt!" She had never had any fancy for the great gawk, a single man with a heart as sour as the salt sea and cold as rain, and she a widow three times over.

"What's the matter with you, ma'am?" he says in his ugly way, not liking her or any of her sort at all, for her last man had hung himself on a plum tree and that's a cold warning to any bachelor.

"Time is time," Mrs. Usher said, "and place is place, and there's a fitness in all things."

"I can say my say," he retorted, "and do my do whether or no. Charity's good teaching but my foot u'll always itch to kick anybody that gives me an offence. You may talk about your coals of fire but I clench fist and feel terrific, and I don't blush for it either."

"Oh, but you should, Mr. Cattermutt, shouldn't you? To blush at sin is no disgrace."

"Sin!" he exclaimed.

"Ah, don't begin quarrelling now," Mrs. Usher pleaded in soft humility; "there's a good man, please don't."

They tramped on, the lot of them, jabbering as though the day was the like of any other day and they were going to the pictures. Whatever the outcome, good or bad, they'd no help for it now but to go on to the end behind Father Raven, and he showed no alarm and never stopped a step but strode out like a great person who was used to getting his own way or else having a large talk about it.

"A diggins of a crowd," he sighed, throwing an eye about him. Away through the trees on the right hand he could see millions, and on the left, along roads crossing green great fields, there were millions more, millions, their footsteps rumbling on and on, voices chattering ever and ever. It delighted Father Raven to see the fine green pastures as close as all that to Paradise. He had a fondness for big fields, to see them any time was good; to walk in them in the springtime when the dandelions were the only flowers in the grass filled him with mute sweet pleasure. The present turn of events had not incommoded him, and if he was not as jubilant as you might think he might have been, at least he was no ways alarmed, and not doubtful of the end, because all this was all very natural. A wondrous marvellous occasion, of course, but always to be expected at some time or other, as certain as the dawn of day; it was the ultimate dream of all, the realization of mortal hopes, the deliverance from evil—and what about a little smoke now as we jog along? Into his pockets he dipped but they were empty, not a pipe or a scroop of tobacco in any of his garments. Oh dear yes! he supposed he would have to give up smoking now, he would have to give it up! And a good thing too, it was bad for the lungs, he spent quite a time every morning hawking the phlegm off his chest. As he lifted his hat and smoothed his grey locks it came upon him that the shining towers were no nearer yet. They had marched that easy highway for hours, the miles were behind them, but the goal, like a mirage, was as far off as ever. Already the sun was drooping down, its low-shot beams had turned the bosoms of trees into sponges of heaving lustre; the hazels twinkled, the poplars inclined, the tall ash was most swayful.

"One gets no nearer by only lifting the sole of the foot," said Father Raven, so he bowed his head and thought good thoughts for his people as he led them along. Not a creature did they meet yet who had turned back, save a man sitting on a rock. He seemed to be in sorrow, for he leaned with his head resting between his hands. As they approached him little Nym tinkled on her triangle and called out gaily: "Hello, mister!"

He looked up and stared in silent sadness.

"Hello!" she rallied him again as they passed.

The man said nothing and turned once more to his brooding.

"D'ye think we are all right?" Mr. Gillingwater asked of the woman alongside him. Winny Cope it was, the mother of two twins though her nuptial finger had not felt the weight of a marriage ring yet. Father Raven had cracked on at her when she made such a fool of herself, but she was never daunted. She was a lissom woman and had a lissom nature. "I'm my son's own mother, or may the seven blessings fail me," was what she answered him, and on their first birthday she dressed up as a Russian and bought a ham and there were flowers and flags "Up the Doublets" all over the parish.

"D'ye think we are all right?" Mr. Gillingwater says to this Winny Cope, for he was always a nervous old spook, harmless as a lamb, not one of your good-for-nothing rob-the-poorbox sort of jokers, but full of fears of this and that or the end of the world and himself altogether.

"D'ye think we are all right?"

"You'll see," was her answer. "Why shouldn't we be?"

"I dunno. You can't tell your luck from the look of anything here, Winny Cope."

"Oh, you's such a 'spicious man."

"Well, it's not my own accord I'm going this stretch, and I'd forfeit all I have in the world to know what's about."

"Don't worry your dear heart. Father Raven puts in all the good prayers for us. Look at him now!" she said.

By and by Gillingwater bent to her again: "How much money you got in the bank, Winny Cope?"

"Huh! I got nothing," she laughed. "But the bank's got plenty!"

So then he held out something under cover of his hand. "Take it," he said.

She took it and gave it a look: a shining sovereign lay in her palm, neat and warm and heavy.

"What'll I do with it?" she asked.

"Trousies and boots for the boys," said Mr. Gillingwater.

Winny's thoughts gave a gobble at that. Well to goodness, didn't he know yet, the old jackass! Fancy offering backsheesh to God—a cat would know better. "Are ye daft!" she cried, and tossed the coin away into the trees. All the same she added: "God bless ye, daddy."

And now it wasn't long till they got nearer and much nearer

to the hill of Paradise. They could see it close and clear. There was a moat around it, all around, of clear water; you could only get over it by crossing a narrow bridge that looked to be made of blue glass—though it might have been sapphire, it glowed very richly in the down-going light. They'd to take their turn now, as Father Raven said, all in order and no crushing. Slowly they moved on. The sun went down until there was no more than twilight around them, but the cross on the topmost tower gleamed with a light that could never be dimmed.

"Halt!" a great voice sounded from the bridge. "Be still," it said.

And when the multitude was hushed, word went round that as time was getting on and the light was gone all the remaining judgments would be made in the mass instead of individually; therefore all the parish priests were requested to go forward alone to answer for their people.

"Come!" said the great voice again.

And there was Father Raven with his cassock kilted up to his knees.

"Why, he wears breeches and stockings!" little Nym cried out.

Father Raven took time by the fetlock, as they say; he flew off towards the bridge and there's no deer could have beat him the way he went on that lick with his two legs twinkling like the spokes of a wheel. And there was no more distress on him when he reached the bridge than would have lifted one bristle of a bee.

A great handsome being was waiting there.

"How many?" he asked Father Raven.

"Forty in all," Father Raven said. "Seven men, twelve women, twenty-one children."

"Sinless?"

"Quite," said he. "Safe and sound, the best in the world."

"All of them?"

"Yes," Father Raven said.

"You have no doubts?"

"None whatever, not a scruple."

"You vouch for them all?"

"For certain sure I do!" he answered sharply.

The handsome being looked solemnly at Father Raven, his red lips were set in a truss of black beard. "You pledge your immortal soul upon it?"

Now, it gave the good priest a bit of a shaking to be asked to pledge his own one soul for the lot of theirs, and no wonder with all the dubious roguery of the Hatfalls and the Boddrills and Cattermutts behind him, not to mention the naughtiness of Winny Cope and one or two others. Yet what did it all amount to anyway? They were good enough for him, kind loving creatures when you got to know them, the salt of the earth really, and if anything in regards of them turned out to be not quite up to snuff he would explain it and smooth it out if they wanted it that way. So he chanced his soul on their spotlessness. "Yes, I will," he declared stoutly, "for certain sure I will."

"They may pass," said the black-bearded men.

Father Raven, all joyful, waved to his people and they rushed up crowding to get on the bridge.

"Get on, on with you, lose no time! Are you there, Winny? And you, Johnny Hatfall? That's right, on you go, Aby. Quickly now, quickly!"

With many pokes and pats Father Raven urged them all safely on to the bridge, but just as he essayed to follow them a barrier was interposed and stopped him only. He protested and tried to break through, but the black-bearded one snapped his finger and thumb with a thick click and waved him off.

"You have done evil! Stand away!"

In a flash of mortal anguish Father Raven realized that he was doomed.

"Sir! Sir!" he pleaded.

"Your pledge is forfeit," the slow voice replied. "Stand away!"

The priest was thrust out, there was no help for him, his fond heart had betrayed him, had stolen the truth from his tongue. He heard the tinkle of little Nym's triangle fading across the bridge, growing fainter and fainter, and when he could hear it no more he felt his soul shrivel out of him.

Ugly Anna (1944)

THE MAN FROM KILSHEELAN

IF you knew the Man from Kilsheelan it was no use saying you did not believe in fairies and secret powers; believe it or no, but believe it you should—there he was! It is true he was in an asylum for the insane, but he was a man with age upon him so he didn't mind; and besides, better men than himself have been in such places, or they ought to be, and if there is justice in the world they will be.

"A cousin of mine," he said to old Tom Tool one night, "is come from Ameriky. A rich person."

He lay in the bed next him, but Tom Tool didn't answer, so he went on again: "In a ship," he said.

"I hear you," answered Tom Tool.

"I see his mother with her bosom open once, and it stuffed with diamonds, bags full."

Tom Tool kept quiet.

"If," said the Man from Kilsheelan, "if I'd the trusty comrade I'd make a break from this and go seek him."

"Was he asking you to do that?"

"How could he an' all and he in a ship?"

"Was he writing fine letters to you, then?"

"How could he, under the Lord? Would he give them to a savage bird or a herring to bring to me so?"

"How did he let on to you?"

"He did not let on," said the Man from Kilsheelan.

Tom Tool lay long silent in the darkness; he had a mistrust of the Man, knowing him to have a forgetful mind; everything slipped through it like rain through the nest of a pigeon. But at last he asked him: "Where is he now?"

"He'll be at Ballygoveen."

"You to know that and you with no word from him?"

"Oh, I know it, I know; and if I'd a trusty comrade I'd walk out of this and to him I would go. Bags of diamonds!"

Then he went to sleep, sudden; but the next night he was at Tom Tool again: "If I'd a trusty comrade," said he; and all that and a lot more.

" 'Tis not convenient to me now," said Tom Tool, "but to-morrow night I might go wid you."

The next night was a wild night, and a dark night, and he would not go to make a break from the asylum, he said: "Fifty miles of journey, and I with no heart for great walking feats! It is not convenient, but tomorrow night I might go wid you."

The night after that he said: "Ah, whisht wid your diamonds and all! Why would you go from the place that is snug and warm into a world that is like a wall for cold dark, and but the thread of a coat to divide you from its mighty clasp, and only one thing blacker under the heaven of God and that's the road you walk on, and only one thing more shy than your heart and that's your two feet worn to a tissue tramping in dung and ditches . . ."

"If I'd a trusty comrade," said the Man from Kilsheelan, "I'd go seek my rich cousin."

" . . . stars gaping at you a few spans away, and the things that have life in them, but cannot see or speak, begin to breathe and bend. If ever your hair stood up it is then it would be, though you've no more than would thatch a thimble, God help you."

"Bags of gold he has," continued the Man, "and his pockets stuffed with the tobacca."

"Tobacca!"

"They were large pockets and well stuffed."

"Do you say, now!"

"And the gold! large bags and rich bags."

"Well, I might do it tomorrow."

And the next day Tom Tool and the Man from Kilsheelan broke from the asylum and crossed the mountains and went on.

Four little nights and four long days they were walking; slow it was, for they were oldish men and lost they were, but the jour-ney was kind and the weather was good weather. On the fourth day Tom Tool said to him: "The Dear knows what way you'd be taking me! Blind it seems, and dazed I am. I could do with a skillet of good soup to steady me and to soothe me."

"Hard it is, and hungry it is," sighed the Man; "starved daft I am for a taste of nourishment, a blind man's dog would pity me. If I see a cat I'll eat it; I could bite the nose off a duck."

They did not converse any more for a time, not until Tom Tool asked him what was the name of his grand cousin, and then the Man from Kilsheelan was in a bedazement, and he was confused.

"I declare, on my soul, I've forgot his little name. Wait now while I think of it."

"Was it McInerney then?"

"No, not it at all."

"Kavanagh? the Grogans? or the Duffys?"

"Wait, wait while I think of it now."

Tom Tool waited; he waited and all until he thought he would burst.

"Ah, what's astray wid you? Was it Phelan—or O'Hara—or Clancy—or Peter Mew?"

"No, not it at all."

"The Murphys—the Sweeneys—the Moores."

"Divil a one. Wait while I think of it now."

And the Man from Kilsheelan sat holding his face as if it hurt him, and his comrade kept saying at him: "Duhy, then? Coman? McGrath?" driving him distracted with his O this and O that, his Mc he's and Mc she's.

Well, he could not think of it; but when they walked on they had not far to go, for they came over a twist of the hills and there was the ocean, and the neat little town of Ballygoveen in a bay of it below, with the wreck of a ship lying sunk near the strand. There was a sharp cliff at either horn of the bay, and between them some bullocks stravaiging on the beach.

"Truth is a fortune," cried the Man from Kilsheelan, "this is it!"

They went down the hill to the strand near the wreck, and just on the wing of the town they saw a paddock full of hemp stretched drying, and a house near it, and a man weaving a rope. He had a great cast of hemp around his loins, and a green apron.

He walked backwards to the sea, and a young girl stood turning a little wheel as he went away from her.

"God save you," said Tom Tool to her, "for who are you weaving this rope?"

"For none but God Himself and the hangman," said she.

Turning the wheel she was, and the man going away from it backwards, and the dead wreck in the rocky bay; a fine sweet girl of good dispose and no ways drifty.

"Long life to you then, young woman," says he. "But that's a strong word, and a sour word, the Lord spare us all."

At that the ropewalker let a shout to her to stop the wheel; then he cut the rope at the end and tied it to a black post. After that he came throwing off his green apron and said he was hungry.

"Denis, avick!" cried the girl. "Come, and I'll get your food." And the two of them went away into the house.

"Brother and sister they are," said the Man from Kilsheelan, "a good appetite to them."

"Very neat she is, and clean she is, and good and sweet and tidy she is," said Tom Tool. They stood in the yard watching some white fowls parading and feeding and conversing in the grass; scratch, peck, peck, ruffle, quarrel, scratch, peck, peck, cock-a-doodle-doo.

"What will we do now, Tom Tool? My belly has a scroop and a screech in it. I could eat the full of Isknagahiny Lake and gape for more, or the Hill of Bawn and not get my enough."

Beyond them was the paddock with the hemp drying across it, long heavy strands, and two big stacks of it beside, dark and sodden, like seaweed. The girl came to the door and called: "Will ye take a bite?" They said they would, and that she should eat with spoons of gold in the heaven of God and Mary. "You're welcome," she said, but no more she said, for while they ate she was sad and silent.

The young man Denis let on that their father, one Horan, was away on his journeys peddling a load of ropes, a long journey, days he had been gone, and he might be back today, or tomorrow, or the day after.

"A great strew of hemp you have," said the Man from Kilsheelan. The young man cast down his eyes; and the young girl cried out: " 'Tis foul hemp, God preserve us all!"

"Do you tell me of that now," he asked; but she would not, and her brother said: "I will tell you. It's a great misfortune, mister man. 'Tis from the wreck in the bay beyant, a good stout ship, but burst on the rocks one dark terror of a night and all the poor sailors tipped in the sea. But the tide was low and they got ashore, ten strong sailor men, with a bird in a cage that was dead drowned."

"The Dear rest its soul," said Tom Tool.

"There was no rest in the ocean for a week, the bay was full of storms, and the vessel burst, and the big bales split, and the hemp was scattered and torn and tangled on the rocks, or it did drift. But at last it soothed, and we gathered it and brought it to the field here. We brought it, and my father did buy it of the salvage man for a price; a Mexican valuer he was, but the deal was bad, and it lies there; going rotten it is, the rain wears it, and the sun's astray, and the wind is gone."

"That's a great misfortune. What is on it?" said the Man from Kilsheelan.

"It is a great misfortune, mister man. Laid out it is, turned it is, hackled it is, but faith it will not dry or sweeten, never a hank of it worth a pig's eye."

"'Tis the devil and all his injury," said Kilsheelan.

The young girl, her name it was Christine, sat grieving. One of her beautiful long hands rested on her knee, and she kept beating it with the other. Then she began to speak.

"The captain of that ship lodged in this house with us while the hemp was recovered and sold; a fine handsome sport he was, but fond of the drink, and very friendly with the Mexican man, very hearty they were, a great greasy man with his hands covered with rings that you'd not believe. Covered! My father had been gone travelling a week or a few days when a dark raging gale came off the bay one night till the hemp was lifted all over the field."

"It would have lifted a bullock," said Denis, "great lumps of it, like trees."

"And we sat waiting the captain, but he didn't come home and we went sleeping. But in the morning the Mexican man was found dead murdered on the strand below, struck in the skull, and the two hands of him gone. 'Twas not long when they came to the house and said he was last seen with the captain, drunk quarrelling; and where was he? I said to them that he didn't come home at all and was away from it. "We'll take a peep at his bed," they said, and I brought them there, and my heart gave a strong twist in me when I see'd the captain stretched on it, snoring to the world, and his face and hands smeared with the blood. So he was brought away and searched, and in his pocket they found one of the poor Mexican's hands, just the one, but none of the riches. Everything to be so black against him and the assizes just coming on in Cork! So they took him there before the judge, and he judged him and said it's to hang he was. And if they asked the captain how he did it, he said he did not do it at all."

"But there was a bit of iron pipe beside the body," said Denis.

"And if they asked him where was the other hand, the one with the rings and the mighty jewels on them, and his budget of riches, he said he knew nothing of that nor how the one hand got into his pocket. Placed there it was by some schemer. It was all he could say, for the drink was on him and nothing he knew.

" 'You to be so drunk,' they said, 'how did you get home to your bed and nothing heard?'

" 'I don't know,' says he. Good sakes, the poor lamb, a gallant strong sailor he was! His mind was a blank, he said. ' 'Tis blank,' said the judge, 'if it's as blank as the head of himself with a gap like that in it, God rest him!' "

"You could have put a pound of cheese in it," said Denis.

"And Peter Corcoran cried like a loony man, for his courage was gone, like a stream of water. To hang him, the judge said, and to hang him well, was their intention. It was a pity, the judge said, to rob a man because he was foreign, and destroy him for riches and the drink on him. And Peter Corcoran swore he was innocent of this crime. 'Put a clean shirt to me back,' says he, 'for it's to heaven I'm going.' "

"And," added Denis, "the peeler at the door said 'Amen.' "

"That was a week ago," said Christine, "and in another he'll be stretched. A handsome sporting sailor boy."

"What—what did you say was the name of him?" gasped the Man from Kilsheelan.

"Peter Corcoran, the poor lamb," said Christine.

"Begod," he cried out as if he was choking, " 'tis me grand cousin from Ameriky!"

True it was, and the grief on him so great that Denis was after giving the two of them a lodge till the execution was over. "Rest here, my dad's away," said he, "and he knowing nothing of the murder, or the robbery, or the hanging that's coming, nothing. Ah, what will we tell him an' all? 'Tis a black story on this house."

"The blessing of God and Mary on you," said Tom Tool. "Maybe we could do a hand's turn for you; me comrade's a great wonder with the miracles, maybe he could do a stroke would free an innocent man."

"Is it joking you are?" asked Christine sternly.

"God deliver him, how would I joke on a man going to his doom and destruction?"

The next day the young girl gave them jobs to do, but the Man from Kilsheelan was destroyed with trouble and he shook like water when a pan of it is struck.

"What is on you?" said Tom Tool.

"Vexed and waxy I am," says he, "in regard of the great journey we's took, and sorra a help in the end of it. Why couldn't he do his bloody murder after we had done with him?"

"Maybe he didn't do it at all."

"Ah, what are you saying now, Tom Tool? Wouldn't anyone do it, a nice, easy, innocent crime? The cranky gossoon to get himself stretched on the head of it, 'tis the drink destroyed him! Sure there's no more justice in the world than you'd find in the craw of a sick pullet. Vexed and waxy I am for me careless cousin. Do it! Who wouldn't do it?"

He went up to the rope that Denis and Christine were weaving together and he put his finger on it.

"Is that the rope," says he, "that will hang my grand cousin?"

"No," said Denis, "it is not. His rope came through the post office yesterday. For the prison master it was, a long new rope— saints preserve us—and Jimmy Fallon, the postman, getting roaring drunk showing it to the scores of creatures would give him a drink for the sight of it. Just coiled it was, and no way hidden, with a label on it, 'O.H.M.S.' "

"The wind's rising, you," said Christine. "Take a couple of

forks now and turn the hemp in the field. Maybe 'twill scour the Satan out of it."

"Stormy it does be, and the bay has darkened in broad noon," said Tom Tool.

"Why wouldn't the whole world be dark and a man to be hung?" said she.

They went to the hemp, so knotted and stinking, and begun raking it and raking it. The wind was roaring from the bay, the hulk twitching and tottering; the gulls came off the wave, and Christine's clothes stretched out from her like the wings of a bird. The hemp heaved upon the paddock like a great beast bursting a snare that was on it, and a strong blast drove a heap of it up on the Man from Kilsheelan, twisting and binding him in its clasp till he thought he would not escape from it and he went falling and yelping. Tom Tool unwound him and sat him in the lew of the stack till he got his strength again, and then he began to moan of his misfortune.

"Stint your shouting," said Tom Tool, "isn't it as hard to cure as a wart on the back of a hedgehog?"

But he wouldn't stint it. " 'Tis large and splendid talk I get from you, Tom Tool, but divil a deed of strength. Vexed and waxy I am. Why couldn't he do his murder after we'd done with him? What a cranky cousin! What a foolish creature! What a silly man, the devil take him!"

"Let you be aisy," the other said, "to heaven he is going."

"And what's the gain of it, he to go with his neck stretched?"

"Indeed, I did know a man went to heaven once," began Tom Tool, "but he did not care for it."

"That's queer," said the Man, "for it couldn't be anything you'd not want, indeed to glory."

"Well, he came back to Ireland on the head of it. I forget what was his name."

"Was it Corcoran, or Tool, or Horan?"

"No, none of those names. He let on it was a lonely place, not fit for living people or dead people, he said; nothing but trees and streams and beasts and birds."

"What beasts and birds?"

"Rabbits and badgers, the elephant, the dromedary, and all

those ancient races; eagles and hawks and cuckoos and magpies. He wandered in a thick forest for nights and days like a flea in a great beard, and the beasts and the birds setting traps and hooks and dangers for a poor feller; the worst villains of all was the sheep."

"The sheep! What could a sheep do, then?" asked Kilsheelan.

"I don't know the right of it, but you'd not believe me if I told you at all. If you went for the little swim you was not seen again."

"I never heard the like of that in Roscommon."

"Not another holy soul was in it but himself, and if he was taken with the thirst he would dip his hand in a stream that flowed with rich wine and put it to his lips, but if he did, it turned into air at once and twisted up in a blue cloud. But grand wine to look at, he said. If he took oranges from a tree, he could not bite them, they were chiny oranges, hard as a plate. But beautiful oranges to look at they were. To pick a flower it burst on you like a gun. What was cold was too cold to touch, and what was warm was too warm to swallow, you must throw it up or die."

"Faith, it's no region for a Christian soul, Tom Tool. Where is it at all?"

"High it may be, low it may be, it may be here, it may be there."

"What could the like of a sheep do? A sheep!"

"A devouring savage creature it is there, the most hard to come at, the most difficult to conquer, with the teeth of a lion and a tiger, the strength of a bear and a half, the deceit of two foxes, the run of a deer, the—"

"Is it heaven you call it! I'd not look twice at a place the like of that."

"No, you would not, no."

"Ah, but wait now," said Kilsheelan, "wait till the Day of Judgment."

"Well, I will not wait then," said Tom Tool sternly. "When the sinners of the world are called to their judgment, scatter they will all over the face of the earth, running like hares till they come to the sea, and there they will perish."

"Ah, the love of God on the world!"

They went raking and raking, till they came to a great stiff hump of it that rolled over, and they could see sticking from the end of it two boots.

"Oh, what is it, in the name of God?" asks Kilsheelan.

"Sorra and all, but I'd not like to look," says Tom Tool, and they called the girl to come see what was it.

"A dead man!" says Christine in a thin voice with a great tremble coming on her, and she white as a tooth. "Unwind him now." They began to unwind him like a tailor with a bale of tweed, and at last they came to a man black in the face. Strangled he was. The girl let a great cry out of her. "Queen of heaven, 'tis my dad; choked he is, the long strands have choked him, my good, pleasant dad!" and she went with a run to the house crying.

"What has he there in his hand?" asked Kilsheelan.

" 'Tis a chopper," says he.

"Do you see what is on it, Tom Tool?"

"Sure I see, and you see, what is on it; blood is on it, and murder is on it. Go fetch a peeler and I'll wait while you bring him."

When his friend was gone for the police Tom Tool took a little squint around him and slid his hand into the dead man's pocket. But as he did so he was nearly struck mad from his senses, for he pulled out a loose dead hand that had been chopped off as neat as the foot of a pig. He looked at the dead man's arms, and there was a hand to each; so he looked at the hand again. The fingers were covered with the rings of gold and diamonds. Covered!

"Glory be to God!" said Tom Tool, and he put his hand in another pocket and fetched a budget full of papers and banknotes.

"Glory be to God!" he said again, and put the hand and the budget back in the pockets and turned his back and said prayers until the peelers came and took them all off to the court.

It was not long, two days or three, until an inquiry was held; grand it was and its judgment was good. And the bigwig asked: "Where is the man that found the body?"

"There are two of him," says the peeler.

"Swear 'em," says he, and Kilsheelan stepped up to a great murdering joker of a clerk, who gave him a book in his hand and roared at him: "I swear by Almighty God—"

"Yes," says Kilsheelan.

"Swear it," says the clerk.

"Indeed I do."

"You must repeat it," says the clerk.

"I will, sir."

"Well, repeat it then," says he.

"And what will I repeat?"

So he told him again and he repeated it. Then the clerk goes on: "—that the evidence I give—"

"Yes," says Kilsheelan.

"Say those words, if you please."

"The words! Och, give me the head of 'em again!"

So he told him again and he repeated it. Then the clerk goes on: "—shall be the truth—"

"It will," says Kilsheelan.

"—and nothing but the truth—"

"Yes, begod, indeed!"

"Say 'nothing but the truth,'" roared the clerk.

"No!" says Kilsheelan.

"Say 'nothing.'"

"All right," says Kilsheelan.

"Can't you say 'nothing but the truth'?"

"Yes," he says.

"Well, say it!"

"I will so," says he, "the scrapings of sense on it all!"

So they swore them both, and their evidence they gave.

"Very good," his lordship said, "a most important and opportune discovery, in the nick of time, by the tracing of God. There is a reward of fifty pounds offered for the finding of this property and jewels; fifty pounds you will get in due course."

They said they were obliged to him, though sorrow a one of them knew what he meant by a due course, nor where it was.

Then a lawyer man got the rights of the whole case; he was the cunningest man ever lived in the city of Cork; no one could match him, and he made it straight and he made it clear.

Old Horan must have returned from his journey unbeknown on the night of the gale when the deed was done. Perhaps he had made a poor profit on his toil, for there was little of his own coin found on his body. He saw the two drunks staggering along the bay—he clove in the head of the one with a bit of pipe—he hit the other a good whack to still or stiffen him—he got an axe from the yard—he shore off the Mexican's two hands, for the rings were grown tight and wouldn't be drawn from his fat fingers. Perhaps he dragged the captain home to his bed—you couldn't be sure of that—but put the hand in the captain's pocket he did, and then went to the paddock to bury the treasure. But a blast of wind whipped and wove some of the hemp strand around his limbs, binding him sudden. He was all huffled and hogled and went mad with the fear struggling, the hemp rolling him and binding him till he was strangled or smothered.

And that is what happened to him, believe it or no, but believe it you should. It was the tracing of God on him for his dark crime.

Within a week of it Peter Corcoran was away out of jail, a stout walking man again, free in Ballygoveen. But on the day of his release he did not go near the ropewalker's house. The Horans were there waiting, and the two old silly men, but he did not go next or near them. The next day Kilsheelan said to her: "Strange it is my cousin not to seek you, and he a sneezer for gallantry."

" 'Tis no wonder at all," replied Christine, "and he with his picture in all the papers."

"But he had a right to have come now and you caring him in his black misfortune," said Tom Tool.

"Well, he will not come then," Christine said in her soft voice, "in regard of the red murder on the soul of my dad. And why should he put a mark on his family, and he the captain of a ship?"

In the afternoon Tom Tool and the other went walking to try if they should see him, and they did see him at a hotel, but he was hurrying from it; he had a frieze coat on him and a bag in his hand.

"Well, who are you at all?" asks Peter Corcoran.

"You are my cousin from Ameriky," says Kilsheelan.

"Is that so? And I never heard it," says Peter. "What's your name?"

The Man from Kilsheelan hung down his old head and couldn't answer him, but Tom Tool said: "Drifty he is, sir, he forgets his little name."

"Astray is he? My mother said I've cousins in Roscommon, d'ye know 'em? the Twingeings—"

"Twingeing! Owen Twingeing it is!" roared Kilsheelan. " 'Tis my name! 'Tis my name! 'Tis my name!" and he danced about squawking like a parrot in a frenzy.

"If it's Owen Twingeing you are, I'll bring you to my mother in Manhattan." The captain grabbed up his bag. "Haste now, come along out of it. I'm going from the cunning town this minute, bad sleep to it for ever and a month! There's a cart waiting to catch me the boat train to Queenstown. Will you go? Now?"

"Holy God contrive it," said Kilsheelan; his voice was wheezy as an old goat, and he made to go off with him. "Good day to you, Tom Tool, you'll get all the reward and endure a rich life from this out, fortune on it all, a fortune on it all!"

And the two of them were gone in a twink.

Tom Tool went back to the Horans then; night was beginning to dusk and to darken. As he went up the ropewalk Christine came to him from her potato gardens and gave him signs, he to be quiet and follow her down to the strand. So he followed her down to the strand and told her all that happened, till she was vexed and full of tender words for the old fool.

"Aren't you the spit of misfortune! It would daunt a saint, so it would, and scrape a tear from silky Satan's eye. Those two deluderers, they've but the drainings of half a heart between 'em. And he not willing to lift the feather of a thought on me? I'd not forget him till there's ten days in a week and every one of 'em lucky. But—but—isn't Peter Corcoran the nice name for a captain man, the very pattern?"

She gave him a little bundle into his hands. "There's a loaf and a cut of meat. You'd best be stirring from here."

"Yes," he said, and stood looking stupid, for his mind was in a dream. The rock at one horn of the bay had a red glow on it like the shawl on the neck of a lady, but the other was black now. A man was dragging a turf boat up the beach.

"Listen, you," said Christine. "There's two upstart men in the house now, seeking you and the other. There's trouble and damage on the head of it. From the asylum they are. To the police they have been, to put an embargo on the reward, and sorra a sixpence you'll receive of the fifty pounds of it: to the expenses of the asylum it must go, they say. The treachery! Devil and all, the blood sweating on every coin of it would rot the palm of a nigger. Do you hear me at all?"

She gave him a little shaking, for he was standing stupid, gazing at the bay, which was dying into grave darkness except for the wash of its broken waves.

"Do you hear me at all? It's quit now you should, my little old man, or they'll be taking you."

"Ah, yes, sure, I hear you, Christine; thank you kindly. Just looking and listening I was. I'll be stirring from it now, and I'll get on and I'll go. Just looking and listening I was, just a wee look."

"Then good-bye to you, Mr. Tool," said Christine Horan, and turning from him she left him in the darkness and went running up the ropewalk to her home.

The Black Dog (1923)

OLIVE AND CAMILLA

THEY had lived and travelled together for twenty years, and this is a part of their history: not much, but all that matters. Ever since reaching marriageable age they had been together, and so neither had married, though Olive had had her two or three occasions of perilous inducement. Being women, they were critical of each other, inseparably critical; being spinsters, they were huffy, tender, sullen, and demure and had quarrelled with each other ten thousand times in a hundred different places during their "wanderings up and down Europe." That was the phrase Camilla used in relating their maidenly Odyssey, which had comprised a multitude of sojourns in the pensions of Belgium, Switzerland, Italy, and France. They quarrelled in Naples and repented in Rome; exploded in anger at Arles, were embittered at Interlaken, parted for ever at Lake Garda, Taormina, and Bruges; but running water never fouls, they had never really been apart, not anywhere. Olive was like that, and so was her friend; such natures could nowise be changed. Camilla Hobbs, slight and prim, had a tiny tinkling mind that tinkled all day long; she was all things to little nothings. The other, Olive Sharples, the portly one, had a mind like a cuckoo-clock; something came out and cried "Cuckoo" now and again, quite sharply, and was done with it. They were moulded thus, one supposes, by the hand of Providence; it could be neither evaded nor altered, it could not even be mitigated, for in Camilla's prim mind and manner there was a prim deprecation of Olive's boorish nature, and for her part Olive resented Camilla's assumption of a superior disposition. Saving a precious month or two in Olive's favour they were both now of a sad age, an age when the path of years slopes downwards to a yawning inexplicable gulf.

"Just fancy!" Camilla said on her forty-fifth birthday—they were at Chamonix then—"we are ninety between us!"

Olive glowered at her friend, though a couple of months really is nothing. "When I am fifty," she declared, "I shall kill myself."

"But why?" Camilla was so interested.

"God, I don't know!" returned Olive.

Camilla brightly brooded for a few moments. "You'll find it very hard to commit suicide; it's not easy, you know, not at all. I've heard time and time again that it's most difficult. . . ."

"Pooh!" snorted Olive.

"But I tell you! I tell you I knew a cook at Leamington who swallowed ground glass in her porridge, pounds and pounds, and nothing came of it."

"Pooh!" Olive was contemptuous. "Never say die."

"Well, that's just what people say who can't do it!"

The stream of their companionship was far from being a rill of peaceful water, but it flowed, more and more like a cataract it flowed, and was like to flow on as it had for those twenty years. Otherwise they were friendless! Olive had had enough money to do as she modestly liked, for though she was impulsive her desires were frugal, but Camilla had had nothing except a grandmother. In the beginning of their friendship Olive had carried the penurious Camilla off to Paris, where they mildly studied art and ardently pursued the practice of water-colour painting. Olive, it might be said, transacted doorways and alleys, very shadowy and grim, but otherwise quite nice; and Camilla did streams with bending willow and cow on bank, really sweet. In a year or two Camilla's grandmother died of dropsy and left her a fortune, much larger than Olive's, in bank stock, insurance stock, distillery, coal—oh, a mass of money! And when something tragical happened to half of Olive's property—it was in salt shares or jute shares, such unstable friable material—it became the little fluttering Camilla's joy to play the fairy godmother in her turn. So there they were in a bondage less sentimental than appeared, but more sentimental than was known.

They returned to England for George V's coronation. In the train from Chamonix a siphon of soda-water that Camilla imported into the carriage—it was an inexplicable thing, that bottle of soda-water, as Olive said after the catastrophe: God alone knew why she had bought it—Camilla's siphon, what with the jolting of the train and its own gasobility, burst on the rack. Just burst! A handsome young Frenchwoman travelling in their compartment was almost convulsed with mirth, but Olive, sitting just below the bottle, was drenched, she declared, to the midriff. Camilla lightly deprecated the coarseness of the expression. How could *she* help it if a bottle took it into its head to burst like that! In abrupt savage tones Olive merely repeated that she was soaked to the midriff, and to Camilla's horror she began to divest herself of some of her clothing. Camilla rushed to the windows, pulled down the blinds, and locked the corridor door. The young Frenchwoman sat smiling while Olive removed her corsets and her wetted linen; Camilla rummaged so feverishly in Olive's suitcase that the compartment began to look as if arranged for a jumble sale; there were garments and furbelows strewn everywhere. But at last Olive completed her toilet, the train stopped at a station, the young Frenchwoman got out. Later in the day, when they were nearing Paris, Olive's corsets could not be found.

"What did you do with them?" Olive asked Camilla.

"But I don't think I touched them, Olive. After you took them off I did not see them again. Where do you think you put them? Can't you remember?"

She helped Olive unpack the suitcase, but the stays were not there. And she helped Olive to repack.

"What am I to do?" asked Olive.

Camilla firmly declared that the young Frenchwoman who had travelled with them in the morning must have stolen them.

"What for?" asked Olive.

"Well, what do people steal things for?" There was an air of pellucid reason in Camilla's question, but Olive was scornful.

"Corsets!" she exclaimed.

"I knew a cripple once," declared Olive, "who stole an ear-trumpet."

"That French girl wasn't a cripple."

"No," said Camilla, "but she was married—at least, she wore a wedding ring. She looked as deep as the sea. I am positive she was up to no good."

"Bosh!" said Olive. "What the devil are you talking about?"

"Well, you should not throw your things about as you do."

"Soda-water," snapped Olive, with ferocious dignity, "is no place for a railway carriage."

"You mean—?" asked Camilla with the darling sweetness of a maid of twenty.

"I mean just what I say."

"Oh no, you don't," purred the triumphant one; and she repeated Olive's topsy-turvy phrase. "Ha, ha, that's what you said."

"I did not! Camilla, why are you such a liar? You know it annoys me."

"But I tell you, Olive—"

"I did not! It's absurd. You're a fool."

Well, they got to England and in a few days it began to appear to them as the most lovely country they had ever seen. It was not only that, it was their homeland. Why have we stayed away so long? Why did we not come back before? It was so marvellously much better than anything else in the world, they were sure of that. So much better, too, than their youthful recollection of it, so much improved; and the cleanness! Why did we never come back? Why have we stayed away so long? They did not know; it was astonishing to find your homeland so lovely. Both felt that they could not bear to leave England again; they would settle down and build a house, it was time; their joint age was ninety! But, alas, it was difficult, it was impossible, to dovetail their idea of a house into one agreeable abode.

"I want," said Olive Sharples, "just an English country cottage with a few conveniences. That's all I can afford and all I want."

So she bought an acre of land at the foot of a green hill in the Chilterns and gave orders for the erection of the house of her dreams. Truly it was a charming spot, pasture and park and glebe and spinney and stream, *deliciously* remote, quite half a mile from *any* village, and only to be reached by a *mere* lane. No sooner had her friend made this decision than Camilla too bought land there, half a dozen acres adjoining Olive's, and began to build the house of *her* dreams, a roomy house with a loggia and a balcony, planting her land with fruit trees. The two houses were built close together, by the same men, and Camilla could call out greetings to Olive from her bedroom window before Olive was up in the morning, and Olive could hear her—though she did not always reply. Had Olive suffered herself to peer steadily into her secret thoughts in order to discover her present feeling about Camilla, she would have been perplexed; she might even have been ashamed, but for the comfort of old acquaintance such telescopic introspection was denied her. The new cottage brought her felicity, halcyon days; even her bedroom contented her, so small and clean and bare it was. Beyond bed, washing-stand, mirror, and rug there was almost nothing, and yet she felt that if she were not exceedingly careful she would break something. The ceiling was virgin white, the walls the colour of butter, the floor the colour of chocolate. The grate had never had a fire in it; not a shovelful of ashes had ever been taken from it, and, please God—so it seemed to indicate—never would be. But the bed was soft and reposeful. Oh, heavenly sleep!

The two friends dwelt thus in isolation; there they were, perhaps this was happiness. The isolation was tempered by the usual rural society, a squire who drank, a magistrate who was mad, and a lime-burner whose daughters had been to college and swore like seamen. There was the agreeable Mr. Kippax, a retired fell-monger, in whom Camilla divined a desire to wed somebody—Olive perhaps. He was sixty and played on the violoncello. Often Olive accompanied him on Camilla's grand piano. Crump, crump, he would go; and primp, primp, Olive would reply. He was a serious man, and once when they were alone he asked Olive why she was always so sad.

"I don't know. Am I?"

"Surely," he said, grinning, running his fingers through his long grey hair. "Why are you?"

And Olive thought and thought. "I suppose I want impossible things."

"Such as—?" he interrogated.

"I do not know. I only know that I shall never find them."

Then there were the vicarage people, a young vicar with a passionate complexion who had once been an actor and was now something of an invalid, having had a number of his ribs removed for some unpleasant purpose; charming Mrs. Vicar and a tiny baby. Oh, and Mrs. Lassiter, the wife of a sea captain far away on the seas; yet she was content, and so by inference was the sea captain, for he never came home. There was a dearth of colour in her cheeks, it had crowded into her lips, her hair, her eyes. So young, so beautiful, so trite, there was a fragrant imbecility about her.

Olive and Camilla seldom went out together: the possession of a house is often as much of a judgment as a joy, and as full of ardours as of raptures. Gardens, servants, and tradespeople were not automata that behaved like eight-day clocks, by no means. Olive had an eight-day clock, a small competent little thing; it had to be small to suit her room, but Camilla had three—three eight-day clocks. And on the top of the one in the drawing-room

—and really Camilla's house seemed a positive little mansion, all crystal and mirror and white pillars and soft carpets, but it wasn't a mansion any more than Olive's was a cottage—well, on the mantelpiece of the drawing-room, on top of Camilla's largest eight-day clock, there stood the bronze image of a dear belligerent little lion copied in miniature from a Roman antique. The most adorable creature it was, looking as if it were about to mew, for it was no bigger than a kitten although a grown-up lion with a mane and an expression of annoyance as if it had been insulted by an ox—a toy ox. The sweep of its tail was august; the pads of its feet were beautiful crumpled cushions, with claws (like the hooks of a tiny ship) laid on the cushions. Simply ecstatic with anger, most adorable, and Olive loved it as it raged there on Camilla's eight-day clock. But clocks are not like servants. No servant would stay there for long, the place was so lonely, they said, dreadful! And in wet weather the surroundings and approach—there was only a green lane, and half a mile of that— were so muddy, dreadful mud; and when the moon was gone everything was steeped in darkness, and that was dreadful too! As neither Camilla nor Olive could mitigate these natural but unpleasing features—they were, of course, the gifts of Providence —the two ladies, Camilla at any rate, suffered from an ever recurrent domestic Hail and Farewell. What, Camilla would inquire, *did* the servants want? There was the village, barely a mile away; if you climbed the hill you could see it spendidly, a fine meek little village; the woods, the hills, the fields, positively thrust their greenness upon it, bathed it as if in a prism—so that the brown chimney-pots looked red and the yellow ones blue. And the church was new, or so nearly new that you might call it a good second-hand; it was made of brown bricks. Although it had no tower, or even what you might call a belfry, it had got a little square fat chimney over the front gable with a cross of yellow bricks worked into the face of the chimney, while just below that was a bell cupboard stuffed with sparrows' nests. And there were unusual advantages in the village—watercress, for instance. But Camilla's servants came and went, only Olive's Quincy Pugh remained. She was a dark young woman with a white amiable face, amiable curves to her body, the elixir of amiability in her

blood, and it was clear to Camilla that *she* only remained because of Luke Feedy. He was the gardener, chiefly employed by
Camilla, but he also undertook the work of Olive's plot. Un-
fortunately Olive's portion was situated immediately under the
hill and, fence it how they would, the rabbits always burrowed
in and stole Olive's vegetables. They never seemed to attack
Camilla's more abundant acreage.

Close beside their houses there was a public footway, but
seldom used, leading up into the hills. Solemn steep hills they
were, covered with long fawn-hued grass that was never cropped
or grazed, and dotted with thousands of pert little juniper
bushes, very dark, and a few whitebeam trees whose foliage when
tossed by the wind shook on the hillside like bushes of entangled
stars. Half-way up the hill path was a bulging bank that tempted
climbers to rest, and here, all unknown to Camilla, Olive caused
an iron bench to be fixed so that tired persons could recline in
comfort and view the grand country that rolled away before
them. Even at midsummer it was cool on that height, just as
in winter it took the sunbeams warmly. The air roving through
the long fawn-hued grass had a soft caressing movement. Darkly
green at the foot of the hill began the trees and hedges that
diminished in the pastoral infinity of the vale, farther and farther
yet, so very far and wide. At times Olive would sit on her iron
bench in clear sunlight and watch a shower swilling over half a
dozen towns while beyond them, seen through the inundating
curtain, very remote indeed lay the last hills of all, brightly glowing and contented. Often Olive would climb to her high seat and
bask in the delight, but soon Camilla discovered that the bench
was the public gift of Olive. Thereupon lower down the hill
Camilla caused a splendid ornate bench of teak with a foot-rest
to be installed in a jolly nook surrounded by tall juniper bushes
like cypresses, and she planted three or four trailing roses thereby.
Whenever Camilla had visitors she would take them up the
hill to sit on her splendid bench; even Olive's visitors preferred
Camilla's bench and remarked upon its superior charm. So much
more handsome it was, and yet Olive could not bear to sit there at
all, never alone. And soon she gave up going even to the iron one.

Thus they lived in their rather solitary houses, supporting the

infirmities of the domestic spirit by mutual commiseration, and
coming to date occasions by the names of those servants—
Georgina, Rose, Elizabeth, Sue—whoever happened to be with
them when such and such an event occurred. These were not remarkable in any way. The name of Emma Tooting, for instance,
only recalled a catastrophe to the parrot. One day she had actually
shut the cockatoo—it was a stupid bird, always like a parson
nosing about in places where it was not wanted—she had ac-
cidentally shut the cockatoo in the oven. The fire had not long
been lit, the oven was not hot, Emma Tooting was brushing it
out, the cockatoo was watching. Emma Tooting was called away
for a few moments by the baker in the yard, came back, saw the
door open, slammed it to with her foot, pulled out blower, went
upstairs to make bed, came down later to make fire, heard most
horrible noises in kitchen, couldn't tell where, didn't know they
came from the oven, thought it was the devil, swooned straight
away—and the cockatoo was baked. The whole thing completely
unnerved Emma Tooting and she gave notice. Such a good cook,
too. Mrs. Lassiter and the lime-burner—that was a mysterious
business—were thought to have been imprudent in Minnie Hop-
plecock's time; at any rate, suspicion was giddily engendered
then.

"I shouldn't be surprised," Camilla had declared, "if they were
all the way, myself. Of course, I don't know, but it would not
surprise me one bit. You see, we've only instinct to go upon,
suspicion, but what else has anyone ever to go upon in such
matters? She is so deep, she's deep as the sea; and as for men—!
No, I've only my intuitions, but they are sufficient, otherwise
what is the use of an intuition? And what *is* the good of shutting
your eyes to the plain facts of life?"

"But why him?" inquired Olive brusquely.

"I suspect him, Olive." Camilla, calmly adjusting a hair-slide,
peered at her yellow carpet, which had a design in it, a hundred
times repeated, of a spool of cord in red and a shuttlecock in
blue. "I suspect him, just as I suspect the man who quotes Plato
to me."

Mr. Kippax that is—thought Olive. "But isn't that what Plato's
for?" she asked.

"I really don't know what Plato is for, Olive; I have never read Plato; in fact I don't read him at all; I can't read him with enjoyment. Poetry, now, is a thing I can enjoy—like a bath—but I can't talk about it. Can you? I never talk about the things that are precious to me; it's natural to be reserved and secretive. I don't blame Maude Lassiter for that; I don't blame her at all, but she'll be lucky if she gets out of this with a whole skin: it will only be by the skin of her teeth."

"I'd always be content," Olive said, "if I could have the skin of my teeth for a means of escape."

"Quite so," agreed Camilla, "I'm entirely with you. Oh, yes."

Among gardeners Luke Feedy was certainly the pearl. He had come from far away, a man of thirty or thirty-five, without a wife or a home in the world, and now he lodged in the village at Mrs. Thrupcott's cottage; the thatch of her roof was the colour of shag tobacco; her husband cut your hair in his vegetable garden for twopence a time. Luke was tall and powerful, fair and red. All the gardening was done by him, both Olive's and Camilla's, and all the odd and difficult jobs from firewood down to the dynamo for electric light that coughed in Camilla's shed. Bluff but comely, a pleasant man, a very conversational man, and a very attractable man; the maids were always uncommon friendly to him. And so even was Olive, Camilla observed, for she had actually bought him a gun to keep the rabbits out of the garden. Of course a gun was no use for that—Luke said so—yet, morning or evening, Olive would perambulate with the gun, inside or outside the gardens, while Luke Feedy taught her the use of it, until one October day, when it was drawing on to evening—bang!—Olive had killed a rabbit. Camilla had rushed to her balcony. "What is it?" she cried in alarm, for the gun had not often been fired before and the explosion was terrifying. Fifty yards away, with her back towards her, Olive in short black fur jacket, red skirt, and the Cossack boots she wore, was standing quite still holding the gun across her breast. The gardener stalked towards a bush at the foot of the hill, picked up a limp contorted bundle by its long ears, and brought it back to Olive. She had no hat on, her hair was ruffled, her face had gone white. The gardener held up the rabbit, a small soft thing, dead, but its eyes still stared, and its forefeet drooped in a gesture that seemed to beseech pity. Olive swayed away, the hills began to twirl, the house turned upside down, the gun fell from her hands. "Hullo!" cried Luke Feedy, catching the swooning woman against his shoulder. Camilla saw it all and flew to their aid, but by the time she had got down to the garden Feedy was there too, carrying Olive to her own door. Quincy ran for a glass of water, Camilla petted her, and soon all was well. The gardener stood in the room holding his hat against his chest with both hands. A huge fellow he looked in Olive's small apartment. He wore breeches and leggings and a grey shirt with the sleeves uprolled, a pleasant comely man, very powerful, his voice seemed to excite a quiver in the air.

"What a fool I am!" said Olive disgustedly.

"Oh, no," commented the gardener. "Oh no, ma'am; it stands to reason—" He turned to go about his business, but said: "I should have a sip o' brandy now, ma'am, if you'll excuse me mentioning it."

"Cognac!" urged Camilla.

"Don't go, Luke," Olive cried.

"I'll fetch that gun in, ma'am, I fancy it's going to rain." He stalked away, found his coat and put it on (for it was time to go home), and then he fetched in the gun. Camilla had gone.

"Take it away, please," cried Olive. "I never want to see it again. Keep it. Do what you like, it's yours."

"Thank you, ma'am," said the imperturbable Feedy. Two small glasses of cognac and a long slim bottle stood upon a table in the alcove. Olive, still a little wan, pushed one towards him.

"Your very good health, ma'am." Feedy tipped the thimbleful of brandy into his mouth, closed his lips, pursed them, gazed at the ceiling, and sighed. Olive now switched on the light, for the room was growing dimmer every moment. Then she sat down on the settee that faced the fire. An elegant little settee in black satin with crimson piping. The big man stood by the shut door and stared at the walls; he could not tell whether they were blue or green or grey, but the skirting was white and the fireplace was tiled with white tiles. Old and dark the furniture was, though, and the mirror over the mantel was egg-shaped in a black frame. In the alcove made by the bow window stood the round table on crinkled legs, and the alcove itself was lined with a bench of tawny velvet cushions. Feedy put his empty glass upon the table.

"Do have some more; help yourself," said Olive, and Luke refilled the glass and drank again amid silence. Olive did not face him—she was staring into the fire—but she could feel his immense presence. There was an aroma, something of earth, something of man, about him, strange and exciting. A shower of rain dashed at the windows.

"You had better sit down until the rain stops." Olive poked a tall hassock to the fireplace with her foot, and Luke, squatting upon it, his huge boots covering quite a large piece of the rug there, twirled the half-empty glass between his finger and thumb.

"Last time I drunk brandy," he mused, "was with a lady in her room, just this way."

Olive could stare at him now.

"She was mad," he explained.

"Oh," said Olive, as if disappointed.

"She's dead now," continued Luke, sipping.

Olive, without uttering a word, seemed to encourage his reminiscence.

"A Yorkshire lady she was, used to live in the manor house, near where I was then; a lonely place. Her brother had bought it because it was lonely, and sent her there to keep her quiet because she had been crossed in love, as they say, and took to drink for the sorrow of it; rich family, bankers, Croxton the name, if you ever heard of them?"

Olive, lolling back and sipping brandy, shook her head.

"A middling-size lady, about forty-five she was, but very nice to look at—you'd never think she was daft—and used to live at the big house with only a lot of servants and a butler in charge of her, name of Scrivens. None of her family ever came near her, nobody ever came to visit her. There was a big motor-car and they kept some horses, but she always liked to be tramping about alone; everybody knew her, poor daft thing, and called her Miss Mary, 'stead of by her surname, Croxton, a rich family; bankers they were. Quite daft. One morning I was going to my work— I was faggoting then in Hanging Copse—and I'd got my bill-hook, my axe, and my saw in a bag on my back, when I see Miss

Mary coming down the road towards me. 'Twas a bright spring morning and cold 'cause 'twas rather early; a rare wind on, and blew sharp enough to shave you; it blew the very pigeons out the trees, but she'd got neither jacket or hat and her hair was wild. 'Good morning, miss,' I said, and she said: 'Good morning,' and stopped. So I stopped, too; I didn't quite know what to be at, so I said: 'Do you know where you are going?'"

"Look here," interrupted Olive, glancing vacantly around the room. "It's still raining; light your pipe."

"Thank you, ma'am," Luke began to prepare his pipe. "'Do you know where you're going?' I asked her, 'No,' she says. 'I've lost my way; where am I?' and she put"—Luke paused to strike a match and ignite the tobacco—"put her arm in my arm and said: 'Take me home.' 'You're walking away from home,' I said, so she turned back with me and we started off to her home. Two miles away or more it was. 'It is kind of you,' she says, and she kept on chattering as if we were two cousins, you might say. 'You ought to be more careful and have your jacket on,' I said to her. 'I didn't think, I can't help it,' she says; 'it's the time 'o love; as soon as the elder leaf is as big as a mouse's ear I want to be blown about the world,' she says. Of course she was thinking to find someone as she'd lost. She dropped a few tears. 'You must take care of yourself these rough mornings,' I said, 'or you'll be catching the inflammation.' Then we come to a public-house, The Bank of England's the name of it, and Miss Mary asks me if we could get some refreshment there. 'That you can't,' I said ('cause I knew about her drinking), 'it's shut,' so on we went as far as Bernard's Bridge. She had to stop a few minutes there to look over in the river, all very blue and crimped with the wind; and there was a boat-house there, and a new boat cocked upside down on some trestles on the landing, and a chap laying on his back blowing in the boat with a pair of bellows. Well, on we goes, and presently she pulls out her purse. 'I'm putting you to a lot of trouble,' she says. 'Not at all, miss,' I said, but she give me a sovereign, then and there, she give me a sovereign."

Olive was staring at the man's hands; the garden soil was chalky, and his hands were covered with fine milky dust that left the skin smooth and the markings very plain.

"I didn't want to take the money, ma'am, but I had to, of course; her being such a grand lady it wasn't my place to refuse."

Olive had heard of such munificence before; the invariable outcome, the denouement of Feedy's stories, the crown, the peak, the apex of them all was that somebody, at some point or other, gave him a sovereign. Neither more nor less. Never anything else. Olive thought it unusual for so *many* people . . .

"—and I says: 'I'm very pleased, miss, to be a help to anyone in trouble.' 'That's most good of you,' she said to me. 'That's most good of you; it's the time of year I must go about the world, or I'd die,' she says. By and by we come to the manor house and we marched arm in arm right up to the front door and I rong the bell. I was just turning away to leave her there, but she laid hold of my arm again. 'I want you to stop,' she says, 'you've been so kind to me.' It was a bright fresh morning, and I rong the bell. 'I want you to stop,' she says. Then the butler opened the door. 'Scrivens,' she says, 'this man has been very kind to me; give him a sovereign, will you.' Scrivens looked very straight at me, but I gave him as good as he sent, and the lady stepped into the hall. I had to follow her. 'Come in,' she says, and there was I in the dining-room, while Scrivens nipped off somewhere to get the money. Well, I had to set down on a chair while she popped out at another door. I hadn't hardly set down when in she come again with a lighted candle in one hand and a silver teapot in the other. She held the teapot up and says: 'Have some?' and then she got two little cups and saucers out of a chiffonier and set them on the table and filled them out of the silver teapot. 'There you are,' she says, and she up with her cup and dronk it right off. I couldn't see no milk and no sugar and I was a bit flabbergasted, but I takes a swig—and what do you think? It was brandy, just raw brandy; nearly made the tears come out of my eyes, 'specially that first cup. All of a sudden she dropped on a sofy and went straight off to sleep, and there was I left with that candle burning on the table in broad daylight. Course I blew it out, and the butler came in and gave me the other sovereign, and I went off to my work. Rare good-hearted lady, ma'am. Pity," sighed the gardener. He sat hunched on the hassock, staring into the fire, and puffing smoke. There was attraction in the lines of his figure squatting beside her hearth, a sort of huge power. Olive wondered if she might sketch him some time, but she had not sketched for years now. He said that the rain had stopped, and got up to go. Glancing at the window Olive saw it was quite dark; the panes were crowded on the outside with moths trying to get in to the light.

"What a lot of mawths there be!" said Luke.

Olive went to the window to watch them. Swarms of fat brown furry moths with large heads pattered and fluttered silently about the shut panes, forming themselves into a kind of curtain on the black window. Now and then one of their eyes would catch a reflection from the light and it would burn with a fiery crimson glow.

"Good night, ma'am," the gardener said, taking the gun away with him. Outside, he picked up the dead rabbit and put it in his pocket. Olive drew the curtains; she did not like the moths' eyes, they were demons' eyes, and they filled her with melancholy. She took the tall brandy bottle from the table and went to replace it in a cabinet. In the cabinet she saw her little silver teapot, a silver teapot on a silver tray with a bowl and a jug. Something impelled her to fill the teapot from the long slim bottle. She poured out a cup and drank it quickly. Another. Then she switched out the light, stumbled to the couch, and fell upon it, laughing stupidly and kicking her heels with playful fury.

That was the beginning of Olive's graceless decline, her pitiable lapse into intemperance. Camilla one May evening had trotted across to Olive's cottage; afterwards she could recall every detail of that tiniest of journeys; rain had fallen and left a sort of crisp humidity in the gloomy air; on the pathway to Olive's door she nearly stepped on a large hairy caterpillar solemnly confronting a sleek nude slug. That lovely tree by Olive's door was desolated, she remembered; the blossoms had fallen from the flowering cherry tree so wonderfully bloomed; its virginal bridal had left only a litter and a breath of despair. And then inside Olive's hall was the absurd old blunderbuss hanging on a strap, its barrel so large that you could slip an egg into it. Camilla fluttered into her friend's drawing-room. "Olive could you lend me your gridiron?" And there was Olive lounging on the settee simply incredibly drunk! In daylight! It was about six o'clock of a May day. And Olive was so indecently jovial that Camilla, smitten with grief, burst into tears and rushed away home again.

She came back of course; she never ceased coming back, hour by hour, day after day; never would she leave Olive alone to her wretched debauches. Camilla was drenched with compunction, filled with divine energy; until she had dragged Olive from her trough, had taken her to live with her again under her own cherishing wings, she would have no rest. But Olive was not always tipsy, and though moved by Camilla's solicitude, she refused to budge, or "make an effort," or do any of the troublesome things so dear to the heart of a friend. Fond as she was of Camilla, she had a disinclination—of course she was fond of her, there was nothing she would not do for Camilla Hobbs—a disinclination to reside with her again. What if they had lived together for twenty years? It is a great nuisance that one's loves are determined not by judgment but by the feelings. There are two simple tests of any friendly relationship: can you happily share your bed with your friend, and can you, without unease, watch him or her partake of food? If you can do either of these things with amiability, to say nothing of joy, it is well between you; if you can do both it is a sign that your affection is rooted in immortal soil. Now, Olive was forthright about food; she just ate it, that was what it was for. But she knew that even at breakfast Camilla would cut her bread into little cubes or little diamonds; if she had been able to she would surely have cut it into little lozenges or little marbles; in fact, the butter was patted into balls the same as you had in restaurants. Every shred of fat would be laboriously shaved from the rasher and discarded. The cube or the diamond would be rolled in what Camilla called the 'jewse'— for her to swallow the grease but not the fat was a horrible mortification to Olive—rolled and rolled and then impaled by the fork. Snip off a wafer of bacon, impale it; a triangle of white egg, impale that; plunge the whole into the yolk. Then, so carefully, with such desperate care, a granule of salt, the merest breath of pepper. Now the knife must pursue with infinite

patience one or two minuscular crumbs idling in the plate and
at last wipe them gloatingly upon the mass. With her fork
lavishly furnished and elegantly poised, Camilla would then
bend to peer at sentences in her correspondence and perhaps
briskly inquire:

"Why are you so glum this morning, Olive?"

Of course Olive would not answer.

"Aren't you feeling well, dear?" Camilla would exasperatingly
persist, still toying with her letters.

"What?" Olive would say.

Camilla would pop the loaded fork into her mouth, her lips
would close tightly upon it, and when she drew the fork slowly
from her encompassing lips it would be empty, quite empty and
quite clean. Repulsive!

"Why are you so glum?"

"I'm not!"

"Sure? Aren't you?" Camilla would impound another little
cube or diamond and glance smilingly at her letters. On that
count alone Olive could not possibly resume life with her.

As for sleeping with Camilla—not that it was suggested that
she should, but it was the test—Olive's distaste for sharing a bed
was ineradicable. In the whole of her life Olive had never known
a woman with whom it would have been anything but an intensely unpleasant experience, neither decent nor comfortable.
Olive was deeply virginal. And yet there had been two or three
men who, perhaps, if it had not been for Camilla—such a prude,
such a killjoy—she might—well, goodness only knew. But
Camilla had been a jealous harpy, always fond, Olive was certain,
of the very men who had been fond of Olive. Even Edgar Salter,
who had dallied with them one whole spring in Venice. Why,
there was one day in a hayfield on the Lido when the grass was
mown in May—it was, oh, fifteen years ago. And before that, in
Paris, Hector Dubonnel, and Willie Macmaster! Camilla had
been such a lynx, such a collar-round-the-neck, that Olive had
found the implications, the necessities of romance quite beyond
her grasp. Or, perhaps, the men themselves—they were not at all
like the bold men you read about, they were only like the oafs

you meet and meet and meet. Years later, in fact not ten years ago, there was the little Italian count in Rouen. They were all dead now, yes, perhaps they were dead. Or married. What was the use? What did it all matter?

Olive would lie abed till midday in torpor and vacancy, and in the afternoon she would mope and mourn in dissolute melancholy. The soul loves to rehearse painful occasions. At evening the shadows cast by the down-going sun would begin to lie aslant the hills and then she would look out of her window, and seeing the bold curves bathed in the last light, she would exclaim upon her folly. "I have not been out in the sunlight all day; it would be nice to go and stand on the hill now and feel the warmth just once." No, she was too weary to climb the hill, but she would certainly go tomorrow, early, and catch the light coming from the opposite heaven. Now it was too late, or too damp, and she was very dull. The weeks idled by until August came with the rattle of the harvest reapers, and then September with the boom of the sportsman's gun in the hollow coombs. Camilla one evening was sitting with her, Camilla who had become a most tender friend, who had realized her extremity, her inexplicable grief; Camilla who was a nuisance, a bore, who knew she was not to be trusted alone with her monstrous weakness for liquor, who constantly urged her to cross the garden and live in peace with her. No, no, she would not. "I should get up in the night and creep away," she thought to herself, "and leave her to hell and the judgment," but all she would reply to Camilla was: "Enjoy your own life, and I'll do mine. Don't want to burden yourself with a drunken old fool like me."

"Olive! Olive! What are you saying?"

"Drunken fool," repeated Olive sourly. "Don't badger me any more, let me alone, leave me as I am. I—I'll—I dunno—perhaps I'll marry Feedy."

"Nonsense," cried Camilla shrilly. She turned on the light and drew the blinds over the alcove window. "Nonsense," she cried again over her shoulder. "Nonsense."

"You let me alone, I ask you," commanded her friend. "Do as I like."

"But you can't—you can't think—why, don't be stupid!"

"I might. Why shouldn't I? He's a proper man; teach me a lot of things."

Camilla shuddered. "But you can't. You can't, he is going to marry somebody else."

"What's that?" sighed Olive. "Who? Oh God, you're not thinking to marry him yourself, are you? You're not going—"

"Stuff! He's going to marry Quincy. He told me so himself. I'd noticed them for some time, and then, once, I came upon them suddenly, and really—! Honest love-making is all very well, but, of course, one has a responsibility to one's servants. I spoke to him most severely, and he told me."

"Told you what?"

"That they were engaged to be married, so what—"

"Quincy?"

"Yes, so what can one do?"

"Do? God above!" cried Olive. She touched a bell and Quincy came in answer. "Is this true?"

Quincy looked blankly at Miss Sharples.

"Are you going to marry Mr. Feedy?"

"Yes'm."

"When are you going to marry Mr. Feedy?" Olive had risen on unsteady legs.

"As soon as we can get a house, ma'am."

"When will that be?"

The girl smiled. She did not know; there were no houses to be had.

"I won't have it!" shouted Olive suddenly, swaying. "But no, I won't, I won't! You wretched devil! Go away, go off. I won't have you whoring about with that man, I tell you. Go off, off with you; pack your box!"

The flushing girl turned savagely and went out, slamming the door.

"Oh, I'm drunk," moaned Olive, falling to the couch again. "I'm sodden. Camilla, what shall I do?"

"Olive, listen! Olive! Now you *must* come to live with me; you won't be able to replace her. What's the good? Shut up the house and let me take care of you."

"No, stupid wretch I am. Don't want to burden yourself with a stupid wretch." With her knuckle Olive brushed a tear from her haggard eyes.

"Nonsense, darling!" cried her friend. "I want you immensely. Just as we once were, when we were so fond of each other. Aren't you fond of me still, Olive? You'll come, and we'll be so happy again. Shall we go abroad?"

Olive fondled her friend's hand with bemused caresses. "You're too good, Camilla, and I ought to adore you. I do, I do, and I'm a beast."

"No, no, listen."

"Yes, I am. I'm a beast. I tell you I have wicked envious feelings about you, and sneer at you, and despise you in a low secret way. And yet you are, oh, Camilla, yes, you are true and honest and kind, and I know it, I know it." She broke off and stared tragically at her friend. "Camilla, were you ever in love?"

The question startled Camilla.

"Were you?" repeated Olive. "I've never known you to be. Were you ever in love?"

"Oh—sometimes—yes—sometimes."

Olive stared for a moment with a look of silent contempt, then almost guffawed.

"Bah! Sometimes! Good Lord, Camilla. Oh no, no, you've never been in love. Oh no, no."

"But yes, of course," Camilla persisted, with a faint giggle.

"Who? Who with?"

"Why, yes, of course, twenty times at least," admitted the astonishing Camilla.

"But listen, tell me," cried Olive, sitting up eagerly as her friend sat down beside her on the couch. "Tell me—it's you and I—tell me. Really in love?"

"Everybody is in love," said Camilla slowly, "some time or another, and I was very solemnly in love—well—four times. Olive, you mustn't reproach yourself for—for all this. I've been —I've been bad, too."

"Four times! Four times! Perhaps you will understand me, Camilla, now. I've been in love all my life. Any man could have had me, but none did, not one."

"Never mind, dear. I was more foolish than you, that's all, Olive."

"Foolish! But how? It never went very far?"

"As far as I could go."

Olive eyed her friend, the mournful, repentant, drooping Camilla.

"What do you mean? How far?"

Camilla shrugged her shoulders. "As far as love takes you," she said.

"Yes, but—" pursued Olive, "do you mean—?"

"I could go no further," Camilla explained quickly.

"But how—what—were you ever really and truly a lover?"

"If you must know—that is what I mean."

"Four times!"

Camilla nodded.

"But I mean, Camilla, were you really, really, a mistress?"

"Olive, only for a very little while. Oh, my dear," she declined on Olive's breast, "you see, you see, I've been worse, much worse than you. And it's all over. And you'll come back and be good too?"

But her friend's eagerness would suffer no caresses; Olive was sobered and alert. "But—this, I can't understand—while we were together—inseparable we were. Who—did I know them? Who were they?"

Camilla, unexpectedly, again fairly giggled. "Well, then, I wonder if you can remember the young man we knew at Venice—?"

"Edgar Salter, was it?" Olive snapped at the name.

"Yes."

"And the others? Willie Macmaster and Hercules and Count Filippo!" Olive was now fairly raging. Camilla sat with folded hands. "Camilla Hobbs, you're a fiend," screamed Olive, "a fiend, a fiend, an impertinent immoral fool. Oh, how I loathe you!"

"Miss Sharples," said Camilla, rising primly, "I can only say I despise you."

"A fool!" shrieked Olive, burying her face in the couch; "an extraordinary person with a horrible temper and intolerant as a —yes, you are. Oh, intolerable beast!"

"I can hardly expect you to realize, in your present state," returned Camilla, walking to the door, "how disgusting you are to me. You are like a dog that barks at every passer."

"There are people whose minds are as brutal as their words. Will you cease annoying me, Camilla!"

"You imagine"—Camilla wrenched open the door—"you imagine that I'm trying to annoy you. How strange!"

"Oh, you've a poisonous tongue and a poisonous manner; I'm dreadfully ashamed of you."

"Indeed." Camilla stopped and faced her friend challengingly.

"Yes." Olive sat up, nodding wrathfully. "I'm ashamed and deceived and disappointed. You've a coarse soul. Oh," she groaned. "I want kindness, friendship, pity, pity, pity, pity, most of all, pity. I cannot bear it." She flung herself again to the couch and sobbed forlornly.

"Very well, Olive, I will leave you. Good night."

Olive did not reply and Camilla passed out of the room to the front door and opened that. Then: "Oh," she said, "how beautiful, Olive!" She came back into Olive's room and stood with one hand grasping the edge of the door, looking timidly at her friend. "There's a new moon and a big star and a thin fog over the barley field. Come and see."

She went out again to the porch and Olive rose and followed her. "See," cried Camilla, "the barley is goosenecked now, it is ripe for cutting."

Olive stood staring out long and silently. It was exquisite as an Eden evening, with a sleek young moon curled in the fondling clouds; it floated into her melancholy heart. Sweet light, shadows, the moon, the seat, the long hills, the barley field, they twirled in her heart with disastrous memories of Willie Macmaster, Edgar Salter, Hercules, and Count Filippo. All lost, all gone now, and Quincy Pugh was going to marry the gardener.

"Shall I come with you, Camilla? Yes, I can't bear it any longer; I'll come with you now, Camilla, if you'll have me."

Camilla's response was tender and solicitous.

"I'll tell Quincy," said Olive. "She and Luke can have this cottage, just as it is. I shan't want it ever again! They can get married at once." Camilla was ecstatic. "And then will you tell me, Camilla," said Olive, taking her friend's arm, "all about—all about—those men!"

"I will, darling; yes, yes, I will," cried Camilla. "Oh, come along."

The Field of Mustard (1926)

CLORINDA WALKS IN HEAVEN

Miss Smith, Clorinda Smith, desired not to die on a wet day. Her speculations on the possibilities of one's demise were quite ingenuous and had their mirth, but she shrunk from that figure of her dim little soul—and it was only dimly that she could figure it at all—approaching the pathways of the boundless in a damp, bedraggled condition.

"But the rain couldn't harm your spirit," declared her comforting friends.

"Why not?" asked Clorinda. "If there is a ghost of me, why not a ghost of the rain?"

There were other aspects, delectable and illusive, of this imagined apotheosis, but Clorinda always hoped—against hope, be it said—that it wouldn't be wet. On three evenings there had been a bow in the sky, and on the day she died rain poured in fury. With a golden key she unlocked the life out of her bosom and moved away without fear, as if a great light had sprung suddenly under her feet in a little dark place, into a region where things became starkly real and one seemed to live like the beams rolling on the tasselled corn in windy acres. There was calmness in those translucent leagues and the undulation amid a vast im-

placable light until she drifted like a feather, fallen from an un-
guessed star, into a place that was extraordinarily like the noonday
world, so green and warm was its valley.

A little coomb lay between some low hills of turf, and on a
green bank beside a few large rocks was a man mending a ladder of white new-shaven willow studded with large brass nails,
mending it with hard knocks that sounded clearly. The horizon
was terraced only just beyond and above him, for the hills rolled
steeply up. Thin pads of wool hung in the arch of the ultimate
heavens, but towards the end of the valley the horizon was
clouded with clouds torn and disbattled. Two cows, a cow of
white and a cow of tan, squatted where one low hill held up, as
it were, the sunken limits of the sky. There were larks—in such
places the lark sings for ever—and thrushes—the wind vaguely
active—seven white ducks—a farm. Each nook was a flounce
of blooms and a bower for birds. Passing close to the man—
he was sad and preoccupied, dressed in a little blue tunic—she
touched his arm as if to inquire a direction, saying: "Jacob!"

She did not know what she would have asked of him, but he
gave her no heed and she again called to him: "Jacob!" He
did not seem even to see her, so she went to the large white gates
at the end of the valley and approached a railway crossing. She
had to wait a long time, for trains of a vastness and grandeur
were passing without sound. Strange advertisements on the
hoardings and curious direction posts gathered some of her attention. She observed that in every possible situation, on any
available post or stone, people had carved initials, sometimes a
whole name, often with a date, and Clorinda experienced a doubt
of the genuineness of some of these, so remote was the antiquity
implied. At last the trains were all gone by, and as the barriers
swung back she crossed the permanent way.

There was neither ambiguity in her movements nor surprise
in her apprehensions. She just crossed over to a group of twenty
or thirty men, who moved to welcome her. They were bare-
legged, sandal-footed, lightly clad in beautiful loose tunics of pea-
cock and cinnamon, which bore not so much the significance of
colour as the quality of light. One of them rushed eagerly forward, crying: "Clorinda!" offering to her a long coloured scarf.

Strangely, as he came closer, he grew less perceivable; Clorinda was aware in a flash that she was viewing him by some other mechanism than that of her two eyes. In a moment he utterly disappeared and she felt herself rapt into his being, caressed with faint caresses, and troubled with dim faded ecstasies and recognitions not wholly agreeable. The other men stood grouped around them, glancing with half-closed cynical eyes. Those who stood farthest away were more clearly seen: in contiguity a presence could only be divined, resting only—but how admirably!—in the nurture of one's mind.

"What is it?" Clorinda asked; and all the voices replied: "Yes, we know you!"

She felt herself released, and the figure of the man rejoined the waiting group. "I was your husband Reuben," said the first man slowly, and Clorinda, who had been a virgin throughout her short life, exclaimed: "Yes, yes, dear Reuben!" with momentary tremors and a queer fugitive drift of doubt. She stood there, a spook of comprehending being, and all the uncharted reefs in the map of her mind were anxiously engaging her. For a time she was absorbed by this new knowledge.

Then another voice spoke:

"I was your husband Raphael!"

"I know, I know," said Clorinda, turning to the speaker, "we lived in Judea."

"And we dwelt in the valley of the Nile," said another, "in the years that are gone."

"And I too . . . and I too . . . and I too," they all clamoured, turning angrily upon themselves.

Clorinda pulled the strange scarf from her shoulders where Reuben had left it, and, handling it so, she became aware of her many fugitive sojournings upon the earth. It seemed that all of her past had become knit in the scarf into a compact pattern of beauty and ugliness of which she was entirely aware, all its multiplexity being immediately resolved . . . the habitations with cave men, and the lesser human unit of the lesser later day, Patagonian, Indian, Cossack, Polynesian, Jew . . . of such stuff the pattern was intimately woven, and there were little plangent perfect moments of the past that fell into order in the web.

Clorinda watching the great seabird with pink feet louting above the billows that roared upon Iceland, or Clorinda hanging her girdle upon the ebony hooks of the image of Tanteelee. She had taken voyaging drafts upon the whole world, cataract, jungle and desert, ingle and pool and strand, ringing the changes upon a whole gamut of masculine endeavour—from a prophet to a haberdasher. She could feel each little life hung now as in a sarsenet of cameos upon her visible breasts: thereby for these— these *men*—she was draped in an eternal wonder. But she could not recall any image of her past life in *these* realms save only that her scarf was given back to her on every return by a man of these men.

She could remember with humility her transient passions for them all. None, not one, had ever given her the measure of her own desire, a strong harsh flame that fashioned and tempered its own body; nothing but a nebulous glow that was riven into embers before its beam had sweetened into pride. She had gone from them childless always and much as a little child.

From the crowd of quarrelling ghosts a new figure detached itself, and in its approach it subdued that vague vanishing which had been so perplexing to Clorinda. Out of the crowd it slipped, and loomed lovingly beside her, took up her thought and the interrogation that came into her mind.

"No," it said gravely, "there is none greater than these. The ultimate reaches of man's mind produce nothing but images of men."

"But," said Clorinda, "do you mean that our ideals, previsions of a *vita nuova*—"

"Just so," it continued, "a mere intoxication. Even here you cannot escape the singular dower of dreams . . . you can be drunk with dreams more easily and more permanently than with drugs."

The group of husbands had ceased their quarrelling to listen; Clorinda swept them with her glances thoughtfully and doubtfully.

"Could mankind be so poor," the angel resumed, "as poor as these, if it housed something greater than itself?"

With a groan the group of outworn husbands drew away.

Clorinda turned to her companion with disappointment and some dismay. . . . "I hardly understand yet—is this all then, just—"

"Yes," it replied, "just the ghost of the world."

She turned unhappily and looked back across the gateway into the fair coomb with its cattle, its fine grass, and the man working diligently therein. A sense of bleak loneliness began to possess her; here, then, was no difference save that there were no correlations, no consequences; nothing had any effect except to produce the ghost of a ghost. There was already in the hinterland of her apprehensions a ghost of her new ghostship: she was to be followed by herself, pursued by figures of her own ceaseless being!

She looked at the one by her side. "Who are you?" she asked, and at the question the group of men drew again very close to them.

"I am your unrealized desires," it said. "Did you think that the dignity of virginhood, rarely and deliberately chosen, could be so brief and barren? Why, that pure idea was my own immaculate birth, and I was born the living mate of you."

The hungry-eyed men shouted with laughter.

"Go away!" screamed Clorinda to them; "I do not want you."

Although they went she could hear the echoes of their sneering as she took the arm of her new lover. "Let us go," she said, pointing to the man in the coomb, "and speak to him." As they approached the man he lifted his ladder hugely in the air and dashed it to the ground so passionately that it broke.

"Angry man! Angry man!" mocked Clorinda. He turned towards her fiercely. Clorinda began to fear him; the muscles and knots of his limbs were uncouth like the gnarl of old trees; she made a little pretence of no more observing him.

"Now what is it like," said she jocularly to the angel at her side, and speaking of her old home, "what is it like now at Weston-super-Mare?"

At that foolish question the man with the ladder reached forth an ugly hand and twitched the scarf from her shoulders.

It cannot now be told to what remoteness she had come, or on what roads her undirected feet had travelled there, but certain it is that in that moment she was gone. . . . Why, where, or how cannot be established: whether she was swung in a blast of annihilation into the uttermost gulfs, or withdrawn for her beauty into that mysterious Nox; into some passionate communion with the eternal husbands, or into some eternal combat with their passionate other wives . . . from our scrutiny at least she passed for ever.

It is true there was a beautiful woman of this name who lay for a month in a deep trance in the west of England. On her recovery she was balladed about in the newspapers and upon the halls for quite a time, and indeed her notoriety brought requests for her autograph from all parts of the world, and an offer of marriage from a Quaker potato merchant. But she tenderly refused him and became one of those faded grey old maids who wear their virginity like antiquated armour.

Clorinda Walks in Heaven (1922)

DOE

THE Reverend Phalarope Doe, fondly referred to by his choir as Sammy, was vicar of a village in the south country. His church and his vicarage, hung over by pastoral elms, were hunched beside a lucid stream near a bridge of stone; the water smiled under its arches, the fish hung dreaming in its tide. Just beyond the bridge the road forked at a triangle of grass where two vast lime trees towered above a tiny tiled hut with a padlocked door; the hut, never opened, and plastered with bills of circuses long remote in time and place, harboured a sort of fire-engine that had never been used, that only a few old men had ever seen. Then you came to the village on the flank of a small hill. It was an undistinguished heap of houses with a burden, no doubt easily assimilated, of the frequent traffic of trains; two long chimney

shafts projected from a lime-kiln that had died in its own pit and
an ironworks that was decaying into rust. The place itself looked
rusty, harassed alike by the roar of passing trains and the poverty
of its trade.

Here, where incentives to virtue were not impressive, though
vice seldom ogled with its alluring eye—at least, not observably
—for forty years the Reverend Phalarope Doe, portly and ruddy,
had ministered, and seldom had a vicar conferred so fair a lustre
on so mean a village.

> His sermon never said or showed
> That Earth is foul, that Heaven is gracious.

For he was kind and wise, and he was *so* forgiving—he could
forgive anything. A pat on the shoulder, and something, somehow—*you* know.

"Now tell me," he would ask some erring maiden, "why were
you so careless?"

"Oh, sir, he decaptivated me!"

"There, there; you shouldn't have done it. I shouldn't do it
again, you know, not that kind of thing, if I were you. It's wrong;
at least, it's not quite right, you know. I shouldn't do it again,
not if I were you."

Sammy's pleasant home was a little too big and his income a
little too small. Too big for what? Too small for what? Well, he
was a bachelor for one thing, and the vicarage—to say nothing of
the garden—was larger than the church, and as he could afford
neither curate nor gardener, he revelled personally in both activities at the expense of muscle and high-mindedness. Kindness was
his hobby, his pastime; he played for the pleasure of giving—and,
in his turn, taking—as one played bridge or golf. And what a
player he was! When his wristbands became frayed he cut off
the ends of his shirt-sleeves. Concealed in his study, behind an
almanac of *The Light of the World,* there hung a certain map of
his own neighbourhood, which he had marked with different-
coloured spots, each spot denoting the homes of agreeable souls
on whom he could rely when rambling afoot. A green spot signified a place where he could be sure of a bed, a red spot meant
lunch, blue merely tea, and so forth.

"Ah, splendid souls!" And, as it were, his very heart would

give them a smile as he took his stick again to trudge the homeward path. At the first tree he came to he might pause awhile. These beautiful leaves! They grew and they died. The trees became bald, like himself, like the aged; their beauty was but skin-deep; yet the *idea* of tree, the spirit manifested in its passion for continuity, its beaming leaves, was eternally beautiful. How unlike man, whose idea here and now was not in life alone, but whose destiny was assured!

One day he received a letter from a man with a vaguely familiar name, who lodged in apartments at Twickenham. Rowfant? Ellis Rowfant? It turned out to be an old college chum he had known forty years ago at Oxford. They had had rooms in the same college, the same scout had served them on the same stair, they had swotted for a degree together, taken it, and had gone down together. And then no more. That was all. Doe had been ordained and disposed of; Rowfant had vanished quite away and he had not heard from him, or of him, until now. The two men began a cordial correspondence, and the long-lost friend soon came to pay Doe a visit of several days.

On the appointed afternoon Doe walked along to the small parched railway station, whose stationmaster had a permanently dazed appearance caused probably by the ignoring rush past of so many trains that never stopped. Its grey granite design seemed to invite the meeting of extremes, for when the weather was at all cold it was colder there than it could decently have been elsewhere, although if warmth were the order of the day it was here that the temperature multiplied.

"What a fine day!" exclaimed Mr. Doe.

"Ah," retorted the stationmaster, "we want plenty of this, and more of it."

"It is sumptuous indeed," said Mr. Doe.

The parson idled up the platform and down the platform, reading every placard quite seriously, even the notice that declared the railway company's resolve to transmit explosives only under the most stringent conditions, and that coal, coke, shoddy, manure, and statuary would be carried only on similar terms.

"Well, well! But really, you know . . ." the parson was reflecting as the train came in.

There could be no doubt that that queer figure was Rowfant.

He was the only passenger to emerge, and he came peeringly up to Mr. Doe.

"My dear friend, do I see you! Good heavens, yes; do you know me?"

"I see you," Doe assured him. "We have trebled the years, but there is little change."

"I fear we shall treble the change in vastly fewer years!" Rowfant rejoined.

"None of your pessimistic whim-whams now, Ellis. I remember you, oh, I remember you very well. You were always a regular Hamlet."

"Deplorable!" grinned Hamlet. "I hope you don't mind me appearing like this? I've come straight off the river—must change directly we get to your place."

"Come on," said the parson. "Come on." And he picked up the traveller's bag.

Ellis Rowfant was an amiably vigorous gentleman in the sixties, with a slight round-shouldered stoop and a large clean-shaven magisterial face. But when you caught his gaze through the round spectacles, you saw that he had quite childish blue eyes. A small pink cap with a monogram was clapped upon his head in a way that seemed to fasten it there; his jacket of navy blue was flashing with buttons, and a pink tie adorned his throat. His trousers of blankety flannel were of such voluminous vastness that they fluttered audibly as he walked along.

"I've no car," explained Doe, "but it is only about ten minutes' walk to the vicarage. I hope you had a pleasant journey down?"

"Most exciting! We had a fellow in our compartment reeking with asthma, and he kept on snorting and spitting out of the window until a lady sitting opposite to him couldn't bear it any longer and complained."

"Dear me. How? What?"

"She asked him to control himself. Ha! Ha!"

"Well, but really—?" the parson said.

"Oh, he was a regular hard-boiled case. He just argued with her."

"Argued! He should have left the carriage."

"That's just what he would *not* do. She hinted at it, then she suggested it, then she bluntly requested him to, but he replied— and very politely, I *must* say—that that alternative was hers."

"By Jove!" the parson said.

"So then she told him that he was the rudest man she had ever met, *and* the most disgusting! But he sat tight, he would not budge, and I am bound to say it got more provoking than ever. At last she burst out again: "This is insupportable! *Cannot* you control yourself?" "Madam," he says, "I can no more control myself than you can control your appearance. There are many things in life we have to put up with, affictions and inflictions all very disagreeable. We are both suffering from the defects of nature. For instance, I do not care for your appearance," he said, "I do not like it at all, it is repellent to me. But do I complain about it? Do I beg you to do something for it, or ask you to leave this compartment? I do *not*," he said, "Heaven forbid! I just mutely suffer." "Well, I wish you would suffer a little *more* mutely," says she. "Madam," he says, "it is impossible to suffer mutely from asthma." And they were still wrangling when I got out here. Ha! ha! By George, he *was* a rascal, he gave her such a dressing-down. I—do you know, I positively rejoiced at it!"

"Oh, but really, Ellis!"

"Can't help it. I'm sure you would have been the same— though I'm not much of a Christian these days. Anyhow, I'd almost bet they are very good friends before they get to their destination."

"Of course, my dear Ellis. I'm sure they will be."

"I wouldn't be too sure—it didn't strike me as a very promising beginning for romance."

"Romance!" echoed the puzzled parson.

"Oh, she wasn't bad-looking," Rowfant explained.

They turned the corner by the lime trees and in a few moments there was the church with its untiring spire, the vicarage trees, the lawn garlanded with peonies and hedged with may, and in the water under the bridge the fish were gliding. A little bow-legged maid with a squint in her eyes took the visitor's bag. Ten minutes later they were drinking tea on the lawn, and Rowfant, admiring the old red wall with its topknots of saxifrage, the squat house and its bow windows, the simple peace of the garden, murmured in envious tones his appreciation.

"You are most welcome here," his host assured him with a beaming look.

"I'm not much of a religieux these days, I'm afraid," Rowfant went on.

"Well—of course—!" Doe smilingly sipped his tea.

"It was never quite in my line, you know," explained Rowfant.

"And I," Doe responded, "I'm a professional. Forty years, my boy. And I rejoice in it. I would not change, I could not."

"Nor could I," said Rowfant, "but I love your home. You never married?"

And Doe answered. "No. That was not in *my* line."

"Nor mine," said Rowfant abruptly.

For many days Rowfant abode there, lingering on and on under pressure from his friend. He soon learned that the parson's familiar name was Sammy, and he too used it fondly. Their old affection had bloomed once more and they were happy. Time and again they rambled in company to spots that were marked red or blue on the vicar's map, and when the parson was otherwise engaged Ellis would lounge for hours in the garden. On Sunday morning he sat there in a dream by the old red wall; the bells had chimed cheerfully, the voices and footsteps of assembling worshippers could be heard passing by. Then there was silence, a silence that itself seemed holy despite the chirping of birds, until the chanting of the choir stole across the road, threaded through the odour of the may, and filled him with melancholy joy. Mysterious melancholy, inexplicable joy! He had not once been into the church during his stay—such a sweet old church! He ought to have gone, at the very least he ought to have gone once. They sang well in there. He would go tonight, it would please Sammy.

When Doe returned, Rowfant warmly praised the singing of the choir.

"Pretty good," the vicar agreed. "Two fine tenors, you know. Jerry has a glorious voice, perfectly topping. Arnold's tone is not so pure perhaps, but it's a shade more ineffable. I like that."

Listening with affectionate amusement to his old friend, Rowfant would forget that there was no disparity of years between them; even when a parishioner came with some trouble, preposterous or profound, Rowfant, noting old Sammy's anxious care, would laugh to see him as a boy might laugh at his funny uncle. When he went visiting in his parish Sammy's pockets bulged with little gifts, the deuce knows what; peppermints for a child, it might be, some crochet cotton for a dame, or a packet of quassia chips for cleaning Sergeant Tullifant's roses. Was Doe working in the garden? Then he would be in his shirt-sleeves and heavy boots, humming as he hoed and sweating as he dug.

"Ellis!" he would bawl across the lawn. "Do you think that poet was sincere when he said: 'The cut worm forgives the plough?'"

"I think he was ignorant."

"Not ignorant, Ellis."

"Well, he can't have known anything about the psychology of worms."

"Oh! Should you think that worms have a psychology, Ellis?"

"They ought to have, Sammy, to carry their forgiveness to such extremes."

"I don't know. It strikes me as a very profound utterance. I do hope it applies to spades, in gardens."

Surely he was a happy man? He had his little life, so neat, so simple; his little desires, so pure, so few; and his little dreams of a very large heaven—while he, Rowfant, what had he got? Even his tragic memories had grown dull, posthumous heaven was a forlorn mirage, he lived in some rooms in Twickenham.

With all his asceticism old Sammy was man enough to enjoy his food to the uttermost—at night—in that low-pitched dining-room with the four Arundel prints on the walls—desperately devout *they* were—and photographs of college teams—*not* so immaculately pious—including one of Rowfant and Doe in a Corpus Christi torpid of eighteen hundred and— Good God, how incredible! No rugs encumbered the polished floor, no cloth the table, and not even a clock on a shelf anywhere, for why have a clock when you've always a watch in your pocket? But there was a huge block of wood in one corner of the room that served as a stand for a tray.

"What *is* that lump of timber?"

"That, Ellis? Oh, that is quite unique. I got hold of it years ago. Do you like it? It's an ancient butcher's block."

"Sweet!" grinned Rowfant.

"Don't you like it?"

"I might—in years to come. I must present you with a pole-axe to go with it."

"Oh, forbear, Ellis! My dear chap, forbear!"

Dinner at night was a ritualistic indulgence by a soul that deserved every hope of the punctual benediction. Each forkful the reverend gentleman shovelled into his mouth caused him to close his eyes and smile. Paradise! He took a gulp of wine and whispered to himself. Having consumed his heap of spaghetti, his piece of mutton, his apple, and his orange, he settled down with a pair of crackers to the nuts and his second glass of wine— white this time in place of red. Selecting the nuts with care, he would rattle them with a frown against his ear and discard some; later his toothpick came into play, raking his hollow teeth with the felicity of a rapier.

"And now, my dear Ellis, what about a game of draughts? Or dominoes? Any little excitement of that kind?"

And they would play on until the nightingales began.

These homely days exercised so beguiling a pressure that Rowfant almost forgot his own creeping age. Though youth was dead and gone, though the future had got all his destiny slyly tucked in its fob, wise old Sammy was friendship's mellowing sign, simple, steady, and devoted, and the prospect of leaving him again for Twickenham's barren complexities filled Rowfant with many qualms. The years ahead of him might be few or they might be many—one could not live for ever—and this lodging alone was a trashy affair; but one could live well with Sammy. Why *not*? Rowfant had a small income that freed him from the embarrassments and futilities of work. The parson's home was large but his income was small, smaller even than Rowfant's own, and with their resources pooled the two of them might dwell in ease for Sammy and some grace and harmony for himself. One night after dinner he spoke of this:

"Sammy, would you care to put up with me?"

"Put up with you?"

"For good. Could you do with a lodger here?"

"A lodger!"

"Yes, me! Tell me truly if the idea fills you with hatred, but I am making you a proposal, Mr. Doe. I want to live with you, to live here, always, and all my worldly goods on thee endow."

The Reverend Phalarope listened intently while his friend dilated, outlining his resources and propounding his hopes.

"What do you think? Would it be possible?"

"It would be terrific!" cried Sammy. "Nothing could be more terrific. It is—good gracious, my *dear* Ellis"—he jumped up to grasp his friend's hand—"a superb idea."

"But could you really bear it?"

"My dear boy! Say no more, it shall be exactly as you wish."

"No, Sammy, it is to be exactly as *you* wish; just as we are now, and you must throw me into the river as soon as you grow sick of it—poison me, pole-axe me, and dump me in a sack!"

"A sack!" shouted Sammy. "I couldn't put you in a sack!"

"Then don't bother about the sack."

"And you really mean it?"

"From the bottom of my heart."

"It is settled, then."

"Settled it is, old friend."

Again they clasped hands upon it. The parson stood for a few moments with closed eyes, and Rowfant knew that some blessing had been invoked on their renewed alliance.

"I must go back to Twickenham, Sammy, for a couple of days, to clear up everything, and then—"

"Then you'll come?"

"I'll come. You don't mind harbouring such a barbarian?"

Doe gazed wildly at his friend. "What do you mean by that, I wonder."

"My not being a church-goer."

"Pooh! You don't object to *my* going!"

"You see—I never could stand that holy capital letter of Holiness."

"Ellis, that is merely a printer's fad."

"Really, my dear Sammy! You'll shock me, you know."

"If I could, my boy, you would be more than half-way to grace!"

"To grace!" Rowfant shook his head sadly. "No, Sammy, I don't think so—ever. But there *is* something I must tell you if I am coming to live with you down here. It is only right that you should know all about it beforehand. I've been going to tell you —but—don't you see—?"

"What *is* it?"

"Well, it will take some little time—shall we sit down?"

"Ellis!" cried the parson protestingly. "Are you going to relate the story of your life?"

"More or less."

"Have you a hideous past?"

"Yes."

"Oh lord! Oh dear!" Sammy wrung his hands and emitted a whimsical sigh.

"I *must* tell you," Rowfant insisted. "And you've *got* to hear it. So just squat down, there's a good chap."

Down they sat, and Rowfant began his story.

II

"When I went down from Oxford forty years ago I lived with an aunt in Gloucestershire. I was an orphan, you know, and my Aunt Susie was a widow; she had looked after me since I was five years old; in fact, she was a mother to me and she adored me. I suppose I was fond of *her*—I hope I was, for she was the soul of goodness—but I am sure that my feeling for her *now* is stronger than it was *then,* all that long time ago. And it isn't exactly love, either; it is more like admiration. Or perhaps it is only gratitude? She gave so much and got so little; somehow there is nothing *inevitable* about such a situation, it is not *always* conducive to love and possibly not very often—what do *you* think?"

"I find it rather hard to think that, Ellis."

"But it *is* so, I am sure. She was not what you call rich—just comfortably off—and we had a small house and garden and one servant maid named Elizabeth—Lizzy Lee. I was supposed to be going into the Government service, but there were all sorts of difficulties and I made a mess of one or two exams. I was a pretty ineffectual sort of creature in those days; my aunt thought I had weak lungs or a heart or something like that, but the truth is it was laziness. I was *born* like it, really lazy. Do you know she never employed a gardener, and the two women—she and Lizzy Lee—managed the garden by themselves, digging and hoeing and so on all at the proper times, and I never stirred a leg or lifted an arm to help them. I love a garden, but I dislike gardening, and they seemed to revel in it. Of course there was nothing physically the matter with me at all—never has been—I've rowed all my life, and still do—but at that time I was reading a lot of poetry and things and I fancied I could make some sort of a shot at composing a poetic drama. There was quite a vogue at that time for poetic dramas, and I went floundering about with my head in a fuzz of fatuous dreaminess, which my Aunt Susie thought was a sign of genius! So did I, but it wasn't—it was mere cheek. Well, after about a year of this my aunt died, and *that* wiped my eye pretty thoroughly because most of her income came from a marriage settlement that ceased on her death. She left me the house though, and a block of shares in some African gold mines that had brought her in about two hundred a year, and she bequeathed thirty pounds to Elizabeth. Of course, I ought to have buckled to then and begun some sort of a career for myself, but I didn't. I decided to carry on the house and write my poetic plays. Oh, dear! I soon got a shock—two shocks, in fact. One came when I found out what wages my aunt had been paying Lizzy Lee—Elizabeth. It was fifteen pounds a year. At that time I was imbued with a lot of radical notions and it seemed to me dreadful to pay anyone such a miserable pittance, especially as Elizabeth was a model domestic. She was young, about my age, and rather pretty, but I assure you it wasn't *that* that did it—it was my Socialism. I was really *shocked,* and I doubled her wages at once."

"Humph! That was rather a jump," exclaimed the vicar.

"Oh, she took it quite as a matter of course; it didn't make any difference, she was as near perfection as a servant could be; but I soon got my second shock. The dividends that year, my dividends on aunt's gold-mine shares, were cut down by a half, and in the end I was only getting a bare hundred pounds. Still, I didn't regret having doubled Lizzy Lee's wages—I was very bigoted in my views in those days—but quite soon, as you may imagine, I was in desperate straits for money, got into debt all round for household necessaries and so on, and at last it came to the point where I decided to *sell* the house, *move* into a cottage somewhere cheap, and get rid of Lizzy Lee. Had I had any sense, I would have told her the truth, but I was too stuck-up to do *that*, I couldn't bring myself to do it, I could *not*, so she knew nothing at all about my financial bust-up and managed the house in the same style she had always done. And I was absolutely on the rocks! So at last I had to tell her that I had arranged to move to a cottage in the Cotswolds and that I shouldn't require her services there. I told her the cottage was very small, that I intended to do all the work myself, in fact I talked a lot of Tolstoyan nonsense—even to her! And I gave her a month's notice. She said: 'Very good, sir.' I can remember it even now. But before the month was up she offered to stay on at her old wages and seemed quite anxious to come to the cottage with me. That was out of the question, of course, and besides I simply could not afford to keep her on—though I didn't tell her *that*. She asked me if she had 'done anything wrong,' but you can understand that as I had donned the high hat by doubling her wages, I was too cocky to own up that I couldn't afford her at any price *now*. Worst of all, it never occurred to me—I was *such* a numskull in those days; I am still, I suppose—it didn't occur to me to ask her what she was going to do, not until the very last day, when she was packed up and about to leave.

"Where shall I send your letters?" I asked her. She said there wouldn't be any. I said I'd better have her address in case anything turned up. She said she was going to London, she didn't quite know whereabouts until she got there.

"Where's your regular home?" I asked her.

"She answered: 'I haven't got one!'

"That was the whole truth of it: her parents were both dead, she had nowhere to go. I hadn't known that, you see, and here was I throwing her out on to the world! Not intentionally, of course, but still I was a thoughtless ass, oozing with fatuous blank verse and having no notion of responsibility. She was about my own age, twenty-four or five, and—did I tell you?—she was really quite beautiful. There were tears in her eyes, but she kept a stiff upper lip and didn't suffer them to fall—not while I was looking. I could see though, and I simply *had* to ask her to stay on. I told her I had had no idea of her circumstances, that of course I could not let her go off like that, and she had better stop with me until she found another situation. Oh, a lot of palaver! But she was rather a proud young woman and her pride wouldn't let her accept my belated offer, and though I wasted a lot of words and remorse on her I could not induce her to change her mind. Away she went, after promising most solemnly to write and let me know how she got on in London. Of course she never kept that promise."

"Didn't she?" asked the parson with a dubious frown.

"No. Well, within a week I moved to my new cottage. I took what I wanted of my aunt's furniture and sold the remainder with the house. And it turned out to be quite a good stroke of business. In a month or two I paid off all my debts and was left with a couple of hundred pounds in the bargain. I saw I had been altogether too hasty. I wished I had had more foresight and kept Lizzy Lee to look after me. I could have managed it easily after all, but, as I say, I did not hear from her, she did not keep her promise to write. By that time she was very much on my mind or my conscience—I don't know which; I expect they are the same thing? It's no use having a conscience unless your mind directs it aright, it's a boat without a compass. I remember that she was a woman, young, good-looking, though possibly my romantic fancy endowed her with ethereal glamours at times, for poetry does really play the deuce with you in your salad days. Quite often I had a cranky notion of trying to find her—goodness knows how! for she did not keep her promise to write to me— but if I could have got into touch with her again I *would* have had her back, for it is not all honey looking after yourself when you're lazy like I was. Besides, I'd got enough money after selling the house to go on paying her her proper wages. What made it more annoying still, in a way, was the fact that in a couple of years those confounded gold-mine shares went soaring up again, so that I could even have kept on my aunt's old house, had I but foreseen it."

Rowfant paused and fixed a musing gaze on the print of some

martyred saint who was being cauterized by demons with a few red-hot harpoons. "It was very tantalizing, you know."

"Well, but Ellis," said the smiling parson, "you have nothing to *reproach* yourself for."

"Oh, haven't I!" exclaimed Rowfant. "I haven't told you yet."

"Oh! Indeed, oh!" Mr. Doe said.

Rowfant went on to describe his efforts to compose poetic dramas, efforts that were frustrated time and again by such trivial impediments. His cottage was on the side of a Cotswold hill; it overlooked a woody valley and a stream. There were horizons too, threaded as it were by long belts of beech trees, a lofty, uplifting view, which so stimulated him that he found it pleasanter to work sitting in his tiny garden rather than at the desk in his room. In that serene and open purview thoughts seemed to flow in him, ideas bubbled, and his imagination became as frisky and glittering as a fountain. But the fountain will not play for ever; bubbles are merely bubbles. The thoughts, although they flowed and flowed, did not flow *out* of him; they swirled, and then they subsided to depths he could never fathom. Ideas came, but they came and went untamed. He imputed this defeat to the languorous airs of summer, the distractions of birds, of bees, of clouds—to anything but his own want of genius. Tomorrow would do, it would go better tomorrow. Every passing cloud or sign of shower was an interruption of his mind's aery play; their exquisite designs were invitations to dally, to postpone. Tomorrow would be time, it would be better tomorrow. When autumn came along he felt a revival of vigour, a glow of renewal, but on the other hand the sharp air made it no longer agreeable to meditate out of doors, and the chill of life got into his mind when the rigour of the season got into his bones and drove him back into his cottage. There with his books he would sit by a drowsing fire, lying in wait for inspiration as a fox waits for a hare, until the idleness bemused him and the tick of the clock became a noisy nuisance past all bearing; he would stop the clock, forget the time, and snooze.

"Ho, ho, my dear fellow!" cried Doe. "You will be able to write *here*. My, yes! Play after play. I believe *I* could write a play. We must do one together, for the village school."

Rowfant smiled wryly. "You know, Sammy, I might have done a real good play if it hadn't been for those infernal shares. You see—they had caused me to do a mean thing, sacking Lizzy Lee, and then they turned on me and gave me all I wanted. It was very significant."

"I don't quite see the—er—significance," remarked the other.

"Don't you! Well, I was selfish—selfish enough, God knows!—but I never really wanted anything at that time except to write my plays. When the shares slumped and I sacked Lizzy Lee I did her a great wrong, it was a vile thing to do. If I had not done that, all would have come right in a few months; but I hadn't the sense, I did the dire thing, and then those shares waxed fat again as though they approved of what I had done. They were certainly cursed; they made me do things I should *not* have done, and they prevented me doing the things I ought to have done. It was over twenty years before I got rid of the brutes—and it was too late then. I sold them in a boom year, I may tell you."
then. I sold them in a boom year, I may tell you."

"Well, ah," Mr. Doe blandly commented, "I'm all for castigating Mammon, but it sounds rather as though you were biting the hand that fed you, Ellis!"

"Wait, Sammy, wait. Let me finish my story!"

"Haven't you finished yet?"

"Good Lord, no. Listen. I went on dithering in the Cotswolds for six or seven years. By then I had got a regular lump of money in the bank; the shares paid hand over fist, and I spent little. I got into the way of dodging up to London fairly often to see plays, and on one such occasion I put up at a private boarding-house in one of those squares just off Holborn. I had been to the theatre and I had gone home to bed. It was one of those places you just blunder upon, goodness knows how. Fate, I suppose. I've never been there since. And I was fast asleep when something woke me up with a great start. It was a cry, a loud cry, it was like the cry of some—well, of some lost soul! I sat up in bed and listened. The room was in darkness, pitch-black. I heard the shriek again. I lit the candle. It was two o'clock. My watch I remember was ticking very loudly and I watched it, almost breathless, for five solid minutes actually, but there wasn't another sound. So I blew out the candle and snuggled down in bed again.

"At that very moment I heard something more, and I half rose up and listened; you know—I listened *furiously*. I heard a voice wailing aloud: 'Oh, won't somebody give me a match? I'm all in the dark and I'm terrified. Can't you hear me? For Christ's sake someone *give* me a match. I want to get up to my own *bed*. I'm all in the *dark!* For God's sake give me a match, can't you! I'm all alone in the dark and I'm frightened. Can't you hear, some-one? For Christ's sake give me a match.' Just like that, on and on, and very loud. I could not make out where the voice was coming from upstairs or downstairs, man or woman, but it was certainly somebody in the house. I waited and trembled and waited, to hear what would come of it, for something to be done, but nobody took any notice. Nobody else seemed to hear it, and that awful wailing went on until I could not bear it a second longer. I *had* to get up and light the candle again and pull on my dressing-gown. When I opened my door I could hear that the noise was downstairs, so I got hold of my candle and crept down the first flight. No one there, so I crept down the second flight to the hall. The crying had stopped directly my light appeared, and half-way down I couldn't see anybody; in fact, at first I only saw a grey skin mat at the foot of the stairs and a pot of very white geraniums shoved under the hatstand, but when I held the candle up high I could see a lady sitting all lopsided on the doormat with her hat cocked askew. And she was tipsy! *That* was it. A handsome woman and elegantly dressed, but tipsy! She said: 'Hullo, I've been here *such* a long time. What the devil's the matter with you all? Nobody ever takes *any* notice in this rotten house. You don't, do you? Who are you?' She seemed to think I was one of the servants. I put the candle on the hatstand and helped her to her feet. Her breath stank of rum and she tottered a little, but she just picked up the candle and made for the stairs. Of course I followed close behind her. She pulled herself together and held the candle up to look at me. 'Rather nice,' she said. 'Haven't seen you before!' She had on a sort of cape, and she walked quite jauntily, carrying the candle in one hand and lifting her skirt with the other. I followed her as she stumbled up two flights of stairs. She opened a door quite close to my own.

"'Come in,' she said; but I stopped in the doorway. She flung off her hat and cape, kicked off her shoes, and then she began to undress. I called out: 'If you've got a candle of your own here I'll light it for you.' 'Don't you trouble, my dear,' she said! In a minute or two she got her own candle alight and brought mine to the door. I said: 'Thank you, good night,' and was walking off with my candle when she hissed out. 'Are you all alone?' I thought it best not to answer, but she bawled: *'Are* you?' So I replied: 'Yes, I am, thank you.' *'Too* bad!' she said. *'So* sorry. Au revoir!' or something like that.

"I didn't get off to sleep again for a very long time. The sight of anybody intoxicated always distresses me, but a young woman beautiful and boozed is simply shocking. I couldn't help wondering who she was, and what she had been doing to get like it, and why no one had answered her cries, for I thought the whole house *must* have heard her. As a matter of fact I found out later that nobody *had* heard her. She had been staying there for quite a long time and had a latch-key. This night she had been out to a party, got fuzzy with rum, and had fallen down in the pitch-dark hall.

"I met her the next morning. I was all alone in the breakfast room when she came in, looking *radiant*. I didn't quite know whether I ought to greet her in such circumstances, but directly she saw me she came bang up to my table and said: 'Thank you for last night.' 'A pleasure!' I said. 'May I sit here?' she asked. 'Do,' I said; 'what will you have for breakfast?' She sat down, she stared at me, and she suddenly exclaimed: 'Mr. Rowfant!' And then I saw it was our Lizzy Lee, dressed in the pink of fashion and looking like a lady. Of course you could have split me with a paper-knife. Such a surprise! 'Why, what ever are you doing here, Elizabeth?' I said. For a long time I couldn't get much information out of her except that she was now a Mrs. Robinson, but we talked and talked and she became quite fascinating, you know. It is extraordinary what nurture and dress does for some women.

"At last I asked what she had to do that morning. She said she had no engagements. 'Shall we go out?' I asked, and she said: 'Yes.' 'Where shall we go?' 'I don't mind.' So off we went and took a hansom as far as the Royal Academy. 'Shall we go in?'

'Yes,' said she. I can remember the details of that visit perfectly, though I have forgotten all about the pictures we looked at. When we got into the courtyard of the Academy there was a baker's cart standing outside the door of the Astronomical Society. The horse had got its nosebag on and some sparrows were waiting and chippering at the horse's feet and Elizabeth had to stop and watch them. It made her laugh because the birds would chirrup and the horse would sneeze, and every time he sneezed he blew a handful of oats out of his nosebag, and the sparrows would snap up the grains and go on chippering encouragingly for more.

"Well, we saw some of the pictures and then we sat down in one of the galleries. I asked her about her marriage and so on, and then it all came out with a vengeance; she wasn't married, she had never been married at all, but, you understand, she *ought* to have been.

"The Mrs. Robinson name was just assumed for propriety's sake and convenience, but she wasn't married. Gradually I got the whole story. It appeared that when she left me and went off to London she was unlucky and could not find another situation. She tried for months and months, until her savings came to an end and she was absolutely on her uppers. Then, of course, the inevitable happened—she was a handsome creature—she went as housekeeper to a certain man who was quite unscrupulous, although he was kind to her in a way. I think he died, and then there were one or two other episodes of that kind. Once, she said, she was an actress, but I discovered that she had only posed in some suggestive tableaux for a threepenny gaff travelling round the fairs. At last she had become the mistress of a rich man who was already married. All this filled me with dreadful remorse, but at the same time I was very angry with her. 'Why in the name of all that's sacred didn't you write to me?' 'Write to *you?*' she said. 'Yes,' I said, 'as you promised?' 'What do you take me for?' she answered (and with a good deal of spirit, by Jove!). 'You had thrown me out, homeless.' 'No, no! I didn't,' I said, 'and you promised faithfully to write.'

" 'Well, it was all your fault,' was her reply, 'but it doesn't matter now.'

"I couldn't believe it of our innocent Lizzy Lee, not for some time. I was appalled to think I had been the unwitting instrument to send her into such a way of life. She was quite insistent that it *was* my fault and of *course* it was, I *saw* that it was—it was only too awfully true.

"She sat on one of those lounges, looking really beautiful, better than any of the paintings I saw, and no one looking at her would have dreamed she had been drunk on the doormat at two o'clock that very morning. She asked me why I had been so anxious to get rid of her and I told her then the reason, the proper reason. That seemed to puzzle her. 'You were hard up! I had no idea,' she said. 'Why didn't you tell me? I did not think it was anything like that at all.' 'What *did* you think it was?' I asked her. 'Oh,' she said, 'I've forgotten now, but I'd have stayed on, of course I would, for nothing if I had known. Instead of that —you just threw me out!' She repeated that it was all *my* fault, as of course it *was,* this mess she was in.

"My fault, my helpless fault! And as I deeply realized it then, my guilt, my imagined guilt if you like, affronted me and I felt it was my solemn duty to get her out of it; I could not rest with a thing like that on my conscience. I told her that I had wanted to get her back again as soon as my affairs had recovered, but that I hadn't known where to find her. 'Do you want me back now?' she ventured. 'Would you come?' I asked. She laughed. 'What wages would you pay me?' Saucy, wasn't it? We didn't say any more about it just then, we just dropped the subject, because in spite of everything she had become a very charming companion. For the next week we were inseparable, went about day after day together, and she behaved well, very well indeed. To cut a long story short, I stayed on in that boarding-house. I got very fond of her and didn't want to leave her, but it wasn't *only* that. I felt overwhelmingly that some reparation had to be made to her, from me, absolute reparation for the hideous harm I had done. Not intentional, of course; I had been careless and it had brought this disaster on her. I felt I had to make amends—if only to redeem myself—and the best way as it seemed to me then would be to marry her.

"I began by asking her to give up this man who was keeping

her. That made her look sad, so sad, I can't describe *how* mournful, yet when I asked her to marry me she just laughed aloud! But she soon realized I was not joking. I was serious, very serious, and I kept on at her until at last she agreed to marry me. And she did marry me, yes, absolutely! I gave up my Cotswold cottage and we took a little house at Brighton. I made Lizzy destroy every stitch she possessed in the way of clothing and personal belongings. She had heaps, but I was very squeamish about her retaining any of those things, and to do her justice she agreed with me. I spent a heap of money on refitting her, and the only thing she retained was a Bible her mother had given her; it had her name inscribed in it: 'To Elizabeth, from her distracted mother on the day of the operation by Dr. Fuller to her nose.'"

"Her nose!" echoed the parson. "What was the matter with her nose?"

"Oh, it wasn't *her* nose," Rowfant explained. "Hers was fine, sort of Grecian, and she had an abundance of bright hair and the bluest eyes. No, it was her mother's nose—a polypus, I think. Lizzy was splendid and for over a year we seemed to be living in Eden itself, but after that things began to go wrong. It may have been my own stupidity, it may have been the cussedness of nature, or it may have been a conflict in myself that betrayed us, for I do know that the more deeply I loved her, the more I came to loathe the thought of that awful life she had once led. I thought I had accepted all that, I had taken my share of the blame and supposed I could dismiss it from my mind, but that was very far from being so—it became a dreadful canker. And Lizzy, too, she had grown used to some of the extremer luxuries, was extravagant, ran into debt, began to drink again. Once more I found it difficult to make ends meet; my savings were all gone, my income was inadequate, and in short I did not know which way to turn. I could not give Lizzy the sack this time, even if I had wished to, and I didn't wish that, though I was horribly hurt by some of the things she was doing, but a climax came when I found out that she was once more corresponding with her old paramour, had actually seen him again, and I guessed she had resumed relations with him. When I taxed her with this, she admitted it, and left me and went back to him. Yes, that's what

Lizzy did. Ah, well, I can't describe the horrible bitterness of it, indeed I couldn't if I wanted to, for thirty years is too long a time to remember a grief. I know that I wanted a divorce. Now, divorces are most expensive affairs, though it *is* so cheap to get married, but I still wanted to get Lizzy on to the right path again. I wanted that very much. This man was a widower now, and I imagined he would be very glad to marry her if she were free as well. Perhaps he would have done so, but as it turned out he did. not. For three years I stinted and starved myself to get money enough to launch proceedings, for I was determined to pay the cost myself, no matter what was the award; it seemed a ghastly immorality to win her redemption—and mine too—with *his* money. Idiot! Fool! Blind besotted owl that I was! Well, at last I got my decree, but it was a sorry businesss, for her man entered a defence and the case lasted several days and those confounded news-butchers made a great to-do in their newspapers. I got my decree, but it didn't avail poor Lizzy very much; within a week of its being absolute she died."

Rowfant stopped at last. Apparently he was finished with his story.

"Dear me," said the parson, "how very sad that is!"

Rowfant blew his nose, using his handkerchief meticulously. The parson coughed. There was a silence lasting several moments. The parson coughed again. At length he said:

"You have had a very sad time, Ellis, a very sad time. But you behaved splendidly. There is something wrong about it all, somewhere, I feel. I don't know. But you behaved splendidly, Ellis, you did, indeed."

"No," said Rowfant. "No. All that starving and stinting to pay the costs was monstrously quixotic, and it was thrown away, wasted in the end. I didn't mind for myself, but for poor Lizzy I *did* mind. Don't you see? If I had been less of a fool, if I had thought more of her and less of my own precious scruples, the poor girl would have been divorced and free a couple of years earlier at least. And she could have been married to that man and it would have put things right for her in a sort of way. But my stupidity prevented even that. And she died, and—well— what about *her*?"

Soon the parson came and bent over his friend:

"All is well, my dear boy, all is well. Believe that. Now—ah—just forget all about it. I wonder," said he, glancing around the room, "I wonder, Ellis—would you care to play a little game of dominoes?"

"Why, yes," Ellis responded brightly. "Yes, I should love to."

"Very well, then."

They played.

III

A few days later Rowfant was installed at the vicarage with his pink cap, his waterproof tobacco pouch, and a lot of books that Sammy declared he would certainly have to look at—some time, later on. From the day he turned his back upon the blandishment of Twickenham and was inducted as it were into the pale of the church Rowfant's heart was aware of revivals and renewals he had not thought to experience again. And there was no betrayal this time. The two old men in friendly bondage shared a home, a life; and they shared their thoughts, snoozing and brooding in the garden under the leaning trees while the sun-inspired brook inched warily by. In some half-maudlin mood Rowfant perhaps would ask: "What is Life?" And Sammy would tell him.

Or Sammy would bridle with domestic ambition:

"We might put up a little greenhouse here, Ellis. I am very partial to cucumbers—do they disturb you?"

Or there would be intimate wanderings over the sleepy fields, for the parson was no longer a lover of the open road.

"I really regret the dust, Ellis, the dust of the old highway. It often gave me real pleasure, thirty years ago, before the roads were so hardened and polished and thousands of wheels going where there were only ten before. Traffic was so small then, and it was genial, too; just a wagon, a butcher's cart, the squire's barouche, or a fleet of bicycles. And you could pad along so softly in the roads with a luxurious inch of fine dust under your foot-soles; rich historical dust, too, gloating over ancient Britain and Julius Cæsar, and the sun flaring at you while the sweat oozed and ran. And then to come to some bosky chestnut tree at the corner of some turn with a pond and a goose deliberating on it! Oh dear, oh dear; the tree and the pond may be there still, but the goose is gone!"

And Rowfant found that he too lamented the dust that had gone to dust indeed. He found that his own divergent thoughts were often of the same cast as his friend's, though *he* seemed to use them as stepping-stones to directions Rowfant had always shunned. Despite his secular bigotries he found that he liked hearing his comrade pronounce the benediction at their meals together. One day Sammy said: "Will *you* say grace, Ellis?" and stood with his venerable head piously bowed, never doubting his friend's response. Rather than grieve him, Rowfant submissively invoked a blessing in which he had no belief. He found that it pleased him immensely to please Sammy; he had no belief in God, but he believed in his friend.

Once he had asked Rowfant to be a good chap and go with him to the church and ring the bell for the evening service.

"Why, what is the matter with the sexton?" Rowfant inquired.

"Drunk," replied Sammy. "He is imperiously drunk."

It seemed such an agreeable quandary for a parson to be in that Rowfant was delighted to oblige—just for once. But somehow things were never done "just for once" with the inexorable Sammy. You were taken for granted, you were inveigled, you were roped in.

"We ought to do a nativity play at Christmas," declared Sammy. "Yes, to be performed in the church. And that's just your line, Ellis, isn't it? You could write something extraordinarily good, it's a beautiful theme, one of the finest the world has ever known—oh, immeasurably! You just knock off the words, not too much spouting, you know, but action and simple piety, and I will find the performers—as many as you like, the more the merrier.

It was a waste of time for Rowfant to plead his entire unfitness; he had to renew his acquaintance with the Gospel according to St. Luke and to plan his Christmas pageant. Naturally, this required—and it was somehow quite, *quite* natural—his occasional attendance in the church where a robin had once had the cheek to build its nest in a hole in Sammy's lectern and put five eggs in it. It ended in Rowfant's becoming a sort of lay clerk to the implacable Mr. Doe, in his sitting below his pulpit and responding to his Amens in no browbeaten manner.

"Wouldn't you like to read the lessons, Ellis?"

"No. You must excuse me, Phalarope."

"I should like you to do that, Ellis."

"I could not do that. I would not *mind,* but I do not feel myself *fitted,* you understand—*fitted.* I am interested in it all, you know that, but the fact remains that I am entirely insusceptible to any sort of religious emotion, utterly and entirely. The ceremonies are quite agreeable, they are pleasant, but beyond that they *mean* nothing to me."

"Why should they? Ellis, what are you afraid of?"

"Afraid! I'm not afraid of anything. But I do miss something, I want some clue. I can't break through the crust of all these ceremonies and contradictions and find the thing I'm after, the thing which sometimes I find in myself, which satisfies *me.* I suppose I can't *find* what you call God. I can't believe in Him."

"It is all very simple, Ellis. The Kingdom of God is within you."

"No, Sammy. The soul is not really man's identification with God, it is merely the possibility of such identification. Now suppose—just listen to me for a moment, Sammy—suppose there is a great Jehovah sitting in the skies, or wherever you like to have Him. That may be true, I won't argue about it, just suppose it. But even then it is quite easy and natural to suppose that this life of ours is the beginning and the end of things for mankind, isn't it? And what then?"

"Suppose! Suppose!" The Reverend Phalarope Doe wagged his head and smiled indulgently. "I am not able to suppose any such thing, Ellis. And you have forgotten Jesus, haven't you?"

"I have not. Even he envisages this world as the centre of the universe."

"Why not?"

"Why not! Don't you realize that our world is but a gnat in the galaxy of a million worlds?"

"I do."

"He had no conception of any other world save heaven."

"Nor have I, Ellis, nor have you. To apprehend omniscience one must have an omniscient mind. All else is impertinence. You could put out your tongue at the Lama of Tibet, but even he would disdain to take notice of the gesture."

"The Lama of Tibet?"

"Yes, you believe in him, although you have never seen him and never will."

"But I *know* of his existence. I have read of him."

"I have read of Jack the Giant-Killer."

"And do you believe in him!"

"No. But I have read of God, and His blessings confront me day by day. God's miracles are numberless, but in face of them all, Ellis, I am sometimes tempted to think that mankind's one stupendous miracle is greater than any of His. I mean the Miracle of Unbelief."

"That's no miracle, Sammy!"

"To me it is. And I would like you to read the lesson sometimes. You could do it beautifully. You read the Bible to yourself and it gives you pleasure, isn't that so? To put it at its lowest, it gives you great pleasure. Now?"

Rowfant sighed. "It's a duodecimo emotion, Sammy; not like yours, a folio in full calf."

"Never mind the binding. Penny plain is no less than twopence coloured, which costs twice as much and means no more. Don't be selfish, Ellis, I'm not asking you to take a Sunday-school class!"

So Rowfant read out the Word of God and feared no evil. He wrote his play, he rang the bell, he did whatever Sammy required him to do. There was no end to their exchanges of belief and unbelief, but there was no division between them; their differences were no more than a crude brush across a surface of velvet, as marked as the advance of a harrow across a pasture— and as fugitive. Sometimes while listening to Sammy's exhortations Rowfant would fall asleep, and when he awoke Sammy would be gone away somewhere, to the garden, to his study, or into the church. "Ah," Rowfant would despondently sigh, "he disapproves of me!" But it was not so, never so. The two old

friends were in bondage to an affection that time and thought had
no wish to subvert.

"Why did you never get married, Sammy? Don't you care for
women?"

"I love mankind."

"But women, Sammy?"

"And their children too."

"Humph! I don't think I love man, really."

"I do."

"Not in the proper human way, not in any *wide* sense. I don't
accept him as an equal, I'm afraid, but still I am content with
him."

"I am not content with him, Ellis, but I love him."

What would have been impossible to Rowfant, or absurd in
him, was so firm and beautiful and appropriate in old Doe, who
was so fond and ever faithful, that Rowfant could not find it in
his heart to oppose him. Against Sammy he could somehow advance his reasoning only with small shuffling steps, like a man on
a tight-rope balancing a rod that was no security against a fall.
The multitudinous permutations of man's mind, its diversity of
measure, its warp that would plait only with the woof of its self-
sown views, left Rowfant without hope of ever sharing his dear
friend's belief and bliss, but he lived gratefully in its reflected
beam. The beam might be a mirage and lead no farther than the
grave—but what then? What pangs and what misery had such
innocence avoided!

The autumn faded upon them and winter eves approached
with the wild cries of those wounded winds that harried every
obstruction, thorn, gulley, barn, garner, fold, and fence. The
sere skeletons of dead herbage were snapped on their fields and
scattered. The clouds that hung above the firmament's meek
frill of light were coloured like the inside of a shell. The surfaces
of flat objects, such as the top of a well or the bar of a gate, had
a grey doubtful lustre, but a rare planet sparkled aloft with a
benignity bland as a prophet's faith. But the heart of a prophet—
thought Rowfant—hears only the echo of its own sighing.

Dunky Fitlow (1933)

FINE FEATHERS

HOMER DODD was a clerk in a brewery and when young had been full of ambition. But what is the use of ambition in a brewery, a country brewery at that? Haggar & Chibnall's Entire was a household word within a radius of ten miles of Humpingden, but at fifteen miles it was only casually appraised. In twenty miles it was rarely met and seldom mentioned. In thirty miles it succumbed to its parochial doom and was unknown. If time or distance or what not could do that to an old malty aromatic conservative brewery, what could it not do to the ideals of a Homer Dodd who had none of those peerless qualities! There was no Haggar now, not a Chibnall even, there was only a Company Limited; there had been a fair number of Haggars and quite a few Chibnalls in days gone by, but all that was left of them was their beautiful old brewery beside its stream that ran past the village that depended largely on the Company Limited, who depended in their counting-house to some trifling extent upon the honesty and exactness of Homer Dodd, son of William Dodd, the under-gardener to Squire Brownsill of Humpingden Hall, Humpingden.

The laggard heavy stream drooled by the brewery wharf, with its barrels, barges, and chimney stack, and office where Homer sat, and Homer had only to lift an eye from his book of accounts to enjoy a vision. On the opposite bank of the river a hill of ground, curved like a young moon and green as Eden, rose up to a vast collar of trees, and amid this stood an abbey of nuns with its belfry and its holy air. Sometimes nuns in couples, with dark robes and absurd white headgear, would be seen strolling about the greensward there, but Homer did not care for nuns, and he had a conviction that they were lazy.

"But they have very sweet knowledge, they nuns," his mother argued.

"They have," commented Homer, "and they have not."

"The kind of knowledge that would get you to heaven," pursued she, "easy."

"It would," Homer replied, "and it wouldn't."

"It must do one or the other." Mrs. Dodd had the sure and certain hope of that, but Homer retorted:

"Not necessarily."

That was Homer all over. He knew that a crushing emphasis of ignorance was often as effective as a crushing weight of knowledge, and he was aware that he had plenty of the one and little of the other. The pursuit of knowledge was difficult for one born and reared in Humpingden, small dull Humpingden.

When Homer left school old Squire Brownsill had offered to take him on as a gardener, under his father, William, but at the first hint of this from his mother the boy had taken himself off to the brewery and got a job in the office. You earned more money in an office than you earned in a garden.

"But I say it's like this. . . ." His father discussed the insurrection with some heat.

"Ho, it is a very good thing for him," interrupted Mrs. Dodd, who had secretly urged her son to this course.

"But what does it all come to, this setting on a stool? A man wants a craft," said the father.

"Well, he is a good scholar at the pen and he's a good hand at the drawing. He done a picture of Marshall Croxford's donkey something beautiful. Like life it was."

"Life! Thass a donkey as near death as ever was. It's starved, you can count the hairs on its tail."

"Ah," sighed Mrs. Dodd, "it do want a bit of a rest."

"Rest! I tell you that donkey wants a relieving officer."

"Well, he's a good scholar," declared Homer's mother, "and it is a good start in life."

"A rum start, adding up other people's money."

"And why not?" snapped she; "that's no worse than growing other people's cauliflower. My brother Bob was a sailor, and proud of it I am. He travelled the world round and saw every one of the King's colonies, but he never did and never could sail his own ship, could he?"

"Thass different," protested her husband.

"Nothing of the kind. Be honest, William. You never knowed a soldier as ever fought his own battles, neither, now did you?"

"Thass different."

"And besides," concluded Mrs. Dodd, "a clurk is more genteel."

That gentility was one of Homer's secret ambitions, though he was never to succeed in shuffling off his country husk and was to talk with the rich utterance of a ploughman all his days.

"Why don't you want to come a-gardening with me, my son?" asked William Dodd. " 'Tain't hard work over yon; the soil's as soft as silk and grows taters as big as my shoe."

It appeared that the boy had a grievance against the squire, who had recently sent him on a long journey, several miles in the rain with a message, and had rewarded him with—what do you think?

"What did he give you?" asked Father William.

"A threepenny bit," answered the boy.

"Humph!" Even the parent was shocked.

"He won't live long," said young Homer scornfully.

The utterance was strangely prophetic. Within a year or two the squire who for half a century had honourably pursued that most agreeable of callings, the three R's of squirearchy—reeving, riding, and rent-collecting—was to the grief of his friends bitten by a pig and died of lockjaw. He was succeeded by his son, recently married to an actress whose face was too pink, too fresh-looking to be fresh. What with the actress and the newfangled fads of the young squire, Humpingden was livened up, the Hall itself renewed its stucco, and even that pleasant spot in front of it where three roads met was transformed and genteelized. It was a triangle of rough green turf where a white signpost grew like a lily and directed you to Pollock's Cross or Peck Common, and loungers sat there on Sunday mornings to gaze at the Vale of Humpingden and smoked and swore with fluent affability. Very pleasant it was. Now the triangle was rolled and mown with such an austerity of virginal tidiness that not a soul had the hardihood to step upon it, and none halted near it lest they should be accused of some violating desire.

With reasonable dispatch the actress gave birth first to a

daughter named Laura and then to a scandal that resulted in her divorcement from the squire.

"Did she love him?" was everybody's wonder when the actress was so tearful and penitent.

"Haw!" chuckled Homer Dodd. "Loved him as a lark loves trees." For Homer was grown up now, and achieving wisdom if not knowledge. Learning was beyond him, there was only his craving for some measure of gentility.

"The parish of Humpingden," he said to his mother, "is full of men who've stuffed their noodles with things they've no mind for and knowledge they don't know how to use. They do not. And the churchyard's full of 'em too."

"And what's the harm of it?" retorted Mrs. Dodd.

"No harm at all that I can see."

"God prosper 'em," she continued.

"But what's the use of it?" he asked. "It's like picking up stones in one corner of a field and marching 'em over to another corner. You begin picking up stones as soon as you're born and by the time you come to your grave there's a tidy bagful to tip into it. Lumber. If you lumber up your brains the cockles of your heart won't grow big enough to get warm. That's my fancy however."

Homer's figure was tallish and slack, but neatly clad, though his feeling for dress was sombre—as befits a clerk. His hair was as light as honey, winter and summer his face was tanned, and though he walked always with his head slightly bowed, it was not dolefully done, he was a lively freehanded man, and liveliness was always as welcome in Humpingden as a plate of cherries. The uncouth ambitions of his boyhood had been sloughed. These had mostly centred on a uniform of some sort—soldier, sailor, constable, porter or page—for early in life he had perceived that a uniform conferred distinction upon the wearer, and if Homer yearned for one thing more than any other—love, money, or sublimity—it was uniqueness. And the uniqueness of Humpingden was that this was impossible there. The only uniform that he regarded now was that of the squire as sheriff of the county. This was beyond his own hope and reach, a mere ideal, but there was still one form of adornment that clad a private man with his own private nobility, no less, and Homer was sworn to the consummation of that dream, though it would have to be done sixpence by sixpence as a slave might hoard for ultimate freedom. This noble attire was an evening dress suit. No common form, no trite or cheapened gear would satisfy his soul; this was no suit of clothes, it was raiment. Nothing was forgotten, the list was drawn and calculated close.

> One coat with tails
> A pair of trousers with stripes
> ? braces
> one white waistcoat
> a hat that lets down
>   black waistcoat
>   pair of shiny shoes (laces)
> and pumps
>   socks (plain and black)
> a pair of white kid gloves
>   white shirt (stiff)
>   collar with wings
>   white tie
>   black ditto
> a muffler
> one opera cloak
> a handkerchief (silk)
>   studs? gold or pearl
>   links?   ditto

Often he would take this list from his desk in the office and brood upon it with so tranced a speculation that when he raised his eyes and looked out across the river the vacancy of his dream was more vivid than the solid texture of stream and field, and he could see neither the abbey nor quiet nuns walking there. The yellow flowers in the grass reminded him then of things like studs, and even the glow of loosestrife bending over the heavy-eyed water was but a shade to line that fabulous cloak. This immortal notion had been conceived when he was twenty. Its realization would cost him a year's salary at the least—but what of that? Year by year the old brewery advanced his salary, some-

times by as much as a shilling a week, and the old brewery bore
this strain with the common fortitude of breweries both ancient
and modern. Steadfastly Homer set aside a tithe of his pocket
money (Account No. 2), and at rare intervals he was able to
add a guinea when the brewery let him repaint an inn sign, The
White Swan, The Black Horse, or The Old Market Tavern.
Homer had that gift, and in the corner of each sign you would
see his name inscribed in clear black letters: H. DODD, ARTIST.
The designation may have been only a claim—it might have been
a challenge—but it is to be feared that the pale object with orange
feet shimmering in a veil of blue liquid was an uncouth creature
for a swan.

His parents knew nothing of this fantastical desire, but he had
told his only sister, Fan. Homer was fond of her. She was a big
girl, with plump country contours, and walked majestically.
Though vague as to expression, her face was agreeable in shape,
and nothing marred the pure perfection of her skin but the one
trifling fleck where she had been bitten on the cheek by a pea-
cock in Kidderminster. Fan was a year or two younger than
Homer, he had no brothers, and he had sworn her to secrecy.
Sometimes his mother would pester him skittishly: when was he
going to marry and settle down?

"Plenty a time for that sort a thing." And this reply of Homer's
would provoke her.

"Pooh," she would scoff, "your unborn children will never
have a father."

And he would answer mildly: "They may—and they may not.
But he'll have a smart suit to his back—eh, Fan?—one day!"

And Fan would smile and look very knowing.

Perhaps it was a mistake for him to have told Fan of his nest
egg, for there came a time when she made a slip with a fellow
she had been engaged to for some years and wanted to get married in a hurry. Her man was quite unprepared, he was a wild
young gamekeeper named Spatkin who wasted his substance on
riotous racehorses, and for a while it looked as if the worst was to
happen to poor Fan. But when Homer heard of her quandary he
behaved as all fond brothers should and bought her a suite of
furniture. That alone cost him fourteen pounds twelve shillings,
and what with the price of linoleum and other odds and ends

his fund (Account No. 2) was terribly depleted. Homer was unconcerned about that, he did not seem to be disappointed in any way, and Fan married her fellow and went to live in a village some way off.

"Well," Homer consoled himself, "if I had that suit now, I'd not have much chance of wearing it, not here in Humpingden. It would be wasted. I can wait!"

In the course of time Fan was blessed with a daughter, Betty Spatkin, and soon afterwards she persuaded her husband to give up gamekeeping and embark on the business of greengrocery. So they moved into a town, where he opened a modest shop and borrowed money for this enterprise. Homer was induced to guarantee some portion of the debt, and he signed a document for this purpose full of a lot of long words that he could not understand; indeed, he could not pronounce some of them, but that only made it seem all the more impressive and legal.

When all this happened he was twenty-six or twenty-seven years old. After a while he began again to consult the list in his desk and to scrutinize, a little despondently, Account No. 2. Across the river the same picture met his gaze; sometimes he would have a playful vision of himself walking under the abbey wall in the marvellous cloak and the hat that let down; at a certain point he would cast open the cloak and, to nobody in particular, reveal his splendid attire.

So he dreamed on for two or three years until he was thirty, and then a bad thing happened—his father died. Like all generous men William Dodd had been improvident and was only lightly insured. To bury him and provide black clothing for himself and his mother cost Homer a pretty penny. He loved his father, he was sorry he had died, but the obsequies took a large sum, an astonishing sum. Then, of course, as head of the family and its only means of support, he had to increase the weekly allowance to his mother, and so his fund for that far-off finery languished and declined. That fund was a special and private one, Account No. 2; it had no connection with his general savings, Account No. 1, which held his reserves against the immediate contingencies of life.

But as time went on, things settled down again and were easy again. His salary at the brewery now amounted to thirty-two shillings a week. Good pay, you know, secure and regular, a nice easy life, rather quiet now and then, but pleasant surroundings. There was the ever rolling stream for ever lapping at the wharf, fair flowers in summer, the fleabane and willow herb frilling the waterside, the smell of malt, the fleet and careless birds. Nothing could impugn the integrity of time, so richly crusted was the old abbey wall, not even those mysterious nuns walking in holiness across the living green of the fields in their dead dark gowns and white fluttering hats. Silly hats, silly women, it was impossible that angels could be anything like them, but somehow they gave a sweet tone to the day and its quiet affairs. You could not judge of sanctity by its clothes, their uniform was but a few secular rags to wrap the spirit in.

Minor troubles, it seemed, grew on Homer Dodd as easily as beans on a vine; they had their punctual season; yet they rested but lightly on him, for he was no complainer, he was a hearty man with an appetite. Food was his delight, he ate it well and paid attention to it. He never looked under the table, there was never anything there but darkness and feet. His mother knew now of his late-concealed ambition, but she began to think he never would buy the suit he had so long desired and for which he had served so long. When she suspected that he had at last amassed sufficient money, and still he did not procure the suit, she began to bother and urge him. Gracious Lord, he was thirty-five years of age!

"True enough," Homer replied. "But if I had 'em now I couldn't wear 'em, I tell you. Where could I wear 'em?"

"Pooh, you can't wear it if you haven't got it, don't you see?" Mrs. Dodd was a very amiable woman, but like all women, amiable or otherwise, she was a compendium of illogicality; yet when it served her purpose she could insist upon logic, and nothing but logic, with the bruising insistence that made one desire sweetly to assassinate her. "So it's stupid saying you don't get it because you can't wear it, Homer."

"I'll get it, I'll get it, I tell you! My mind's set on that."

"Well then, why don't you? Homer, my boy, why not buy just a good little second-hand suit? It would be much cheaper and serve you just as well."

"Pah!" snorted the horrified man.

"And at least you would *have* it, even if you didn't wear it."

"I tell you I *will* wear it! Of course I will."

"Well," sighed his mother, "I'd like to see you in it."

"You may do that, sooner than you think for. Go slow as you can is what I think, always, but do it with a rush when the time belongs to you."

And at last Homer did it with a rush. A week of his annual holiday, spent in London, provided the opportunity, and from top to toe all the glory of his choice was regarded and approved. The suit came to Humpingden, and when it came it was laid with care, like a robe of sanctity, in a roomy chest and there it remained, locked up. Account No. 2 was closed, the list was destroyed, and yet . . . ? Homer came to wonder vaguely whether a final accomplishment might not create another void as big almost as that it all so handsomely filled. Somehow he was not at the journey's end, although he had arrived; but there was now no other end for him to travel to.

He kept the suit idle for a year; two years. It lay buried in the roomy chest, invested with tissue paper and packets of perfumed moth-killer. Sometimes he inspected it to see that all was well, and after the bath in his bedroom on Sunday mornings he would occasionally try on some part of it—the squash hat was so very alluring. Nothing more than that. So again his aging mother began to bother and urge him.

"It's a sin and a shame, my boy. Why don't you wear it? That beautiful suit! You know it is."

"I know," he said.

"Well then? You'll never have another one. It's a sin and a shame."

"There's nought to wear it to."

"There are dances, Homer, dozens."

"You know I can't dance, mother."

"Of course you can, you stupid thing! Go and learn."

"That's all very fine," said Homer Dodd.

"Or join the Freemasons. I can't think why you don't go to church in it sometimes."

"You know I never go to church."

"But you ought to go to church, Homer."

"Indeed to glory! What sort of a scarecrow d'you want to make of me? Go yourself!"

"I do go."

"Tcha! Why do you go?"

"Well, I go to encourage the vicar. He don't get much congregation, but he's such a nice man."

"You know, mother, you're not a religious woman at all."

"Homer! I am."

"You're not."

"I am!"

"And you never have been, so there."

"Oh yes, my boy, I have. I was brought up to it, thank God. And it's the way you're brought up. Our mother always made me go to church. I used to quarrel with her about it, dreadful I used to quarrel with our mother, but it was quite right, you know, for if you weren't brought up to it and made to go to church, why, you never would go, would you? You must have your photograph taken in it, Homer; and I'll tell you another thing: if you an't going to wear it yourself, why don't you hire it out to those as would be glad of it for dances and weddings? You could make a tidy bit of money that way. . . ."

"Mother, you don't understand."

"It's a sin and a shame!"

"You don't understand anything at all, not a damn scrap. But I'll tell you one thing about that suit." His manner was impressive. "I want you to give me your solemn promise about it."

"What?" asked Mrs. Dodd.

Homer gave a preliminary cough, and then plunged: "When I die, you're to see that I'm buried in that dress suit, all of it."

The old woman glared speechless at him.

"That's all, mother, just buried in it. Promise me that."

"That I shall not." Mrs. Dodd indignantly bristled. "The idea!"

"Why not? I want your solemn promise."

"For one thing," said she, "you'll outlive me, please God, many and many a year. And besides that, you can't be buried in a suit of clothes, Homer."

"Why not?"

"Not with trousers on and all! Certainly not! Homer Dodd, what are you thinking of!"

Now her son displayed some thoughtful cunning. "Mother, I shall make a will, I shall make a will straight away and leave instructions for to be buried in my dress suit. And that you'll have to do, whether or no."

Mrs. Dodd remained a block of contemptuous adamant. "You may say what you like, my boy, but I shall have nothing to do with it, that I shall not, nothing at all."

"You can't," said Homer hotly, "go against a man's last will and testament, signed and sealed. A dead man's instructions must and shall be carried out. It's law."

"We shall see about that," was Mrs. Dodd's rejoinder. "You an't dead yet."

Dodd was not the first to whom possession was something more than a challenge to envy or a prop to peculiar pride. Save for one pollution his robe of sanctity was to remain what it had become—the pure heaven of his desire. He had simply no wish to wear it. The ardours of the quest had perhaps exhausted him, as though a man with a fondness for Hesperidian apples had ground out his teeth in the search. Well, many's the man has bought a thing and a few things that are of no service to him, and locked them in a cabinet for to be stared at. It is so indeed. The things people will put into a cabinet! Why, one of them once hung a copper warming pan in the hall of his house. For ornament! Astounding! There was never a red cinder ever seen in it. And between the doormat and the barometer was also a brass soup-ladle, big enough to convey half a pint—but empty! Impossible to tell whether it was there to mortify the postman or to signify a descent from Bumble, but it is certain that neither spoon nor pan ever suffered in service. The honour of disuse was theirs and they were accorded reverence. Two ideas, however, requited Homer Dodd: first, although he might be content for ever with the mere possibility, he *could* wear his suit whenever he had a mind to; second, its possession marked him off quietly and impeccably from the half-baked, insufficiently fledged clerks who shared his office, and from those crabbed countrymen his neighbours. What an uncouth world they occupy! On Sundays the countryman changes his shirt. If he be a young man he changes all his clothes and gets into a pair of extraordinarily polished sacred shoes that are worn only on the Sabbath. But a middle-aged man is with difficulty persuaded to indulge in such diversity. At noon he may drag a crumpled suit from a damp box and put it on, but not all the arts of Helen could move him to wear a collar, and he goes off to the inn in an old hat and a pair of mouldy boots; walking slowly, not because of his deliberating nature but because his limbs have for so long been anchored to the soil.

> Pride and ambition here
> Only in far-fetched metaphors appear.

It is enough if the day provide him with meat and drink; there are few things he loves. He may wish for a little more money, a little more leisure, a little more joy, but these deficiencies are not tragic to him. As often as the sun of heaven shines he whistles at his work and touches his hat to his master without envy, for truly no one has a claim that is likely to disturb his natural rights —so low is their level.

Homer's father had been much like that, but not for Homer was such rude inadequate scale, and the unworn suit was as significant to him as the inner revelation may be to every divergent mystic. It made him *feel* himself a gentleman, made him even cast an audacious eye on Laura Brownsill, the daughter of the squire.

When that lovely girl celebrated her twenty-first birthday the squire invited all the village folk to a tea on his lawns, and Laura had certainly singled Homer out for some attention. This was on a warm Sunday in mid-April, when the formal garden was gay with yellow sprays on its deciduous shrubs, with pink blossoms on saplings that hadn't any leaves—and papas were explaining that those trees were foreigners, from Japan. All the idle families in the world seemed to be congregated there, strolling about the grassy pathways, clothed with propriety and behaving with sedateness, aping an enjoyment they were desirous of really feeling. Yet although the verdure of the lawns invited them to loll, to bask, to meditate, to play, they were too inhibited to accept. They stared at the fountain with eight jets, at the labels in the lake announcing the names of lilies that were to flourish there later on, and looked timid and admonished their children. Homer surprisingly found himself in the yew pleasaunce, alone with Laura. He apologized to her for his mother's absence. (Really he had not wanted her to accompany him, she looked so "dowdy.") And Laura was explaining to him the pleasant features of the grounds.

"Yes, I know," he said, "my father worked here once upon a time."

"I can just remember him." Laura smiled.

"And I nearly took a job here meself once."

"Indeed," said Laura. Bright brown hair she had, a round pink face, a charming bust, and her white clothing gave her a fragrant blossomy appearance.

"But I never cared for manual work," he went on. "If you've got a headpiece you want something more mental."

"Of course." Her recognitions were perfect. "And now?"

"I'm at the brewery."

"Ah, yes," said Laura.

"In the office," he explained.

"Ah, yes," Laura repeated, "that gives you more scope."

"Well, it does and it doesn't," said he.

"Yes," she sighed, "that is so." And for some time they were silent. At last he ventured:

"We are going to have a beautiful summer."

"You think so?"

"Yes. The kind of summer you'd wish for if you knew it was to be your last."

"It is a splendid day. I shall always remember it."

"So shall I," he returned, meaningly. Laura smiled at him with such frankness that the whole richness of her being and influence was demoralizing. They were quite alone, unseen.

"I am now my own mistress," the adorable creature chattered.

"I wish you were mine," said he. She did not seem to notice the remark, it glided over and past her, and Homer idiotically hoped she would give him the opening again so that he might repeat it.

"Yes, it's a day to remember"—stupid how husky your voice got sometimes—"and I'll remember it too."

That was useless. Ah, but she was a grand creature!

"Now let me get you some tea," she said, and they went back to the lawn. "Johnson!" Laura called out to her butler. Johnson was dressed in a suit something like Homer's evening dress suit, but not quite. The boots were all wrong, and the trousers. Waiters always fell away at footgear, but in his sacred chest there was a pair of shiny shoes the squire himself might wear, but not old Bill Johnson, who pretended he did not know him and called him "sir."

When, later on, Laura said: "Good afternoon" and shook hands with Homer, she gave him a smile that seemed to invite, to anticipate, something further. But what could he anticipate, or she invite?

Ah, the endless futilities of desire! Yet he did not really desire Laura Brownsill, at least not so much as he desired her peculiar recognition. And she had devoted a special graciousness to him. He thought of her a great deal one way and another, and on the rare occasions when they met in the village she would stop and chat to him for a few moments. How was his mother? And his work? And was life pleasant? Mother was quite well, he told her. And work was simple, nothing to put a strain on a man's headpiece, you know. And life was pleasant enough if you were satisfied with your lot . . . but . . . of course. "Ah yes," Laura would say; "is it not a fine day?" and "Good morning" or "Good evening," as the case might be.

So two or three years went by, and then, one day, she had called at his home and asked for him. The Dodds lived in a corner cottage that had a fine chestnut tree in the front garden and a row of irises under the window. He was not home yet, Mrs. Dodd told her.

"Oh," temporized the beautiful woman. "We are having a dance at the Hall next week and I wondered—I am told he has some dress clothes?"

"Yes, he has," replied Mrs. Dodd, "this long time."

"I thought—perhaps—but I'd better call and ask him myself. Tomorrow. What time?"

Dodd's mother told her what time Homer would be at home.

When Homer heard the tremendous news he was smitten with exquisite qualms. Why in the name of fortune had he never learned to dance? Why this? Why that? How was she looking? And even as he debated the matter with his mother a knock came at the door. He leaped to answer it, and there was Laura again.

"Oh, I thought I would catch you this evening," she explained.

"Come in," cried Homer Dodd, throwing wide the door.

The lovely creature hesitated. "I hope I am not disturbing you?"

"Come in, come in," he repeated. "Present company is always accepted."

She went into the little parlour and plunged straightway into the matter of her visit. They were giving a ball in the following week, she wondered if he would be disengaged that night.

"Well, yes, but—" said Homer Dodd timorously.

"We are expecting a lot of people. Would you be able to come along and help Johnson?"

"Help? How? What Johnson?"

"The butler," she smiled explicatively, and then gazed away from him with a trifle of shyness. "We have to get extra help and we'd rather have someone we know and can trust. You have a dress suit?"

"Ah! You mean for me to come and wait on the visitors?"

"Yes. You would be paid of course."

"Help the butler?"

"Yes. We want someone we know and can trust."

For a moment he thought he would go away and thoroughly die. "But I know nothing about such work," he protested. "I've never done such a thing in my life. I couldn't do that, I wouldn't do it."

Laura looked disappointed, perplexed even.

"I thought you said, once—it was at my birthday party—that you would like to work at the Hall."

In a flash Homer realized that she had not comprehended his

daring then. "I wish you were mine," he had said, and she had thought he had wanted to come and look after her fowls, he supposed. And the clatter his mother was making with those dishes in the kitchen almost demented him. He uttered a mirthless laugh.

"Oh no, no, I never meant anything like that. No, I meant— Oh, very different."

It began to gleam upon her that something was wrong, vitally wrong, but for the life of her she could not fathom the blunder.

"I am sorry, Mr. Dodd," she said. "I see. Please excuse me." And she held out her hand, adorably tender. Homer held her hand, smiling again. He was a whimsical fellow. The devastating proposal had swept him in its cold clasp like an avalanche, but having escaped this death, he got up and began to pelt the avalanche with snowballs. He said:

"What time would you like me to come?"

Laura, still more mystified, answered:

"Would you really care to?"

"Yes," he said.

"You are sure? You can spare the time?"

"Yes," he said.

So she gave him all particulars and instructions.

"It will be rather a long night for you."

"The longer the better," retorted Homer.

"And—er"—it was delicately uttered—"how much am I to pay you?"

"Nothing. Nothing at all," said proud Mr. Dodd.

"Shall we say a sovereign?" she pursued, suavely.

"Very well, thank you," he submittingly agreed.

"Good night."

Homer went into the kitchen and told his mother what it was that Miss Brownsill required of him. Mrs. Dodd was elated when she heard he was to get so much money for such a little service. Homer went upstairs and took the moth-killer out of his dress clothes. Then he went to bed early and dreamed that he was frying hundreds of eggs in a large ballroom. Each egg had to be fried singly and laid carefully and neatly in lines on the ballroom floor until the initials H D and L B had been formed and then encircled by a heart. It took a long time.

On the evening of the ball Mrs. Dodd prepared her son's dress clothes, put the magnificent shoes beside the fire, set the squash hat acock upon the dresser, and hung the rich cloak across the armchair.

"Don't want those shoes," he exclaimed when he came in, "shall wear my old 'uns. You can put that white vest away, shall wear the black. What a fool of a woman you are, mother! D'ye think I can wear that hat and the gloves up to Brownsill's kitchen? God bless my soul! Nor that cloak neither."

Wasn't he a queer fellow! It disturbed the poor woman that he should go, as you might say, only half-dressed. He looked grand in the tailed jacket and the starched shirt and things. It only wanted that hat, and the cloak hung over his arm, to finish him off properly. But no, he covered himself up in an old top-coat and went off wearing a cap. Wilful, foolish, but a good son. Never a moment's uneasiness, never a pang.

He was still a fairish-looking man, with a tolerable figure, though he was getting on towards forty. His hair had thinned and there was an austerity in his gait, but still he was a lively man, freehanded, and was liked by Humpingden men.

Mother Dodd sat up dozing, hour after hour, during his absence. Ah, she was sleepy, but she could not sleep. She wrote a letter to her daughter, Fan, and another to a friend in a distant town. The fire slackened and was renewed. There were nibbling mice under the floor; she smote the floor with a brush, but they took no heed. At midnight there was three parts of a moon shining in the sky, and the wind blew cold. The clock ticked on and on; if you could keep pace with that ticking you would not notice time. Time smoothed all things. The clock ticked on, the chestnut tree in the garden heaved its mournful sigh, the dawn came. And with it came her son.

"Well?" said she.

"You ought to been abed," he replied.

"I've got a nice cup of cocoa for you, Homer."

"Don't want it. I'm half tight as it is." He sat down, looking around the kitchen as if it were a place he scarcely recognized, and drummed on the table with his fingers. "Champagne," he said. "She's going to be married."

"Who?"

"Laura Brownsill."

"Laura Brownsill! Is she, then?"

"Aw. Some rich old foxhunter. The squire gave it out at the ball. That's what this ball was for. Sir John Swells. Lady Laura, huh!"

"That's nice," commented Mrs. Dodd.

"Why?"

"Well, of course it is."

"He's old enough to be her father! Silly girl."

"That don't matter," said Mrs. Dodd, "not nowadays. And she must do as her father bids her. I wouldn't mind being an old man's darling."

"Well, I should," said her son.

"I suppose he's got a lot of money?"

"I'd hope so! He ain't got much else, 'cept a bald head and a spongy sort of nose to look at. I pity her, I do indeed."

"Humph." Mrs. Dodd was non-committal. "I suppose the squire wants it so."

"He wants a lot of other things, I may tell you," said Homer sardonically. "I overheard him and Mrs. Sansonny spooning together. They weren't aware of me, they were so hot."

"Mrs. Sansonny!" exclaimed his mother. "That fat sarah!"

"Ah. She's wide as a barn door, and he's lean as a sheet, but there they were. Fat as she is, she'd no more on than would clothe a child. And he says to her: 'I worship you, you devil!'"

"My God, murmured Mrs. Dodd, "what a wicked thing to say!"

"Wicked?"

"Well, he's a Christian, or he ought to be. And what did she say? Where was her husband?"

"Dunno," Homer yawned, and began to unlace his boots. "I crept away. And it's bed for me now."

"Drink up this cocoa," said his mother. "And what did they all say about your suit?"

"Why, nothing."

"Oh, but they must have said something, Homer!"

"Nobody didn't, not to me."

"Nobody?"

"Nobody and nothing. Why should they?"

"Lord!" Mrs. Dodd muttered. "I think I should have said something."

"Well, I say bed. Where's candle?"

She lit a candle. "Drink your cocoa."

"Damn the cocoa," said Homer Dodd.

Upstairs in his small bedroom he flung off the grand suit and let it lie on the floor. It was a low-pitched room with beams in the ceiling that would brain you if you were not wary, and it was hung with pestering white muslin. Muslin for the window, for the chair-back, the mirror, for the valance of the bed, and muslin skirts (as if it were a female) for the washstand. He stood swaying in his nightshirt until he trod upon the clothes; then he picked up the coat and, holding it at arm's length, muttered: "Who'll buy it? Fourpence!"

Nothing answered, from nowhere.

"Fourpence!" he repeated.

On the shoulder of the coat he then observed a pale thread gleaming, a fine single golden hair, and he remembered. . . . In the Hall kitchen the servants had snatched from time to time their own fandango—drinking, dancing, and bantering—and Homer had been beguiled by Polly, the parlour-maid. He had hugged her, and she him, they grown quite fond and daring. Homer picked the hair from his coat and gazed at it ironically.

"Keep that!" he mumbled, letting the coat slip to the floor again. Carefully laying the hair on the washing-table, he set the box of matches atop of it, so that he should find it in the morning. Then he lurched into bed and slept a sleep free of care and dreams.

On rising late he was still so tired that he forgot all about the golden hair under the matchbox, and in tidying up the room afterwards his mother swept it away. Homer did not remember it for two days. It was gone then, and he could not ask his mother if she had noticed such a thing under a box of matches. A pity! But after all it was not fitting to make a sally with the maid whose mistress had befooled you. That would indeed be the action of a poor-minded man. Having been a servant by romantic proxy for a few hours, now let it drop.

In a few months Laura married and went to dwell in Scotland, and within a year she had a child. Though she paid visits to her old home occasionally, it so happened that Homer never saw her again. And Homer, musing upon his unborn romance, came to believe that Laura was not happy, that she had once had for him, not love perhaps, not quite that, but a loving feeling, and in time this conception accrued and brightened until it appeared that he and she had been separated only by the stern decree of her father! To charge with such fragrant lustre such faint seeming is a debility of any mind; we frame and bring to life the delusions we desire to cherish, lest in the void of our fancies we decline in pride and the soul faint in the shadow of its being.

One day is much like another day in general, but at times something may befall that is not diurnal: it clinches an epoch, stability is gone, time has begotten a monster. The monster took the form of a letter to Homer from the money-lenders who had befriended Charley Spatkin, to whom Homer was inescapably bound as a surety for the Spatkin loan, and whom a defaulting Spatkin had altogether displeased. They wanted forty pounds! They wanted it immediately, and they wanted it from Homer. Oh, the misfortune! Homer had not got so much money, he could not pay it. And if he had got it, he would not pay! He stormed at the contrite Spatkin, he wrote to the placid lenders, the unrelenting lawyers, the adamantine bailiffs; there was no useless thing to be done that he did not do, but he could not escape the consequences of his sponsorship. So finally he hauled the dress suit from its chest and directed his mother to pack it carefully.

"I don't ever want to see it again," he said.

There was no help for it, it was packed and sent to a Jew dealer in London who bought the entire panoply—the jacket, the cloak, the hat, shoes, socks, linen, studs, and trousers—for a moiety of its cost. There was no help for it.

"I don't ever want to see it again."

Mrs. Dodd was cloven to the soul.

"As God sees me, it's wicked!" she cried. "You might just as well ha' been a gardener, like your father."

"Yes," said Homer, "I might. The suit's no use to me now."

"And never has been," she added ruefully; " 'twas all a foolish fancy, Homer. You've never even worn it."

"I wore it once," he said. That had been his only chance of sporting these fine feathers.

Mrs. Dodd recalled the occasion: "Why, so you did, and it paid you well that time."

The money received for the suit, with the rest of his savings, discharged the Spatkins of their dilemma.

"I will repay," the poor greengrocer wrote, "trust me for that, Homer."

Trust was far indeed from Homer, but at least the Spatkins, Fan, Charley and their Elizabeth, were on their feet once more. Yet not for long. One night in their town there was a great fire and Charley Spatkin, always a daredevil, in saving some children, lost his own life.

Mrs. Dodd took train and went to the aid of her daughter. After a few days she returned to Humpingden bringing with her the ten-year-old Elizabeth for a short holiday.

"Poor Charley," said Mrs. Dodd through her tears, "he done prodigals of bravery."

Fan remained in her home to wind up the greengrocery business and look around for some new opportunity to live. Soon she had an offer from a kindly rich couple who desired a servant, and then she came home to sound her mother and brother on her project of leaving Betty in their care. No obstacle to this plan interposed, and so Fan went off to service, leaving Betty at Humpingden.

Homer never took a liking to this child. Blood may be thicker than water, but the blood was unattractive. Betty had a round greyish face and ashen hair tied tightly with a ribbon. She was thin and untidy and terribly plebeian. Though spiteful and stupid, she quickly conceived a morose desire to become a nun, like those she often saw walking from the abbey.

"But you are cruel," says Homer. "You have a cruel nature. Why is that?"

Betty stares with silent hatred into her uncle's eyes.

"Sometimes you are cruel to the cat, ain't you?"

"Yes, I am."

"Now mind," says he severely, "you are not to ill-treat that cat any more."

The child says nothing, intimates nothing.

"You understand me, Betty?"

"Yes."

"All right, then."

Betty goes away. In a little while she returns to Homer and says: "I've been banging the cat."

"You have!"

"I threw it down the stairs."

"What for?"

The child contemptuously grins at him.

"You're a bad thing, Elizabeth. Tit is good for tat, you know. I fear I shall have to serve you the same."

They were silently unpleasant to each other. The child grew but she did not improve, and as the months wore on, Homer's heart ached for that time to come when Betty could rejoin her mother. That happy event he began to fear was yet far off—as far as his forty pounds—and so at last, in despair, he wrote to his sister Fan, making her a fair proposal. His salary was now really a good one, he had been promoted head clerk, some day he might even be manager, but their mother was getting old and the child was something of an anxiety to her. So would it not be fine now if she, Fan, would come back to Humpingden and live with them once more, to help their old mother and look after Elizabeth, who was　good child in many ways but still needed a parent's guiding hand?

Homer wrote like that, and Fan replied to his "welcome letter," saying how pleased she was to hear of his progress, he had worked hard for it, he ought to have been made manager years ago, but she was sorry she could not do what he wanted now and she implored her brother to keep the child. Indeed, she was thinking of getting married again, her sweetheart would marry her at once if only some arrangement about Betty could be made. No man liked to have the care of another's child, etc., etc. If Homer would only keep her in Humpingden she would know the child was in safe hands; and she, Fan, would contribute to her support. And she pointed out that soon Betsy would be old enough to go out to work, into service; they would employ her at the Hall for certain, and so on. It was a hard thing to ask him to do, but he must remember that she was only a widow and had not had the best of luck in life. He had always been a good brother to her and she would be staunch to him.

"The best of luck in life!" he mused over the letter. "No, no one has that, for no one deserves it."

But was he to have nothing in life that he really desired? Or deserved? Nothing—though his hopes were not high nor his deeds remarkable. Age came upon you, it had come upon him: younger men could go uphill now faster than he could come down. And yet what would he have if he had but the power, what mortal desire for which he could still suffer and endure? He felt there was little enough to make a stir about at the best of times, luck or no luck. If only he could look forward now, as he had been wont to do, to some fine promise of the future—but no, no, there was nothing that age did not wither. His mother was old, and he could only look forward to the time when he would be left to the care and mercy of the hateful Elizabeth. That seemed to be his doom—not love, but loathing.

"It's bad," he said, folding up the letter. "Why, I might just as well have been born a fool."

Silver Circus (1928)

CHRISTINE'S LETTER

CHRISTINE was vexed. A charming waitress; she wore a wedding ring, but she was the most attractive girl at the Café Tee To Tum, always deft and alert, with beauty that cheered you, good sense that satisfied, a gentle dignity that pleased; now she was vexed, fuming. The girl at the cash desk had given her a letter, it had come by the afternoon post, a fat letter, it had been redirected once or twice, and Christine was anxious to read it. She had read snatches of it, she burned to read more, the whole of it, it was so long and beseeching, and it so gilded her triumph, because it was from her husband, living in the country. Christine had not seen him for three or four months, she had not even heard from him since she had left him, this was the first letter that had reached her, and it began: "Come, it was not nice of you to run away and leave me so, but I do not reproach you." The phrases were in the very spirit of the namby unmasterful creature she had so unhappily married, but hating him though she did, she was eager to know how much her lightning severance of their bond had wounded him. Did he want her to return; was he sorry, or angry, or what? Not that she cared now: he was in the south, she was in the north, there were hundreds of miles between them. Sick to loathing she had run from him and put herself to work, mean work. Christine did not like working for her living, but it was heaven compared to living with *that*. She read: "I wish I had never married you, it was my mother's fault, she urged me to it."

"Oh, it is not true; how he enrages me! Lies, lies, lies! He besieged me, swore he would kill himself with . . ."

"Some bread and butter," said the clergyman she was called to attend. "Household bread, and stale if you have got it." His voice seemed to threaten the very food he was ordering. Old, tottery, and abrupt he was, with a vague warp of rufous hairs combed from left to right across his poll, which was coloured like a pine board.

"He is a hound, you know," ruminated Christine. "As if his mother had anything to do with it!"

At the buffet she filled a pot of tea, clapped bread and butter upon a plate, knife, spoon, milk, and conveyed her tray to the clergyman.

"China tea?" he inquired, peering up. "No? I said China. I can't drink this." He was very ugly for a man of God.

"I do not reproach you. Indeed! Oh, thanks!" and with a hoity-toity aria in her soul Christine replaced the Indian beverage with Chinese potion. "He wants me back and promises not to grumble! Jam, sir? Pastry?"

"No. I detest pastry. Oh—I don't know, what else have you got; where's the card? I'd like to see it, though I shan't want anything else. Mum . . . mum . . . mum . . . bananas. I suppose there is no cream for threepence each? No. Yes, a banana." And he pushed a fold of bread and butter into his mouth without offering a grace.

Christine served him with a small plump banana on a little white dish and for some reason pushed a cruet towards him. But people continued to pour in and she could not find a corner or a moment in which to read another line of her letter. So distracting it was, she could hardly grasp what the customers said to her, and she gazed with a lost gaze through the great windows with those white letters stamped upon it backwards:

ƎƎꟻꟻO   TA⅃OƆOƆ   AƎT

Flittings of experience came to and fro in her mind: conjugal life in their hamlet, so quiet, so empty, so dull, and therefore so exhausting; a husband who wanted to be a poet, whose pensive melancholy would have blackened the soul of an angel; their incompatible association, his serenity, her despair, and her suppressed fury at it all.

The tottery clergyman went, went without offering a God-bless-it, Christine was sure; a stout matron with a green parasol desired a glass of water, some cracknels, and the loan of the time-table; a little fat-legged girl lolling with her toes on a table rail fell with her chair backwards and screamed.

"I hate the things you think, and the things you have done to me." Well, it was his own fault; she had not loved him, she never could have loved him, for he stifled her, his very goodness mangled every fibre of her self-respect, so that, at last, to be in the same room with him submitted her to a sort of ghostly asphyxiation. They had never quarrelled, not really quarrelled, but oh, how often she had longed to shatter with some blasphemy the contentment of his eyes! The wildcat was in Christine, hidden, it had never been tamed, he had never known of it—how *was* he to know of it?—propriety had swamped him in such billows. And yet the place had been beautiful, ah, the hills, the woods, the sky like holy balm—if only, oh, if only . . . !

Christine kept stealing the letter from her breast, it began: "Beloved," but she could not win two moments of repose, it would have to wait, it was a long, long letter, pages and pages. So Christine went on serving; there was a shower of rain outside and the people lingered on. But the rain stopped at last and the people began to go, soon they were nearly all gone and then — Then Arabella Barnes came up with her knuckle bleeding, to beg Christine to bind it up for her, and there and then Phyllis Wicks began to beguile them with stories of her own true love. He was a bus-conductor, and had violet eyes; they made Phyllis reckless, and she lavished her pocket money upon him.

"What's mine is his," Phyllis said to Arabella, "and what's his is mine."

"But not," Arabella sniffed, "not that boil on the back of his neck?"

"There's no such thing! His flesh is as sweet as a lamb."

Faugh! Christine almost shrieked, but she only said: "Excuse me!" and ran off to the only place where she could be free from unceasing interruptions—the lavatory. Oh, blessed inviolable refuge! Instantly she began to read her letter.

"Beloved,

"Come, it was not nice to run away and leave me so, but I will not reproach you. No, nor for anything. But still, why did you? Why did you? It is hard for me to account for your absence, you know, I am in a false position, a stupid position, I am a fish out of water, I am like a fish that some tidal wave has left upon an ironmonger's counter. People, the neighbours, your friends, the very tradesmen, imagine painful things. They must know, they can see it, they smirk and pity me. How am I to explain? It is not possible. Perhaps you have gone off with another man. Of course we had ceased to love each other, though we had only been married a year, a little long year; our life together was stifling, unbearable, though I never told you so—you would not have understood. We stung and annoyed each other—but, what of that? Excuse me, my dear, what of it?

This then is life,
This is what has come to the surface after so many throes and convulsions.

And you have gone, have gone without a good-bye, without a quarrel, without even a kiss-my-behind, and left me only some of your old shoes and a bottle of aspirin tablets. Did you think I suffered from headaches? I have never suffered from headaches. I shall throw them away soon and give the shoes to that girl with the blue eyes who brings the washing. After these months of silence what am I to think, or do? Why have you not written? I wish I had never married you, it was my mother's fault, she urged me to it. And you were pretty. I liked that, though I did not like your irreligion, or your ideas, or the friends you favoured. They were foolish people, they were, believe me, my dear, I know, I know, all of them unworthy of you. Was I too? And yet, without boasting, I could have done great and marvellous things if you had cared for them, yes, in time I could; but you were restless, you were artistic I suppose, bohemian, and the long slow months exhausted you. For myself I was content in the little house in this sweet country place, yet often I envied riches. Oh, my goodness, yes; you did not guess that! I envied riches for you, so that we could have gone, well, where *could* we have gone? Now perhaps you are gone with some man. That is not right or fitting, but if you would come home again, I should not say anything about it. One forgets, it is lonely here, foolish here, but I dare not go away lest you come suddenly home again. Oh, I wish you would. You were always wanting to travel, to blaze out, to 'do' things; even on your last birthday you said bitterly: 'A quarter of a century and nothing done.' What is it you want to do? You will not have children. Let us travel together. We will give up this little house, it is too isolated and unspacious, there is not enough room in it for you and I together, it makes us melancholy and mean and full of evil. It is true, yes, though you did not believe there was any evil in me—and that used to annoy you. I'll take a mistress, I will, I swear it, and what will you say to that? Oh, forgive me, my blessed one, I wish you would come back, it is lonely here, foolish here. Sometimes I am singing quite happily and loudly all by myself, and then in the midst of a song, without any reason at all I stop and burst into tears. Why, why is this? Oh, tell me, dear one, come and tell. When first you left me I did not mind, I was unmoved. It was summer, and in summer what is now monotony was almost ideal. Unless you lay and stared at the sky everything you saw was green leaves and grass, grass and leaves. The birds were all those friendly fellows of one or two notes, chiff-chaffs calling for hours, the tom-tit sawing, the magpie rattling a box of peas, and the cuckoo, whose company always stirred the small birds to such rages. All gone now. And at night there were nightjars, and out on the down the curlew. The boughs of the trees would just float in the hot air, and the leaves would hum like gnats. Time really existed, a thick accreting medium, without lapse. Pine needles filled our watershoot, there were cobwebs everywhere. And now the garden has run to waste, all except the bed of parsley, it *has* grown. I do not use it, but you were so fond of parsley. How it did annoy me when you sent me out at night into the dark garden to gather a sprig or two for some fish cakes or something! I would grope about and light matches endlessly in the wind until I'd picked a handful and then I would bring it to you. The grass of the lawn is getting long and rough. Do you remember one day last April when it snowed and you stripped yourself naked and went out on the lawn and danced in the white flakes? So reckless of you, anybody passing might have seen you, but I did not say anything. I did not even watch you. I got out some towels and warmed them for you, but somehow you did not like that. Why not? It always pleased you greatly to be displeased. I wish you believed in God. How can you not—there is Christ? You believed only in the things that concerned you, you said: death was death and you knew nothing about it and could not know. Oh, false, dreadful, trivial spirit of the age, so flippant and so fleeting; every year a new Abraham prepares to sacrifice a new Isaac. The everlasting wanders in the void, for half the truths we know can never be told, they are too divine for speech. But God is freedom from evil—is it not so? I told my mother that you were gone abroad with friends, I have not told her the truth, I dare not tell myself. Besides, it may not be true. Sometimes I have a conviction, sweet and lovely one, that it is not true, that it never can be true. Not today, alas, no, for it rains, it rains all over the world. There is melancholy in my mind and gloom in everything, in the straggled forlorn briars and the scoops of dark leaves shrinking from the wind on the common. I have just been walking there, along by the pond. The tiny pond shivered as the lorn drops fell upon it, some sheep lay under the blackthorn, the wind was cold. The misty hills with their dying woods were far away, too far. There was a horse tied to the white palings beside the inn, and it lifted its head and neighed as I came by. I bowed my own head and almost wept, wept for nothing save that life was gloomy and chill. And yet a mile above those clouds that cling to the land the sunlight must be everlastingly beautiful; even in the next county the day may be bright and warm, and perhaps on some happy seacoast, blue and golden a hundred miles away, little white yachts are gliding, and people sit and snooze and declare that life is splendid. Yet here my misery fits me as tightly as a new hat that I cannot discard, it is my clothing, my element, my doom. Oh, you are right, my darling, this is no place for a beautiful woman. You were a bright pin stuck in a cushion of mud, it was right to go and leave me. But I might find you again and take you far away. Every time I come home my glance leaps to the hallrack to see if your hat and coat are there. No, not today, certainly not today. I do not even know whether this letter will reach you. Perhaps I shall not send it after all. I have written others, many, and I have not sent them, so you do not reply; but I go on writing and writing, and perhaps some day I will show them all to you. But no, you are harsh and evil, I hate the things you think and the thing you have done to me—it is just crude cruelty. And there is hatred in me too, and evil, for I know you will never come back, never, never, never. You will find another lover who may deserve you more than I, though he could not love you better. But, however that may fall, you will deserve him as little as you deserved me, poor thing as I am. For you had no generosity of spirit, all you had was a beautiful alluring body, nothing more on which a man could anchor his deep feeling. I suppose I could go on abusing you for a long, long page. It is sad to have to say the last thing between us. I know I shall go on loving you. Perhaps I shall find a true friend who will love me better than you, and I shall love her—until I remember. Then I suppose I shall tell her of a lover I once had, far sweeter than she, who used me well, was beautiful beyond all, was forbearing and kind and understanding. Listening, she will vainly envy you, not, oh, not for your love of me, but because of your surpassing excellence.

"Christine, my wife, do not believe it ever. I am a bird in your heart that will sing when you remember me."

"The hound! The hound!" gasped Christine, clenching the letter with fury. As for a moment she stood with it crushed between her hands her wry glance caught one word at the beginning of the letter. "Beloved." So she began to read it again, opening it until she came to the lines: "I wish I had not married you, it was my mother's fault, she urged me to it." Once more she crushed the detestable pages together, and this time she cast them into the lavatory. A gesture of the hand, and they were swirled away.

"I want," called the girl at the cash desk when Christine returned, "twopence from you."

"Twopence?"

"Please. It was surcharged, that letter of yours. Didn't you notice the envelope? It had been redirected or something. I paid the postman. Twopence it was."

"Oh, dear," Christine said. "It wasn't of the slightest consequence. I wish you hadn't. It was from—from someone I didn't know."

The Field of Mustard (1926)

AHOY, SAILOR BOY!

ARCHY MALIN, a young sailor just off the sea, rambled into a tavern one summer evening with a bundle under his arm. There was hearty company, and sawdust on the floor, but he was looking for a night's lodging and they could not do with him there, so they sent him along to the widow Silvertough who keeps a button and bull's-eye shop down by the shore. (You would know her again: she's a mulatto, with a restive eye.) And could she give him a night's lodging? He would be off by the first train in the morning—would 'a' gone tonight only the last train had beat it —just a bed? She could; so he threw down his bundle, bought a packet of butterscotch, and went off back to the tavern, the Cherry Tree. Outside it was a swing-sign showing about forty painted cherries as fat as tomatoes on a few twigs with no more than a leaf apiece. Inside there was singing, and hearty company, and sawdust on the floor.

"Happy days!" said the sailor, drinking and doing as others do.

Well, this fair young stranger, you must know, was not just a common seaman; he wore a dressy uniform with badges on his arm and looked a dandy. He could swop tales with any of them there, and he sang a song in a pleasant country voice, but at times his face was sad and his eyes mournful. Been to Sitka, so he said, but said in such a way that nobody liked to ask him where that was, or where he was bound for now. They thought, indeed, that maybe some of his family had grief or misfortune come upon them, and no one wanted to go blundering into the sort of private matters that put a man down; but when someone spoke about the numbers of people dying in the neighbourhood just then, the sailor became rather contentious.

"Baw! Plenty of people die every hour, but you don't know any of them. There's thousands die every day, but devil a one of them all is known to you or to me. I don't know them, and you do not know them, and if you don't know them it's all the same, death or life. Of course, when a big one falls—like President Roosevelt, it might be, or old Charley the linendraper over at Crofters—you hear about that; but else you don't know them, so what does it matter to you—if you ain't acquainted with them? I tell you what, it is very curious how few of the people you *do* know ever seem to die; but it's true—they don't. I knew my own father, of course, as died; and a friend or two that died was well known to me; but I don't know any of these other corpses, nor what becomes of them I do not care. And that's as true as the dust on the road."

"Young feller," an oldish man, drinking rum, said, "you are young yet. When you get to my age you will find your friends a-tumbling off like tiles from a roof."

"And what becomes of them?"

"They'll get their true sleep."

"That all there is to it, then?"

"Oh, there's goodly mercy everywhere. Accorden to your goings-on before, so it is. Whatsoever you does here must be paid for there."

"Ay," said the sailor, with a general wink, "even up yonder money talks, I suppose?"

"God help you! To be thinking of that!" the old man cried. "Money talks, 'tis true; but there's only two ways it gives you any satisfaction: one is earning it, the other spending it."

"There's many though," the sailor said, "as spends a lot they don't earn."

"Ah, that's their own look-out," said the other, with his glass of rum in his hand. "And you can take your mighty oath it's the sacramental truth. You can't thread a camel through a needle's eye. Dust to dust, you know; ashes to ashes."

"Here!" growled the landlord. "Tip us a lively song, some-one. I feels like I was going to be haunted."

So they persuaded the young sailor to sing his song.

"What's become of all the lassies used to smile up on a hearty?
    Luck my lay, luck my laddie, heave and ho!

"What's the news of Jane and Katy with their mi-ra-fah-so-lah-ty?
    I dunno, Archy Malin, I dunno.

"Where's the lass as swore she'd wed me when I shipped again
        this way?
    Luck my lay, luck my laddie, heave and ho!

"Was it booze, or was it blarney? Was it just my bit of pay?
    I dunno, Archy Malin, I dunno.

"Oh, young men are fond of pleasure, but the girls are full of vice.
    Luck my lay, luck my laddie, heave and ho!

"Is there ne'er a pretty creature who's as simple as she's nice?
    I dunno, Archy Malin, I dunno."

They gave him a hearty clap for singing it, though it wasn't very lively.

"I never heard that ballad before," the old rum man said.

"You wouldn't," replied the sailor.

"And I thought I knew most every song as ever was, most of 'em!"

"You wouldn't know that one," the sailor said, "because I made it myself."

"Ah!" the other gleefully cried, "I knew; I knew there was some craft about it."

"And it's true," added the singer, "true as the dust in the road."

With that he got up, pushed his drink back on the table, and away he went.

With a bit of a lurch now and then he strode moodily along the sea wall of the little harbour. Most of the shops were closed, and a calm midsummer dusk was nestling on street and sea. At the end of a rocky mole protruding seawards he was quite alone and leaned on a parapet. The moon rose drowsily over the bay, whose silent waters only moved when near the shore; the waves frilled pettishly on grey rocks veined with silica. A ship passed over the sad evening sea, its lamps faintly glowing, and a few houses on shore beamed with lights as well. The mountains around were black already, though the sky behind them was pearly. Somewhere a bell was ringing.

He wished himself gone out of the dull little town, but he was bound to stay until morning, and so after sighing away a half-hour or more he turned at ten o'clock to ramble back to his lodging, but on the border of the town he took a turn up on to a little rampart of the hills, a place newly laid out on its banks in municipal fashion with shrubs and young birch trees and seats on winding paths. Up there he lounged down on one of the seats under the slim birches, between whose branches he saw the now risen moon over a darker bay, the harbour with its red and green lights, one or two funnels, a few masts and spars. And he could hear, though he could not see, a motor passing below and the clatter of a trolley. Half full of beer and melancholy, he began to drowse, until someone passed quietly by him like a shadow. The night was come, and despite the moon's rays he only took in the impression of a lady, richly dressed and walking with a grand air. There was a waft of curious perfume.

Now, the handsome sailor had a romantic nature, he was inclined to gallantry, but the lady was gone before he could collect his hazy senses. He had not seen her face, but she seemed to be wearing a dark cloak that might have been of velvet. He stared until he could no longer see her. "Smells like an actress," he mused, and yawned. Leaning back on the seat again, he soon fell into a light slumber, until roused once more by a feeling that someone had just gone past. The path was empty, up and down, but though he could see no one, or hear anything, that strange perfume hung in the air. Then he caught sight of a little thing on the seat beside him. In the chequered moonlight it looked white, but it was not white. The stranger knew it was unlucky to pick up a strange handkerchief, but he did pick it up. He found it was charged with that elegant smell he had imputed to actresses.

The moon glittered on his buttons, the patterns of slim boughs and leaves lay across him. *I dunno, Archy Malin, I dunno!* he hummed, and stuffing the scented handkerchief into his breast pocket he sat blinking in the direction he had seen the mysterious lady take. It was late, she had gone *up* the hill; she ought to be coming *down* again soon.

"That's a nice smell, so help me," he observed, and pulled the handkerchief from his pocket again. "I bet it's hers." While twiddling it musingly in his fingers, he maintained an expectant gaze along the upward path. "Couldn't have been any handkerchief there when I sat down, or I'd have seen it." As he replaced it in his pocket he concluded: "I bet a crown she dropped it here on purpose. Well, you done it, Jane; *you* done it." Leaning with his arm along the back of the seat, he sat so that he would be facing her when she came down the hill again. And he waited for her.

It was in his mind that he ought to have followed her—she might be waiting for him somewhere up there. But she would be coming back—they always did!—and he felt a little unwilling to move now. Time passed very slowly. In the gloss of the moon his brass buttons shone like tiny stars; the patterns of leaves and branches were draped solemnly across his body and seemed to cling to his knees. He held his breath and strained his ears to catch a sound of her returning footsteps. As still as death it was. And then the shock came; the sudden feeling that there, round about him, just behind, some malignant thing was watching, was about to pounce and rend him, and he shrank at once like a touched nerve, waiting for some certainty of horror —or relief. And it gave him a breathless tremble when his eyes swivelled round and he *did* see something there, sitting on the seat behind him. But it was all right—it was her!

Calmly he said: "Hello! How did you get here?" (God Almighty, his brain had been on the point of bursting!)

She did not reply. She sat gracefully, but still and silent, in a black velvet cloak, one knee linked over the other. Whether she had a hat or not he could not tell, there was a dark veil covering her head and face. But none the less he could tell she was a handsome woman all right. Her arms were folded under the cloak, where her fingers must have been clinging to hold it tight around her.

"I saw you go by," began the young sailor, "but I didn't hear you come back."

Well, she did not answer him then, she did not utter a word, but she certainly did pay a lot of attention to what he said to her, and her eyes gleamed quite friendly under her veil. So Archy kept on chaffing her, because he was sure she had not dumped herself down there beside him in that lonely spot, at that time of night, for nothing; and of course he felt quite gay. She nodded a lot at the things he said to her, but it was quite some time before she opened her mouth to him, and then he was rather surprised. Because she was a fine well-built girl, with a lovely bosom and all that, but her voice really did surprise him.

"I have never been here before," was what she said, but her voice was thin and reedy, as if she had asthma or something. "I happened to see you—so I came along."

"Oh, that's dandy," said Archy, and he hauled up to her and was for putting his arm around her straight away.

"No! You must not do that!"

And although she did not move or shrink away she spoke so sadly that somehow that jaunty sailor was baffled; she was a perfect lady! He sat up and behaved himself.

The girl stared through the trees at the lights down in the harbour, and you could not hear a whisper down there, or anywhere else in the world.

She said: "I was lonely."

"I bet you was!" was his uncouth reply, and he kept his own arms folded. This was the queerest piece he had met for a long time.

"Please don't be angry," she said, turning to him.

"No. Sure," he answered heartily. "I'd like to know your name, though. Mine's Archy Malin. I'm a sailor."

"My name?" She gave a sigh. "It was Freda Listowell."

"Well, ain't it now?" he quizzed her.

She shook her head.

"Married?" pursued the sailor.

"No." The question seemed faintly to amuse her.

"You lost it, then?"

"Yes," was the grave reply.

The young man was beginning to enjoy these exchanges. That sort of chit-chat was part of the fun of making up to girls like Jane and Katy. This one was a lady—you could not doubt that—and so it surprised him a bit. But all the same, he liked it.

"Freda Listowell! That's a nice name, too good to lose."

She shivered, the moonlight had grown cold.

"Shall have to help you find it again," he continued.

"You could not do that."

"Could I not! Are you staying in this burgh for long?"

"I am not stopping anywhere at all. I must go back soon."

"You can't get far tonight—it's late. Where are you stopping, then?"

"You would not believe me if I told you."

"Me! Not! I'd believe you if you said you was an angel from heaven. Unless you've got a car?"

She slowly shook her head.

He began to feel he was not getting on very well with her, after all. Somehow they were making a poor show together.

But he could tell she was an actress; it was not the things she said so much as the way she spoke them. Taking a cigarette from a packet, he lit it.

"I've never seen anything like him in my wanderings!" He held the packet towards her, indicating the picture of a fathead seaman with whiskers and the word HERO on his hat. "Have one?" he asked her, but she declined. So he leaned his elbows on his knees and puffed smoke at the ground between his boots. And she had very elegant shoes on, and silk stockings on her fine legs—he couldn't take his eyes off them. But what was she trying to put across? Where did she live, then? Without turning, he spoke towards the ground at his feet.

"Are you all right?"

"No," she replied, and there was despair in her voice that woke an instant sympathy in him. He sat up and faced her.

"What's wrong, Miss Freda? Can I butt in at all?"

For the first time she seemed to relax her grave airs, and echoed: "Can—you—butt—in!" It almost amused her. "Oh no. Thank you, thank you, thank you; but no!"

The refusal was so definite that he could not hope to prevail against it; he could only murmur half-apologetically:

"Well, if you wanted my help, I'd do my best. You know—say the word."

"Ah, I was sure of that!" was the almost caressing rejoinder. "My dear, dear friend—but you—" In agitation she sat up, her hands, clasped together, slipping out from her cloak. He saw them for the first time, they were gloved. Then she parted her hands and almost hissed: "What do you think I am?"

It startled him; there was certainly something the matter with her.

"You'd better let me see you home. Serious, Miss Freda."

"But I have nowhere to go," she cried.

"What are you going to do, then?"

"Nothing."

"But you *must* do something."

Raising her veiled face, she gestured with one hand towards the moon and said:

"I am going to vanish."

"Oh, ho!" In a flash of a second the sailor perceived that he was not dealing with an actress at all: she was dotty! She was going to commit suicide! That was what had baffled him—she was a lunatic! A pretty fine lot to drop in for!

"You see, I am what you call a ghost!" she solemnly said.

Well, that clinched it; the poor things generally got worse at the time of the moon. He was keeping a wary eye on her; he liked women, got very fond of them, especially nice young women on moonlight nights, but he did not like them mad.

"You don't believe that?" she asked.

He tried to humour her. "It's a funny thing that I was having an argument about ghosts with a fellow once before tonight. And now here you are, the second one that's trying to persuade me. As a matter of fact, take it or leave it, just as you like, I wouldn't believe in ghosts not even if I *saw* one!"

Very calmly she said: "What do you think I am doing here?"

Archy fidgeted for a moment or two before replying:

"Quite honest, then, I never thought you were a ghost. First I thought you were—you know—a nice girl out for a bit of a lark."

He paused for her comment on this. It was a very cold one.

"Go on," she said.

"Ah well. Then I thought you were an actress."

"I'm not." There was a flash of petulance.

"But then I saw you must be in a bit of trouble of some sort."

With hesitation she agreed: "Yes, I am."

"You know—lost your memory, or—"

"No," she sharply interposed. "I've lost my life."

"Well, something like that," he said pacifyingly. "Do you come from—or—from down there?" He nodded towards the town.

Quietly she answered: "I come from heaven."

The poor fellow was almost suffering with bewilderment; a sailor lacks subtlety, and he was adrift, so he almost leaped at his little bit of a joke:

"Ah! That's it! You're an angel—I guessed that."

"There are no angels in heaven," cried the girl. ——

"Ain't!" said he.

"No. I have never seen one there."

Archy mumbled that that would be a great disappointment to him later on.

"What do you think heaven is?" the lady asked.

He was obliged to admit that he had not up to that moment been able to give very much thought to the matter.

"I can tell you," she said gravely.

"Do." She was so patient that somehow he was giving up that notion of her being just mad—and anyway he did not know how to deal with a lunatic.

"When I died about three years ago—" she began.

"You know"—the sailor turned laughing towards her—"you *would* make a blooming good actress!"

Wearily she stirred. "Listen!"

"What were you before you died?" he jeered; he was not going to let her mesmerize him like that.

"I was young and rich and foolish then. I had only one thought or passion in my life. I doted on clothes, fine clothes. I suppose I must have been mad. Nothing else ever really interested me, though I pretended it did. I lived simply to dress myself in quantities of beautiful garments. I think I was beautiful, too—perhaps you would have thought so. . . ."

"Let me see!" Archy made a snatch at her veil.

"No!" There was such a tone in her denial that his marauding arm shrank back on him, and it seemed as if the echo of her cry fluttered for a moment up among the faint stars.

"Take care!" Her gravity quelled him. "That was my life, that and nothing else: day by day, even hour by hour, to array myself in the richest gowns I could procure. What vanity! And I believed that I was thus honouring my body and delighting my soul. What madness! In everything I did my only thought was of the clothes I might wear, what scope the occasion would give me thus to shine. That was all my joy. Life seemed to have no other care, meaning, or end; no other desire, no other bliss. I poured out fortunes on silk, satin, and brocades, and imagined that by doing so I was a benefactor to all."

"Oh, but damn it!" interjected Archy. She stopped him with a gesture and then sank back in the corner of the seat, wholly wrapped in her velvet cloak. The sailor leaned with his arm on the back of the seat and surveyed her very wearily, thinking that if she did not go very soon he would have to clear himself off and leave her to her trouble. He felt like yawning, but somehow he did not dare. As far as he could make out she was the picture of misery, and he was veering once more to the belief that she was crazy. Harmless enough, but what could *he* do with a daft woman?

"Then I died, suddenly," she went on. "Imagine my disgust when I realized, as I soon did, that I was buried in a stupid ugly gown of cheap cotton, much too big for me! Ugh!" The lady shuddered. "For a long time I seemed to be hanging in a void, like a cloud of matter motionless in some chemical solution, alone and utterly unapproachable. My sight was keen, but I could *see* nothing. All was dim and featureless as though I was staring at a sky dingy with a half-dead moon.

"Then my thoughts began to swirl around and come back to me, my worldly thoughts; and though I knew I was dead, a waif of infinity, my thoughts were only of what I had prized in life itself—my wonderful clothes. And while I thought of them, they too began to drift around me, the comforting ghosts of them all—gowns, petticoats, stockings, shoes."

The sailor sighed and lit another cigarette. The lady waited until he composed himself again.

"But there they were, as real as I was, real to me. Ah, what joy that was! I tore off my hideous cotton shroud and dressed myself in one of those darling frocks. But I soon tired of it. When I took it off, it disappeared, and never came back again. I remembered other things I had enjoyed in life, but none of those ever came to me—only the clothes. They had been my ideal, they became my only heaven; in them I resumed the old illusions."

"Christ!" muttered the sailor. "I shall! I shall have to clout her in a minute."

"Pardon?" cried the lady.

"I said: Time's getting on, late, you know," he replied.

In the ensuing silence he could almost *feel* her hurt surprise, so he turned to her quite jocularly:

"Well, you *are* giving me a sermon, Miss Freda. What I'd like to know is how you dropped on *me* like this!"

"They all disappeared after I had worn them once; one by one they left again. I did not realize that for a long while, and in my joy at getting them back I wore them and changed and wore others, just as I had done in life; but at last all had departed except these you see me in now. When these are gone, I think something strange is going to happen to me—"

"Huh!" said Archy.

"—but I cannot tell."

When she stopped speaking the sailor wriggled his cigarette with his lips; the smoke troubled his nose and he sniffed.

"There ought to be *something* else, don't you think?" she sorrowfully asked.

There was moonlight in the buckles of her shoes, the leaf patterns lay across her neat legs and graceful body.

"Sure!" he answered consolingly. "It will be all right in the morning. Have a good night's sleep and you'll be as gay as Conky's kitten tomorrow."

The lady did not speak or move for some minutes, and when the silence became too tiresome the sailor had to ask:

"Well, what are you going to do now?"

"I wish," she sighed, "I could be buried very deep, under the floor of the sea."

"Haw! You'll get over that!" he heartily assured her.

Then she seemed to be summing him up, as if he only irritated her now: "But I am dead, I tell you. I am nothing but a wraith in the ghosts of my old clothes."

Her persistence annoyed him; he could not believe she was a lunatic, and this other business was the sort of lark he did not take kindly to.

"Oh, cheese it, Freda! Where do you live? Come on. You've been trying to put the dreary on me all this time, but I'm not that type of jacko. I'm a sailor, I am. So suppose you give us a kiss and say night-night and toddle off home like a good girl."

And yet—he waited for that gesture from her. It did not come.

"You do not believe me?" she asked.

"No. I've been doing my best, and you're a blooming fine actress—aren't you?—but I can't bite in. Can't!"

Up he stood, almost indignant. The girl sat where she was and the sailor lingered. For, to tell the truth, he still did not want to leave her; after all, she *might* be queer, he was still adrift; perhaps if he walked off she would follow him. He had taken but one step away when he heard her voice murmuring. With a frown he listened:

"I could prove it very easily."

"How?" He swung round.

"By taking off my clothes," she said.

My! Wasn't that a good one!

"Your clothes off! Here!"

A silent nod was the answer, and it revived at once all his extravagant fancies.

"Aw, now you're talking, Freda!"

He flung himself back on the bench beside her again. "Will you? Come on!" He knew she was going to do it, he awaited her restlessly. "What about it?" he urged, glancing up and down the paths. "It's all right. Come on. There's no one about."

At last she got up, and as he moved too, she hissed: "Sit down, you fool!"

For a moment or two she stood there in the path, guarded by the bushes and little trees, fumbling with her clothes, under the cloak. And she was very cunning, because before he knew how it happened, all the clothes dropped and lay in a heap there.

And that was all.

There was no slender naked girl awaiting his embrace. Freda Listowell was gone, dissolved, vanished; he had seen nothing of her, not even her hands. Only her ghostly garments lay in the path with the moon shining on them; the cloak and the shoes, the veil, the stockings, flounces, frills, green garters, and a vanity bag with a white comb slipping out of it. So cleanly swift and yet so casual was her proof that he was frightened almost before he knew.

"She was there. She did not move!" he whispered. "I could pawn my soul on that!"

For a space the doubting sailor dared not rise from the seat; his hands clung to it as a castaway's to a spar, as he turned his fearing eyes to right, to left, and behind him.

"I don't believe it!" he muttered stoutly, and tearing himself away from the bench he cringed in the path.

"Ahoy there!" he whispered. "Where are you?"

Sternly he straightened himself and walked erect among the near bushes. She was not there. Nowhere. When he spun round again, her clothes had gone too. "Hoi! Stop it!" he shouted, but he knew she was not hiding—there was nothing of her to hide. With his heart threshing like a flail he breathed appalling air. What was it? He wanted to fly for his life, but could not. His nails were grinding into his palms as he braced himself to grapple with his shocked brain.

"Foo!" he gasped, twining himself round and round, not daring to stand still. "Foo!" Sweat was blinding him, and thrusting one hand to his pocket he pulled out a handkerchief. It was the perfumed wisp he had found on the seat an hour before. As he caught its scent again, he remembered. He held it out in the moonlight and stared at it, muttering: "I don't fancy that. I don't. . . ."

Something invisible in the air plucked it from his fingers.

Dunky Fitlow (1933)

NINEPENNY FLUTE

HARRY DUNNING sold me his flute for ninepence. I didn't pay him the money all at once because at that time I was working for two horrible blokes and they didn't do me right. One was a Scotchman, and very Scotch, and the other a Jew, one of these 'ere Jews, and a credit to his race I must say. So I give Harry Dunning a tanner down and promised him the other as soon as I could. And this flute—I mean it was a fife—had a little crack in it near the top, only Harry Dunning said that didn't injure the tune at all because the crack was above the mouth-hole and the noise had to come out the bottom end. He said he'd get me into his fife and drum band if I bought it, and as it was no good him getting me in the band if I hadn't got any flute, I said I'd give him all the ninepence as soon as I could. So that's how I began to get real musical. My ma was very musical and after our dad pegged out she used to sing in the streets along of the Salvation Army. I didn't care much about that but she wanted me to get musical too, so I bought this fife and practised on *The Wild Scottish Bluebells* till Harry Dunning took me one night to the instructor's class in Scrase's basement, after I'd paid him twopence more off the ninepence.

Mrs. Scrase always used to go out on the practice nights. She was a fat woman and their sitting-room wasn't very big and when old Scrase got the big drum in there she said it overpowered her. I suppose that's only woman-like, but all the same I really reckon it was because she didn't care much about music; in fact, I don't think she liked it. Well, there was about a dozen of us there besides old Scrase; one of 'em had a kettledrum all polished up like gold and a lot of little screw taps on it to screw the skin up tighter or not. But it cost a fearful lot and it was only such chaps as Hubert Fossdyke could go in for a drum, his father being a master butcher as sold his own meat and cooked sheep's heads and had a horse and cart. Old Scrase instructed Hubert some way I couldn't get the gauge of. "Daddy—mummy" he used to keep on saying to him, "daddy—mummy," and Hubert would make a roll on the kettledrum that blooming near deafened you. Daddy meant tap it one way with one stick and mummy meant tap it some other way—I couldn't cotton on to it —and it was a treat to hear. I'd much rather have had a kettledrum, they've got more dash than these flutes, only they cost such a fearful lot. And it's Eyes Front for drummers, always, none of your looking to the right or left—Eyes Front! The fifers had little brass gadgets to fit on the flutes and put the music cards in, and old Scrase comes up to me. He was a paperhanger by trade, with a cast in his eye. Not half the size of his missus and he'd got a medal pinned on his lapel for life-saving somebody out of the sea that was drowning, and I made up my mind I'd have a go at learning to swim too, because it's healthy for you and I like medals. There's something about medals, especially when you've got four or five all in a row. And Scrase says to me:

"Can't you read music?"

"I ought to," I says, "I was in a church choir once."

"Yah, but can you *play* it? Let's hear you."

I had a go at some card he give me, but as a matter of fact I was absolutely bamfoozled, because as a matter of fact I never could make anything of this old notation. So I told him I could really play anything if only I heard it once or twice. I'd a good ear for music.

"Oh!" he says; "how'd you get in the church choir if you couldn't read music?"

"I got in all right," I told him.

"Yes, but how?"

"I dunno—I did. But it's this flute, I can't do with it yet, not properly."

"No," he says, "you can't."

"I never played before."

"No," he says, "you ain't."

All the same, after about an hour, off we all goes out for a route march slap up the High Street playing hallelujah on the *Wild Scottish Bluebells,* Hubert in front blurring away on his kettledrum (grand it was) and old Scrase bringing up the rear—whump, whump—on the big 'un. Half the time I didn't know what else we was playing, but I give 'em *Bluebells,* and we kept in step, everybody on the pavements stopping and staring at us and some bits of kids stepping out behind whistling the tune.

I dunno what it is, but there's something in a band makes you want to sock anybody that sauces you, and there was a couple of chaps as gave us a nasty bit of lip. They did; but you mustn't step out of the ranks when you're playing on the march, not without orders. You're all together, doing your best, and you get no thanks for it, no thanks at all. There was these two chaps I made a note of—I know 'em—and when I sees 'em again—! I wonder what they'll have to say then! I shall stipulate for one at a time, of course.

After we had done our route march we finished up outside Scrase's and he give us the dismiss.

"But step inside a minute, boys, will you?" he said. "Just a minute, I'm not satisfied; there's something wrong tonight."

So in we goes. "Shan't keep you a minute," he says, and we all tumbled after him down the basement stairs, and there was Mrs. Scrase frying something hot for supper.

"My God!" she says. "Albert, you ain't going to bring that ruddy drum in here again, are you?"

"No," he says, "I ain't going to do that, Min." And half of us was already in the sitting-room when she says: "What's all these blooming mohawks want here for?"

It was enough to make poor old Albert set about her, but he only said: "They don't want anything to eat, Min. There was something not quite all si-garney about 'em tonight, and I'm just a-trying 'em. Now, boys, I want a bar or two of *The Wild Scottish Bluebells.*"

So we ups and tootles a few.

Poor old Albert shook his blooming head. "Damme, whatever is it? Play it again, right through."

We does so.

"God!" he says then. "Play it singly."

So Fashy played it by himself, and Billy Wigg played it, and then it came to my turn and I played it.

"Ar! I thought so!" says Albert. "It's you, is it!"

And so it was. My flute was a different pitch to theirn; not much, only half a note or so, but it properly upset Albert. He grabbed hold of my flute and unscrewed it.

"It's cracked!" he said. "Where'd you get this thing?"

I told him I bought it off Harry Dunning. Harry Dunning said it was quite all right when he sold it to me. I said no it wasn't. "It was cracked," I said, "and you said that didn't matter as I could play alto on it." But Harry Dunning denied that; he denied it. And it surprised me a lot and I didn't like him any the more. I never did like him much, he was only a plasterer's boy though he always made out to be apprenticed to a mason, and I never did like the shape of his nose, it looked bad somehow. He denied it.

"Well, it's no good," Albert said. "Don't you come here with that thing any more."

I tell you, I went red in the face about it, and then, when we got outside again, Harry Dunning asked me for the penny I still owed him on it.

"Not much!" I says. "It's broke, it's out of tune, and Albert says it's no good—you heard him."

"That flute's all right," Harry Dunning says. "Only you can't play it yet."

"I could play it," I says, "if it was a good 'un."

He said: "No, you couldn't do that even. And what do you expect for eight penn'orth?"

"You take it," I says, "and give me back my eightpence."

"Gives nothing," he says. "It cost two and ninepence original—what could you have better than that? Two bob I'm giving you! The flute's perfect. All you got to do is poke a bit of wood up in the top of the mouthpiece part and that will make the pitch same as all ours."

Of course I didn't like him at all, but he was bigger than me. Next day I cut out a round piece of wood and shoved it up in the top of the mouthpiece part. It sounded worse than awful. I must have put up too much. And the worst of it was I couldn't get it down again, so there I was, dished. But I didn't give Harry Dunning the penny I owed him. Not me!

I couldn't afford no more on fifes and drums then, so I didn't go again, I give it up, but my ma was struck more than ever on me getting musical ideas. She even wanted me to be confirmed, but that was the doings of some old priest called Father Isinglass. She'd gone up very high-church all of a sudden and chucked the Salvation Army for the Roman Catholics because she liked confessing her sins. Well, I don't, but she did—only she was very forgetful. She wrote out what she was going to tell Father Isinglass on a little bit of paper, just to remind herself at the end of the week, only she would leave this bit of paper knocking about all over the room, and when I used to read it I couldn't help laughing. Poor old ma! I'm blessed if she didn't forget to take it with her sometimes!

So she wanted me to be confirmed and she wanted me to get some musical ideas, but I said I couldn't contend with 'em both. She said I ought to do one or the other, and I said music was as good as confirmation any day. She said it wasn't *quite* as good, but still it *was* very good and so she let me off being confirmed. To tell you the truth, I did not much care for this holy father she was struck on; his breath smelt rotten, and he brought us some Jerusalem artichokes once that nearly did me in. I got rather keen on the volunteers, only I wasn't grown up enough to join them. They used to go round about our town lugging four great cannons behind some horses and chaps on 'em dressed up like soldiers. They didn't look *quite* like soldiers, not quite, but the drivers had whips and helmets and jackboots with spurs on; and there'd be a squad of volunteers on foot, all dressed up like soldiers, only as it happened our town was a garrison town and had a barracks full of regulars like the Inniskilling Dragoons or the Lancers, and you couldn't help noticing the difference. Especially on Sunday mornings when the proper army turned out from the barracks to go to St. Martin's Church for the service, with the band playing. Hundreds of 'em, all of 'em with swords and spurs and tight trousers with yellow stripes down the leg, dead in step from the front rank to the back one—plonk, plonk, plonk, plonk! When you watched 'em sideways from behind, it looked like one long scorpion with thousands of legs. Going under the railway arch by the pill factory you couldn't hear yourself speak, especially if there was a train going over. And when any of 'em died they did have some grand funerals. Grand and solemn, the poor corpse on the gun carriage leading the regiment for the only time, Union Jack on the corpse, his helmet on top of that, and his old horse walking behind him without a rider. Ma always cried when she saw the horse. There'd be all the regiment following, very slow step, carbines upside down, and the "Dead March." Lord, it made you feel good! And when they'd finished burying him in the cemetery on the hill, they'd fire a few shots up in the air and blow on the bugles. So long, old pal, so long. Then they'd all turn home again, quick march, quick as you like now, with the band playing something lively, like *Biddy Mc-Grah*:

> Biddy McGrah, the colonel said,
> Would you like a soldier made of your son Fred,

With a sword by his side and a fine cocked hat—
Biddy McGrah, how would you like that?

and everybody would be laughing—nearly everybody—whistling
and laughing and jolly like.

Still, the volunteers was quite nice. They was all right. One of
the volunteers' wives (he was a sergeant) knew my ma and knew
I was musical, so her husband asked us if I would like to join
them as a bugle boy. Course, there wasn't any chance of ever going to any wars—I shouldn't have cared a lot for that sort of thing
—but I thought it 'ud be grand to have red stripes and a bugle
with white cord and tassels. My! So I told my ma to say as I
wouldn't mind being a bugler boy as long as there wasn't anything to pay, because I tell you straight you can't keep on for
ever buying, buying, buying these here instruments. So this
sergeant comes along one evening and takes me with him down
to the drill hall to try and see how I could get on with bugles. It
was a big hall where these four cannon was kept, but the sergeant
took me up some wooden steps to a loft where the practice was
going on and set me down on a box and left me there among a
lot of chaps dressed anyhow in their ordinary clothes, but they
had all got helmets on and I watched 'em blowing on bugles
enough to deafen a Greek. Then they had a go on some trumpets
made of brass, larger than the bugles and very pretty. I liked 'em
much better; there's more music in a trumpet, you know; it
makes a nicer kind of noise, much grander and looks more nice.
It's the proper thing you have to blow before the King when he
goes out, or these judges when they go to assizes, not like these
fat little bugles which only give a kind of a moo—there's no
comparison.

After about an hour the bandmaster come up to me and asked
me what I wanted. Of course, I didn't really know, because the
sergeant hadn't told me what to say—they do mess you about,
these chaps, and all for nothing. This bandmaster was a posh
fellow, all got up with black braid on his tunic and a quiff. Well,
I told him something, and he says:

"You're not very big."

"But I'm tough," I says.

"How old are you?"

I told him, and he said I wasn't old enough, but anyway he went and fetched me a bugle to try on. I wasn't half surprised when I found I couldn't blow the thing at all, not a sound, not in five minutes! I hurt my face trying. So then he gets me a trumpet, and the trumpet was no better than the bugle—not for me. And it looked so easy! Well, the result was he said I was too young (of course I knew that already) and too little, and said I should have to eat a lot more pudden for a year or two and then try again. I tell you, I was ashamed about the whole blessed lot of these volunteers. I was quite angry, too. It gets you that way, messing about over sizes and ages when you been left school and out to work for nearly two years. If a chap's old enough to go out to work he's old enough to go bugling. I should say so, and you couldn't expect a nipper like me to play *Annie Lorry* on the thing the very first time. I should say not. Anyhow, I gives him a salute and says: "Good night, sir."

I couldn't find the sergeant, he'd mizzled, so I started off home by myself. It was dark outside and the gas lamps were all alight. Mind you, I was in a great wax, but it somehow made me feel as if I wanted to cry. My ma's a bit that way too, only she cries about nothing at all. This drill hall was in a quiet street, but not far off I sees a crowd where there was a row on. I like a bit of a shindy so I wedges my way in. The row was over a couple of drunken soldiers out in the middle of the road challenging anyone to fight, and nobody 'ud take 'em on! There they was, the crowd all standing on the pavement each side, and the two soldiers prancing up and down the middle of the road offering to pay anyone who'd fight 'em. They'd got forage caps on and spurs and canes in their hands, both of 'em half canned, but one of 'em a bit more mad than the other. He kept on yelling out:

"Come on, ye bastards, I'm the ten-stone champion of Belfast! Forty men I've killed and I've eaten tigers alive!"

Not a soul in that crowd said a word or blinked an eye—he sounded too awful. The second soldier walked behind the other and kept swishing his own leg with his cane and asking everybody very quiet-like: "D'ye want to fight? D'ye want to fight? He's the cock of the world."

As if they would! But it made you feel angry though, it does make you get angry, that kind of thing. I could feel my savage blood surging up, but I thought I'd better keep quiet. Nobody wanted to tackle this champion and he got angrier and angrier, going up to fellows and grabbing them by the lapel of their coats.

"Come on, come on," he said, "it'll do ye the world of good." But the chaps all dodged away from him.

"Almighty God!" the soldier yells, "I must kill somebody. Come on, ye yeller guts, all of ye!" And he picked hold of another chap and spit in his face. Then the people in the back of the crowd started calling out: "Send for the picket. Where's the police?" And I'm blessed if this champion didn't come up to me and say: "D'ye want a bit of a brish?"

I thought to myself: "Lord, shall I have just one good sock at his eye!" but before I knew what I was thinking of I said: "No, thank you, sir," and he passed on to someone else. We all stood silent there like a flock of sheep waiting to be pole-axed and not daring to say a word. I was ashamed, but still, if anyone had tried to move away he'd 'a' been pounced on by this soldier and corpsed straight there. And this pal of his kept swishing his own leg with his cane: "D'ye want to fight? He's the cock of the world."

Now, standing just by the crowd was a deaf and dumb bloke known as Dummy—but I didn't know his right name. Everybody knew him because he *was* dumb and couldn't speak or hear, but these two soldiers didn't know him. Old Dummy stood there with his bowler hat on, but he couldn't 'a' known much about what was going on, being deaf, and anyway he couldn't say anything 'cause he couldn't speak, and this fighting soldier seemed to take a regular fancy to Old Dummy.

"Come on," he roars out at him; "come on, you'll do!" and prances in front of him, wagging his fists. Old Dummy never said a thing—well, he couldn't, you see. But this soldier didn't know that and kept prancing at him till some woman at the back shrieks out:

"Don't you hit him! He's dumb, he is. Let him alone, you dirty coward!"

When the soldier heard that he stopped still and looked all over the crowd. Everybody shivered in their shoes, you could 'a' heard a pin drop.

"What did I hear? Me? Who said that? Who said it?" And he didn't half swear. He chucked his cane to his pal and marched right into the crowd and banged poor Dummy's hat hard down on his ears.

"Will ye fight?" he says, and poked his ugly face out to Dummy and tells him: "Come on, hit me, hit me here."

Old Dummy could only make a funny noise with his mouth— "Mum . . . um . . . um . . . um . . . um"—and he put up his hands to save his hat. That only made the soldier madder still. He rushed at Dummy and fetched him a terrible slosh across the jaw with his right and followed it up with another biff in the neck with his left. Talk about wallop, I never seen anything like it—and really, there's something grand about this scientific art of boxing. Poor old Dummy went down like a sow, full stretch on his side with his nose in the gutter. The blood was coming out of his face. He didn't move and he didn't say a word—well, of course, he couldn't. And that did seem to stir up one or two of these people. They began shouting at the soldiers and some picked Dummy up and carried him across into a pub called the Corporation Arms—I could see its gold letters shining sideways because of the gas lamp farther up. When the two soldiers saw the damage they done and the crowd getting so threatening, they went to clear off. The champion got his cane from his pal and marched away like a lord, but his pal stopped to argue with some of the people, and while he was arguing who should come out of the Corporation Arms but Arthur Lark! He was a tough nut, was Arthur Lark, a carriage-cleaner up at the railway; only just left off work, because he still had his uniform on, green corduroys, and was having a drink when they took Dummy in the pub where Arthur was. He come walking up to the crowd very quiet and says: "Is this him?"

They says: "That's one of 'em," they says, and without any more ado Arthur knocked the soldier's pal senseless with one punch. Oh gosh!

"Where's the other?" says Arthur.

Of course he'd gone off, but we all pelted after him, this champion one, and except for a couple of women no one took any notice of that blooming soldier lying in the road like a dead 'un. We soon saw the champion of Belfast staggering along and wagging his cane about, but just then a bobby pops round a corner, sees our crowd, and steps in the road and stops us. A big chap, fifteen stone I bet he was, and I could tell you his number only that wouldn't do! Stops us: "What's all this? What's going on here?"

Arthur Lark never budged an inch. He up and told the bobby what was on and what had happened, what the soldier had done to Dummy. The bobby said: "I'll run the bleeder in."

"That's no good, no," says Arthur, "what's the use a doing that! Soon as you got him the picket 'ull come and fetch him away! You let me have a word or two with him now, just five minutes. Shan't want any more. You turn your eyes another way, you go on up the street for a walk, it's a nice evening, ain't it?"

I can see old Arthur now, a fine bloke with a funny bent face. After a bit more palaver the bobby did a grin. "All right, go on," he says, "but hurry up, and don't forget—I ain't *seen* you, I ain't seen *anything!*"

We went off with a whoop again, and the bobby shouted: "Not so much noise there, please!"

Coughdrop, he was.

When that soldier heard us all coming after him he turned and gave one look and then bolted for his life. We youngsters headed him off a side turning. Arthur got up with him at the bottom of the street, where there's a row of houses with gardens and iron railings facing you. The soldier didn't know whether to run to the right or the left, and Arthur caught him wallop in the gutter. I never saw such a blow in my life, right in the guts, and lifted him fair across the pavement bang into the iron railings. And so help me God, the railings cracked and broke, fair crumbled up, and when the soldier fell the bits fell all over him. He lay down there quiet as a lamb. We gathered round and picked up the bits of iron railing.

"Get up!" says Arthur.

But the soldier wouldn't get up, he said he couldn't, he said it was a foul blow: "It's damn near killed me!"

"Foul!" Arthur says, and he shoved his fist right in front of this soldier's nose: "D'ye see that! Was it a foul blow? Was it?"

"You let me alone," the soldier said, "or you'll be sorry for it." And you could see he was real bad.

"You got that for striking a harmless dumb man what couldn't help hisself," said Arthur.

"How did I know he was dumb?" the soldier said.

"How did you *know!* Couldn't you *see* it? And deaf, too!"

"How did I know he was deaf?" the swaddy said. He was sweating like a stoker and his face was the colour of suet. Anyone could see he was real bad. So Arthur said: "Here, some of you chaps, just fold him up and put him in a tram for the barracks. With my compliments, say." And off goes Arthur as calm as a cucumber! He left us to it. That's what I liked so much about Arthur; so quiet with his old bent face, and no fuss; he just put this soldier out of mess and left us to it. Presently we saw the policeman coming towards us again.

"Come on, soldier," we says, "here's a rozzer coming, you better get up now."

He managed to sit up all right after a bit, and then he says: "Go away or I'll blind the lot of ye to hell!" So we mooched off and left him, because of this rozzer. But I think he was all right— anyways I never heard no more about him nor any of 'em. I suppose he must have been all right, because you don't half cop it for killing a soldier. He was supposed to be the true champion of Belfast, but he didn't like the way Arthur cooked his eggs for him. My God! But there's no doubt about it, boxing is the most patriotic thing after all. To my mind it's absolutely noble. I mean what's the good of these here bugles, blowing your insides out? Give me a pair of dukes like Arthur Lark.

Well, after all my blooming trouble this musical business didn't come to anything again, so I give up the idea altogether. Somebody showed me a pipe called a oboe, but it cost a fearful lot. Besides, I couldn't make any sound come out of it. I dunno why everything you wants to go in for costs so much. I can't make it out and I can't stand it neither, so I give up these musical ideas and bought a rabbit off a fellow as said he was going to learn me all the doings of the noble art of self-defence.

Ninepenny Flute (1937)

A LITTLE BOY LOST

"The boy ought to have a cricket bat, Tom," said Eva Grieve to her husband one summer evening. He was a farm labourer, very industrious, very poor, and both were so proud of their only child that they sometimes quarrelled about him. They all lived together in a tiny field that was shaped like a harp and full of sweet grass. There was an ash tree in it, a water splash, a garden with green things, and currant bushes in corners; and of course their little cottage.

"He can't play cricket," Tom Grieve replied.

"Not without a bat, he can't; he ought to have a bat, like other boys."

"Well, I can't buy him no cricket bats and so he can't have it," said Tom.

"Why, you mean wretch—" began Eva with maternal belligerence.

"For one thing," continued her mate, "he ain't old enough—only five; and for another thing, I can't afford no cricket bat."

"If you had the true spirit of a father"—very scornful Eva was—"you'd make him one, yourself."

So Tom chopped a cricket bat out of a slice of willow bough and presented it to his son. The child hardly looked at it.

"Course not," snapped Eva to her sarcastic husband, "he wants a ball, too, don't he?"

"You'll be wanting some flannel duds for him next."

"I'll make him a ball," cried Eva.

Eva went into the fields and collected wisps of sheep's wool off the briars for her firstborn and bound them firmly into a ball with pieces of twine. But the child hardly looked at that either. His mother tossed the ball to him, but he let it fall. She pelted him playfully with it, and it made his nose bleed.

"He's got no one to play with," explained Eva, so she cut three sticks for a wicket, and in the evenings she and Tom would take the child out into the harp-shaped field. But the tiny Grieve did not care for cricket; it was not timid, it simply did not care. So Eva and Tom would play while David stood watching them with grave eyes; and at last Tom became very proficient indeed, and so enamoured of the game of cricket that he went and joined the village club and no longer played with Eva; and the child wouldn't, so she was unhappy.

"He likes looking at things, but he doesn't want to *do* anything himself. What he ought to have is a telescope," said Eva. But how to get a telescope? She did not know. The village store had stocks of hobnailed boots and shovels and peppermint drops, but optical instruments were not in demand, and Eva might for ever have indulged in dreams—as she constantly did—of telescopes that brought the interior of heaven itself close up to you as clear as Crystal Palace. But one day she went to a farm auction, and there had the luck to meet a great strapper of a gypsy man, with a husky voice, a long ragged coat, and a depressed bowler hat, who had bought a bucketful of crockery and coathooks and odds and ends, including a little telescope.

"Here," Eva approached the gaunt man, "is that telescope a good one?"

"Good!" he growled. "Course it's a good 'un, and when I say it's a good 'un I mean the gentleman's gone to Canada, ain't he? And he don't want it. Ho, ho!" he yelled, extending the instrument and tilting it against his solemn eye. "Ho, ho! I give you my oath it's good. I can see right clean into the insides of that cow over there!" Forty people turned to observe that animal, even the auctioneer and his clerk and his myrmidons. "I can see his liver, I can. Ho, what a liver he has got—I never see such a liver in my life! Here"—he dropped the glass into Eva's hand—"two shillings."

Eva turned it over and over. It looked perfect. "Have a squint at me!"

Eva was too dashed in public to do any such thing.

"How much do you want?"

"Look here, ma'am, no talk for talk's sake. Two bob."

Eva quickly gave him back the telescope.

"Eighteenpence, then," wailed he.

She turned away.

"Come here, a shilling."

Eva took the telescope and gave the gypsy a shilling. Home she went, and David received the telescope on his birthday. It occupied him for an hour, but he did not seem able to focus it properly, and so he only cared to look through it from the wrong end. He would sit on one side of the table and stare through the cylinder at his mother on the other side. She seemed miles away, and that appeared to amuse him. But Eva was always taking peeps with it and carried it with her wherever she went. She would look at the trees or the neighbouring hill and discover that those grey bushes were really whitebeam; or tell you what old woman had been tiggling after firewood in the hanging copse and was bringing a burden home; or who that man was riding on the slow horse through the shocks of barley. Once when she surveyed the moon she saw a big hole in the planet that no one had ever mentioned to her before; and there wasn't a man in the moon at all. But David could not contrive to see any of these wonders, and after a while the telescope was laid by.

A singularly disinterested child was David; not exactly morose, and certainly never peevish, but how quiet he was! Quiet as an old cat. "He'll twine away!" sighed his mother. Gay patient Eva would take him into the spring woods to gather flowers, but he never picked a bloom and only waited silently for her.

"Look at this, I declare!" cried she, kneeling down in a timber lane before a strange plant. When its green shoots had first peered into light they pushed themselves up through a hole in a dead leaf that had lain upon them. They had grown up now to four or five inches, but they still carried the dead constricting leaf as if it were a collar that bound them together; it made them bulge underneath it, like a lettuce tied with bast, only it was much smaller.

Eva pulled at the dead leaf; it split, and behold! the five released spears shot apart and stretched themselves flat on the ground.

"They're so pleased now," cried she. "It's a bluebell plant."

And Eva, singular woman, delighted in slugs! At a threat of rain the grass path in the harplike field would be strewn with them, great fat creatures, ivory or black, with such delicate horns. Eva liked the black ones most.

"See!" she would say to her son. "It's got a hole in its neck, that little white hole, you can see right into it. There!" And she would take a stalk of grass and tickle the slug. At once the hole would disappear and the horns collapse. "That's where it breathes." She would trot about tickling slugs to make them shut those curious valves. David was neither disgusted nor bored; he just did not care for such things, neither flowers, nor herbs, nor fine weather, nor the bloom of trees.

One day they met a sharp little man with grey eyebrows that reminded you of a goat's horns. There was a white tie to his collar, shiny brown gaiters to his legs, and an umbrella slanted through his arm as if it were a gun.

"How is your cherry tree doing this year, Mr. Barnaby?"

Mr. Barnaby wagged his head and gazed critically down at Eva's son.

"There was a mazing lot of bloom, Eva; it hung on the tree like—like fury, till it come a cold wind and a sniggling frost. That coopered it. A nightingale used to sing there; my word it could sing, it didn't half used to chop it off!" Then he addressed the lad. "Ever you see a nightingale part its hair?"

David gazed stolidly at Mr. Barnaby.

"Say no," commanded Eva, shaking him.

The boy only shook his head.

"No, you wouldn't," concluded the man.

"There's no life in him. I'm feared he'll twine away," said Eva.

For David's ninth birthday she procured him a box of paints and a book with outlines of pigs and wheelbarrows and such things, to be coloured. David fiddled about with them for a while and then put them aside. It was Eva who filled up the book with magnificent wheelbarrows and cherubic pigs. She coloured a black-and-white engraving of *The Miraculous Draught of*

Fishes, every fish of a different hue, in a monstrous gamboge ocean; a coloured portrait of David himself was accomplished, which made her husband weep with laughter; and a text, extravagantly illuminated, *I am the Way, the Truth, and the Life,* which was hung above David's bed. To what ambitious lengths this art might have carried her it is impossible to say, the intervention of another birthday effecting a complete diversion. This time the lad was given a small melodeon by his fond parents, but its harmonic complications embarrassed him, baffled him; even the interpretations of *All hail the power* or *My Highland Laddie* which Eva wrung from its desperate bosom were enough to unhinge the mind of a dog, let alone poor David.

David seemed to be a good scholar, he was obedient and clean, and by the time he was due to leave school at the age of fourteen he had won the right to a free apprenticeship with an engineer who specialized in steam-rollers. How proud Eva was! Tom too, how proud!

Yet he had not been at work three months when he was stricken with a spinal infirmity that obliged him to take to his bed. There he remained a long time. The doctor prescribed rest, and David rested and rested and rested, but he did not get better. At the end of a year he was still as helpless. There was no painful manifestation of disease, but it seemed as if his will were paralysed, as if he had surrendered a claim on life which he did not care to press. Two years, three years rolled on, and four years went by. The long thin youth, prematurely nipped, and helpless, was a burden like the young cuckoo that usurps a dunnock's nest. But even the cuckoo flits, and David Grieve did not. For seven years thus he lay. There were ill-speaking folk who hinted that he was less ill than lazy, that his parents were too easy with him, that he wanted not rest but a stick. At times Tom, who had begun to feel the heavy burden of years, seemed to agree, for there was nothing the brooding invalid was interested in save brandy in lieu of medicine, and a long row of bottles in Eva's kitchen testified that the treatment had been generous. It had, to the point of sacrifice. Decent steady-going people the Grieves had been, with the most innocent vices—for vice comes to all—but at last Tom had to sink the remnant of his savings in a specialist doctor from London. To the joy of the devoted parents the doctor declared that a certain operation might effect a cure.

So David was bundled off to the county hospital and operated upon. For a while Eva breathed with gaiety, an incubus was gone; it was almost as if she herself had been successfully operated upon. But soon, like a plant that flourishes best in shade, she began to miss not only David but the fixed order his poor life had imposed on her. His twenty-second birthday occurred as he was beginning to recover, and so they sent him a brand-new suit of clothes, the first he had had since boyhood.

Dear Son, [Eva wrote to him]
We are pleased to hear of you getting so well thank God we are very pleased and miss you a lot but cant expect no other you being our only little pipit. Your father has bought you a suit for you to ware when you get up and you can walk a drak serge like himself. what a tof. And will send them by the parcel post off next week. Look careful in the pockets.
And God bless love from
TOM *and* EVA

He looked careful in the pockets—and found a halfcrown.

It was on an April day that he returned to his parents, very much enfeebled, neither man nor child. Seven years of youth he had forgone, his large bones seemed too cumbersome for him, and adult thoughts still hung beyond his undeveloped flight. But even to him the absence had taught something: his mother had lost her sprightly bloom, his father was setting towards the sere. Both of them kissed him with joy, and Eva hung upon his neck in an ecstasy of tears that made him gasp and stagger to a chair.

Restoration to vigour was still far off. Sometimes a villager would come in of an evening and chat with him, or invite him to a party or a "do" of some sort, but David did not go; he was frail, and as it were immobile. He was on his feet again, but hardly more than enough to convey him about the harplike field. Restless and irritable he grew; his life was empty, quite empty, totally irremediably empty. The weather, too, also unmanned him; summer though it was, the storms of rain were unending and he would sit and sigh.

"What is that you're saying?" asks Eva.

"Rain again!"

"Oh lord," says his mother, "so it is. Well!"

The grass was lush in the field, the corn grew green and high, but the bloom of the flowering trees was scattered and squandered. Whole locks of laburnum would lie in the lane, the blossomy cream of the quicken trees was consumed, and the chestnut flowers were no more than rusty cages.

But on one brighter eve he suddenly took a stick and hobbled off for to take a walk. The wrath of the morning had gone like the anger of a good woman. The sky was not wholly clear, but what was seen was radiant, and the shadows were august. Trees hummed in the bright glow, bees scoured the blooms without sound, and a tiny bird uttered its one appealing note—Please! For half an hour he strolled along a road amid woods and hills; then the sky overdarkened quickly again, and he waited under a thick tree to watch a storm pass over. Clouds seemed to embrace the hills, and the woods reeled in a desperate envy. Rain fell across the meads in drooping curtains, and died to nothing. Then, in a vast surprise, heaven's blue waves rocked upon a reef all gold, and with a rainbow's coming the hills shone, so silent, while the trees shone and sung.

There was no song in the heart of the desolate man; his life was empty, and even its emptiness had a weight, a huge pressure; it was a fearful burden—the burden of nothingness. Grieve turned back, and when he came to an inn he entered and drank some brandy. Others there who knew him offered him ale, and he sat with them until his sorrow fell away. But when he got up to go, the world too seemed to fall away, his legs could not support him, nor his mind guide him. Two companions took him and with his arms around their necks conveyed him home.

"He's drunk, then?" uttered Tom harshly.

"No, it's the weakness," cried Eva.

"That's it," corrected one of the men. "That beer at the Drover ain't worth gut room. If you has five or six pints you be giddy as a goose."

For a week David could not rise from his bed, but as soon as he was up he went out again, and as often as he went out, he was carried home, tipsy. Tom took his money away from him, but that did not cure him.

"He's mad," said the father, and at last Tom took the suit of clothes, too, rolled them into a bundle, and went and sold them to a neighbour.

So David Grieve lies on his bed, and his mother cherishes him. Sometimes he talks to her of his childhood and of school-treats he remembers on days that smelt—so he says—like coconut. Eva has ransacked her cupboards and found a melodeon and a box of paints and a telescope. The sick man watches for her to come and feed him, and then he sleeps; or, propped against a pillow, he hugs the melodeon to his breast and puffs mad airs. Or he takes the telescope and through the reverse end stares at a world that is not so far away as it looks. Eva has taught him to paint inscriptions, but he repeats himself and never does any other than *Lead Kindly Light,* because it is easy to do, and the letters are mostly straight ones.

Fishmonger's Fiddle (1925)

THE LITTLE MISTRESS

SMALL as it was, and amply shaded by maple trees, the little villa was hidden in a garden wholly enclosed by a high wall of brick. There was a bright green door with a latch in one corner of the wall, its lintel and sill painted white; near the top of the door was a white word *Sackville,* and in the middle of the door was a brass plate.

Curious travellers on the tops of passing omnibuses could just glance into the two lower rooms of the house; they had no time

to observe much, but they could see in the first room a fireplace framed with marble in the back wall, with a tall mirror
upon the mantel and a gilt clock under a glass dome. In the
second room they could see the same features meticulously repeated, nothing but fireplace, white mantel, large mirror, gilt
clock. Once inside the garden you felt that the modest little
house took on, or seemed to take on, a watching self-conscious
air, an impression not at all lessened by the dark door which confronted you with a large knocker of very conscious brass, three
separate bell pulls—one marked NIGHT, one marked DAY, the
third not marked at all but possibly for use in times of an eclipse
—a brass-mouthed letter-box, a brass speaking-tube, and a new
glistening name plate of much brass inscribed *HUGH HARPER
Physician*. Visiting consultants would be ushered into the right-
hand room—all marbled and gilt-clocked and mirrored—by a
more or less spruce maid-servant, and chronic patients, not too far
lapsed from the arts of observation, might have remarked a
changing succession of these domestics. The Harpers never had
more than one; they came, they served, they departed; they did
not *continue* to serve at Sackville. After a month or two of the
discomposure induced by each of them the young doctor would
say to his wife in a soft meditative voice: "Francesca, I shall discharge her."

In contrast to his wife Harper was of quite distinctive avoirdu-
pois, almost a colossus, with crisp hair, brown moustache growing
tightly on a round fresh face, and a lot of pleasant teeth. He always dressed in grey, and a watch-guard of gold and black silk
always stretched from pocket to pocket of his vest in a broad
grin. His hands lived in the pockets of his trousers like rabbits in
a burrow; he was never seen to stretch himself. Harper and his
wife Francesca might be defined typographically, the one a
capital O and the other as asterisk: there was always an implied
footnote about Francesca, who was small and dusky and lovely.

"Yes, I shall discharge her now."

Harper always discharged the servant, quietly, after a few
weeks. He had no liking for such an office, it was disagreeable to
him, but somehow or other, sooner or later, like a domestic Henry
VIII he discharged everybody—even his friends—and he always ·

had a reason for that course. Maggie Taproe committed unmentionable indiscretions, Eva Lodden developed incurable boils, Lena Hughes would spill oil into the bath and neglect that business of the cat: they were discharged without a gramme of compunction or gratitude; service was service, and if you paid for it it should be worth paying for. Each departing menial was a vicious unspeakable hog, while her successor—for how brief a date!—was a peerless angel. But the doctor's antipathies, though vast, were superficial; his sympathy and kindness in their narrower range were deep and prodigious.

In the fullness of time and dissatisfaction he prepared to discharge Fanny Hackbut, who had been engaged by him without a recommendation of any sort, human, devilish, or divine. It appeared that her last mistress had indulged in a most scandalous affiair with a fascinating gentleman, a Perugian from South America. Miss Hackbut's moral pride had revolted and demanded recognition; she had prudently left. That was good enough for Harper, who admired (amongst a heap of other things) conscience and character; he engaged her: "She's a howling prude, but I think she'll do."

And she didn't do at all. He met her more than once descending the stairs. There was nothing more unendurable to him than the sight of a woman wearing a man's boots—and they were his own boots!

"I shall discharge her," he told Francesca.

"What has she done?" asked his gentle wife, who was as delightful as an antelope.

"Oh, curse the girl, she's a great female elephant!"

Fanny Hackbut had features—God made them, it is true, but you could not think of that, said Francesca—which were too improbable for description; and she had a mind like a devitalized fowl—God inscrutably made that, too. In times gone by she had been engaged (providentially engaged, Francesca couldn't help thinking) to the thin youth with the physique of a hairdresser, who came round upon a bicycle carrying a large tin that had once (according to Francesca) contained pounds and pounds of jam and was now used to convey pints and pints of milk. That was all over. So few virtues and so few vices had she that the whole lot might have been collected like half a dozen buttons, black and white ones, left unnoticed on the corner of a large dark table; there might once have been more of them but they had dropped off. The rest of the large dark table was the rest of Fanny.

Meals were late, or if not late, were badly served, or if not badly served, were poorly conceived. Everything was left to Fanny, for Francesca—the doctor confided it to himself—though dainty and adorable was so capricious; she was all brains and apprehension, but she hadn't any sense; they might talk of a thing for a week, and she would forget it in five minutes. Piles of unclean dishes languished in the kitchen sink from morn to eve. Those brooms on the dark places of the stairs, those pails in the passage corners —they were man-traps, deliberate traps, diabolical! Fanny's one grace was a devotion to her little mistress, who, unlike the huge master, had the tiniest of shoes, of hats, of gloves, indeed, of every-thing. Those personal belongings delighted Fanny in the way that a doll's things delight a child. Francesca's room was always a pattern of brightness and discretion, the buckles on her shoes most perspiringly shone, hose and linen had the perfect sequence and spontaneity of a packet of new envelopes; brushes and combs never lost their pristine order; while the silver trinkets of the dressing-table, sconces and caskets and phials, beamed as in the days when they adorned some jeweller's window. But as for the young doctor, it appeared that not a thing was ever in place, or rightly done, or punctually performed. A clean shirt was as rare as a gift from the King! Socks! He had no socks, once there had been millions! She was a squab, a sprout!

Like the servant, he, too, adored the little mistress and could deny her nothing, not even the lover whose blue-grey letters, strangely inscribed, so often appeared in the letter-box. Even Fanny had noticed their impressive caligraphy, a battalion of half-dressed letters flung boldly across the solitude of the en-velope and left at astonished attention.

After the usual couple of months Fanny had become insup-portable to Harper. On a warm September eve he and Francesca had concluded a disillusioning dinner. Windows and doors were open, the thrush in the garden was trying to recapture its old gamut, lamps were yet unlit, though it was growing a little dim.

"I shall give her notice now, I think," he mumbled. At the door that led to the kitchen he stood for a moment—listening.

"She's singing, Frances, singing to herself, the fool!"

Playfully Francesca grimaced at him.

"Can't sack a person who is singing," he growled.

"But why not?"

"Well, I dunno, you can't somehow." He lumbered about the room and grinned apologetically at Francesca. He shook his fist at the door.

"Minx, elephant! Stop it, will you!" he chuckled. "Dash it, she'll stop soon." He grew very serious. "I'll tell her then, presently. If not—tomorrow. Go she must, the Kaffir!"

He sat down and began to play a game of dominoes with his wife.

"Now she's not singing," remarked Francesca presently.

"No, she's stopped, hasn't she?" Harper gazed at his wife. "Yes, she's stopped, but let's finish this game and then I'll sack her. Presently will do, or tomorrow. You know, she's *so* ugly; I didn't notice that at first, did you?"

"Oh, yes," replied Francesca.

"You did! You didn't tell me! I thought she was going to be so good. She was good at first, damn her, wasn't she?"

"Oh, I think she does rather well; she dotes on doing things for me," Francesca said. "My room is immaculate, I'm almost pained to touch anything, and when I tell her to get my bath ready she's enchanted; I have to shove her out of the room while I undress, for I can't take off so much as a shoe while she's there, she gloats so."

"Yes, she would," cried Hugh, "just gloat and gloat. That's good of her though, I'll give her one more chance. You talk to her, look after her, and be firm with her, Frances, will you?"

"Yes, Hugh." Francesca's eyes dropped under their lids. "But do you know what I've heard?—she's got a baby."

"Baby! A baby!" The doctor was incredulous. "How?"

"She keeps it at Tappingham and goes over to see it whenever she can."

"At Tappingham! Does she know?"

"Know?" Frances was puzzled.

"I mean does she know that *you* know?"

"She thinks we don't know."

"What a devil! How *did* you come to know?"

"The grocer's wife told me. Oh, such a fool I am! That grocer muddled me up about the candles I ordered; the beast has sent packets and packets, there are four hundred and thirty-two candles in the kitchen and Fanny can't find anywhere to put them. What can we do with them all, Hugh?"

"Burn 'em," said the doctor. "How old is this kid?"

"Only a few months. I like her much better now, don't you? I'm rather pleased, aren't you? She's not our fool of a Fanny now. It's such an enlightening surprise, Hugh; I'm rather pleased."

"Pleased! And all that pious reason of hers for leaving her last situation was just bunkum. What a libellous cat! She was thrown out because of this."

"Oh, Hugh, do you think so? How shameful! I'd rather liked what she told me about that mistress. Hugh, our Fanny was too good for such people!"

"I shall discharge her now certainly."

"No, Hugh, not now! What difference does it make?"

"On the spot!" he cried, rising and approaching the door leading to the kitchen. "She's a liar, a baggage, an immoral fool!" But he paused doubtfully. "Shall I? Shall I sack her? Now?"

After a moment or two he turned back with a tortured grin. "She's singing again!" he meditated. "Well, at any rate I can tell her to stop that, and if she don't stop it I'll sack her on the spot. And if she does stop it—well, I can sack her presently. Do you know, I *like* the word 'sack.'" He went and sat down by Francesca. "It's such a satisfactory word, it's like a funnel; you pour your feeling into it—sack—and it swirls and swishes down through the pipe—sack—such a beautiful jolt."

"Hm! Sack, sack, sack, sack—yes," said Francesca, "but I think the loveliest word of all is 'cotton.'"

"Cotton!" he cried.

"No, say it cot'n: the 'cot' hard, mute the next 't,' and then gulp the 'n.'"

"Cot'n, cot'n, cot'n, cot'n. Oh my, yes, isn't it delicious!" cried the doctor. "Cot'n, cot'n, cot'n!"

II

For a few days longer some baffling protector seemed to ward from Fanny the menace of dismissal—Harper's tremors, his absences, or the servant's temporary disappearance. It was a task the young doctor would not delegate to his wife, for whom he strove to maintain an atmosphere of congruity and peace, with no disturbing elements crossing her apprehension of what life meant to her. Whether that was much or little mattered not at all so long as the mild air of its enchantments engrossed and sustained her. Francesca was moulded less by her acts than by her intentions; her will was so much less strong than her desires that life was coloured more by the intensity of her moods than by its misuse of her aims.

But even Francesca, indifferent, forbearing, pounced with anger one morning, just as she had pounced, like a cat, into her own room, for there she beheld the execrable Fanny perusing with eminent delight a bundle of those blue-grey letters which usually reposed in a locked drawer. So engrossed was the culprit that she did not hear her mistress until, venting a sigh of appreciation, she suddenly realized that she was observed. Guilty Fanny dropped the letters to the table and turned briskly to her broom and brushes. Francesca closed the door behind her and said very disgustedly: "Yes, Fanny?" The servant with pained innocence murmured: "What, ma'am?"

Francesca directed at her a gaze that mutely fulminated. "I suspected this. You read my private letters! You *do* read them," insisted the trembling Francesca. "You've read them all, I know you."

There was no answer; there were just the broom, the brushes, and Fanny, and as Francesca scuffled the letters back into their drawer and turned the key Fanny went towards the door.

"Where are you going?" hissed Francesca.

"Downstairs, ma'am," the lost sheep whispered.

"You abominable thing! What have you to say?"

"Oh, for sure, I'd never say anything, ma'am," said the astonishing culprit, "never anything to anybody I shouldn't say, not to anyone, ma'am."

"What do you mean—what is there to say? You wicked eaves-dropping girl! It's the wickedest thing in the world to do, the most wicked."

"I didn't mean to, ma'am. . . ."

"Of course not, of course you didn't—they bit you, I suppose."

"I saw them lying about."

"Where? Where did you see them?"

"Just there, on the table."

"When?" Francesca had to repeat it. "When were they lying on the table?"

"When I came here, the first week."

"So you read them before, all of them! I guessed that! How horrible and vulgar! When did you read them since?"

"Every day, ma'am, I think."

"But it's impossible, I lock them up."

"You leave the key in the drawer, ma'am. (You have now, ma'am.) But I didn't do it sneakily."

"No?"

"I didn't, ma'am; you leave 'em lying about. And you see he calls you by the name of Dear Fan, and that's my name—it's the same as me."

"Absurd devil!" commented Francesca. "You've read them all?"

"That's no harm, ma'am. I shan't make any trouble, ma'am," wailed unhappy Fanny. "I like you too much, I do, and him too."

The women gazed at each other curiously for a few moments until Fanny was moved to say: "It's rather—it's so—" The ghost of a smile seemed to chase the ghost of a word from the girl's lips.

"So what?" snapped the little mistress.

Fanny let it surprisingly fall at last. "Funny!" she said, and the indignant flush on Francesca's cheeks deepened as the domestic continued. "His name is just like my friend's who I used to walk out with; he used to write to me, just like that. It was rude of me to read your letters, ma'am, and me so fond of you, but my name's Fan too, and it didn't seem rude, not with the same names. I'm stupid, ma'am, I don't know everything sometimes, ma'am."

Fanny's eyes glimmered ruefully in her yellow face, and her small nose exhibited a perfect stupidity of pink that almost disarmed Francesca.

"Oh, I don't mind your having read them, though of course I don't like it, really; it's loutish. But it's the beastly furtiveness you've imported into my private affairs that I resent. If my private affairs aren't safe from this— Oh, you cursed devil, you've spoiled everything now, you've made everything ridiculous, you beastly clammy Hackbut! I suppose"—she gleamed ironically at the stricken servant—"you spied on your last mistress just the same? And then you left her, didn't you, proper Hackbut? I shall never call you Fanny again, never; never anything but Hackbut until you go, for of course you would not dream of stopping here now, would you?"

"I don't want to leave you, ma'am."

"Oh," raged Francesca, "I must tell Dr. Harper at once." And she ran angrily out of the room.

Fanny returned to the kitchen, full of musing tremors, but with just one gleam of confidence: her mistress couldn't tell the doctor —she would not dare! Why, the letters . . . Oh, but they were so—so—they were like what you read about, like the Bible, they were like plays. If she only had a lover like that she'd go with him and do things and things, all sorts of things. She would do whatever she liked, and he would do what he wanted, and they'd go all over the world together—the Isle of Wight and Tappingham Woods, Tappingham, Tap . . ." Hackbut drooped forlornly upon the kitchen table and broke into tears. There her mistress found her again.

"Why, what's the matter? Don't be such a fool, Fanny! I'm going out to tea this afternoon and I want you to—"

"It's my afternoon off." Fanny interjected with sullen promptitude, through her tears.

"Oh!" exclaimed Francesca, sullenly too. "Dear me, yes."

"I've got an appointment," explained Fanny.

"I see. All right, then," agreed her mistress.

Having prepared lunch, Fanny hurried from the house, dressed in her brown jacket and the flaunting hat with green bow as large as a lamp shade. Francesca hated it, she always wore small hats herself, like the socket of an acorn.

After lunch the little mistress cycled away to a country friend, five miles off. You couldn't help staring at Francesca, always, and now she was dressed in white she was more beguiling than ever—all white from head to foot except the gold ring on her finger and the strip of crimson ribbon hanging from her hat. The hat was not quite white, perhaps; shaped like the moon in its first quarter, it curved round her dark fringed hair as if it loved her, and the points almost brushed her pink cheeks. You couldn't help staring at Francesca.

Stopping at the Tappingham café on the way for a cup of coffee, she sat at a table opposite a nun who was eating three sausages. Three! But Francesca did not stare at the nun; no, she only sipped her coffee and glanced out of the window at the passers-by, or looked at the other customers. There were two ladies with a youngish man who took snuff frequently. Disgusting! Presently the ladies retired to the lavatory and left the youngish man alone at the table. He did not look very merry; small squeezed eyes he had, thin mouse-coloured hair, and was painfully shaven. Francesca could see in the mirror behind him that a bald patch as large as a teacup had already established itself upon his oily skull. And what a squab nose! But it must have smelt money, Francesca thought, for he looked, indefinably, quite rich. He took the small box again from his pocket, tapped it, opened it, took a pinch between finger and thumb, shook the surplus to the floor (how filthy!) pressed the thumb into his right nostril, the forefinger into the left, replaced the box, and drew out his handkerchief. There followed a mild dextrous conclusion.

But oh, how happy little Francesca was! There was nothing in life so exciting as one's interest in one's self, and she had nothing to do but sit and see her own life glide sweetly by, like—like a yacht. Indeed, it was she herself that seemed to glide and glide, with infinite gentleness, like a little yawl sliding to its moorings in a green crystal bay, with a yard-long burgee of crimson galloon. She could rest apart, as it were, and behold herself living and acting as something beautifully strange. Some day, soon, she was to go on a cruise with a friend whose yacht was called the *Francesca*.

Well, she must get on, so on she goes. She pays for her coffee, and as she steps into the street a clergyman crosses the road towards her, dressed in his cassock, and hatless. In his arms he carries a pile of six or seven money-boxes for missionaries, and as he is about to enter the ironmonger's shop next door to the café one of the boxes tumbles from his arms and clutters along the pavement to Francesca's feet. Francesca picks it up for him. "Thank you," he intones solemnly, but as he replaces it another box falls. Francesca with a gleam of gaiety restores this too, the clerical gentleman says solemnly: "I am much obliged to you," and then dives into the doorway.

"Fop!" mutters Francesca, turning to her bicycle. But again she is interrupted, she almost bumps into two passing women, one old and one young. Francesca draws back sharply, for the young one, in black attire, carries in her arms before her a little white coffin. She does not wear the appearance of grief; indeed, she seems secretly to enjoy the surprise of the staring people. The older woman is weeping. With a little chilling shock Francesca recognizes the girl with the coffin; it is Fanny Hackbut, in a borrowed black hat and cloak. The two mourning women pass along the pavement for some distance and then cross the road into the churchyard at the end of the street. The clergyman comes out of the ironmonger's shop and hurries after them.

Francesca rode away to her friend, a little quenched in spirit.

"So miserable I am," she wailed to Goneril Stroove, "I passed a funeral, and I hate funerals."

Miss Stroove dwelt in a village that was but a higgledy-piggledy street with an inn at each end. One, the Crown, had lost the sign from its tall white pole; the other was the King's Head. Her tiny house was higgledy-piggledy too. It had a rather large bakery on one side, a rather small post office on the other, and behind was a blacksmith's yard—she could hear the anvil chiming all day long. Her front door, painted deep blue, had a disk of glass as large as a coal plate above the black knocker. The ground floor was a little below the level of the street, and visitors had accordingly to descend two stone steps and crank themselves through the doorway straight into a room where the ceiling was altogether too low for the lofty thoughts encouraged there. Its two front windows each had six bulbous panes that defeated inquisitive scrutineers and left even the dweller herself in a state of hapless speculation about passing identities. A clear window at the back revealed the yard of the smith.

Goneril was a plump, grey lady, spruce as a crested lark, with wavery eyes the colour of zinc. She dabbled a little in occultism and other sidereal quackery, but her ideas, good or bad, were never indifferent, were pungently expressed, and her pathetic belief in human brotherhood—as if the whole of mankind might be turned into a joint-stock soul company with herself as private secretary—infected her hearers with the charm of her sincerity. For some years now she had been compiling a history of history.

While Goneril went into her kitchen to prepare tea Francesca sat and listened to the ching of the anvil. The smith was shoeing a horse, and the smell of its burning hoofs came unpleasantly through the open window. Neither men nor horse could be seen, but gruff voices of the smith and a carter in charge of the horse carried on a conversation much broken by violent admonitions to the animal. Pit, pit, pit, went the hammer on the new shoe.

"Whuppah!" yelled the smith. It startled Francesca at first; she thought the horse must have bitten somebody, but it was not so. "Git over, Dragon. Doh-wee-yock boy," cried the very affable carter. Pit, pit, pit, went the hammer again.

"How much they give for this hoss, Archie?" puffed the smith.

"Sixty pounds," replied Archie. "He cost sixty golden (whoa!) sovrins, Ted."

"Too much, that," gurgled the smith. "Whoa, Dragon! Whoa, boy!"

"Bought him from a man as had the whooping cough or summat."

"Git up, there! roared the smith. To Francesca his voice sounded fearfully brutal.

Over some rather intense muffins and cups of China tea Goneril discoursed to Francesca for some time upon universal space, of the way to raise sunken ships, and lastly of dual personality.

"Yes, Goneril," said Francesca at length. "There is nothing in life so exciting to me as my own interest in myself. I suppose I am an egoist."

"I dare say—if one only knew them—the things other people think about you would be quite as exciting."

"Oh, but . . ." objected Francesca.

"Almost everything one person *thinks* of another," persisted Goneril, "is likely to be bad rather than good. We are all of us at once delicate and brutal, wise and wanton, courageous and procrastinating. But well then, our virtues are taken for granted, or what is pleasanter, they are generally known; but it is what is unknown in others that offers itself to our crooked furtive speculations. Fortunately these indecencies are seldom expressed. It's a sublime reticence."

"Aren't we foul!" ejaculated Francesca. "And yet I was thinking only as I came along that there is nothing in life so fascinating as one's own view of oneself. Do you ever stand apart, as it were, and observe yourself living and acting as some enchanting thing, beautifully strange?"

The zinc eyes wavered about the visitor's visible daintiness. "I never see myself in that way, no, but sometimes I do feel my being as a kind of labyrinth, with my spirit wandering in it lost and sighing, in search of something, I don't know what—I wish I did. Yes, take that piece of muffin, please. I'm not a romantic, you see; I can only probe into myself, make dissections of my tendencies, my impulses." Francesca had a fleeting vision of numberless rashers of bacon. "It is very hopeless, though disillusioning," continued Goneril. "The person I really am is the person I understand least of all. I never do see myself. No, Nimrod, no; you are a bad cat!"

Nimrod's stiff upstanding tabby tail reminded her, Miss Stroove said, of the Tower of Babel: she was debarred for ever from understanding even him. Whenever it ceased to prowl, the tabby imp continued to lift its paws in apparent trepidation, as though it could feel the fire which is said to lie in the heart of the earth. Silently for a few moments they watched him do this; then the voices from the smithy broke upon them again.

"He's a queer hoss, Ted," the carter was saying. "If he've bin in mud and his fetlocks be all mired up he'll stand to the brush and let a child groom him; but if you want to lay a finger on him when he was clean he'd kick a fly's eye out. Now then, Dragon! What be at? Git over!"

"Yes," Francesca resumed, "I suppose the average person is romantic?"

"The average person!" said Goneril with a whimsical frown. "What is that? There was once an Average Man, and his good and bad deeds were mingled in such equal proportions, so absolutely balanced, that no one could determine whether he had any goodness at all. In consequence, everybody believed him to be bad. When he was swayed by his bad desires they called him Sinner and Monster. When he had his good ones, they could not believe the evidence of their senses, it was too good to be true; they called him Hypocrite, Impostor, Liar. When he did things neither good nor bad, they said he was trivial—and wished him dead."

She was interrupted by renewed uproar from the smithy.

"What a hubbub!" cried Francesca, "it must annoy you dreadfully."

"No, no," cried Goneril, "I like it, I like it. I expect it's a difficult horse to shoe."

"Git over, Dragon!" shouted Archie, "you lolloping badger, you! I'll gie you a drench tomorrow." The silent women peered a little apprehensively at the back window.

"He's not up to much," the smith growled and puffed, "what you been feeding him on—unction?"

"Oh, they has to be fed, we know. Horses have to be fed, we knows that. He's too fat now, but not so—"

"Whoa up, there! Gee whoa, Dragon!" roared the smith, "gee whoa."

Pit, pit, pit, went the hammer again.

"He ain't—whoa, Dragon, good boy," said Archie, "he ain't so—"

"Yah, whuppah!" the smith again momentarily raged. The horse subsided, it was bearing its ordeal with fortitude, the hammer resumed its pit, pit, pit.

"What was that you was a-going to say, Archie?"

"To say, Ted?" the carter questioned, "to say? What *was* I a-going to say?"

"Ah, I can't tell you, Archie, but it were summat about this 'ere hoss, I believe."

"Oh, ah, I know!" Archie cried. "I was only going to say as how he ain't so fat as he was, not near."

The smith made no reply, the shoeing was finished. "So long, Ted."

"So long, Archie." A great horse, with a man on its back, clumped past Goneril's little window.

"I am romantic, you know," continued Francesca at last, "I am too romantic, such a fool I am!"

"No, no, don't say too romantic," protested Goneril; "all romantic souls have compassion. One of the most beautiful things in life is mankind's pity for its own sinfulness."

"Do you think so?" Francesca said. "It sounds rather maudlin to me. But it is you who are compassionate, Goneril. Nobody could be more compassionate than you. And you're not a *bit* romantic! Too, too compassionate you are, you never find fault with the world, the flesh, or the devil, or anything else—if there is anything else!"

"If there are faults to find, Francesca"— Goneril's gaze seemed to pierce her visitor's—"it is not my business to find them, and I don't want to find them. True, this is an entirely inexplicable existence: we may be living in a fool's paradise, but it *is* paradise. You see," she went on as Francesca did not speak, "romance is a bridge between mysticism and reality. To the mystic nothing is impossible save reality, which is vanity and vexation of spirit; while to the realist all things are possible, except mysticism. You are neither, dear little Francesca, you are like love itself, and love's only duty is to be delightful."

"Dear Goneril," protested the other, "you rush over me like a cataract, terrifying! And I don't understand your axioms one bit—I never do, though I like them enormously—they seem to me to be just sufficiently comprehensive to be either true or untrue. So puzzled I am! Surely love, now, should be faithful, that is its duty, surely?"

"Faithful to what?"

"To what it loves."

"It can only be faithful or unfaithful to itself, Francesca, to its own genius of delight. Yes, yes, and to that faith I know we all prove false: men are ungrateful and women are unwise. Blessed are the pure in heart, for they shall see God; but isn't that just too hard a price to pay—even for heaven!"

"Ah, yes," said Francesca, "we always know what we can do until we try!"

Goneril had brought their talk to an altitude at which (as happened with the Tower of Babel) neither knew what to do with it. It stood there, tempting time, until Francesca put on her yellow gloves and Goneril declared that it—the weather—was blowing up for rain.

So Francesca departed: she kissed her friend in the sunken doorway.

"Good-bye, Goneril, you will come in to tea soon?"

"Yes, I will. Have you got rid of your tiresome servant yet?"

"No," Francesca deliberated, with one leg over the cycle saddle, "we've not, no. She's begun to be satisfactory. We are keeping her on."

"Indeed!"

"Oh, she's quite a friend of the family now—she reads our letters! Good-bye!"

"Dear me! Good-bye, Francesca."

Francesca cycled away quite swiftly, for she was exhilarated. "What a curious day it keeps on being!" she breathlessly mused. Goneril always excited her. She felt like a tiny plant, recently parched, that had just been cheered by soft copious streams from a pot that had brass sprayer, very large and shiny, with very little holes in it.

"And it's not half over yet. Oh, all sorts of things I've got to tell Hugh."

She came to the railway crossing and abated her speed.

"I'm sure it is not going to rain, it is only splendidly dull. I think that railway station is quite beautiful, too. Railway stations can be, and they are. Oh, isn't it! It must be charming to live there."

It was a very, very small station—there were only two advertisements even; one that promised soft white hands and a good complexion (Francesca had both), the other a gall cure for horses. One bench, one window, one lamp, and one fox-terrier dog that dashed from the booking office six times a day to bark at a train coming almost silently from the tunnel in the green hills and then sliding through the lime works that sprawled in a white pit with six black cupolas and a high pink chimney.

"Goneril's talk is so stimulating. And yet that's strange, too, for it's no more like real life than a topic of conversation in a train. I don't know, I can't think she can have been in love many times; perhaps not more than once—everybody has loved once. In men it is an art, she says, and in women it is a gift. That's very true, only how can one keep on giving one's gift away? As one does?"

Back through Tappingham she rode with undiminished spirit. The ironmonger's shop was closing; the baths and shovels had been taken down so that she could now see the name above the window, *Kitchen, late Kettle*. The churchyard was very still. Francesca glanced over the wall as she sped by, but she could see nothing disquieting. She was glad. It would be nice when one died to have a very beautiful quotation on one's gravestone, something quite distinctive that no one else had ever thought of; she determined to make notes of suitable mottoes.

In the park under Tappingham Woods scores of deer were browsing under the trellising trees, and close to the metal palings there was a small but emphatic lake, its ambulant swan covering the beholder with the shrewd eye of a strumpet.

"Goneril doesn't help me in the least, really. She makes everything one hopes for seem impossible. And one always longs for the impossible—there's nothing else to wish for. Oh, but I love days like this, they are so exciting."

On reaching home Francesca ran first to peep in the kitchen. Nobody there, but it smelled of dinner—divinely. Stuffed hare, forced meat balls, fried whiting—lovely! How pathetic the fishes would look under their little sprigs of parsley. How delicious! How tantalizing! Oh, hunger was quite the most heavenly thing in the world. Nobody in the dining-room either, no letters by the afternoon post, the gilt clock had stopped at twenty-five minutes past six. It often stopped between six and seven—so stupid of it. Then, through an open doorway that led into the garden, she could see and hear her husband talking to Fanny, a very quenched Fanny, standing with a bowl of corn in her hands. Hugh had the appearance of a virtuous man about to convict a despicable scoundrel of some misdemeanour.

"Stupid," he said softly, but disagreeably, "you needn't do that, I've already fed them; besides, some of them are broody and mustn't be fed at all. You are a fool, you know nothing about chickens, do you, no, you know nothing about chickens!"

"Hugh, Hugh," cried Francesca from the doorway, "come in quickly, please, I want you."

"Hello, hello!" He came at once, and Francesca closed the door.

"You mustn't do it, Hugh, not now. You mustn't do it at all."

"Do what?"

"Mustn't discharge her, her baby is dead."

"Oh," he said blankly, "well they always do die, I'm rather glad."

"But, Hugh, you mustn't discharge her at all now, she only buried it today, this afternoon. I saw her carrying the coffin in her arms, in the street, Hugh!"

They sat down side by side and she told him all about it. Later on, after dinner, as they sat in the gathering dusk still harping upon Fanny, Francesca said: "She's been reading my letters."

Hugh made no comment.

"My private ones," Francesca proceeded. "I caught her at them, all of them!"

"Your private letters? From—him?"

Francesca nodded with a playful grimace.

"Well," said he slowly, "that's a reason the more for getting rid of her, isn't it, not that we want any more, when there are already nine hundred and ninety-nine, the slut."

"Reasons? Yes, but perhaps—we must let this blow over. You mustn't do it now, Hugh, at least, you mustn't do it yet, must you?"

"Oh, because of the letters! I see, I see, yes, I see. Damn her," he added softly, but after a few seconds he burst out petulantly: "I wish you'd give up this confounded flirtation. You've let yourself in for something now, if she goes tattling—as of course she will!"

"But you said I could."

"Could?" he snapped.

"Have a friend."

"Heavens! You say that as if I had said that you might have a cake."

"Well," Francesca said, a little hardly, and it seemed the only thing to say: "What about it?"

"About it! I did say so, yes, I did say it, yes, certainly; but if he writes you letters which horrify our scullion—"

"Oh, but they don't, Hugh; she revels in them, she's in love with them, her imbecility is quite touching."

"He's a philanderer," replied her husband severely, "a posturer, a scandal-maker, and a liar. Besides I don't approve of him. I liked him once, but I loathe him now. I warn you, he has a crooked bawdy mind and is not to be trusted or believed."

"Does all that matter, Hugh?"

"Doesn't it?"

"No, his only duty is to be delightful."

"And is he?"

She nodded again. "It's so odd, Hugh, I'm very fond of him." Her small white hands groped their way into the doctor's large fist. "I shall be seeing him again—soon."

"When?"

Francesca did not reply.

"Well," he said, releasing her, "he's not in love with me, nor I with him. I don't like him. His clothes always look too large for him, and his hats too small."

"Oh, Hugh, Hugh!" Francesca shuddered.

"I used to like him once, very much, but he hasn't a scrap of conscience, not a scrap. Everybody has some sort of conscience, but he has none; I couldn't exist without it. One forgets it, it's true, same as one forgets the collar stud at the back of one's neck —but it's *there!* When are you going to see him?"

He gleamed at her with all his pleasant teeth.

"Tomorrow, Hugh."

Again she groped her way into his unresponsive hands. He

could enjoy the perfume of her dark fine hair, carelessly combed, but never dishevelled. Ah, she was most lovely, most discerning, and yet still most fantastic.

They were silent for a very long time. He could hear the maple trees in their garden swishing and sighing. He thought Francesca had gone to sleep, she fell asleep so easily; he got up, groping his way towards the door, and put on a hat. Her voice at last broke drowsily into the darkness that had grown chill about them.

"Good night, Hugh," she said; and he said: "Good night" and went out to walk in the dark streets. The wind had roughened and he tramped in freshened airs as far as the borders of the town, where there were no public lights, only a few scattered villas with long hedged gardens and lines of trees. There seemed to be light as well as sound in the windy sky, but earth remained all one streaming blackness, and he stepped along timidly. His soul was full of doubt, mournful as the dark seething trees. The gates in the gardens rattled their loose latches, dim lights shone through most of the upper windows, each casting the shadow of a looking-glass upon its drawn blind—symbol of curiosity and care, vanity and love. What a world it would be without looking-glasses, wherein we see ourselves as others do *not* see us! The wind blows; upon its unknown course rolls this vast surprising world; how idle is sorrow, how vain is faith, how slight a thing is love! Nothing, nothing (his mind chattered) but a little fervid dust peering into a mirror that reflects only its own gazing face.

"It's beginning to rain," sighed Harper, "I must go back home," and he returned home to find an urgent summons from an old colleague desiring his assistance in a critical case some fifteen miles away.

On several nights he was away from home, it was the desperate case of an unimportant but wealthy woman, and for many days he scarcely saw Francesca at all except that always on his tired return she would meet him, beautifully sympathetic, and minister to him.

But she made no further confidences, his almost frenzied desire to be assured of her romantic infidelity was never satisfied. As to that the absurdest inhibition possessed him, he could not muster the will to ask her and discover. He knew Francesca too well to be too hopeful, she had a curious ruthlessness. Yet he was puzzled, and he kept the puzzle lying in his hands like some useless, intricate ingenuity that he could neither conquer nor discard. And there was some sort of solace in mere doubt—doubt and hope were just two sides of the same coin—it left him a margin on which he could still precariously, though so intolerably, live. How serious Francesca intended this affair to be he did not know, he could only guess. She had opportunity for anything, everything, but opportunity was nothing unless time, or chance, or the devil himself, transfigured it.

"Why, oh why," he groaned, "doesn't she go and see him? Or does she? She ought to go, it's the thing to do. She is fond of him. I wish it were not true. What a thing love is! Well, well, but if it's got to be borne! Oh, I wish it were not true!"

If he could only be certain of something, good or bad! He would feel better, even if it were bad; he would indeed welcome the ignominy of that relief. But he dared not for the peace of his soul ask the simple question of Francesca. Let sleeping dogs lie—he remembered the adage, only he wanted to be sure that they *were* sleeping and not shamming for some infernal purpose. Francesca was quite blameless; he envisioned her always, always, as a tender flower; but she had to grow in the way God made her. "All brains and apprehension—but she hasn't any sense," he confided to himself, and in that state of mind he moodily waited, and only frigidly fingered the distractions of duty, of scene, of appetite.

One afternoon, three weeks having gone by, he came home and found her kneeling in front of the fire with a pile of blue-grey letters in her lap.

"Hello." He squatted down beside her. "What's all this?"

"Junk!" said Francesca. "Do you see, Hugh?" She smiled at him and continued idly throwing the letters by twos and threes into the flames. "Junk!" Francesca repeated, "throw some on, Hugh, quickly."

He began to throw letters upon the fire.

"Do you think I'm faithless, Hugh?"

"Well, he hasn't much to congratulate himself upon, how long did it last?"

"Oh, I don't mean faithless to him. Besides, it doesn't matter how long, does it?"

"Not as long as it was long enough," said he.

"Enough for what?" Francesca shot a glance at him, but he was not looking at her.

"Enough to get tired of," he rejoined.

She seized some of the remaining letters and began to peruse them silently, even sullenly.

"These will do," at last she cried, throwing the rest away, "they are not too wicked, they won't corrupt her, they couldn't demoralize anyone, even me; they wouldn't agitate a nun. I'm keeping these for Fanny," she explained, "I shall leave them about on purpose for her to read."

"Humph!" grinned the doctor. "Tell me what happened."

"Oh, it was too silly. She read them all and revelled in them."

"Fanny?"

"Yes, it spoilt everything and made it ridiculous. I could see myself in such an absurd light, like a housemaid! Do you ever see yourself, Hugh, living and acting very strangely, apart from your real self? No? I suppose I am too sensitive, but it seemed as if Fanny and I had changed places, that the letters were more hers than mine—she liked them better than I did—and that *he* was, too. Preposterous situation! Have you ever felt like that, Hugh?"

"Yes," murmured the doctor, gazing at his wife, "I think, yes."

"Too preposterous, isn't it? But it was you who were so right, Hugh. It's incredible—but you are always so incredibly right. You aren't ever right in the ordinary way. You are really rather wrong about him generally, he is just like Goneril's average man, so very balanced that he's just trivial. But what I do see so absurdly now—I can see nothing else and it's horribly ridiculous—is that his clothes *are* too big, and his hats *are* too small!"

The doctor grinned as generously as his somewhat strained apprehension allowed. Francesca clasped her white hands and gazed at the paper ashes; the doctor gathered her tiny fists into his own.

"Hugh, am I a faithless being?"

"Well," he replied, "isn't that just what I want to know?"

"Dear Hugh!" and then Francesca irrelevantly said: "Fanny's such an impossible fool!"

"Now isn't she!" the doctor softly groaned. "I shall sack her at once."

"Hugh," Francesca murmured, "why don't you ever want to sack me?"

Fishmonger's Fiddle (1925)

FISHMONGER'S FIDDLE

Maxie. Morrisarde was not of the generation of Morrisardes; what they were doesn't matter, save that one of them was a vendor of cheroots. Her paternal ancestry was Vole, her father and her father's father were Voles, but neither does that matter, for her mother had been a Crump. Here and now, for better or for worse, she was a Morrisarde set in a dominion of Voles. Aunt Vole and Uncle Vole. They had Christian names, of course—Ethelbert and Ida—but they were the sort of people who never sported their Christian plumes, you always thought of them patronymically, and Maxie addressed them simply—Uncle, Aunt. And those respectable elderly retired Voles dwelt in a villa called Crag Dhu, half a mile from the sea front. It had blood-red bricks and a white gate. There was also a laburnum tree that never flowered, so it might just as well have been a pincushion; but still, it was a tree and it stood in the gate-corner of a plot of grass that framed an escarpment of mould whereon a dozen geraniums took seasonal holiday. And Crag Dhu seemed to hover over its garden, its gravel, and its coal plate with benignity and pride. The next villa was in the occupation of a horse-doctor, and was called Phædra. Except for this it was just like Crag Dhu, where the Voles lived: where Maxie Morrisarde was now living, and feeling much like one of those geraniums. That was absurd, for Maxie was married—in a kind of a way. She had been married truly and honourably to a one-time amiable tobacconist, who, however, after six months had untruly and shamefully forsaken her by bolting to America, leaving Maxie without any tangible means of subsistence until she was rescued by her uncle and aunt. A ruffian, a serpent, he was; he had married her for her little fortune; a swindler he was, pimp, bloodsucker, criminal, and sponge; and he was doomed to the gallows; these things Aunt Vole so constantly avowed, vociferated, and vouched for that in time even Maxie came to believe them. In her heart, too, Mrs. Vole believed him to be a bigamist, but of this she never breathed a hint to the deserted girl.

Mrs. Morrisarde had been a school-teacher, a slight fair pretty creature, helpless, charming, delicate, and an orphan, when she married, quite suddenly, the first man who had made love to her —this scoundrelly tobacco fellow. Since she had no other friends in the world, her gratitude to the Voles when they, as it were, adopted her was profound. Uncle Vole was a retired cattle dealer, hearty, connubial, and a nonconformist. Aunt Vole was neither hearty (saving as to appetite) nor connubial (except by implication), but she was rather deaf and she was very nonconformist. Life to her was the world, the flesh, and repentance; packed with tribulation from birth to burial, with snares by the scheming of Satan in every hour of the twenty-four. All by the scheming of Satan. Mercy enough if you were alive, and miracle beyond belief if you were sinless. Aunt Vole sewed and sewed and glowered.

Now, the Voles had a great rough hufty of a dog, with the name of Toots and the manners of a buffalo.

"What breed is she?" Maxie once asked, and Aunt Vole quivered all over as if Maxie had sworn at her. "Breed!" she repeated, with hushing depreciation. And really, when her aunt said it thus, it did sound like something not quite nice.

"Oh, I only mean what sort," floundered the flushed Maxie.

"Toots is a very good dog and bold as a lion. You must take

her with you whenever you go out; you're safer with a dog, always."

But Maxie did not go out alone, not at first; for a while her aunt always accompanied her with Toots, and indoors the colloquy of Aunt Vole was as constant as the clock-ticks. Sometimes she felt a vague unease, would have liked to go out by herself to some quiet place by the shore and think her own timid thoughts for a while, but she was shy and unresisting. She did not know that freedom is never to be given, but only to be taken; she was like a child for ever beckoning to the things that did not come—tobacconists, perhaps. The tobacconist was never heard of more, and in time Maxie's freedom was enlarged, but there was generally a catechism.

"Well?" her aunt said at tea-time.

"Been a beautiful day," bayed Mr. Vole, "turned out capital well."

"What do you think," laughed Maxie, "I saw a man with a cello going into a fishmonger's shop."

Mr. Vole genially grinned.

"With a what?" Aunt Vole gazed curiously at the girl.

"Cello!" cried her husband.

"A great big fiddle." Maxie made a gesture in the air with her two hands to indicate its gigantic size.

"Fiddle! Oh, I thought—humph." And a silence followed in which the powerful crunching of lettuce became audible as an earthquake. Then Aunt Vole took up her cup and you could hear her gulping her tea—gallons of it. So Maxie took up her cup, and Uncle Vole his, and they all gulped together.

"What shop did you say?" inquired Aunt Vole.

"Fish shop!" shouted her husband.

"A fish shop," said Maxie too. "It looked funny, you know."

"Fish shop," echoed the elder lady, with a puzzled frown. "What were you in a fish shop for?"

"I wasn't, aunt; I only saw him go in."

"Where?"

"In Stamboul Street, I think it was. I was just passing by the fish shop and this man went in with a great big fiddle." Again Maxie made a curve in the air with her hands.

"Did he say anything to you?"

"No, no, aunt, of course not." A faint blush grew in Maxie's cheek. "He didn't see me," she added.

"What did they want with a fiddle in there?"

"Oh, I don't suppose he was anything to *do* with the shop," explained the girl.

"They don't go into a fish shop for nothing," Aunt Vole pursued, "fiddle or no fiddle."

"No, he must have gone in to buy some fish," ventured her flurried niece.

"Oh," rejoined aunt, "Roman Catholic, I dare say. I shouldn't go that way again."

Maxie felt as if she had been admonished for some questionable behaviour.

"The best fiddler ever I heard was old Fishel Ayres. Up at Cadmer End, t'other side of Kent, mother," mused Uncle Vole. "The master hand! He hadn't got no sense, and he wouldn't be told no sense. But he was the masterpiece with a fiddle; ah, good ocean! Never had an overcoat on or an umbrella, not if it rained bullock's blood. The last words he ever said to me was: 'I shan't last many more years.' 'No,' I said, 'you won't if you don't take care of yourself.' He'd only got an old policeman's jacket coat on, and believe you me he was dead in a week. Played the fiddle capital well, but you know: break out—and you break down. Those were his last words to me. Now, that's a funny thing, ain't it?"

Aunt Vole had no pity for those roving customers. "They are all for self, and no responsibility; they're no good, and you can't trust them. A man should settle down, he should settle down and bear his burdens, bear his burdens properly. That's what a burden's for."

One morning Maxie took the dog with her and went to the pier. It stretched out into the sea quite a long way and was dotted with little cabins where you had your horoscope told or your photograph taken. Delicious it was on sunny mornings to hear the thumps of your own feet and those of people with parasols and fine-scented cigars all assembling to hear the musicians, or to fish, or to dive, or to go little journeys in rollicking little

steamers. Maxie had no wish to indulge in these accessory joys;
she was content to stroll up and down the long planked pier, or
to sit and divide the passing people into those she liked—how
few they were!—and those she did not.

A small group stood silently staring at a man sitting on a bench.
He was covered with wild pigeons, the birds hopping upon his
head, his shoulders, his knees, or picking peas from his hands
outstretched on either side of him. Only a few were enjoying this
vision of man and trusting birds; a tiny boy with a hoop and a
black velvet tam-o'-shanter hat; a dame with a hare-lip and the
austerity of a judge; a stout gentleman in grey with a malacca
cane and a white hat; some sweethearts. Pigeons pattered at the
man's feet; he had a gentle face. As Maxie came by, the dog
Toots bounded into the group and snapped one of the birds in
her jaws. The other pigeons swooped away on thick flapping
wings, everybody shouted "Brrr!" and the stout gentleman
fetched the wretched Toots such a blow with his malacca stick
that she yelped and dropped the bird at Maxie's feet. It was dead.

"Oh, oh! What can I do?" cried Maxie to the man, who sprang
up and confronted her. "Is it dead, was it yours?"

He picked up the dead bird and felt its breast, and then turned
and dropped in into the sea. The boy in the velvet hat leaned over
the railing to watch the feathered body floating and lifting with
the waves. The man—he was not very old, he might have been
thirty or thereabouts, with a pale face and thick brown hair—
turned and stared at Maxie.

"I am so very sorry," she stammered, trembling with apprehension, or disgust, or pity. Toots had vanished. "You had better
apologize to God," the young man sourly said, walking away.
Maxie was then still more abashed, for the people glowered at
her; the little boy looked as if he was about to weep, and the
stout gentleman swore that the dog ought to be shot or poisoned
or cut in half; then he went stumping off after the young man,
thumping his malacca stick dreadfully. Maxie fled off the pier,
deeply angry with the young man. It was wicked of him to say
such a thing to her, and she thought him quite nasty; but Aunt
Vole, when the quivering girl related the misadventure to her,
said it was only what you might expect from such people, that it

was a dog's nature, and people ought to look after their birds better. So emphatic was she that a flame of forgiveness at once began to flicker in Maxie's heart for the young man whom the birds seemed to love.

In a few days she ventured on the pier again. It was afternoon, and she did not take Toots with her, but still she had a faint fear that some passer-by would remember her as the girl whose dog killed the pigeon. In that episode it seemed to her as if she had shared in a crime, dreadful and pitiful, and that it would be long before the stout gentleman with a cane and the velvet-hatted boy with a hoop would cease to arraign her. Of the young man himself she had come to think that he might even protect her from them. None of these appeared, and no one else affronted her. Then she audaciously paid twopence to sit in a chair close to the band. At that moment a solo was being played, a piece called *Wiegenlied* by a composer named Schubert; so dreamy and beautiful it was that Maxie at the close even clapped her hands with delight. Everybody else applauded too, and so the player had to stand up in the midst of the band and bow and smile. Bowing and smiling, with his arm cuddling the neck of a violoncello, stood the young man of the pigeons.

Maxie knew at once. In the act of clapping she stayed as if she had been turned into that pillar of salt, her two hands still raised, her lips parted, and her eyes very wide open, for he was looking at her now. She remembered his sad serious gaze when he had reproached her about the dead bird; she remembered his going into that fishmonger's shop; remembered too her aunt's warning words when she had spoken to her of that. How strange! and how clever of Aunt Vole! It was exhilarating, and yet almost terrifying, to know he was that same man.

But nothing could have been less terrifying than their conjunction as she was leaving the pier. The music was over, people were sauntering off to tea, and suddenly he walked at her side, lifted his hat, and chaffed her about her savage dog—where was it? Had it been shot yet, or poisoned yet, or had she chopped it in half! No, yes; yes, no; confused delight allowed her no more indulgent replies; but when they parted at the pier gates she knew that she would meet him again as surely as if he had asked her to

—which he did not—that he was splendid and clever, and that she must be careful not to let Aunt Vole know anything at all about it.

At their second meeting, as they took tea together on the pier, she told him of her marriage and her misfortune. Blackburne smiled: sympathetically, but he appeared to think it was funny. He was rather queer, but irresistibly friendly, and Aunt Vole had been quite wrong about him: nothing to do with any fishmonger at all, he only bought fish to eat. It was a pity, but all musicians had to, and he vowed that he ate like a horse. Each day he played on the pier three times, day in and day out; he was like a cart-horse, never free, and he would rather be a fishmonger, and he envied Maxie.

"Oh, but that is quite a mistake," said the girl. "I haven't any freedom."

"Stuff!" cried Blackburne, so loudly that the waitresses turned and stared at him. In lower tones he went on: "You married and so achieved a status. That's an important truth about marriage—for the woman. She links herself with a man and *ipso facto* becomes an individual. Until then she has only been a nuisance, bullied by her mother, badgered by her sisters, and spanked by her brothers—possibly even by her pa. You were freed of all those affectionate ties, and then your man obligingly left you, so now you are more free than ever."

"He has left me alone, but not free," murmured Mrs. Morrisarde.

"Are you still fond of him?"

She shook her head. "No, he is wicked."

"Forget him, then."

"I have forgotten."

And he did not go to church at all, how could he? And he wasn't a Roman Catholic or anything like that.

"But Roman Catholics," he declared, "do at least confess their sins to some real person; it's more than the other sort ever do."

"That's because they've got," ventured Maxie, "such a lot to confess."

"All the more to their credit, then," grinned Blackburne (whose other name was Arnold).

"No," Maxie was positive, "they confess, and then they go and sin the more."

· "Well, if their consciences are clear! Of course," he jested.

"The only one who can forgive is God."

"Who's He?" the implacable musician returned.

"You told me to apologize to Him."

"And did you?"

"It was so rude of you, I thought."

"There you are, you didn't!" laughed Blackburne, but noting her solemnity, he quickly added: "No, no, forgive me; you were not to blame. And you would never have anything to confess, nothing worth hearing."

"It isn't so," cried she, "no."

"What! Shameful, shameful, Mrs. Morrisarde!" And he swore he would kiss her sins away—let her begin telling him at once!

He did not, he could not, give her those kisses then and there, but Maxie imagined them, and was secretly thrilled to be treated as a woman. Aunt Vole never would forget that her husband had run away, and her air imputed a blame to Maxie for that loss, as if she had been silly and overlooked something, something about his socks or his taste in cheese; without the anchorage of a husband of some sort she was a ship drifting, menaced by hazards all too dreadful to name but not too ambiguous to signify.

Maxie Morrisarde continued to meet her friend, to meet him daily, and to keep her aunt in ignorance of him. Concealment was like a "worm i' the bud," but still there *was* a bud, and it was opening, for although Arnold was absurd and tempestuous and spoke foolishly of God, he was handsome and careless and tender, and all her thoughts were of him.

Days of the week were days of timid bliss, but Sunday was a wretch for dullness. In the Voles' creed a visit to the pier on the Sabbath day was an act verging on blasphemy, and their niece was no blasphemer, and no rebel. She had had a black serge father and a mother full of hymns; they died young, but they had not died soon enough—Maxie was no rebel.

Aunt Vole had put on her Sunday afternoon bodice; though her proportions were inelegant she knew she was a woman with refined ideas. Uncle Vole snoozed in his easy chair; Maxie hymned at the piano, with the soft pedal down; Toots wandered disconsolately about the room until Uncle Vole opened his eyes and commanded her to lie down.

"Lie down, Toots," whispered Maxie, and aunt, glaring up from a book, said: "Toots!" so sharply that it sounded like a sneeze. The dog complied, and silence settled on them all like a mist in a vacant garden. Ping . . . ping . . . ping chimed the timepiece bell.

"Ah," Uncle Vole mistily murmured, "it's three o'clock."

"Humph," sighed his wife, and Maxie sighed too, and went out into the garden to look at the geraniums. The thought of her marriage, so disturbing, so disillusioning, so inescapable, had lately begun to sadden her. She was filled with longings, as restless as a bee in a window, for the afternoon was fair and languorous, the pier would be full of gaiety, and the music would be sweet. How tiny, harsh, and ridiculous the garden looked, how vast and blue the sky! Some clouds, in a small remote line, inched along the horizon; dark and flat underneath, but white and convoluted above, they were like travelling snails.

"Aunt," said she on returning to the parlour, "is it hard to get a divorce?"

As if the word were foul, fouler even than the word "breed," Aunt Vole flung it away from her. And from Maxie too.

"I just wondered," temporized the niece.

"How could you! No modest Christian girl could wonder or talk or think of such a wicked thing. At least I hope not. What ever did you get married for?"

"It costs a bushel of money." Uncle Vole sat up. "Good ocean! It costs a fortune, my girl!"

"We may thank God for that," his wife added.

"I could go to work."

"What? I can't hear!" shouted Mrs. Vole. "What could you work at?"

"I could work at something, I could save. I don't like him, and he doesn't want me."

"That makes no odds, you've been joined," declared Uncle Vole, "it's in the Book."

"Besides, you're separated *now*." Her aunt was quite impatient with her.

"He doesn't want me, he has been so bad to me."

"Suppose," cried Aunt Vole, "suppose he came back again?"

"I couldn't bear it, he has been bad to me."

"Or suppose he sent for you, as of course he might as soon as he settles down and pays his debts? Then you would be together again, and just as happy as ever you were." Aunt Vole could travel upside down as easily as a wasp on a ceiling, and you dared not remind her of this for she could just as easily sting you.

"Aunt, I believe I hate him."

"No, you don't. You can't, not your own husband! I never heard of such nonsense. I don't know why the Almighty allowed a Christian girl to marry such a wretch—but He did; and you've got to carry your burden. That's what a burden's for! Oh, Maxie, no, no, no!"

"Listen to me for a minute, my dear," began her uncle. "One of our leading butchers died last Tuesday, Roland Dean. I spent many a happy half-hour with him. And he used to keep a dog called Brisket chained up in his yard, very savage it was. There lived close by a soft-hearted man who wanted to persuade Roland Dean to let it off the chain, just for an hour now and again. Well, every dog has his day, and so after a lot of jaw-tackle Roland Dean did let it off, and the first thing Brisket did—what do you think? Flew at him! Flew at the soft-hearted man—Budge his name was—and nearly limbed him. That's a fact. And always afterwards that Brisket was so savage whenever she saw Budge that he had to give up going past there altogether. So you see! Things should be left alone. Stay as you are, my girl, you're safer. Break out, and you break down."

Maxie, timid and unfortunate, felt like an insect caught in a web that the spider had forsaken. But her delicate beauty throve, for in those hours snatched almost daily with Arnold was all the life and wonder she desired. Morning or afternoon—she could not meet him at night—in the intervals of his playing they would sit together and murmur and smile, and he would say the most absurd, the most delightful things. And coming or going, the lively streets crowded with people crudely gay or graciously dignified, the very dust on the worn pavements printed with a thousand footfalls, the sweet air, the wide sea rolling a collar of milky surf along the shore, were full of an enchanting savour;

her soul seemed to caress all these things, and her dark fancies were lulled.

"Look!" he cried one day as he greeted her, "tomorrow I'm to have a holiday. You must spend it with me. We'll go along the shore, miles and miles. . . ."

But already she was shaking her head, denying him. It would have been difficult in any circumstances, but tomorrow would be Sunday.

"But you must!" he cried. "What! I've a hundred things to tell you and ask you. Are you afraid?"

"Yes," she answered meekly.

"Afraid of those wretched Voles! Pouf! I'll teach you!" And he was so contemptuous and jocular and headstrong that she had to consent. She dared not tell her aunt, and it was impossible to think of an excuse for such an absence—on a Sunday, too! How it was to be done she did not know, but she did not care now; she had promised. In the morning she slipped guiltily out of Crag Dhu before her aunt could interrogate her, and ran to meet Blackburne waiting by the sea.

They made off in a westerly direction far along the sands. The air was windily bright, the tide was low, but the waters were dull dark green except for the tufts of foam the wind tossed upon the strand. All over the soft wet shore were wormlike knots of sand, and tiny recesses beside them like sunken cups with a hole in the middle.

When Arnold asked her what excuse she had made to the Voles she answered that she had not told them at all and did not know what the outcome would be.

"Tell them the truth," he said, "I will come with you."

And he kept on singing, or beating stones into the sea with his stick. "Tell them the truth."

By and by they came to a village, all cabins and nets and husky canvas-clad fishermen. Beyond the village was a river, with an old wooden bridge crossing it. The river was wide and they sat down upon its grassy margin before going over. Some way off was a chalk pit scooped out of a green down, so white that it dazzled the eyes, and beside it were tall black chimneys. Nearer there were fields, vacant save for a few writhen trees. And in the middle of the river, where it widened to take the sea, lay a pear-shaped island of sand uncovered by the ebb; nearly an acre of flat smooth sand, like bleached gold, washed by blue crinkled waves. On that silent isle hundreds of snowy gulls were scattered, standing motionless, snoozing in the sun, intensely white, like a drift of divine flowers, and among them a few rooks intensely black.

"Enchanting," murmured Blackburne, "how lovely!"

"They are like crocuses growing," Maxie said.

"Yes indeed," the man replied. "That is how our sense of beauty sometimes drugs us—by analogies; by things that in their beautiful deceit remind us of things different but in their like-ness. The voice of the forest is like the voice of the sea, the rhythm of a hill is the green wave, the torrent of storm is the anger of God, and so on. Here are birds that make you think of flowers. Pure nonsense! It is all unnatural; it is only man's strange faculty for making an ass of himself."

One of the gulls came soaring above them, and as it slid by on motionless wings it lifted one of its pink feet and scratched gravely at its tilted neck. Arnold lounged beside Maxie and med-itated solemnly. She did not understand him, but the sunny solitude was sweet, and she was happy.

"You cannot catch beauty," he went on. "She never affirms herself or asserts herself. Beauty is that which is denied—isn't it so?"

"I don't know," said the girl, "I know so little."

"Ignorance is bliss, my dear, truly. What makes for happiness? Not knowledge. Knowledge only realizes that it doesn't know very much, and that what little it does know it doesn't know very well. You just take up life and opportunity, learn the way to do things, and keep life in order—that's all."

"It seems to me God does all that *for* you."

A deeper pink flush spread in her cheeks as she said it. "He is wise. To pray for them that hate you and to forgive your enemies is noble, and that is wise too. You pretend not to believe in Him, but in spite of it your spirit *knows*."

"Perhaps, my dear priestess, perhaps. For a man's emotions are exposed not merely in his relations with his fellows; they are most nobly expressed in his denial of the world in which he lives, and in his sense of his soul's relation with—its perceptions, its concurrences with—that ideal kingdom of which he only dreams and wonders. Yes," he mused, but as if not speaking to her and communing only with himself as he gazed at the vision of the birds, "beauty is that which is denied. Man so loves the world that he craves this unbegotten beauty, not as a sign of his mystical relationship to God, but as a sequel and a solace to his own mute misgivings. Without this we are but stocks and stones." He turned to her, smiling. "You may not understand this. I hope you don't."

"I do! And it means that you are a Christian."

"Oh, chuck, chuck! You've no more brains than a frying-pan. But oh, Mrs. Morrisarde," he leaned on his elbow closer to her, "I'm deeply fond of you."

Her blush deepened as she slipped off her wedding ring and tossed it into the river. "Don't call me that," and she put her arms around him. He swore that she had a soul as sweet as any of the white birds, and the body of a queen—which was going rather far, perhaps, but not really absurd, maybe.

The wind had fallen and the heat was increasing when they journeyed over the bridge. A mile or two along the road they found an inn and a haughty barmaid with bedevilled eyes and lustrous hair, who said she could not provide them with lunch but that they might have sandwiches. They sat down in the bar and ate them. Arnold drank beer and Maxie drank wine. Presently they heard steps approaching the open door and a voice lustily singing a song about the Queen of Poland. An elegantly dressed man and a lad came in together, flushed from swift walking, their boots covered with dust.

"Foo!" said the gentleman to the barmaid, "Foo, hot! The barometer is—ah—quite a lot, I think. In the shade, you know. Foo, dash it, yes!"

He had a large freckled face and triangular eyebrows, with a tough chestnut moustache; his voice was large and angular, too.

"What can we have to drink? How's that blister, Jamie?"

The sylph of the barrels replied: "Anything you care for."

"Well, yes; it must be something we care for. You haven't any

egg flip? No, you haven't any egg flip. Then a bottle of melodi-
ous beer, if you please, with a few chromatic splinters in it."

Leaning upon his walking-stick, he crossed a leg and sung
again:

> "Oh, the Queen of Poland is my queen
> And I'm her Salamander."

"Jamie, have a bun? Isn't it hot, foo! What have you done
with your orange? Jamie, spotless treasure, they haven't any
buns, so what now, eh? Cocoa! Oh, but Jamie, you can't; it's
Sunday, it's rude. No, what you want for your complaint, my
darling, is, is—"

"I said some ginger beer," the boy interrupted loudly.

"Ginger beer! Oh, God bless me, yes. If you please, madam.

> "Oh, the Queen of Poland is my queen,"

sang the gentleman, winking—or appearing to wink—at Mrs.
Morrisarde.

Arnold and she walked in the fields again, inland, far from the
sea, towards a town where they could catch an evening train for
home. Fragrant and alluring their track was, fragrant and
tender those untiring hours, with the glimpse of a kingfisher as it
dashed from a rock into the bosom of the stream; rabbits, water-
voles, ducks; the forlorn beggars who all cajoled pence from
Blackburne; "I'm powerless, abject," he cried to her, "they conduct their peaceful raids upon my charitable emotions"; the
cottage where they got tea from a widow whose man had been
massacred by Zulus; the churchyard stone to a sailor who had
been "done to death by Neptune"; Maxie felt she could go on
roving thus for ever in so bright and free a world, to hear and see
all the absurd things and all the beautiful things with the man
she loved.

But in the cool of the evening: "Tell me," Blackburne suddenly urged, "what can we do about this husband of yours?
Can't you divorce him?"

She stopped quite still, facing him; not looking at him, but
staring back along their travelled road. So far they had come already, so very far! They were in a long thin white rambling

road, its herby borders fringed with ragwort and succory. A willow brook dribbled along one side, and endless fields ranked with stooks of corn stretched on and on. The sun was going down, the daylight moon, which had ghosted in the sky for hours, was triumphantly hovering. So alone they were, so quiet it was, that their very footsteps had seemed to crunch the peaceful air. Her hand was laid upon his sleeve in a slow caress.

"No," she said, "it's impossible, Arnold." She had come to accept her aunt's horror of divorce; not for its hideous publicity, but because it defamed God's will. Like all timid people she took a reason that had not been hers and made it her own, multiplying its intensity. Never, never, never! And with that dark question hopelessly argued there and then between them she felt she was a miserable woman, deeply sinning. Blackburne pleaded and scoffed and stormed, but she cried on his breast and declared she must never see him again.

"I believe, you know," said he, "that in seven years you are free to marry again provided you hear nothing of him in that time; you are free."

"Is that true?"

"I have heard so, in seven years, yes."

"How strange!" She was smiling, almost placidly. "That's not long."

"Oh, no—the week after next!" But his sarcasm crumbled at her gaze. "Dear love, I want you."

"Yes, yes," she murmured.

"Do you know? Do you want it, too?"

She was bewildered by his caresses. "Oh, what do you want, Arnold?"

"A lover, a wife, a mistress," he whispered, "whatever you can be to me."

"If I gave you everything it would not be enough."

"Come and live with me, Maxie. I'll care for you dearer than any husband."

Her refusal was the softest ever uttered, but it was the ultimate answer.

With her arm linked in his they walked on rapidly until they got to the railway station, where they sat and waited for their train.

"Don't hate me, Arnold."

"No, of course not," he returned moodily. "Isn't this an ugly, rackety, exasperating hole? And that cursed engine hoasting and heaving and crashing with its millions of empty trucks!"

Half an hour later they parted at the gate of Crag Dhu. Should he wait to see if she were flung from the door? No. In the gathered gloom she pressed him to her as if bidding an eternal farewell.

"Don't go, Maxie. Come away now!"

"It has been a sweet little holiday," she whispered, and then ran off along the garden path.

As she entered the house Aunt Vole appeared in the passage, bonneted and cloaked and wild-eyed. With a stupid shriek she heaved herself upon the errant girl and burst into tears. "Oh, Maxie, darling child!" Little Mary Fitchew, the servant, stared from the end of the passage, like an owl.

"We thought you were dead!" sobbed the extraordinary, the surprising Aunt Vole. "Dead drowned!"

"Oh, aunt! I'm all right, I've only been out with a friend."

"Or that you had run away!"

"No, no, aunt, I'm all right." At this unexpected reception she almost wept herself; but she patted her hysterical aunt and hushed her. "I ought not to have gone, I know; I ought to have told you, didn't I?"

"Tell me, come into the parlour and tell me everything," adjured Aunt Vole. And there Maxie told her everything.

"Dear, dear!" was her aunt's comment. "And your uncle is scouring the town after you."

"Let me go to bed," said the distracted girl.

"Oh, but wait for your uncle, won't you?"

"No, you tell him, aunt."

"If you wish it, child. But promise me, promise me this, promise you will never see that man again."

Maxie sat silent for a few moments. "I'll go away, aunt, a long way away, and get work."

"Oh, your uncle wouldn't hear of that. Do you want to leave us? We are fond of you. And what work could you do now? And your husband—don't forget him—what would your husband think of this?"

The pretty sinner bowed her head in tears, while Aunt Vole, who envisaged a soul tottering on the brink of damnation, went to a shelf and reached down a large heavy book.

"You will promise?" she urged, with strange unfamiliar gentleness.

"Yes," said Maxie.

"Lay your hand on the book."

Maxie laid her hand on the open book. She was the creature of her environment, always. With her lover she had no fears, for he was fearless. With the Voles she laid down her pride; and she swore on the book as Aunt Vole directed her. There at the end of one of her fingers a verse met her glance:

"My heart panteth, my strength faileth me: as for the light of mine eyes, it also is gone from me."

Her aunt kissed her and then startlingly knelt down as if in silent prayer. But Maxie did not join her. She sat staring at invisible things, a wonderful sunset shining with eternity, and far-off ineffable joys. Seven years! Seven years! And there was a stupid man with triangular eyebrows who kept winking at her and singing:

> Oh, the Queen of Poland is my queen,
> And I'm her Salamander.

Fishmonger's Fiddle (1925)

THE HURLY BURLY

THE Weetmans—mother, son, and daughter—lived on a thriving farm. It was small enough, God knows; but it had always been a turbulent place of abode. For the servant it was "Phemy, do this," or "Phemy, have you done that?" from dawn to dark, and even from dark to dawn there was a hovering of unrest. The Widow Weetman, a partial invalid, was the only figure that manifested any semblance of tranquillity; and it was a misleading one, for she sat day after day on her large hams, knitting and nodding, and lifting her grey face only to grumble, her spectacled eyes transfixing the culprit with a basilisk glare. And her daughter, Alice, the housekeeper, who had a large face, a dominating face, in some respects she was all face, was like a blast in a corridor with her "Maize for the hens, Phemy!—More firewood, Phemy!—Who has set the trap in the harness room?—Come along!—Have you scoured the skimming-pans?—Why not?—Where are you idling?—Come along, Phemy, I have no time to waste this morning; you really must help me!" It was not only in the house that this cataract of industry flowed; outside there was activity enough for a regiment. A master farmer's work consists largely in a series of conversations with other master farmers, a long-winded way of doing long-headed things; but Glastonbury Weetman, the son, was not like that at all; he was the incarnation of energy, always doing and doing, chock-full of orders, adjurations, objurgatives, blame, and blasphemy. That was the kind of place Phemy Madigan worked at. No one could rest on laurels there. The farm and the home possessed everybody, lock, stock, and barrel; work was like a tiger, it ate you up implacably. The Weetmans did not mind—they liked being eaten by such a tiger.

After six or seven years of this, Alice went back to marry an old sweetheart in Canada, where the Weetmans had originally come from; but Phemy's burden was in no way lessened thereby. There were as many things to wash and sew and darn; there was always a cart of churns about to dash for a train it could not possibly catch, or a horse to shoe that could not possibly be spared. Weetman hated to see his people merely walking. "Run over to the barn for that hayfork!" or "Slip across to the ricks, quick, now!" he would cry; and if ever an unwary hen hampered his path it only did so once—and no more. His labourers were mere things of flesh and blood, but they occasionally resented his ceaseless flagellations. Glas Weetman did not like to be impeded or controverted; one day in a rage he had smashed that lumbering loon of a carter called Gathercole. For this he was sent to jail for a month.

The day after he had been sentenced Phemy Madigan, alone in the house with Mrs. Weetman, had waked at the usual early hour. It was a foggy September morning; Sampson and his boy Daniel were clattering pails in the dairy shed. The girl felt sick and gloomy as she dressed; it was a wretched house to work in, crickets in the kitchen, cockroaches in the garret, spiders and mice everywhere. It was an old long low house; she knew that when she descended the stairs the walls would be stained with autumnal dampness, the banisters and rails oozing with moisture. She wished she was a lady and married, and living in a palace fifteen stories high.

It was fortunate that she was big and strong, though she had only been a charity girl taken from the workhouse by the Weetmans, when she was fourteen years old. That was seven years ago. It was fortunate that she was fed well at the farm, very well indeed; it was the one virtue of the place. But her meals did not counterbalance things; that farm ate up the body and blood of people. And at times the pressure was charged with a special excitation, as if a taut elastic thong had been plucked and released with a reverberating ping.

It was so on this morning. Mrs. Weetman was dead in her bed.

At that crisis a new sense descended upon the girl, a sense of responsibility. She was not in fear, she felt no grief or surprise. It concerned her in some way, but she herself was unconcerned, and she slid without effort into the position of mistress of the farm. She opened a window and looked out of doors. A little way off a boy with a red scarf stood by an open gate.

"Oi—oi, kup, kup, kup!" he cried to the cows in that field. Some of the cows, having got up, stared amiably at him, others sat on ignoring his hail, while one or two plodded deliberately towards him. "Oi—oi, kup, kup, kup!"

"Lazy rascal, that boy," remarked Phemy; "we shall have to get rid of him. Dan'l! Come here, Dan'l!" she screamed, waving her arm wildly. "Quick!"

She sent him away for police and doctor. At the inquest there were no relatives in England who could be called upon, no other witnesses than Phemy. After the funeral she wrote a letter to

Glastonbury Weetman in jail, informing him of his bereavement, but to this he made no reply. Meanwhile the work of the farm was pressed forward under her control; for though she was revelling in her personal release from the torment, she would not permit others to share her intermission. She had got Mrs. Weetman's keys and her box of money. She paid the two men and the boy their wages week by week. The last of the barley was reaped, the oats stacked, the roots hoed, the churns sent daily under her supervision. And always she was bustling the men.

"Oh dear me, these lazy rogues!" she would complain to the empty rooms. "They waste time, so it's robbery—it *is* robbery. You may wear yourself to the bone, and what does it signify to such as them? All the responsibility too! They would take your skin if they could get it off you—and they can't!"

She kept such a sharp eye on the corn and meal and eggs that Sampson grew surly. She placated him by handing him Mr. Weetman's gun and a few cartridges, saying: "Just shoot me a couple of rabbits over in the warren when you get time." At the end of the day Mr. Sampson had not succeeded in killing a rabbit, so he kept the gun and the cartridges many more days. Phemy was really happy. The gloom of the farm had disappeared. The farm and everything about it looked beautiful, beautiful indeed with its yard full of ricks, the pond full of ducks, the fields full of sheep and cattle, and the trees still full of leaves and birds. She flung maize about the yard; the hens scampered towards it and the young pigs galloped, quarrelling over the grains which they groped and snuffled for, grinding each one separately in their iron jaws, while the white pullets stalked delicately among them, picked up the maize seeds—one, two, three—and swallowed them like ladies. Sometimes on cold mornings she would go outside and give an apple to the fat bay pony when he galloped back from the station. He would stand puffing with a kind of rapture, the wind from his nostrils discharging in the frosty air vague shapes like smoky trumpets. Presently, upon his hide, a little ball of liquid mysteriously suspired, grew, slid, dropped from his flanks into the road. And then drops would begin to come from all parts of him until the road beneath was dabbled by a shower from his dew-distilling outline. Phemy would say:

"The wretches! They were so late they drove him near distracted, poor thing. Lazy rogues, but wait till master comes back, they'd better be careful!"

And if any friendly person in the village asked her: "How are you getting on up there, Phemy?" she would reply: "Oh, as well as you can expect with so much to be done—and such men!" The interlocutor might hint that there was no occasion in the circumstances to distress oneself, but then Phemy would be vexed. To her, honesty was as holy as the Sabbath to a little child. Behind her back they jested about her foolishness; but, after all, wisdom isn't a process, it's a result, it's the fruit of the tree. One can't be wise, one can only be fortunate.

On the last day of her elysium the workhouse master and the chaplain had stalked over the farm, shooting partridges. In the afternoon she met them and asked for a couple of birds for Weetman's return on the morrow. The workhouse was not far away, it was on a hill facing west, and at sunset-time its windows would often catch the glare so powerfully that the whole building seemed to burn like a box of contained and smokeless fire. Very beautiful it looked to Phemy.

II

The men had come to work punctually, and Phemy herself found so much to do that she had no time to give the pony an apple. She cleared the kitchen once and for all of the pails, guns, harness, and implements that so hampered its domestic intention, and there were abundant signs elsewhere of a new impulse at work in the establishment. She did not know at what hour to expect the prisoner, so she often went to the garden gate and glanced up the road. The night had been wild with windy rain, but morn was sparklingly clear though breezy still. Crisp leaves rustled along the road where the polished chestnuts beside the parted husks lay in numbers, mixed with coral buds of the yews. The sycamore leaves were black rags, but the delicate elm foliage fluttered down like yellow stars. There was a brown field neatly adorned with white coned heaps of turnips, behind it a small upland of deeply green lucerne, behind that nothing but blue sky and rolling cloud. The turnips, washed by the rain, were creamy polished globes.

When at last he appeared she scarcely knew him. Glas Weetman was a big, though not fleshy, man of thirty, with a large boyish face and a flat bald head. Now he had a thick dark beard. He was hungry, but his first desire was to be shaved. He stood before the kitchen mirror, first clipping the beard away with scissors, and as he lathered the remainder he said:

"Well, it's a bad state of things, this—my sister dead and my mother gone to America. What shall us do?"

He perceived in the glass that she was smiling.

"There's nought funny in it, my comic gal!" he bawled indignantly. "What are you laughing at?"

"I wer'n't laughing. It's your mother that's dead."

"My mother that's dead, I know."

"And Miss Alice that's gone to America."

"To America, I know, I know, so you can stop making your bullock's eyes and get me something to eat. What's been going on here?"

She gave him an outline of affairs. He looked at her sternly when he asked her about his sweetheart.

"Has Rosa Beauchamp been along here?"

"No," said Phemy, and he was silent. She was surprised at the question. The Beauchamps were such respectable high-up people that to Phemy's simple mind they could not possibly favour an alliance now with a man that had been in prison; it was absurd, but she did not say so to him. And she was bewildered to find that her conviction was wrong, for Rosa came along later in the day and everything between her master and his sweetheart was just as before; Phemy had not divined so much love and forgiveness in high-up people.

It was the same with everything else. The old harsh rushing life was resumed, Weetman turned to his farm with an accelerated vigour to make up for lost time, and the girl's golden week or two of ease became an unforgotten dream. The pails, the guns, the harness crept back into the kitchen. Spiders, cockroaches, and mice were more noticeable than ever before, and Weetman himself seemed embittered, harsher. Time alone could never still him, there was a force in his frame, a buzzing in his blood. But there was a difference between them now; Phemy no longer feared him. She obeyed him, it is true, with eagerness, she worked in the house like a woman and in the fields like a man. They ate their meals together, and from this dissonant comradeship the girl, in a dumb kind of way, began to love him.

One April evening, on coming in from the fields, he found her lying on the couch beneath the window, dead plumb fast asleep, with no meal ready at all. He flung his bundle of harness to the flags and bawled angrily to her. To his surprise she did not stir. He was somewhat abashed; he stepped over to look at her. She was lying on her side. There was a large rent in her bodice between sleeve and shoulder; her flesh looked soft and agreeable to him. Her shoes had slipped off to the floor; her lips were folded in a pout.

"Why, she's quite a pretty cob," he murmured. "She's all right, she's just tired, the Lord above knows what for."

But he could not rouse the sluggard. Then a fancy moved him to lift her in his arms; he carried her from the kitchen and, staggering up the stairs, laid the sleeping girl on her own bed. He then went downstairs and ate pie and drank beer in the candlelight, guffawing once or twice: "A pretty cob, rather." As he stretched himself after the meal a new notion amused him: he put a plateful of food upon a tray, together with a mug of beer and the candle. Doffing his heavy boots and leggings, he carried the tray into Phemy's room. And he stopped there.

III

The new circumstance that thus slipped into her life did not effect any noticeable alteration of its general contour and progress. Weetman did not change towards her. Phemy accepted his mastership not alone because she loved him, but because her powerful sense of loyalty covered all the possible opprobrium. She did not seem to mind his continued relations with Rosa.

Towards midsummer one evening Glastonbury came in in the late dusk. Phemy was there in the darkened kitchen. "Master!" she said immediately he entered. He stopped before her. She continued: "Something's happened."

"Huh, while the world goes popping round something sall always happen!"

"It's me—I'm took—a baby, master," she said. He stood chock-still. His back was to the light, she could not see the expression on his face, perhaps he wanted to embrace her.

"Let's have a light, sharp," he said in his brusque way. "The supper smells good, but I can't see what I'm smelling, and I can only fancy what I be looking at."

She lit the candles and they ate supper in silence. Afterwards he sat away from the table with his legs outstretched and crossed, hands sunk into pockets, pondering while the girl cleared the table. Soon he put his powerful arm around her waist and drew her to sit on his knees.

"Are you sure o' that?" he demanded.

She was sure.

"Quite?"

She was quite sure.

"Ah, well, then," he sighed conclusively, "we'll be married!"

The girl sprang to her feet. "No, no, no! How can you be married? You don't mean that—not married—there's Miss Beauchamp!" She paused and added a little unsteadily: "She's your true love, master."

"Ay, but I'll not wed her!" he cried sternly. "If there's no gainsaying this that's come on you I'll stand to my guns. It's right and proper for we to have a marriage."

His great thick-fingered hands rested upon his knees; the candles threw a wash of light upon his polished leggings; he stared into the fireless grate.

"But we do not want to do that," said the girl dully and doubtfully. "You have given your ring to her, you've given her your word. I don't want you to do this for me. It's all right, master, it's all right."

"Are ye daft?" he cried. "I tell you we'll wed. Don't keep clacking about Rosa—I'll stand to my guns." He paused before adding, "She'd gimme the rightabout, fine now—don't you see, stupid—but I'll not give her the chance."

Her eyes were lowered. "She's your true love, master."

"What would become of you and your child? Ye couldn't bide here!"

"No," said the trembling girl.

"I'm telling you what we must do, modest and proper; there's naught else to be done, and I'm middling glad of it, I am. Life's a seesaw affair. I'm middling glad of this."

So, soon, without a warning to anyone, least of all to Rosa Beauchamp, they were married by the registrar. The change in her domestic status produced no other change; in marrying Weetman she but married all his ardour, she was swept into its current. She helped to milk cows, she boiled nauseating messes for pigs, chopped mangolds, mixed meal, and sometimes drove a harrow in his windy fields. Though they slept together, she was still his servant. Sometimes he called her his "pretty little cob," and then she knew he was fond of her. But in general his custom was disillusioning. His way with her was his way with his beasts; he knew what he wanted, it was easy to get. If for a brief space a little romantic flower began to bud in her breast it was frozen as a bud, and the vague longing disappeared at length from her eyes. And she became aware that Rosa Beauchamp was not yet done with; somewhere in the darkness of the fields Glastonbury still met her. Phemy did not mind.

In the new year she bore him a son that died as it came to life. Glas was angry at that, as angry as if he had lost a horse. He felt that he had been duped, that the marriage had been a stupid sacrifice, and in this he was savagely supported by Rosa. And yet Phemy did not mind; the farm had got its grip upon her, it was consuming her body and blood.

Weetman was just going to drive into town; he sat fuming in the trap behind the fat bay pony.

"Bring me that whip from the passage!" he shouted. "There's never a dam thing handy!"

Phemy appeared with the whip. "Take me with you," she said.

"God-a-mighty! What for? I be comen back in an hour. They ducks want looking over, and you've all the taties to grade."

She stared at him irresolutely.

"And whose to look after the house? You know it won't lock up—the key's lost. Get up there!"

He cracked his whip in the air as the pony dashed away.

In the summer Phemy fell sick, her arm swelled enormously. The doctor came again and again. It was blood-poisoning, caught from a diseased cow that she had milked with a cut finger. A nurse arrived, but Phemy knew she was doomed, and though tortured with pain she was for once vexed and protestant. For it was a June night, soft and nubile, with a marvellous moon; a nightingale threw its impetuous garland into the air. She lay listening to it and thinking with sad pleasure of the time when Glastonbury was in prison, how grand she was in her solitude, ordering everything for the best and working superbly. She wanted to go on and on for evermore, though she knew she had never known peace in maidenhood or marriage. The troubled waters of the world never ceased to flow; in the night there was no rest—only darkness. Nothing could emerge now. She was leaving it all to Rosa Beauchamp. Glastonbury was gone out somewhere—perhaps to meet Rosa in the fields. There was the nightingale, and it was very bright outside.

"Nurse," moaned the dying girl, "what was I born into the world at all for?"

Clorinda Walks in Heaven (1922)

THE FIELD OF MUSTARD

On a windy afternoon in November they were gathering kindling in the Black Wood, Dinah Lock, Amy Hardwick, and Rose Olliver, three sere disvirgined women from Pollock's Cross. Mrs. Lock wore clothes of dull butcher's blue, with a short jacket that affirmed her plumpness, but Rose and Amy had on long grey ulsters. All of them were about forty years old, and the wind and twigs had tousled their gaunt locks, for none had a hat upon her head. They did not go far beyond the margin of the wood, for the forest ahead of them swept high over a hill and was gloomy; behind them the slim trunks of beech, set in a sweet ruin of hoar and scattered leaf, and green briar nimbly fluttering made a sort of palisade against the light of the open, which was grey, and a wide field of mustard, which was yellow. The three women peered up into the trees for dead branches, and when they found any Dinah Lock, the vivacious woman full of shrill laughter, with a bosom as massive as her haunches, would heave up a rope with an iron bolt tied to one end. The bolted end would twine itself around the dead branch, the three women would tug, and after a sharp crack the quarry would fall; as often as not the women would topple over too. By and by they met an old hedger with a round belly belted low, and thin legs tied at each knee, who told them the time by his ancient watch, a stout timepiece which the women sportively admired.

"Come Christmas I'll have me a watch like that!" Mrs. Lock called out. The old man looked a little dazed as he fumblingly replaced his chronometer. "I will," she continued, "if the Lord spares me and the pig don't pine."

"You—you don't know what you're talking about," he said. "That watch was my uncle's watch."

"Who was he? I'd like one like it."

"Was a sergeant-major in the lancers, fought under Sir Garnet Wolseley, and it was given to him."

"What for?"

The hedger stopped and turned on them. "Doing of his duty."

"That all?" cried Dinah Lock. "Well, I never got no watch for that a-much. Do you know what I see when I went to London? I see'd a watch in a bowl of water, it was glass, and there was a fish swimming round it. . . ."

"I don't believe it."

"There was a fish swimming round it. . . ."

"I tell you I don't believe it. . . ."

"And the little hand was going on like Clackford Mill. That's the sort of watch I'll have me; none of your Sir Garney Wolsey's!"

"He was a noble Christian man, that was."

"Ah! I suppose he slept wid Jesus?" yawped Dinah.

"No, he didn't," the old man disdainfully spluttered. "He never did. What a God's the matter wid ye?" Dinah cackled with laughter. "Pah!" he cried, going away, "great fat thing! Can't tell your guts from your elbows."

Fifty yards farther on he turned and shouted some obscenity back at them, but they did not heed him; they had begun to make three faggots of the wood they had collected, so he put his fingers to his nose at them and shambled out to the road.

By the time Rose and Dinah were ready, Amy Hardwick, a small, slow, silent woman, had not finished bundling her faggot together.

"Come on, Amy," urged Rose.

"Come on," Dinah said.

"All right, wait a minute," she replied listlessly.

"Oh God, that's death!" cried Dinah Lock, and heaving a great faggot to her shoulders she trudged off, followed by Rose with a like burden. Soon they were out of the wood, and crossing a highway they entered a footpath that strayed in a diagonal wriggle to the far corner of the field of mustard. In silence they journeyed until they came to that far corner, where there was a hedged bank. Here they flung their faggots down and sat upon them to wait for Amy Hardwick.

In front of them lay the field they had crossed, a sour scent rising faintly from its yellow blooms, which quivered in the wind. Day was dull, the air chill, and the place most solitary. Beyond the field of mustard the eye could see little but forest. There were hills there, a vast curving trunk, but the Black Wood heaved itself effortlessly upon them and lay like a dark pall over the outline of a corpse. Huge and gloomy, the purple woods draped it all completely. A white necklace of a road curved below, where a score of telegraph poles, each crossed with a multitude of white florets, were dwarfed by the hugeness to effigies that resembled hyacinths. Dinah Lock gazed upon this scene whose melancholy, and not its grandeur, had suddenly invaded her; with elbows sunk in her fat thighs, and nursing her cheeks in her hands, she puffed the gloomy air, saying:

"Oh God, cradle and grave is all there is for we."

"Where's Amy got to?" asked Rose.

"I could never make a companion of her, you know," Dinah declared.

"Nor I," said Rose, "she's too sour and slow."

"Her disposition's too serious. Of course, your friends are never what you want them to be, Rose. Sometimes they're better—most often they're worse. But it's such a mercy to have a friend at all; I like you, Rose; I wish you was a man."

"I might just as well ha' been," returned the other woman.

"Well, you'd ha' done better; but if you had a tidy little family like me you'd wish you hadn't got 'em."

"And if you'd never had 'em you'd ha' wished you had."

"Rose, that's the cussedness of nature, it makes a mock of you. I don't believe it's the Almighty at all, Rose. I'm sure it's the devil, Rose. Dear heart, my corn's a-giving me what-for; I wonder what that bodes."

"It's restless weather," said Rose. She was dark, tall, and not unbeautiful still, though her skin was harsh and her limbs angular. "Get another month or two over—there's so many of these long dreary hours."

"Ah, your time's too long, or it's too short, or it's just right but you're too old. Cradle and grave's my portion. Fat old thing! he called me."

Dinah's brown hair was ruffled across her pleasant face and she looked a little forlorn, but corpulence dispossessed her of tragedy. "I be thin enough a-summer-times, for I lives light and sweats like a bridesmaid, but winters I'm fat as a hog."

"What all have you to grumble at, then?" asked Rose, who had slid to the ground and lay on her stomach staring up at her friend.

"My heart's young, Rose."

"You've your husband."

"He's no man at all since he was ill. A long time ill, he was. When he coughed, you know, his insides come up out of him like coffee grouts. Can you ever understand the meaning of that? Coffee! I'm growing old, but my heart's young."

"So is mine, too; but you got a family, four children grown or growing." Rose had snapped off a sprig of the mustard flower and was pressing and pulling the bloom in and out of her mouth. "I've none, and never will have." Suddenly she sat up, fumbled in her pocket, and produced her purse. She slipped the elastic band from it, and it gaped open. There were a few coins there and a scrap of paper folded. Rose took out the paper and smoothed it open under Dinah's curious gaze. "I found something lying about at home the other day, and I cut this bit out of it." In soft tones she began to read:

The day was void, vapid; time itself seemed empty. Come evening it rained softly. I sat by my fire turning over the leaves of a book, and I was dejected, until I came upon a little old-fashioned engraving at the bottom of a page. It imaged a procession of some angelic children in a garden, little placidly-naked substantial babes, with tiny bird-wings. One carried a bow, others a horn of plenty, or a hamper of fruit, or a set of reed-pipes. They were garlanded and full of grave joys. And at the sight of them a strange bliss flowed into me such as I had never known, and I thought this world was all a garden, though its light was hidden and its children not yet born.

Rose did not fold the paper up; she crushed it in her hand and lay down again without a word.

"Huh, I tell you, Rose, a family's a torment. I never wanted mine. God love, Rose, I'd lay down my life for 'em; I'd cut myself into fourpenny pieces so they shouldn't come to harm; if one of 'em was to die I'd sorrow to my grave. But I know, I know, I know I never wanted 'em, they were not for me, I was just an excuse for their blundering into the world. Somehow I've been duped, and every woman born is duped so, one ways or another in the end. I had my sport with my man, but I ought never to have married. Now I'd love to begin all over again, and as God's my maker, if it weren't for those children, I'd be gone off out into the world again tomorrow, Rose. But I dunno what 'ud become o' me."

The wind blew strongly athwart the yellow field, and the odour of mustard rushed upon the brooding women. Protestingly the breeze flung itself upon the forest; there was a gliding cry among the rocking pinions as of some lost wave seeking a forgotten shore. The angular faggot under Dinah Lock had begun to vex her; she too sunk to the ground and lay beside Rose Olliver, who asked:

"And what 'ud become of your old man?"

For a few moments Dinah Lock paused. She too took a sprig of the mustard and fondled it with her lips. "He's no man now, the illness feebled him, and the virtue's gone; no man at all since two years, and bald as a piece of cheese—I like a hairy man, like —do you remember Rufus Blackthorn, used to be gamekeeper here?"

Rose stopped playing with her flower. "Yes, I knew Rufus Blackthorn."

"A fine bold man that was! Never another like him hereabouts, not in England neither; not in the whole world—though I've heard some queer talk of those foreigners, Australians, Chinymen. Well!"

"Well?" said Rose.

"He was a devil." Dinah Lock began to whisper. "A perfect devil; I can't say no fairer than that. I wish I could, but I can't."

"Oh come," protested Rose, "he was a kind man. He'd never see anybody want for a thing."

"No," there was playful scorn in Dinah's voice; "he'd shut his eyes first!"

"Not to a woman he wouldn't, Dinah."

"Ah! Well—perhaps—he was good to women."

"I could tell you things as would surprise you," murmured Rose.

"You! But—well—no, no. I could tell *you* things as you wouldn't believe. Me and Rufus! We was—oh my—yes!"

"He *was* handsome."

"Oh, a pretty man!" Dinah acceded warmly. "Black as coal and bold as a fox. I'd been married nigh on ten years when he first set foot in these parts. I'd got three children then. He used to give me a saucy word whenever he saw me, for I liked him and he knew it. One Whitsun Monday I was home all alone, the children were gone somewheres, and Tom was away boozing. I was putting some plants in our garden—I loved a good flower in those days—I wish the world was all a garden, but now my Tom he digs 'em up, digs everything up proper and never puts 'em back. Why, we had a crocus once! And as I was doing that planting someone walked by the garden in such a hurry. I looked up and there was Rufus, all dressed up to the nines, and something made me call out to him. "Where be you off to in that flaming hurry?" I says. "Going to a wedding," says he. "Shall I come with 'ee?" I says. "Ah yes," he says, very glad; "but hurry up, for I be sharp set and all." So I run in-a-doors and popped on my things and off we went to Jim Pickering's wedding over at Clackford Mill. When Jim brought the bride home from church that Rufus got hold of a gun and fired it off up chimney, and down come the soot, bushels of it! All over the room, and a chimney-pot burst and rattled down the tiles into a prambulator. What a rumbullion that was! But no one got angry—there was plenty of drink and we danced all the afternoon. Then we come home together again through the woods. Oh lord, I said to myself, I shan't come out with you ever again, and that's what I said to Rufus Blackthorn. But I did, you know! I woke up in bed that night, and the moon shone on me dreadful—I thought the place was afire. But there was Tom snoring, and I lay and thought of me and Rufus in the wood, till I could have jumped out into the moonlight, stark, and flown over the chimney. I didn't sleep any more. And I saw Rufus the next night, and the night after that, often, often. Whenever I went out I left Tom the cupboardful—that's all he troubled about. I was mad after Rufus, and while that caper was on I couldn't love my husband. No."

"No?" queried Rose.

"Well, I pretended I was ill, and I took my young Katey to sleep with me, and give Tom her bed. He didn't seem to mind, but after a while I found he was gallivanting after other women. Course, I soon put a stopper on that. And then—what do you think? Bless me if Rufus weren't up to the same tricks! Deep as the sea, that man. Faithless, you know, but such a bold one."

Rose lay silent, plucking wisps of grass; there was a wry smile on her face.

"Did ever he tell you the story of the man who was drowned?" she asked at length. Dinah shook her head. Rose continued. "Before he came here he was keeper over in that Oxfordshire, where the river goes right through the woods, and he slept in a boathouse moored to the bank. Some gentleman was drowned near there, an accident it was, but they couldn't find the body. So they offered a reward of ten pound for it to be found."

"Ten, ten pounds!"

"Yes. Well, all the watermen said the body wouldn't come up for ten days."

"No, more they do."

"It didn't. And so late one night—it was moonlight—some men in a boat kept on hauling and poking round the house where Rufus was, and he heard 'em say: "It must be here, it must be here," and Rufus shouts out to them: "Course he's here! I got him in bed with me!""

"Aw!" chuckled Dinah.

"Yes, and next day he got the ten pounds, because he *had* found the body and hidden it away."

"Feared nothing," said Dinah, "nothing at all; he'd have been rude to Satan. But he was very delicate with his hands, sewing and things like that. I used to say to him: 'Come, let me mend your coat,' or whatever it was, but he never would, always did such things of himself. 'I don't allow no female to patch my clothes,' he'd say, ' 'cos they works with a red-hot needle and a burning thread.' And he used to make fine little slippers out of reeds."

"Yes," Rose concurred, "he made me a pair."

"You!" Dinah cried. "What—were you—?"

Rose turned her head away. "We was all cheap to him," she said softly, "cheap as old rags; we was like chaff before him."

Dinah Lock lay still, very still, ruminating; but whether in old grief or new rancour Rose was not aware, and she probed no further. Both were quiet, voiceless, recalling the past delirium. They shivered, but did not rise. The wind increased in the forest, its hoarse breath sorrowed in the yellow field, and swift masses of cloud flowed and twirled in a sky without end and full of gloom.

"Hallo!" cried a voice, and there was Amy beside them, with a faggot almost overwhelming her. "Shan't stop now," she said, "for I've got this faggot perched just right, and I shouldn't ever get it up again. I found a shilling in the 'ood, you," she continued shrilly and gleefully. "Come along to my house after tea, and we'll have a quart of stout."

"A shilling, Amy!" cried Rose.

"Yes," called Mrs. Hardwick, trudging steadily on. "I tried to find the fellow to it, but no more luck. Come and wet it after tea!"

"Rose," said Dinah, "come on." She and Rose with much circumstance heaved up their faggots and tottered after, but by then Amy had turned out of sight down the little lane to Pollock's Cross.

"Your children will be home," said Rose as they went along, "they'll be looking out for you."

"Ah, they'll want their bellies filling!"

"It must be lovely a-winter's nights, you setting round your fire with 'em, telling tales, and brushing their hair."

"Ain't you got a fire of your own indoors?" grumbled Dinah.

"Yes."

"Well, why don't you set by it then!" Dinah's faggot caught the briars of a hedge that overhung, and she tilted round with a mild oath. A covey of partridges feeding beyond scurried away with ruckling cries. One foolish bird dashed into the telegraph wires and dropped dead.

"They're good children, Dinah, yours are. And they make you a valentine, and give you a ribbon on your birthday, I expect?"

"They're naught but a racket from cockcrow till the old man snores—and then it's worse!"

"Oh, but the creatures, Dinah!"

"You—you got your quiet trim house, and only your man to look after, a kind man, and you'll set with him in the evenings and play your dominoes or your draughts, and he'll look at you—the nice man—over the board, and stroke your hand now and again."

The wind hustled the two women close together, and as they stumbled under their burdens Dinah Lock stretched out a hand and touched the other woman's arm. "I like you, Rose, I wish you was a man."

Rose did not reply. Again they were quiet, voiceless, and thus in fading light they came to their homes. But how windy, dispossessed, and ravaged roved the darkening world! Clouds were borne frantically across the heavens, as if in a rout of battle, and the lovely earth seemed to sigh in grief at some calamity all unknown to men.

The Field of Mustard (1926)

THE THIRD PRIZE

NABOTH BIRD and George Robins were very fond of footracing. Neither of them was a champion runner, but each loved to train and to race; that was their pastime, their passion, their principal absorption and topic of conversation; occasionally it brought one or the other of them some sort of trophy.

One August bank holiday in the late nineties they travelled fifty miles to compete in a town where prizes of solid cash were to be given instead of the usual objects of glittering inutility. The town was a big town with a garrison and a dockyard. It ought to have been a city, and it would have been a city had not the only available cathedral been just inside an annoying little snob of a borough that kept itself (and its cathedral: admission sixpence) to itself just outside the boundaries of the real and proper town. On their arrival they found almost the entire populace wending to the carnival of games in a long stream of soldiers, sailors, and quite ordinary people, harried by pertinacious and vociferous little boys who yelled: "Program?" and blind beggars who just stood in the way and said nothing. Out of this crowd two jolly girls, Margery and Minnie, by some pleasant alchemy soon attached themselves to our two runners. Margery and Minnie were very different from each other. Why young maidens who hunt in couples and invariably dress alike should differ as much in character and temperament as Boadicea and Mrs. Hemans affords a speculation as fantastic as it is futile. They were different from each other, as different as a sherry cobbler and pineapple syrup, but they were not more different than were the two lads. The short snub one was Nab Bird; a mechanic by trade, with the ambition of a bus-conductor, he sold bicycle tires and did odd things to perambulators in a shed at the corner of a street; the demure Minnie became his friend. George Robins, a cute good-looking clerk, devoted his gifts of gallantry to Margery, and none the less readily because she displayed some qualities not commonly associated with demureness.

"From London you come!" exclaimed George. "How'd you get here?"

The young lady crisply testified that she came in a train—did the fathead think she had swum? They were jolly glad when they got here, too and all. Carriage full, and ructions all the way.

"Ructions! What ructions?"

"Boozy men! Half of 'em trying to cuddle you."

Mr. Robins intimated that he could well understand such desires. Miss Margery retorted that then he was understanding much more than was good for him. Mr. Robins thought not, he hoped not. Miss Margery indicated that he could hope for much more than he was likely to get. Mr. Robins replied that, he would do that, and then double it. And he asserted, with all respect, that had he but happily been in that train he too might have, etc. and so on. Whereupon Miss Margery snapped, Would he? and Mr. Robins felt bound to say Sure!

"Would you—well, I'll tell you what I did to one of them." And she told him. It was quite unpleasant.

"Lady!" cried George sternly, "I hope you won't serve me like that."

"'Pends on how you behave."

"How do you want me to behave?"

"Well, how *should* you behave to a lady?"

"'Pends on what's expected of me." George delivered it with a flash of satisfaction.

"Oh, go on," she retorted, "you're as bad as the rest of 'em. It depends really on what is expected of me, don't it?"

"Oh, you're all right," he replied, "you're as good as they make 'em."

"How do you know?"

"Well, ain't you?"

"I'm as good as I *can* be. Is that good enough for you?"

" 'Pends on how good that is."

Margery declared her unqualified abhorrence of his sort of goodness.

"I'm all right when I *am* all right," George assured her.

"I know all about you!" There was a twinkle in her eyes.

"Do you!" interjected Nab; "then you know more than he'd like his mother to know."

They arrived at the sports field. Already there were ten thousand people there, and the bookmakers, having assembled their easels, cards, and boxes, were surrounded by betting men. The space adjacent to the arena was occupied by a gala fair with roundabouts, shies, booths, swings, and other uproarious seductions. The track was encircled by a wedge of onlookers ironic or enthusiastic, the sports began, runners came and went, the bookmakers stayed and roared, the hurdy gurdies lamented or rejoiced, the vanquished explained their defeats in terms that brought grins of commiseration to the faces of the victors, who explained their successes in terms that brought gleams of pride and triumph into the eyes of all who attended them. Very beautiful and bright the day was; the air smelt of grass, fusees, and cokernuts. Amongst those scantily garbed figures on the track Margery and Minnie scarcely recognized the young men they had accompanied, and for a long time they were unaware that George had won the third prize in a mile race.

Like all the other prize-winners he was subjected to the extravagant cajoleries of Jerry Chambers, a cockney ruffian living by his wits, a calling that afforded him no very great margin of security. He had lost his money, he was without a penny, and in the dressing-room he fastened himself upon Robins and Bird in an effort to obtain something or other, little or much, from each or either.

"I tell you," he darkly whispered, "the winner of the mile is a stiff un."

"What's a stiff un?" inquired Nab Bird.

"A stiff un! What a stiff un is!" Chambers's amusement at this youth's boundless ignorance was shrill and genuine. "Why, he's run under an assumed name and got about sixty yards the best of the handicap. You was third in that race, Robins, and the winner was a stiff un. Make it worth my while and I'll get him pinched for impersonation. Know him!—I knew his father! I'll tell you what I'll do, I'll get the second man disqualified as well —how will that stand you? Give me a dollar now so I can lodge the objection at once and the first prize must be awarded to you, it must. A five-pound note ain't it? I backed you to win myself and I don't like losing my money to a stiff un—I took ten pound to two about you. Now half a dollar won't hurt you. You won't! Well, good God Almighty!"—Chambers tilted his hat over one eye and scratched his neck—"don't let me try to persuade you. Lend us a tanner."

"To hell with you!"

"Make it eighteen pence, then."

They did not. At the distribution of the prize money, there was much ringing of a bell, shouting of names, and some factitious applause as a pert and portly lady of title appeared at a table in front of the pavilion to perform the ceremony. It was the only titled person our friends had ever seen, and the announcement of her grand name and the sound of her voice despite her appearance—for though she was a countess she had a stomach like a publican's wife—affected them occultly. A very gentlemanly steward, in private life a vendor of fish, bawled out the names of the prize-winners, and when it came to the turn of George Robins he was surprised to hear:

"Third prize in the mile race: W. Ballantyne."

He hesitated.

"It's wrong, O George!" gasped Nab Bird, "it's a mistake."

Nobody responding to the call for W. Ballantyne, George suddenly exchanged hats with his friend. Giving Nab his tweed cap he seized Nab's bowler hat and, although it was far too small, put it on his own head, where it looked much as it would have done on the bust of Homer.

"What—George, what?" asked his bewildered friend amid the

chuckles of the two girls, but without stopping to explain, George Robins pushed his way through the crowd, advanced to the table, and received in the name of W. Ballantyne his own prize of a sovereign, which he acknowledged by just raising his terrible headgear and blowing his nose with a large handkerchief.

"Thanks, Nab," said he, returning to his friends. "I'll have my cap again."

The presentation concluded, the lady of title shook hands with the gentleman fishmonger and they went, presumably, their separate ways, while part of the crowd drifted gaily over to the fair booths and the rest went home to tea. With a mysterious preoccupied air George directed Nab to take the girls into a tent for tea and await him there.

"We'll look after him," declared Minnie, linking her arm with Nab's.

"But where you going, O George?" exclaimed the puzzled one, as Margery, too, linked an arm in his.

"See you later, five minutes, only five minutes. Take him away," shouted the departing George to the girls, "give him a bun and don't let him make his face jammy."

So Nab went to tea with the girls, and says he:

"I wonder what he's up to."

"Didn't he run well?" said Minnie.

"Beautiful," agreed Margery.

"I don't want no tea," declared Nab, "I'm 'ot, but I'll have a couple of them saveloys, and then for a glass of ice cream-o. But you have just what you like, Minnie and Margery."

They had what they could get, and then, as Nab for the twentieth time was audibly wondering what George was "up to" and Margery for the dozenth time was realizing how splendidly he had run, George himself reappeared beaming with satisfaction.

"Where you been to, O George?"

"Been to get my prize."

"What prize?"

"In the mile."

"Third prize?"

"Didn't I win it?"

"But you got that before, didn't you?"

"Did I?"

"Well, 'aven't you?"

"Have I?"

Nab was mystified, George was triumphant: "I'll explain it to you. Listen, O Little Naboth. That third prize was awarded by some mischance to a chap the name of Ballantyne. Well, there wasn't any Ballantyne won that prize. The winner was G. Robins, that's me."

"Yes."

"So I go to the secretary of the sports and I say to him: 'Excuse me, sir, I'm George Robins, I won third prize in the mile, but there has been a mistake, and the prize has been given to some-one called Ballantyne. What am I to do?' Well, there was a lot of palavering and running about and seeing stewards, but at last they found out that what I said was absolutely true and so they gave me another sovereign."

"Two lots of prize money you got, then!" ejaculated Nab, "two quid!"

George nodded modestly. "And they apologized for the mistake!"

"My goodness, isn't he—!" remarked Margery admiringly to Minnie, and Minnie too appeared to think he was—! But Nab was perturbed. Margery's observation—"All's fair in love and war!"—did not seem very pertinent to Nab and he corrected her:

"Love and war's one thing, sport's another."

"Sport!" exclaimed George. "But you know what these professionals are, you daren't trust 'em. Jerry Chambers, now, how about him if you met him on a dark night, eh? Any of these professionals would cut your throat for fivepence. They'd bag your boots and bone your bag and your skin too if you wasn't chained up inside it."

"Yes, O George, I know, but it wasn't them you done it to, it's the committee."

"Their look-out, ain't it? Their own mistake, not mine! It wasn't my mistake, now was it?"

"Well, no, but it's a bit like what Jerry Chambers might have done himself."

Margery interposed: "I think it was jolly smart, but you were a confederate—you lent him your hat."

"Of course! I borrowed that for disguise, see! But you shall share the swag, little Naboth, so don't keep grumbling and grumbling. Here's your half-a-james." Saying which, George stretched out a hand to his friend, who saw lying upon his palm a glittering sovereign. "Give me change for half of that!"

The girls sparklingly approved this offer of the magnanimous one, but Nab, a little confused, turned away saying:

"No, thanks, George O man, no, thanks."

Although they all surrounded Nab and tried to cajole him into acceptance, the little man was adamant—very kind of George, but he'd rather not. However, they all went away very amiably together, and it was apparent to Naboth Bird that his friend's questionable manœuvre was acclaimed by the girls as an admirable exploit, while his own qualms were regarded as an indecent exhibition of an honesty no less questionable.

Moving idly down a hill amongst the stream of people, they were brought to a standstill at the edge of a crowd surrounding an old blind beggar and his wife. The man was playing a hymn tune on a tin pipe. Tall and ragged, with white thin beard and clerical hat, there was the strange dignity inseparable from blindness in his erect figure, but his shuffling wife, older, and very feeble, held his arm with one hand and outstretched the other for the few pitying pence that came to them. George and his friends were astonished to perceive the ruffian Jerry Chambers standing mockingly in front of the beggars. His arms were spread out to the halting people, his hat had been flung upon the ground before him, he was making excruciating gestures and noises with his hands and mouth, yodelling like a costermonger and performing ridiculous antics to gain their attention. He was entirely successful; the good-natured holiday folk assembled and stretched across the road in a great crowd. With an ironical gesture of the hand Chambers directed the attention of the onlookers to the forlorn couple behind him.

"Look at 'em," he yelled, "look at 'em—roll, bowl, or pitch—but look at 'em! Did ever you see such a thing in your lives?"

He paused for a moment and then recommenced very gently: "People, men of my own fraternity! I ain't doing this bit of a job for myself—nor for no barney—nor for no bank-holiday rag. I'm a-doing this—just five minutes—for my compatriarch and his noble consort. Look at 'em, I say. I bin a-looking at 'em—I 'ad to —and it just breaks my heart. Well, you're not a brass-bellied lot —you don't look it—*your* hearts ain't made of tripe. So that's where I've pushed in."

The old man had forborne his solemn piping; he blinked the sightless eyes unobjectively upon the people, while his partner clung to him with both arms, bewildered and a little terrified.

"I am going," Chambers began to roar again, "to sing you a comical song. Shall then, if my old compatriarch will oblige with a tootle on his bangalorum, shall then dance you a jig. Shall then crawl upon my hands and knees, barking like a tiger, with my cady in me mouth to collect bullion for this suffering fambly. Look at 'em, lord alive, look at 'em!"

After singing so raucous and ridiculous a song that his kindly intentions were nearly defeated Chambers poised himself for the jig:

"Righto, play up, uncle!"

But the old beggar could only repeat the one tune, his hymn called *Marching to Zion.*

"God A'mighty! 'ark at 'im!" cried the baffled Chambers. "Well, you people, men of my own fraternity, it's no go; 'ere's my cadging 'at—give us a good whip round for those two old bits of mutton!"

So the old man piped his hymn while the cockney ruffian begged and bullied a handful of money for them. Chaffing and scolding, he approached George; Margery was searching for a coin.

"It's all right," whispered George to her, "it's all right." He showed her the coin already in his fingers, the glittering questionable sovereign. She clutched his arm to prevent such a sacrifice, but she was too late, George dropped the coin into Chambers's hat and then, curiously shamefaced, at once walked away in a little drift of pleased excitement.

"Min, Min, d'you know what he's done!" cried Margery to the friends as they all followed after him, "he's given 'em that sovereign."

In the eyes of the dazzled girls the gesture crowned George with the last uttermost grace, and even Nab was mute before its sublimity. They hurried away as if the devil himself might be coming to thrust the sovereign back upon them.

And Chambers? His triumph, too, was great, the well-used occasion had won its well-devised reward, and his pleasure, though modestly expressed, was sincere.

"Ladies and gennermen," cried the jolly ruffian a few minutes later as he counted up the coin. "I thank you one and all for your kindness to this old couple and the very handsome collection (here y'are, uncle," he whispered, "it's splendid, eight shillings and fo'pence). All correct, thank you, ladies and gennermen. God bless the lot of yer," and then, leaving the delighted beggars to their gains, and murmuring to himself "Beau-tiful beautiful Zi-on!" he hurried rapidly away.

Silver Circus (1928)

THE WATERCRESS GIRL

WHEN Mary McDowall was brought to the assize court the place was crowded, Mr. O'Kane said, "inside out." It was a serious trial, as everybody—even the prisoner—well knew; twelve tons of straw had been thrown down on the roads outside the hall to deaden the noise of carts passing and suchlike pandemoniums, and when the judge drove up in his coach with jockeys on the horses, a couple of young trumpeters from the barracks stiffened on the steps and blew a terrible fanfare up into heaven. "For a sort of a warning, I should think," said Mr. O'Kane.

The prisoner's father, having been kicked by a horse, was unable to attend the trial, and so he had enlisted Mr. O'Kane to go and fetch him the news of it; and Mr. O'Kane in obliging his friend suffered annoyances and was abused in the court itself by a great fat geezer of a fellow with a long staff. "If you remained on your haunches when the judge came in," complained Mr. O'Kane, "you were poked up, and if you stood up to get a look at the prisoner when *she* came in you were poked down. Surely to God we didn't go to look at the judge!"

Short was her trial, for the evidence was clear, and the guilt not denied. Prisoner neither sorrowed for her crime nor bemoaned her fate; passive and casual she stood there at the willing of the court for a thing she had done, and there were no tears now in Mary McDowall. Most always she dressed in black, and she was in black then, with masses of black hair; a pale face with a dark mole on the chin, and rich red lips; a big girl of twenty-five, not coarsely big, and you could guess she was strong. A passionate girl, caring nothing or not much for this justice; unimpressed by the solemn court, nor moved to smile at its absurdities; for all that passion concerns with is love—or its absence—love that gives its only gift by giving all. If you could have read her mind, not now but in its calm before the stress of her misfortune, you would have learned this much, although she herself could not have formulated it: I will give to love all it is in me to give; I shall desire of love all I can ever dream of and receive.

And because another woman had taken what Mary McDowall wanted, Mary had flung a corrosive acid in the face of her enemy, and Elizabeth Plantney's good looks were gone, gone for certain and for ever. So here was Mary McDowall and over there was Frank Oppidan; not a very fine one to mislead the handsome girl in the dock, but he had done it, and he too had suffered and the women in court had pity for him, and the men—envy. Tall, with light oiled hair and pink sleepy features (a pink heart, too, you might think, though you could not see it), he gave evidence against her in a nasal tone with a confident manner, and she did not waste a look on him. A wood-turner he was, and for about four years had "kept company" with the prisoner, who lived near a village a mile or two away from his home. He had often urged her to marry him, but she would not, so a little while ago he told her he was going to marry Elizabeth Plantney. A few evenings láter he had been strolling with Elizabeth Plantney on the road outside the town. It was not yet dark, about eight o'clock, but they had not observed the prisoner, who must have been dogging them, for she came slyly up and passed by them, turned, splashed something in his companion's face, and then walked on. She didn't run; at first they thought it was some stupid joke, and he was for going after the prisoner, whom he had recognized.

"I was mad angry," declared Oppidan, "I could have choked her. But Miss Plantney began to scream that she was blinded and burning, and I had to carry and drag her some ways back along the road until we came to the first house, Mr. Blackfriar's, where they took her in and I ran off for the doctor." The witness added savagely: "I wish I *had* choked her."

There was full corroboration, prisoner had admitted guilt, and the counsel briefed by her father could only plead for a lenient sentence. A big man he was with a drooping yellow moustache and terrific teeth; his cheeks and hands were pink as salmon.

"Accused," he said, "is the only child of Fergus McDowall. She lives with her father, a respectable widower, at a somewhat retired cottage in the valley of Trinkel, assisting him in the conduct of his business—a small holding by the river where he cultivates watercress, and keeps bees and hens and things of that kind. The witness Oppidan had been in the habit of cycling from his town to the McDowalls' home to buy bunches of watercress, a delicacy of which, in season, he seems to have been—um—in-ordinately fond, for he would go twice, thrice, and often four times a week. His visits were not confined to the purchase of watercress, and he seems to have made himself agreeable to the daughter of the house; but I am in possession of no information as to the nature of their intercourse beyond that tendered by the witness Oppidan. Against my advice the prisoner, who is a very reticent, even a remarkable, woman, has insisted on pleading guilty and accepting her punishment without any—um—chance of mitigation, in a spirit, I hope, of contrition, which is not—um—entirely unadmirable. My lord, I trust . . ."

While the brutal story was being recounted, the prisoner had stood with closed eyes, leaning her hands upon the rail of the dock; stood and dreamed of what she had not revealed:

Of her father, Fergus McDowall; his child she was, although he had never married. That much she knew, but who her mother had been he never told her, and it did not seem to matter; she guessed rather than knew that at her birth she had died, or soon afterwards, and the man had fostered her. He and she had always been together, alone, ever since she could remember, always together, always happy, he was so kind; and so splendid in the great boots that drew up to his thighs when he worked in the watercress beds, cutting bunches deftly or cleaning the weeds from the water. And there were her beehives, her flock of hens, the young pigs, and a calf that knelt and rubbed its neck on the rich mead with a lavishing movement just as the ducks did when the grass was dewy. She had seen the young pigs, no bigger than rabbits, race across the patch of greensward to the blue-roan calf standing nodding in the shade; they would prowl beneath the calf, clustering round its feet, and begin to gnaw the calf's hoof until, full of patience, she would gently lift her leg and shake it, but would not move away. Save for a wildness of mood that sometimes flashed through her, Mary was content, and loved the life that she could not know was lonely with her father beside the watercress streams. He was uncommunicative, like Mary, but as he worked he hummed to himself or whistled the soft tunes that at night he played on the clarinet. Tall and strong, a handsome man. Sometimes he would put his arms around her and say: "Well, my dear." And she would kiss him. She had vowed to herself that she would never leave him, but then—Frank had come. In this mortal conflict we seek not only that pleasure may not divide us from duty, but that duty may not detach us from life. He was not the first man or youth she could or would have loved, but he was the one who had wooed her; first-love's enlightening delight, in the long summer eyes, in those enticing fields! How easily she was won! All his offers of marriage she had put off with the answer: "No, it would never do for me," or "I shall never marry," but then, if he angrily swore or accused her of not loving him enough, her fire and freedom would awe him almost as much as it enchanted. And she might have married Frank if she could only have told him of her dubious origin, but whether from some vagrant modesty, loyalty to her father, or some reason whatever, she could not bring herself to do that. Often these steady refusals enraged her lover, and after such occasions he would not seek her again for weeks, but in the end he always returned, although his absences grew longer as their friendship lengthened. Ah, when the way to your lover is long, there's but a short cut to the end. Came a time when he did not return at all and then, soon, Mary found she was going to have a child. "Oh, I wondered where you were, Frank, and why you were there, wherever it was, instead of where I could find you." But the fact was portentous enough to depose her grief at his fickleness, and after a while she took no further care or thought for Oppidan, for she feared that like her own mother she would die of her child. Soon these fears left her and she rejoiced. Certainly she need not scruple to tell him of her own origin now, he could never reproach her now. Had he come once more, had he come then, she would have married him. But although he might have been hers for the lifting of a finger, as they say, her pride kept her from calling him into the trouble, and she did not call him and he never sought her again. When her father realized her condition he merely said "Frank?" and she nodded.

The child was early born, and she was not prepared; it came and died. Her father took it and buried it in the garden. It was a boy, dead. No one else knew, not even Frank, but when she was recovered, her pride wavered and she wrote a loving letter to him, still keeping her secret. Not until she had written three times did she hear from him, and then he only answered that he should not see her any more. He did not tell her why, but she knew. He was going to marry Elizabeth Plantney, whose parents had died and left her five hundred pounds. To Mary's mind that presented itself as a treachery to their child, the tiny body buried under a beehive in the garden. That Frank was unaware made no difference to the girl's fierce mood; it was treachery. Maternal anger stormed in her breast, it could only be allayed by an injury, a deep admonishing injury to that treacherous man. In her sleepless nights the little crumpled corpse seemed to plead for this much, and her own heart clamoured, just as those bees murmured against him day by day.

So then she got some vitriol. Rushing past her old lover on the night of the crime, she turned upon him with the lifted jar, but the sudden confrontation dazed and tormented her; in momentary hesitation she had dashed the acid, not into *his* faithless eyes, but at the prim creature linked to his arm. Walking away, she heard the crying of the wounded girl. After a while she had turned back to the town and given herself up to the police.

To her mind, as she stood leaning against the dock rail, it was all huddled and contorted, but that was her story set in its order. The trial went droning on beside her remembered grief like a dull stream neighbouring a clear one, two parallel streams that would meet in the end, were meeting now, surely, as the judge began to speak. And at the crisis, as if in exculpation, she suffered a whisper to escape her lips, though none heard it.

" 'Twas him made me a parent, but he was never a man himself. He took advantage; it was mean, I love Christianity." She heard the judge deliver her sentence: for six calendar months she was to be locked in a jail. "Oh Christ!" she breathed, for it was the lovely spring; lilac, laburnum, and father wading the brooks in those boots drawn up to his thighs to rake the dark sprigs and comb out the green scum.

They took her away. "I wanted to come out then," said Mr. O'Kane, "for the next case was only about a contractor defrauding the corporation—good luck to him, but he got three years—and I tried to get out of it, but if I did that geezer with the stick poked me down and said I'd not to stir out of it till the court rose. I said to him I'd kill him, but there was a lot of peelers about so I suppose he didn't hear it."

II

Towards the end of the year Oppidan had made up his mind what he would do to Mary McDowall when she came out of prison. Poor Liz was marred for life, spoiled, cut off from the joys they had intended together. Not for all the world would he marry her now; he had tried to bring himself to that issue of chivalry, of decency, but it was impossible; he had failed in the point of grace. No man could love Elizabeth Plantney now, Frank could not visit her without shuddering, and she herself, poor generous wretch, had given him back his promise. Apart from his ruined fondness for her, they had planned to do much with the five hundred pounds; it was to have set him up in a secure and easy way of trade, they would have been established in a year or two as solid as a rock. All that chance was gone, no such chance ever came twice in a man's lifetime, and he was left with Liz upon his conscience. He would have to be kind to her for as long as he could stand it. That was a disgust to his mind, for he wanted to be faithful. Even the most unstable man wishes he had been faithful—but to which woman he is never quite sure. And then that bitch Mary McDowall would come out of her prison and be a mockery to him of what he had forgone, of what he had been deprived. Savagely he believed in the balance wrought by an act of vengeance—he, too!—eye for eye, tooth for tooth; it had a threefold charm, simplicity, relief, triumph. The McDowall girl, so his fierce meditations ran, miked in prison for six months and then came out no worse than when she went in. It was no punishment at all, they did no hurt to women in prison; the court hadn't set wrong right at all, it never did; and he was a loser whichever way he turned. But there was still a thing he could do (Jove had slumbered, he would steal Jove's lightning) and a project lay troubling his mind like a gnat in the eye, he would have no peace until it was wiped away.

On an October evening, then, about a week after Mary Mc-Dowall's release, Oppidan set off towards Trinkel. Through Trinkel he went and a furlong past it until he came to their lane. Down the lane too, and then he could hear the water ruttling over the cataracts of the cress-beds. Not yet in winter, the year's decline was harbouring splendour everywhere. Whitebeam was a dissolute tangle of rags covering ruby drops, the service trees were sallow as lemons, the oak resisted decay, but most confident of all the tender-tressed ashes. The man walked quietly to a point where, unobserved, he could view the McDowall dwelling, with its overbowering walnut tree littering the yard with husks and leaves, its small adjacent field with banks that stooped in the glazed water. The house was heavy and small, but there were signs of grace in the garden, of thrift in the orderly painted sheds. The conical peak of a tiny stack was pitched in the afterglow, the elms sighed like tired old matrons, wisdom and content lingered here. Oppidan crept along the hedges until he was in a field at the back of the house, a hedge still hiding him. He was trembling. There was a light already in the back window; one leaf of the window stood open and he saw their black cat jump down from it into the garden and slink away under some shrubs. From his standpoint he could not see into the lighted room, but he knew enough of Fergus's habits to be sure he was not within; it was his day for driving into the town. Thus it could only be Mary who had lit that lamp. Trembling still! Just beyond him was a heap of dung from the stable, and a cock was standing silent on the dunghill while two hens, a white one and a black, bickered around him over some voided grains. Presently the cock seized the black hen, and the white scurried away; but though his grasp was fierce and he bit at her red comb, the black hen went on gobbling morsels from the manure heap, and when at last he released her she did not intermit her steady pecking. Then Oppidan was startled by a flock of starlings that slid across the evening with the steady movement of a cloud; the noise of their wings was like showers of rain upon trees.

"Wait till it's darker," he muttered, and skulking back to the lane he walked sharply for half a mile. Then, slowly, he returned. Unseen, he reached the grass that grew under the lighted window, and stooped warily against the wall; one hand rested on the wall, the other in his pocket. For some time he hesitated but he knew what he had to do and what did it matter! He stepped in front of the window.

In a moment, and for several moments longer, he was rigid with surprise. It was Mary all right (the bitch!), washing her hair, drying it in front of the kitchen fire, the thick locks pouring over her face as she knelt with her hands resting on her thighs. So long was their black flow that the ends lay in a small heap inside the fender. Her bodice hung on the back of a chair beside her, and her only upper clothing was a loose and disarrayed chemise that did not hide her bosom. Then, gathering the hair in her hands, she held the tresses closer to the fire, her face peeped through, and to herself she was smiling. Dazzling fair were her arms and the one breast he astonishingly saw. It was Mary; but not the Mary, dull ugly creature, whom his long rancour had conjured for him. Lord, what had he forgotten! Absence and resentment had pared away her loveliness from his recollection, but this was the old Mary of their passionate days, transfigured and marvellous.

Stepping back from the window into shadow again, he could feel his heart pound like a frantic hammer; every pulse was hurrying at the summons. In those breathless moments Oppidan gazed as it were at himself, or at his mad intention, gazed wonderingly, ashamed and awed. Fingering the thing in his pocket, turning it over as a coin whose toss has deceived him, he was aware of a revulsion; gone revenge, gone rancour, gone all thought of Elizabeth, and there was left in his soul what had not gone and could never go. A brute she had been—it was bloody cruelty—but, but—but what? Seen thus, in her innocent occupation, the grim fact of her crime had somehow thrown a conquering glamour over her hair, the pale pride of her face, the intimacy of her bosom. Her very punishment was a triumph; on what account had she suffered if not for love of him? He could feel that chastening distinction melting now; she had suffered for his love.

There and then shrill cries burst upon them. The cat leaped from the garden to the window-sill; there was a thrush in its mouth, shrieking. The cat paused on the sill, furtive and hesitant. Without a thought Oppidan plunged forward, seized the cat, and with his free hand clutched what he could of the thrush. In a second the cat released it and dropped into the room, while the crushed bird fluttered away to the darkened shrubs, leaving its tail feathers in the hand of the man.

Mary sprang up and rushed to the window. "Is it you?" was all she said. Hastily she left the window, and Oppidan with a grin saw her shuffling into her bodice. One hand fumbled at the buttons, the other unlatched the door. "Frank." There was neither surprise nor elation. He walked in. Only then did he open his fist and the thrush's feathers floated in the air and idled to the floor. Neither of them remembered any more of the cat or the bird.

In silence they stood, not looking at each other.

"What do you want?" at length she asked. "You're hindering me."

"Am I?" He grinned. His face was pink and shaven, his hair

was almost as smooth as a brass bowl. "Well, I'll tell you." His hat was cumbering his hands, so he put it carefully on the table.

"I come here wanting to do a bad thing, I own up to that. I had it in my mind to serve you same as you served her—you know who I mean. Directly I knew you had come home, that's what I meant to do. I been waiting about out there a good while until I saw you. And then I saw you. I hadn't seen you for a long, long time, and somehow, I dunno, when I saw you—"

Mary was standing with her hands on her hips; the black cascades of her hair rolled over her arms; some of the strands were gathered under her fingers, looped to her waist; dark weeping hair.

"I didn't mean to harm her!" she burst out. "I never meant that for her, not what I did. Something happened to me that I'd not told you of then, and it doesn't matter now, and I shall never tell you. It was you I wanted to put a mark on, but directly I was in front of you I went all swavy, and I couldn't. But I had to throw it, I had to throw it."

He sat down on a chair, and she stared at him across the table. "All along it was meant for you, and that's God's truth."

"Why?" he asked. She did not give him an answer then, but stood rubbing the fingers of one hand on the finely scrubbed boards of the table, tracing circles and watching them vacantly. At last she put a question:

"Did you get married soon?"

"No," he said.

"Aren't you? But of course it's no business of mine."

"I'm not going to marry her."

"Not?"

"No, I tell you I wouldn't marry her for five thousand pounds, nor for fifty thousand, I wouldn't." He got up and walked up and down before the fire. "She's—aw! You don't know, you don't know what you done to her! She'd frighten you. It's rotten, like a leper. A veil on indoors and out, has to wear it always. She don't often go out, but whether or no, she must wear it. Ah, it's cruel."

There was a shock of horror as well as the throb of tears in her passionate compunction. "And you're not marrying her!"

"No," he said bluntly, "I'm not marrying her."

Mary covered her face with her hands and stood quivering under her dark weeping hair.

"God forgive me, how pitiful I'm shamed!" Her voice rose in a sharp cry. "Marry her, Frank! Oh, you marry her now, you must!"

"Not for a million, I'd sooner be in my grave."

"Frank Oppidan, you're no man, no man at all. You never had the courage to be strong, nor the courage to be evil; you've only the strength to be mean."

"Oh, dry up!" he said testily; but something overpowered her and she went leaning her head sobbing against the chimney-piece.

"Come on, girl!" he was instantly tender, his arms were around her, he had kissed her.

"Go your ways!" She was loudly resentful. "I want no more of you."

"It's all right, Mary. Mary, I'm coming to you again, just as I used to."

"You . . ." She swung out of his embrace. "What for? D'ye think I want you now? Go off to Elizabeth Plantney . . ." She faltered. "Poor thing, poor thing, it shames me pitiful; I'd sooner have done it to myself. Oh, I wish I had."

With a meek grin Oppidan took from his pocket a bottle with a glass stopper. "Do you know what that is?"

It looked like a flask of scent. Mary did not answer. "Sulphuric," continued he, "same as you threw at her."

The girl silently stared while he moved his hand as if he were weighing the bottle. "When I saw what a mess you'd made of her, I reckoned you'd got off too light, it ought to have been seven years for you. I only saw it once, and my inside turned right over, you've no idea. And I thought: there's she—done for. Nobody could marry her, less he was blind. And there's you, just a six months and out you come right as ever. That's how I thought and I wanted to get even with you then, for her sake, not for mine, so I got this, the same stuff, and I came thinking to give you a touch of it."

Mary drew herself up with a sharp breath. "You mean—throw it at me?"

"That's what I meant, honour bright, but I couldn't—not now." He went on weighing the bottle in his hand.

"Oh, throw it, throw it!" she cried in bitter grief, but covering her face with her hands—perhaps in shame, perhaps fear.

"No, no, no, no." He slipped the bottle back into his pocket. "But why did you do it? She wouldn't hurt a fly. What good could it do you?"

"Throw it," she screamed, "throw it, Frank, let it blast me!"

"Easy, easy now. I wouldn't even throw it at a rat. See!" he cried. The bottle was in his hand again as he went to the open window and withdrew the stopper. He held it outside while the fluid bubbled to the grass; the empty bottle he tossed into the shrubs.

He sat down, his head bowed in his hands, and for some time neither spoke. Then he was aware that she had come to him, was standing there, waiting. "Frank," she said softly, "there's something I got to tell you." And she told him about the babe.

At first he was incredulous. No, no, that was too much for him to stomach! Very stupid and ironical he was until the girl's pale sincerity glowed through the darkness of his unbelief: "You don't believe! How could it not be true!"

"But I can't make heads or tails of it yet, Mary. You a mother, and I were a father!" Eagerly and yet mournfully he brooded. "If I'd 'a' known—I can't hardly believe it, Mary—so help me God, if I'd 'a' known—"

"You could done nothing, Frank."

"Ah, but I'd 'a' known! A man's never a man till that's come to him."

"Nor a woman's a woman, neither; that's true, I'm different now."

"I'd 'a' been his father, I tell you. Now I'm nothing. I didn't know of his coming, I never see, and I didn't know of his going, so I'm nothing still."

"You kept away from me. I was afraid at first and I wanted you, but you was no help to me, you kept away."

"I'd a right to know, didn't I? You could 'a' wrote and told me."

"I did write to you."

"But you didn't tell me nothing."

"You could 'a' come and see me," she returned austerely, "then you'd known. How could I write down a thing like that in a letter as anybody might open? Any dog or devil could play tricks with it when you was boozed or something."

"I ought 'a bin told, I ought 'a bin told." Stubbornly he maintained it. " 'Twasn't fair, you."

" 'Twasn't kind, you. You ought to 'a' come; I asked you, but you was sick o' me, Frank, sick o' me and mine. I didn't want any help, neither, 'twasn't that I wanted."

"Would you 'a' married me then?" Sharply but persuasively he probed for what she neither admitted nor denied. "Yes, yes, you would, Mary. 'Twould 'a' bin a scandal if I'd gone and married someone else."

When at last the truth about her own birth came out between them, oh, how ironically protestant he was! "God a'mighty, girl, what did you take me for! There's no sense in you. I'll marry you now, for good and all (this minute if we could), honour bright, and you know it, for I love you always and always. You were his mother, Mary, and I were his father! What was he like, that little son?"

Sadly the girl mused. "It was very small."

"Light hair?"

"No, like mine, dark it was."

"What colour eyes?"

She drew her fingers down through the long streams of hair. "It never opened its eyes." And her voice moved him so that he cried out: "My love, my love, life's before us; there's a many good fish in the sea. When shall us marry?"

"Let me go, Frank. And you'd better go now, you're hindering me, and father will be coming in, and—and—the cakes are burning!"

Snatching up a cloth, she opened the oven door and an odour of caraway rushed into the air. Inside the oven was a shelf full of little cakes in pans.

"Give us one," he begged, "and then I'll be off."

"You shall have two," she said, kneeling down by the oven. "One for you—mind, it's hot!" He seized it from the cloth and quickly dropped it into his pocket. "And another, from me," continued Mary. Taking the second cake, he knelt down and embraced the huddled girl.

"I wants another one," he whispered.

A quick intelligence swam in her eyes: "For?"

"Ah, for what's between us, dear Mary."

The third cake was given him, and they stood up. They moved towards the door. She lifted the latch.

"Good night, my love." Passively she received his kiss. "I'll come again tomorrow."

"No, Frank, don't ever come any more."

"Aw, I'm coming right enough," he cried cheerily and confidently as he stepped away.

And I suppose we must conclude that he did.

Fishmonger's Fiddle (1925)

FIFTY POUNDS

AFTER tea Phillip Repton and Eulalia Burnes discussed their gloomy circumstances. Repton was the precarious sort of London journalist, a dark deliberating man, lean and drooping, full of genteel unprosperity, who wrote articles about Single Tax, Diet and Reason, The Futility of this that and the other, or The Significance of the other that and this; all done with a bleak care and signed P. Stick Repton. Eulalia was brown-haired and hardy, undeliberating and intuitive; she had been milliner, clerk, domestic help, and something in a canteen; and P. Stick Repton had, as one commonly says, picked her up at a time when she was drifting about London without a penny in her purse, without even a purse, and he had not yet put her down.

"I can't understand! It's sickening, monstrous!" Lally was fumbling with a match before the penny gas fire, for when it was evening, in September, it always got chilly on a floor so high up. Their flat was a fourth-floor one and there was—oh, fifteen thousand stairs! Out of the window and beyond the chimney you could see the long glare from lights in High Holborn and hear the hums and hoots of buses. And that was a comfort.

"Lower! Turn it lower!" yelled Phillip. The gas had ignited with an astounding thump; the kneeling Lally had thrown up her hands and dropped the matchbox saying "Damn" in the same tone as one might say good morning to a milkman.

"You shouldn't do it, you know," grumbled Repton. "You'll blow us to the deuce." And that was just like Lally, that was Lally all over, always: the gas, the nobs of sugar in his tea, the way she . . . and the, the . . . oh dear, dear! In their early life together, begun so abruptly and illicitly six months before, her simple hidden beauties had delighted him by their surprises; they had peered and shone brighter, had waned and recurred; she was less the one star in his universe than a faint galaxy.

This room of theirs was a dingy room, very small but very high. A lanky gas tube swooped from the middle of the ceiling towards the middle of the tablecloth as if burning to discover whether that was pink or saffron or fawn—and it *was* hard to tell—but on perceiving that the cloth, whatever its tint, was disturbingly spangled with dozens of cup-stains and several large envelopes, the gas tube in the violence of its disappointment contorted itself abruptly, assumed a lateral bend, and put out its tongue of flame at an oleograph of Mona Lisa which hung above the fireplace.

Those envelopes were the torment to Lally; they were the sickening monstrous manifestations which she could not understand. There were always some of them lying there, or about the room, bulging with manuscripts that no editors—they *couldn't* have perused them—wanted; and so it had come to the desperate point when, as Lally was saying, something had to be done about things. Repton had done all *he* could; he wrote unceasingly, all day, all night, but all his projects insolvently withered, and morning, noon, and evening brought his manuscripts back as unwanted as snow in summer. He was depressed and baffled and weary. And there was simply nothing else he could do, nothing in the world. Apart from his own wonderful gift he was useless, Lally knew, and he was being steadily and stupidly murdered by those editors. It was weeks since they had eaten a proper meal. Whenever they obtained any real nice food now, they sat down to it silently, intently, and destructively. As far as Lally could tell, there seemed to be no prospect of any such meals again in life or time, and the worst of it all was Phillip's pride—he was actually too proud to ask anyone for assistance! Not that he would be too proud to accept help if it were offered to him: oh no, if it came he would rejoice at it! But still, he had that nervous shrinking pride that coiled upon itself, and he would not ask; he was like a wounded animal that hid its woe far away from the rest of the world. Only Lally knew his need, but why could not other people see it—those villainous editors! His own wants were so modest and he had a generous mind.

"Phil," Lally said, seating herself at the table. Repton was lolling in a wicker armchair beside the gas fire. "I'm not going on waiting and waiting any longer, I must go and get a job. Yes, I must. We get poorer and poorer. We can't go on like it any longer, there's no use, and I can't bear it."

"No, no, I can't have that, my dear . . ."

"But I will!" she cried. "Oh, why are you so proud?"

"Proud! Proud!" He stared into the gas fire, his tired arms hanging limp over the arms of the chair. "You don't understand. There are things the flesh has to endure, and things the spirit too must endure. . . ." Lally loved to hear him talk like that; and it was just as well, for Repton was much given to such discoursing. Deep in her mind was the conviction that he had simple access to profound, almost unimaginable wisdom. "It isn't pride, it is just that there is a certain order in life, in my life, that it would not do for. I could not bear it, I could never rest; I can't explain that, but just believe it, Lally." His head was empty but unbowed; he spoke quickly and finished almost angrily. "If only I had money! It's not for myself. I can stand all this, any amount of it. I've done so before, and I shall do so again and again I've no doubt. But I have to think of you."

That was fiercely annoying. Lally got up and went and stood over him.

"Why are you so stupid? I can think for myself and fend for myself. I'm not married to you. You have your pride, but I can't starve for it. And I've a pride, too. I'm a burden to you. If you won't let me work now while we're together, then I must leave you and work for myself."

"Leave! Leave me now? When things are so bad?" His white face gleamed his perturbation up at her. "Oh well, go, go." But then, mournfully moved, he took her hands and fondled them. "Don't be a fool, Lally; it's only a passing depression, this. I've known worse before, and it never lasts long, something turns up, always does. There's good and bad in it all, but there's more goodness than anything else. You see."

"I don't want to wait for ever, even for goodness. I don't believe in it, I never see it, never feel it, it is no use to me. I could go and steal, or walk the streets, or do any dirty thing—easily. What's the good of goodness if it isn't any use?"

"But, but," Repton stammered, "what's the use of bad, if it isn't any better?"

"I mean—" began Lally.

"You don't mean anything, my dear girl."

"I mean, when you haven't any choice it's no use talking moral, or having pride; it's stupid. Oh, my darling"—she slid down to him and lay against his breast—"it's not you, you are everything to me; that's why it angers me so, this treatment of you, all hard blows and no comfort. It will never be any different. I feel it will never be different now, and it terrifies me."

"Pooh!" Repton kissed her and comforted her: she was his beloved. "When things are wrong with us our fancies take their tone from our misfortunes, badness, evil. I sometimes have a queer stray feeling that one day I shall be hanged. Yes, I don't know what for, what *could* I be hanged for? And, do you know, at other times I've had a kind of intuition that one day I shall be— what do you think?—Prime Minister of the country! Yes, well, you can't reason against such things. I know what I should do, I've my plans, I've even made a list of the men for my Cabinet. Yes, well, there you are."

But Lally had made up her mind to leave him; she would leave him for a while and earn her own living. When things took a turn for the better she would join him again. She told him this. She had friends who were going to get her some work.

"But what are you going to do, Lally? I—"

"I'm going away to Glasgow," said she.

"Glasgow?" He had heard things about Glasgow! "Good heavens!"

"I've some friends there," the girl went on steadily. She had got up and was sitting on the arm of his chair. "I wrote to them last week. They can get me a job almost any when, and I can stay with them. They want me to go—they've sent the money for my fare. I think I shall have to go."

"You don't love me, then!" said the man.

Lally kissed him.

"But *do* you? Tell me!"

"Yes, my dear," said Lally, "of course."

An uneasiness possessed him; he released her moodily. Where was their wild passion flown to? She was staring at him intently, then she tenderly said: "My love, don't you be melancholy, don't take it to heart so. I'd cross the world to find you a pin."

"No, no, you mustn't do that," he exclaimed idiotically. At her indulgent smile he grimly laughed too, and then sank back in his chair. The girl stood up and went about the room doing vague nothings, until he spoke again.

"So you are tired of me?"

Lally went to him steadily and knelt down by his chair. "If I was tired of you, Phil, I'd kill myself."

Moodily he ignored her. "I suppose it had to end like this. But I've loved you desperately." Lally was now weeping on his shoulder and he began to twirl a lock of her rich brown hair absently with his fingers as if it were a seal on a watch-chain. "I'd been thinking that we might as well get married, as soon as things had turned round."

"I'll come back, Phil"—she clasped him so tenderly—"as soon as you want me."

"But you are not really going?"

"Yes," said Lally.

"You're not to go!"

"I wouldn't go if—if anything—if you had any luck. But as we are now I must go away, to give you a chance. You see that, darling Phil?"

"You're not to go; I object. I just love you, Lally, that's all, and of course I want to keep you here."

"Then what are we to do?"

"I—don't—know. Things drop out of the sky, but we must be together. You're not to go."

Lally sighed: he was stupid. And Repton began to turn over in his mind the dismal knowledge that she had taken this step in secret, she had not told him while she was trying to get to Glasgow. Now here she was with the fare, and as good as gone! Yes, it was all over.

"When do you propose to go?"

"Not for a few days, nearly a fortnight."

"Good God," he moaned. Yes, it was all over, then. He had never dreamed that this would be the end, that she would be the first to break away. He had always envisaged a tender scene in which he could tell her, with dignity and gentle humour that— Well, he never had quite hit upon the words he would use, but that was the kind of setting. And now here she was with her fare to Glasgow, her heart towards Glasgow, and she as good as gone to Glasgow! No dignity, no gentle humour—in fact he was enraged—sullen but enraged, he boiled furtively. But he said with mournful calm:

"I've so many misfortunes, I suppose I can bear this too."

Gloomy and tragic he was.

"Dear, darling Phil, it's for your own sake I'm going."

Repton sniffed derisively. "We are always mistaken in the reasons for our commonest actions; Nature derides us all. You are sick of me; I can't blame you."

Eulalia was so moved that she could only weep again. Nevertheless she wrote to her friends in Glasgow promising to be with them by a stated date.

Towards the evening of the following day, at a time when she was alone, a letter arrived addressed to herself. It was from a firm of solicitors in Cornhill inviting her to call upon them. A flame leaped up in Lally's heart: it might mean the offer of some work that would keep her in London after all! If only it were so she would accept it on the spot, and Phillip would have to be made to see the reasonability of it. But at the office in Cornhill a more astonishing outcome awaited her. There she showed her letter to a little office boy with scarcely any fingernails and very little nose, and he took it to an elderly man who had a superabundance of both. Smiling affably, the long-nosed man led her upstairs into the sombre den of a gentleman who had some white hair and a lumpy yellow complexion. Having put to her a number of questions relating to her family history, and appearing to be satisfied and not at all surprised by her answers, this gentleman revealed to Lally the overpowering tidings that she was entitled to a legacy of eighty pounds by the will of a forgotten and recently deceased aunt. Subject to certain formalities, proofs of identity and so forth, he promised Lally the possession of the money within about a week.

Lally's descent to the street, her emergence into the clamouring atmosphere, her walk along to Holborn, were accomplished in a state of blessedness and trance, a trance in which life became a thousand times aerially enlarged, movement was a delight, and thought a rapture. She would give all the money to Phillip, and if he very much wanted it she would even marry him now. Perhaps, thought, she would save ten pounds of it for herself. The other seventy would keep them for . . . it was impossible to say how long it would keep them. They could have a little holiday somewhere in the country together, he was so worn and weary. Perhaps she had better not tell Phillip anything at all about it until her lovely money was really in her hand. Nothing in life, at least nothing about money, was ever certain; something horrible might happen at the crucial moment and the money be snatched from her very fingers. Oh, she would go mad then! So for some days she kept her wonderful secret.

Their imminent separation had given Repton a tender sadness that was very moving. "Eulalia," he would say, for he had suddenly adopted the formal version of her name; "Eulalia, we've had a great time together, a wonderful time, there will never be anything like it again." She often shed tears, but she kept the grand secret still locked in her heart. Indeed, it occurred to her very forcibly that even now his stupid pride might cause him to reject her money altogether. Silly, silly Phillip! Of course, it would have been different if they had married; he would naturally have taken it then, and really it would have *been* his. She would have to think out some dodge to overcome his scruples. Scruples were *such* a nuisance, but then it was very noble of him: there were not many men who wouldn't take money from a girl they were living with.

Well, a week later she was summoned again to the office in Cornhill and received from the white-haired gentleman a cheque for eighty pounds drawn on the Bank of England to the order of Eulalia Burnes. Miss Burnes desired to cash the cheque straightway, so the large-nosed elderly clerk was deputed to accompany her to the Bank of England close by and assist in procuring the money.

"A very nice errand!" exclaimed that gentleman as they crossed to Threadneedle Street past the Royal Exchange. Miss Burnes smiled her acknowledgment, and he began to tell her of other windfalls that had been disbursed in his time—but vast sums, very great persons—until she began to infer that Blackbean, Carp & Ransome were universal dispensers of largesse.

"Yes, but," said the clerk, hawking a good deal from an affliction of catarrh, "I never got any myself, and never will. If I did, do you know what I would do with it?" But at that moment they entered the portals of the bank, and in the excitement of the business Miss Burnes forgot to ask the clerk how he would use a legacy, and thus she possibly lost a most valuable slice of knowledge. With one fifty-pound note and six five-pound notes clasped in her handbag she bade good-bye to the long-nosed clerk, who shook her fervently by the hand and assured her that Blackbean, Carp & Ransome would be delighted at all times to undertake any commissions on her behalf. Then she fled along the pavement, blithe as a bird, until she was breathless with her flight. Presently she came opposite the window of a typewriter agency. Tripping airily into its office, she laid a scrap of paper before a lovely Hebe who was typing there.

"I want this typed, if you please," said Lally.

The beautiful typist read the words of the scrap of paper and stared at the heiress.

"I don't want any address to appear," said Lally. "Just a plain sheet, please."

A few moments later she received a neatly typed page folded in an envelope, and after paying the charge she hurried off to a district messenger office. Here she addressed the envelope in a disguised hand to P. Stick Repton, Esq., at the address in Holborn. She read the typed letter through again:

Dear Sir,

In common with many others I entertain the greatest admiration for your literary abilities, and I therefore beg you to accept this tangible expression of that admiration from a constant reader of your articles, who for purely private reasons, desires to remain anonymous.

Your very sincere
Wellwisher

Placing the fifty-pound note upon the letter Lally carefully folded them together and put them both into the envelope. The attendant then gave it to a uniformed lad, who sauntered off whistling very casually, somewhat to Lally's alarm—he looked so small and careless to be entrusted with fifty pounds. Then Lally went out, changed one of her five-pound notes, and had a lunch—half a crown, but it was worth it. Oh, how enchanting and exciting London was! In two days more she would have been gone; now she would have to write off at once to her Glasgow friends and tell them she had changed her mind, that she was now settled in London. Oh, how enchanting and delightful! And tonight he would take her out to dine in some fine restaurant, and they would do a theatre. She did not really want to marry Phil, they had got on so well without it, but if he wanted that too she did not mind—much. They would go away into the country for a whole week. What money would do! Marvellous! And looking round the restaurant she felt sure that no other woman there, no matter how well-dressed, had as much as thirty pounds in her handbag.

Returning home in the afternoon she became conscious of her own betraying radiance; very demure and subdued and usual she would have to be, or he might guess the cause of it. Though she danced up the long flight of stairs, she entered their room quietly, but the sight of Repton staring out of the window, forlorn as a drowsy horse, overcame her and she rushed to embrace him, crying: "Darling!"

"Hullo, hullo!" he smiled.

"I'm so fond of you, Phil dear."

"But—but you're deserting me!"

"Oh, no," she cried archly; "I'm not—not deserting you."

"All right." Repton shrugged his shoulders, but he seemed happier. He did not mention the fifty pounds then; perhaps it had not come yet—or perhaps he was thinking to surprise her.

"Let's go for a walk, it's a screaming lovely day," said Lally.

"Oh, I dunno," he yawned and stretched. "Nearly tea-time, isn't it?"

"Well, we—" Lally was about to suggest having tea out somewhere, but she bethought herself in time. "I suppose it is. Yes, it is."

So they stayed in for tea. No sooner was tea over than Repton remarked that he had an engagement somewhere. Off he went, leaving Lally disturbed and anxious. Why had he not mentioned the fifty pounds? Surely it had not gone to the wrong address? This suspicion once formed, Lally soon became certain, tragically sure, that she had misaddressed the envelope herself. A conviction that she had put No. 17 instead of No. 71 was almost overpowering, and she fancied that she hadn't even put London on the envelope—but Glasgow. That was impossible, though, but— oh, the horror!—somebody else was enjoying their fifty pounds. The girl's fears were not allayed by the running visit she paid to the messengers' office that evening, for the rash imp who had been entrusted with her letter had gone home and therefore could not be interrogated until the morrow. By now she was sure that he had blundered; he had been so casual with an important letter like that! Lally never did, and never would again, trust any little boys who wore their hats so much on one side, were so glossy with hair-oil, and went about whistling just to madden you. She burned to ask where the boy lived but in spite of her desperate desire she could not do so. She dared not, it would expose her to—to something or other she could only feel, not name; you had to keep cool, to let nothing, not even curiosity, master you.

Hurrying home again, though hurrying was not her custom and there was no occasion for it, she wrote the letter to her Glasgow friends. Then it crossed her mind that it would be wiser not to post the letter that night; better wait until the morning, after she had discovered what the horrible little messenger had done with her letter. Bed was a poor refuge from her thoughts, but she accepted it, and when Phil came home she was not sleeping. While he undressed he told her of the lecture he had been to, something about Agrarian Depopulation it was, but even after he had stretched himself beside her, he did not speak about the fifty pounds. Nothing, not even curiosity, should master her, and she calmed herself, and in time fitfully slept.

At breakfast next morning he asked her what she was going to do that day.

"Oh," replied Lally offhandedly, "I've a lot of things to see to, you know; I must go out. I'm sorry the porridge is so awful this morning, Phil, but—"

"Awful?" he broke in. "But it's nicer than usual! Where are you going? I thought—our last day, you know—we might go out somewhere together."

"Dear Phil!" Lovingly she stretched out a hand to be caressed across the table. "But I've several things to do. I'll come back early, eh?" She got up and hurried round to embrace him.

"All right," he said. "Don't be long."

Off went Lally to the messenger office, at first as happy as a bird, but on approaching the building the old tremors assailed her. Inside the room was the cocky little boy who bade her "Good morning" with laconic assurance. Lally at once questioned him, and when he triumphantly produced a delivery book she grew limp with her suppressed fear, one fear above all others. For a moment she did not want to look at it: truth hung by a hair, and as long as it so hung she might swear it was a lie. But there it was, written right across the page, an entry of a letter delivered, signed for in the well-known hand, P. Stick Repton. There was no more doubt, only a sharp indignant agony as though she had been stabbed with a dagger of ice.

"Oh yes, thank you," said Lally calmly. "Did you hand it to him yourself?"

"Yes'm," replied the boy, and he described Phillip.

"Did he open the letter?"

"Yes'm."

"There was no answer?"

"No'm."

"All right." Fumbling in her bag, she added: "I think I've got a sixpence for you."

Out in the street again she tremblingly chuckled to herself. "So that is what he is like, after all. Cruel and mean! He was going to let her go and keep the money in secret to himself!" How despicable! Cruel and mean, cruel and mean! She hummed it to herself. "Cruel and mean, cruel and mean!" It eased her tortured bosom. "Cruel and mean!" And he was waiting at home for her, waiting with a smile for their last day together. It would *have* to be their last day. She tore up the letter to her Glasgow friends, for now she *must* go to them. So cruel and mean! Let him wait! A bus stopped beside her, and she stepped on to it, climbing to the top and sitting there while the air chilled her burning features. The bus made a long journey to Plaistow. She knew nothing of Plaistow, she wanted to know nothing of Plaistow, but she did not care where the bus took her; she only wanted to keep moving and moving away, as far away as possible from Holborn and from him, and not once let those hovering tears down fall.

From Plaistow she turned and walked back as far as the Mile End Road. Thereabouts wherever she went she met clergymen, dozens of them. There must be a conference, about charity or something, Lally thought. With a vague desire to confide her trouble to someone, she observed them; it would relieve the strain. But there was none she could tell her sorrow to, and failing that, when she came to a neat restaurant she entered it and consumed a fish. Just beyond her, three sleek parsons were lunching, sleek and pink; bald, affable, consoling men, all very much alike.

"I saw Carter yesterday," she heard one say. Lally liked listening to the conversation of strangers, and she had often wondered what clergymen talked about among themselves.

"What, Carter! Indeed. Nice fellow, Carter. How was he?"

"Carter loves preaching, you know!" cried the third.

"Oh yes, he loves preaching!"

"Ha, ha, ha, yes."

"Ha, ha, ha, oom."

"Awf'ly good preacher, though."

"Yes, awf'ly good."

"And he's awf'ly good at comic songs, too."

"Yes?"

"Yes!"

Three glasses of water, a crumbling of bread, a silence suggestive of prayer.

"How long has he been married?"

"Twelve years," returned the cleric who had met Carter.

"Oh, twelve years!"

"I've only been married twelve years myself," said the oldest of them.

"Indeed!"

"Yes, I tarried very long."

"Ha, ha, ha, yes."

"Ha, ha, ha, oom."

"Er—have you any family?"

"No."

Very delicate and dainty in handling their food they were; very delicate and dainty.

"My rectory is a magnificent old house," continued the recently married one. "Built originally 1700. Burnt down. Rebuilt 1784."

"Indeed!"

"Humph!"

"Seventeen bedrooms and two delightful tennis courts."

"Oh, well done!" the others cried, and then they all fell with genteel gusto upon a pale blancmange.

From the restaurant the girl sauntered about for a while, and then there was a cinema wherein, seated warm and comfortable in the twitching darkness, she partially stilled her misery. Some nervous fancy kept her roaming in that district for most of the evening. She knew that if she left it she would go home, and she did not want to go home. The naphtha lamps of the booths at Mile End were bright and distracting, and the hum of the evening business was good despite the smell. A man was weaving sweetstuffs from a pliant roll of warm toffee that he wrestled with as the athlete wrestles with the python. There were stalls with things of iron, with fruit or fish, pots and pans, leather, string, nails. Watches for use—or for ornament—what d'ye lack? A sailor told naughty stories while selling bunches of green grapes out of barrels of cork dust which he swore he had stolen from the Queen of Honolulu. People clamoured for them both. You could buy back numbers of the comic papers at four a penny, rolls of linoleum for very little more—and use either for the other's purpose.

"At thrippence per foot, mesdames," cried the sweating cheapjack, lashing himself into ecstatic furies, "that's a piece of fabric weft and woven with triple-strength Andalusian jute, double-hot-pressed with rubber from the island of Pagama, and stencilled by an artist as poisoned his grandfather's cook. That's a piece of fabric, mesdames, as the king of heaven himself wouldn't mind to put down in his parlour—if he had the chance. Do I ask thrippence a foot for that piece of fabric? Mesdames, I was never a daring chap."

Lally watched it all, she looked and listened; then looked and did not see, listened and did not hear. Her misery was not the mere disappointment of love, not that kind of misery alone; it was the crushing of an ideal in which love had had its home, a treachery cruel and mean. The sky of night, so smooth, so bestarred, looked wrinkled through her screen of unshed tears; her sorrow was a wild cloud that troubled the moon with darkness.

In miserable desultory wanderings she had spent her day, their last day, and now, returning to Holborn in the late evening, she suddenly began to hurry, for a new possibility had come to lighten her dejection. Perhaps, after all, so whimsical he was, he was keeping his "revelation" until the last day, or even the last hour, when (nothing being known to her, as he imagined) all hopes being gone and they had come to the last kiss, he would take her in his arms and laughingly kill all grief, waving the succour of a flimsy bank-note like a flag of triumph. Perhaps even, in fact surely, that was why he wanted to take her out to-day! Oh, what a blind, wicked, stupid girl she was, and in a perfect frenzy of bubbling faith she panted homewards for his revealing sign.

From the pavement below she could see that their room was lit. Weakly she climbed the stairs and opened the door. Phil was standing up, staring so strangely at her. Helplessly and half-guilty she began to smile. Without a word said he came quickly to her and crushed her in his arms, her burning silent man, loving and exciting her. Lying against his breast in that constraining embrace, their passionate disaster was gone, her doubts were flown; all perception of the feud was torn from her and deeply drowned in a gulf of bliss. She was aware only of the consoling delight of their reunion, of his amorous kisses, of his tongue tingling the soft down on her upper lip that she disliked and he admired. All the soft wanton endearments that she so loved to hear him speak were singing in her ears, and then he suddenly swung and lifted her up, snapped out the gaslight, and carried her off to bed.

Life that is born of love feeds on love; if the wherewithal be hidden, how shall we stay our hunger? The galaxy may grow dim, or the stars drop in a wandering void; you can neither keep them in your hands nor crumble them in your mind.

What was it Phil had once called her? Numskull! After all it was his own fifty pounds, she had given it to him freely, it was his to do as he liked with. A gift was a gift, it was poor spirit to send money to anyone with the covetous expectation that it would return to you. She would surely go tomorrow.

The next morning he awoke her early and kissed her.

"What time does your train go?" said he.

"Train!" Lally scrambled from his arms and out of bed.

A fine day, a glowing day. Oh, bright, sharp air! Quickly she dressed and went into the other room to prepare their breakfast. Soon he followed, and they ate silently together, although whenever they were near each other he caressed her tenderly. Afterwards she went into the bedroom and packed her bag; there was nothing more to be done, he was beyond hope. No woman waits to be sacrificed, least of all those who sacrifice themselves with courage and a quiet mind. When she was ready to go she took her portmanteau into the sitting-room; he, too, made to put on his hat and coat.

"No," murmured Lally, "you're not to come with me."

"Pooh, my dear!" he protested; "nonsense!"

"I won't have you come," cried Lally with an asperity that impressed him.

"But you can't carry that bag to the station by yourself!"

"I shall take a taxi." She buttoned her gloves.

"My dear!" His humorous deprecation annoyed her.

"Oh, bosh!" Putting her gloved hands around his neck she kissed him coolly. "Good-bye. Write to me often. Let me know how you thrive, won't you, Phil? And"—a little wavering—"love me always." She stared queerly at the two dimples in his cheeks; each dimple was a nest of hair that could never be shaved.

"Lally, darling, beloved girl! I never loved you more than now, this moment. You are more precious than ever to me!"

At that, she knew her moment of sardonic revelation had come—but she dared not use it, she let it go. She could not so deeply humiliate him by revealing her knowledge of his perfidy. A compassionate divinity smiles at our puny sins. She knew his perfidy, but to triumph in it would defeat her own pride. Let him keep his gracious, mournful airs to the last, false though they were. It was better to part so, better from such a figure than from an abject scarecrow, even though both were the same inside. And something capriciously reminded her, for a flying moment, of elephants she had seen swaying with the grand movement of tidal water—and groping for monkey nuts.

Lally tripped down the stairs alone. At the end of the street she turned for a last glance. There he was, high up in the window, waving good-byes. And she waved back at him.

The Field of Mustard (1926)